READER'S DIGEST

CONDENSED BOOKS

FIRST EDITION
Published by
THE READER'S DIGEST ASSOCIATION LIMITED
25 Berkeley Square, London W1X 6AB

THE READER'S DIGEST ASSOCIATION LIMITED
Nedbank Centre, Strand Street, Cape Town

Typeset in 10 on 12 pt. Highland Lumitype Roman
and printed in Great Britain by Petty & Sons Ltd., of Leeds
on paper made by Kymmene, in Finland.

Original cover design by Jeffery Matthews.

For information as to ownership
of copyright in the material in this book see last page.

ISBN 0 340 16595 2

READER'S DIGEST
CONDENSED BOOKS

THE ODESSA FILE
Frederick Forsyth

THE WALTZ KINGS
Hans Fantel

RENDEZVOUS – SOUTH ATLANTIC
Douglas Reeman

THE UNEXPECTED MRS. POLLIFAX
Dorothy Gilman

COLLECTOR'S LIBRARY
EDITION

In this volume

THE ODESSA FILE *by Frederick Forsyth (p.11)*

This is the amazing story of a journalist's crusade against the last legacy of Hitler. It began in 1963 when Peter Miller investigated the suicide of an old German Jew and so stumbled on the trail of the notorious "Butcher of Riga", SS Captain Roschmann.

Miller's inquiries brought him into direct confrontation with Odessa, the infamous organization that was set up at the end of the last war not only to protect all Nazis from Allied justice but also to keep alight the embers of their lost cause. . . .

Using the same meticulous research and factual techniques that made *The Day of the Jackal* the outstanding best-seller of 1971, Frederick Forsyth tells us how Miller laid bare the complex world of Odessa's machinations. Here—or so it seems—must be the truth behind the facts reported in the newspapers at the time and, as the last page is turned, the inevitable question will be asked: *can* this be fiction?

THE WALTZ KINGS
by Hans Fantel (p.173)

This is the tale of Johann Strauss, the undoubted king of the waltz, and his son, also Johann, who carried on the tradition with such classics as "The Blue Danube" and "Tales from the Vienna Woods". Hans Fantel, Viennese by birth, is uniquely qualified to present the lives of these flamboyant personalities whose struggles, successes, and bitter rivalries are as memorable as the music they created.

RENDEZVOUS— SOUTH ATLANTIC
by Douglas Reeman (p.269)

This epic story of *Benbecula*, an ageing passenger liner that is converted into an armed merchant cruiser, has all that authenticity that has established Reeman as today's master of naval fiction. "You are there, in the icy hell of the Atlantic," said the *Daily Telegraph*, "fighting against dreadful odds and cursing the Admiralty."

THE UNEXPECTED MRS. POLLIFAX
by Dorothy Gilman (p.437)

When Emily Pollifax, a spry little grandmother, volunteers to become a spy for the CIA, *everything* is unexpected. For a start, she is accepted. And from that moment on, fiction's most unlikely and lovable secret agent is more trouble than her bosses—or anyone else—bargained for.

THE ODESSA FILE
Frederick Forsyth

the Odessa file

a condensation of the book by
FREDERICK FORSYTH

Published by Hutchinson, Lon

The secret
lifeline for
ex-Nazis
on the run

Germany

Odessa

Illustrations by Roy Houlihan

In a recent interview with *The Sunday Times*, Dr. Simon Wiesenthal, the man who brought Adolf Eichmann to justice, had this to say about the current hunt for Hitler's deputy, Martin Bormann: "The tracking down of a single man using eight to ten aliases, who has unlimited funds, and who is surrounded by friends anxious to protect him, has no precedent, except in the case of Eichmann."

But was he right? Or was there another manhunt for a Nazi which was every bit as gruelling and even more disturbing in its implications? That is the theme of this brilliant successor to *The Day of the Jackal*.

According to Frederick Forsyth, the year was 1963 and the hunt began when a young German journalist, Peter Miller, set out to trace the "Butcher of Riga", concentration camp commandant Captain Roschmann of the Waffen-SS. Miller's search led him, via such men as Simon Wiesenthal and Lord Russell of Liverpool, into the heart of the Odessa, the organization that protected Eichmann, guards Bormann and, as the reader will discover, still spreads its tentacles throughout the Western World.

Frederick Forsyth, himself an ex-journalist, has already built a stunning reputation for revealing unpleasant realities in the guise of fiction. Significantly, he dedicated this full-scale exposé of Odessa's power and sinister influence to all journalists "who would not take 'Drop it' for an answer."

Foreword

The Odessa of the title is neither the city in southern Russia nor the small town in America. It is a word composed of the six initial letters of *"Organisation Der Ehemaligen SS-Angehörigen"*. In English this means "Organization of Former Members of the SS".

The SS, as most readers will know, was the army within an army, devised by Adolf Hitler, and charged with special tasks under the Nazis who ruled Germany from 1933 to 1945. These tasks were supposedly concerned with the security of the Third Reich; in effect they included the carrying out of Hitler's ambition to rid Europe of all elements he considered to be "unworthy of life".

Under Heinrich Himmler, the SS organized the murder of some fourteen million human beings, comprising roughly six million Jews, five million Russians, two million Poles, half a million gipsies and half a million others, including, though it is seldom mentioned, close to two hundred thousand non-Jewish Germans and Austrians. These were either mentally or physically handi-capped unfortunates or so-called enemies of the Reich, like Communists, Social Democrats, Liberals, editors, reporters and priests who spoke out too inconveniently, men of conscience and courage, and later army officers suspected of lack of loyalty to Hitler.

In carrying out these tasks, the SS made the two initials of its name, and the twin-lightning symbol of its standard, synonymous with inhumanity in a way that no other organization before or since has been able to do.

Towards the end of the war its senior members, under no illusions as to how civilized men would regard their actions when the reckoning came, made secret provision to disappear to a new life, leaving the entire German people to carry the blame for the vanished culprits. Vast sums of SS gold were smuggled out and deposited in numbered bank accounts, false identity papers were prepared, escape channels opened up. Consequently, when the Allies finally conquered Germany, the bulk of the mass-murderers had gone under cover within Germany, suitably protected by new identities, while the top men had escaped to more hospitable climes where, from the safety of a comfortable exile, they proceeded to manipulate the organization they called Odessa.

The aim of the Odessa was and remains five-fold: to rehabilitate former SS men into the professions of the new Federal Republic, to infiltrate at least the lower echelons of political party activity, to pay for the very best legal defence for any SS killer hauled before a court, to establish former SS men in commerce and industry, and finally to propagandize the German people to the viewpoint that the SS killers were in fact none other than patriotic soldiers doing their duty to the Fatherland.

In all these tasks, backed by their considerable funds, they have been measurably successful, but despite this, the Odessa does occasionally take a defeat. The worst it ever suffered occurred in the early spring of 1964 when a package of documents arrived unannounced and anonymously at the Ministry of Justice in Bonn. To the very few officials who saw it, the package became known as "The Odessa File".

Chapter One

Everyone seems to remember with great clarity what he was doing on November 22nd, 1963, at the moment he heard President Kennedy was dead. The President was hit at 12:22 in the afternoon, Dallas time, and the announcement that he was dead came at half-past one in the same time zone. It was two-thirty in New York, seven-thirty in the evening in London and eight-thirty on a chilly, sleet-swept night in Hamburg.

Peter Miller was driving back into town after visiting his mother at her home in Osdorf, a suburb of the city. He always visited her on Friday evenings. He would have telephoned her if she had a telephone, but as she did not, he drove out to see her. That was why she refused to have a telephone.

He had the radio on and was listening to music broadcast by North-West German Radio. At half-past eight the music stopped and the voice of the announcer came through, taut with tension.

"*Achtung*. Here is an announcement. President Kennedy is dead. I repeat, President Kennedy is dead."

"My God," Miller breathed, eased down on the brake pedal and swung into the right-hand side of the road. Right down the broad, straight highway other drivers were also pulling in to the side of the road as if driving and listening to the radio had suddenly become mutually exclusive, which in a way they had.

The light music on the radio was replaced by the Funeral March, and at intervals the announcer read snippets of further information as they were brought in from the newsroom. The details began to fill in: the open car ride into Dallas, the rifleman in the window of the School Book Depository. No mention of an arrest.

As a reporter, Miller could imagine the chaos sweeping across the newspaper offices of the country as every staff man was called back to help put out a crash edition. He wished in a way he were back on the staff of a daily newspaper, but since he had become a freelance three years earlier he had specialized in news features inside Germany, mainly connected with crime, the police, the underworld. His mother accused him of mixing with "nasty people" and his argument that he was becoming one of Germany's most sought-after reporter-investigators availed nothing.

As the reports came through, Miller leaned back in the comfortable leather upholstery of his Jaguar, trying to think of an "angle" that could be chased up inside Germany. The reaction of the Bonn government would be covered out of Bonn by the staff men, the memories of Kennedy's visit to Berlin the previous June would be covered from there. He didn't see anything he could ferret out to sell to the picture magazines that were his best customers.

It is always tempting to wonder what would have happened if.... Usually it is a futile exercise, but it is probably accurate to say that if Miller had not pulled in to the side of the road for half an hour, he would not have seen the ambulance, nor heard of Salomon Tauber or Eduard Roschmann, and forty months later the republic of Israel would probably have ceased to exist.

He finished his cigarette and threw the stub away. At a touch of the button the 3.8 litre engine beneath the long sloping bonnet of the Jaguar XK 150 S thundered once and settled down to its habitual and comforting rumble. Miller flicked on the two head-lights and swung out into the growing traffic along Osdorf Way.

He had got as far as the traffic lights on Stresemann Strasse when he heard the ambulance behind him. It came past on the left, the wail of the siren rising and falling, then it swung across Miller's nose and sped on towards Daimler Strasse. Miller reacted on his reflexes alone. He let in the clutch and the Jaguar surged after the ambulance twenty metres behind it.

It was probably nothing, but one never knew. Ambulances meant trouble and trouble could mean a story, particularly if one were first on the scene, and Miller always carried a small Yashica camera with flash attachment in the glove compartment of his car.

The ambulance twisted into the narrow, ill-lit streets of Altona, and drew up in front of a crumbling rooming house where a police car already stood. Its blue roof-light sent a ghostly glow across the faces of a knot of bystanders grouped round the door.

A burly police sergeant in a rain cape roared at the crowd to stand back and make a gap in front of the door for the ambulance. Its driver and attendant climbed down, ran round to the back and eased out an empty stretcher. After a brief word with the sergeant the pair hastened upstairs.

Miller pulled the Jaguar to the opposite kerb twenty yards down the road. He climbed out and strolled over to the sergeant.

14

"Mind if I go up? I'm Press." He waved his Press card.

"And I'm police," said the sergeant. "Nobody goes up. Those stairs are narrow enough as it is, and none too safe. The ambulance men will be down directly."

"What's up then?" asked Miller.

"Can't make statements. Check at the station later."

A man Miller recognized came down the stairs and emerged onto the pavement. They had been at school together and Karl Brandt was now a junior detective inspector in the Hamburg police, stationed at Altona Central.

"Hey, Karl."

The young inspector caught sight of Miller and his face broke into a grin. He nodded to the sergeant.

"It's all right, Sergeant. He's more or less harmless."

Miller shook hands with Karl Brandt.

"What are you doing here?" Brandt asked.

"Followed the ambulance."

"Bloody vulture. What are you up to these days?"

"Same as usual. Freelancing."

"Making quite a packet out of it by the look of it. I keep seeing your name in the picture magazines."

"It's a living. Hear about Kennedy?"

"Yes. Hell of a thing. They must be turning Dallas inside out tonight. Glad it wasn't on my patch."

Miller nodded towards the hallway of the rooming house.

"A suicide. Gas. Neighbours smelled it coming under the door."

"Not a film star by any chance?" asked Miller.

"Yeah. Sure. They always live in places like this. No, it was an old man. Looked as if he had been dead for years anyway."

The inspector turned as the two ambulance men came down the hallway with their burden. Brandt turned round.

"Make a bit of room. Let them through."

The two men walked out to the pavement and round to the open doors of the ambulance. Brandt followed them, with Miller at his heels. As the ambulance men reached the door of the vehicle Brandt said, "Hold it," and flicked back the corner of the blanket

15

from the dead man's face. He remarked over his shoulder, "Just a formality. My report has to say I accompanied the body to the ambulance and back to the morgue."

The interior lights of the ambulance were bright, and Miller caught a two-second look at the face of the suicide. His only impression was that he had never seen anything so old and ugly. A few strands of lank hair were plastered over the otherwise naked scalp and the face was hollowed out to the point of emaciation. The lips hardly existed and both upper and lower were lined with vertical creases. To cap the effect two pale and jagged scars ran down the man's face, from the temple to the corner of the mouth.

After a quick glance, Brandt stepped back and the ambulance attendant rammed the stretcher into its berth. The ambulance surged away and the crowd started to disperse.

Miller looked at Brandt and raised his eyebrows. "Charming."

"Yeah. Well, I must get back to the station. See you, Peter."

Miller drove back towards Altona station, picked up the main road into the city centre and twenty minutes later swung into the underground car park off the Hansa Square, two hundred yards from the house where he had his rooftop flat.

Keeping the car in an underground car park all winter was one of the extravagances he permitted himself. Also, he liked his fairly expensive flat because it was high and he could look down on the bustling boulevard of the Steindamm. Of his clothes and food he thought nothing, and at twenty-nine, just under six feet, with the rumpled brown hair and brown eyes that women go for, he didn't need expensive clothes.

The real passions of his life were sports cars, reporting and Sigrid, though he sometimes shamefacedly admitted that if it came to a choice between Sigi and the Jaguar, Sigi might have to find her loving somewhere else.

He stood and looked at the Jaguar in the lights of the garage after he had parked it. He could seldom get enough of looking at that car. Even approaching it in the street he would stop and admire it, occasionally joined by a passer-by who would stop also and remark, "Some motor, that."

Normally a young freelance reporter does not drive a Jaguar XK 150 S. Spare parts were almost impossible to come by in Hamburg, the more so as the XK series had gone out of production in 1960. He maintained it himself, spending hours on Sunday in overalls beneath the chassis or half-buried in the engine. He had hardened up the independent suspension on the two front wheels, and as the car had stiff suspension at the back it took corners as steady as a rock. Just after buying it he had had it resprayed black with a long wasp-yellow streak down each side.

He left the car and walked up the ramp to the street and back to his flat. Although his mother had fed him at six, he was hungry again. He scrambled some eggs and listened to the late night news. It was all about Kennedy and heavily accented on the German angles, since there was little more news coming through from Dallas. The police were still searching for the killer. He switched it off and went to bed, wishing Sigi were home. He always wanted to snuggle up to her when he felt depressed. But the cabaret at which she danced did not close till nearly four in the morning, often later on Friday nights when the provincials and tourists were thick down the Reeperbahn.

So he smoked another cigarette and fell asleep to dream of the hideous face of the old gassed man in the slums of Altona.

WHILE Peter Miller was eating his scrambled eggs in Hamburg five men were sitting drinking in a house attached to a riding school outside Cairo.

The five men were in a jovial mood because of the news from Dallas. Two of the guests and the host were Germans, the other two Egyptians. The host was proprietor of the riding school, a favourite meeting place of the cream of Cairo society and the several-thousand-strong German colony.

Sitting in the leather easy chair by the shuttered window was Hans Appler, formerly an expert on Jews in the Nazi Propaganda Ministry of Dr. Joseph Goebbels. Appler had taken the Egyptian name of Salah Chaffar. On his left was another Goebbels man, Ludwig Heiden. Both were still fanatical Nazis. Of the Egyptians, one was Colonel Chams Edine Badrane, personal aide to Marshal Abdel Hakim Amer, later to become Egyptian Defence Minister. The other was Colonel Ali Samir, head of the Moukhabarat, the Egyptian Secret Intelligence Service.

Hans Appler raised his glass. "So Kennedy the Jew-lover is dead. Gentlemen, I give you a toast."

The reference to Kennedy as a Jew-lover baffled none of the five men in the room. On the 14th of March 1960, while Dwight Eisenhower was still President of the United States, the Premier of Israel, David Ben-Gurion, and the Chancellor of Germany, Konrad Adenauer, had met secretly at the Waldorf-Astoria hotel in New York.

The two statesmen had signed an agreement whereby West Germany agreed to open a credit account for Israel to the tune of fifty million dollars a year. Ben-Gurion, however, soon discovered that to have money was one thing, to have a secure and certain source of arms was quite another. Six months later the Waldorf agreement was topped off with another, signed by the defence ministers of Germany and Israel, under which Israel would be able to use the money to buy weapons in Germany.

Adenauer, aware of the vastly more controversial nature of the second agreement, delayed implementing it for months. Then, in November 1961 he was in New York to meet the new President, John Fitzgerald Kennedy, and Kennedy put the pressure on. He did not wish arms to be delivered to Israel from the U.S.A., but he wanted them to arrive somehow. Israel needed fighters, transport planes, Howitzer 105mm. artillery pieces, armoured cars, armoured personnel carriers and tanks. And Germany had all of these, mainly of American make.

So the deal was pushed through.

German tanks started to arrive at Haifa in late June 1963. When the Odessa found out it promptly informed the Egyptians, with whom its agents in Cairo had the closest links.

In late 1963 things started to change. On October 15th, Adenauer, "the Granite Chancellor", resigned and went into retirement. His place was taken by Ludwig Erhard, a good vote-catcher as the

18

father of the German economic miracle, but weak in matters of foreign policy.

Even when Adenauer was in office there had been a vociferous group inside the West German cabinet in favour of shelving the Israeli arms deal. The old Chancellor had silenced them with a few terse sentences, and such was his power they stayed silent. But as soon as Erhard took the chair, they opened up again. Erhard dithered. But the determination of John Kennedy that Israel should get her arms via Germany was unremitting. Now that Kennedy had been shot, there were high hopes in Cairo that President Lyndon Johnson would take the American pressure off Germany and let the indecisive chancellor in Bonn renege on the deal.

The host at the convivial meeting outside Cairo that night, having filled his guests' glasses, turned back to the sideboard for his own. Wolfgang Lutz, born at Mannheim in 1921, was a former major in the German army who had emigrated to Cairo in 1961 and started his riding academy. Blond, blue-eyed, hawk-faced, he was a favourite among both the influential political figures of Cairo and the expatriate German and mainly Nazi community along the banks of the Nile.

He turned to face the room and gave them a broad smile. If there was anything false about that smile no one noticed. But it was false. He had been born in Mannheim, a Jew, but had emigrated to Palestine at the age of twelve. He was a major, but in the Israeli army. He was also the top agent of Israeli Intelligence in Egypt.

Lutz could hardly wait for his guests to depart, for he desperately wished to get his transmitter out of the bathroom scales and send a message to Tel Aviv. He raised his glass to the four smiling faces. "Death to the Jew-lovers," he toasted, forcing his own smile. "*Sieg Heil!*"

PETER MILLER woke the next morning just before nine and shifted luxuriously under the enormous feather cushion that covered the double bed. Even half-awake he could feel the warmth of the sleeping figure of Sigi and he snuggled closer to her.

Sigi, still fast asleep after only four hours in bed, grunted in annoyance. "Go away," she muttered. Miller sighed, slipped out of bed and padded into the living room to pull back the curtains. The steely November light washed across the room. He yawned and went into the kitchen to brew the first of his innumerable cups of coffee.

Sigi was twenty-two and at school had been a champion gymnast who, so she said, could have gone on to Olympic standard if her bust had not developed to the point where it got in the way. Instead, she trained to become a teacher of physical training at a girls' school. The change to striptease dancing came for the simplest of reasons: it paid five times a teacher's salary.

Miller had seen her by chance on a visit to Madam Kokett's bar just below the Café Keese on the Reeperbahn. She was a big girl, five feet nine, with a figure to match. She stripped to the music with her face set in the usual bedroom pout of strippers. Miller had sipped his drink without batting an eyelid.

But when the applause started, the girl had bobbed a shy, half-embarrassed little bow and given a big sloppy grin like a half-trained bird dog which against all the betting has brought back a downed partridge. It was the grin that got Miller. He asked if she would like a drink, and she was sent for.

To his surprise Miller found she was a very nice person to be around, and asked if he might take her home after the show. With obvious reservations she agreed. She emerged from the cabaret clad in a most unglamorous duffel coat.

Miller played his cards coolly. They just had coffee and talked. She finally unwound and began chatting gaily. He learned that she liked pop music, art, walking along the banks of the Alster, keeping house and children. They started, then, going out together on her one free night.

After three months Miller took her to his bed and later suggested that she move in. Sigi, who had a single-minded attitude to the important things in life, had already decided she wanted to marry Peter Miller and the only problem was whether she should try to get him by sleeping in his bed or not. Noticing his ability to fill the other half of his mattress with other girls if the need arose, she decided to accept his invitation and make his life so comfortable that he would want to marry her. They had been together for six months by this late November morning.

Miller carried the radio into the bathroom and listened to the news while he showered and shaved. A man had been arrested for the murder of President Kennedy. There were no news items on the entire programme but those connected with the assassination.

After drying off from his shower, he went back to the kitchen and made more coffee. He was halfway to the living room with it when the phone rang. It was Karl Brandt.

"Peter? Look, it's about this dead Jew."

Miller was baffled. "What dead Jew?"

"The one who gassed himself last night in Altona."

"I didn't know he was Jewish," said Miller. "What about him?"

"I want to talk to you. Not on the phone. Can we meet?"

Miller's reporter's mind clicked into gear immediately. "Are you free for lunch?" He mentioned a small restaurant on the Goose Market.

"Good," said Brandt. "I'll be there at one o'clock."

Throughout lunch Karl avoided his subject, but when the coffee came he said simply. "The man last night."

"Yes," said Miller. "What about him?"

"You must have heard, we all have, about what the Nazis did to the Jews during the war and even before it?"

"Of course. They rammed it down our throats at school."

Miller was puzzled and embarrassed. Like most young Germans at school in the immediate post-war period, he had been told that his countrymen had been guilty of massive war crimes, but something inside him had persuaded him it was nothing to do with Peter Miller. It was another time, another place, a long way away. He wondered why Brandt should be bringing the subject up.

Brandt stirred his coffee, not knowing how to go on.

"That old man last night," he said at length. "He was a German Jew. He was in a concentration camp."

Miller thought back to the death's head on the stretcher the

21

previous evening. Was that what they ended up like? He had never seen anyone who had been in a camp before, at least, not knowingly. For that matter he had never met one of the SS mass-killers, he was sure of that. One would notice, after all. The man would be different. But then his mind strayed back to the publicity surrounding the Eichmann trial in Jerusalem two years earlier, and he remembered how ordinary had been that face in the glass booth, so depressingly ordinary.

He brought his thoughts back to the present and the sense of unease Brandt's line of talk aroused in him.

"What about it?" he asked the detective.

For answer Brandt took a brown paper-wrapped parcel out of his attaché case and pushed it across the table.

"The old man left a diary. Actually, he wasn't so old. Fifty-six. It seems he wrote notes at the time and stored them in his foot-wrappings. After the war he transcribed them all."

Miller looked at the parcel with scant interest. "Where did you find it?"

"It was lying next to the body. I picked it up and took it home. I read it last night."

Miller looked at his former schoolfriend quizzically. "It was bad?"

"Horrible. I had no idea of the things they did to them."

"Why bring it to me?"

Now Brandt was embarrassed. He shrugged. "I thought it might make a story."

"Who does it belong to now?"

"Technically, Tauber's heirs. But we'll never find them. So I suppose it belongs to the Police Department. But they'd just file it. You can have it, if you want it."

Miller paid the bill and the pair walked outside.

"All right, I'll read it. But I don't promise to get steamed up about it."

Brandt turned to him with a half-smile.

"You're a cynical bastard," he said.

"No," said Miller. "It's just that like most people I'm concerned with the here and now."

Brandt was serious again. He looked at the parcel under Miller's arm and nodded slowly.

"Yes, but it's not all past history. That story ended here in Hamburg last night. Good-bye Peter."

The detective turned and walked away, not knowing how wrong he was.

Chapter Two

Peter Miller took the brown paper parcel home and arrived there just after three. Settled in his favourite armchair, with the inevitable cup of coffee at his elbow and a cigarette going, he opened it. The diary consisted of a hundred and fifty typewritten pages in a loose-leaf folder. It had apparently been banged out on an old machine, for some of the letters were distorted or faint; and it seemed to have been typed over a period of years, for most of the pages bore the unmistakable tinting of old paper. But there was a preface of new pages at the front of the typescript and a sort of epilogue at the back. Both were dated November 21st, two days previously.

Miller's first glance at the opening paragraphs surprised him, for the language was clear and precise German, the writing of a well-educated and cultured man. On the outside of the front cover a square of white paper had been gummed, and on it had been written in large capitals THE DIARY OF SALOMON TAUBER.

Miller settled deeper in his chair and began to read.

DIARY OF SALOMON TAUBER

PREFACE

My name is Salomon Tauber, I am a Jew and about to die. I have decided to end my own life because it has no more value. Those things that I have tried to do with my life have come to nothing; for the evil that I have seen has survived and flourished and only the good has departed. The friends that I have known, the sufferers and the victims, are all dead and only the persecutors are all around me. I see their faces on the streets in the daytime, and in the night I see the face of my wife Esther who died long ago.

I have stayed alive this long only because there was one thing I wished to do, and now I know I never shall.

I bear no hatred nor bitterness towards the German people, for they are a good people. Peoples are not evil; only individuals are evil. The English philosopher Burke was right when he said, "I do not know the means for drawing up the indictment of an entire nation". The Bible relates how the Lord wished to destroy Sodom and Gomorrah for the evil of those men who lived there, but among them was one righteous man, and because he was righteous he was spared. Therefore guilt is individual like salvation.

When I came out of the concentration camps of Riga and Stutthof, when I survived the Death March to Magdeburg, when the British soldiers liberated my body there in April 1945, leaving only my soul in chains, I hated the Germans. I asked then as I had asked many times over the previous four years why the Lord did not strike them down, every last man, woman and child. And when He did not, I hated Him too, crying that He had deserted me and my people.

But with the passing of time I have learned again to love; to love the rocks and the trees, the sky above and the river flowing past the city, the stray dogs and the cats, and the children who run away from me because I am so ugly. They are not to blame. There is a French adage, "To understand everything is to forgive everything". When one can understand people's fear and greed and ignorance, one can forgive. But there are some men whose crimes surpass comprehension and therefore forgiveness. They are still among us, in the cities, in the offices, lunching in the canteens, smiling, shaking hands, calling decent men *Kamerad*. That these should live on, to smear a whole nation in perpetuity with their individual evil is your failure, and my failure. We have all failed, and failed miserably.

Lastly, as time passed, I have come again to love the Lord, and to ask His forgiveness for the things I have done against His Laws, and they are many.

Shema Yisroel, Adonai elohenu, Adonai ehad.

Hear, O Israel, the Lord is our God, the Lord is One.

The diary began with twenty pages in which Tauber described his boyhood in Hamburg. By the late thirties he was married to a girl called Esther, was working in Hamburg as an architect, and was spared being rounded up before 1941 due to the intervention of his employer. Finally he was taken in Berlin, on a journey to see a client. After a period in a transit camp he was packed with other Jews into a boxcar on a cattle train bound for the east.

I cannot remember the date the train finally rumbled to a halt in a railway station. I think it was six days and seven nights after we were shut up in the truck in Berlin. Suddenly the train was stationary, the slits of white light told me it was daytime outside, and my head swam from exhaustion and the stench.

There were shouts outside, the sound of bolts being drawn back, and the doors were flung open. As brilliant daylight rushed into the car men threw arms over their eyes and screamed with the pain. Half the truck emptied itself onto the platform in a tumbling mass of stinking humanity. As I had been standing at the rear of the car to one side of the centrally placed doors, I avoided this and stepped down upright to the platform.

The SS guards who had opened the doors, mean-faced, brutal men who jabbered and roared in a language I could not understand, stood back with expressions of disgust. Inside the boxcar thirty-one men lay trampled on the floor. They would never get up again. The remainder, starved, half-blind, reeking from head to foot, struggled upright on the platform. From thirst our tongues were gummed to the roof of the mouth, and our lips were split and parched.

Down the platform forty other carriages from Berlin and eighteen from Vienna were disgorging their occupants, about half of them women and children. Many of the women and most of the children were naked and smeared with excrement as we were. Some women carried the lifeless bodies of their children in their arms as they stumbled out into the light.

The guards ran up and down the platform, clubbing the deportees into a sort of column, prior to marching us into the town. But what town? And what was the language these men were speaking? Later I was to discover this town was Riga and the SS guards were local Latvians, as fiercely anti-Semitic as the SS from Germany, but of a much lower intelligence, virtually animals in human form.

There were a few German SS officers standing in the shade of the station awning. One stood aloof on a packing crate, surveying the human skeletons who emptied themselves from the train with a thin but satisfied smile. He was tall and lanky, with pale hair and washed-out blue eyes. It was my first sight of Waffen SS-Captain Eduard Roschmann—the Butcher of Riga.

At 5 a.m. on the morning of June 22nd, 1941, Hitler's one hundred and thirty divisions, divided into three army groups, had rolled across the border to invade Russia. Behind each army group came SS extermination squads, charged by Hitler, Himmler and Heydrich with wiping out the Communist commissars and the rural-dwelling Jewish communities and penning the large urban Jewish communities into the ghettos of each major town. The army took Riga, capital of Latvia, on July 1st. By August 1st the SS had begun the extermination programme that would make Ostland (as the Germans re-named the three occupied Baltic states) Jew-free. Then it was decided in Berlin to use Riga as the transit camp to death for the Jews of Germany and Austria. In 1938 there were 320,000 German Jews and 180,000 Austrians, a round half-million. By July 1941 tens of thousands had been dealt with in the concentration camps, notably Sachsenhausen, Mauthausen, Ravensbrück, Dachau, Buchenwald, Belsen, and Theresienstadt in Bohemia. But the camps were getting overcrowded. Work was begun to expand or begin the six extermination centres of Auschwitz, Treblinka, Belzec, Sobibor, Chelmno and Maidanek. Until they were ready, however, a place had to be found to finish off as many Jews as possible and "store" the rest. The obscure lands of the east seemed an excellent choice for the purpose. Tauber's transport was the first into Riga from Reich Germany, and reached there at 3.45 in the afternoon of August 18th, 1941.

The Riga ghetto lay at the northern edge of the city, with open countryside to the north. There was a wall along the south face, the other three sides were sealed off with rows of barbed wire. There was one gate, on the northern face, through which all exits and entries had to pass. From this gate running down the centre of the ghetto was Mase Kalnu Iela, or Little Hill Street. To the right-hand side of this (looking from south to north) was the Blech Platz, or Tin Square, where selections for execution took place, along with roll call, selection of slave-labour parties, floggings and hangings. The gallows with its eight steel hooks and permanent nooses swinging in the wind stood in the centre of this. It was occupied every night, and frequently several shifts had to be effected before Roschmann was satisfied with his day's work.

The whole ghetto must have been just under two square miles, a township that had once housed 12,000 to 15,000 people. After we arrived transports continued to come day after day until the population of our part of the ghetto soared to 30,000 to 40,000 and with the arrival of each new transport a number of the existing inhabitants had to be executed to make room for the newcomers.

As summer merged into autumn and autumn into winter conditions grew worse. Each morning the entire population was assembled on Tin Square. These were mainly men, for women and children were exterminated on arrival in far greater percentages than the work-fit males. We were divided into work groups which left the ghetto each day in columns to work twelve hours at forced labour in the growing host of workshops nearby.

I had said early on that I was a carpenter, which was not true, but as an architect I had seen carpenters at work and knew enough to get by. I guessed, correctly, that there would always be a need for carpenters, and I was sent to work in a nearby lumber mill.

Before marching to work in the mornings, we were given a half-litre of so-called soup, mainly water, sometimes with a knob of potato in it. We had another half-litre, with a slice of black bread and a mouldy potato on return to the ghetto at night. Bringing food into the ghetto was punishable by hanging at evening roll call on Tin Square. Nevertheless, to take that risk was the only way to stay alive.

As the columns trudged back through the gate each evening, Roschmann and his cronies would do spot checks. At random, they would order people to strip. If food was found, the person would stay behind while the others marched to Tin Square for roll call.

When they were all assembled Roschmann and the other SS guards would stalk down the road, followed by the condemned people. The males among them would mount the gallows and wait with ropes round their necks during roll call. Then Roschmann would walk along the line, grinning up at the faces above him and kicking the chairs out from under them, one by one. Sometimes he would pretend to kick the chair away, only to pull his foot back in time, laughing uproariously.

Sometimes the condemned men would pray to the Lord, sometimes they would cry for mercy. Roschmann liked this. He would pretend he was slightly deaf, cocking an ear and asking, "Can you speak up a little? What was that you said?"

When it was a woman who was caught with food, she was made to watch the hangings first, especially if one was her husband or brother. Afterwards, Roschmann made her kneel in front of the rest of us while the camp barber shaved her bald, and then she was taken to the cemetery outside the wire, made to dig a shallow grave, then kneel beside it while Roschmann fired a bullet from his Lüger into the base of her skull. Word came from the Latvian guards that he would often fire past the woman's ear. She would fall into the grave with shock, only to have to climb out and go through it all again. The Latvians were brutes, but Roschmann managed to amaze them for all that. . . .

There was one certain girl at Riga who helped the prisoners at her own risk. She was Olli Adler, from Munich, I believe. Her sister

Gerda had already been shot in the cemetery for bringing in food. Olli was a girl of surpassing beauty, and took Roschmann's fancy. He made her his concubine. The official term was housemaid, because relations between an SS man and a Jewess were banned. She used to smuggle medicines into the ghetto when she was allowed to visit it, having stolen them from the SS stores. This of course was punishable by death. The last I saw of her was when we boarded the ship at Riga Docks. . . .

By the end of that first winter I was certain I could not survive the hunger and cold and damp, the overwork and the constant brutalities. My strong frame had been whittled down to skin and bones. In the mirror I saw a haggard, stubbled old man. I was just thirty-five and I looked double that. My will to live had dissipated; and then something happened in March that gave me another year of willpower.

I remember the date even now. It was March 3rd, 1942, the day of the second Dünamünde convoy. About a month earlier we had seen the arrival of a strange van. It was about the size of a long single-decker bus, but without windows. It parked just outside the ghetto gates, and at morning roll call Roschmann announced that there was a new fish-pickling factory just started at the town of Dünamünde, about eight miles from Riga. It involved light work, he said, good food and good living conditions. Because the work was so light the opportunity was open only to old men and women, the frail, the sick and the small children.

Roschmann walked down the lines selecting those to go, and the old and sick were eager to show themselves. Finally over a hundred were selected, and all climbed into the van. The doors were slammed shut, and the van rolled away, emitting no exhaust fumes. Later word filtered back that there was no fish-pickling factory at Dünamünde; the van was a gassing van.

On March 3rd the whisper went round that there was to be another Dünamünde convoy and, sure enough, at morning roll call Roschmann announced it. But there was no pressing forward to volunteer, so with a wide grin Roschmann began to stroll along the ranks, tapping on the chest with his quirt those who were to go. He started at the rear rank, where he expected to find the weak and the old. There was one old woman who had foreseen this and stood in the front rank. She must have been sixty-five, but she had rouged her cheeks and painted her lips hoping to pass for a young girl.

Reaching her, Roschmann stopped, stared, then grinned.

"Well, what have we here?" he cried. "Don't you want a nice little ride to Dünamünde, young lady?"

Trembling with fear, the old woman whispered, "No, sir."

"And how old are you then?" boomed Roschmann as his SS friends began to giggle. "Seventeen, twenty?"

The old woman's knees began to tremble. "Yes, sir," she whispered.

"Well, I always like a pretty girl," cried Roschmann. "Come out into the centre so we can all admire your beauty."

He hustled her to the centre of Tin Square. "Well now, since you're so young and pretty, perhaps you'll dance for us, eh?"

The woman shook her head. Roschmann's smile vanished. "Dance," he snarled.

She made a few little shuffling movements, then stopped. Roschmann fired his Lüger into the sand an inch from her feet.

"Dance . . . dance . . . dance you hideous Jewish bitch," he shouted, firing each time he said "dance". He made her leap higher and higher, until at last she fell to the sand, unable to rise. He fired his last three slugs in front of her face, blasting the sand up into her eyes. Then, with no ammunition left, he shouted "dance" again and slammed his boot into her belly.

All this had happened in complete silence, until the man next to me started to pray. He was a Hassid, small and bearded, in the rags of his long black coat. He began to recite the Shema in a quavering voice that grew steadily louder. I too began to pray, silently, that the Hassid would be quiet. But he would not.

"Hear O Israel . . . ."

"Shut up," I hissed out of the corner of my mouth.

"*Adonai elohenu* . . . the Lord is our God . . . ."

"Will you be quiet. You'll get us all killed."

"The Lord is One . . . *Adonai Eha-a-a-ad.*"

Like a cantor he drew out the last syllable in the traditional way. Just at that moment Roschmann stopped shouting at the old woman and lifted his head like an animal scenting the wind.

"Who was that talking?" he screamed, striding towards me. "You . . . step out of line." I stepped forward. His face, twitching like a maniac's, changed as he looked at me and he gave his quiet, wolfish smile that struck terror into even the Latvian SS men.

His hand moved so quickly no one could see it. I felt only a thump down one side of my face, and a tremendous bang as if a bomb had gone off next to my eardrum. Then the quite distinct but detached feeling of my own skin splitting like rotten calico from temple to mouth. His hand moved again, and the other side of my face ripped open. He had a two-foot quirt, a steel core at the handle end, the remaining foot of plaited leather thongs. It could split hide like tissue paper.

Warm blood was dripping off my chin in two red fountains. Roschmann pointed to the old woman sobbing in the Square.

"Pick up that old hag and take her to the van," he barked.

And so it was that I picked up the old woman and carried her to the van, the blood pouring onto her from my face.

As I set her down in the van she gripped my wrist with a strength I would not have thought she still possessed. She pulled me down and with a handkerchief that must have come from better days, she staunched some of my flowing blood. She looked up at me, her face streaked with mascara, tears and sand, but with dark eyes as bright as stars.

"Jew, my son," she hissed. "Swear to me that you will live. You must live, so that you can tell them outside what happened to our people here. Promise me, swear it by Sefer Torah."

And so I swore that I would live somehow. Then I stumbled back down the road into the ghetto, and half-way down I fainted. . . .

Shortly thereafter I made two decisions. One was to keep a secret diary, nightly tattooing words and dates into the skin of my feet and legs, so that one day I would be able to give precise evidence against those responsible for what was happening.

The second decision was to become a Kapo. The decision was

hard, for Kapos were camp police who herded their fellow Jews to work, and often to execution. They carried pickaxe handles and sometimes under the eye of an SS officer, used them to beat their fellow Jews to work harder. Nevertheless, on April 1st, 1942, I went to the chief of the Kapos and volunteered, thus becoming an outcast. There was no point in explaining why I had done it: that one Kapo more or less would make no difference; but that one single surviving witness might make all the difference, not to save the Jews of Germany, but to avenge them. . . .

I should describe here the method of execution of those unfit for labour, for in this manner between 70,000 and 80,000 Jews were exterminated under Roschmann's orders at Riga. When the cattle train arrived with a new consignment of prisoners, usually about five thousand strong, close to a thousand were already dead from the journey. The new arrivals were lined up on Tin Square and the selections for extermination took place, not merely among them, but among us all. Among the new arrivals the old, the diseased, most of the women and almost all the children, were set on one side as unfit. The remainder were then counted. If there were two thousand of them, then two thousand of the existing inmates whose health had been worked to ruins would be picked out by Roschmann's quirt to die. In that way there was no overcrowding.

These victims were marched to the High Forest, just outside the town, where they dug the enormous open ditches into which they fell when the Latvian SS mowed them down. The remaining Riga Jews then filled in enough earth to cover the bodies, adding one more layer of corpses to those underneath until the ditch was full. Then a new one was started. All those killed on execution hill were stripped at the graveside. The gold, silver and jewellery was taken in charge by Roschmann personally.

In August 1942, I was standing on Tin Square as Roschmann went round making his selections from a transport that had just come in from Bohemia. The new arrivals were already shaved bald, and it was not easy to tell the men from the women, except for the shift dresses the women wore. There was one woman, as thin as a rake and coughing continuously, who caught my attention. Something about her rang a bell in my mind.

Arriving opposite her, Roschmann tapped her on the chest and passed on. Most of those selected that evening were marched to the High Forest. But there was a gassing van at the gates, and a group of about a hundred of the frailest was detached from the crowd. SS Lieutenant Krause pointed to four or five of the Kapos. "You lot," he shouted, "take these to the Dünamünde convoy."

Among the limping, crawling, coughing people we escorted to the van was the thin woman. She knew where she was going, they all did, but like the rest she stumbled obediently to the rear of the van. She was too weak to climb up, for the tailboard was high off the ground, so she turned to me for help. We stood and looked at each other in stunned amazement. Behind me I heard somebody approach, and the two Kapos at the tailboard straightened to attention, scraping their caps off with one hand. Realizing it must be an SS officer, I did the same. The woman just stared at me unblinking. The man behind me came forward. It was Captain Roschmann. Those pale blue eyes glared at me, then flickered to the woman, and his slow wolfish smile spread across his face.

"Do you know this woman?" he asked.

"Yes, Herr Captain," I answered.

"Who is she?" he asked. I could not reply.

"Is she your wife?" he went on. I nodded dumbly.

He grinned even wider. "Well now, my dear Tauber, where are your manners? Help the lady up into the van."

I stood there unable to move. He put his face closer to mine. "You have ten seconds to pack her in. Then you go yourself."

Slowly I held out my arm and Esther leaned upon it. With this assistance she climbed into the van. She looked down at me, and two tears rolled down her cheeks. She did not say anything, we never spoke throughout. Then the doors were slammed and the van rolled away. The last thing I saw were her eyes looking at me.

I have spent twenty years trying to understand the look in her eyes. Was it love or hatred, contempt or pity, bewilderment or understanding? I shall never know.

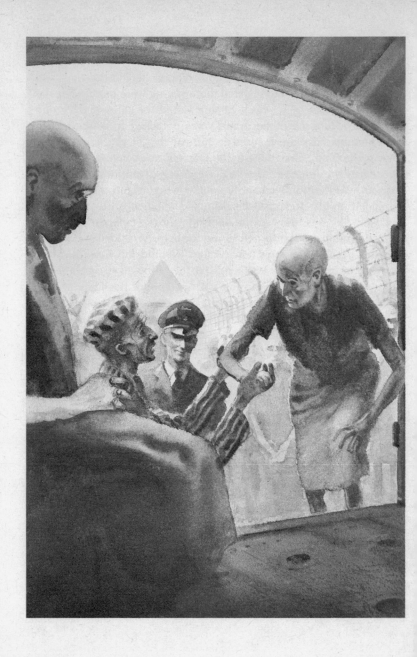

Roschmann turned to me, still grinning. "You may go on living until we finish you off, Tauber. But you are dead as of now."

And he was right. That was the day my soul died inside me. It was August 29th, 1942.

Peter Miller read on late into the night. Several times he sat back in his chair and breathed deeply for a few minutes to regain his calm. Once, close to midnight, he laid the book down and made more coffee. Tauber had now come to the spring of 1944, to the moment when Soviet troops had cut the whole of Ostland off from the Reich, marching south of the Baltic states right through to the Baltic Sea. The Wehrmacht generals, who had seen the trap closing on them, had argued and pleaded with Hitler to pull back the forty-five divisions inside the enclave. Hitler's reply had been his parrot-cry, "Death or Victory". Cut off from re-supply, 500,000 soldiers fought with dwindling ammunition to delay a certain fate.

That spring, when the Russians were pushing westward, Riga ghetto was finally liquidated. Most of its 30,000 remaining inhabitants were marched to the High Forest. About 5000 were transferred to the camp of Kaiserwald while behind them the ghetto was fired, then bulldozed. Of what had been there nothing was left but hundreds of acres of ashes.

For twenty pages Tauber described his struggle to survive starvation, disease and brutality in Kaiserwald. Roschmann was not there. Apparently he was still in the town of Riga, for Tauber went on to tell how in October of 1944 the SS, panic-stricken at the thought of being taken alive by the Russians, prepared for a desperate evacuation of Riga by sea, taking along a handful of the surviving prisoners as their passage-ticket back to the Reich.

It was during the afternoon of October 11th that we arrived, by now barely 4000 strong, at the Riga docks. In the distance we could hear a strange crump as if of thunder—Russian mortars landing in the suburbs. The dock area was crawling with officers and men of the SS. There must have been more of them than there were of us. We were lined up in rows against one of the warehouses and thought we were to die under the machine guns. But apparently the SS were going to use us as their alibi to escape from the Russian advance. Berthed alongside Quay Six was a freighter, the last one out of the encircled enclave. As we watched, the loading began of some of the hundreds of German wounded who were lying on stretchers in warehouses farther along the quay.

It was almost dark when Captain Roschmann arrived. He stopped short when he saw the Army wounded being taken aboard. "Stop that!" he shouted to the stretcher bearers. He strode across to the quay and slapped one of them in the face, then rounded on us prisoners. "You scum," he roared. "Get up on that ship and get these men off. That ship is ours."

Prodded by the gun barrels of the SS we were about to begin carrying the stretchers back ashore when another shout stopped us. An army captain was running down the quay. "Who ordered these men to be off-loaded?"

Roschmann walked up behind him. "I did. This boat is ours."

The captain spun round. "This ship was sent to pick up Army wounded," he said. "And Army wounded is what it will take."

He shouted to the Army orderlies to resume the loading.

Roschmann was trembling, I thought with anger. Then I saw he was scared. He began to scream, "Leave them alone. I have commandeered this ship in the name of the Reich." But the orderlies obeyed the Wehrmacht captain. I could see the captain's face, grey with exhaustion. He made to march past Roschmann to supervise the loading. As he did so I heard from one of the stretchers a voice shout, in Hamburg dialect, "Good on you captain. You tell the swine." Then he was abreast of Roschmann. The SS officer grabbed his arm and slapped him across the face. I had seen Roschmann slap men a thousand times, but never with the same result. The captain shook his head, bunched his fist and landed a haymaker of a right-fisted punch on Roschmann's jaw. Roschmann went flat on his back in the snow, a small trickle of blood coming from his mouth, and the captain moved on towards his orderlies.

As I watched, Roschmann drew his Lüger and fired between the captain's shoulders. Everything stopped at the crash from the pistol. The captain staggered and turned. Roschmann fired again, and the bullet caught the captain in the throat. He was dead before he hit the quay. I saw something fly off from round his neck as the bullet struck. I never knew the captain's name, but what he had worn was the Knight's Cross with Oak Leaf Cluster.

Miller read this page a dozen times with growing astonishment, turning to deep anger. Then he resumed reading the diary. Tauber recorded that Roschmann ordered the prisoners back to unload the Wehrmacht wounded. Then 4,000 survivors of Riga were packed into the ship's two holds, so cramped they could hardly move. The hatches were battened down above them, the SS streamed aboard, and the ship sailed hastily before the Russian dawn patrol could spot and bomb it. It took three days to reach Danzig, well behind German lines. Three days in a pitching, tossing hell below decks, without food and water, during which a quarter of the prisoners died.

Riga fell to the Russians on October 14th, while they were at sea.

From Danzig the prisoners were taken by barge to the concentration camp of Stutthof. There thousands more died of malnutrition, but somehow Tauber stayed alive. Then, in January 1945, as the Russians closed in, the survivors of Stutthof were driven through winter snow on the notorious Magdeburg Death March. Tauber survived even this, and finally at Magdeburg, west of Berlin, the SS ran for safety and abandoned the remaining prisoners to the care of the bewildered old men of the Home Guard. Unable to feed the prisoners, and terrified of what the advancing Allies would say when they found them starving, the Home Guard permitted them to go scrounging for food in the surrounding countryside.

The last time I had seen Eduard Roschmann was on the Danzig quayside [Tauber wrote]. But I was to see him once again. It was on April 3rd, 1945. I had been out that day towards Gardelegen and had gathered a small sackful of potatoes with three others. We were trudging back with our booty when a car came up behind. Inside were four SS officers, evidently making their escape to the west. Sitting beside the driver, pulling on the uniform jacket of an army corporal, was Eduard Roschmann.

He did not see me. But I saw him. There was no doubt about it. All four men were apparently changing their uniforms. As the car disappeared past us down the road a garment was thrown from a window. We reached the spot a few minutes later and stooped to examine it. It was the jacket of an SS officer, bearing the silver twin-lightning symbols of the Waffen-SS and the rank of captain. Roschmann of the SS had disappeared.

Twenty-four days after this, there was a hammering on the locked gates of the prison. The old Home Guard went to open them. The man who stepped through, cautiously, with a revolver in his hand, was evidently an officer, in a uniform I had never seen before. He was accompanied by a soldier in a flat round tin hat who carried a rifle. They just stood there in silence, looking around the courtyard. In one corner were stacked about fifty corpses, those who had died in the past two weeks and whom no one had the strength to bury. Others, half-alive, lay around the walls trying to soak up a little of the spring sunshine, their sores festering.

The two men looked at each other, then at the seventy-year-old Home Guard. He looked back, embarrassed. Then he said, "Hello, Tommy."

The officer looked back at him and said quite clearly in English, "You bastard Kraut pig."

And suddenly I began to cry.

The English put me in hospital but I left and hitchhiked home. When I saw there was nothing of it left, I finally, belatedly, collapsed completely.

The book ended with a further two clean, white sheets of paper, evidently recently typed, which formed the epilogue.

I have lived in this little room in Altona since 1947. After I came out of hospital I began to write the story of what happened to me and to the others at Riga. Looking back, it was all a waste of time and energy, the battle to survive and to be able to write down the evidence. Others have already done it so much better. I wish now I had died in Riga with Esther.

I know now I will never see Eduard Roschmann stand before a court, never give evidence to that court about what he did.

Once a woman came to see me. She said she was from the Reparations Office and that I was entitled to money. That it was my right to be recompensed for what was done. I said I did not want money. They sent someone else to see me, and I refused again. I only take from them what is due to me.

One of the British doctors asked me why I did not emigrate to Israel. How could I explain that I can never go up to the Land, not after what I did to Esther, my wife? I think about it often, but I am not worthy to go.

But if ever these lines should be read in Israel, will someone there please say khaddish for me?

SALOMON TAUBER,
Altona, Hamburg
21st November, 1963

PETER MILLER lay back in his chair for a long time, staring at the ceiling and smoking.

Just before five in the morning, Sigi came in from work. She was startled to find him awake.

"What are you doing up so late?" she asked.

"Been reading," said Miller

Later they lay in bed as the first glint of dawn picked out the spire of St. Michaelis, Sigi drowsy, Miller silent and preoccupied.

"Penny for them," said Sigi after a while.

"Just thinking."

"I know. What about?"

"The next story I'm going to cover."

"What are you going to do?" she asked. Miller leaned over and stubbed out his cigarette.

"I'm going to track a man down," he said.

Chapter Three

While Peter Miller and Sigi slept in Hamburg, a giant Coronado of Argentine Airlines entered final approach for a landing at Barajas Airport, Madrid. Sitting in a window seat in the third row back of the first-class passenger section was a man in his early sixties with iron-grey hair and a trim moustache.

His passport identified him as Señor Ricardo Suertes, citizen of Argentina, and the name was his own grim joke against the world. For *suerte* in Spanish means "luck", and luck in German is *glueck*. The airline passenger had been born Richard Gluecks, later to become a full general of the SS, head of the Reich Economic Administration Main Office and Hitler's Inspector-General of Concentration Camps. On the wanted lists of West Germany and Israel, he was number three after Martin Bormann and the former chief of the Gestapo, Heinrich Müller.

The role Gluecks had played was unique. He had been a senior mastermind of the holocaust, and yet had never pulled a trigger.

Of the crimes against humanity committed on the German side between 1933 and 1945, probably ninety-five per cent can be laid at the door of the SS. Of these, nearly ninety per cent can be attributed to two SS departments: These were the Reich Security Main Office (the RSHA) and the Reich Economic Administration Main Office. The economic bureau was involved because the intention was not only to exterminate every Jew on the face of Europe, and most of the Slavic races with them, but also to make them pay for the privilege.

First, the Jews were robbed of their businesses, houses, bank accounts, furniture, cars and clothes. They were shipped to slave labour camps and death camps with what they could carry, assured they were destined for resettlement. On the camp square their suitcases were taken from them, along with the clothes they wore. Out of the luggage of six million people thousands of millions of dollars worth of booty was extracted, for the European Jews of the time habitually travelled with their wealth upon them. From the camps entire trainloads of gold trinkets, jewels, silver ingots, gold dollars, and banknotes of every description were shipped back to the SS headquarters inside Germany. Throughout its history the SS made a profit on its operations. A part of this profit formed the fortune on which the Odessa was later based. Much of this gold still lies in vaults beneath the streets of Zurich.

The second stage of the exploitation lay in the living bodies of the victims. Those unfit for work were exterminated. Those able to work were hired out, either to the SS's own factories or to German industrial concerns like Krupp, Thyssen, von Opel, at three marks a day for unskilled workers, four marks for artisans. As much work as possible was abstracted from them for as little food as possible. Hundreds of thousands died in this manner.

The third stage of the exploitation lay in the corpses of the dead. These left behind wagonloads of shoes, socks, shaving brushes, spectacles, jackets and trousers. They also left their hair, which was turned into felt boots for the winter fighting and their gold teeth fillings, which were later melted down to be deposited as gold bars in Zurich.

In charge of the entire economic, or profit-making, side of the extermination of fourteen million people was the man in seat 3-B on the airliner that night.

Gluecks preferred not to chance his liberty by returning to Germany after his escape at the end of the war. He had no need to. Handsomely provided for out of the secret funds, he could live out his days comfortably in South America. His dedication to the Nazi ideal secured him a high and honoured place among the fugitive Nazis of Argentina, whence the Odessa was ruled.

From the airport Gluecks took a cab to the Zurburan Hotel. He had showered and shaved and had ordered breakfast when at nine o'clock on the dot three soft knocks, followed after a pause by two more, sounded at his door. He opened it, and quickly closed it behind the new arrival.

"*Sieg Heil!*" The man flashed up his right arm in salute.

General Gluecks raised his own right hand. "*Sieg Heil!*" He waved his visitor to a seat. The man facing him was at present the

41

chief of the Odessa network inside West Germany. To the citizens of his city he was a brilliantly successful lawyer in private practice. His Odessa code name was the Werwolf.

General Gluecks finished a cup of coffee and lit a large Corona. "You have probably guessed the reason for this sudden visit," he said. "As I dislike remaining on this continent longer than necessary I will get to the point. Kennedy is now dead, and there must be no failure to extract the utmost advantage from this event. Do you follow me?"

"Certainly, in principle, Herr General. But specifically . . . ?"

"I refer to the secret arms deal between Bonn and Tel Aviv. You know about the weaponry flowing from Germany to Israel?"

"Yes, of course."

"And you know also that our organization is doing everything in its power to assist the Egyptian cause?"

"Certainly. We have organized the recruiting of numerous German scientists to that end."

General Gluecks nodded. "Good. Now, Arab protests have led to the formation of a group in Germany strongly opposed to the arms deal. So far Erhard has not called off the shipments. What Kennedy wants, Erhard gives him. But Kennedy is now dead." The SS general jabbed the glowing tip of his cigar at his subordinate. "For the rest of this year therefore, our main political action within Germany will be to whip up public opinion against this arms deal and in favour of Germany's true and traditional friends, the Arabs."

"Yes, yes, that can be done."

"Your job will be to coordinate press publicity through the pamphlets and magazines we secretly support, advertisements in major newspapers, lobbying of civil servants and politicians."

"To promote feelings against Israel today will be difficult."

"The angle," said Gluecks tartly, "is simply that Germany must not alienate eighty million Arabs—a perfectly permissible, practical viewpoint. Funds, of course will be made available. Erhard must be subjected to constant pressure at every level. If we can cause policy in Bonn to change course, our stock in Cairo will rise sharply."

The Werwolf nodded, already seeing his plan of campaign taking shape before him. "It shall be done," he said.

"Excellent," replied General Gluecks.

"Herr General, we spoke of our German scientists in Egypt . . ."

"Ah yes, the second prong in our plan to destroy the Jews once and for all. You know about the rockets of Helwan, of course? Do you know what they are really for?"

"Well, I assumed of course . . ."

"That they would be used to throw high explosive onto Israel?" General Gluecks smiled broadly. "You could not be more wrong. I think the time is ripe to tell you why the rockets and the scientists are so vitally important."

General Gluecks leaned back, and told his subordinate the *real* story behind the rockets of Helwan.

AFTER the war, when King Farouk still ruled Egypt, thousands of Nazis and former members of the SS had found a sure refuge along the sands of the Nile. Among these were a number of scientists. Even before the *coup d'état* that dislodged Farouk, two German professors, Paul Goerke and Rolf Engel, were charged with studies for a rocket factory. The project went into abeyance when Nasser took power. After the defeat of Egypt in the 1956 Sinai campaign, the new dictator vowed that one day Israel would be totally destroyed. But it wasn't until 1961 when he got Moscow's final "No" on heavy rockets that the Goerke/Engel project was revitalized, and with a vengeance. Within the year Factory 333 was built and opened at Helwan, north of Cairo.

To open a factory is one thing; to design and build rockets is another. Long since, the senior supporters of Nasser, mostly with pro-Nazi backgrounds, had been in touch with the Odessa. And from the Odessa came the answer to the Egyptians' problem. What Nasser needed, they pointed out, was something remarkably similar to the V.2s that Werner von Braun and his team had once built at Peenemünde to pulverize London. And many of the Peenemünde team were still available.

Late in 1961, the Odessa appointed as a recruiting officer in

Germany a former major of the SS, Dr. Ferdinand Brandner, who employed as leg-man an ex-SS sergeant, Heinz Krug. With the salaries he could offer he was not short of choice recruits. Many of the scientists who worked at the Institute for Aerospace in Stuttgart were frustrated because the Paris Treaty of 1954 forbade Germany's undertaking research or manufacture in the realms of nuclear physics and rocketry. The prospect of research money and the chance to design real rockets was too tempting. Notable among those who left for Egypt in early 1962 were several experts in propulsion fuels and techniques.

GENERAL Gluecks paused, drew on his cigar, and returned to the immediate problem. "The key of a guided missile, however, lies in the tele-guidance system, and *that* we have been unable to furnish to the Egyptians. By ill-luck, we could not persuade a single expert in guidance systems to emigrate to Egypt.

"But we promised Egypt rockets and have them she will. President Nasser is determined there will one day be war between Egypt and Israel, and war there will be. Just think. If, when all the Soviet weaponry had failed, our scientists' rockets won that war, we would have achieved the double coup of ensuring a safe home for our people in an eternally grateful Middle East, and the final destruction of the Jew-pig State—thus fulfilling the last wish of the dying Fuehrer. It is a mighty challenge, and we must not fail."

The Werwolf watched his senior officer pacing the room, with awe and some puzzlement. "Forgive me, Herr General, but will four hundred medium warheads really finish off the Jews once and for all?"

Gluecks gazed at the younger man with a triumphant smile. "But what warheads! You do not think we are going to waste mere high explosive on these swine! Some will contain concentrated cultures of bubonic plague. Others will shower Israel with irradiated Strontium 90. Within hours they will all be dying of the plague or of gamma-ray sickness. *That* is what we have in store for them."

"It's brilliant," the Werwolf breathed.

44

"Brilliant, yes, and inevitable, provided we of the Odessa can equip those rockets with the necessary tele-guidance systems. To this end we have started a factory in West Germany, run by a man whose code name is Vulkan. It manufactures transistor radios as a front. And in its research department a group of scientists is devising the tele-guidance systems that will one day be fitted to the rockets of Helwan."

"Why don't they simply go to Egypt?" asked the other.

Gluecks smiled again. "There's the stroke of genius. I told you that no German guidance experts would emigrate. The men who now work in Vulkan's factory believe they're on a contract for the Defence Ministry in Bonn."

"God in heaven. How on earth was that arranged?"

"Quite simply. The Paris Treaty forbids Germany to do rocket research, so the men under Vulkan were sworn to secrecy by a genuine official of the Defence Ministry in Bonn, who also happens to be one of us. Of course, the cost of such research is stupendous. It has made enormous inroads into our secret funds. Now do you understand the importance of Vulkan?"

"Of course," replied the Odessa chief from Germany.

"Vulkan is chairman and managing director of the company, sole shareholder and paymaster. No one else knows the true nature of the over-large research section. The men in the closed-off section are believed to be working on micro-wave circuits for the transistor market. The secrecy is explained as a precaution against industrial espionage. The only link between the factory and the research is Vulkan. If he went, the entire project would collapse."

"Can you tell me the name of the factory?"

General Gluecks mentioned a name. The other man stared at him in astonishment. "But I know those radios," he protested.

"Of course. It's a bona fide radio factory. Here, look!"

General Gluecks handed the man from Germany a photograph. The Werwolf stared at it, then turned it over and read the name on the back. "Good God, I thought he was in South America."

"On the contrary. He is Vulkan. Now, your instructions. If you should get a whisper of anyone asking inconvenient questions about this man, that person is to be . . . discouraged. One warning and then a permanent solution. Do you follow me, *Kamerad*? No one, repeat, no one is to get anywhere near exposing Vulkan.''

The SS general rose. His visitor did likewise.

''That will be all,'' said Gluecks. ''You know what to do.''

Chapter Four

''But you don't even know if he's alive.''

Peter Miller and Karl Brandt were sitting in Miller's car outside Brandt's house.

''No. So that's the first thing I have to find out. If Roschmann's dead, obviously that's the end of it. Can you help me?''

Brandt slowly shook his head. ''Sorry, I can't.''

''Why not?''

''Look, why can't you just make a story out of the diary?''

''Because there's no story in it,'' said Miller. ''What am I supposed to say? 'Surprise, surprise, I've found a loose-leaf folder in which an old man who just gassed himself describes what he went through during the war'? There have been hundreds of memoirs written since the war. No editor in Germany would buy it.''

''So what are you going on about?'' asked Brandt.

''Simply this. Get a major police hunt started for Roschmann on the basis of the diary, and I *have* got a story.''

Brandt tapped his ash into the dashboard tray. ''There won't be a major police hunt. Look Peter, you may know journalism, but I know the Hamburg police. Our job is to keep Hamburg crime-free now, in 1963. Nobody's going to detach overworked detectives to hunt a man for what he did in Riga twenty years ago.''

''But you could at least raise the matter?'' said Miller.

''No. Not me. I don't intend to jeopardize my career.''

''Why should this jeopardize your career? Roschmann's a criminal isn't he? Police forces are supposed to hunt criminals.''

Brandt crushed out his stub. ''There's a sort of feeling in the police that to start probing into the war crimes of the SS can do a young policeman's career a power of no-good. Nothing comes of it anyway. The request would simply be denied. But the fact that it was made goes into a file. Then bang goes your chance of promotion. Nobody mentions it, but everyone knows it."

Miller sat and stared through the windscreen. "All right. If that's the way it is," he said at last. "But I've got to start somewhere. Did Tauber leave anything else behind when he died?"

"Well, there was a brief note, in which he said he left his effects to a friend of his, a Herr Marx."

"Well, that's a start. Where's this Marx?"

"How the hell should I know?" said Brandt.

"Didn't you look for him?"

Brandt sighed. "Have you any idea how many Marxes there are in Hamburg? Anyway, what the old man left wasn't worth ten pfennigs."

"That's all then?" asked·Miller. "Nothing else."

"Not a thing. If you want to find Marx you're welcome to try."

"Thanks. I will," said Miller.

THE next morning Miller visited the house where Tauber had lived. The door was opened by a middle-aged man wearing a collarless shirt and a pair of stained trousers supported by string.

"'Morning. Are you the landlord?"

The man looked Miller up and down and nodded.

"A man gassed himself here a few nights back," said Miller.

"Are you from the police?"

"No. The Press." Miller showed his Press card.

"I ain't got nothing to say."

Miller waved a ten-mark note. "I only want to look at his room."

"I've re-let it."

"What did you do with his stuff?"'

"It's in the back yard."

The pile of junk was lying in a heap under the thin rain. There was a battered typewriter, a few clothes, some books, a fringed white silk shawl. But there was no address book.

"Is that the lot?" he asked.

"That's the lot," said the man, regarding him sourly.

"Do you have any tenant by the name of Marx?" Miller asked.

"Nope."

"Did you ever see Tauber with anybody? With a friend?"

"No. Not surprised, the way he kept mumbling to himself. Barmy."

For the next three days, Miller quartered the area asking up and down the street, checking tradesmen, the milkman and the postman. Most people remembered seeing the old man, shuffling along, head down, wrapped in an ankle-length greatcoat. But no one had seen him talk to anyone else.

It was Wednesday afternoon when he found some urchins playing football.

"What, that old Jew? Mad Solly?" said one of them in answer to Miller's question. "Yes, I seen him once with a man. Talking they was. Sitting and talking."

"Where was that?"

"On the grass bank along the river. On one of the benches."

"How old was he, the other one?"

"Very old. Lot of white hair. Stuck out all over his head."

Miller wandered to the Elbe and stared down the length of the grass bank. There were a dozen benches, all empty. In the summer they'd be full of people watching the ocean liners come in and out. Now on his left half a dozen North Sea trawlers were drawn up at the wharves discharging their fresh-caught mackerel and herring. As a boy he had loved this fishing port. He liked the fishermen, gruff, kindly men. He thought of Roschmann, and wondered how the same country could produce them both.

His mind came back to Tauber. Where could he have met his friend Marx? It was not until he was back in his car and had stopped for petrol that the answer came—as so often from a chance remark. The pump attendant pointed out there had been a price increase in petrol and added that money went less and less far these days. He left Miller staring at the open wallet in his hand.

Money. Where did Tauber get his money? He didn't work, he

had refused payment by the Reparations Office, yet he paid his rent and had not starved. A disability pension, perhaps.

Miller drove to the local Post Office.

"Can you tell me when the pensioners collect their money?" he asked the lady behind the grill.

"Last day of the month, of course," she said.

MILLER was back on Friday morning, watching the old men and women begin to filter through the doors of the Post Office when it opened. Just before eleven an old man with a shock of white hair like candy floss came out and looked round as if searching for someone. After a few minutes he turned and began to walk in the direction of the river bank. Miller followed.

The old man settled himself on a bench. Miller approached slowly from behind. "Herr Marx?"

The old man turned. "Yes," he said gravely, "I am Marx."

"My name is Miller."

Marx inclined his head gravely.

"Are you . . . er . . . waiting for Herr Tauber?"

"Yes, I am," said the old man.

"May I sit down?"

"Please."

Miller sat beside him. "I'm afraid Herr Tauber is dead."

"I see," the old man said simply.

Miller told him about the events of the previous Friday night.

"You don't seem surprised. That he killed himself."

"No," said Marx, "he was a very unhappy man."

"He left a diary, you know."

"Yes, he told me once about that."

"Were you in Riga too?"

The man looked at him with sad, old eyes. "I was in Dachau."

"Look, Herr Marx, I need your help. In his diary your friend mentioned a man, an SS officer, called Roschmann. Captain Eduard Roschmann. Did he ever mention him to you?"

"Oh, yes. That was really what kept him alive. Hoping one day to give evidence against Roschmann."

"That's what he said in his diary. I read it after his death. I'm a reporter. I want to try and find Roschmann. Bring him to trial. Do you understand?"

"Yes."

"But there's no point if Roschmann is already dead. Can you remember if Herr Tauber ever learned whether Roschmann was still alive and free?"

"Captain Roschmann is alive," Marx said simply. "And free."

Miller leaned forward earnestly. "How do you know?"

"Because Tauber saw him last month."

For several minutes there was silence.

"Last month?" repeated Miller at length. "Did he say how?"

Marx sighed. "Yes. He was walking late at night as he used to do when he could not sleep. He was walking past the State Opera House just as people came out. Wealthy people, men in dinner jackets, women in furs and jewels. One was Roschmann. He climbed into a taxi with two others and drove off."

"Now, listen, Herr Marx, this is very important. Was he absolutely sure it was Roschmann?"

"Yes, he said he was."

"He hadn't seen him for nineteen years. How could he be sure?"

"He said he smiled."

"That is significant?"

Marx nodded. "He said once you had seen Roschmann smile that way you never forgot it. He could not describe that smile, but just said he would recognize it among a million others, anywhere."

Miller stood up and sighed.

"You must realize that nobody would ever believe this story?"

Marx shifted his gaze off the river and looked up at the reporter.

"Oh yes," he said softly, "he knew that. You see, that was why he killed himself."

THAT evening Peter Miller paid his usual Friday visit to his mother. She was a short, plump, matronly person who had never quite resigned herself to the idea that all her only son wanted to be was a reporter. When he told her of his intention to track down

50

Eduard Roschmann, she was aghast. "It's bad enough your covering the doings of criminals without getting mixed up with those Nazi people. I don't know what your dear father would have thought. . . ."

Peter Miller was facing the mantelpiece, dominated by a photograph of his dead father in captain's uniform. He stared out of the frame with the kind, rather sad smile that Peter remembered. He remembered too how his father came home after enlisting in 1940, how his mother had cried, and how he had thought how stupid women were to cry over such a wonderful thing as a father in uniform; and the day in 1944—he was eleven then—when an Army officer had come to tell his mother that her war-hero husband had been killed.

The black-edged column of names in the newspaper was different that day in late October, for halfway down was the entry:

"Fallen for Fuehrer and Fatherland. Miller, Erwin, Captain, on October 11th. In Ostland."

"I mean," said his mother behind him, "do you think your father'd want his son digging into the past, trying to drag up another war crimes trial? Do you think that's what he'd want?"

Miller kissed her lightly on the forehead.

"Yes, Mutti," he said. "I think that's exactly what he'd want."

HANS HOFFMANN was one of West Germany's wealthiest and most successful magazine publishers. His formula was simple—tell it in words and make it shocking, then back it up with pictures that make competitors look like novices with their first box Brownie. It worked. His chain of eight magazines had made him a multimillionaire. But *Kosmos*, the news and current affairs magazine, was still his favourite, his baby.

That Wednesday afternoon Hoffmann closed the diary of Salomon Tauber after reading the preface, leaned back and looked at the young reporter. "I can guess the rest. What do you want?"

"There's a man mentioned in there called Eduard Roschmann," said Miller. "SS Captain and Commandant of the Riga ghetto. Killed eighty thousand men, women and children. I want to find him."

51

"How do you know he's alive?"

Miller told him briefly. Hoffmann pursed his lips.

"Pretty thin evidence."

"True. But I've brought home stories that started on less."

Hoffmann grinned, recalling Miller's talent for ferreting out stories that hurt the establishment. "If the police can't find this man Roschmann, what makes you think you can?"

"Are the police really looking?" said Miller.

Hoffmann shrugged, "So what do you want from me?"

"A commission to give it a try. If nothing comes of it, I drop it."

"Miller, you're a good reporter. I like the way you cover a story, you've got style. That's why you get a lot of work from me. But you don't get this one."

"But why? It's a good story."

"Listen, you think this is a story everyone will want to read. No one will want to, and I'll tell you why. Before the war just about everyone in Germany knew one Jew. The fact is, before Hitler we didn't hate Jews. We had the best record of treatment of our Jewish minority of any country in Europe. Better than France or Spain, infinitely better than Poland and Russia.

"Then Hitler started. Telling people the Jews were to blame for the first war, unemployment, and everything else that was wrong. People didn't know what to believe. So when the vans took the Jews away, they kept quiet. They even got to believing the voice that shouted the loudest. Because that's the way people are, particularly Germans. We're a very obedient people.

"For years people haven't asked what happened to the Jews. They just disappeared. Now you want to tell them chapter and verse what happened to their next door neighbours. These Jews"— he tapped the diary—"were people they knew, and they stood around while they were taken away for your Herr Roschmann to deal with. You couldn't have picked a story they'd want to read less."

Miller sat and digested this. "There's another reason you want me to drop it, isn't there?"

Hoffmann eyed him keenly. "Yes," he said.

53

"Are you afraid of them—still?" asked Miller.

"No. I just don't go looking for trouble. That's all."

"What kind of trouble?"

"Have you ever heard of a man called Hans Habe?"

"The novelist? Yes, what about him."

"He used to run a magazine, in the early fifties. A good one too; *Echo of the Week* it was called. He ran a series of exposures of former SS men living in freedom in Munich."

"What happened to him?"

"One day he got more mail than usual. Half the letters were from his advertisers, withdrawing their custom. Another was from his bank saying it was foreclosing on his overdraft, as of that minute. Within a week the magazine was out of business."

"So what do the rest of us do? Keep running scared?"

"I don't have to take that from you, Miller," Hoffmann's eyes snapped. "I hated the bastards then. I do now. But I know my readers. They don't want to know about Eduard Roschmann."

"All right. I'm sorry. But I'm still going to cover it."

"If I didn't know you, Miller, I'd think there was something personal in this. Anyway, how are you going to finance yourself?"

"I've got some savings." Miller rose to go.

"Best of luck," said Hoffmann, rising. "I tell you what I'll do. The day Roschmann is arrested, I'll commission you to cover the story. But while you're digging for him, you're not carrying the letterhead of my magazine around as your authority."

Miller nodded.

"I'll be back," he said.

Chapter Five

That same Wednesday morning, December 4th, in Tel Aviv, the heads of the five branches of the Israeli Intelligence *apparat*, the Mossad, met for their regular informal weekly discussion.

On his way to this meeting the Controller of the Mossad, General Meir Amit, was a deeply worried man.

The cause of his worry was a piece of information that had reached him in the small hours. A fragment of knowledge to be added to the immense file on the rockets of Helwan. The general leaned back in his limousine and considered the history of those rockets.

The Mossad had learned of their existence in 1961. From the moment the first dispatch came through from Egypt, they had kept Factory 333 under constant surveillance. They were perfectly well aware of the influx of German scientists. It was a serious matter then; it became infinitely more serious in the spring of 1962.

In May that year Heinz Krug, the German recruiter of the scientists, approached the Austrian physicist, Doctor Otto Yoklek in Vienna. Instead of allowing himself to be recruited, the Austrian made contact with the Israelis. What he had to say electrified Tel Aviv. He told the Mossad that the Egyptians intended to arm their rockets with warheads containing irradiated nuclear waste and cultures of bubonic plague.

So important was the news that the then Controller of the Mossad, General Isser Harel, flew to Vienna to talk to Yoklek himself. He was convinced the professor was right, a conviction corroborated by the news that the Cairo Government had just purchased a quantity of radio-active cobalt equal to twenty-five times their possible requirement for medical purposes.

Isser Harel urged Premier David Ben-Gurion that he be allowed to begin a campaign of reprisals against the German scientists who were either working in Egypt or about to go there. The old premier was in a quandary. On the one hand he realized the hideous danger the new rockets presented; on the other hand, precious German tanks and guns were due to arrive in Israel at any moment. Israeli reprisals on the streets of Germany might just persuade Adenauer to shut off the arms deal. Ben-Gurion compromised. He authorized Harel to undertake a discreet campaign to discourage German scientists from going to Cairo.

But Harel went beyond his brief. On September 11th, 1962, recruiter Heinz Krug disappeared. His wife claimed he had been kidnapped by Israeli agents, but the Munich police found no evidence. In fact, a group led by a shadowy figure called Leon had abducted him and dumped his body in the lake.

The campaign then turned against the Germans already in Egypt. On November 27th a registered package addressed to Professor Wolfgang Pilz arrived in Cairo. It was opened by his secretary, and in the ensuing explosion the girl was maimed and blinded for life. On November 28th another package arrived at Factory 333. Five dead and ten wounded. On the 29th a third was defused without an explosion.

By February, 1963, the reprisal campaign was making headlines in Germany. In March, Heidi Goerke, daughter of Professor Paul Goerke, pioneer of Nasser's rockets, received a telephone call at her home in Freiburg, Germany. A voice suggested she meet the caller at a hotel in Basel, just over the Swiss border.

Heidi informed the German police, who tipped off the Swiss. They planted a bugging device in the room and heard two men warn Heidi and her brother to persuade their father to get out of Egypt if he valued his life. The two men were arrested in Zurich the same night. The chief was Yossef Ben Gal, Israeli citizen. The two men went on trial on June 10th, 1963. It was an international scandal.

The trial went well. Professor Yoklek testified as to the warheads and the Egyptian intent to commit genocide. Shocked, the judge acquitted the two accused.

But back in Israel, there was a reckoning. In a rage, Ben-Gurion rebuked General Harel for the lengths to which he had gone. Harel, who had become a legend in his own time, and realized it, handed in his resignation. To his surprise, Ben-Gurion accepted it. At the end of June General Meir Amit became Controller of Intelligence. His instructions remained the same. With no alternative, he turned the terror campaign against the scientists inside Egypt.

Guarded by Egyptian troops, these Germans lived in the suburb of Meadi, seven miles south of Cairo. To get at them Meir Amit used his top agent, the riding-school owner, Wolfgang Lutz, who began in September 1963 taking suicidal risks that would lead to his eventual undoing.

The German scientists, already badly shaken, began to get death threats posted from inside Cairo.

On September 27th, a letter blew up in the face of a Dr. Kirmayer. For Dr. Pitz, this was the last straw. He left Cairo for Germany. Others followed, and the furious Egyptians were unable to stop them.

The man in the limousine that December morning knew, of course, that his agent, the supposed Nazi Lutz, was the sender of the explosives.

But he also knew that the genocide programme was not being halted. General Amit flicked his eye over the decoded message he had just received. It confirmed simply that a virulent strain of bubonic bacillus had been isolated in the Contagious Diseases laboratory of Cairo Medical Institute, and that the budget of the department involved had been increased tenfold.

HAD Hans Hoffmann been watching he would have been forced to give Miller full marks for cheek. Leaving the penthouse office he took the lift down to the fifth floor and dropped in to see Max Kahn, the magazine's Legal Affairs Correspondent.

"I've just been up to see Herr Hoffmann," he said. "Now I need some background. Mind if I pick your brains?"

"Go ahead," said Kahn, assuming Miller was on a *Kosmos* story.

"Who investigates war crimes in Germany?"

"Well, basically it's the various Attorney Generals' offices of the provinces of West Germany."

"You mean, they *all* do it?"

Kahn leaned back in his chair. "There are sixteen provinces in West Germany. In each State Attorney General's office there is a department responsible for investigation into what are called 'crimes of violence committed during the Nazi era'. Each state capital is allocated a certain area as its special responsibility. Munich, for instance, is responsible for Dachau, Buchenwald, Belzec and Flossenberg. Most crimes in the Soviet Ukraine and the Lodz area of former Poland come under Hanover. And so on."

"Who do the Baltic States comes under?" Miller asked.

"Hamburg," said Kahn promptly.

"You mean that if there had ever been a trial of anyone guilty of crimes in Riga, it would have been here?"

"Yes, though the arrest could have been made anywhere."

"Has there ever been a Riga trial in Hamburg?" Miller asked.

"Not that I remember," said Kahn.

"Would it be in the cuttings library?"

"Sure. If it happened since 1950 when we started the cuttings."

"Mind if we look?" asked Miller.

"No problem."

The library was in the basement, tended by five archivists in grey smocks. It was almost half an acre of grey steel shelves and filing cabinets.

"What do you want?" asked Kahn as the librarian appeared.

"Roschmann, Eduard," said Miller.

"Personal Index section," said the librarian. He opened a cabinet door and flicked through it. "Nothing on Roschmann, Eduard."

"Do you have anything on war crimes?" Miller asked.

"Yes," said the librarian. "This way." They went along a hundred yards of cabinets.

"Look under Riga," said Miller.

The librarian mounted a ladder and came back with a red folder labelled 'Riga—War Crimes Trial'. Miller opened it. Two pieces of newsprint from the summer of 1950 fluttered out. One recorded that three SS privates went on trial for brutalities committed at Riga between 1941 and 1944. The other recorded they had all three been sentenced to long terms of imprisonment.

"Is that it?" asked Miller.

"That's it," said the librarian.

IT WAS a week before Miller could get an appointment in the Hamburg Attorney General's office.

The man he confronted was nervous, ill at ease.

"You must understand I have only agreed to see you as a result of your persistent inquiries," he began.

"That's nice of you all the same," said Miller. "I want to

inquire about a man whom I assume your department must have under permanent investigation, called Eduard Roschmann."

"Roschmann?" said the lawyer.

"Roschmann, Captain of the SS. Commandant of Riga ghetto from 1941 to 1944. I want to know if he's alive, if he has ever been arrested and if he has ever been on trial."

The lawyer was shaken. "Good Lord, I can't tell you that."

"Why not? It's a matter of public interest."

"I hardly think so," the lawyer said. "Otherwise we would be receiving constant inquiries of this nature. Actually, so far as I can recall, yours is the first inquiry we've ever had from . . . a member of the public."

"Actually, I'm a member of the Press," said Miller.

"That may be. But I'm afraid we are not empowered to give information regarding the progress of our inquiries."

"Well, that's not right to start with," said Miller.

"Oh, come now, Herr Miller, you would hardly expect the police to give you such information about *their* criminal cases."

"I would. In fact, I do. The police are customarily very helpful in issuing bulletins on whether an early arrest may be expected. Certainly they'd tell a Press inquiry if their main suspect was to their knowledge alive or dead."

The lawyer smiled thinly. "All I can say is that all matters concerning the area of responsibility of my department are under constant inquiry. *Constant*, I repeat. And now I really think, Herr Miller, there is nothing more I can do to help you."

IT TOOK Miller a week to get ready for his next move. He spent it reading books concerned with the war along the eastern front and the camps in the occupied eastern territories. It was the librarian at his local library who mentioned the Z-Commission.

"It's in Ludwigsburg," he told Miller. "I read about it in a magazine. Z-Commission is short for *Zentrale Stelle*. It's the only organization in the country that hunts Nazis on a nationwide, even an international level."

"Thanks," said Miller. "I'll see if they can help me."

Miller went to his bank the next morning and drew out all he had, leaving a ten-mark note to keep the account open.

He kissed Sigi before she went off to work, telling her he would be gone for a week, maybe more. Then he took the Jaguar from its underground home and headed south towards the Rhineland. The first snows were whistling in off the North Sea, slicing in flurries across the autobahn as it swept into Lower Saxony. He paused once for coffee, then pressed on across North Rhine/Westphalia. He stuck to the fast lane as always, pushing the Jag close to one-hundred miles an hour, watching the growling hulks of the heavy lorries swish past to his right as he overtook.

By six in the evening he was beyond the Hamm Junction and the glowing lights of the Ruhr began to be dimly discernible to his right through the darkness. When the autobahn went into an over-pass he could look down and see factories and chimneys stretching away into the December night, lights aglow from a thousand furnaces churning out the wealth of the economic miracle. Fourteen years ago as he travelled through it by train towards his school holiday in Paris, it had been rubble.

LUDWIGSBURG is a little market town set in the rolling, pleasant hills of Württemberg, fifteen miles north of Stuttgart. Set in a quiet road off the High Street is the home of the Z-Commission, an underpaid, overworked group of men dedicated to hunting down the Nazis and the SS who were guilty of mass-murder. Even though the Statute of Limitations had eliminated all SS crimes with the exception of murder and mass-murder, the Z-Commission still had 170,000 names in its files.

There were eighty detectives on the staff and fifty investigating attorneys. The lawyers were mainly taken from private practice, to which they would one day return. The detectives knew their careers were finished. For detectives prepared to hunt the SS in West Germany, promotion was finished in any other police force in the country.

Quite accustomed to having their requests for co-operation ignored, to seeing their loaned files go unaccountably missing, or their quarry disappear after an anonymous tip-off, the Z-Men worked on at a task they realized was not in accordance with the wishes of the majority of their fellow countrymen.

Miller found the Commission at 58, Schorndorfer Strasse, a large house inside an eight-foot-high wall. Two massive steel gates barred the way up the drive. When he pulled the bell handle a shutter slid back and a face appeared. "Please?"

"I would like to speak to one of your investigating attorneys," said Miller.

"Which one," said the face.

"Anyone will do. Here is my Press card."

The man shut the hatch and went away. When he came back it was to open the gate, lead Miller to the front door, and pass him over to another porter who showed him into a small waiting room. "Someone will be with you directly," he said and shut the door.

The man who came three minutes later was in his early fifties, mild-mannered and courteous. He handed Miller back his Press card and asked, "What can I do for you?"

Miller explained briefly about Tauber and Eduard Roschmann.

"Fascinating," the lawyer said.

"The point is, can you help me?"

"I wish I could," said the man, and for the first time since he had started asking questions, Miller believed him. "But I am bound hand and foot by the rules that govern our continued existence here. Which are that no information may be given out about any wanted SS criminal to anyone other than a person officially backed by one of a specific number of authorities."

"In other words, you can tell me nothing?" said Miller.

"Please understand," said the lawyer, "this office is under constant attack. Not openly, no one would dare. But privately, within the corridors of power, we are incessantly being sniped at. We are allowed no latitude where the rules are concerned."

"Have you, then, a newspaper cuttings reference library?"

"No, we don't."

"Is there in Germany any cuttings library open to the public?"

"Only those compiled by the newspapers and magazines. *Der Spiegel* is reputed to have the most comprehensive. And *Kosmos* has a very good one."

"I find this rather odd," said Miller. "Where in Germany today does a citizen inquire about investigation into war crimes, and get material on wanted SS criminals?"

"I'm afraid the citizen can't," the lawyer said uncomfortably.

"All right," said Miller, "where are the archives in Germany that refer to the men of the SS?"

"There's one set here, in the basement," said the lawyer. "All photostats. The originals of the entire card index of the SS were captured in 1945 by an American unit. At the last minute a group of the SS tried to burn their records. They got through about ten per cent before the American soldiers stopped them. The rest were all mixed up. It took two years to sort them out. Since then the entire SS-Index has remained in Berlin, under American direction."

"And that's it? Just two sets in the whole country?"

"That's it. I repeat, I wish I could help. If you should get anything on Roschmann, we'd be delighted to have it."

Miller thought. "If I find anything, there are only two authorities that can do anything with it. The Attorney General's Office in Hamburg, and you. Right?"

"Yes, that's all," said the lawyer.

"And you're more likely to do something positive with it than Hamburg." Miller made it a flat statement.

The lawyer gazed fixedly at the ceiling. "Nothing that comes here that is of real value gathers dust on a shelf."

"O.K. Point taken," said Miller and rose. "One thing, between ourselves, are you still looking for Eduard Roschmann?"

"Between ourselves, yes."

"And if he were caught, there'd be no problems about getting a conviction?"

"None at all."

"Give me your phone number," said Miller.

The lawyer took out a card and wrote on it. "My name and two phone numbers. Home and office. You can get me day or night. In every state police force there are men I can call and know I'll get action. There are others to avoid. So call me first, right?"

Miller pocketed the card. "I'll remember that," he said.

"Good luck," said the lawyer.

IT'S A long drive from Stuttgart to Berlin and it took Miller most of the following day. Fortunately it was dry and crisp and the Jaguar ate the miles northward past the sprawling carpet of Frankfurt to Hanover. Here Miller followed the branch-off to the border with East Germany. There was an hour's delay at the Marienborn checkpoint while he filled out the inevitable forms, and while the customs men and the green-coated People's Police poked around, in and under the Jaguar. There was a further delay at the entry into West Berlin where again the car was searched and his overnight case emptied onto the customs bench. Eventually he was through and the Jaguar roared towards the glittering ribbon of the Kurfurstendamm, brilliant with Christmas decorations. It was the evening of December 17th.

He decided not to go blundering into the American Document Centre the way he had in the Attorney General's office and the Z-Commission. Without official backing, he had come to realize, no one got anywhere with Nazi files in Germany.

So in the morning he called Karl Brandt in Hamburg for help.

Brandt was aghast. "I don't know anyone in Berlin."

"Well, think. You must have come across someone from the West Berlin force at one of the colleges you went to. I need him to vouch for me."

"I told you I didn't want to get involved."

"Well, you are involved. Either I get a look at that archive officially, or I blow in and say you sent me."

"I'll have to think," said Brandt, stalling for time.

"I'll give you an hour," said Miller, and he slammed down the receiver. When he called back Brandt was angry, and frightened, clearly wishing he had kept the diary to himself.

"There's a man I was at detective college with. I didn't know him well, but he's with Bureau One of the West Berlin force."

"What's his name?"

"Schiller. Volkmar Schiller, detective inspector."

To Miller's great relief Detective Inspector Volkmar Schiller was about his own age, and seemed to have his own cavalier attitude to red tape. Miller explained briefly what he wanted.

"I don't see why not," said Schiller. "The Americans are pretty helpful to us. Because we're charged with investigating Nazi crimes, we're in there almost every day."

They drove Miller's Jaguar to Number One, Wasserkäfersteig, in the suburb of Zehlendorf, Berlin 37. The building was a long, low, single-storey affair set amid the trees.

"Is that it?" said Miller incredulously.

"That's it," said Schiller. "Not much, is it? The point is, there are eight floors below ground level. That's where the archives are stored, in fireproof vaults."

Inside the front door was the inevitable porter's lodge. The detective proffered his police card. He was handed a form which he filled out and they were led into a larger room, set out with rows of tables and chairs. After a quarter of an hour a clerk quietly brought them a file. It was about an inch thick, stamped with the single title "Roschmann, Eduard." Volkmar Schiller rose.

"If you don't mind I'll be on my way," he said. "If you want anything photo-statted, ask the clerk." Miller rose and shook hands.

"Many thanks."

"Not at all."

Ignoring the other three or four readers hunched over their desks, Miller put his head between his hands and started to peruse the SS dossier on Eduard Roschmann.

It was all there. Nazi Party number, SS number, application forms, filled out and signed by the man himself, medical record, self-written life story, officer's commission, promotion certificates, right up to April 1945. There were also two photographs, one full-face, one profile. They showed a man with close shorn hair, a pointed nose, a lipless slit of a mouth, and a grim expression. Miller began to read. . . .

Eduard Roschmann was born on August 25th, 1908, in the

Austrian town of Graz, son of a highly respectable and honest brewery worker. He attended college to study law but failed. In 1931 at the age of twenty-three he began work in the brewery and in 1937 rose to an administrative job. That year he joined the Austrian Nazi Party and the SS, both then banned organizations in neutral Austria. A year later Hitler annexed Austria and rewarded the Austrian Nazis with swift promotions all round.

In 1939, at the outbreak of war, he volunteered for the Waffen-SS, was trained in Germany, served in a Waffen-SS unit in the overrunning of France. In December 1940 he was sent back to Berlin— here somebody had written in the margin the word "cowardice?"— and in January 1941 was seconded to the RSHA.

In August 1941 he became commandant of Riga ghetto. He returned to Germany by ship in October 1944 and after handing over the remaining Jews of Riga, reported to Berlin.

The file ended there, presumably because the SS clerk in Berlin re-assigned himself rather quickly in May 1945.

Attached to the back of the bunch of documents was a sheet bearing the typewritten words: "Inquiry made about this file by the British occupation authorities in December 1947."

Miller took from the file the self-written life story, the two photographs and the last sheet. With these he approached the clerk.

"Could I have these photo-copied please?"

"Certainly." A grey-coated man who had been reading in the room also tendered two sheets for copying.

Ten minutes later there was a rustle behind the clerk and two envelopes slid through an aperture. The clerk glanced quickly inside one of the envelopes.

"The file on Eduard Roschmann?" he queried.

"For me," said Miller and extended his hand.

"These must be for you," he said to the grey-coated man, who was glancing sideways at Miller. The other man took his own envelope and they walked to the door. Outside Miller ran down the steps and climbed into the Jaguar. An hour later he rang Sigi.

"I'm coming home for Christmas," he told her.

Two hours later he was on his way.

As Miller's Jaguar headed for home, the other man sat in his tidy flat off Savignyplatz, dialling a number in West Germany.

"I was in the Document Centre today. There was a man in there reading the file of Eduard Roschmann. He had three sheets photo-copied. After the message that went round recently, I thought I'd better tell you."

There was a burst of questions from the other end.

"No, I couldn't get his name. He drove away in a long black sports car. Yes. It was a Hamburg number plate."

He recited the number slowly for the man at the other end.

"Well, I thought I'd better. I mean, one never knows with these snoopers. Yes, thank you. Happy Christmas, *Kamerad*."

Chapter Six

Christmas Day was on the Wednesday of that week and it was not until after the Christmas period that the man in West Germany who had received the news about Miller in the Document Centre passed it on. When he did so, it was to his ultimate superior.

The man who took the call on a strictly private wire thanked his informant, put down the phone, leaned back in his leather-padded chair and gazed out of the window at the snow-covered rooftops.

"*Verdammt* and once again *verdammt*," he whispered. "Why now?"

The Werwolf thought back to his meeting with SS-General Gluecks in Madrid thirty-five days earlier, and to the importance of maintaining at any cost the security of the radio factory owner now preparing, under the code name Vulkan, the guidance systems for the Egyptian rockets. Alone in Germany, the Werwolf also knew that Vulkan was Eduard Roschmann.

He glanced down at the jotting pad on which he had scribbled the number of Miller's car and pressed a buzzer on his desk. His secretary's voice came through from the next room.

"Hilda, what was the name of that private investigator we employed last month on the divorce case?"

"One moment. . . . It was Memmers, Heinz Memmers."

"Give me his telephone number, will you? No, don't ring it. Just give me the number."

He noted it down then rose and crossed the room to a wall-safe. From the safe he took a thick book and flicked through the pages until he came to Memmers. There were only two listed, Heinrich and Walter. He ran his finger along the page opposite Heinrich, usually shortened to Heinz. He noted the date of birth, worked out the age of the man in late 1963 and recalled the face of the private investigator. The ages fitted.

He jotted down two other numbers listed against Heinz Memmers and picked up the telephone.

After a dozen rings, a gruff voice said, "Memmers Private Inquiries."

"Is that Herr Heinz Memmers?"

"Yes, who is that speaking?"

"Tell me, does the number 245.718 mean anything to you."

There was dead silence as Memmers digested the fact that his SS number had just been quoted at him. His voice came back, harsh with suspicion. "Should it?"

"Would it mean anything to you if I said that my own number had only five figures in it. . . . *Kamerad*?"

The change was electric. Five figures meant a very senior officer indeed.

"Yes, sir," said Memmers.

"Good," said the Werwolf. "Now. Some snooper has been inquiring into one of the *Kameraden*. I need to find out who he is. I have his car number." The Werwolf read it slowly. "Got that?"

"Yes, *Kamerad*."

"I want the name, address, profession, family, social standing . . . the normal rundown. How long would that take you?"

"About forty-eight hours," said Memmers.

"There is to be no approach made to the subject. He must not know any inquiry has been made. Is that clear?"

"Certainly. It's no problem."

"Very well then. I'll ring you back in two days."

MILLER set off from Hamburg the same afternoon. This time his destination was Bonn, the small town on the river's edge that Konrad Adenauer had chosen as the capital of the Federal Republic. Just south of Bremen his Jaguar crossed Memmer's Opel speeding north to Hamburg. Oblivious to each other, the two men flashed past on their separate missions.

It was dark when Miller entered the single long main street of Bonn and drew up beside a traffic policeman.

"How can I get to the British Embassy?" he asked.

The policeman pointed straight down the road. "Follow the tramlines," he said. "As you are about to leave Bonn and enter Bad Godesberg, you'll see it on your left."

Miller nodded his thanks and drove on. Outside the embassy he parked in one of the slots provided for visitors.

He walked through the glass doors and into a small foyer. "I would like to speak with the Press attaché, please," he said in his halting English. He proffered his Press card to the receptionist.

"I don't know if he's still here. I'll try him." She dialled a number on her house telephone. Miller was in luck.

The Press attaché, he was glad to see, seemed eager to help.

"What can I do for you?"

"I am investigating a story for a news magazine," Miller lied. "It's about a former SS captain, one of the worst, a man still sought by our own authorities. Can you tell me how I can check whether the British ever captured him, and if so what happened to him?"

The young diplomat was perplexed.

"Good Lord, I'm sure I don't know. I mean, we handed over all our records and files to your Government in 1949."

Miller decided to avoid mentioning that the German authorities had all declined to help.

"True," he said. "Very true. But my inquiries so far indicate he has not been put on trial in the Federal Republic since 1949. However, the American Document Centre in West Berlin reveals that a copy of the man's file was requested by the British in 1947. There must have been a reason for that, surely?"

"Yes, one would indeed suppose so,"said the attaché. His brow furrowed in thought.

"Who would your investigating authority have been?"

"Well, the investigations were carried out by the Provost Marshal and the trials were prepared by the Legal Branch. But the files of both were handed over in 1949. Do you see?"

"But surely copies must have been kept by the British?"

"I suppose they were," said the diplomat. "But they'd be filed away in the archives of the Army by now."

"Would it be possible to look at them?"

The attaché appeared shocked. "Oh, I very much doubt it. I suppose bona fide research scholars . . . but I don't think a reporter would be allowed to see them. No offence meant you understand?"

"I understand," said Miller. He rose, and so did the attaché.

"I don't really think the Embassy can help you."

"O.K. One last thing. Was there anybody here then who is still here now?"

"Oh no, they've all changed many times. Wait a minute, though, there's Cadbury. The sort of senior British Press chap. Married a German girl. He was here just after the war. You might ask him."

"Fine," said Miller. "Where do I find him?"

"Well, it's Friday. He'll probably be at his favourite place by the bar in the Cercle Français. Do you know it?"

"No, I've never been here before."

"Yes, well, it's in Bad Godesberg, just down the road."

MILLER found it, a hundred yards from the bank of the Rhine. Cadbury was not there, but the barman told Miller that if he did not come in that evening, he would almost certainly be there for pre-lunch drinks the following day.

Miller checked into the Dreesen Hotel down the road, then he dined at the Cercle Français hoping the Englishman would turn up. At eleven, he went back to the hotel to sleep.

Cadbury walked into the bar of the Cercle Français a few minutes before twelve the following morning, greeted a few acquaintances and seated himself at his favourite corner stool.

Miller rose and went over to him. "Mr. Cadbury?"

Bright blue eyes under shaggy grey eyebrows surveyed Miller warily. "Yes."

"My name is Miller. Peter Miller. I'm a reporter from Hamburg. May I talk with you a moment please?"

Anthony Cadbury gestured to the stool beside him.

"I think we had better talk in German, don't you?" he said, dropping into the language. "What can I do for you?"

Starting at the beginning, Miller told Cadbury the story from the moment of Tauber's death. The London man did not interrupt once. When Miller had finished he gestured to the barman to fill his own glass and bring another beer for Miller.

"Cheers," said Cadbury. "Well now, you've got quite a problem. I must say I admire your nerve."

"Nerve?" said Miller.

"It's not the most popular story to investigate among your countrymen in their present state of mind—as you have found out." The Englishman grinned. "A spot of lunch? My wife's away for the day."

Over lunch Miller asked about Cadbury's years in Germany.

"I came in as a war correspondent with Montgomery's army. About your age then. The headquarters was at Lüneburg. Covered the end of the war, all that. Then the paper asked me to remain. From then on, I just sort of stayed."

"Did you cover the Zonal War Crimes trials?" asked Miller.

Cadbury nodded while he chewed his steak.

"The ones held in the British Zone. The star criminals in our Zone were Josef Kramer and Irma Grese. Heard of them?"

"No, never."

"The Beast and Beastess of Belsen. Did you hear about Belsen?"

"Only vaguely," said Miller. "My generation wasn't told much about all that."

Cadbury shot him a shrewd glance. "But you want to know now?"

"We have to know sooner or later. May I ask you something? Do you hate the Germans?"

70

Cadbury considered the question for a minute.

"Just after the discovery of Belsen, a crowd of journalists went up for a look. I've never been so sickened in my life. In war you see terrible things. But nothing like Belsen. I think at that moment, yes, I hated them all."

"And now?"

"No. Not any longer. I married a German girl in 1948, and I live here. I wouldn't if I still felt the way I did in 1945."

"What caused the change?"

"Time. The passage of time. And the realization that not all Germans were Josef Kramers. Or Roschmanns. Mind you, I still can't get over a sneaking sense of mistrust for people of my own generation among your nation."

"And my generation?" Miller twirled his wine glass.

"They're better," said Cadbury. "Let's face it, you have to be better."

"Will you help me on Roschmann? Nobody else will."

"If I can," said Cadbury. "What do you want to know?"

"Do you recall him being put on trial in the British Zone?"

"No, I'm certain there was no trial against Roschmann in the British Zone of Germany. I'd remember the name."

"But why would the British authorities request a photo-copy of his career from the Americans in Berlin?"

"I don't know how he would have come to the attention of the British. At that time nobody knew about Riga. We got no information from the east. Yet that was where the overwhelming majority of the mass-murders took place. We were in an odd position. Eighty per cent of the crimes against humanity were committed east of what is now the Iron Curtain, but about ninety per cent of the men responsible were in the three western zones. Hundreds of guilty men slipped through our hands because we didn't know what they had done a thousand miles to the east."

"With Roschmann," said Miller, "where would one start to look? Among the British records?"

"Well, we can start with my own files. They're back at my house. Come on, it's a short walk."

Cadbury's study was lined with box files along two walls. Besides these, there were two grey filing cabinets in one corner.

"This cabinet is people, in alphabetical order. The other concerns subjects listed under subject headings. We'll start with the first one."

There was no folder with Roschmann's name on it.

"All right," said Cadbury. "Now for subject headings. There's one called Nazis, another for SS. A large section headed Justice has subsections about trials. Then there's War Crimes. Let's start."

It took them until nightfall to wade through those four files. Eventually Cadbury rose with a sigh.

"I'm afraid I have to go out to dinner tonight," he said. "The only things left to look through are these." He gestured to the box files along two of the walls.

Miller closed the file he was holding. "What are those?"

"Those," said Cadbury, "are nineteen years of dispatches from me to the paper. That's the top row. Below them are nineteen years of cuttings from the paper of news stories and articles about Germany and Austria. That's quite a lot to get through. Fortunately tomorrow is Sunday."

"It's very kind of you to take so much trouble," said Miller.

Cadbury shrugged. "I have nothing else to do this weekend. Meet me for a drink in the Cercle Français about eleven-thirty."

It was in the middle of Sunday afternoon that they found it. Anthony Cadbury suddenly shouted "Eureka!" It was one of his own dispatches headed "23rd December 1947".

"The paper didn't use it," he said. "Who wants to know about a captured SS man just before Christmas." He laid the sheet on the desk for Miller to read.

"British Military Government, Hanover, 23rd Dec—A former captain of the notorious SS has been arrested by British military authorities at Graz, Austria, and is being held pending further investigation.

"The man, Eduard Roschmann, was recognized on the streets of the Austrian town by a former inmate of a concentration camp, who alleged Roschmann had been the commandant of the camp in Latvia. After identification, Roschmann was arrested by members of the British Field Security Service in Graz.

"A request has been made to Soviet Zonal headquarters at Potsdam for further information about the concentration camp in Riga, Latvia, and a search for further witnesses is under way, the spokesman said. Meanwhile the captured man has been positively identified as Eduard Roschmann from his personal file, stored by the American authorities in their SS Index in Berlin."

"You got him," Miller breathed.

"I think this calls for a drink," said Cadbury.

MEMMERS was in his office on Monday morning at nine sharp. The call from the Werwolf came through at half-past.

"So glad you called, *Kamerad*," said Memmers. "I got back from Hamburg late last night."

"You have the information?"

"Certainly." Memmers began to read from his notes. "The owner of the car is a freelance reporter, one Peter Miller. Aged twenty-nine, about six feet tall, brown hair, brown eyes. Widowed mother lives in Osdorf, outside Hamburg. He lives in a flat in central Hamburg."

Memmers read off Miller's address and telephone number.

"He lives there with a girl, a striptease dancer, Miss Sigrid Rahn. He works mainly for the picture magazines. Apparently does very well. Specializes in investigative journalism. Like you said, *Kamerad*, a snooper."

"Any idea who commissioned him on this inquiry?"

"No, that's the funny thing. Nobody seems to know what he is doing at the moment. I checked with the girl by phone, claiming to be from a magazine. She said she did not know where he was, but expected a call this afternoon."

"Anything else?"

"Just the car. It's very distinctive. A black Jaguar, British model, with a yellow stripe down the side."

The Werwolf thought for a minute.

"Could you find out where he is now?" he asked.

"I think so," said Memmers. "I could ring the girl back this afternoon, saying I needed to contact Miller urgently. She sounded a simple girl on the phone."

"Yes, do that," said the Werwolf. "I'll ring you at four."

CADBURY rang Miller at the Dreesen Hotel at ten-thirty on Monday morning.

"Glad to get you before you left," he said. "I've got an idea. Meet me at the Cercle Français this afternoon around four."

At noon, Miller rang Sigi to tell her where he was.

When they met, Cadbury ordered tea. "If Roschmann was captured and identified as a wanted criminal," he said, "his case would have come under the eyes of the British authorities in our zone of Germany at the time. Have you ever heard of a man called Lord Russell of Liverpool?"

"No, never," said Miller.

"He was the legal adviser in all our war crimes trials during the occupation. Later he wrote a book called *The Scourge of the Swastika*. Didn't make him terribly popular in Germany, but it was quite accurate. He's retired now, lives in Wimbledon. I could give you a letter of introduction."

"Would he remember so far back?"

"He was reputed to have a memory like a filing cabinet. If he prosecuted the Roschmann case I'm sure he'd remember every detail."

Miller nodded. "Yes, I could fly to London to talk to him."

Cadbury stood up, reached into his pocket and produced an envelope. "I have the letter ready. Good luck."

THE WERWOLF'S phone rang just after four.

"His girl-friend got a call from him," said Memmers. "He's in Bad Godesberg, staying at the Dreesen Hotel."

The Werwolf put the phone down and thumbed through an address book. In a moment he picked up the phone again and rang a number in Bonn/Bad Godesberg.

74

MILLER went back to the hotel to book a flight from Cologne to London for the following day, Tuesday, December 31st. The receptionist pointed to a chair in the bay window.

"There's a gentleman to see you, Herr Miller."

Miller saw a middle-aged man holding a black Homburg and a rolled umbrella. He strolled over. "You wanted to see me?"

The man sprang up. "Herr Peter Miller?"

"Yes."

The man inclined his head in the short, jerky bow of old-fashioned Germans. "My name is Schmidt. Doctor Schmidt."

"What can I do for you?"

"I am told you are a journalist. Yes?" Dr. Schmidt smiled brightly. "You have a reputation for being very tenacious."

Miller remained silent.

"Some friends of mine heard you are engaged on an inquiry into events that happened . . . well, let us say . . . a long time ago. A very long time ago."

Miller stiffened and his mind raced. "An inquiry about a certain Eduard Roschmann," he said tersely. "So?"

"I just thought I might be able to help you." The man fixed his eyes kindly on Miller. "Captain Roschmann is dead."

"Indeed?" said Miller. "Can you tell me when he died?"

"Ah yes, of course." Dr. Schmidt seemed happy to oblige. "He was killed in Austria fighting the Americans in early 1945. His body was identified by several people who had known him."

"He must have been a remarkable man," said Miller.

Dr. Schmidt nodded. "Well, indeed, some of us thought so."

"Remarkable," Miller said, "to have been the first man since Jesus Christ to rise from the dead. He was captured alive by the British on December 20th, 1947, at Graz in Austria."

The doctor's eyes reflected the glittering snow along the balustrade outside the window.

"Miller, you are being very foolish. Permit me to give you a word of advice. Drop this inquiry."

Miller began to get angry.

"You make me sick, Herr Doktor. You and your whole stinking

gang. You are filth on the face of my country. So far as I am concerned I'll go on asking questions till I find him."

He turned to go, but the older man grabbed his arm. They stared at each other from a range of two inches.

"You're not stupid, Miller. But you're behaving as if you were. It's almost as if you had something personal in this matter."

"Perhaps I have," said Miller and walked away.

Chapter Seven

Miller knocked on the door of a house in a quiet street in Wimbledon. Lord Russell himself answered, a man in his late sixties wearing a cardigan and a bow tie.

"Mr. Anthony Cadbury gave me a letter of introduction to you," Miller said. "I hoped I might have a talk with you, sir."

Lord Russell gazed at him with perplexity. "Cadbury?"

"A British newspaper correspondent," said Miller. "He covered the war crimes trials at which you were Deputy Judge Advocate."

"Yes, Cadbury, newspaper chap. I remember now. Haven't seen him in years. Well, don't let's stand here. Come in, come in."

He turned and walked back down the hall and Miller followed. He hung his coat on a hook in the hall at Lord Russell's bidding and followed him into the back of the house where a welcoming fire burned in the sitting-room grate.

Miller held out the letter from Cadbury. Lord Russell took it, read it quickly and raised his eyebrows.

"Humph. Help in tracking down a Nazi? Is that what you came about? Well, sit down, sit down. No good standing around."

They sat in armchairs on either side of the fire.

"How come a young German reporter is chasing Nazis?"

"I'd better explain from the beginning," said Miller.

"I think you had better," said the peer. He filled his pipe and was puffing contentedly away when the German had finished.

"I hope my English is good enough," said Miller at last, when no reaction came from the retired prosecutor.

Lord Russell seemed to wake from a private reverie.

"Oh, yes, yes, interesting, very interesting. And you want to try and find Roschmann. Why?" He shot the question, and Miller found the old man's eyes boring into his own.

"The man should be brought to trial," he said stiffly.

"Humph. We all agree. The question is, will he be?"

Miller played it straight back. "If I can find him, he will be. The point is, sir, do you remember him?"

"Oh yes, I remember him. Or at least the name. Wish I could put a face to the name. There were so many of them."

Miller took the two photo-copies of Roschmann's picture from his breast pocket. Lord Russell gazed at the pictures, then rose and began to pace the sitting-room.

"Yes," he said at last, "I've got him. I can see him now. We got him in Graz. His file was sent on to me in Hanover. And you say that your man Tauber saw him in April 1945 driving west through Magdeburg in a car with several others?"

"That's what he said in his diary."

"All right young man, I'll fill in what I can. . . ."

ROSCHMANN and his SS colleagues in their army corporal uniforms made it as far as Munich, then split up. The American Army columns now sweeping through Bavaria were concerned with rumours that the Nazi hierarchy intended to shut themselves up in a fortress at Berchtesgaden and fight it out to the last man, so they paid scant attention to the hundreds of wandering German soldiers. Travelling by night across country, hiding by day in woodmen's huts and barns, Roschmann crossed into Austria and headed for the sanctuary of his home town. He had almost made it to Graz when he was challenged by a British patrol on May 6th. Foolishly he tried to run for it. As he dived into the undergrowth by the roadside a hail of bullets cut through the brushwood, and one passed clean through his chest, piercing one lung. After a quick search in the darkness the British Tommies passed on, leaving him undiscovered in a thicket. From there he crawled to a farmer's house half a mile away. Still conscious, he told the farmer the name

77

of a doctor in Graz, and for three months he was tended by friends, first at the farmer's house and then in the town itself. When he was fit enough to walk, the war was three months over and Austria under four-power occupation. Graz was in the heart of the British Zone.

All captured German soldiers were held by the British for two years in prisoner-of-war camps, and Roschmann, deeming a British camp the safest place to be, gave himself up. So from August 1945 to August 1947, while the hunt for the worst of the wanted SS murderers went on, he remained there at ease. He was using the name of a friend who had been killed in North Africa. Since the Allies had neither the time nor facilities to conduct a probing examination of Army corporals, the name was accepted as genuine. By the summer of 1947 Roschmann felt it safe to leave the custody of the camp. He was wrong.

One of the survivors of Riga had sworn his own vendetta. This old man haunted the streets of Graz, waiting for Roschmann to return to his home, the parents he had left in 1939 and the wife he had married while on leave in 1943, Hella Roschmann.

From his release in August Roschmann worked as a labourer in the fields outside Graz. Then on December 20th, 1947, he went home for Christmas.

The old man was waiting.

Within an hour two British sergeants of the Field Security Service, puzzled and sceptical, arrived at the house and knocked. After a quick search Roschmann was discovered under a bed. Had he brazened it out, he might easily have persuaded the sergeants that the old man was wrong. But hiding was the giveaway. He was led off to be interviewed by Major Hardy of the FSS, who promptly had him locked up while a request went off to Berlin for the American index of the SS.

Confirmation arrived in forty-eight hours, and the Americans asked for Roschmann to be transferred to Munich to give evidence at Dachau. The British agreed, and on January 8th, 1948, Roschmann, accompanied by two British sergeants, was put on a train bound for Salzburg and Munich.

LORD RUSSELL paused in his pacing and knocked out his pipe.

"Then what happened?" asked Miller.

"He escaped," said Lord Russell.

"He *what*?"

"He escaped. He jumped from the lavatory window of the moving train, after complaining the prison diet had given him diarrhoea. By the time his two escorts had smashed in the lavatory door, he was gone into the snow. They never found him. He had evidently made contact with one of the organizations which helped ex-Nazis escape."

"So—where does one go from here?" Miller asked.

Lord Russell blew out his cheeks. "Your own people, I suppose."

"Which ones?" asked Miller, fearing he knew the answer.

"As it concerns Riga, it should be the Hamburg Attorney General's office," said Lord Russell.

"I've been there, they didn't help."

Lord Russell grinned. "Not surprised, not surprised. Have you tried Ludwigsburg?"

"Yes. They were nice, but not helpful. Against the rules."

"Well, that exhausts the official lines of inquiry. There's only one other man. Have you ever heard of Simon Wiesenthal?"

"Wiesenthal? No."

"He lives in Vienna. Jewish chap who spent four years in a series of concentration camps, twelve in all. Decided to spend the rest of his days tracking down Nazi criminals. No rough-stuff, mind you. He just keeps collecting information. When he's convinced he has found one, he informs the police. If they don't act, he gives a Press conference and puts them in a spot. Needless to say, he's not terribly popular with officialdom."

"The name rings a bell now. Wasn't he the man who found Adolf Eichmann?" asked Miller.

Lord Russell nodded. "And several hundred others. If anything is known about your Eduard Roschmann, he'll know it. I'd better give you an introduction. He gets a lot of visitors."

He went to the writing desk and swiftly wrote a few lines.

"Good luck; you'll need it," he said as he showed Miller out.

THE NEXT morning Miller flew back to Cologne, picked up his car and set off on the two-day run to Vienna.

He made it to Vienna in the midafternoon of January 4th. He drove straight into the city centre and asked his way to Rudolf Square.

At number seven the list of tenants showed "Documentation Centre" to be on the third floor. He mounted and knocked at the cream-painted wooden door. From behind it someone looked through the peephole before the lock was drawn back. A pretty blonde girl stood in the doorway.

"Please?"

"My name is Miller. Peter Miller. I would like to speak with Herr Wiesenthal. I have a letter of introduction."

He gave it to the girl who smiled and asked him to wait.

A minute later she reappeared. "Please come this way."

Miller followed her down the passage to an open door. As he entered a man rose to greet him.

Simon Wiesenthal was a burly man over six feet tall, wearing a thick tweed jacket. Lord Russell's letter was in his hand.

The office was small and crammed with books. The desk stood away from the window, and Miller took the visitor's chair in front of it. The Nazi-hunter of Vienna seated himself behind it.

"My friend Lord Russell tells me you are trying to hunt down a former SS killer," he began without preamble.

"Yes, that's true."

"May I have his name?"

"Roschmann. Captain Eduard Roschmann."

Simon Wiesenthal exhaled in a whistle. "The Butcher of Riga? One of my top fifty wanted men. May I ask why you are interested in him?"

Miller started to explain briefly, but Wiesenthal held up his hand. "I think you had better begin at the beginning. What about this diary?"

This made the fourth time Miller had had to tell his tale. Each time it grew a little longer, another period having been added to his knowledge of Roschmann's life story. "What I have to know

80

now," he ended, "is where did he go when he jumped from the train?"

"Have you got the diary?" Wiesenthal asked. Miller took it out of his briefcase and laid it on the desk. Wiesenthal examined it appreciatively. "Fascinating." He looked up and smiled. "All right, I accept the story."

"Was there any doubt?" Miller asked.

Simon Wiesenthal eyed him keenly. "There is always a little doubt, Herr Miller. Yours is a very strange story. I still cannot follow your motive for wanting to track Roschmann down. Are you sure there's nothing personal in this?"

Miller ducked the question. "People keep suggesting that. Why should it be personal? I'm only twenty-nine years old. All this was before my time."

"Of course." Wiesenthal glanced at his watch and rose. "It is five o'clock, and I would like to get home to my wife. Would you let me read the diary overnight?"

"Yes. Of course," said Miller.

"Good. Then please come back tomorrow morning and I will fill in what I know of the Roschmann story."

MILLER arrived the next day at ten and found Simon Wiesenthal attacking a pile of letters. He gestured the reporter to a seat. "I read the diary. Remarkable document."

"Were you surprised?" asked Miller.

"Not by the contents. We all went through much the same sort of thing. But it's so precise. Tauber would have made a perfect witness. He noticed everything, even the small details. And noted them – at the time. That is very important to get a conviction before German or Austrian courts. And now he's dead."

"Herr Wiesenthal, you're the first Jew I have ever had a long talk with who went through all that. Tauber said there was no such thing as collective guilt. But we Germans have been told for twenty years that we are all guilty. Do you believe that?"

"No," said the Nazi-hunter flatly. "Tauber was right."

"How can you say that, if we killed all those millions?"

"You, personally, were not there. You did not kill anyone."
Wiesenthal regarded him intently. "Those who really were responsible for the killing were two sections of the SS. The Reich Economic Administration Main Office was charged with exploiting the victims before they died. Then when the economic exploitation was over, finishing the victims off was the task of the RSHA, the Reich Security Main Office. The rather odd use of the word 'Security' stems from the quaint Nazi idea that the victims posed a threat to the Reich, which had to be made secure against them."

Roschmann, Miller remembered, had been in the RSHA.

"If one is going to specify guilt, therefore," Wiesenthal went on, "that's where it rests—on those Economic and Security Offices of the SS, and the numbers involved are thousands, not the millions who make up contemporary Germany. The theory of the collective guilt of sixty million Germans suits the SS extremely well. Even today they hide behind it. They realize that so long as it's accepted nobody will start to look for specific murderers, at least, not look hard enough."

Miller digested this. "The reason Tauber apparently had for killing himself, do you believe it?"

"I believe he was right in thinking no one would believe him, that he saw Roschmann on the steps of the Opera."

"But he didn't even go to the police," said Miller.

After a pause Simon Wiesenthal replied. "No. I don't think it would have done any good. Not in Hamburg at any rate."

"What's wrong with Hamburg?"

"You went to the State Attorney General's office there?"

"Yes, I did. They weren't terribly helpful."

"I'm afraid the Attorney General's department in Hamburg has a certain reputation in this office," Wiesenthal said. "Take for example Gestapo chief and SS General Bruno Streckenbach. In 1940 he was head of the Security sections of the SS for the whole of Nazi-occupied Poland. Thousands were exterminated during that period. Just before the invasion of Russia he helped to organize the extermination squads that went in behind the Army.

"Then he was given the all-embracing responsibility for the

extermination squads throughout the Nazi-occupied Eastern
Territories until the end of the war."

"So where is he now?" asked Miller.

"Walking around Hamburg, as free as air," said Wiesenthal.

Miller looked stunned. "They haven't arrested him?"

Simon Wiesenthal rummaged in a drawer and produced a sheet
of paper. He folded it down from top to bottom, and handed it to
Miller so that ten names showed on the left side. "Do you recognize
those names?"

Miller scanned the list with a frown. "Of course. These are all
senior police officers of the Hamburg force. Why?"

"Spread the paper out," said Wiesenthal.

Miller did so. Fully expanded, the sheet read:

Name	Nazi Pty. No.	SS-No.	Rank	Promotion Date
A.	—	455,336	Capt.	1.3.43
B.	5,451,195	429,339	1st Lt.	9.11.42
C.	—	353,004	1st Lt.	1.11.41
D.	7,039,564	421,176	Capt.	21.6.44
E.	—	421,445	1st Lt.	9.11.42
F.	7,040,308	174,902	Major	21.6.44
G.	—	426,553	Capt.	1.9.42
H.	3,138,798	311,870	Capt.	30.1.42
I.	1,867,976	424,361	1st Lt.	20.4.44
J.	5,063,331	309,825	Major	9.11.43

Miller looked up. "My God," he said.

"Now do you begin to understand why a lieutenant-general of
the SS is walking around Hamburg today?"

AFTER the lunchtime break, Wiesenthal took up the Roschmann
story from the day he escaped from British custody, January 8th,
1948.

Roschmann had already been in touch with a Nazi escape
organization called the "Six-Point Star", so called because it had
tentacles in six major Austrian cities. After jumping from the train

into deep snow he had staggered as far as a peasant's cottage and taken refuge there. The following day he walked across the border of Upper Austria into Salzburg province and contacted the Six-Point Star. They took him to a brick factory where he passed as a labourer while arrangements were made with the Odessa for a passage to the south and Italy.

At that time the Odessa was in close contact with the French Foreign Legion, into which scores of former SS soldiers had fled. Four days after contact was made, a car with French number plates drove Roschmann and five other Nazi escapers over the Italian border to Merano, where the Odessa representative paid the driver, in cash, a hefty sum per head.

From Merano Roschmann was taken to Rimini, where he had the five toes of his right foot amputated, for they were rotten with frostbite he had picked up wandering through the snowy night of January 8th. His wife in Graz got a letter in October from Rimini in which for the first time he used the new name he had been given, Fritz Bernd Wegener.

Shortly afterwards he was transferred to the Franciscan Monastery in Rome. When his papers were ready he set sail from Naples for Buenos Aires. There he was received by the Odessa and lodged with a German family called Vidmar. Early in 1949 he was advanced the sum of 50,000 American dollars out of the Bormann funds in Switzerland, and went into business as an exporter of South American hardwood timber to Western Europe. The firm was called Stemmler and Wegener.

He engaged a German girl as his secretary, Irmtraud Sigrid Muller, and in early 1955 he married her, although his first wife, Hella, still lived in Graz. Soon afterwards, Eva Peron, the power behind the throne of Argentina, died of cancer. Roschmann saw that the writing was on the wall for the Peron régime, and that if Peron fell, much of the protection accorded to ex-Nazis might be removed. So, with his new wife, Roschmann left for Egypt.

He spent three months there in the summer of 1955, and came to West Germany in the autumn. Nobody would have known a thing but for the anger of a woman betrayed. Hella Roschmann had

written to her husband in care of the Vidmar family in Buenos
Aires. The Vidmars replied that he had gone back to Germany and
had married his secretary. Furious, the wife informed the police,
and asked for the arrest of Fritz Wegener on a charge of bigamy.

"Did they get him?" asked Miller.

Wiesenthal shook his head. "No, he disappeared again. Almost
certainly under a new set of papers, and almost certainly in
Germany. You see, that's why I believe Tauber could have seen
him."

"Is it worth contacting Hella Roschmann?" asked Miller.

"I doubt it," Wiesenthal said. "Roschmann is not likely to
reveal his whereabouts to her again. Or his new name. He must
have acquired his new papers in a devil of a hurry."

"Who would have got them for him?" asked Miller.

"The Odessa, certainly."

"Just what is the Odessa? You've mentioned it several times."

"You've never heard of them?" asked Wiesenthal.

"No. Not until now."

"Then you'd better come back tomorrow morning. I'll tell you all
about them."

Chapter Eight

Miller returned to Wiesenthal's office the following morning.
"You promised to tell me about the Odessa," he said, "but first
there is something that I forgot to tell you yesterday." And Peter
Miller went on to recount the incident of Doctor Schmidt who had
accosted him at the Dreesen Hotel and warned him off the
Roschmann inquiry.

Wiesenthal pursed his lips and nodded. "You're up against
them, all right. It's most unusual for them to take a step like that
with a reporter, particularly at such an early stage. I wonder what
Roschmann is up to that could be so important."

Then for two hours the Nazi-hunter told Miller about the
organization known as the Odessa.

WHEN the Allies stormed into Germany in 1945 and found the concentration camps with their hideous contents, they not unnaturally rounded on the German people to demand who had carried out the atrocities. The answer was "The SS"—but the SS were nowhere to be found.

Where had they gone? Either underground, or abroad. And it was no spur-of-the-moment flight. While the Nazis and the SS were screaming at the German people to fight on until the "wonder weapons" were delivered, they themselves prepared for comfortable exile. The SS bullied the German Army to take unbelievable casualties from the Russians for six months after defeat was inevitable, to give them time to complete their own escape plans. The SS stood behind the Army, shooting and hanging some of the Army men who took a step backward. Thousands of the Wehrmacht died in this way. It casts an interesting light on the so-called SS patriotism that from Heinrich Himmler down each of them tried to save his own skin at the expense of other Germans.

Just before the final collapse, the leaders of the SS all over the country quit their posts, stuffed their beautifully forged papers into the pockets of new civilian clothes, and vanished. They left the granddads of the Home Guard to meet the British and Americans at the gates of the concentration camps and the exhausted Wehrmacht to go into prisoner-of-war camps.

The Odessa was formed just before the end of the war to take charge of this mass disappearance. Those who were too well known to go underground had to flee abroad. To this end, the Odessa had established close links with Juan Peron. Argentina issued seven thousand passports "in blank" so that the refugee merely had to fill in a false name, his own photograph, get it stamped by the Argentine consul, and board a ship for Buenos Aires or the Middle East. SS refugees poured into the South Tyrol province of Italy and were shuttled to Genoa or, like Roschmann, to Rimini and the Franciscan Monastery in Rome. In some cases they travelled on Red Cross travel documents issued through the intervention of the Church, and in many cases the charitable organization Caritas paid for the tickets.

Just how many SS murderers passed to safety will never be known, but it was well over eighty per cent of those who would have faced death sentences.

The Odessa had succeeded in its first job. Now, having established itself comfortably on the proceeds of mass murder, transferred from Swiss banks, it sat back and watched the deterioration of relations between the Allies of 1945. With the establishment in May 1949 of a new Republic of West Germany, the leaders of the Odessa set out to infiltrate former Nazis into every facet of life in the new Germany.

Throughout the late forties and fifties former members of the Nazis slipped into lawyers' offices, onto judges' benches, into the police forces, local government and doctors' surgeries. From these positions they were able to protect each other from investigation and arrest, advance each others' interests and generally ensure that investigation and prosecution of former comrades—they call each other *"Kamerad"*—went forward as slowly as possible, if at all.

In politics, avoiding the high levels, former Nazis slipped into the grass roots of the ruling party at ward level. It may be a coincidence, but no politician with a record of calling for vigorous investigation of Nazi crimes has ever been elected in the CDU or the CSU (the Christian Democrat or Christian Socialist parties). One politician expressed it with crisp simplicity: "It's a question of election mathematics. Six million dead Jews don't vote. Five million former Nazis can and do, at every election."

The aim of this infiltration was simple. It was to slow down or stop the prosecution of former members of the Nazis. In this the Odessa had a great ally. This was the secret knowledge in the minds of hundreds and thousands that they had either helped in what was done, albeit in a small way, or had known what was going on and remained silent. Years later, respected in their communities, they could hardly relish the mention of their names in a faraway courtroom where a Nazi was on trial.

Odessa has also infiltrated business and industry in order to take full advantage of the staggering "economic miracle" of the fifties and sixties. Bankrolled from the Zürich deposits, former Nazis have developed businesses of their own whose profits help keep Odessa's funds flourishing. As a result, if any Nazi is forced to stand trial, his defence lawyers are among the most brilliant and the most expensive in Germany, regardless of the defendant's income.

The profits from these businesses also pay for propaganda. This takes many forms, from lobbying for the Statute of Limitations, which would end all legal culpability of the Nazis, to assuring the Germans of today that the death figures of Jews, Russians, Poles and others in the camps were but a tiny fraction of those quoted by the Allies—a hundred thousand dead Jews is the usual figure mentioned.

But the main object of Odessa propaganda is to persuade the seventy million Germans of today—and with a large degree of success—that the SS were patriotic soldiers like the Wehrmacht and that solidarity between the former comrades must be upheld. This is the weirdest ploy of them all, for the Wehrmacht regarded the SS with repugnance, while the SS treated the Wehrmacht with contempt. How former members of the Army, Navy, and Air Force can conceivably regard ex-SS men as *Kameraden* is a mystery. Yet herein lies the real success of the Odessa, which has, by and large, succeeded in impeding West German efforts to bring to trial the mass-murderers.

WHEN Simon Wiesenthal had finished, Miller laid down the pencil with which he had made notes. "I hadn't the faintest idea," he said.

"Few people have," conceded Wiesenthal. "The term Odessa is not used much nowadays. The new name is 'The Comradeship', just as the Mafia in America is called the 'Cosa Nostra'. But the Odessa is still there, and will be while there is still an SS criminal to protect."

"And you think these are the men I'm up against?"

"I'm sure of it. Dr. Schmidt's warning could not have come from anyone else. Be careful, these men can be dangerous."

Miller's mind was on something else.

"When Roschmann's first wife gave away the Wegener name, how would the Odessa get him the new passport you said he must now have?"

"They probably have a forger somewhere who turns them out."

"So if one found the passport forger, one might find Roschmann."

Wiesenthal shrugged.

"One might. But to do that one would have to penetrate the Odessa. Only an ex-SS man could do that."

"Then where do I go from here?" said Miller.

"I should think your best bet would be to try and contact some of the survivors of Riga. Look. . . ." He flicked open Tauber's diary. "There's reference here to an Olli Adler from Munich, who was in Roschmann's company during the war. It may be she survived and came home to Munich."

Miller nodded. "If she did, where would she register?"

"At the Jewish Community Centre. It contains the archives of the Jewish Community of Munich. I should try there."

"Do you have the address?"

"Reichenbachstrasse, number twenty-seven, Munich," said Wiesenthal.

He rose and escorted Miller to the front door.

"Good luck," he said, "and let me know how you get on."

Chapter Nine

The next morning, Miller found himself at an inquiry desk on the third floor of 27, Reichenbachstrasse in Munich. The room was lined with books, all new, for the original library had long since been burnt by the Nazis. There was a rack of newspapers, some in German, others in Hebrew. A short dark man was scanning the front page of one of the latter.

"Can I help you?" The inquiry desk was occupied by a dark-eyed woman in her mid-forties.

Miller made his request: any trace of Olli Adler, who might have reported back to Munich after the war?

"Where would she have returned from?" asked the woman.

"From Riga."

"Oh dear," said the woman. "I don't think we have anyone listed who came back here from Riga. But I'll look."

She went into a back room and returned after five minutes.

"I'm sorry. There is nobody listed under that name."

"Would there be anybody else left in Munich who was at Riga? The man I'm really trying to find is the former commandant."

There was silence in the room. Miller sensed that the man by the newspaper rack had turned round to look at him.

"It is possible there might be someone. But I'd have to go through the whole list of survivors. Could you come back tomorrow?"

"Yes," Miller said. "I'll come back. Thank you."

He was in the street, reaching for his car keys, when he heard a step behind him.

"Excuse me," said a voice. He turned. The man behind him was the one who had been reading the newspaper.

"You are inquiring about the commandant of Riga?" asked the man. "Would that be Captain Roschmann?"

"Yes, it would," said Miller. "Why?"

"I was at Riga." The man was short and wiry, somewhere in his mid-forties, with button-bright brown eyes. "My name is Mordechai, but people call me Motti. Shall we have a coffee and talk?"

They adjourned to a nearby coffee-shop. Miller described his hunt. The man listened quietly.

"Mmmm," he said finally. "Why should you, a German, want to track down Roschmann?"

"Why shouldn't a German be angry at what was done?"

Motti shrugged. "It's unusual for a man to go to such lengths, that's all. About Roschmann's last disappearance—D'you really think he has a passport provided by the Odessa?"

"I've been told so. And it seems that the only way to find the man who forged it would be to penetrate the Odessa."

Motti considered the young man in front of him for some time.

90

"What hotel are you staying at?" he asked, at length.

Miller told him he had not checked in yet, but planned to go to one he had stayed in before. At Motti's request he went to the telephone and called the hotel.

When he got back to the table Motti had gone. There was a note under the coffee cup. It said, "Whether you get a room there or not, be in the lounge at eight tonight."

Miller paid for the coffees and left.

THAT same afternoon the Werwolf read once again the written report that had come in from his "Doctor Schmidt" in Bonn. The last words General Gluecks had spoken in Madrid virtually robbed him of freedom of action. "A permanent solution" had been the order, and he knew what that meant.

Nor did the phraseology of "Dr. Schmidt" leave him any more room for manoeuvre: "A stubborn young man, truculent and headstrong, and with an undercurrent of personal hatred for the *Kamerad* in question, Eduard Roschmann, for which no explanation seems to exist. Unlikely to listen to reason, even in the face of personal threat. . . ."

The Werwolf sighed and reached for the phone. He dialled a number in Düsseldorf.

After several rings a voice said simply, "Yes."

"There's a call for Herr Mackensen," said the Werwolf.

The voice at the other end said, "Who wants him?"

"Werwolf," replied the chief of the Odessa. "There is work to be done. Get over here by tomorrow morning."

"What time?" asked Mackensen.

"Be here at ten," said the Werwolf. "Tell my secretary your name is Keller."

In Düsseldorf, Mackensen went into his bathroom to shower and shave. He was a big, powerful man, a former sergeant of the Das Reich division of the SS, who had learned his killing when hanging French hostages in Tulle and Limoges, back in 1944. After the war he had driven a truck for the Odessa, running human cargoes into the South Tyrol. In 1946, stopped by an American patrol, he had slain all four occupants of the Jeep, two of them with his bare hands.

He had been employed later as a bodyguard for senior men of the Odessa and in the mid-fifties he had become the Odessa executioner. By January 1964 he had fulfilled twelve assignments.

THE CALL came on the dot of eight. It was taken by the reception clerk who put his head round the corner of the hotel lounge, where Miller sat watching television.

He recognized the voice on the phone.

"Herr Miller? It's me, Motti. I have friends who may be able to help you. Would you like to meet them?"

"I'll meet anybody who can help me," said Miller.

"Good," said Motti. "Turn left down Schillerstrasse for two blocks. Meet me at Lindemann's coffee-shop right away."

Miller took his coat and walked out through the doors. Half a block from the hotel something was jabbed into his ribs from behind, and a car slid up to the kerb.

"Get into the back seat, Herr Miller," a voice breathed.

The door nearest him swung open, and Miller ducked his head and got in. In the back seat another man slid over to make room. He felt the man behind him enter the car also.

His heart was thumping as the car slid from the kerb. He recognized none of the men. The one to his right said, "I am going to bind your eyes."

Miller felt a sort of black sock pulled over his head until it covered his nose. He recalled what Simon Wiesenthal had told him: Be careful, the men of the Odessa can be dangerous.

They drove for twenty-five minutes then the car slowed and stopped. He was eased out of the back seat, and with a man on each side was led across some cobblestones. For a moment he felt the cool night air on his face, then he was back inside again. A voice said, "Take off the blindfold," and the sock over his head was removed.

The room he was in was evidently below ground for there were no windows. It was well decorated and comfortable. There was a

long table close to the far wall with eight chairs around it. Motti stood smiling almost apologetically beside the table. The two men who had brought Miller in offered him a chair and sat down at his left and right. Across the table was another man, about sixty, Miller thought, lean and bony, with a hollow-cheeked, hook-nosed face. It was he who spoke.

"Welcome, Herr Miller. I apologize for the strange way in which you were brought to my home. The reason for it was that if you decide to turn down my proposal, you can return to your hotel and never see any of us again.

"My friend here," he gestured to Motti, "informs me that for reasons of your own you are hunting a certain Eduard Roschmann. And that to get closer to him you might be prepared to attempt to penetrate the Odessa. We might be prepared to help you."

Miller stared at him in astonishment.

"Are you telling me you are not from the Odessa?" he said.

The man leaned forward and drew back the sleeve of his left wrist. On the forearm was tattooed a number in blue ink. "Auschwitz." He pointed to the men at Miller's sides. "Buchenwald and Dachau." He pointed to Motti. "Riga and Treblinka. Herr Miller, there are some who think the murderers of our people should be brought to trial. I and my group do not agree. We stayed on in Germany after 1945 with one object and one only in mind. Revenge. We don't arrest them, Herr Miller, we kill them like the swine they are. My name is Leon."

LEON interrogated Miller for four hours before he was satisfied with the reporter's genuineness. When he had finished, he leaned back and surveyed the younger man. "Are you aware how risky it is to try and penetrate the Odessa?"

"I can guess," said Miller. "For one thing I'm too young."

"There would be no question of using your own identity, of course. There is a list of former SS men and Peter Miller's name is not on it. And you will, as you say, have to age ten years at least. You will have to take on, completely, the identity of a man who really was in the SS."

94

"Do you think you can find such a man?" asked Miller.

Leon shrugged. "It would have to be one whose death cannot be checked out by the Odessa. In addition you will have to pass all the Odessa tests. That means living for five or six weeks with a former SS man who can teach you the phraseology, the behaviour patterns. Fortunately we know such a man."

Miller was amazed. "Why should he do such a thing?"

"He is a former SS captain who sincerely regretted what was done. He was inside the Odessa, and passed information about wanted Nazis to the authorities. He would be doing so yet, but he was 'shopped' and was lucky to escape with his life. Now he lives under a new name, in a house outside Bayreuth."

"What else would I have to learn?"

"Everything about your new identity. Where the man was born, his date of birth, how he got into the SS, where he trained, where he served, his unit, his commanding officer, his entire history from the end of the war onward. You will also have to be vouched for by a guarantor. That will not be easy. A lot of time and trouble will have to be spent on you, Herr Miller."

"What's in this for you?" asked Miller suspiciously.

Leon rose and paced the carpet. "The worst of the SS killers are living under false names," he said. "Those names are on file. We want those names. There's one other thing. We need to know who is the new recruiting officer of the Odessa for German rocket scientists to work in Egypt."

"Have you ever tried to get your own men inside the Odessa?"

Leon nodded. "Twice," he said.

"What happened?"

"The first was found floating in a canal without fingernails. The second disappeared without trace. Do you still want to go ahead?"

Miller ignored the question.

"If you are so efficient, why were they caught?"

"They were both Jewish," said Leon shortly. "We tried to get the tattoos off their arms, but they left scars. Besides, they were both circumcised. By the way, are you circumcised?"

"Does it matter?" inquired Miller.

"Of course. If a man is circumcised it does not prove he's a Jew. Many Germans are circumcised as well. But if he is not, it more or less proves he is not a Jew."

"I'm not," said Miller shortly.

Leon breathed a long sigh.

"This time, I think we may be able to get away with it."

It was long past midnight. Leon looked at his watch. "Motti, I think a little food for our guest."

Motti grinned and disappeared through the door.

"You'll have to spend the night here," said Leon to Miller. "Give me your car keys and I'll have your car brought round. It will be better out of sight. We'll take care of your hotel bill and luggage. You must write to your mother and girl-friend, explaining that you'll be out of contact for several weeks. Understood?"

Miller nodded and handed over his car keys.

"In the morning we will drive you to Bayreuth and you will meet our SS officer. His name is Alfred Oster. Meanwhile, excuse me. I have to start looking for your new identity."

As he ate the cold chicken and potato salad that Motti brought him, Miller wondered what he had let himself in for.

FAR away to the north, in the General Hospital of Bremen, an orderly was patrolling his ward in the small hours of the morning. At the end of the room was a screen. The orderly, a man called Hartstein, peered round at the man in bed behind it. He lay very still. The orderly checked the patient's pulse. There was none.

Something the patient had said in delirium caused the orderly to lift his left arm. Inside the armpit a number was tattooed—his blood group, a sure sign of an ex-SS.

Orderly Hartstein covered the dead man's face and glanced into the drawer of the bedside table. He drew out the driving licence that had been placed there along with the man's other personal possessions. It showed a man of thirty-eight, date of birth June 18th, 1925; name, Rolf Gunther Kolb.

The orderly slipped the driving licence into his pocket and went off to report the death to the night physician.

Chapter Ten

Shortly before noon Peter Miller and Motti, accompanied by the driver of the previous night, set off for Bayreuth. Once in the back of the car the black sock was again pulled over his head. He was pushed to the floor and kept blindfolded until they were well clear of Munich. They lunched at a wayside inn at Ingolstadt and were at Bayreuth an hour later.

In January Bayreuth is a quiet little town, blanketed by snow. They found the cottage of Alfred Oster on a by-road a mile beyond the town and there was not another car in sight as the small party went to the front door.

The former SS officer was a big bluff man with blue eyes and a fuzz of ginger hair. Despite the season, he had the healthy tan of men who live in the sun and the mountain air.

Motti handed Oster a letter from Leon. The Bavarian read it, glancing sharply at Miller. "Well, we can always try," he said. "How long can I have him?"

"Until he's ready," said Motti, "and until we can devise a new identity for him. We will let you know."

A few minutes later he was gone.

Oster led Miller into the sitting-room. "So, you want to be able to pass as a former SS man, do you?" he asked.

Miller nodded. "That's right."

"Well, we'll start by getting a few basic facts right. I don't know where you did your military service, but I suspect in that ill-disciplined, democratic, wet-nursing shambles that calls itself the new German Army. Here's the first fact. The new German Army would have lasted exactly ten seconds against any crack regiment of the British, American or Russians during the last war.

"Here's the second fact. The Waffen-SS were the toughest, best-disciplined, fittest bunch of soldiers who ever went into battle in the history of this planet. Whatever they did can't change that. *So smarten up, Miller.* So long as you remain in this house this is the procedure.

"When I walk into a room you leap to attention. And I mean *leap*. You smack those heels together and remain at attention until I am five paces beyond you. When I say something to you that needs an answer, you reply: '*Jawohl*, Herr Hauptsturmfuehrer.' And when I give an order or an instruction, you reply: '*Zu Befehl*, Herr Hauptsturmfuehrer.' Is that clearly understood?"

Miller nodded in amazement.

"Heels together," roared Oster. "I want to hear the leather smack. All right, since we may not have much time, we'll press on. Before supper we'll tackle the ranks, from private up to full general. You'll learn the titles, mode of address, uniform and collar insignia of every SS rank that ever existed in any branch of the SS.

"After that I'll put you through the full political-ideological course that you would have undergone at Dachau SS training camp. Then you'll learn the marching songs, the drinking songs and the various unit songs. I can get you as far as your departure from training camp for your first posting. Beyond that Leon has to tell me what unit you were supposed to have joined, who was your commanding officer, what happened to you at the end of the war, how you have passed your time since 1945. However, the first part of the training will take from two to three weeks.

"By the way, don't think this is a joke. Once inside the Odessa, if you make one slip you'll end up in a canal. Believe me, I'm no milksop, but after betraying the Odessa, even I am running scared. That's why I live here under a new name."

For the first time since he had set off on his one-man hunt for Eduard Roschmann, Miller wondered if he had not gone too far.

MACKENSEN, the Odessa executioner, reported to the Werwolf on the dot of ten. The Werwolf seated him in the client's chair opposite his desk and lit a cigar.

"There is a certain person, a newspaper reporter, inquiring about the whereabouts of one of our comrades," he began. The liquidator nodded. Other briefings had begun in the same way.

"The man he is seeking is of absolutely vital importance to us and to our long-term planning. The reporter himself seems to be intelligent, tenacious, ingenious, and wholly committed to extracting a sort of personal vengeance from the *Kamerad*."

"Any motive?" asked Mackensen. The Werwolf's puzzlement showed in his frown. He tapped ash from his cigar before replying.

"We cannot understand why there should be, but evidently there is," he murmured. "The man he is looking for commanded a ghetto in Ostland. Some, mainly foreigners, refused to acknowledge our justification for what was done there. The odd thing about this reporter is that he is neither foreign nor Jewish. He's a young German, Aryan, son of a war hero, nothing in his background to suggest such a depth of hatred towards us. It gives me some regret to order his death. Yet he leaves me no alternative."

"Whereabouts?"

"Not known. A good place to start would be his own flat, where his girl-friend lives with him. If you present yourself as a man sent by one of the magazines for which he works, the girl will probably talk to you. He drives a noticeable car. You'll find the details here." The Werwolf handed him a sheet of paper.

"I'll need money," said Mackensen. The Werwolf pushed a wad of 10,000 marks across the desk.

"And the orders?" asked the killer.

"Locate and liquidate," said the Werwolf.

IT was January 13th before news of the death in Bremen hospital of Rolf Gunther Kolb reached Leon in Munich. The letter from his north-German representative included the dead man's driving licence. Leon checked that Kolb was on the SS list, and that he was *not* on the West German "wanted" list, then he called Motti.

"Here's the man we need," he said, handing him Kolb's driving licence. "He was a staff-sergeant at the age of nineteen, promoted just before the war ended. They must have been very short of material. Kolb's face and Miller's don't match, but the height and build fit. So we'll need a new photograph. That can wait. To cover the photograph we'll need a replica of the stamp of the Bremen Police Traffic Department. See to it."

When Motti had gone, Leon dialled a number in Bremen.

99

"ALL RIGHT," said Alfred Oster to his pupil. "Now we'll start on the songs. You've heard of the Horst Wessel? I'll have to teach you about a dozen songs, but this is the most important. Not to know it would be a death sentence. Now, after me. . . .

> "The flags are high,
>   The ranks are tightly closed . . ."

It was January 18th.

MACKENSEN sipped a cocktail in the Schweizer Hof hotel in Munich and considered his problem: Miller and his car had vanished.

Inquiries at his flat had led to a conversation with the handsome and cheerful girl-friend. She had produced a letter postmarked Munich, saying Miller would be staying there for a while.

Mackensen had checked every Munich hotel, public and private parking space, and petrol station. There was nothing. The man he sought had disappeared as if from the face of the earth.

Finishing his drink Mackensen eased himself off his bar stool and went to telephone the Werwolf. Although he did not know it, he stood just twelve hundred metres from the black Jaguar with the yellow stripe, parked in the courtyard of the antique shop where Leon lived and ran his small and fanatic organization.

IN Bremen General Hospital a man in a white coat strolled into the Registrar's Office. He had a stethoscope round his neck, almost the badge of a new intern.

"I need a look at the medical file on one of our patients, Rolf Gunther Kolb," he told the filing clerk.

The woman did not recognize the intern, but there were scores of them working in the hospital. She found the Kolb dossier and handed it to him. The phone rang and she went to answer it.

The intern sat down and flicked through the dossier. It revealed simply that Kolb had collapsed in the street and been brought in by ambulance. An examination had diagnosed cancer of the stomach. A decision had been made not to operate. The patient had been put on a series of drugs, and later on pain-killers. The last sheet in the file stated simply: "Patient deceased on the night of 8th/9th

January. Cause of death: carcinoma of the large intestine. *Corpus delicti* delivered to the municipal mortuary 10th January."

The new intern eased the last sheet out of the file and inserted in its place one of his own. This one read:

"Despite serious condition of patient the carcinoma responded to treatment and went into remission. On 16th January, patient was transferred at his own request to the Arkadia Klinik, Delmenhorst, for convalescence."

The intern gave the file back to the clerk, thanked her with a smile and left.

It was January 22nd.

THREE days later Leon filled in the last section of his private jigsaw puzzle.

A ticket agent reported that a certain bakery proprietor in Bremerhaven had booked a winter cruise for himself and his wife. The pair would tour the Caribbean for four weeks, leaving from Bremerhaven on Sunday, February 16th. Leon knew the man to have been a colonel of the SS during the war, and a member of Odessa after it. He ordered Motti to go out and buy a book of instructions on the art of making bread.

THE Werwolf was puzzled. For nearly three weeks he had had his representatives in the major cities of Germany on the lookout for a man called Miller and a black Jaguar sports car. Several telephone calls had been made to a girl called Sigi, purporting to come from the editor of a major picture magazine, but the girl had said she did not know where her boy-friend was. Inquiries had been made at his bank. He had cashed no cheques since November. In short, he had disappeared.

It was already January 28th, and the Werwolf felt obliged to make a phone call.

HALF AN HOUR later, far away, high in the mountains, a man put down his telephone and swore softly. It was a Friday evening and he had returned to his weekend manor for two days of rest.

He walked to the window of his elegantly appointed study and looked out. The light from the window spread over the thick carpet of snow on the lawn, the glow reaching away towards the pine trees that covered most of the estate.

The call he had taken disturbed him. He had told the caller there had been no one spotted near his house, no one hanging around his factory; but he was worried. Miller? Who the hell was Miller? The assurances on the phone that the reporter would be taken care of only partly assuaged his anxiety. The seriousness with which the caller and his colleagues took the threat posed by Miller was indicated by the decision to send him a personal bodyguard the next day, to stay with him until further notice.

He drew the curtains of the study, shutting out the winter landscape. The thickly padded door cut out all sounds from the rest of the house. The only sound in the room was the crackle of fresh pine logs in the hearth, the cheerful glow framed by the great fireplace with its wrought-iron vine leaves and curlicues.

The door opened and his wife put her head round.

"Dinner's ready," she said.

"Coming, dear," said Eduard Roschmann.

THE next morning, Saturday, a party from Munich arrived at Oster's house. The car contained Leon and Motti, the driver and a man with a black bag.

Leon said to the man with the bag. "You'd better get up to the bathroom and set out your gear."

They all sat at the table and Leon asked, "How is he so far?" Miller might as well not have existed.

"Pretty good," said Oster. "I gave him a two-hour interrogation yesterday and he could pass."

Leon passed a driving licence over to Miller. Where the photograph had been was a blank.

"That's who you are going to become," he said. "Rolf Gunther Kolb, born June 18th, 1925. That would make you nineteen at the end of the war, and thirty-eight now. You were born and brought up in Bremen. You joined the Hitler Youth at the age of ten and the SS in January 1944 at eighteen. Both your parents were killed in an air raid in 1944."

"What about his career in the SS?" asked Oster.

"We don't know Kolb's career with the SS," Leon said. "It couldn't have been much, for he's not on any wanted list and nobody's ever heard of him. In a way that's just as well, for the chances are the Odessa have never heard of him either. But he'd have no reason to seek help from the Odessa unless he was being pursued. So we have invented a career for him. Here it is."

When he had finished reading the papers Leon gave him, Oster nodded. "It's good. It would be enough to get him arrested if he were exposed."

Leon grunted with satisfaction. "We have also found a guarantor for him. A former SS colonel in Bremerhaven is going on a sea-cruise on February 16th. He owns a bakery. When Miller presents himself as Kolb after February 16th, he will have a letter from this man assuring the Odessa that Kolb, his employee, is genuinely a former SS man and genuinely in trouble. By that time the bakery owner will be on the high seas and uncontactable. By the way," he handed Miller a book, "you can learn baking as well."

He did not mention that the bakery owner would be away for only four weeks and that after that Miller's life would hang by a thread.

"Now my friend the barber is going to change your appearance somewhat," Leon told Miller. "After that we'll take a new photograph for the driving licence."

In the upstairs bathroom the barber cut Miller's hair until his white scalp gleamed through the stubble. The rumpled look was gone. His eyebrows, too, were plucked until they were almost gone.

"Bare eyebrows make the age almost unguessable within six or seven years," said the barber. "There's one last thing. We'll fake a moustache for the photograph. It adds years, you know. Can you grow one to match in three weeks?"

"Sure," Miller said, gazing at his reflection. He looked in his mid-thirties already.

When they got downstairs Miller stood up against a white sheet, and Motti took several photographs of him.

"I'll have the licence ready within three days," he said.

The party left and Oster turned to Miller.

"Right, Kolb," he said, having long ceased to refer to him in any other way, "you were trained at Dachau, seconded to Flossenbürg in July 1944. In April 1945 you commanded the squad that executed Admiral Canaris and other Army officers suspected of complicity in the July 1944 assassination attempt on Hitler. O.K. lets get down to work, Staff Sergeant."

THE man who sat in the window seat of the Olympic Airways flight from Athens to Munich seemed quiet and withdrawn. He had been born in Germany thirty-three years earlier, as Josef Kaplan, son of a Jewish tailor, in Karlsruhe. Three years old when Hitler came to power, seven when his parents had been taken away in a black van, he had been hidden in an attic for another three years until, at the age of ten in 1940, he too had been discovered and taken away. He had used the resilience and ingenuity of youth to survive in a series of concentration camps until 1945.

Two years later, aged seventeen and as hungry as a rat, with that creature's mistrust of everyone and everything, he had come on a ship to a new shore many miles from Karlsruhe and Dachau. There he had taken the name of Uri Ben Shaul.

The passing years had given him a wife and two children and a major's commission in the army, but never eliminated the hatred he felt for the country to which he was travelling that day. He had agreed to swallow his feelings, to take up again as he had done twice before the façade of easy amiability that was necessary to effect his transformation back into a German. The Mossad Service had provided the other necessities, the passport, letters, cards, all the documentary paraphernalia of a citizen of a West European country, and the clothes and luggage of a German commercial traveller.

As the heavy clouds of Europe engulfed the plane he reconsidered his mission. To follow a man. To keep an eye on a young German four years his junior while that man sought to do what several others had tried to do and failed, to infiltrate the Odessa. To check on the young man's findings and ascertain if he could trace the recruiter of the new wave of German scientists headed for Egypt to work on the rockets. Then to report back with the sum total of what the young man had discovered before he was "blown", as he was bound to be. He would do it; he did not have to enjoy doing it. Fortunately no one asked him to like becoming a German again.

ON February 16th, Oster and Miller had their last visit from Leon. Apart from Leon and Motti, there was a new man who was introduced simply as Josef.

"By the way," Motti told Miller, "I drove your car up here today. I've left it on a public parking lot down in the town, by the market square."

He tossed Miller the keys, adding, "Don't use it when you go to meet the Odessa. It's too conspicuous."

Miller nodded, but privately he regretted being separated from his beloved Jaguar.

"Here is your driving licence, complete with your photograph as you now look. You can tell anyone who asks that you drive a Volkswagen, but you have left it in Bremen, as the number could identify you to the police.

"The man who, unbeknown to him, is your guarantor, left from Bremerhaven on a cruise ship this morning. His name is Joachim Eberhardt. Here is a letter from him to the man you are going to see. The paper was taken from his office. The signature is a perfect forgery. The letter tells its recipient that you are a good former SS man now fallen on misfortune, and asks him to help you acquire a new identity."

"Who's the man I have to present myself to?" Miller asked.

Leon handed him a sheet of paper.

"That is his name and his address in Nuremberg. We are certain that he is very high up in the Odessa. He may have met Eberhardt, who is a big wheel in the Odessa in North Germany. Here is

Eberhardt's photograph. Study it, in case your man asks for a description of him. I think you should probably present yourself on Thursday morning next."

Miller nodded. "All right. Thursday it is."

"Remember," said Leon, "that we want to know who is recruiting rocket scientists for Egypt. And we want the Odessa's list of their top men in Germany. One last thing. Stay in touch. Use public telephones and phone this number whenever you get anything. The number will always be manned, even if I am not there."

He passed Miller a card.

"Memorize and destroy it."

Twenty minutes later the group was gone.

ON the way back to Munich, Leon and Josef sat in silence, the Israeli agent hunched in his corner.

"Why so gloomy?" Leon asked finally. "Everything is going well."

Josef glanced at him.

"How reliable is this man Miller?"

"Reliable? He's the best chance we've ever had for penetrating the Odessa. You heard Oster. He can pass for a former SS man anywhere, provided he keeps his head."

"My brief was to watch him at all times," Josef grumbled. "I ought to be reporting back on every man he talks to. I wish I'd never agreed to let him go off alone. He's an amateur. Supposing he doesn't check in?"

Leon's anger was barely controlled. It was evident they had been through this before. "Now listen one more time. This man is *my* agent. I've waited years to get someone where he is now—a non-Jew. I'm not having him exposed by someone tagging along behind him."

BACK in Bayreuth, Miller stared out of the window at the falling snow. Privately he had no intention of checking in by phone. He had no interest in rocket scientists. He had only one objective— Eduard Roschmann.

Chapter Eleven

On the evening of Wednesday, February 19th, Peter Miller bade farewell to Alfred Oster and headed for Nuremberg. He walked the mile to the railway station, and once there bought a single ticket to Nuremberg. It was only as he passed through the barrier towards the platform that the ticket collector told him: "I'm afraid the Nuremberg train will be quite late tonight."

"What's happened?" Miller asked. The ticket collector nodded up the line where the track disappeared into the hills.

"There's been a heavy snowfall down the track. And now the snow plough's gone on the blink."

In the small station buffet Miller sipped a cup of coffee and looked at his ticket. It had already been clipped. His mind went back to his car parked up the hill.

Surely, if he parked it on the other side of Nuremberg, several miles from the address he had been given . . . ? He could even park it in a garage, out of sight. No one would ever find it. Not before the job was done. . . . Besides, he reasoned, it wouldn't be a bad thing to have another way of getting out fast if the occasion required. There was no reason for him to think anyone in Bavaria had ever heard of him or his car.

He thought of Motti's warning about the Jaguar being too noticeable. To use it was a risk, of course, but then so was the possibility of being stranded on foot. He gave the prospect another five minutes, walked out of the station and back up the hill. Within ten minutes he was behind the wheel of the Jaguar and heading out of town.

It was a short trip to Nuremberg. Miller checked into a small hotel near the main station, and walked through the King's Gate into the old walled city.

Lights from the streets and windows lit up the quaint pointed roofs and decorated gables of the medieval town. It was hard to realize that almost every brick and stone of what he saw around him had been meticulously reconstructed since the end of the war.

He found the house he was looking for two streets from the main market square, almost under the spires of St. Sebald's Church.

He walked back to the market square, looking for a place to have supper. After strolling past two or three traditional eating houses he noticed smoke curling up into the frosty night sky from the red-tiled roof of a small sausage house. It was a pretty little place. He ordered the speciality of the house, the small, spiced Nuremberg sausages, and treated himself to a bottle of wine to wash them down.

After his meal he dawdled over his coffee, gazing at the logs flickering in the open fire. For a long time he wondered why he should risk his life in the quest for a man who had committed his crimes twenty years before. He almost decided to shave off his moustache, grow his hair and go back to Hamburg and the bed warmed by Sigi. Then when the bill came he reached into his pocket for his wallet and his fingers touched a photograph. He pulled it out, glanced at the rat-trap mouth and the pale eyes that stared back at him above the collar with those silver lightning symbols. He would recognize the face when he saw it.

MACKENSEN was confronting an angry and baffled Werwolf at about the same time.

"How the hell can he be missing?" snapped the Odessa chief. "He can't vanish off the face of the earth. His car must be one of the most distinctive in Germany, visible half a mile off, and all you can tell me is that he hasn't been seen. . . ."

Mackensen waited until the outburst was over. "Nevertheless, it's true. I've had his girl-friend and his mother and his colleagues interviewed. They all know nothing."

"We have to find him," repeated the Werwolf. "He must not get near to this comrade. It would be a disaster."

"He'll show up," said Mackensen with conviction. "Sooner or later he has to break cover. Then we'll have him."

The Werwolf considered the logic of the professional hunter and nodded slowly. "Very well. Stay close to me. Check into a hotel here in town and we'll wait it out."

JUST before nine the following morning Miller rang the brilliantly polished bell. The door was opened by a maid, who showed him into the sitting-room and went to fetch her employer.

The man who entered the sitting-room ten minutes later was in his mid-fifties, his medium-brown hair touched with silver at the temple. He was self-possessed and elegant and gazed at his visitor without curiosity, assessing at a glance the inexpensive trousers and jacket of a working-class man.

"And what can I do for you?" he inquired calmly.

"Well, Herr Doktor, I hoped you might be able to help me."

"Come now," said the Odessa man, "I'm sure you know my working chambers are not far from here. Perhaps you should go there and ask my secretary for an appointment."

"Well, it's not actually professional help I need," said Miller. He had dropped into the vernacular of Hamburg working people. He was obviously ill at ease. "I brought a letter from the man who suggested I come, sir."

The Odessa man took the letter without a word, and cast his eyes quickly down it. He stiffened slightly.

"I see, Herr Kolb. Perhaps we had better sit down."

He spent several minutes looking speculatively at his guest. Suddenly he snapped, "What did you say your name was?"

"Kolb, sir."

"First names?"

"Rolf Gunther, sir."

"Do you have any identification on you?"

"Only my driving licence."

"Let me see it please."

The lawyer considered the driving licence for another few minutes.

"Wait here," he said suddenly.

He left the room, traversed the house and entered his office at the rear, which was reached by clients from a back street. He went in, opened a wall safe, and took out a thick book.

He knew the name of Joachim Eberhardt, but had never met the man. He was not completely certain of Eberhardt's last rank in the SS. The book confirmed the letter. Joachim Eberhardt, promoted colonel of the Waffen-SS on January 10th, 1945. He flicked over several more pages and checked against Kolb. Rolf Gunther, Staff Sergeant as from April 1945. Date of birth 18.6.25. He closed the book, replaced it and locked the safe. Then he returned to the sitting-room and settled himself again.

"It may not be possible for me to help you, you realize that, don't you?"

Miller bit his lip and nodded. "I've nowhere else to go, sir. Herr Eberhardt said if you couldn't help me no one could."

The lawyer sighed. "You'd better tell me how you got into this mess in the first place."

"Well, sir, I was in Bremen. I live there, and I worked for Herr Eberhardt in the bakery. Well, I was walking in the street one day about four months back, and I came over very queer. I felt terribly ill, with stomach pains. I fainted on the pavement. So they took me away to hospital."

"Which hospital?"

"Bremen General, sir. They did some tests, and they said I'd got cancer. In the stomach. Only apparently it was caught at an early stage. They put me on a course of drugs, and after some time the cancer went into remission."

"So far as I can see, you're a lucky man."

"Yes. Well, then this Jewish hospital orderly kept staring at me. It was a funny sort of look, see? He had a sort of 'I know you' look on his face."

"Go on." The lawyer was showing increasing interest.

"So about a month ago they said I was fit to be transferred to a convalescent clinic. But before I left the hospital I remembered the Jew-boy. He was an inmate at Flossenburg."

The lawyer sat upright. "You were at Flossenburg?"

"Yes, and I remembered this orderly from then. He was in the party of inmates that we used to burn the bodies of Admiral Canaris and the others what tried to assassinate the Fuehrer."

"You were one of those who executed Canaris and the others?"

Miller shrugged. "I commanded the execution squad."

The lawyer smiled. "That certainly would get you into bad trouble with the present authorities. Go on with your story."

"I was transferred to this clinic and I didn't see the Jewish orderly again. Then last Friday I got a telephone call. The man wouldn't give his name. He just said that a certain person had informed those swine at Ludwigsburg who I was, and there was a warrant being prepared for my arrest."

"Probably a friend on the police force of Bremen," the lawyer said. "What did you do?"

Miller looked surprised.

"Well, I got out. I didn't go home in case they were waiting for me there. I didn't even go and pick up my Volkswagen. On Saturday I went to see the boss, Herr Eberhardt. He was real nice to me. He said he was leaving for a winter cruise the next morning, so he gave me the letter and told me to come to you."

"Why did you think Herr Eberhardt would help you?"

"Well, I didn't know that he had been in the war till about two years back when we was having the staff party. We all got a bit drunk, see? And I went to the men's room. There was Herr Eberhardt washing his hands and singing the 'Horst Wessel'. So I joined in. There we was, singing it in the men's room. Then he clapped me on the back, and said, 'Not a word, Kolb,' and went out. I didn't think no more about it till I got into trouble. Then I thought, well, he might have been in the SS like me."

"What was the name of the Jewish orderly."

"Hartstein, sir."

"And the convalescent clinic you were sent to?"

"The Arkadia Klinik, at Delmenhorst."

The lawyer made a few notes on a sheet of paper and rose.

"Stay here," he said, and crossed the passage to his study. He rang the Eberhardt bakery first.

Eberhardt's secretary was most helpful.

"I'm afraid Herr Eberhardt is away. No, he can't be contacted, sir, he has gone on his usual winter cruise to the Caribbean. Yes, for four weeks, sir."

The lawyer thought briefly of asking her if Kolb had worked

there, or of checking with some assistant manager, but dismissed it as unwise to risk arousing curiosity if Kolb was who he said he was. So he called the Bremen General Hospital instead and asked for the Personnel office.

"This is the Department of Social Security, Pensions Section," he said. "I wanted to confirm that you have a ward orderly on the staff by the name of Hartstein."

There was a pause while the girl at the other end went through the staff file. "Yes, we do," she said. "David Hartstein."

"Thank you," said the lawyer and hung up. He dialled the same number again and asked for the Registrar's Office.

"This is the secretary of the Eberhardt Baking Company here," he said. "I want to check on the progress of one of our staff who has been in your hospital with a tumour in the stomach. His name is Rolf Gunther Kolb."

There was another pause. "He's been discharged," the caller was told. "He was transferred to a convalescent clinic."

"Excellent," said the lawyer. "Can you tell me which clinic?"

"The Arkadia, at Delmenhorst," said the girl.

The lawyer next dialled the Arkadia Klinik. A girl answered. After hearing the request she covered the mouthpiece and murmured to the doctor by her side. "There's an inquiry about Kolb," she said.

The doctor took the telephone. "This is the Chief of the Clinic, Dr. Braun," he said. "Can I help you?"

At the name of Braun the secretary shot a puzzled glance at her employer. Without batting an eyelid he listened to the voice from Nuremberg and replied smoothly, "Herr Kolb discharged himself last Friday afternoon. Most irregular, but there was nothing I could do to prevent him. Yes, he was transferred here from the Bremen General. A stomach tumour, well on the mend."

He listened for a moment, then said, "Not at all. Glad I could be of help to you."

The doctor, whose real name was Rosemayer, hung up and then dialled Munich. Without preamble he said, "Someone's been on the phone asking about Kolb. The checking-up has started."

Back in Nuremberg the lawyer replaced the phone and returned
to the sitting-room.

"Right, Kolb, you evidently are who you say you are. However,
I have a few more questions. Are you circumcised?"

Miller stared back blankly. "No, I'm not," he said.

"Show me, Staff Sergeant," snapped the lawyer.

Miller shot out of his chair, ramrodding to attention.

"*Zu Befehl!*" he responded. He held the attention position for
three seconds, then unzipped his fly.

"Well, at least you're not Jewish," the lawyer said amiably.

Miller goggled at him. "Of course I'm not Jewish."

The lawyer smiled. "There have been cases of Jews trying to pass
themselves off as *Kameraden*. They don't last long. Now I'm going
to shoot some questions at you. Where were you born?"

"Bremen, sir."

"Were you in the Hitler Youth?"

"Yes, sir. Entered at the age of ten in 1935, sir."

"When were you inducted into the SS?"

"January 1944, sir. Age eighteen."

"Where did you train?"

"Dachau SS training camp, sir."

"You had your blood group tattooed under your right armpit?"

"No, sir. And it would have been the left armpit."

"Why weren't you tattooed?"

"Well, sir, we were due to pass out of training camp in August
1944. But in July a group of Army officers involved in the plot
against the Fuehrer were sent down to Flossenbürg. Flossenbürg
asked for immediate draftings from Dachau to increase their staff.
Me and about a dozen others were posted straight there. We
missed our tattooing, and the commandant said it was not
necessary, as we would never get to the front, sir."

The lawyer nodded. No doubt the commandant had been aware
in July 1944 that the war was drawing to a close.

"Did you get your dagger?"

"Yes, sir. From the hands of the commandant."

"What are the words on it?"

"Blood and Honour, sir."

"What was the book of marching songs from which the '*Horst Wessel*' was drawn?"

"The album *Time of Struggle for the Nation*, sir."

"What was your uniform?"

"Grey-green tunic and breeches, jackboots, black collar lapels, black belt and gunmetal buckle, sir."

"The motto on the buckle?"

"A swastika ringed with the words 'My Honour is Loyalty', sir."

The lawyer lit a cigar and strolled to the window.

"Now you'll tell me about Flossenbürg Camp, Staff Sergeant Kolb. How large was it?"

"When I was there, sir, three hundred metres by three hundred. It had a roll-call square one hundred and twenty metres by one hundred and forty. God we had fun there with them Yids . . ."

"Stick to the point," snapped the lawyer. "What was the population in late 1944?"

"Oh, about sixteen thousand inmates, sir."

"Where was the commandant's office?"

"Outside the wire, sir, on a slope overlooking the camp."

"Which was the number of the political department?"

"Department Two, sir."

"Where was it?"

"In the commandant's block."

"One last question, Staff Sergeant. When you looked up, from anywhere in the camp, what did you see?"

Miller looked puzzled. "The sky," he said.

"Fool, I mean what dominated the horizon?"

"Oh, you mean the hill with the ruined castle keep on it?"

The lawyer nodded and smiled. "All right, Kolb, you were at Flossenbürg. Now, how did you get away?"

"Well, sir, it was on the march. We all broke up. I found an army private wandering around, so I hit him on the head and took his uniform. The Yanks caught me two days later. I did two years in a prisoner-of-war camp. They thought I was in the Army, sir."

The lawyer exhaled cigar smoke. "Did you change your name?"

"No, sir. I threw my papers away, because they identified me as SS. But I didn't think to change the name. I didn't think anyone would look for a staff sergeant. Nothing would have happened if that orderly hadn't spotted me, and after that it wouldn't have mattered what I called myself."

"True. Now repeat the oath of loyalty to the Fuehrer."

It went on for another three hours. It was past lunchtime when at last the lawyer professed himself satisfied.

"Just what do you want?" he asked Miller.

"Well, sir, with them all looking for me, I'm going to need a set of papers showing I am not Rolf Gunther Kolb. I can grow my hair and moustache long, and get a job in Bavaria or somewhere. I mean, I'm a skilled baker, and people need bread, don't they?"

The lawyer threw back his head and laughed.

"Yes, my good Kolb, people need bread. Very well, I'll do what I can. You need a new passport. Have you got any money?"

"No, sir. I'm flush out. I've been hitchhiking."

The lawyer gave him a hundred-mark note. "I'll send you to a friend of mine in Stuttgart who will get you a passport. Check into a commercial hotel, then go and see him. He's called Ludwig Bayer and here's his address. If you need a little more money, he'll help you out. But stay under cover until you have the passport. Then we'll find you a job in southern Germany."

Miller took the hundred marks and the address of Bayer with embarrassed thanks. "Oh, thank you, Herr Doktor. Thank you."

The maid showed him out and he walked back to his car. An hour later he was speeding towards Stuttgart, while the lawyer rang Bayer and told him to expect Rolf Gunther Kolb in the early evening.

Miller arrived after dark and found a small hotel in the outer city that had a garage round the back for the car. From the hall porter he got a town plan and found Bayer's street in the suburb of Ostheim. Following the map he drove the car away from the centre of Stuttgart, and parked his car half a mile from Bayer's house. As he stooped to lock the driver's door he failed to notice a middle-aged lady passing by on her way home from her weekly meeting of the Hospital Visitors' Committee.

AT EIGHT that evening the lawyer in Nuremberg thought he had better ring Bayer and make sure Kolb had arrived safely. It was Bayer's wife who answered.

"Oh, yes, the young man and my husband have gone out to dinner somewhere. Such a nice young man," Frau Bayer burbled on, "and such a lovely car!"

"Excuse me, Frau Bayer," the lawyer cut in. "The man had not got his Volkswagen with him. He came by train."

"No, no," said Frau Bayer. "He came by car, I passed him as he was parking it, a long black sports car, with a yellow stripe down the side. . . ."

The lawyer slammed down the phone, then raised it and dialled a hotel in Nuremberg. He was sweating slightly. He asked for a room number, and a familiar voice said, "Hello."

"Mackensen," barked the Werwolf, "get over here fast. We've found Miller."

IT WAS at least a two-hour drive from Nuremberg to Stuttgart, even if one pushed the car hard. And Mackensen pushed that night. He arrived at Bayer's house at half-past ten.

Frau Bayer, alerted by another call from the Werwolf, was a trembling and frightened woman. Mackensen's manner was hardly calculated to put her at ease. "When did they leave?" he asked.

"About a quarter past eight," she quavered.

"Did they say where they were going?"

"No. Ludwig just said he was taking the young man into town for a meal. Ludwig loves dining out. His favourite place is the Three Moors on Friedrich Strasse," she said.

"What did the young man look like?"

"Oh, brown hair and moustache. Tall, I'd say."

"You said you saw him parking his car. Where was this?"

She described the location of the Jaguar.

"So they left in your husband's car? Its make and number?"

Armed with all the information he needed, Mackensen left and drove to the parked Jaguar. He examined it closely, then climbed back into his Mercedes and headed for the centre of town.

116

IN A small hotel in the back streets of Munich a cable was delivered to Josef in his room. He slit the envelope and scanned the lengthy contents. It began:

"Here are the prices we are able to accept for commodities about which the customer has inquired:

      Celery: 481 marks, 53 pfennigs
      Melons: 362 marks, 17 pfennigs
      Oranges: 627 marks, 24 pfennigs. . . ."

Ignoring the words, Josef wrote down the figures in a long line, then split them into groups of six figures. From each six-figure group he subtracted the date, 20th February, 1964, which he wrote as 20264. In each case the result was another six-figure group. It was a simple book code, based on the paperback edition of Webster's *New World Dictionary*. The first three figures in the group represented the page in the dictionary; the fourth figure could be anything from one to nine. An odd number meant column one, an even number column two. The last two figures indicated the number of words down the column from the top.

He worked steadily for half an hour, then slowly read the message through.

Thirty minutes later he was in Leon's cellar. The revenge-group leader read the message and swore. "I'm sorry," he said at last. "I couldn't have known."

Unknown to either man three fragments of information had come into the possession of the Mossad in the previous six days. One, from the resident Israeli agent in Buenos Aires, was to the effect that someone had authorized the payment of one million German marks to a figure called Vulkan "to enable him to complete the next stage of his research project".

The second, from a Jewish employee of a Swiss bank known to handle transfers of Nazi funds, noted that one million marks had been collected from a Beirut bank by a man named Fritz Wegener.

The third item came from an Egyptian colonel in a security position at Factory 333 in Cairo. He reported that the rocket project was lacking only a reliable tele-guidance system, and that this was being constructed in a factory in West Germany and was costing the Odessa millions of marks.

The three fragments, among thousands of others, had been processed by the computer. Where a human memory might have failed, the whirring micro-circuits had linked the three items, and in addition had recalled that up to his exposure by his wife in 1955 Eduard Roschmann had used the name of Fritz Wegener.

Josef rounded on Leon. "I'm not moving out of range of that telephone from now on. Get me a powerful motorcycle and protective clothing. Have both ready within the hour. If and when your precious Miller checks in, I'll have to get to him fast."

"If he's exposed, you won't get there fast enough," said Leon. "They'll kill him if he gets within a mile of his man."

As Leon left the cellar Josef ran his eye over the cable from Tel Aviv again:

RED ALERT NEW INFORMATION INDICATES VITAL KEY ROCKET SUCCESS GERMAN INDUSTRIALIST YOUR TERRITORY STOP CODE NAME VULKAN STOP PROBABLY ROSCHMANN STOP USE MILLER INSTANTLY STOP TRACE AND ELIMINATE STOP CORMORANT

Josef sat at the table and meticulously began to clean and arm his Walther PPK automatic.

OVER dinner Bayer had been the genial host, roaring with laughter as he told his favourite jokes. Every time Miller tried to get the talk round to his passport, Bayer clapped him on the back. "Leave it to me, old boy, leave it to old Ludwig."

One thing Miller had acquired from eight years as a reporter was the ability to drink and keep a clear head. By the dessert course they had demolished two bottles of excellent hock, and Bayer, squeezed into his tight, horn-buttoned jacket, was perspiring in torrents. He called for a third bottle of wine.

Miller pretended to be worried that it would prove impossible to get a passport. "You'll need photographs of me, won't you?"

Bayer guffawed. "Yes, a couple of them. No problem. You can get them taken in one of the booths at the station."

"What happens then?" asked Miller.

Bayer leaned over and placed a fat arm round his shoulders.

"Then I send them away to a friend of mine, and a week later back comes the passport. No problem, old chap, stop worrying."

Miller was afraid to push him further. The fat man paid for the meal finally and they headed for the door. It was half-past ten.

"I suppose that's the end of what Stuttgart has to offer in the way of night life," observed Miller.

"Ha, silly boy. That's all you know. There's the Moulin Rouge, the Balzac, the Imperial and the Sayonara. Then there's the Madeleine in Eberhard Strasse. . . ." Bayer led the way to his car.

MACKENSEN reached the Three Moors at quarter past eleven.

"Herr Bayer?" said the headwaiter. "Yes, he left a while ago."

"Had he a guest? Tall with a brown moustache?"

"That's right."

Mackensen slipped a twenty-mark note into the man's hand without difficulty. "It's vitally important that I find him. Do you know where they went from here?"

"I confess I don't," said the headwaiter. He called to one of the junior waiters. "Hans, you served Herr Bayer and his guest. Did they mention if they were going on anywhere?"

"No," said Hans. "I didn't hear anything."

Mackensen asked for a copy of the tourist booklet, *What's On In Stuttgart*. He headed for the first cabaret on the list.

MILLER and Bayer sat at a table for two in the Madeleine. Bayer, on his second large whisky, stared with pop eyes at a generously-endowed young woman gyrating her hips in the centre of the floor. It was well after midnight and he was very drunk.

"Look, Herr Bayer," whispered Miller. "How soon can you—"

Bayer draped his arm round Miller's shoulders. "Look, Rolf, old buddy, I've told you. You don't have to worry, see? Just leave it to Ludwig, see?" He flapped a pudgy hand in the air. "Waiter, another round."

When Miller finally got the Odessa man away from the club it was after one in the morning and Bayer was unsteady on his feet.

"I'd better drive you home," Miller said as they approached Bayer's car. He took the car keys from Bayer's coat pocket and helped the unprotesting fat man into the passenger seat. Slamming the door, he walked round to the driver's side and climbed in. At that moment a grey Mercedes slewed round the corner behind them and stopped twenty yards up the road.

Mackensen, who had visited five nightclubs, stared at the number plate of the car moving away from the kerb. It was the number Frau Bayer had given him. He let in his clutch and followed.

Miller drove, not back to Bayer's house, but to his own hotel. On the way Bayer dozed, his head nodding forward. Outside the hotel Miller nudged him awake.

"Come on, Ludwig old mate, let's have a night-cap."

The fat man stared about him.

"Must get home," he mumbled. "Wife waiting."

"Come on, just a little drink to finish the evening. We can have a noggin in my room and talk about the old times."

Bayer grinned drunkenly. "Great times we had, Rolf."

"Great," Miller said as he helped Bayer through the door.

Down the street the Mercedes had doused its lights and merged with the grey shadows.

Behind his desk the night porter seemed to be dozing. Bayer mumbled. "Ssssh," said Miller, "got to be quiet."

"Got to be quiet," repeated Bayer, tiptoeing like an elephant towards the stairs. Fortunately for Miller, his room was on the first floor, or Bayer would never have made it. He opened the door, flicked on the light, and helped Bayer into a wooden armchair.

Outside in the street Mackensen stood across from the hotel. When Miller's light came on he noted it was on the first floor, on the right side of the hotel. He debated whether to go up and hit Miller as he opened his bedroom door. Two things decided him against it. The night porter, woken by Bayer's heavy tread, was pottering around the foyer. And the fat man was too drunk to be capable of getting out of the hotel in a hurry. If the police got

Bayer, there would be bad trouble with the Werwolf. Despite appearances Bayer was a much-wanted man under his real name and important in the Odessa.

Across from the hotel was a building halfway through construction. The frame and the floors were in place, with a rough concrete stairway leading up to the first floor. He could wait there and go for a window-shot. Mackensen walked purposefully back to his car and the Remington locked in the boot.

BAYER was taken completely by surprise when the blow came. Miller had never had occasion to use the blows he had learned in the Army and he was not entirely certain how effective they were. The vast bulk of Bayer's neck caused him to hit as hard as he could.

It was hard enough. By the time Bayer had cleared the dizziness from his brain both his wrists were lashed tightly to the arms of the wooden chair with two of Miller's ties and his own tie had been pulled off his neck to secure his left ankle to the foot of the chair.

"What the . . .?" he growled thickly, as Miller bound the right ankle with the telephone wire.

Comprehension began to dawn. He looked up owlishly at Miller. Like all of his kind, Bayer had one nightmare that never quite left him.

"You'll never get me to Tel Aviv. You can't prove anything. I never touched you people. . . ."

The words were cut off as rolled-up socks were stuffed in his mouth and Miller's woollen scarf was wound round his face.

Miller drew up a chair and sat astride it, his face two feet from his prisoner.

"Listen, you fat slug. I'm not an Israeli agent. And you're going to talk. Understand?"

For answer Ludwig Bayer stared back above the scarf. His eyes were red-tinged, like those of an angry boar.

Miller looked round, spotted the bedside lamp, and brought it over. "Now, Bayer, or whatever your name is, I'm going to take the gag off. You are going to tell me the name and address of the man who makes the passports for the Odessa. If you attempt to yell, you get this right across the head."

He eased off the scarf and pulled the socks out of Bayer's mouth, keeping the lamp poised in his right hand.

"You bastard," hissed Bayer. "You'll get nothing out of me."

He hardly got the words out before the socks went back into his bulging cheeks. The scarf was replaced.

"No?" said Miller. "We'll see. I'll start on your fingers."

He took the little finger and ring finger of Bayer's right hand and bent them backward. Bayer threw himself about in the chair and Miller took off the gag again.

"I can break every finger on both your hands, Bayer," he whispered. "After that I'll take the bulb out of the table lamp, and you know what I'll do with the socket."

Sweat rolled in torrents off Bayer's face. "No! Not the electrodes!"

"You know what it's like, don't you?"

Bayer closed his eyes and moaned softly. He knew very well what it was like, but not on the receiving end.

"Talk," hissed Miller. "The forger, his name and address."

Bayer slowly shook his head.

"I can't," he whispered. "They'll kill me."

Miller replaced the gag. He took Bayer's little finger, closed his eyes and jerked once. The bone snapped. Bayer heaved in his chair and vomited into the gag. Miller whipped it off before the fat man could drown in the evening's highly expensive food and drink. "Talk," he said. "You've got nine fingers to go."

Bayer swallowed, eyes closed. "Winzer, Klaus Winzer."

"He's a professional forger?"

"He's a printer."

"Where? Which town?"

"They'll kill me."

"I'll kill you if you don't tell me. Which town?"

"Osnabrück," whispered Bayer.

Miller replaced the gag. He went to his attaché case and took out a road map. Osnabrück was a four or five-hour drive to the north.

It was already nearly three o'clock in the morning of February 21st.

Across the road Mackensen shivered in the half-completed building. The light still shone in the room over the road. He flicked his eyes constantly from the illuminated window to the front door. If only Bayer would come out, he thought, he could take Miller alone. Or if Miller came out, he could take him farther down the street.

In his room Miller quietly packed his things. He needed Bayer quiescent for at least six hours, so he spent a few minutes tightening the bonds that held Bayer immobile and silent, then eased the chair onto its side so that the fat man could not raise attention by rolling the chair over with a crash. The telephone cord was already ripped out. He took a last look round and left the room, locking the door behind him.

He was almost at the top of the stairs when a thought came to him. The night porter might have been awake enough to have seen them both mount the stairs. What would he think if only one came down, paid his bill and left? Miller retreated and headed for the back of the hotel. At the end of the corridor was a window looking out on the fire-escape. He slipped the catch and stepped out on the ladder. A second later he was in an alley at the back of the hotel, and off at a stride to where he had parked his Jaguar. He was desperately tired, but he had to reach Winzer before the alarm was raised. By four in the morning he was out on the autobahn, streaking north.

Almost as soon as he had gone, Bayer, by now completely sober, began to struggle to get free. He tried to lean forward far enough to use his teeth on the ties that bound his wrists, but his fatness prevented his head getting low enough, and the sock in his mouth forced his teeth apart. Finally, he spotted the table lamp lying on the floor. The bulb was still in it. It took him an hour to inch the overturned chair across the floor and crush the light bulb.

It isn't easy to use a piece of broken glass to cut wrist-bonds. It was seven in the morning, and light was beginning to filter over the roofs of the town, before the first strands parted. It was nearly eight when Bayer's left wrist came free.

By that time Miller's Jaguar was boring round the Cologne Ring to the east of the city with another hundred miles before Osnabrück. It had started to rain, an evil sleet running in curtains across the slippery autobahn, and the mesmeric effect of the windscreen wipers almost put him to sleep. He slowed down to a steady eighty m.p.h. rather than risk running off the road into the muddy fields on either side.

WITH his left hand free, Bayer took only a few minutes to rip off his gag and release his feet. Then he lay for several minutes whooping in great gulps of air. His first thought was the door, but it was locked. Then he staggered to the window, ripped back the curtains and jerked the window open.

In his shooting niche across the road Mackensen saw the curtains of Miller's room pulled back. Snapping the Remington up he fired straight into the face of the figure.

Without waiting to cast a second look into the room across the road, Mackensen ran. He regained his car within sixty seconds of firing, stowed the gun in the boot and drove off.

He suspected he had made a mistake. The man he was briefed to kill was tall and lean. The mind's eye impression of the figure at the window was of a fat man. He was sure that it was Bayer he had hit.

Not that it was too serious a problem as far as Miller was concerned. Seeing Bayer dead on his carpet, Miller would be bound to flee. Therefore he would run to his Jaguar, parked three miles away. Mackensen only began to worry badly when he saw the empty space where the Jaguar had stood the previous evening.

Mackensen would not have been the chief executioner for the Odessa if he had been the sort who panics easily. He sat at the wheel of the Mercedes for several minutes while he digested the fact that Miller could now be hundreds of miles away. If Miller had left Bayer alive, he reasoned, it could be because he had got nothing from him. Or because he *had* got something. In the first case there was no harm done; he could take Miller later. If Miller had got something from Bayer, the Werwolf alone would know

what information Bayer had to give. There was nothing to do but call Nuremberg.

When he heard the news the Werwolf went into the transports of rage that Mackensen feared. "You'd better find him, you oaf, and quickly."

Mackensen explained that to find Miller he needed to know what kind of information Bayer could have supplied.

"Dear God," the Werwolf breathed, "the forger."

"What forger, Chief?" asked Mackensen.

The Werwolf pulled himself together. "I'll get on to the man and warn him," he said crisply. "This is where Miller has gone." He dictated an address to Mackensen. "You get the hell up to Osnabrück like you've never moved before. If Miller's not at that address, keep searching the town for the Jaguar. And this time, don't leave that car. It's the one place he always returns to."

He slammed down the phone and then dialled Osnabrück.

Chapter Twelve

Klaus Winzer had had one of the strangest careers of any man to wear the uniform of the SS. Born in 1924, he was the son of a pork butcher of Wiesbaden, a large, boisterous man who from the early twenties onward was a trusting follower of Adolf Hitler and the Nazi party.

To his father's disgust Klaus grew up small, weak, short-sighted and peaceful. At only one thing did he excel; in his early teens he fell in love with the art of handwriting and the preparation of illuminated manuscripts, an activity his disgusted father regarded as an occupation for cissies.

The war came, and in the spring of 1942 Klaus turned eighteen years old, the age of call-up. Failing even to pass the medical for an Army desk job, he was sent home. For his father this was the last straw.

He went to Berlin to see an old friend who had risen high in the SS, in hopes the man might obtain for his son an entry into some

branch of service to the Reich. The man asked if there was anything the young Klaus could do well. Shamefacedly, his father
admitted he could prepare illuminated manuscripts, and the friend
asked if Klaus would prepare an illuminated address on parchment,
in honour of an SS major.

At the handing-over ceremony in Berlin, everyone admired the
beautiful manuscript. An officer of the RSHA asked who had done
it and requested that young Klaus Winzer be brought to Berlin.
Before he knew what was happening, Klaus was inducted into the
SS, made to swear oaths of loyalty and secrecy, and told he would
be transferred to a top-secret project. His father, bewildered, was
in seventh heaven.

The project was basically simple. The SS was trying to forge
hundreds of thousands of British five-pound notes and American
hundred-dollar bills. It was for his knowledge of papers and inks
that they wanted Klaus.

The idea was to flood Britain and America with phoney money,
thus ruining the economies of both countries. In early 1943, when
the watermark for the British fivers had been achieved, the printing
project was transferred to Block 19, Sachsenhausen concentration
camp, where graphic artists among the inmates worked under the
direction of the SS. Winzer's job was quality control, for the SS
feared their prisoners might make deliberate errors in their work.
Towards the end of 1944 the project in Block 19 was also used to
prepare the forged identity cards that the SS officers would use
when Germany collapsed.

At the end of the war Klaus Winzer went back to Wiesbaden and
home. To his astonishment, having never lacked for a meal in the
SS, he found civilians almost starving. His mother explained that
all food had to be bought on ration cards issued by the Americans.
Klaus took a handful to his room for a few days and when he
emerged it was to hand over to his astonished mother enough
ration cards to feed them all for six months.

A month later Klaus Winzer met Otto Klops, the king of the
black market of Wiesbaden, and they were in business. Winzer
turned out ration cards, petrol coupons, driving licences, PX cards;

Klops used them to buy food, petrol, tyres, soap, cosmetics, and clothing, which he sold at black market prices. By the summer of 1948, Klaus Winzer was a rich man.

But that October the authorities reformed the currency, and the populace, no longer needing the black marketeers as goods came on the open market, denounced Klops, and Winzer, ruined, had to flee. Taking one of his own zonal passes and some forged references, he went to the headquarters of the British Zone at Hanover and applied for, and got, a job in the passport office of the Military Government.

Two months later he was in a beer hall when he got into conversation with a man named Molders. Molders confided to Winzer that he was being sought by the British for war crimes and needed to get out of Germany. But only the British could supply passports to Germans, and he dared not apply. Winzer murmured that it might be arranged, but would cost money.

Molders produced a diamond necklace which he had obtained from a concentration camp and a week later Winzer prepared the passport. He did not even forge it. He did not need to.

The system at the passport office was simple. In Section One, applicants turned up with all their documentation and filled out a form. In Section Two documents were checked against the "wanted" list and examined for forgery. If the application was approved the documents, signed by the Head of the Department were passed to Section Three. Section Three, on receipt of the note of approval from Section Two, took a blank passport from the safe where they were stored, filled it out, and stuck in the applicant's photograph.

Winzer got himself transferred to Section Three. He filled out an application form for Molders in a new name, wrote out an "Application Approved" slip from the head of Section Two, forging that British officer's signature. Then he walked into Section Two, picked up the application forms and approval slips waiting to go on to Section Three—there were nineteen that day—and slipped the Molders forms in with them. In the routine way he took the sheaf of papers to Major Johnstone of Section Three. The Major checked that there were twenty approval slips, so he took twenty passports from his safe and handed them to Winzer. Winzer duly stamped them, passed on nineteen of them to nineteen happy applicants, and put the twentieth in his pocket.

That evening Klaus gave Molders his new passport and went home with a diamond necklace. He had found his new métier.

Each week thereafter, armed with a photograph of one nonentity, Winzer carefully filled out a passport application, and slipped it in with the regular sheaf of forms and approval slips. So long as the number tallied, he got a bunch of blank passports in return. All but one went to genuine applicants. The blank one went home with Klaus. All he needed then was the official stamp. He took it for one night, and by morning had his own casting of the stamp of the Passport Office of the State Government of Lower Saxony.

In sixty weeks he had sixty blank passports. He resigned his job, sold the diamond necklace in Antwerp and started a nice little printing business in Osnabrück.

He would never had got involved with the Odessa if Molders had kept his mouth shut. But once in Madrid, Molders boasted of his contact. From then on, whenever an Odessa man was in trouble, Winzer supplied the new West German passport. Once the passport was obtained, the wanted SS man could acquire a fresh driving licence, social security card, bank account, credit card, in short an entire new identity.

By the spring of 1964 Winzer had used forty-two out of his stock of sixty passports.

But the cunning little man had taken one precaution. It occurred to him that one day the Odessa might wish to dispose of his services, and of him. So he kept a record. He never knew the real names of his clients; to make out a false passport in a new name it was not necessary. But he made a copy of every photograph sent to him, pasted the original in the passport he was sending back, and kept the copy. Each photograph was pasted to a sheet of paper, and beside it was typed the new name, the address and the new passport number.

This file was his life insurance. There was one in his house, and a copy with a lawyer in Zurich. If the Odessa ever threatened him he would warn them that if anything happened to him his lawyer would send the copy to the German authorities. They, armed with a photograph, would soon compare it with their "Rogues Gallery", and exposure would take no more than a week. It was a foolproof scheme to ensure that Klaus Winzer stayed alive and in good health.

This then was the man who sat quietly munching toast and jam that Friday morning when the phone rang. The voice at the other end was first peremptory, then reassuring.

"There is no question of your being in any trouble with us at all," the Werwolf assured him. "It's just this damn reporter. We have a tip he's coming to see you. It's all right. We have one of our men coming up behind him and the whole affair will be taken care of within the day. But you must get out of there within ten minutes. Now here's what I want you to do. . . ."

Thirty minutes later a very flustered Klaus Winzer explained to his housemaid that instead of going to the printing works that morning he had decided to take a holiday in the Austrian Alps.

MILLER found a petrol station at the Saar Platz at the western entrance to Osnabrück. He pulled up and climbed wearily out.

"Fill her up," he told the boy and headed for the phone booth. He found two listings for Klaus Winzer, one marked "Printer" the second "res." for residence. As it was nine-twenty he rang the printing works.

The man who answered said, "I'm sorry, he's not in yet. He'll no doubt be along directly. Call back in half an hour."

Miller thanked him and considered dialling the house. Better not. If he was at home, Miller wanted him personally.

The house was in an obviously prosperous area. Miller left the Jaguar at the end of the drive and walked to the front door.

The maid who answered it smiled brightly at him.

"Good morning. I've come to see Herr Winzer," he told her.

"Oooh, he's left, sir. You just missed him by about twenty minutes. He's gone off on holiday."

Miller fought down a feeling of panic. "Holiday? That's odd," he said. "We had an appointment this morning."

"Oh, what a shame," said the girl. "And he went off so sudden. He got this phone call in the library, then tells me, Barbara, I'm off on holiday. Tells me to ring the works and say he's not coming in for a week. Not like Herr Winzer at all."

"Do you know where he went?" Inside Miller hope began to die.

"No. He just said he was going to the Austrian Alps."

"No forwarding address? No way of getting in touch with him?"

"No, that's what's so strange."

"Could I speak to Frau Winzer please?" Miller asked.

Barbara looked at him archly. "There ain't no Frau Winzer."

"So he lives here alone then?"

"Well, except for me. I mean, I live in. Mind you, it's quite safe. From that point of view." She giggled.

"I see. Thank you," said Miller and turned to go.

"You're welcome," said the girl, and watched him go down the drive and climb into the Jaguar, which had already caught her attention. She sighed for what might have been and closed the door.

Miller felt the weariness creeping over him, accentuated by this final disappointment. He had got so close, only fifteen minutes from his target. Bayer must have wriggled free and rung Winzer. Desperate for sleep, Miller drove to the Theodor Heuss Platz, parked in front of the station and checked into the Hohenzollern Hotel across the square.

They had a room available at once, so he went upstairs, undressed and lay on the bed. There was something nagging in the back of his mind, some tiny detail of inquiry he had left unasked. It was still unsolved when he fell asleep at half-past ten.

MACKENSEN made it to the centre of Osnabrück at half-past one. On the way into town he had checked Winzer's house, but there was no sign of a Jaguar. At the Theodor Heuss Platz his face split in a grin. The Jaguar he sought was in front of the town's main hotel. He phoned the Werwolf and found him in a better mood.

131

"It's all right, I reached Winzer in time," he told Mackensen. "I just phoned his house again. The maid told me he had left town barely fifteen minutes before a man with a black sports car came inquiring after him."

"I've got some news too," said Mackensen. "The Jaguar is parked right here on the square. Chances are he's sleeping it off in the hotel, and I can take him in his room."

"Hold it," warned the Werwolf. "For one thing he must not get it in Osnabrück. The maid has seen him and would probably report to the police. I can't have any attention directed to our forger. One other thing. Does Miller carry a document case?"

"Yes," said Mackensen. "He had it with him last night."

"The point is," said the Werwolf, "he has now seen me and knows my name and address. He knows of the connection with Bayer and the forger. And reporters write things down. That document case must not fall into the hands of the police."

"I've got you. You want the case as well?"

"Either get it, or destroy it."

Mackensen thought for a moment. "The best way to do both would be for me to plant a bomb in the car. Linked to the suspension, so it will detonate when he hits a bump at high speed."

"Excellent," said the Werwolf. "Can you do it?"

Mackensen grinned. The killing kit in the boot of his car was an assassin's dream. It included nearly a pound of plastic explosive and two electric detonators. "Sure, no problem. I'll have to wait until dark—" He stopped talking, gazed out of the call box and barked down the phone, "Call you back."

He called back in five minutes.

"Sorry. I just saw Miller, attaché case in hand, climb into his car and drive off. I checked the hotel and he's left his luggage, so he'll be back. I'll get on with the bomb and plant it tonight."

MILLER had woken up just before one, mildly elated. He had remembered what was troubling him. He drove back to Winzer's house.

"Hello, you again?" the maid beamed.

132

"I was just passing on my way back home," said Miller, "and I wondered, how long have you been in service here?"

"Oh, about ten months. Why?"

"Well, who looked after Herr Winzer before you came?"

"His housekeeper. Fräulein Wendel."

"Where is she now?"

"Oh, in hospital sir. Dying of cancer, I'm afraid. That's another thing makes it so funny Herr Winzer dashing off like that. He goes to visit her every day. Devoted to her he is. She was with him for ever such a long time, since 1950 I think."

"What hospital is she in?" asked Miller.

She gave him the name of an exclusive private sanatorium just beyond the outskirts of town.

Miller presented himself there at three in the afternoon.

MACKENSEN spent the early afternoon buying the rest of the ingredients for his bomb. "The secret of sabotage," his instructor had once told him, "is to keep the requirements simple. The sort of thing you can buy in any shop."

With his purchases made, he took a room in the Hohenzollern Hotel overlooking the square, so that he could keep an eye on the parking area to which he was certain Miller would return.

Seated at the table in front of the window, with a pot of strong black coffee to stave off his tiredness, he went to work on his bomb. The trigger mechanism consisted of two six-inch lengths of hacksaw blade, bound parallel to each other one and a quarter inches apart. To ensure that there was a little more resistance than air to prevent their touching, he lodged a light-bulb between the open jaws, fixing it in place with a generous blob of glue. Should the trigger be subjected to sudden pressure, the bulb would shatter, the two lengths of steel would close together, and the electric circuit contained within the plastic explosive would be complete.

His device finished, he stowed it in the bottom of the wardrobe along with the materials he'd need to fix it to Miller's car. Then he settled down to wait. He was prepared to be patient. He knew Miller would return sooner or later.

Chapter Thirteen

The doctor glanced with little favour at the visitor. Miller, who hated wearing collars and ties and avoided them whenever he could, had on a white nylon polo-necked sweater and over it a black pullover with a turtle neck. Over both he wore a black blazer. For hospital-visiting, the doctor's expression clearly said, a collar and tie would be more appropriate.

"Her nephew?" he repeated with surprise. "I had no idea Fräulein Wendel had a nephew."

"Obviously I would have come sooner, had I known of my aunt's condition, but Herr Winzer only rang me this morning."

"Herr Winzer is usually here himself about this hour."

"I understand he's been called away for some days," said Miller blandly. "He asked me on the phone to visit my aunt in his stead."

"Strange," the doctor murmured. "He has been regular as clockwork since she was brought in. Well, he had better be quick if he wishes to see her again. She is very far gone, you know."

Miller looked sad. "So he told me on the phone," he said.

"As her relative, of course you may spend a short time with her. But I must ask you to be brief. Come this way."

The doctor led Miller down several passages and stopped at a door which he opened. "She's in here. Don't be long, please."

The room was in semi-darkness and until his eyes had become accustomed to the dull light Miller failed to distinguish the shrivelled form of the woman in the bed. So pale was her face that she almost merged with the bedclothes. Her eyes were closed.

"Fräulein Wendel," he whispered, and her eyelids fluttered open.

They closed again and she began to mutter incoherently. Something about "all dressed in white, so very pretty".

Miller leaned closer. "Fräulein Wendel, can you hear me?"

The dying woman was still muttering. ". . . carrying a prayer book, so innocent. . . ."

Miller frowned in thought before he understood. In delirium

she was trying to recall her first Communion. Like himself she had once been a Roman Catholic.

She opened her eyes again and stared at him, taking in the white band round his neck, the black material over his chest and the black jacket. To his astonishment two tears rolled down the parchment cheeks. With surprising strength her hand gripped his wrist, and she said quite distinctly, "Bless me, Father, for I have sinned."

For a few seconds Miller failed to understand, then a glance at his shirt-front made him realize the mistake the woman had made. He debated for two minutes whether to leave her or to risk his immortal soul and have one last try at Eduard Roschmann. He leaned forward.

"My child, I am prepared to hear your confession."

In a tired mumble her life story came out: how she had grown up ugly, had realized there would be no marriage for her, and in 1939 had been posted, an embittered woman, as a wardress in a camp called Ravensbrück. As she told of her days of power and cruelty, tears rolled down her cheeks.

"And after the war?" Miller asked softly.

There had been years of wandering, abandoned by the SS, hunted by the Allies, working as a scullery-maid, and sleeping in Salvation Army hostels. Then in 1950 she met Winzer, staying in a hotel in Osnabrück where she was a waitress, while he looked for a house to buy. He asked her to keep house for him.

"Is that all?" asked Miller when she stopped.

"Yes, Father."

"My child, you know I cannot give you absolution if you have not confessed all your sins."

"That is all, Father."

Miller drew a deep breath.

"And what about the forged passports for the SS men?"

"I did not make them, Father," she said.

"But you knew about them, about the work Klaus Winzer did."

"Yes." The word was a low whisper.

"He has gone now. He has gone away," said Miller.

"No. Not gone. Klaus would not leave me."

"He has been forced to run away. Think, my child. Where would he go?"

The emaciated head shook slowly. "I don't know, Father. If they threaten him, he will use the file. He told me he would."

Miller tensed. "What file, my child?"

They talked for another five minutes, then there was a soft tap on the door and Miller rose to go.

"Father. . . ." The voice was plaintive, pleading.

He turned. She was staring at him, her eyes wide open.

"Bless me, Father." The tone was imploring.

Miller sighed. It was a mortal sin. He hoped somebody somewhere would understand. He made the sign of the cross. *"In nomine Patris, et Filii, et Spiritus Sancti, Ego te absolvo a peccatis tuis."*

The woman sighed deeply, closed her eyes and passed into unconsciousness.

The doctor escorted him back to the entrance hall.

"Thank you for letting me see her," said Miller at the front door. "There is one thing, Doctor. We are Catholics in our family. She asked me for a priest. Will you see to it?"

"Certainly," said the doctor. "Thank you for telling me."

It was late afternoon when Miller drove back into the Theodor Heuss Platz and parked the Jaguar. He crossed the road and went up to his room. From two floors above, Mackensen had watched his arrival. Taking his bomb in his handgrip he went out to his car. He manoeuvred it into a place where he could watch the hotel entrance and the Jaguar, and settled down to another wait.

In his room, Miller began telephoning friends in the underworld of Hamburg, trying to locate a man called Viktor Koppel, a skilful safe-cracker whose court case he had once covered.

He found him at half-past seven, in a bar with a crowd of friends, and it took a bit of prompting before he remembered Miller.

"I need a spot of help," said Miller.

The man in Hamburg sounded wary.

"I ain't got much on me, Herr Miller."

136

"I don't want a loan," said Miller. "I want to pay you for a job. Just a small one."

Koppel's voice was full of relief.

"Oh, I see, sure. Where are you?"

Miller gave him his instructions.

OUTSIDE, Mackensen decided to start on the Jaguar at midnight if Miller had not emerged.

But Miller walked out of the hotel at quarter past eleven, crossed the square and entered the station. Mackensen was surprised. He wondered idly why Miller should want to take a train.

At eleven thirty-five his problem was solved. Miller came back out of the station accompanied by a small, shabby man carrying a black leather grip. The pair approached a taxi, climbed in and drove off. Mackensen decided to give them twenty minutes and then start on the Jaguar.

At midnight the square was almost empty. Mackensen slipped across to the Jaguar, opened the hood and lashed an explosive charge to the inside of the engine bay, directly in front of the driving position. Sliding under the car he wired the rear end of the trigger mechanism to a handy bracing-bar. The trigger mechanism was connected to the main charge by two wires eight feet long. The open jaws of the trigger, held apart by the glass bulb, he jammed between two coils of the stout spring that formed the front nearside suspension.

When it was firmly in place, unable to be shaken free by normal jolting, he came out from under. He estimated the first time the car hit a bump or a normal pot-hole at speed, the retracting suspension on the front nearside wheel would force the open jaws of the trigger together, crushing the glass bulb, and make contact between the two electrically-charged hacksaw blades. When that happened, Miller and his incriminating documents would be blown to pieces.

Returning to the back seat of the Mercedes, Mackensen curled up and dozed.

He had done, he reckoned, a good night's work.

137

"TO the Saar Platz," Miller told the taxi driver.

It was only when they had dismounted and the taxi had disappeared that Koppel opened his mouth. "I hope you know what you're doing, Herr Miller. It's odd a reporter being on a caper like this."

"Koppel, there's no need to worry. What I'm after is a bunch of documents, kept in a safe inside the house. I'll take them, you get anything else there is to hand. O.K?"

"Well, all right. Let's get on with it."

"There's one last thing. The place has a living-in maid," said Miller. "So we'll wait until we know she's asleep."

They walked the mile to Winzer's house, cast a quick look around and darted through the gate. They hid in rhododendron bushes facing what looked like the study.

Koppel made a tour round the house, leaving Miller to watch the bag of tools. When he came back he whispered, "The maid's still got her light on. Window at the back under the eaves."

For an hour they sat shivering in the bushes. Then Koppel made another tour, and reported the girl's light was out. They sat for another ninety minutes before Koppel squeezed Miller's wrist, took his bag and padded through moonlight towards the study windows.

Fortunately for them, the area beneath the windows was in shadow. Koppel flicked on a pencil torch and ran it round the window frame. There was a good burglar-proof window catch but no alarm system. He opened his tool bag.

With remarkable skill he cut a perfect circle on the surface of the glass just below the window catch, performed some quick magic with sticky tape and a suction pad, and then with a rubber hammer he gave the cut circle of window pane a sharp tap. At the second tap the disc fell in towards the room. They waited for a moment then, still gripping the end of the sucker to which the glass disc was attached inside the window, Koppel reached through the hole, unscrewed the burglar catch and eased up the lower window. He was through it as nimble as a fly; Miller followed more cautiously.

Koppel hissed, "Keep still," and Miller froze while the burglar

138

closed the window, drew the curtains, and shut the door to the passage. Only then did he flick on his torch. It swept round the room, picking out a desk, a wall of bookshelves, a deep armchair, and a fireplace surrounded with red brick.

"This must be the study, guv," Koppel muttered. "Where's the lever that opens the brickwork?"

"I don't know," muttered Miller back, imitating the burglar who had learned the hard way that a murmur is far more difficult to detect than a whisper. "You'll have to find it."

"Gor blimey. It could take ages," said Koppel.

He sat Miller in the chair, warning him to keep his gloves on. He slipped a headband round his head with the pencil torch fixed into it, and inch by inch, he went over the whole of the brickwork, feeling with sensitive fingers for bumps or cracks. Then he started again, probing this time with a palette knife. He found it at half-past three. The blade slipped between two bricks, there was a low click, and a section of brick, two feet by two feet in size, swung an inch outward. Behind it the thin beam of Koppel's headlamp picked out a small wall safe.

Koppel slipped a stethoscope on, held the listening end where he judged the tumblers would be, and began to ease the first ring through its combinations.

It took forty minutes before the last tumbler fell over. Gently Koppel eased the safe door back and turned to Miller, the beam from his head darting over a table holding a pair of silver candlesticks and a heavy old snuff box.

Without a word, Miller took the torch from Koppel's headband and used it to probe the safe. On the bottom shelf were several bundles of bank notes which he passed to the grateful burglar. The upper shelf contained only one object, a buff manila folder. Miller pulled it out and riffled through the sheets inside. There were about forty of them. Each contained a photograph and several lines of type. At the eighteenth he paused and said out loud, "Good God."

"Quiet," muttered Koppel, with urgency.

Miller handed the torch back to Koppel. "Close it."

Koppel stuffed the banknotes in his pocket and twirled the dial until the figures were in the original order. Then he eased the brickwork back into place and pressed it firmly home.

He put the candlesticks and snuff-box gently into his black leather holdall, then switching off his light, he slid the window up and hopped through. Miller, with the file stuffed inside his sweater, joined him. He pulled the window down and headed for the shrubbery. When they emerged on the road, Miller had an urge to run.

"Walk slowly," said Koppel. "Just walk and talk like we was coming home from a party."

It was close to five o'clock, but the streets were not wholly deserted, for the German working man rises early to go about his business.

There was no train to Hamburg before seven, but Koppel said he would wait in the station and warm himself with a coffee.

"A very nice little tickle, Herr Miller," he said. "I hope you got what you wanted."

"Oh, yes, thanks. I got it all right," said Miller.

"Well, mum's the word. Bye-bye, Herr Miller." The little burglar nodded and strolled into the station. Miller crossed the square to the hotel, unaware of the red-rimmed eyes that watched him from a parked Mercedes.

It was early to make the calls he needed to, so Miller allowed himself three hours sleep and asked to be wakened at nine-thirty. The phone shrilled at the exact hour, and he ordered breakfast, then took a hot shower. Over coffee he sat and studied the Odessa file, recognizing about half a dozen of the faces.

Sheet eighteen was the one he came back to. The man was older, the hair longer, a sporting moustache covered the upper lip. But the ears were the same—that feature that is more individual than any other—and the narrow nostrils, the tilt of the head, the pale eyes. The name was a common one. What fixed his attention was the address. From the postal district, it had to be the centre of the city, and that would probably mean an apartment building.

Just on ten o'clock he rang telephone information for the city named on the sheet of paper. He asked for the number of the

140

manager for the apartment building at that address. It was a gamble, and it came off. It *was* a block of flats.

He rang the block manager, and explained that he had been trying to get one of the tenants but there was no reply, which was odd because he had been asked to call at that hour. Was the phone out of order?

The man at the other end was most helpful. The Herr Direktor would probably be at the factory. What factory? Why his own, of course. The radio factory. He mentioned its name. Oh, yes, of course, how stupid of me, said Miller.

The girl who answered Miller's call to the factory gave him the boss's secretary who told him that the Herr Direktor was at his country house and would be back on Monday. No, sorry, the house number was private.

The man who finally gave Miller the country address and private telephone number was an old contact, the industrial correspondent of a Hamburg newspaper.

Miller took out his map of Germany and located the area where the estate must be. He got out Winzer's photo of Roschmann and stared at it. He'd heard of the man, a big Ruhr industrialist. And he'd seen his radios in the shops.

It was past twelve o'clock when he packed and settled his bill. He was famished, so he treated himself to a large steak in the hotel dining room. Over his meal he decided to drive the last section of the chase that afternoon and confront his target the next morning. He still had the private telephone number of the lawyer with the Z-Commission in Ludwigsburg. He could have rung him then, but he wanted to face Roschmann first.

It was nearly two when he emerged, stowed his suitcase in the boot of the Jaguar, tossed the document case on the passenger seat and climbed behind the wheel.

He failed to notice the Mercedes that tailed him to the edge of Osnabrück. Mackensen watched the Jaguar accelerate down the autobahn, then he went to a roadside telephone booth. "He's on his way," he told the Werwolf. "Within fifty miles he'll be in pieces you couldn't identify."

141

"Excellent," purred the man in Nuremberg. "You must be tired, my dear *Kamerad*. Go and get some sleep."

Miller made those fifty miles, and more. For Mackensen had overlooked one thing. His trigger device would certainly have detonated quickly if it had been jammed into the cushion suspension system of a continental saloon car. But the Jaguar was a British sports car, with a far harder suspension system. As it tore down the autobahn towards Frankfurt the heavy springs above the front wheels retracted slightly, crushing the light bulb between the jaws of the bomb-trigger. But the electrically-charged lengths of steel failed to touch each other. On the hard bumps they flickered to within a millimetre of each other before springing apart.

Unaware of how close to death he was, Miller made the trip past Munster and Dortmund to Bad Homberg in just under three hours, then turned off towards Königstein and the wild, snow-thick forests of the Taunus mountains.

Chapter Fourteen

It was dark when the Jaguar slid into the small spa town. Miller found he was less than twenty miles from his goal. He decided to find a hotel and wait till morning. Just to the north lay the mountains, quiet and white under a thick carpet of snow. An icy wind gave promise of more snow during the night.

At the corner of Hauptstrasse and Frankfurt Strasse, Miller found a hotel, the Park, and asked for a room.

It was over supper that the nervousness set in. He noticed that his hands were shaking as he raised his wine glass. Part of the condition was exhaustion; part delayed reaction from the tension of the break-in with Koppel. But most, he knew, was the sense of the impending end of the chase, the confrontation with the man he had sought through so many by-ways, and with the fear that something might still go wrong.

He thought of the doctor in Bad Godesberg who had warned him off the pursuit; and of the Nazi-hunter who had said "these men

142

can be dangerous". He wondered why they had not struck at him yet. Perhaps they had lost him, or decided that, with the forger in hiding, he would get nowhere.

And yet he had the file, Winzer's secret, explosive evidence. And he had pulled off the greatest journalistic coup he had ever heard of, and was about to settle a score as well.

He grinned to himself, and the passing waitress thought it was for her. She swung her bottom as she passed his table next time, and he thought of Sigi. He felt that he needed her as he never had before.

He ran over his plan as he finished his wine. A simple confrontation, a telephone call to the Z-commission lawyer at Ludwigsburg, the arrival thirty minutes later of a police van to take the man away for imprisonment, trial, and a life sentence.

He thought it over, and realized he was unarmed. Would Roschmann really be alone, confident that his new name would protect him? Supposing he had a bodyguard?

During his military service one of Miller's friends had stolen a pair of handcuffs from the military police and had given them to him as a trophy of a wild night's roistering in the Army. They were at the bottom of a trunk in the Hamburg flat. He also had a gun, locked in a desk drawer, a small Sauer automatic, bought quite legally when he had been covering an exposé of Hamburg's vice rackets in 1960.

He found a public phone—safer than the hotel, he thought—and called Sigi at the club where she worked. Above the clamour of the band in the background, he had to shout to make her hear. He cut short her stream of questions and told her what he wanted. She protested that she couldn't get away, but something in his voice stopped her.

"Are you all right?" she shouted.

"Yes. I'm fine. But I need your help. Please, darling, don't let me down. Not now, not tonight."

"I'll come," she said simply. "I'll say it's an emergency."

He told her to call an all-night car-hire firm he had used.

"How far is it?" she asked.

"Five hundred kilometres. You can make it in five hours. Or six. You'll arrive about five in the morning."

"All right, expect me." There was a pause. "Peter darling . . . ."

"What?"

"Are you frightened of something?"

"Yes," he said and hung up the receiver.

In the foyer of the hotel he asked the night porter if he could have a large envelope, and after some hunting around the man produced a stiff brown one. Miller also bought enough stamps to cover the cost of sending the envelope by first class mail.

Back in his room he opened his attaché case, which he had carried throughout the evening, and took out Tauber's diary, the sheaf of papers from Winzer's safe, and two photographs. He read again the pages in the diary that had sent him off on this hunt.

Finally he wrote on a sheet of plain paper a brief message, explaining the sheaf of documents. The note, along with the file from Winzer's safe and one of the photographs, he placed inside the envelope, addressed it to the Ministry of Justice in Bonn, sealed and stamped it. The envelope and the diary went back into his attaché case, which he slid under the bed. The other photograph he put into the breast pocket of his jacket.

He carried a small flask of brandy in his suitcase, and he poured a measure into his tooth-glass. His hands were trembling, but the fiery liquid relaxed him. He lay down on the bed, his head spinning slightly, and dozed off.

IN THE underground room in Munich, Josef paced the floor angrily. At the table Leon and Motti gazed at their hands. It was forty-eight hours since the cable had come from Tel Aviv. Their attempts to trace Miller had brought no result. A friend in Stuttgart had informed Leon that the local police were looking for a young man in connection with the murder of a citizen called Bayer. The description fitted Miller.

"He must have known after killing Bayer that he had blown his cover," reasoned Leon, "and so abandoned the search. Unless he got something out of Bayer that took him to Roschmann."

"Then why the hell doesn't he check in," snapped Josef. "Does the fool think he can take Roschmann on his own?"

Motti coughed quietly. "He doesn't know Roschmann has any real importance to the Odessa," he pointed out.

"Well, if he gets close enough, he'll find out," said Leon.

"And by then he'll be a dead man," snapped Josef. "Why doesn't the idiot ring in?"

THE phone lines were busy elsewhere that night. Klaus Winzer had rung the Werwolf, and the news was reassuring.

"Yes, I think it's safe for you to return home," the Werwolf had said. "The reporter has been taken care of."

The Odessa forger had thanked the Odessa chief, and set off for the comfort of his large bed at home in Osnabrück.

MILLER was awakened by a knock at the bedroom door. When he opened it the night porter stood there, Sigi behind him. Miller explained that the lady was his wife who had brought him some important papers from home. The porter took his tip and left.

Sigi threw her arms round him as he shut the door. "Where have you been? What are you doing here?"

He silenced her in the simplest way, and by the time they parted Sigi's cold cheeks were flushed and burning.

He took her coat and hung it on the hook behind the door. She started to ask more questions.

"First things first," he said and pulled her down on the bed with its thick feather cushion.

She giggled. "You haven't changed."

An hour later Miller filled the tooth-glass with brandy and water. Sigi sipped a little, and Miller took the rest.

"So," said Sigi, "would you mind telling me why the mysterious letter, why the six-week absence, why that awful skinhead haircut and why a room in an obscure hotel in Hesse?"

Miller rose, crossed the room and came back with his attaché case.

He seated himself on the edge of the bed, and talked for

145

nearly an hour, starting with the discovery of the diary. As he talked she grew more and more horrified.

"You're mad," she said when he had finished. "Stark, staring, raving mad. All this to get a rotten old Nazi? Why, Peter? Why on earth?"

"I just had to do it," he said defiantly.

She sighed heavily. "All right, so now you know who he is and where he is. You just come back to Hamburg, pick up the phone and ring the police. They'll do the rest."

Miller did not know how to answer her. "It's not that simple," he said. "I'm going up there this morning."

"To his house?" Her eyes widened in horror.

"Yes. Don't ask me why, because I can't tell you. It's just something I have to do."

Her reaction startled him. She sat up with a jerk and glared down at him. "That's what you wanted the gun for," she threw at him. "You're going to kill him . . . ."

"I'm not going to kill him . . . ."

"Well, then, he'll kill you. You're going up there alone against him and his mob, all to make a story for your idiot magazine readers. You don't even think about me, you rotten, horrible . . . ." She had started crying. "Look at me, you great stupid oaf. I want to get married. I want to be Frau Miller. I want to have babies. And you're going to get yourself killed . . . Oh, God. . . ."

She jumped off the bed and ran into the bathroom, slamming the door behind her.

Miller lay there, his cigarette burning down to his fingers. He had never seen her so angry, and it had shocked him. Stubbing out the cigarette he crossed to the bathroom door. "Sigi."

There was no answer. Just the sound of water running.

"Sigi."

Taps were turned off.

"Sigi, please open the door."

There was a pause, then the door was unlocked. "What do you want?" she asked.

"Sigrid Rahn, will you marry me?"

"Do you mean it?" She looked as if she didn't believe it.

"Yes, I do. I never really thought of it before. But then you never got angry before."

"Gosh," she said. "I'll have to get angry more often."

HALF an hour later Klaus Winzer rolled up to his house. He was stiff and tired, but glad to be home.

The maid, Barbara, was not yet up. When she did appear, she told him of her discovery on Saturday morning of the broken window and the missing silverware. She had called the police, and they had been positive the neat, circular hole was the work of a professional burglar. She had told them Winzer was away, and they said they wanted to know when he returned, just for routine questions, about the missing items.

Winzer listened, his face paling, a single vein throbbing steadily in his temple. He dismissed Barbara to the kitchen to prepare coffee, went into his study and locked the door. It took him thirty seconds of frantic scratching inside the empty safe to convince himself that the file of forty Odessa criminals was gone.

For two hours Winzer sat in his chair before the unlit fire, oblivious to the cold seeping in through the newspaper-stuffed hole in the window. Barbara's repeated calls that breakfast was ready went unheeded. Through the keyhole she could hear him muttering, "Not my fault, not my fault at all."

AT NINE Miller showered, finishing off with several minutes under the ice-cold spray. The depression and anxiety of the night before had vanished. He felt fit and confident.

He dressed in ankle-boots and slacks, a thick pullover and his blue duffel jacket. It had deep slit pockets at each side, big enough for the gun and handcuffs, and a breast pocket for the photograph. He took the handcuffs from Sigi's bag and examined them. There was no key and the manacles were self-locking.

He opened and examined the gun. The magazine was full; he kept it that way. He worked the breech several times, smacked the magazine into the grip, pushed a round into the chamber and set the safety catch to "On". He stuffed the telephone number of the lawyer in Ludwigsburg into his trouser pocket.

Sigi was fast asleep, and he wrote a message for her to read when she awoke. "My darling. I am going now to see the man I have been hunting. I have reason for wanting to look into his face, and be present when the police take him. This afternoon I will tell you why. But just in case, here is what I want you to do. . . ."

The instructions were precise. He wrote down the telephone number in Munich she was to ring, and the message she was to give. He ended: "Do not under any circumstances follow me. You could only make matters worse. If I am not back by noon, or have not rung you in this room by then, call that number, give that message, check out of the hotel, post the envelope at any box in Frankfurt, then drive back to Hamburg. Don't get engaged to anyone else in the meantime. All my love, Peter."

On the bedside table he propped the note, the large envelope containing the Odessa file, and three fifty-mark bills. Tucking Tauber's diary under his arm, he slipped out. At the reception desk he asked the porter to give his room a call at eleven-thirty.

Miller went to the car park at the back of the hotel, climbed into the Jaguar, and pressed the starter. While the engine was warming up he brushed the snow off the bonnet, roof and windscreen.

Back behind the wheel he slipped into gear and drove out onto the main road. The thick layer of snow that had fallen during the night acted as a sort of cushion under the wheels. After a glance at the map, he set off down the road towards Limburg.

Chapter Fifteen

The morning was grey and overcast and the wind keened off the mountains. The road wound upward out of town and was soon lost in the sea of trees that make up the Romberg Forest. Miller turned off towards Glashütten, skirted the flanks of the towering Feldberg mountain, on down to the village of Schmitten. In another twenty minutes of careful driving he began to look for the

The Odessa File

gateway to a private estate. When he found it, he headed into the drive.

Two hundred yards on a branch from a massive oak had come down in the night. It had brought down with it a thin black pole which lay square across the drive. Rather than get out and move the pole, Miller drove carefully forward, feeling the bumps as it passed under the front and then the rear wheels.

He moved on and emerged into a clearing which contained a villa, fronted by a circular area of gravel. He climbed out of the car in front of the main door and rang the bell.

WHILE Miller was climbing out of his car, Klaus Winzer made his decision and rang the Werwolf. The Odessa chief was irritable, for it was long past the time he should have heard of a sports car being blown to pieces on the autobahn south of Osnabrück. As he listened his mouth tightened in a thin, hard line.

"You fool, you unbelievable, stupid little cretin. Do you know what's going to happen to you if that file is not recovered? . . ."

Calmly Klaus Winzer replaced the receiver. Taking an old, but serviceable Lüger from the bottom drawer of his desk, he placed the end in his mouth, and fired.

THE WERWOLF sat and gazed in something close to horror at the silent telephone. He thought of the men for whom Klaus Winzer had provided passports and that each of them was destined for arrest and trial if caught. The prospect was appalling.

But his first priority was the protection of Roschmann. Three times he dialled and three times he got the 'unobtainable' signal. Finally, the operator told him the line must be out of order.

So he rang the Hohenzollern Hotel in Osnabrück and caught Mackensen about to leave. In a few sentences he told the killer of the latest disaster and where Roschmann lived. "It looks as if your bomb hasn't worked," he told him. "Get down there faster than you've ever driven. Hide your car and stick close to Roschmann. There's a bodyguard called Oskar as well. If Miller goes straight to the police, we've all had it. But if he comes to Roschmann, take him alive and make him talk. We must know what he's done with those papers before he dies."

"I'll be there at one o'clock," Mackensen said.

THE DOOR opened at the second ring.

Years of good living had put weight on the once-lanky SS officer. He looked the picture of middle-aged, upper-middle-class, prosperous good health. He surveyed Miller without enthusiasm.

"Yes?" he said.

It was several seconds before Miller could speak.

"My name is Miller," he said, "and yours is Eduard Roschmann."

Something flickered through the man's eyes, but he spoke smoothly. "This is preposterous. I've never heard of Eduard Roschmann."

Behind his calm façade the former SS man's mind was racing. Recalling his conversations with the Werwolf, he overcame his first impulse to shut the door in Miller's face.

"Are you alone in the house?" asked Miller.

"Yes," said Roschmann, truthfully.

"I'm coming in," said Miller flatly.

Roschmann turned on his heel and strode back down the hallway and through an open door, with Miller at his heels. It was a comfortable room, evidently a study, with a thick padded door which Miller closed behind him. A log fire burned in the grate.

"Is your wife here?" asked Miller.

Roschmann shook his head. "She has gone away for the weekend to visit relatives," he said. This much was true. And she had taken one of the cars. What Roschmann did not mention was that the other car was in the garage for repairs, and that his chauffeur/ bodyguard, Oskar, had cycled down to the village half an hour earlier to report the telephone out of order. He had to keep Miller talking until Oskar returned.

When he turned to face Miller the young reporter's right hand held an automatic pointed straight at his belly.

Roschmann covered his fright with bluster. "You threaten me with a gun in my own house?"

150

"Then call the police," said Miller. "They'll identify you, Herr Direktor. The face is still the same, also the bullet wound in the chest and the scar under the left armpit where you no doubt tried to remove the Waffen-SS blood group tattoo."

Roschmann let out the air in his lungs in a long sigh.

"What do you want, Miller,"

"Sit down," said the reporter. "And keep your hands on the armrests. Don't give me an excuse to shoot, because I'd dearly love to."

Roschmann sat in the armchair, his eyes on the gun. Miller perched on the edge of the desk facing him. "So now we talk," he said.

"About what?"

"About Riga. About eighty thousand people, men, women and children, whom you had slaughtered up there."

Roschmann began to regain his confidence. "That's a lie. There were never eighty thousand disposed of in Riga."

"Seventy thousand? Sixty?" asked Miller. "Do you really think it matters precisely how many thousands you killed."

"That's the point," said Roschmann eagerly. "It doesn't matter. Look, young man, I don't know why you've come after me. But I can guess. Someone's been filling your head with a lot of sentimental clap-trap about so-called war crimes and the like. It's all nonsense. How old are you?"

"Twenty-nine."

"Then you were in the Army for military service?"

"Yes."

"Then you know. In the Army a man's given orders, he obeys them. He doesn't ask whether they are right or wrong."

"You weren't a soldier," said Miller quietly. "You were an executioner. A murderer. Don't compare yourself with soldiers."

"Nonsense," said Roschmann. "We were soldiers like the rest. You young Germans—you don't know what it was like. . . ."

"So tell me, what was it like?"

Roschmann leaned back, the immediate danger past. "What was it like? We ruled the world, we Germans. We had beaten every

151

army they could throw at us. For years they had done us down, and then we showed them we were a great people. You youngsters don't realize what it is to be proud of being a German.

"It lights a fire inside you. When the flags were waving and the whole nation was united behind one man, we could have marched to the ends of the world. That is greatness, young Miller. And we of the SS were the élite, still are the élite.

"They say a lot of stupid things about what happened to a few Jews in a few camps a sensible world would have forgotten. They make a big cry because we had to clean up the pollution of the Jewish filth that impregnated German life. We had to, I tell you. It was a mere sideshow in the great design of a German people, pure in blood and ideals, ruling the world as is their right, *our* right, Miller, *our* destiny. For make no bones about it, we are the greatest people in the world."

Despite the gun, he rose from his chair and paced the carpet.

"You want proof? Look at Germany today. In 1945, utterly destroyed. And now? Rising again, increasing each year in her industrial and economic power. Yes, and military power. One day we will be as mighty as ever. It will take time, but the ideals will be the same, and the glory the same. And what brings this about? Discipline, harsh discipline, the harder the better. And management. For we can manage things. Look at our factories, churning out power and strength each day to build Germany's might.

"And who do you think did all this? People who mouth platitudes over a few miserable Jews? Or cowards who try to persecute patriotic German soldiers? *We* did this, the same men we had twenty, thirty years ago, we brought this prosperity back to Germany."

He turned from the window and faced Miller, his eyes alight. But he also measured the distance to the heavy iron poker by the fire. Miller had noticed the glance.

"Now, you come here, full of your idealism, hunting me down with a gun. You think that's what they want, the people of Germany?"

Miller shook his head. "No, I don't," he said shortly.

"Well, there you are then. If you turn me in to the police, they might make a trial out of it, but that is not certain, with all the witnesses scattered or dead. So put your gun away and go home. Read the true history of those days, learn that Germany's greatness stems from patriots like me."

Miller had sat through the tirade mute, observing with rising disgust the man who paced the carpet, seeking to convert him. After some seconds he asked, "Have you ever heard of a man called Tauber?"

"Who?"

"Salomon Tauber. He was a German too. Jewish. He was in Riga from the beginning to the end."

Roschmann shrugged. "I can't remember him. Who was he?"

"Sit down," said Miller. "And this time stay down."

Roschmann went back to the armchair. Confident now that Miller would not shoot, his mind was concerned with how to trap him before he could get away.

"Tauber died in Hamburg on November 22nd last year," Miller said. "He gassed himself. Are you listening?"

"Yes. If I must."

"He left behind a diary. It was an account of what happened to him, what you and others did to him, in Riga and elsewhere. But mainly in Riga. He came back to Hamburg, and he lived there for eighteen years because he was convinced you were alive and would never stand trial. I got hold of his diary."

"The diary of a dead man is not evidence," growled Roschmann.

"It is for me. There's a page of it I want you to read."

Miller opened the diary and pushed it into Roschmann's lap.

"Pick it up," he ordered, "and read it—aloud."

Roschmann read the passage in which Tauber described Roschmann's murder of a German Army officer wearing the Knight's Cross with Oak Leaf cluster.

"So what?" he said, at the end of it. "The man struck me. He disobeyed orders. I had the right to commandeer that ship."

Miller tossed a photograph onto Roschmann's lap.

"Is that the man you killed?"

153

Roschmann shrugged. "How should I know? It was twenty years ago."

There was a slow click as Miller thumbed the hammer back and pointed the gun at Roschmann's face.

"Was that the man?"

Roschmann looked at the photograph again.

"So it was. So what?"

"That was my father," said Miller.

The colour drained out of Roschmann's face. "Oh dear God," he whispered, "you didn't come about the Jews at all."

"No. I'm sorry for them, but not that sorry."

"But how could you know from that diary who the man was?"

"My father was killed on October 11th, 1944, in Ostland," said Miller. "For twenty years that was all I knew. Then I read the diary. It was the same day, the same area, the two men had the same rank. Above all, both men wore the Knights Cross with Oak Leaf cluster, the highest award for bravery in the field. There weren't that many of those awarded, and very few to Army captains."

Roschmann stared at the gun as if mesmerized.

"You're going to kill me. You mustn't do that, not in cold blood. You wouldn't do that. Please, Miller, I don't want to die."

Miller leaned forward and began to talk. "I've listened to your twisted mouthings till I'm sick to my guts. Now you're going to listen to me while I make up my mind whether you die here or rot in some jail.

"You had the nerve, the crass bloody nerve, to tell me that you, you of all people, were a patriotic German. I'll tell you what you are. You and all your kind are the worst filth that was ever elevated from the gutters in this country to positions of power. And for twelve years you smeared my country with your dirt.

"What you did sickened and revolted the whole of civilized mankind and left my generation a heritage of shame that's going to take us all our lives to live down. You used the German people until they could not be used any more and then you quit while the going was good. You weren't even brave. You were the most sickening cowards ever born. You murdered millions for your own profit and in the name of your maniac power-lust, and then you ran and hid like the dogs you are. And as for daring to call Army soldiers and others who really fought for Germany '*Kamerad*', it's a bloody obscenity. Patriotism! You don't know what the word means. I'll tell you one other thing, as a German of a generation you so despise. This prosperity we have, it's nothing to do with you. It's got to do with millions who work a hard day and never murdered anyone in their lives."

Miller pulled the telephone over, took the receiver off the cradle, and dialled. "There's a man in Ludwigsburg who wants to have a chat with you," he said. He put the telephone to his ear.

"Have you cut this off? If you have I'll drill you here and now." Roschmann shook his head. "I haven't touched it."

Miller remembered the fallen branch on the drive. He swore softly.

Roschmann gave a small smile. "The lines must be down. You'll have to go into the village. What are you going to do now?"

"I'm going to put a bullet through you unless you do as you're told," Miller snapped. He dragged the handcuffs out of his pocket and tossed them over to Roschmann." Take these to the fireplace," he ordered. "I'm going to lock you to it while I go and find a phone."

He was scanning the wrought-iron scroll work that surrounded the fireplace when Roschmann dropped the handcuffs at his feet and bent as though to pick them up. Instead he gripped the poker and swung it viciously at Miller's kneecaps. Miller stepped swiftly back and whipped the barrel of his pistol across Roschmann's head.

"Try that again and I'll kill you," he said.

Roschmann straightened up, wincing from the blow.

"Clip one of the handcuffs round your right wrist," Miller commanded, and Roschmann did as he was told. "You see that metal branch in front of you? Lock the other bracelet to that."

When Roschmann had snapped the second link, Miller cleared the area around him of all objects he could reach.

Outside in the driveway the man called Oskar pedalled towards

the door, his errand to report the broken phone line accomplished. He paused in surprise on seeing the Jaguar. No one had been expected.

Quietly he let himself in the front door. Then stood irresolute, hearing nothing through the padded door to the study.

Miller took a last look round and was satisfied.

"Incidentally," he told the glaring Roschmann, "it wouldn't have done you any good if you had hit me. I left the complete dossier of evidence on you in the hands of my accomplice, to drop into the post box, addressed to the right authorities, if I have not returned or phoned by midday. As it is I'm going to phone the police from the village. I'll be back in twenty minutes and the police will be no more than thirty minutes behind me. You couldn't be out of there in twenty minutes, even if you had a hacksaw, and I haven't got a key."

As he talked Roschmann's hopes flickered. He knew he only had one chance—for the returning Oskar to take Miller alive so that he could be forced to make the phone call at their demand and keep the documents from reaching the post box. The clock on the mantelpiece read ten-forty.

Miller swung open the door and found himself staring at a man a full head taller than he was.

Roschmann screamed, "Hold him!"

Miller jerked up the gun he'd been replacing in his pocket. He was too slow. A swinging left backhander from Oskar's paw swept it out of his grasp. At the same time Oskar's right crashed into Miller's jaw and lifted all one hundred and seventy pounds of him off his feet. As he fell, his head slammed into the corner of a bookcase. Crumpling like a rag doll, his body slid to the carpet and rolled on its side. From the back of his head a trickle of blood flowed onto the floor.

"You fool!" yelled Roschmann when he had taken in what had happened. Oskar looked baffled. "Get over here."

The giant lumbered across the room.

"Get me out of these handcuffs. Use the fire-irons."

But the fireplace had been built in an age when craftsmen

intended their handiwork to last for a long time. Oskar's efforts merely bent the poker and a pair of tongs.

"Bring him over here," Roschmann told Oskar at last. While Oskar held Miller up, he felt the reporter's pulse.

"He's still alive," he said. "But he'll need a doctor to make him come round. Bring me a pencil and paper."

He scribbled two phone numbers while Oskar went for a hacksaw blade. "Get down to the village as fast as you can. Take the Jaguar," he told Oskar. "Ring this Nuremberg number and tell the man who answers it what has happened. Ring this local number and get the doctor up here immediately. Now hurry."

As Oskar ran from the room Roschmann looked at the clock. Ten-fifty. If Oskar made the village by eleven, and was back with the doctor by eleven-fifteen, they might get Miller to a phone in time. Urgently, he began to saw at his handcuffs.

In front of the door Oskar peered through the window of the Jaguar. The key was in the ignition. He climbed behind the wheel and gunned it into life. He had got up into third gear and was boring down the slippery track as fast as he could take it when he slid round a curve in a spurt of gravel and hit the telegraph pole.

Roschmann was still sawing at the chain linking the two bracelets when the shattering roar in the pine forest stopped. Straining to one side he could peer through the French windows and although the car and the driveway were out of sight, the plume of smoke drifting across the sky told him at least that the car had been destroyed by an explosion. He recalled the assurance he had been given that Miller would be taken care of. But Miller was on the carpet a few feet away from him, his bodyguard was certainly dead, and time was running out. He leaned his head against the fireplace and closed his eyes.

"Then it's over," he murmured quietly. After several minutes he continued sawing. It was over an hour before the specially hardened steel of the military handcuffs parted. As he stepped free, the clock chimed midday.

If he had had time he might have paused to kick the body on the carpet, but he was a man in a hurry.

From the wall safe he took a passport and several fat bundles of new, high-denomination banknotes. Twenty minutes later, he was cycling down the track, round the shattered hulk of the Jaguar and the still smouldering remnants of a body in the snow, past scorched and broken pines, towards the village. From there, he took a taxi to Frankfurt airport. He walked to the Flight Information desk.

"What time is the next flight for Argentina, preferably within an hour? Failing that. . . ."

Chapter Sixteen

It was ten past one when Mackensen's Mercedes turned off the country road into the gate of the estate. Halfway up the drive he found the way blocked.

The Jaguar had evidently been blown apart from inside, but its wheels had not left the road. It was slewed slantwise across the drive. The centre section was completely missing.

Mackensen walked over to the car's skeleton with a grim smile. Then he stooped over the corpse. Something about its size caught his attention. Then he straightened and ran up to the house.

He tried the front door handle. It opened and he went into the hallway. For several seconds he listened, sensing the atmosphere for danger. There was no sound. He reached under his left armpit and brought out a Lüger automatic, flicked off the safety catch and started to open the doors leading off the hall.

The first was the dining room, the second the study. Although he saw the body on the hearth-rug at once, he did not move from the half-open door before he had covered the rest of the room. Warily he glanced through the crack between the door's hinges to make sure no one waited behind it, then entered.

Miller was lying on his back with his head turned to one side. For several seconds Mackensen stared down into the chalky white face. The matted blood on the back of the head told him roughly what had happened.

He scoured the house, noting the open drawers in the bedroom, the missing shaving tackle from the bathroom. Back in the study, he glanced into the empty wall-safe, then picked up the telephone. He sat listening for several seconds, swore under his breath and replaced it. He found the tool chest, took what he needed and went back down the drive, leaving by the French windows.

It took him almost an hour to find the parted strands of the telephone line and connect them. When he was finished he walked back to the house and rang his chief in Nuremberg.

He had expected the Werwolf to be eager to hear from him, but the man sounded tired and only half-interested. Mackensen reported what he had found, the car, the corpse of the bodyguard, Miller unconscious on the floor. He finished with the absent owner.

"He hasn't taken much, Chief. Overnight things. I can clear up and he can come back if he wants to."

"No, he won't come back," the Werwolf told him. "He called me from Frankfurt airport. He's booked on a flight to Madrid, connection this evening to Buenos Aires. . . ."

"But there's no need," protested Mackensen. "I'll make Miller talk, we can find where he left his papers. There was no document case in the car wreckage, and nothing on him, except a sort of diary lying on the floor. But the rest of his stuff must be somewhere not far away."

"Far enough," replied Werwolf. "In a post box."

Wearily he told Mackensen what Miller had stolen from the forger, and what Roschmann had told him on the phone. "Those papers will be in the hands of the authorities in the morning, or Tuesday at the latest. After that everyone on that list is on borrowed time. I've spent the whole morning trying to warn everyone concerned to get out of the country inside twenty-four hours."

"So where do we go from here?" asked Mackensen.

"You get lost," replied his chief. "You're not on that list. I am, so I have to get out. Go back to your flat and wait until my successor contacts you. For the rest, it's over. With Vulkan's departure his whole operation is going to fall apart unless someone new can come in and take over the project.

"Since it's over, you might as well know. Vulkan was the name for Roschmann . . ." and in a few sentences Werwolf explained to Mackensen why he was supposed to have eliminated Miller. When he had finished, Mackensen uttered a low whistle.

The Werwolf seemed to pull himself together and some of the old authority returned to his voice. "*Kamerad*, you must clear up the mess over there. You remember that disposal squad you used once before?"

"Yes, they're not far from here."

"Have them leave the place without a trace of what happened. The man's wife must never know what happened. Understand?"

"It'll be done," said Mackensen.

"Then make yourself scarce. One last thing. Before you go, finish that bastard Miller. Once and for all."

Mackensen looked across at the unconscious reporter with narrowed eyes. "It'll be a pleasure."

"Then goodbye and good luck."

Mackensen took out an address book, thumbed through it and dialled a number. He introduced himself to the man who answered and told him where to come, and what he would find.

"The car and the body beside it have to go into a deep gorge off a mountain road. Plenty of petrol over it, a real big blaze. Leave nothing identifiable on the man—take everything."

"Got it," said the voice. "I'll bring a trailer and winch."

"There's one last thing. In the study of the house you'll find another stiff on the floor. Get rid of it. A long cold drop to the bottom of a long cold lake. Well weighted."

"No problem. We'll be there by five and gone by seven. I don't like to move that kind of cargo in daylight."

"Fine," said Mackensen. "I'll be gone before you get here."

He hung up, slid off the desk and walked over to Miller. He pulled out his Lüger and held the gun at arm's length pointing downward, lined up on the forehead.

Years of living like a predatory animal had given Mackensen the senses of a leopard. He didn't see the shadow that fell on the carpet from the open French window; he felt it. He spun round.

161

The man stood in the French window, dressed in the black leather leggings and jacket of a motor-cyclist. In his left hand he held his crash helmet across his stomach. The man flicked a glance at the body at Mackensen's feet and the gun in his hand.

"Who the hell are you?" Mackensen kept him covered.

"I was sent for," he said innocently.

"Who by?" said Mackensen.

"Vulkan," replied the man. "My *Kamerad*, Roschmann."

Mackensen lowered the gun. "Well, he's gone."

"Gone?"

"Heading for South America. The project's off—thanks to this bastard reporter." He jerked the gun towards Miller.

"You going to finish him?" asked the man.

"Sure. The Werwolf's orders."

"The Werwolf?"

Something sounded an alarm inside Mackensen. How could a man know Vulkan and not know Werwolf? His eyes narrowed.

"You're from Buenos Aires?" he asked.

"No."

"Where from then?"

"Jerusalem."

It was half a second before this made sense to Mackensen. Then he swung up his Lüger. But half a second is a long time, long enough to die.

The foam rubber inside the crash helmet was scorched when the Walther PPK went off. The slug went through the fibreglass and took Mackensen high in the breastbone with the force of a kicking mule. The helmet dropped to the ground to reveal Josef's right hand, and from inside the cloud of blue smoke the PPK fired again.

Mackensen was a strong man. Despite the bullet in his chest he would have fired, but the second slug entering his head above the right eyebrow spoiled his aim. It also killed him.

MILLER awoke on Monday afternoon in a private ward in Frankfurt General Hospital. He lay for half an hour, becoming slowly aware that his head was swathed in bandages. He found a buzzer and pressed it, but the nurse who came told him to lie quietly because he had severe concussion. So he lay, and piece by piece recollected the events of the previous day. He dozed off and when he woke a man was sitting by his bed. Miller stared at him.

"I've seen you," he said at length. "You were in Oster's house. With Leon and Motti. Josef, they called you."

"That's right. What else do you remember?"

"Almost everything. Roschmann?"

"Roschmann's gone. Fled back to South America. The whole affair's over. Finished. Do you understand?"

Miller slowly shook his head. "Not quite. I've got one hell of a story. And I'm going to write it."

Josef leaned forward. "Listen Miller. You're a bloody amateur, and you're lucky to be alive. You're going to write nothing. For one thing you've got nothing to write. I've got Tauber's diary and it's going back home with me, where it belongs. I read it last night. There was a photograph of an Army captain in your jacket pocket. Your father?"

Miller nodded.

"So that was what it was really all about?" asked the agent.

"Yes."

"Well, in a way I'm sorry. About your father I mean. I never thought I'd say that to any German. Now about the file. Why the hell couldn't you have let us have it? We could have used that information to best advantage."

"I had to send it to someone through Sigi. That meant by mail. You're so clever, you never let me have Leon's address."

Josef nodded. "All right. But either way, you have no story to tell. You have no evidence. The diary's gone, the file is gone. If you insist on talking nobody will believe you except the Odessa, and they'll come for you. Or rather, they'll hit Sigi or your mother. They play rough, remember?"

Miller thought for a while. "What about my car?"

Josef told Miller about the bomb. "I told you they play rough. The car has been found gutted by fire in a ravine. The body in it is unidentified, but not yours. Your story is that you were flagged

163

down by a hitchhiker, he knocked you out and went off in your car. The hospital will confirm you were brought in by a passing motor-cyclist who called an ambulance when he saw you by the roadside. That's the official version. To make sure it will stick, I rang the German Press Agency, claiming to be the hospital, and gave them the story."

Josef stood up and looked down at Miller. "I wonder if you realize how lucky you are. I got the message from your girl-friend at midday yesterday, and by riding like a maniac I made it from Munich to Roschmann's house in two and a half hours dead. Which was what you almost were—dead."

He turned, hand on the doorknob.

"Take some advice. Go back to Hamburg, marry Sigi, have kids and stick to reporting. Don't tangle with professionals again."

Half an hour after he had gone the nurse came back.

"There's a phone call for you," she said.

It was Sigi, crying and laughing. An anonymous call had told her where Peter was. "I'm on my way this minute."

The phone rang again. "Miller? This is Hoffman. I just saw a piece on the agency tapes. You got a bang on the head. Are you all right?"

"I'm fine, Herr Hoffman," said Miller.

"Great. When are you going to be fit to work?"

Miller thought. "Next week. Why?"

"I've got a story that's right up your street. By the way, that Nazi-hunt you were on. Was there a story at all?"

"No, Herr Hoffmann," said Miller slowly. "No story."

"Didn't think so. Hurry up and get well. See you in Hamburg."

JOSEF'S plane came into Lod Airport, Tel Aviv, as dusk was settling on Tuesday. He was met and taken to headquarters for debriefing by the man who had signed the cable from Cormorant. They talked until almost two in the morning, a stenographer noting it all down. When it was over Cormorant leaned back, smiled, and offered his agent a cigarette.

"Well done," he said simply. "We've checked on the factory

and tipped off the authorities—anonymously of course. The research section will be dismantled. We'll see to that, even if the German authorities don't. The scientists apparently didn't know who they were working for. Most will destroy their records. The weight of opinion in Germany today is pro-Israeli, so they'll keep their mouths shut. What about Miller?"

"He'll do the same. What about those rockets?"

The colonel blew a column of smoke and gazed at the stars in the night sky outside. "I have a feeling they'll never fly now. Nasser has to be ready by the summer of '67 at the latest, and without the tele-guidance work from that Vulkan factory they'll never mount an operation in time."

"Then the danger's over," said the agent.

Cormorant smiled. "The danger's never over. It just changes shape. This particular danger may be over. The big one goes on. Anyway, you must be tired. You can go home now." At the door they shook hands. "Welcome home, Major Uri Ben Shaul."

The major took a taxi to his flat in the suburbs and let himself in. In the darkened bedroom he could make out the sleeping form of Rivka, his wife. He peeked into the children's room and looked down at their two boys, Shlomo who was six, and the two-year-old baby, Dov.

He wanted badly to climb into bed, but there was one more job to be done. He quietly undressed, then put on his uniform. His trousers were cleaned and pressed as they always were when he came home. His khaki shirts had razor-sharp creases where the hot iron had pressed. He slipped on his battle jacket, adorned only with the glinting steel wings of a paratroop officer and the five campaign ribbons he had earned in Sinai and in raids across the borders.

The final article was his red beret. When he had dressed he took several articles and stuffed them into a small bag. There was already a dim glint in the east when he got back outside and found his small car parked where he had left it a month before.

He drove eastward out of Tel Aviv and took the road to Jerusalem. There was a stillness about the dawn that he loved, a peace and a cleanness that never ceased to cause him wonder. He had seen it a thousand times on patrol in the desert, the phenomenon of a sunrise, cool and beautiful, before the onset of a day of blistering heat.

When he had climbed up the last hills to Jerusalem the sun had cleared the eastern horizon and glinted off the Dome of the Rock in the Arab section of the divided city.

He parked his car a quarter of a mile from his destination, the mausoleum of Yad Vashem, and walked down the avenue flanked by trees, planted in memory of the gentiles who had tried to help, and to the great bronze doors that guard the shrine to six million Jews who died in the holocaust.

The old gatekeeper told him it was not open so early, but he explained what he wanted and the man let him in. He passed through into the hall of remembrance, and walked forward to the rail.

By the light of the Eternal Flame he could see the names written across the floor, in Hebrew and Roman letters: Auschwitz, Treblinka, Belsen, Ravensbrück, Buchenwald . . . There were too many to count, but he found the one he sought. Riga.

He did not need a yarmulka to cover his head, for he wore his red beret. From his bag he took a fringed silk shawl, the tallith, the same kind of shawl Miller had found among Tauber's effects. This he draped around his shoulders.

He took a prayer book from his bag and opened it. He advanced to the brass rail, gripped it with one hand and gazed across it at the flame in front of him. Because he was not a religious man he had to consult his prayer book frequently.

> *Yisgaddal,*
> *Veyiskaddash,*
> *Shemay rabbah. . . .*

And so it was that a major of paratroops of the Army of Israel, standing on a hill in the Promised Land, finally said kaddish for the soul of Salomon Tauber.

Author's Note

It would be agreeable if things in this world always finished with the ends neatly tied up. That is very seldom the case. People go on, to live and die at their own appointed time and place. For instance, of those characters who appear in my book under their own names, Simon Wiesenthal still lives and works in Vienna, gathering a fact here, a tip there, slowly tracking down the whereabouts of wanted SS murderers, and each month and year brings him a crop of successes. Lord Russell also is alive and well and living in Dinard. As for Eduard Roschmann, so far as it has been possible to establish, he is still in Argentina.

The rockets of Helwan never flew. The fuselages were ready, along with the rocket fuel, but all forty pre-production rockets, helpless for want of the electronic systems necessary to guide them to their targets in Israel, were still standing in the deserted factory at Helwan when they were destroyed by bombers during the Six-Day War. Before that the German scientists had disconsolately returned to Germany.

Recently a lawyer and investigator of the Z-Commission in Ludwigsburg was able to say, "1964 was a good year for us, yes, a very good year". At the end of 1964 Chancellor Erhard himself issued a nation-wide and international appeal for all those having knowledge of the whereabouts of wanted SS criminals to come forward and tell the authorities. The response was considerable and the work of the men of Ludwigsburg received an enormous fillip.

Of course many characters in the book could not appear under their own names, but they and all those who helped me get the information I needed are entitled to my heartfelt thanks. If I do not name them all it is for three reasons.

Some, being former members of the SS, were not aware at the time that what they said would end up in a book. Others have specifically asked that their names never be mentioned as sources of information about the SS. In the case of others still, the decision not to mention their names is mine alone, and taken I hope for their sakes rather than for mine.

F.F.

THE WALTZ KINGS
Hans Fantel

The Waltz Kings

by
HANS FANTEL

a condensation of the book
Johann Strauss: Father and Son,
and Their Era

Illustrated by David McCall Johnston
Published by David & Charles, Newton Abbot

They were truly monarchs of music. From humble beginnings, the first Johann Strauss became the composer and conductor who introduced the waltz to the world. His son, also called Johann Strauss, immortalized this most romantic of all dances with such melodies as "The Blue Danube", "The Emperor Waltz", and "Tales from the Vienna Woods".

In a family torn by fierce loyalties and tragic jealousies, their lives were rich in drama and not untouched by scandal. Yet from country inn to the great halls of the royal palace, their music caught the spirit of a people and of the vibrant, fairy-tale city of Vienna.

It has been said that the meaning of any music lies not only in *what* it is but, often more importantly, in *why* it is. By recreating so vividly the fantastic personalities of the Waltz Kings and their era, Hans Fantel takes us into the world of musical genius, enabling us to understand their work better and thus to appreciate it all the more.

CHAPTER ONE

BEFORE it reaches the city the western wind sweeps over vast Alpine forests, taking from them a fragrance that makes Vienna's summer air as heady as its wine. But in winter the wind carries the chill from snowy peaks. On March 14, 1804, when the first Johann Strauss was born, the midwife was delayed by glare ice. She arrived just in time to keep the frail little boy from by-passing this world altogether.

The scene of his arrival was a shabby tavern called The Good Shepherd, on an island bounded by two branches of the Danube. Johann's father and mother, Franz and Barbara Strauss, as owners of the dank, low-ceilinged inn which offered shelter and beer to riverboat sailors, were counted among the lower, but still respectable, class of citizens. Little is known of Franz Strauss except that he was uncommonly moody, which gave rise to rumours of suicide when shortly after a second marriage his body was found in the Danube.

Johann's mother had died when he was seven, and after his father's drowning he had stayed on at The Good Shepherd with his stepmother, who eventually remarried. Johann's stepfather, a genial man named Golder who was genuinely fond of the boy, soon changed the dour atmosphere of the tavern. Strolling musicians, who groped through the dark lanes from alehouse to alehouse by the dim light of pig-fat lanterns, were invited to play a few tunes for the customers before moving on.

A pair of violins, a cello, and a zither made up the more imposing of these groups. At other times, a solitary "beer fiddler" might scratch out a dance in exchange for some goulash. Whatever the level of the performance, the very sound of music created a paradise for Johann. Night after night the child huddled in the background among barrels and ham hocks, listening.

Golder noticed the boy's entrancement, and on Johann's saint's day he made him the present of a violin. It was little more than a toy, but Johann soon discovered that he could improve its dry, buzzy tone by pouring beer into its "f" holes.

He taught himself to play the tunes he heard from the strolling players, and the beer-soaked fiddle became the focus of his life. At school he did poorly because the fiddle distracted him. He always kept it under his desk, and played it in the yard during recess. What Golder had given as a toy had become an obsession, and his stepfather cursed the violin. Then a perceptive schoolmaster suggested music lessons for Johann. But Golder had seen too many besotted fiddlers at his inn. His boy was to learn a solid trade.

At the age of thirteen Johann was apprenticed to a bookbinder. He detested the smelly glue, boiled down from animal bones. He refused to work, and once, weeping and shouting, he dashed the glue pot to the ground. The usual whipping had no effect so the bookbinder resorted to incarceration. But his wife took pity on the wild boy and, in her husband's absence, opened the door to the dark storeroom where he was kept. Johann dashed out, grabbed his fiddle, and ran off.

He headed west, towards the Vienna Woods. There, he knew, were the vintners' inns with shady courtyards, where the Viennese came every afternoon to sample new wine. Surely a young man of fourteen who played as well as he could earn his keep with his

174

violin. But when he reached the *Heurigen* district he felt too shy to enter the guest-filled gardens. He walked on towards the slopes of the Kahlenberg, that last gentle echo of the Alps rising above Vienna like a huge hand cradling the city in its palm.

Along the way Johann may have met a leonine man striding with his hands behind his back, whose tortured face suggested that he was not native to this genial land. Those who encountered Ludwig van Beethoven shied away from the gruff northerner who refused companionship rather than admit his deafness. But the landscape sang in Beethoven's ears: vineyards and gardens and brooks patterning the hills and the meadows. And in the distance where the ribbon of the Danube unites mountain and plain, Vienna lay like a jewel in its setting. Beethoven, on his daily walks, distilled from Vienna's landscape the sublime music of the "Pastoral" Symphony.

Other musicians, too, had been profoundly affected by the spell of this singular region. Schubert, too chubby to do much hiking through the countryside, liked to spend his afternoons at the inn here, sharing a jug of *Nussberger* with friends, flirting with the waitress, and—in the absence of napkins—jotting down music on his cuffs. Some years later, Robert Schumann, on visiting Vienna, wrote at length in his diary how the vista from the Kahlenberg had stirred his mind.

Indeed, the view from the Kahlenberg encompasses the regions from which Vienna, the heart of Europe, draws its lifeblood: the Alpine west lent Germanic influence; the eastern plains, stretching towards Asia, added Slavic and Magyar elements to the Viennese mix; and to the south, beyond the mountain pass of Semmering, was the outpost of Mediterranean culture.

Slowly Johann climbed towards the small castle at the crest of the mountain, making his way among the weather cannon in the vineyards. The sole purpose of these enormous guns was to make loud noises which, as everyone knew, shook up the clouds and scared off hailstorms that might damage the grapes.

But on that balmy afternoon in 1818 the weather cannon lay silent. By the time Johann gained the heights above the vineyards

the sun stood low, illuminating the red tile roofs and green copper domes of the city below. The runaway was tired from walking and excitement. He fell asleep by the wayside with his fiddle in his arms as the warm summer night settled over him.

BY A fateful coincidence, it was a professional musician, a certain Herr Polischansky who, while taking his evening walk, found the boy. Curious about the fiddle, he wakened Johann, and soon the two were chatting happily about music. For the first time in his life, Johann spoke with a man who understood the mysteries of tone that so entranced him. How different he was from those inarticulate beer fiddlers at the tavern!

Polischansky was able to persuade Johann to return home. Convinced of the boy's talent, he promised to give him free lessons and to talk with his stepfather about his following a musical career.

Meanwhile, the bookbinder had told Johann's step-parents everything about the boy's behaviour at the bindery and of the drastic measures taken to discipline him. The couple were desolate; they felt sure that the boy had inherited his father's bent towards self-destruction, and had done himself harm.

In his joy and relief at Johann's safe return, Golder readily accepted Polischansky's offer, though he insisted that his stepson should also continue his bookbinding apprenticeship. But now that Johann could devote himself mainly to music, he no longer detested that glue pot and eventually won his journeyman's papers.

As a violinist, Johann surmounted the problems of technique with a sort of natural knack, and soon outgrew Polischansky's ability to teach him. At the age of fifteen, after only one year of formal study, he became a violist in Michael Pamer's string orchestra—Vienna's most famous dance-music ensemble.

Pamer was a capable musician, but a drunkard who suffered from the curious delusion that he had somehow swallowed a Capuchin monk alive. He also had fits of foul-mouthed drunken rage which he vented on his musicians. Yet for all his failings, it was largely through Pamer that the waltz gained a foothold in Vienna's glittering ballrooms.

Three-quarter time dances seem to have originated in the Black Forest and the Danube uplands, where the strong beat formed the basis of rustic tunes, rollicking with the persuasive *oom-pah-pah* that impelled dancers to turn, turn, and keep turning.

The swirling music reached Vienna on ships that plied the Danube between there and the upstream city of Linz. Of course, to the Austrians a boat ride without music would have been inadequate, and every ship had a deck orchestra. Docking in Vienna, the musicians would pick up extra money by playing their upland dances in the riverfront taverns.

Jumping was the salient feature of outdoor folk dances, for heavy boots and rough ground made it necessary for the dancers to be up in the air while turning. These leaps were too strenuous for the fashionable Viennese, and the precursors of the waltz were banished to the suburban inns. It was Napoleon who unwittingly prepared the triumph of the waltz.

In 1809 French troops stood at Vienna's gates. The Viennese, far too fond of their city to expose even a single plaster cherub to Napoleon's cannonballs, surrendered.

But it was Napoleon who was conquered. The Viennese treated him with the cheerful courtesy they would have shown any visiting monarch. Napoleon, in turn, showed the Viennese every consideration. He further endeared himself to them by his fondness for music, his frequent visits to concerts and the opera, and by posting a guard of honour at the house of Vienna's most revered musician, the septuagenarian Haydn.

Rumours that the French emperor breakfasted on newborn children soon lost their credibility. The Viennese even began to take pride in Napoleon's admiration of their city, and the General soon found that he could move about Vienna without special security provisions. In fact, when a young German radical tried to kill Napoleon, the Viennese were outraged at such an unmannerly breach of decency and hospitality. While Napoleon urged clemency for his would-be assassin, the Viennese insisted on executing the young man.

This strange relationship between conqueror and conquered

culminated in 1810, when Napoleon married the Austrian Arch-duchess Marie Louise, thereby becoming an in-law of the House of Habsburg. But Napoleon was too restless to become Viennese. His devouring ambition drove him eastward against Russia. By 1814 he had been exiled to Elba, and his enemies were gathering at the Congress of Vienna under the aegis of his royal father-in-law to forge a Holy Alliance against him.

The Congress had a hard time getting down to business. In fact, it never really did. There were simply too many distractions in Vienna. When one of the delegates, Prince de Ligne, was asked, "How goes the Congress?" he replied tartly, "It doesn't go; it dances."

The Viennese thoroughly enjoyed the panache and pageantry, grumbling only faintly about the extra taxes imposed to pay for it all. They were rewarded by the colourful sight of six royal delegations and their retinues riding daily through the streets, and by the seven hundred foreign diplomats who took up local residence. The Viennese watched the miserly King of Denmark haggle with shopkeepers, wondered at the quirks of Talleyrand, who always travelled with his own pianist to play for him. Everyone knew that furtive man with the big round hat drawn over his face who nightly walked certain streets in obvious search of company was really the Grand Duke of Baden. And they heard about the dinner party at Count Zichy's, where the Tsar engaged the sprightly young Countess Wrbna-Kageneck in an argument as to whether men or women spent longer over their toilettes. To settle the question, they withdrew together to undress and dress again, an incident often discussed by the papal nuncio, Monsignor Severoli, who disapproved. History does not record the results of the experiment.

Parties, plays, parades, concerts, horseshows, and fireworks crowded the calendar. And in the wake of the dignitaries trundled an army of courtiers, servitors, adventurers, pickpockets, and mothers anxious to peddle their daughters to the highest title or the highest bidder. In its expectant holiday mood, this motley horde displayed an almost pathological craving for entertainment.

Night after night, dance-mad crowds filled Vienna's ballrooms.

It was in the largest, most ornate and resplendent of these, the famous Sperl, that Michael Pamer's orchestra played. To satisfy the public's demand for new and more exciting music, Pamer borrowed some of those three-quarter-time dances from the outlying inns, slowing the tempo so that the Viennese could replace rural hops and leaps with a gliding step. As in the country dances, the couples kept turning. And because swirling is easier when you have something to hold on to, the town dancers soon copied the old country trick of embracing one another.

This startling change from the minuet made the new dance instantly notorious. But moral outcries in Vienna were stifled in the licentious atmosphere of the Congress. The new dance swept the city, and an obvious name for it soon gained currency: *Walzer*— revolving dance.

Vienna's waltz fever continued even after the Congress disbanded in alarm at the chilling news that Napoleon had escaped from Elba, his island exile, and was reconquering France. But imminent disaster never kept the Viennese from their pleasures. They continued to build splendid ballrooms until the total capacity was more than fifty thousand. Since they were invariably sold out, this meant that every fourth adult in Vienna was out dancing every evening.

The popular Apollo-Säle, for example, held four thousand dancers in five huge halls with graceful marble pillars lined against mirrored walls that multiplied the brilliant crystal chandeliers. There were forty-four intimate drawing-rooms, three flower-filled garden pavilions domed with glass, artificial grottoes with water-falls and live swans, and thirteen kitchens.

Even the humblest inn had to have an orchestra of sorts to attract trade. In this ready and constantly shifting market for musicians, it is hardly surprising that young Johann Strauss did not stay long in Pamer's orchestra. When he had first joined it, he had shared a desk with Josef Lanner, a glover's son and talented musician only three years older than he. Lanner had been playing with Pamer since he was twelve, but revolted by Pamer's alcoholic coarseness, he had left to form a trio of two fiddles and a guitar. This modest ensemble's meagre bookings in small coffee-houses hardly kept its members alive, so Lanner resolved to expand it into a quartet and asked Johann Strauss to join as violist.

As the junior member of the group, it was Strauss's job to pass the tin plate among the patrons at the end of each concert, a painful chore. But the sheer exhilaration of making music with a congenial group made up for the hardships of his life. To cut overheads, he and Lanner moved into the same room, which also enabled each to deny the other's presence to pursuing creditors. By August 1821 they were so impoverished that they took turns wearing the only shirt they had between them. When they went out together, one of them, despite the summer heat, had to wear his coat buttoned to the neck and his collar turned up.

From this nadir their fortunes rose swiftly. Joining Lanner's sweetness of tone to Strauss's rhythmic verve, they fashioned a distinctive and captivating style of music that was quickly recognized and rewarded. In their ascent from the small coffee-houses to the great ballrooms they expanded their group to a well-drilled orchestra of some twenty players and became Vienna's most celebrated musical attraction. As if to compensate for the time of shared shirts, both now lived in comfortable apartments, and their colourful tailcoats and cravats were always in the latest fashion.

The orchestra owed much of its popularity to the waltzes Lanner composed. Vienna had never heard such music before. Lanner interlaced several distinct and contrasting waltz melodies into a garland of tunes framed by a formal introduction and ending. He was in the habit of composing a new number for every special occasion, usually jotting down a sketchy score the evening before the concert and rehearsing the new piece in the morning. One evening he felt ill and asked Strauss to take over the morning rehearsal.

"But what about the new number for tomorrow?" Strauss exclaimed.

"Why don't you think of something?" Lanner suggested.

That, according to his own account, is how Johann Strauss became a composer.

Strauss's first waltzes appeared on the programmes under Lanner's name. But the audience's enthusiasm encouraged him to acknowledge his own work. Soon he and Lanner ruled Vienna's musical life on equal terms.

They took turns in conducting the orchestra, and jointly revised not merely the form but the attitude to the waltz. By the eighteen twenties romanticism was in early bloom. The unvarnished sensualist of the Congress period had welcomed Pamer's quick-stepping waltzes as a pretext for getting a tight grip on a girl. But the flowery swain of the next decade wanted romance garnished with illusion and ceremony.

Of the two composers, Lanner was more lyrical. A man of quiet, matter-of-fact piety, he inscribed each new score: "With God— Josef Lanner". Although less tender than Lanner's, Strauss's tunes were catchier. One contemporary critic pinpointed the difference: "With Lanner, it's, 'Please dance, I entreat you!' With Strauss, it's, 'You must dance, I command you!'"

The Viennese public delighted in the contrast of the two personalities. The slender, flaxen-haired, fine-featured Lanner projected romantic delicacy. The dark Strauss, now nearing twenty, with his burning eyes and jet-black curls, embodied romantic passion. They were dubbed "Flaxhead" and "Blackamoor" respectively, and their admirers split into fiercely partisan camps. The distinctive qualities of the two composers were constantly mulled over in the Press, in coffee-houses, and on the street. And by treating them as rivals, the public subverted their friendship.

The inevitable clash came in the autumn of 1825. Strauss and Lanner were playing at The Ram, an inn they favoured for the excellent acoustics of its arcaded courtyard. It was long past midnight and everyone was tired and nervous. Suddenly the hot-tempered Strauss took exception to what he considered a slighting remark by Lanner. In front of the audience, he leapt at his friend. The musicians, trying to separate their leaders, became themselves embroiled, duelling with flutes and clarinets, splintering cellos and basses. Even the inn's great gilt-framed mirror was shattered. Fortunately, casualties were confined to a few bruises.

A few days later Strauss composed a "Reconciliation Waltz" dedicated to Lanner. Lanner countered with a "Separation Waltz" that opened with a lament. Both men retained their personal fondness for each other, but never again did they appear together. At the age of twenty-one Strauss was on his own.

THE dark-haired girl who seated herself next to the orchestra nearly every night was pretty enough to have caught Strauss's eye even if she hadn't so obviously sought his attention. Of course, there were always pert little girls flirting with Strauss and he made the most of it. But with Anna Streim things were different.

When he finally spoke to her, he discovered to his surprise that she had a critical intelligence and was unafraid to show it. At twenty-four she had no more education than other lower-class women, but her frankness and perceptivity must have been striking at a time when the fashion called for women to swoon rather than think.

Strauss was also impressed by Anna's musicality. She was an excellent guitarist and had keen musical judgment. When she praised one of Strauss's waltzes she could give precise reasons for liking it. For Strauss, who had known only blind adulation and empty badinage from women, the combined attraction of sex and shoptalk proved irresistible. They were married in July. The fight with Lanner left Strauss jobless in September, and their baby was due in October. He needed money, but could expect no dowry with his bride, who was the daughter of an ex-coachman turned innkeeper. Anna liked to embellish her prosaic descent. Her mother, she claimed, was the child of a Spanish grandee who had fled from Spain after killing a member of the royal family in a duel, found refuge at a Bohemian estate, where he changed his name, became a cook, and soon died from his sorrows—a story which is lovingly detailed in the Strauss family papers.

Anna's dark complexion, jet-black hair, full lips, and almond eyes might well have been Iberian. She owned a beautiful guitar unquestionably of Spanish origin, which she said had been her grandfather's. But, on balance, the story of her noble descent

Left, Johann Strauss, Sr.; above,
Frau Anna Strauss; right, Josef
Lanner, and a Viennese court
ball of the period.

attests mainly to the quality of her imagination. Certainly, the invention of such a pedigree is in keeping with the character of a girl whose high spirits and resolute ambition were as much a factor in establishing a dynasty of the waltz as the genius of her husband and sons.

The child was born on October 25, 1825. If the young father could have known that his son's fame would one day surpass his own, he might not have christened him Johann, also.

Strauss had little time to devote to his new family. He was busy building an orchestra of his own, and raiding Lanner's. He booked his group, which included fourteen of his former colleagues, under his own name at the Two Pigeons inn.

Success there was by no means assured. He was known, after all, as Lanner's partner. The owner of the Two Pigeons was taking a chance on Strauss alone and said so. To mollify him, Strauss wrote the "Pigeon Waltz" for his début, a tune replete with phrases inspired by the cooing of Vienna's abundant turtledoves.

Whatever apprehensions the innkeeper may have felt vanished

in the shouts and applause as Strauss leapt to the podium and signalled the downbeat. With demonic intensity, he fiddled along with his players indicating rhythm and phrasing with his hips and shoulders, magically welding the audience into a single swaying body.

From that day on Strauss always had more offers than he could handle. If only he could be in two places at once, then he could collect two fees. To implement this idea he divided the orchestra, hired extra musicians, appointed assistant conductors, booked two halls, and appeared in each for half the evening.

With mounting demand for his appearance at private balls as well as public functions, this process of division continued until, by 1830, he had two hundred musicians under contract, and eight orchestras. On a typical evening he would race by cab from place to place, conduct the same meticulously rehearsed sequence of waltzes in each location, fight his way out through adoring crowds, and hurry on to the next assignment.

By about three in the morning he would arrive home, not

exhausted but tingling with excitement. In this state of feverish stimulation he would cover his notebooks with ideas for the new waltzes his public constantly demanded. A brief sleep around daybreak sufficed to refresh him for the next rehearsal.

Lanner, lacking the taste and stamina for this type of big-business operation, might well have felt envy. But his more patient merit was rewarded in 1829 by his appointment as director of the imperial court balls. Not to be outdone, Strauss entered into an exclusive contract, at an unprecedented fee, with Sperl. As a boy of fifteen he had played viola there under Pamer. Now, in 1833, at the age of twenty-nine, Strauss was on view to the world, for Sperl's was Vienna's tourist showplace.

The constant flow of foreign visitors to the hall included Richard Wagner, a nineteen-year-old youngster from Saxony who had already composed two operas. "I shall never forget the almost hysterical response evoked by every piece of Strauss's in these curious people," Wagner wrote. "A demon within the Viennese populace seems to be summoned anew at the beginning of every waltz. The shudders of sheer pleasure in the audience are unquestionably due to the music rather than the wine, and the frenzied enthusiasm for the magic music master struck me as frightening."

Wagner was astonished that all this merrymaking continued right through a cholera epidemic in which hundreds died daily. "Nobody dreams of altering his life and the places of amusement are crowded," he reported. The waltzing soon sweated his fears out of him. Night after night, Richard Wagner defied death at Sperl's to the music of Johann Strauss, and ran up bills so high that he eventually had to skip town.

One visitor in particular spread the fame of Strauss beyond Austrian borders. He was Heinrich Laube, a roving journalist from Leipzig, who filed with his paper, the *Elegante Zeitung*, a remarkable piece of reportage:

> Under illuminated trees and in open arcades people are seated
> at innumerable tables, eating, drinking, laughing, and listening.
> In their midst is the orchestra from which come the new waltzes

that stir the blood like the bite of a tarantula. On the orchestra platform stands the Napoleon of Austria, the musical director Johann Strauss. The Strauss waltzes are to the Viennese what the Napoleonic victories were to the French, and if only the Viennese possessed cannons, they would erect a Vendôme pillar to him at Sperl. The father shows him to his child, the Viennese lady shows him to her foreign lover, the host points him out to his guest.

The power wielded by the black-haired musician is potentially very dangerous; it is his especial good fortune that no censorship can be exercised over waltz music and the thoughts and emotions it arouses. He is a man who could do a great deal of harm if he were to play Rousseau's ideas on his violin.

Very characteristic is the beginning of each dance. Strauss intones his trembling preludes. The Viennese male partner tucks his girl deep in his arm and in the strangest way they sway themselves into the measure. The actual dance begins with whirling rapidity. The couples waltz straight through any accidental hindrances in their joyful frenzy; no god holds them back.

It is a notable fact that Austrian sensuality is neither vulgar nor sinful; it is that of mankind before the fall, before the tree of knowledge. These orgies last till the early morning when the heated couples stream out into the warm night airs of Vienna and disappear with fond giggles in all directions.

Flamboyance was the literary fashion of the day and does not detract from Laube's credibility. Particularly significant is his reference to the French thinker, Rousseau; for in Vienna the waltz was clearly a political phenomenon. Not the least reason for the overwhelming importance of this unconventional music to the Viennese was its use as an escape from the prevailing political climate.

During the Biedermeier period—the span from the Congress of Vienna to the revolution of 1848—Austria's throne was occupied successively by Franz I and Ferdinand I, two notably incompetent emperors. Both placed the affairs of state in the hands of a capable chancellor, the lean-faced, elegant Prince Clemens von Metternich.

This steward of the crown conceived of himself as guardian of the divine right of kings and devoted his ample executive talent to that cause. For nearly four decades Metternich managed to keep Austria politically in the Middle Ages. Liberalism, he perceived, was the road to democracy, which, to him, was the ultimate blasphemy.

Beyond Austria's borders a new age had emerged. Consent of the governed and their participation in the governing process were already accepted in England and France. To guard Austria from the contagion of such ideas, Metternich imposed a censorship so strict as to choke off nearly all public intellectual life. To deal with private dissent, he relied on secret police.

But Metternich's subtlest and most insidious ally was Johann Strauss. He provided the chief instrument of pacification: music to *not* think by.

"If I were a despot," wrote the contemporary Viennese poet Glasbrenner, "I would award a ton of gold to Strauss and Lanner to lull the heads of my subjects and halt all public discussion."

The music of the people became the tool of reaction. Or, to paraphrase a later social critic, the waltz was their opium, the antidote to the stifling air of a country where not too many questions could be asked. It was better to dance.

CHAPTER TWO

AFTER Johann junior, Anna bore her husband five more children: Josef (1827), Anna (1829), Therese (1831), Eduard (1835), and Ferdinand, who died shortly after birth. It is remarkable that she managed to be so fecund. It wasn't just work that kept her husband away. There was also Emilie Trampusch.

What he saw in her is a puzzle. Strauss, who could have had his pick among women, enmeshed himself with a plain-faced, ill-spoken, graceless and stupid hatmaker. Her shabby flat in the Kumpfgasse, a dank medieval alley, must have been insufferably drab. Yet it was with Emilie in the Kumpfgasse that Strauss found repose.

All Emilie asked of him was money to fritter away on silly luxuries. Anna asked for things that were harder to give. She demanded more of life than glitter and pretty tunes. Strauss, perhaps drained by his frenzied pace, was apparently unprepared to meet these demands. Whatever Anna's merits, Emilie was easier.

Anna was accustomed to other women's pursuit of her celebrated husband, and appears to have kept prudent silence about many a passing fling. She would have understood Johann's attraction to any of the elegant and witty women who fawned upon him. But to see the man she loved, and of whom she was deeply proud, involved with a dull and ugly creature was very distressing to her.

She kept her composure in the face of gossip, devoting herself to her children and the management of her spacious home in the new *Hirschenhaus*, Vienna's first large apartment building. When malicious friends informed her that Emilie flaunted herself at Strauss's concerts, her response was quiet and appropriate. She no longer appeared in public with her husband. Even the eagerly reported news of a spectacular diamond clasp Strauss had given his mistress failed to shake Anna's self-possession.

But her endurance reached its limit when Emilie, who bore Johann as many children as she, named one of them Johann. To Anna this was blasphemy. She confronted her husband with an ultimatum, whereupon he simply packed up and moved into the Kumpfgasse. From then on his relations with his family consisted mostly of sending them a monthly allowance of five hundred gulden. Emilie added her own grace note to the situation by announcing that Anna evidently lacked the awareness of "the liberty needed by Strauss of the Waltz".

Supporting ten children, and keeping Emilie in her kind of pin money, strained the finances of even the fabulous Strauss. Throughout the late 1830s he took one group of musicians on extended concert tours while the rest remained in Vienna under assistant conductor Franz Ammon. In these journeys Strauss found surcease from his almost pathological restlessness. He needed the challenge of conquering strange audiences.

Travelling itself was still a risk. The newly invented railways with their tiny wood-burning locomotives and their open-sided cars were a splendid adventure. The Viennese, who had their own way of looking at progress, regarded railways as a new form of entertainment, in a class with such excellent innovations as the steam-driven merry-go-round. The government declined to support such frivolities, and only Baron Rothschild seemed to see any future in rail travel. He financed the first Austrian rail lines and is said to have employed dachshunds which, tied near refuelling stops, could hear approaching trains long before human ears, and announced imminent arrivals with frenetic barking. According to report, the dachshunds were official railway employees, with pension rights and the resounding title of *Zugsvormeldehund*.

At the time, most railways ran but a few miles beyond the major cities. For long distances Strauss and his thirty-man orchestra still depended on hard-sprung stagecoaches. With luck, these "accommodations" bouncing over cobbled streets or lurching through mud, covered fifty miles each day.

The first of his longer journeys—in November 1834—took Strauss to Berlin, where the sober public was by no means predisposed towards any artistic import from Vienna. However, after a concert on November 12, 1834, the well-known Berlin critic Oettinger seemed to lose control of his pen:"I am so happy, so joyful, so glad that I want to kiss the heavens with their stars; so recklessly, deliriously happy that I want to embrace the whole world and press it to my heart! And why? Because I have heard him! Because I have heard Johann Strauss!"

On November 25 Strauss and his whole orchestra were virtually kidnapped after a public concert, bundled into carriages, and whisked off to the royal palace at Potsdam. The visiting Tsar Nicholas of Russia and his Tsarina had expressed the wish to hear Strauss play. After the music, the Tsar made amends for abducting Strauss by presenting him with a magnificent gold cigarette box, and then inviting him and his musicians to St. Petersburg, an honour Strauss declined.

On his return trip to Vienna, Strauss gave concerts in Leipzig, Dresden, and Prague. At this last stop he encountered the polka, a new dance that had just sprung up in Bohemia and that he later introduced, with his own tunes, to Viennese ballrooms. According to local hearsay, the polka had been invented by a pretty peasant girl in a village near Prague. Whatever the source of the dance, during Strauss's journey sweet-tootling brass bands were pumping out polkas for farm boys and girls in every arcaded village square.

By mid-December Strauss was at Sperl's, celebrating his return to Vienna. But within a year he had again set off on an extended tour that included many quaint capitals of the small ducal states that later were to form a unified Germany. Not everyone in these cities welcomed Strauss. Especially in the Protestant north the waltz was decried as "an incitement to sinful passion", and as "demoralizing and lewd". Some of the opposition circulated a treatise splendidly titled, "Proof That the Waltz is a Main Cause of the Weakness of Body and Mind of Our Generation. Most Urgently Recommended to German Sons and Daughters".

Although medically the treatise was spurious, the new dance, in its more bacchanalian forms, occasionally did induce fainting, and was dangerous to the elderly or hypertense. A few fatalities occurred, and several German towns passed health ordinances against waltzing. Others simply issued police edicts against the "improper and horrible turning of women by men", particularly if done in a manner to "make skirts fly up and reveal too much".

But such statutes failed to stem the Straussian avalanche, and Strauss began to realize that he was not merely a travelling entertainer. His music represented the Viennese spirit, and his travels seemed to become a mission. As a Hamburg newspaper observed: "Vienna is wherever Strauss is".

Strauss relished the role of cultural ambassador. He returned to Vienna to prepare himself for his toughest assignment—the journey to Paris and London.

AT FIVE o'clock in the afternoon of October 4, 1837, Strauss and twenty-eight musicians climbed into the coaches that were to take them to Paris. But an almost hysterical crowd refused to make way for the horses in the narrow street. The Viennese seemed afraid to let Strauss go. Women pushed small bouquets of flowers and their tear-stained handkerchiefs through the open carriage windows. It was nearly an hour before the caravan rolled through the city gate.

When he arrived in Paris on October 27 Strauss's confidence wavered for the first time. He was tackling the intellectual and artistic capital of the world, a critical city surfeited with excellence in every field. How would the Parisians react to the sentimental sweep of his waltzes? Their own popular music, dominated by the quadrille, tended to be crisp and pointed. Besides, in Vienna it was generally understood that, in a mystic sort of way, love and the waltz were the same thing. No such amiable association existed among the French.

No sooner had Strauss taken up residence at the Hôtel Violette than his chief rival, the fabled M. Musard, politely called to welcome him to Paris. Soon the two musicians were engrossed in shop-talk and their rivalry receded before their liking for each other. Later in the season they would give joint concerts with immediate success, but this visit left Strauss wondering uneasily how his own puny group would sound to a public conditioned by Musard's orchestra of ninety-six men, which included a floor-shaking row of double basses and an oboe player with seemingly endless breath.

Strauss was noticeably nervous when, on November 1, 1837, he mounted the podium for his sold-out opening concert. The luminaries of French music had shown up *en masse*: Meyerbeer, Auber, Cherubini, Adam, Halévy. And looking down from the stage Strauss recognized the wild carrot-coloured hair of Hector Berlioz, the man who had revolutionized orchestration.

As tribute to France, the concert began with Auber's prelude to *"Les Faux-Monnayeurs"*. The composer, obviously pleased, tossed Strauss a bunch of violets at the end. Then Strauss launched into his own waltzes. His physical abandon in conducting seemed exotic to the Parisians. But they were carried away by his obvious musicality and the charm of his waltzes. Long before the concert was over, Strauss knew that Paris was his.

Berlioz recorded his impressions of the concert in an essay analysing the contrast in Viennese and Parisian styles of orchestral playing. Admiring the wide range of tonal nuance Strauss drew from his relatively small orchestra, he also said: "Strauss's musicians had more practice in overcoming the difficulties of rhythmic change than our artists. Their waltzes in which the melody, self-intoxicated, chases and whips up the tempo, are difficult to play; but how easily the Viennese accomplish it, how they charm us with their piquant rhythmic coquetry!"

Four days later Strauss and his orchestra played at the Tuileries for King Louis Philippe. They were alarmed, on entering the palace, to have to pass through a long hall filled with armed troops, and other aspects of the French court seemed equally perplexing. When his group was finally admitted to the royal presence, Strauss made a deep bow and remained in that position, just as he would have before a Habsburg emperor, awaiting the touch of a chamberlain before straightening up. But Louis Philippe, the Bourgeois King, expected no obeisance and had no one ready to straighten Strauss. He remained bent until a genial bystander ambled over to him and suggested that he might as well start the music. Later on, the democratic monarch mortified Strauss by saying to him graciously, in German: "Herr Strauss, you have done me an honour by appearing here personally." It was a strange country where a musician could do honour to the king.

After the concert Louis Philippe invited the orchestra to mix socially with members of the court! The Duke of Orléans took the violin from Strauss and scratched a few tunes on it, and the visiting King and Queen of the Belgians, a pleasant young couple, casually engaged Strauss in conversation. The world was changing, but Strauss, like most Viennese, did not understand it.

He himself was an absolute ruler to his musicians. He enforced personal discipline and proper public deportment as rigidly as good musicianship, and if his men did not necessarily love him, they were deeply loyal and proud of their share in his glory. The only thing ever to undermine the orchestra's morale was homesickness, which, predictably, broke out at Christmas. The French didn't even have Christmas trees! And instead of going to midnight Mass, they were dancing in the streets. One orchestra member indignantly wrote home that he had seen a nun whirling about in the arms of a Capuchin monk. It took all the persuasion Strauss could muster, along with a massive pay boost, to keep his band from straggling back to Austria in the middle of winter.

Strauss was under contract to remain in Paris for some time, giving public concerts and playing in fashionable private mansions. It was in one of these that he was approached by an ancient man who was treated deferentially by everyone. The old man silently took Strauss's hand, smiled, and left again. Strauss had been greeted by Talleyrand, who years before had dominated the Congress of Vienna.

The Comte de la Garde captures the mood of these gatherings: "It has a mysterious power, this waltz. As soon as the first measures ring out, a smile steals upon the faces, the eyes light up, and all feel some inward expectation. The graceful pairs form and begin to move, interweaving their paths. One must observe the beauty of the women as they are carried along by this irresistible music, leaning on the arms of their partners, with the glossy silk and delicate gauze of their dresses sharing their every move in caressing waves . . . ."

Strauss's most memorable encounter in Paris involved another old man who rarely went to concerts any more. At one of Strauss's, he sat inconspicuously in a back row, but the audience spotted him and escorted him to a quickly vacated place of honour. Strauss, about to begin the concert, recognized Nicolò Paganini and hurried down from the stage to greet him. Paganini rose and embraced Strauss. Then he spoke into the silence that had fallen on the audience: "I am glad to meet a man who has brought so much joy into the world."

At the end of the season Strauss would not hear of returning to Vienna. The young Princess Victoria was to be crowned Queen of

England that spring, and he would not forgo the chance to play in London at that festive time. Again he raised his players' pay, and to mollify their grumblings made every possible provision for their comfort. "We have every kind of convenience," one of the players wrote home, "equal to anything enjoyed by rich travellers."

Yet the British venture started badly. The London hotel in which the orchestra was booked fell short of Strauss's standard of luxury. With typical impatience he gathered his men and marched out. They did not get far. The irate hotelkeeper had Strauss arrested for breach of contract, and it took the intervention of the Austrian ambassador to get him free.

There was more trouble in store. Strauss and his band had found suitable lodgings at the Hotel Commerce in Leicester Street. The proprietor, sharing the customary British opinion of artists, suddenly demanded advance payment. When Strauss went to his room for the money he found that a thief had broken in and taken all his cash. He could not even pay expenses already incurred. Under British law, his entire entourage might have been marched off to debtor's prison, had not a certain Mr. Cock turned up. If Mr. Strauss would be so kind as promptly to write a waltz for him, said Mr. Cock, he would take care of everything. Strauss sat down and wrote a short waltz. Cock paid the bill and, being a music publisher, recouped his investment many times over.

As earlier in Germany, Strauss also enjoyed a great deal of free publicity in England, thanks to the outrage of self-appointed moral guardians. One London observer wrote that he "could not help reflecting how uneasy an English mother would be to see her daughter so familiarly treated, and still more to witness the obliging manner in which the freedom is returned by the female".

This sort of notoriety as well as the competent reviews of his concerts, soon helped fill the halls that had at first been more than half empty. But his most telling support came from the graceful nineteen-year-old girl who soon would be Queen of England. At the great court ball at Buckingham Palace preceding Victoria's coronation, she waltzed with charming restraint to the music played for her by Johann Strauss.

Now that he had played before the Queen, the Defender of the Faith, it was presumably safe for the good people of the English provinces to hear Strauss, and he left London for a tour which turned out to be highly successful. At the farthest point of his great journey, he stood on the Irish shore and looked westward over the sea. Beyond lay new land—America—a curious country without kings and castles, a land where everything was yet to be. Across the water lay the last challenge. That was where he now wanted to go.

The clarinettist Reichmann, his trusted confidant among the musicians, tried to dissuade him. The men were homesick. Besides, the small wooden ships then in transatlantic service made the ocean seem doubly dreadful. Rumours sprang up among his players: Strauss, having broken with his family, never really intended to return to Vienna, and planned to drag his troupe into the murderous wilds of the United States.

One night the orchestra confronted Strauss with its suspicions and refused outright to go onstage. It was an open revolt, and only Reichmann's mediation prevented a walkout. Grudgingly the players agreed to complete the scheduled tour of Britain on condition that they would then go directly to Vienna.

They were home sooner than promised. A seven-day spell of rain overtook them in Scotland as they travelled in unheated coaches up to the axles in mud. Repeatedly the entire orchestra had to get out in the downpour to lift their carriages from the mire. By the time they reached Edinburgh a fever had spread among them. A local doctor prescribed plenty of claret, nutmeg, and ginger "hot enough to wake the dead". The men shivered with fever and sweated from the medicine, but they played as scheduled.

At Derby, Strauss found himself unable to go onstage. A doctor tried to still his coughing spasms with a massive dose of opium, the latest all-purpose medicine. Strauss almost died. Frightened, he fled England, crossing to France. In Calais he collapsed in a hotel corridor.

For days he lay in intermittent coma. Finally his orchestra took desolate farewell of the man who had led them to worldwide fame and set off for Vienna. Only Reichmann remained with the sick leader. Again and again Strauss begged his doctors to let him go home. At last they permitted the presumably moribund man to attempt the long trip in a coach fitted with a cot. Only rugs shielded him from the cold. Sometimes the coachman tried to keep him warm by piling trampled straw from the stables on top of him.

The carriage limped from hospital to hospital with Strauss delirious. At Strasbourg physicians despaired of his survival. But when he crossed to Austrian soil at Linz and once again heard familiar accents about him, he became alert and his condition improved.

At the town of Purkersdorf in the Vienna Woods, something frightened the horses. They bolted and splintered the coach against a great acacia tree. Miraculously the sick man was uninjured. Anna came from Vienna to fetch him, and Johann Strauss returned to his wife and family.

Under Anna's patient care he gradually regained his health. The whole city rejoiced at his recovery. He was back at Sperl's as soon as he was able to stand on his feet.

One reason for his eagerness to resume concerts may have been that the huge profits from his tour had been mysteriously dissipated. Not even his astute manager could figure out where it all went. Quite possibly the loss was only a ruse to deceive Anna. When he no longer depended on her care, Strauss left her once more for Emilie. He never again set foot in his own home.

As before, Strauss enraptured his city and everything seemed as it once was. But the Vienna of the early 1840s was no longer quite the same city Strauss had left. Beneath the bland harmonies a new note was heard. Students, poets, and playwrights were passing forbidden books among themselves, whispering "freedom of thought". And though Vienna was still a joyous panoply for the celebration of life, the silvery innocence had passed.

The scent of scandal, Vienna's favourite perfume, hung in the air and aroused the city. The Waltz King had been challenged by his own son. Johann junior, barely nineteen, had hired a hall, assembled an orchestra, and plastered the town with placards.

Agitated groups quickly formed around the posters, discussing the announcement as if it were a political proclamation. Lately there had been rumours that Strauss was pathologically jealous of his son's musical talent.

At the age of six little Johann had picked out a waltz tune all his own on the family's piano. This first hint of his son's musicality had so disturbed the older Strauss that he forbade the child all musical activity. But Anna, proud of her boy's precocity, secretly noted down his first composition.

That may have been the day Anna Strauss, consciously or not, conceived a plan to revenge herself on her husband. She would pinch kreuzer from her household allowance to pay for secret music lessons and train little Johann to rival his father as Waltz King. Young Johann, who like most Viennese boys of that name was called Schani, was a willing accomplice. Franz Ammon, Strauss's assistant conductor, recognizing the boy's unusual gifts, agreed to teach him.

It was from Ammon that Schani absorbed every nuance of the musical style his father had created. Secretly practising the violin, he not only copied his father's mannerisms but developed his father's knack for striking that seductive balance between gaiety and yearning. He was hardly more than a child when his playing

198

already had what the Viennese call *Schmiss*—a curious witchery that makes music propelling, ravishing, yet at the same time smiling and innocent.

When Ammon felt that Schani needed more solid grounding in music theory than he could give him, the boy studied counterpoint and harmony with Joseph Drexler, a renowned organist and composer of church music. Schani knew but one kind of music— the waltz—and this gentle old musician was horrified to see the boy's talent wasted on what he considered a vulgar dance. He was also taken aback by Schani's playing waltzes on the church organ, occasionally confounding the worshippers in the dimly lit nave. "I meant to play a fugue," the boy would explain, "but somehow it slipped."

To break Schani of such habits, Drexler made him write a church cantata on the text *Tu qui regis totum orbem* (Thou Who Rulest the Whole World). But the assignment went clearly against the boy's grain, and Anna, too, would have none of it. Schani was to challenge his father on his own ground—not in the church, but in the dance hall.

Paradoxically it was this cantata that cleared the way for Schani's defiance of the Waltz King. Before playing in public he had to have a licence, and no magistrate was likely to grant one to a minor whose famous father was known to object to such a venture. Surprisingly Drexler helped Schani clear this hurdle. This gentle sixty-year-old music master would not stand in the way of young talent, even though he deplored the manner of its expression. He endorsed Schani's licence application, assuring the authorities that young Strauss was a "most modest and highly cultured youth", and he clinched the case by presenting the manuscript of *Tu qui regis totum orbem* as proof of the boy's serious musical intentions. Impressed by Drexler's reputation, the magistrate at last authorized the first public appearance of "Johann Strauss the son".

As had been rumoured, Schani's entry into the musical profession did not take his famous father entirely by surprise. Years before, on one of his rare visits to his family, the elder Strauss had caught Schani practising the violin. He had whipped the boy brutally, shouting that he was going to beat the music out of him, until Anna had torn the whip from his hands.

From that day on the elder Strauss had been gnawed by suspicions. Lately his business manager, Carl Friedrich Hirsch, a tall, hook-nosed man with a manner of elegant lassitude, had been making the rounds of Vienna's great ballrooms. He intimated that if that young whelp, Schani, were ever permitted to play in one of them, the Waltz King himself would boycott the place. As a result the luxurious ballrooms of the inner city were closed to Schani.

But out in the forest-ringed suburb of Hietzing, near the emperor's summer palace of Schönbrunn, stood Dommayer's Casino—an elegant café with a large, tree-shaded garden that was the frequent site of outdoor concerts. Since father Strauss confined most of his appearances to the inner city, it is likely that Hirsch had not yet delivered his threat to the outlying districts. At any rate Schani succeeded in signing up Dommayer's for his début.

The next problem was to recruit an orchestra and weld its players into a cohesive group. Schani was short of cash, but he knew he could find his men at the City of Belgrade, a rather disreputable inn frequented by unemployed musicians. During days and nights of frantic rehearsing, he hired and fired musicians with calm self-assurance. Within four weeks he had smoothed his ragtag fifteen-man group into a reasonably polished ensemble. The date was set. The posters went up.

Gossip had already carried the news of Schani's rehearsals to the Waltz King. Now, in a rage, he announced that he would give a concert of his own on the same night. According to one report, he abandoned the plan when he heard that scalpers were quoting higher prices for Schani's concert than for his own. Whatever the case, his fury made him ill and he took to his bed, suffering a deep depression. Two days before Schani's concert he said to Tobias Haslinger, his publisher, "I hope to die before then."

Deeply worried about the Waltz King's health, the loyal Hirsch conceived a dramatic plan for cheering him up. He organized a group of rowdies to disrupt Schani's concert at his signal.

Hirsch was not alone in his enmity to the young Johann. Many

Viennese, learning of the condition of their adored Waltz King, condemned the youngster's impertinence. Had he no respect for his father's greatness? Why his ruthless insistence on grieving a man loved by everyone? Others felt that the older Strauss was getting a well-deserved come-uppance from his mistreated family. They knew that young Johann, by the exercise of his musical talent, hoped to earn back for his mother some of the money the father had squandered on his mistress. In the music-mad city nearly everyone took sides. The Strauss family quarrel exploded into a public issue.

Hours before the concert the exodus began. Through the majestic city gates thousands poured out to the Glacis, the garden-like meadows outside the walls, which by imperial edict were to remain free of encroachments. The Viennese penchant for making any occasion into a fashion show was abetted by the sunny October day. Top-hatted burghers with their silver-tipped walking sticks and heavy watch chains looked almost as festive as their ladies in feathers and lace.

The wealthier families rode in lacquered landaus and cabriolets, driven by liveried coachmen. Others travelled less elegantly, though just as comfortably, in graceful cabs drawn by high-stepping pairs. The majority, however, came via *Zeiserlwagen*—a farm wagon fitted with rough benches.

Of the thousands who made the four-mile trek to Hietzing only a fraction would hear the music. On the spacious square outside Dommayer's an impatient ticketless crowd milled about, pressing for entrance, until mounted police sealed off the café.

Inside Dommayer's little of Vienna's usual *Gemütlichkeit* prevailed. Unable to make their way through the audience, the waiters soon abandoned attempts to serve food and wine—a privation not borne lightly in Vienna. Not even the clear, cool evening air rolling in from the hillsides brought much comfort to the stifling crowd. And the rival factions in the audience made the mood even more ominous. Hirsch and Haslinger sat surrounded by a loyal following, all with studiously bored faces that bespoke their expectations.

Far in the back of the garden in one of its trellised arcades sat Anna Strauss. She seemed to be praying.

The nervous murmur of the crowd quieted as the orchestra filed into the bandstand and began to tune up. Behind the scenes, young Johann stood before a mirror, fussing with his cravat. He had tried to grow a moustache, but little more than a tuft appeared on his lip. None of his new clothes had yet been paid for, but they were certainly in the latest fashion. A flowing blue tailcoat with silver buttons was cut away at the waist and draped over a silk waistcoat embroidered with tiny Alpine flowers. Uncreased grey trousers clung tightly to his legs, fastened with loops stretched under the soles of his buckled shoes. Lace cuffs dangled from his sleeves to lend dash to his arm movements. And to heighten the effect of his gestures, Johann resorted to a trick he would retain for years: on his right wrist flashed a thin gold bracelet. Yet all this finery could not bolster his confidence. As he admitted later, he was sick with stage fright. No amount of acclaim would ever rid him of that fear.

Whatever his doubts, none showed as the dark, intense young man jumped nimbly to the podium. But as he turned to bow to the audience, the booings of Hirsch's hirelings mixed with the hurrahs of his own faction. Quickly Johann sought refuge in the music.

The first selection was the popular overture to *The Mute of Portici* by François Auber. The elder Strauss had opened his first Paris concert with an Auber overture, so Schani was following a family custom. Besides it was not unusual for a cafe concert to include a sprinkling of operatic and symphonic pieces. The Viennese made no sharp distinction between "serious" and "popular" music, and they liked something solid to listen to while catching their breath between dances.

Johann was undismayed by the perfunctory applause. He knew that the audience had come to judge him as a composer, to compare his waltzes with his father's. The crucial moment would come with the next number, a waltz of his own which he had originally titled *"Das Mutterherz"* ("The Mother's Heart") as a tribute to the woman whose self-denying faith in him had made this evening possible. But Anna Strauss had thought this dedicatory title too sentimental and had suggested *"Die Gunstwerber"* which translates roughly as "Those Who Seek To Please". The title was a coy bid for favour, but there was nothing coy about Johann's music. The mesmerizing, willowy rhythm, the sweeping melody, and the bold, capricious accents that marked his later works were already evident.

Almost visibly the music enraptured the crowd. Overwhelming applause drowned the catcalls from the Hirsch contingent, and Strauss had to repeat the waltz. The second time all constraint fell from him. Astonished, the orchestra responded to the new freedom of his gestures, pouring out those swaying, lambent cadences that have since become the hallmark of Vienna's music.

An ovation followed. People climbed on their chairs, waving hats, shawls, and handkerchiefs, shouting until Strauss played the waltz again. And again. After the fourth repetition, he forestalled demand for another by immediately signalling the start of his new polka: *"Herzenslust"*—"Heart's Delight". The orchestra, bewitched by the frenzied audience as much as by the conductor, played it with an effervescent lightness that seemed to defy gravity.

To the bewilderment of his hirelings, Hirsch joined in the jubilant applause. True, he was the father's friend and had a financial stake in him. But he had a greater loyalty: to music. He, a former pupil of Beethoven, would not withhold approbation from any artist who deserved it.

Another new waltz by young Strauss came next: *"Sinngedichte"* —"Poems of the Senses". The title says it all, and the raving audience demanded and got nineteen repeats. Nothing like that had ever happened before.

The hours passed. One by one the newspaper critics left the concert, clattering back to town in their cabs to dictate last-minute notices directly to the printers. Johann Nepomuk Vogt, the most influential critic, noted: "Talent is the monopoly of no single individual. This young man is fully as melodious, as piquant, as effective in his instrumentation as his father. . . . Nevertheless, he is no slavish imitator of the latter's methods of composition."

Another reviewer, L. Wiest of the *Wanderer*, felt that young Strauss's compositions were not superior to his father's, but pointed out that at the age of nineteen the elder Strauss had had nothing like the musical competence and aplomb of his son. And he ended his review with words that were to echo through Vienna for weeks: "Good evening, Father Strauss! Good morning to you, Strauss Junior!"

Long before the morning papers carried the news, the crowd at Dommayer's knew that Vienna had a new Waltz King. In the midst of his triumph young Johann—his face flushed and radiant—signalled for silence. Softly the orchestra began. This music had not been listed on the programme. As its measures floated into the night, listeners looked at each other in disbelief. Wasn't this *"Lorelei Rheinklänge"*, the most famous of all the waltzes by the elder Strauss? And how the boy conducted it! Into the lyric parts he infused something other than the customary sweetness. This went beyond the boundaries of a dance. Gradually, as the music unfolded, the audience sensed the meaning of this interpretation. Young Strauss was playing his father's music not merely as a filial tribute. He was playing it as a supplication—to beg his father's forgiveness.

There were tears in the audience, even among the men.

THAT concert in Dommayer's trellised garden marked the ascent of the man who would bring the Viennese waltz to its culmination. Yet it took place at a time when the social roots that had so far nourished the waltz were already decaying.

A handful of journeymen who had picked up socialist notions in France and Switzerland carried them into the Viennese working class. Even members of the very proper bourgeoisie became infected by foreign intellectuals with subversive ideas about constitutional freedoms. By the mid-forties a fairly receptive soil had been prepared for the seeds of revolution.

The first factories were already springing up. When some of these new enterprises failed, Vienna had its first taste of industrial unemployment. Moreover, one kept hearing odd tales about the

provinces. In the east a tax rebellion by Galician landowners had been put down by the district governor, who had expediently encouraged local farmhands to cut down their masters with their scythes. In the south Venice protested a tariff on salt drawn from the sea. To the north, in Prague, Bohemian textile workers had to be dissuaded by bullets from wrecking the new automatic looms that threatened their jobs.

On the surface Vienna remained merry and calm. The only intimation of disaffection was to be found on the stage. Plays like *Einen Jux will er sich machen* by Johann Nestroy (which re-emerged a little over a century later in America as *Hello, Dolly!*) came as close to social criticism as censorship permitted. Since Nestroy's humour was homey and his thrust oblique, even the police laughed. But if one listened closely, one sensed that the Biedermeier idyll, the dream of pleasured tranquillity, had begun to rot.

THE revolution in Austria took its cue from France. In February 1848 revolutionaries had stormed the Tuileries, toppled the throne of France and shouted the republic from the barricades.

But in Vienna even revolutions begin with proper decorum. On the morning of March 13, 1848, an orderly delegation of university students in their colourful fraternity costumes, led by frock-coated professors and top-hatted gentlemen from a merchants' association, approached Metternich's palace to present a petition. They did not even mention the unspeakable word, "Constitution". But they formally demanded freedom of the Press, public accounting of state budgets, a municipal charter, and participation of the middle class in appointed councils.

All might have gone well had not the middle-class liberals invited a group of factory workers to come along. Metternich might possibly have negotiated with professors and businessmen. But the sight of the workers in their blouses and caps—officially described in a state document as "brutal and licentious trade and factory people"—had an unfortunate effect on the fastidious prince. To him, they were *canaille*—corrosive dregs of Robespierre's Reign of

Terror. Seeing them advance on his palace in common cause with proper burghers confounded Metternich's usually cool judgment. His reply to the petition was a volley fired into the waiting assemblage.

Metternich came from the Rhineland. Germans, he knew, could be cowed by terror. What he didn't know about the Viennese was that in the face of bald outrage their *Gemütlichkeit* changes to stubborn courage. Within hours after the crack of his muskets the unthinkable happened: Austria's capital rose in revolt, and from March to October 1848, the rebels held the city.

Like Vienna itself, the Strauss family was now torn by forces beyond its comprehension. Johann senior sided with the Royalists; Johann junior with the rebels. Ironically, neither had strong political convictions. The elder man was a Royalist mainly because he felt a loyalty to the past. Besides, royalism was convenient for a musician who often played before kings.

Young Johann was a revolutionary for equally flimsy reasons. As far as one can judge, his stand was based on a generous sympathy for his liberal young friends, many of whom merely hoped for the removal of Metternich and would have been happy to see the Habsburgs return as constitutional rulers.

During the upheaval the two Waltz Kings held official positions as regimental composer-conductors. Strauss senior bucked up the Royalists with sprightly military marches. One of these became his most famous work, the "Radetzky March", and was written in honour of an imperial field marshal. Young Strauss also switched from waltzes to marches. But his compositions had revolutionary titles: "Freedom March", "Songs of the Barricades", and "March of the Students".

Holding military rank while siding with rebels did not seem to disturb young Johann. On one occasion he resolved a potential conflict in characteristic fashion. On August 22, while he stood guard on the Karmeliterplatz in the inner city, a courier warned him of a new uprising in the Leopoldstadt. If the mob marched on the inner city there might be skirmishes, Strauss knew, and he certainly did not want to shoot or be shot by people who had danced to his music. With eminent practicality he simply left his post, went home to his mother, ate supper, and did a little composing until all was quiet again.

Fighting in the city was rare, and during much of the seven months of the revolution, the Viennese were able to lead a normal life. Metternich had fled to London, where he made long speeches to himself, and played cadenzas on his violin to calm his nerves. The Emperor and his court had run off to the Tyrol. Without them the revolutionary struggle in Vienna became a political seesaw with more shouting than shooting.

Since public entertainments were curtailed, the Viennese slaked their musical appetite with private concerts and dances. The elder Strauss with his established entrée to the great town houses was often the centre of such evenings. The splendour of these bright occasions was enhanced by a new Viennese invention: the dripless candle. The new "Apollos" were nearly smoke-free, which permitted more chandeliers to be lit without polluting the air or blackening the ceiling. Strauss, who spent most his working life by artificial light, promptly wrote his "Apollo Waltz". When the end of the revolution finally came, it proved unexpectedly painful. All summer long the Emperor's troops had been massing in the provinces. In October they encircled Vienna and during the night of October 30, after negotiations had failed, they cannonaded the city.

One suspects that young Johann spent that night in a relatively safe and comfortable place. His brother Josef, a more ardent revolutionist, bravely stood on the barricades, ready to fight. Frau Anna Strauss and her youngest son Eduard watched in terror as fires spread through the city, lighting the sky so brightly that in the middle of the night they could read the time from a clock in a nearby tower.

At dawn the cannon fell silent, and the Viennese stared in stunned dismay into the ruins. The loveliest of cities had been damaged. Rather than risk further destruction the liberals capitulated.

Yet the revolution was not truly lost. Metternich was gone. More importantly, the weak-minded Emperor Ferdinand was persuaded to relinquish his throne to his eighteen-year-old nephew, Franz Josef. As the boy kneeled before his uncle to receive Europe's most venerable crown on December 2, 1848, the simple old Emperor was heard to whisper to him: "Just be good and all will be well."

Franz Josef seems to have heeded this plain advice. Under his benevolent sixty-eight-year reign Vienna saw the apogee of its distinctive civilization. In this period the city radiated a sunburst of achievements in the arts, in science, in literature, and in medicine.

Most of the Strauss family got through the aftermath of the revolution with only minor difficulty. Only young Johann, still unreconciled to defeat, got into trouble. On December 3, the day after the new Emperor's coronation, Johann conducted a performance of the *"Marseillaise"* at a public concert. Predictably the police asked him to explain his taste for the republican hymn.

According to the record of his interrogation, he claimed that, as a musician, he was totally indifferent to the political associations of any piece and judged it only on musical merit. Such arguments rarely carry weight in police courts. But at twenty-three Johann was already far too famous to be gaoled without causing further political uproar. He signed a written promise henceforth to consider the political as well as the aesthetic aspects of music, and the charge against him was dismissed.

ONE who never quite recovered from the effects of the revolution was the elder Johann Strauss. He couldn't understand why nobody really felt like dancing any more. Neither could he understand the decline of his personal popularity. Many Viennese were angry at his support of their city's vanquishers and reproved him by letter for having written that march in honour of Radetzsky.

Helpless in his confusion, Strauss brooded. What he now needed Emilie could not supply. Desperate for reassurance, he left Vienna with his orchestra in search of the only real love he had ever known—public adoration. Whatever may have poisoned the Viennese against him, surely his loyal admirers would welcome him elsewhere.

Even that hope came to nothing. In Prague protesting students howled all night in front of his hotel. In Munich, Heilbronn, and Heidelberg, the composer of anti-revolutionary marches found only resentment.

"What do I care about politics," he muttered to one of his players, "I only want to make music."

Almost like a fugitive, Strauss travelled to England. On reaching London in April 1849, his first visit was to Prince Metternich, who, with his wife and daughter, received him. When Princess Metternich saw Strauss approaching she could utter only one word, "Vienna!" then broke into sobs.

Like Strauss himself, the old chancellor had little comprehension of what had happened to him and why. "Thirty years of peace I gave the Austrians," he said bitterly. "And this is their gratitude!"

At first it seemed that Strauss's injured ego might heal in England. The Queen and her court received him, the aristocracy showered him with honours. But often the concert halls were half-empty. The Liberals stayed away, and even in England, the mail brought threats and abuses. The whole world had become political. Strauss no longer felt at home in it. He did not feel well and wrote to Emilie that this would perhaps be his last tour.

Yet at the end of his troubled journey, the great and generous city of London softened all political discord to give Vienna's Waltz King what he most needed: an affectionate farewell. As Strauss's ship sailed down the Thames, a flotilla of boats filled with well-wishers escorted him towards the estuary. As the Channel steamer headed for open water, leaving the smaller ships behind, the orchestra members stood on deck, softly singing Vienna's traditional leave-taking: "So Fare Thee Well, Thou Silent House".

When he returned to Vienna the political situation had improved. The volatile Viennese don't bear grudges long, and they gave him so warm a welcome that he promptly scheduled a concert at Unger's Casino for July 15. Tickets sold briskly and the evening promised the mood of cheerful festivity he had missed for so long.

In his usual manner Strauss alternately played the violin and conducted with his bow. But during the very first number his bow snapped. For a moment he stood dazed. Then he reached for another bow and continued his part. But throughout the evening he was visibly disturbed. The broken bow seemed an ill omen.

All summer long he was moody and withdrawn. The musician of laughter seemed overwhelmed by fears and doubts he could not express. The tough, passionate energy devoted to the pursuit of his career, the flashing vivacity that mesmerized audiences, seemed suddenly drained from him.

Strauss's attitude towards young Johann also altered. He had no personal contact with him or any other member of his legitimate family. Yet acquaintances noticed that the bitterness was gone. He no longer resented the "competition" of the young man's burgeoning career. On the contrary, he seemed secretly proud of his son's musical achievements and followed with evident concern the newspaper accounts of Johann's musical forays into Serbia and Rumania, regions where brigands still robbed unwary travellers. Strauss may even have wished for a reconciliation with his son, but in his stubborn pride he found no way to admit this even to himself.

Towards the end of summer a new prospect lifted him from his melancholy. Field Marshal Radetzsky was to return from Italy, and a great banquet was planned in his honour. He had saved the Italian provinces for Austria—at least for a while—and very few Viennese would begrudge him a hero's welcome. Strauss would have been delighted to play for the field marshal's homecoming.

But on September 22, the night of the banquet, he lay in his mistress's flat in the Kumpfgasse, fighting the scarlet fever he had caught from one of his bastard children. He had always liked to end his waltzes with a fast coda—a brief and unexpected febrile swirl. So also ended his life. Within four days, on September 25, 1849, in his forty-sixth year, the disease killed him.

Presumably Emilie had been with him at his death. She certainly wasn't there when the corpse was discovered by a grocer's delivery boy, who ran to Anna Strauss with the news.

Josef was sent to investigate and he found his father's naked body on the floor, tumbled from a stripped bed. Chests and drawers gaped open. Everything was in disarray. Emilie had packed up what she could, including the dead man's nightshirt and bedding, and scattered the rest. Then she had gathered up her children and fled.

"Strauss died like a dog," wrote the essayist Hans Weigel, "but he was buried like a king."

On September 27 he was carried in his coffin from the dank Kumpfgasse to the gothic grandeur of St. Stephen's. Candles transformed the dusk of the cathedral into golden brightness, and the high-vaulted nave gleamed like the ballrooms at Sperl's. A hundred thousand people, one-fifth of Vienna's population, filled the cathedral, crowded the Stefansplatz and Graben, and lined the funeral route to the city limits. The death of Strauss, more than the new emperor's hopeful proclamations, drew the divided capital together once again. It was with the funeral of the Waltz King that the revolution really ended.

The spirit of conciliation swept over remnant bitterness and the Viennese were once again able to make contact with the gentle and cheerful tradition which Strauss has distilled into music. They would again tap the wellspring, and the earth in which Johann Strauss was laid would sing again.

Slowly the cortège drew westward against the red autumn sky, traversing the city from St. Stephen's to the outlying vineyards. Hundreds of bells from all the towers resounded in the air. The cortège halted at the foothills of the Vienna Woods. The last part of the way Strauss did not ride in the tall, resplendent funeral coach drawn by four black horses. Instead, the grieving men of the orchestra took the coffin on their shoulders. So Strauss reached the churchyard at Döbling, where he lies beneath the green slopes of the Kahlenberg, the mountain he had climbed as a runaway bookbinder's apprentice, determined to be a musician.

At the tomb Anna and her children mourned the husband and father they had lost long before. The other family was not to be seen. Only once more did Emilie attract notice. Years later the police caught her stealing a bronze lantern from the grave of Johann Strauss.

CHAPTER THREE

WHEN Johann Strauss the younger scheduled his first concert after his father's death, he may already have sensed that his musical destiny lay in going far beyond the traditional limits of dance music. On October 11 he conducted his father's orchestra and a group of vocalists in a memorial performance of Mozart's *Requiem*. For a young dance musician to direct Mozart's sombre score was remarkable. But Johann's choice is all the more noteworthy, because, at the time, Mozart, Austria's greatest composer, was half-forgotten.

Aside from proving his musical scope, the memorial concert gave Johann a chance to establish contact with his father's orchestra. Instead of making enemies by disbanding it he combined it with his own, and though a dozen or so men were dismissed in the process, he handled the dismissals impartially on the basis of musical competence. As a result the orchestra gained not only in size—now numbering nearly fifty—but also in quality. Franz Ammon, the concertmaster of the older Strauss's orchestra who had secretly given Johann his first music lessons, now helped him win the personal loyalty of the men who had formerly worked for his father.

Winning the loyalty of the Viennese public proved unexpectedly difficult. As a young man defying a tyrannical father, Strauss could count on widespread public sympathy. But people were muttering that his ruthlessness in pursuit of his own career had hastened his father's death. The Viennese had been quite shaken on discovering that young Strauss had once secretly commissioned a series of articles in a leading Hungarian newspaper, attacking his father on both musical and personal grounds. They had also felt distressed when he had so brazenly cheated his father in matters of exclusive performance rights that he had been threatened by legal action. Feelings against Johann ran so high after his father's death that he felt impelled to publish a kind of apologia in the prestigious *Wiener Zeitung*.

213

Pitiable is every son who here below weeps at his father's grave; but still more pitiable is he whose divided home forces him to hear from the severely judging lips of his opponents a sentence passed on himself and those who have remained loyal to him; for him there remain no other weapons of defence than to make reference to a deserted mother and younger brothers and sisters. I decided to apply my simple talents to the support and nourishment of these. It was not my purpose, as hostile opponents believe, to brazenly challenge my father's superior gifts. May God be my witness, no!

My father died, and I now stand alone in the midst of my weeping dear ones. I intend to earn a portion, even though it be very small, of the favour that my deserving father so richly harvested. If I should succeed in showing myself not unworthy of my artistic profession and thus be enabled to fulfil my duty towards my mother and my brothers and sisters, I believe that my blessed father will be reconciled to me in his grave and this will give me the greatest possible happiness.

Having been restored to public favour by this ritual of self-abjection, Strauss found still another reconciliation was due before he could assume the royal succession in the realm of the waltz. He had to atone to the Emperor of Austria for his revolutionary capers of 1848, and an excellent occasion for such a gesture presented itself in 1854 at the marriage of Franz Josef to Elisabeth von Wittelsbach, Princess of Bavaria. Elisabeth was sixteen when the young Emperor first saw her at the little Alpine city of Ischl. The setting alone was like a love potion, but in the case of Elisabeth, no scenery was needed.

The Princess was like those porcelain figurines made in her land. Her tiny waist and graceful posture inspired comparisons with swans, lilies, and gazelles. Those fortunate enough to see her at close quarters marvelled at the ethereal fineness of her oval face in its frame of long, dark hair.

Franz Josef was too smitten, and perhaps too young, to perceive that this fairy princess was but a child, and that her spontaneous and sometimes wilful nature—so charming in a girl—would make her a tragic failure as an empress. He could not know that his love would doom her to a life of mounting futility, of incessant travel to escape the strictures of her court, or that, in the end, an Italian anarchist would murder her with a rusty file on the boat dock at Geneva.

No hint of this future clouded her radiant face as Elisabeth sailed down the Danube to Vienna to become the Empress of Austria. Her ship was garlanded with roses from the royal park at Schönbrunn, and a great gilded coach drawn by twelve of Vienna's famous milk-white Lippizaner horses took her through the jubilant streets of her capital to the Hofburg.

On April 26, 1854, two days after the imperial marriage, a great court ball was to celebrate the event. An archduchess had expressed the wish to hear Strauss's "*Annen-Polka*", a sprightly bit of melodic fluff that was the rage of Vienna. But Strauss, wanting to keep the piece exclusively for his orchestra, had not published the score and the court music director was unable to obtain it. The only solution was to invite Strauss himself to play it. Thus it happened that on the evening of the coronation ball, the court musicians shared the flower-laden stage of the Ceremonial Hall in the Hofburg with young Strauss, and the beautiful Empress danced with her new husband to the music of the former revolutionary.

Pressing his advantage, Strauss shortly afterwards sought to gain for himself the prestigious title of Imperial Court Ball Music Director, which his father had held before him. But the shadows of 1848 still clung to him and he met with a curt rebuff.

In the course of processing his bid for the exalted title, the office of the court chamberlain conducted a character investigation of the applicant. After noting Strauss's role in the revolution, the investigator added, "Since becoming a successful music director, he has adopted a prodigal and unseemly mode of life and has only recently shown any tendency towards a more orderly existence."

Presumably the office of the court chamberlain was referring to the succession of girls passing through Strauss's life. Another clue to such private matters is a note in the diary of Strauss's first wife, whom he apparently told about his earlier affairs. She puts their number at thirteen. With the marital tragedy of his parents etched in his mind, it is not surprising that Strauss, until middle age, preferred light amours.

Vienna in the nineteenth century tacitly permitted certain artistic and upper-class young people a delightful and distinctive style of romance that had nothing in common with the furtive encounters by which other Europeans circumvented the mores of their times. Affection and sweetness was the expected essence of a Viennese *Liebelei*, and what was lightly given and lightly taken was not really expected to last longer than the bloom of a flower.

The dominant woman in Strauss's life was still his mother. Her plan had worked. She wanted a Johann Strauss—a Waltz King—and now at last she had one.

With his dark curly hair, intense gaze, generous moustache, and graceful movements, Johann recalled his father even in physical appearance, and Anna made her son the surrogate for her faithless husband. She handled all of Johann's business arrangements, leaving him free for his artistic and personal pursuits. She saw to it that her younger son Josef, deeply fascinated by the new wonders of steam-driven engines, received an excellent engineering education at the *Technik*, where everyone was wondering what practical uses there might be for electricity.

What is perhaps most remarkable about Anna is that she never ceased to expand her own musical perception. In particular she was captivated by the radically new compositions that made Richard Wagner the most controversial musician of his time. While Europe's most sophisticated listeners still balked at such outrages as *Lohengrin* and *The Flying Dutchman*, Anna took these scores calmly in her musical stride. It was she who first drew Johann's attention to the chromatic marvels of Wagnerian harmony and thus planted the seed in Johann's musical imagination that, long after her death, matured into the tonal opulence of his later works.

DURING the 1850s the focus of Vienna's night life shifted from Sperl's to the even more splendid Sophien-Saal, a creation that had started out as a huge indoor swimming pool in a steambath establishment. When that enterprise had failed because the Viennese just couldn't stand the steam, and swam only in summer, the owner had let out the water, put in parquet, and turned it into Vienna's most famous entertainment palace.

Tiers of loggias surrounded the glittering dance floor and could be used as private boxes by elegant spectators, who dined while watching the dancing throng below. The great vaulting roof of the pool turned out to be an acoustic wonder that made any singer or orchestra sound bigger and better—a quality that a century later was to make the Sophien-Saal a favourite location for recording sessions.

It was at the Sophien-Saal that Strauss enraptured the Viennese with countless compositions deftly turned out for special occasions. He would oblige associations and prominent clubs with pieces named in their honour. The engineers' club would dance the "Electromagnetic Polka". Jurists would be set in motion with the "Due Process Polka", while the men of the medical association and their ladies responded nicely to "Heightened Pulses" and even the "Paroxysm Waltz".

Luckily, however, the titles bear no relation to the music. The "Transaction Waltz", written for stockbrokers, doesn't sound very different from a waltz written for the traditional ball of Vienna's laundry girls. Nearly three hundred such occasional pieces came into existence in the twenty years between Strauss's début and his retirement as a regular dance-hall conductor. "The melodies gush out like water," he wrote to a friend. The incessant flow of invention filled stacks of notebooks, which Strauss regarded as a hoard on which to draw if his imagination ever ran dry. Only a fraction of these notes were ever worked into finished compositions.

"Accelerations" and "Morning Papers"—the latter dedicated to the Concordia, a famous club of writers and journalists—mark the culmination of Strauss's work during this period. For the first time, in "Morning Papers", Strauss achieves the free inventive range of a concert piece. The melodic phrases grow longer, arching sweetly over the support of the three-quarter beat and the listener senses that Strauss—perhaps without conscious intent—had now fixed the course that would ultimately take him to the concert hall.

The creative intensity of these formative years, added to the physical strain of daily rehearsals and performances, finally took its toll. One early morning, as he was returning from a concert, Strauss fell unconscious at his door. The doctors spoke of *Nervenzerrütterung*, a typical nineteenth-century diagnosis that translates vernacularly as "shook-up nerves", and recommended a rest cure in southern Styria. Strauss was twenty-eight years old.

A sanatorium bed is a good place for stock-taking. In the quiet of the Styrian Alps, Strauss sorted out his dual functions of composer and conductor. Up to then he had uncritically accepted the two as inseparable. Now it occurred to him that they were not necessarily linked, that he would prefer to devote himself mainly to composition. Unlike his father, who was at his best before the public, he was not an entertainer by temperament. He liked solitude and the inner silence from which all music springs.

Yet to abandon public performances would be economic suicide. His concerts were a family business—the main support of his mother, Anna, Josef, Eduard, and his sisters Therese and Anna. What the Waltz King needed was a working "prince" to assume some of the burden. His brother Josef who, like all of Anna's children was musically literate, would have to be drafted as substitute conductor.

Johann asked his mother, as head of the family, to prevail upon Josef to abandon engineering for music, but Josef dismissed the suggestion outright. Once before, when his father had wanted him to become an army officer, he had defied a parent.

"Let me be what I am," Josef had written in refusal. "Do not force me into that crude occupation of soldiering that destroys all feeling for humanity. . . . I do not want to learn how to kill people, and I do not want to be rewarded with high rank for having hunted human beings. I want to be useful to mankind."

218

Josef's idea of usefulness was engineering. With a naïve optimism shared by many of his contemporaries, he looked on the emergent technology as the main road to human happiness. Two years younger than Johann, he had already distinguished himself in his field, above all by inventing the first mechanical street-sweeper, the pride of Vienna's sanitation department. He had no intention of trading his excellent professional prospects for the chancy, semi-itinerant life of a musician.

Johann listened from his bed as Josef itemized his shortcomings.

"I'm too ugly," he said.

That was better than trying to explain. And, in fact, Josef lacked Johann's compelling vividness. His usual expression was a bit glum. His movements were often clumsy, a severe handicap for the prospective conductor of the world's most evanescent music. Then Johann turned on his pillow, looked at his brother, and said without smiling:

"But you have the most talent of us all. You would be a greater musician than either myself or our father."

It never occurred to the good-hearted Josef that his brother might say this to gain his assent. He *was* a talented pianist, and he believed that Johann spoke the truth as he saw it. Johann may have believed the same thing.

Overcome by his brother's faith in him, Josef left his accustomed life and under the tutorship of the now-ancient Franz Ammon, soon achieved a passable conducting technique. His self-conscious awkwardness was a striking contrast to his brother's fluid, impassioned conducting style, but the public affection lavished on Johann seemed to include Josef simply as a member of the family. Besides, his shyness appealed to the protective instincts of his lady listeners.

From a purely musical point of view Josef's conducting had its own distinction and markedly influenced the development of the waltz. He slowed the tempo to an almost hypnotic, insinuating songfulness that revealed new expressive possibilities in the dance, and led towards the broad, pliant performance style that is known as the Viennese tradition. Josef's reflective music-making also

Johann Strauss, Jr., made the waltz a command to dance, whether at court or in a Viennese dance hall, right.

influenced Johann, turning him increasingly towards a mellowed lyricism.

There was no rivalry between the brothers. Josef led the orchestra whenever Johann went on tour or, as happened more and more often, simply wanted time off. Posters announced concerts by "J. Strauss", leaving which "J" was to direct them to the convenience of the moment. Josef even edged into Johann's preserve by becoming a composer. The stimulus of conducting emboldened him to compose and play a work of his own, titled with typical diffidence, "The First and Last Waltzes of Josef Strauss". Deserved success made it impossible to keep the promise implied in the title, and his next composition was called "The First Waltz After the Last".

By 1857 Josef felt confident enough as a musician to marry. The girl was a childhood sweetheart, Karoline Pruckmayr—his beloved "Lintscherl"—a quiet, gentle girl who gave him a treasured domestic tranquillity. But Josef did not know the meaning of leisure. In the moments he could spare from the orchestra, he

completed no less than 283 musical compositions, maintained an informed interest in science and engineering, became an accomplished amateur painter, wrote passable poetry, and a tragic drama about a supposed maternal ancestor. He slept little, rarely relaxed, and smoked twenty cigars a day.

His health, never robust, eroded under this régime. He began to suffer fainting spells, and mounting nervous tension impaired his dealings with the orchestra. He had none of the innate coolness and authority that enabled Johann to lead it without emotional friction. Josef also suffered deeply from being away from his wife and small daughter during concert tours.

On one of those tours, in April 1870, seven of his key players failed to arrive in Warsaw in time for a gala concert in the presence of the Russian Tsarevich. When local substitutes proved less than satisfactory in rehearsal, Josef told the leading violinist to skip a difficult passage. But the man's pride was hurt. At the concert he attempted to play the passage anyway—and threw the orchestra into chaos. Trying frantically to pull it together, Josef fainted. He

221

tumbled from the podium, then rolled off the high stage, his head crashing against the floor.

Blood running from his ears indicated skull fracture and possible brain damage, but by the time Karoline and Johann arrived from Vienna, Josef was fully conscious again, which inspired hope for his recovery. From April to July Karoline sat at her husband's bedside in the strange city, while Johann, often in tears, conducted the orchestra to fulfil its obligations. The considerable proceeds of 14,000 gulden he immediately put at Karoline's disposal.

In July Josef's condition began to deteriorate. Yet despite lapses of consciousness and spasmodic breathing he kept asking to be taken to Vienna so that he could once more see his little daughter. It would have been easier to bring the child to Warsaw, but Karoline, placing her sinking hope in the superior skill of Viennese doctors, arranged for Josef's return. He died a few days after his homecoming, at the age of forty-three.

Three eminent Viennese doctors had examined Josef immediately on his arrival and suspected that his fainting spells had been symptoms of a brain tumour. They asked for an autopsy, but Karoline could not bring herself to grant permission. Her refusal sparked a bevy of rumours among the gullible Viennese. Russian officers in Warsaw, it was said, had killed Josef with their sabres for declining to play a chauvinistic Russian tune. One tabloid insisted that, instead of the corpse, the Russians had shipped a big wax doll to Vienna, that Karoline had been bribed into secrecy.

To prevent a new issue in the already strained Austro-Russian relations, Karoline asked the priest who had given Josef the last rites to declare publicly that he was still alive at the time. Even that did not still the rumours.

Because Josef left no posthumous works, one story accused Johann of having stolen his deceased brother's notebooks—suggesting that his later works were really purloined from Josef. Why, asked his detractors, would Johann have given such large sums to his widowed sister-in-law except to soothe his conscience? In the tight, gossipy world of Vienna's music-makers it was impossible to shield Johann from hearing such talk, which must have deeply embittered him. Yet with an innate nobility, he never uttered a single word on the subject.

As if to prove the spurious rumour, time itself has melded the music of the two brothers. It is a measure of Josef's talent that his works are almost invariably confused with those of Johann. Listening to such enduring masterpieces as "Village Swallows" or "Music of the Spheres" it is hard to believe that anyone but the Waltz King himself could have been inspired with such melody. Yet a certain sweet gravity distinguishes Josef's melodies from those of his brother.

One lasting favourite, the "Pizzicato Polka", bears the signature of both Johann and Josef, who collaborated in its composition. It is a common monument to the two brothers, a rare moment of pure laughter transmuted into music.

BY THE middle of the nineteenth century, rails stretched all across Europe. With the new ease and speed of travel, concert tours, considered adventures in the day of the older Strauss, had become routine. This was no comfort to Johann, who had a horror of trains. "Going on the railway is for me like going to be hanged," he complained.

He was haunted by the idea of a wreck. When travelling he never looked at the landscape. It seemed to move—and that increased his fright. The blinds of his compartment were always drawn, and he spent most of the journey stretched out under the seat, which he considered the safest position. He also carried with him ample supplies of champagne to loosen the rigour of his fear.

In this peculiar manner Strauss reached Badgastein in the Salzburgian Alps in a tranquil summer long before Josef's death. Johann had come to "take the air", unsuspecting that his Alpine sojourn would get him more than ever involved with railways.

As he sat on the terrace of his hotel, a tall, heavily bearded man approached him, and in fluent French introduced himself as the director general of the Tsarskoje-Selo Railway Company, a Russian line. To induce people to travel on its trains, the company was developing an elegant resort at Pavlovsk, within easy reach of St. Petersburg. A splendid music pavilion had been erected, and it only remained for Monsieur Strauss to please come and play there. The board of directors felt that only he could fill up the excursion trains. Of course, a private villa, fully staffed, would be at his disposal. And, oh yes, if Monsieur Strauss cared to discuss the more mundane arrangements, his stipend would be . . . . The Russian named a sum beyond all dreams of greed. Strauss, never averse to a rapid rouble, signed a contract to play at Pavlovsk for several summers

Actually, it was not his musicianship alone that made him so attractive to the railway men and their highly placed government backers. The Crimean War had been a profound embarrassment, and it seemed advisable to keep the population of the capital pleasantly entertained. Dancing was the favourite diversion because one didn't have to talk much. Talking was always risky in Russia, and since the upper classes disdained their native language and spoke only French in public, conversation rarely extended beyond a formal exchange of pleasantries.

At the time of Strauss's visit the country, with its fiefdoms, its serfs and icons, still lay in Byzantine torpor. It was a brutal and incongruous place for a Waltz King—as his very first experience on Russian soil showed him.

No sooner had Strauss and his musicians crossed the Russian border from Silesia than questions arose as to the validity of their travel documents. At a sign from the border guard, Russian soldiers rudely pulled them out of the carriages, herded them like cattle across open fields, and locked them overnight in a freezing barn. From there, the local commander dispatched them to General Abramovich, the Russian commandant of occupied Warsaw, with the standard explanation that they were suspected spies. Like a good military man, Abramovich accepted this at face value. Obsessed with fear of conspirators, he operated on the precept, when in doubt shoot them dead, or at least lock them up.

A local friend of Strauss's, the music dealer Friedlein, attempted to intercede with Abramovich, and was threatened with exile to Siberia. Even the Austrian consul was no help. Doubting that he could provide effective protection against the whim of a Russian officer, he took no action.

But Strauss had another way of showing who he was. He and the orchestra offered to play a private concert for Abramovich as proof of their identity. His music would be his passport.

Intrigued by this proposal, the general agreed, and the concert was held at police headquarters. Later Strauss recalled: "It was one of the best concerts we ever played. Every man did his best."

Abramovich was equally appreciative. "Very well done," he said. "Truly well done." Then, suddenly, his voice changed to a bellow: "But it is a fraud! Everything can be faked! A deliberate trick! Spies! Robbers!"

Strauss and the orchestra were packed off to a dingy hotel, held under arrest there, and told to surrender their clothes.

At this juncture the faithful Friedlein once more risked his liberty, and possibly his life. He knew that the Tsarina was visiting Castle Laschenski near Warsaw, and managed to get word of Strauss's predicament to her chief chamberlain. The reply was an imperial command: Strauss was to give a gala performance before Her Majesty the following week at the Théâtre-Paré, the city's showplace.

General Abramovich attended the concert and afterwards went to Strauss's dressing room to pay his respects.

Strauss asked Abramovich if he had liked the playing as much as at the police station. The general managed an urbane answer: "You must forgive me, dear master. We are living here between two revolutions, one past and one future. You and your men might have been political conspirators. And if that had been the case, I might have been banished to Siberia. You must not take it amiss that I would rather have had *you* deported."

PAVLOVSK offered a friendlier welcome. The ovations of the audience, demanding encore after encore, often lasted until the early hours of the morning. People simply refused to leave.

No music like this had ever been heard in Russia. The Viennese waltz—expansive without being emotional, sensuous without passion, and filled with delight and spontaneity—gave many listeners a first inkling of a more volatile and amiable world outside their borders. As a result, all summer long, the excursion trains from St. Petersburg were packed with starched and crinolined excursionists whose day in the country would be topped off by a Strauss concert.

For a good many visitors the attraction to Pavlovsk was not purely musical. Going there was simply the social thing to do. Best of all, the summer festival offered middle-class Russians a rare opportunity to enter the presence of princes. The Tsar himself attended often and would honour Strauss with a nod of his be-whiskered head. At his side in the imperial box, the teenage girl with the fragile features and the shining hair was, as everyone knew, Princess Katherine Dolgoruky, with whom the Tsar had fallen in love when she was still a child, and now made his constant companion.

By far the most ardent of Strauss's royal admirers was the Tsar's brother, Grand Duke Konstantin. An avid musical amateur and a passable cellist, Konstantin was so taken with the Viennese music that he asked Strauss for permission to play with the orchestra. That St. Petersburg was quietly scandalized at such *lèse-majesté*, troubled neither Strauss nor Konstantin. The Grand Duke fitted himself into the cello section of the orchestra with casual ease, and he and his professional colleagues seemed to enjoy each other's company.

Such democratic behaviour, rare among the Romanovs, seemed fitting for the brother of Russia's remarkable ruler. The reign of Alexander II was a uniquely humane interlude in Russia's harsh history. Alexander instituted many reforms, and voluntarily limited his own power by giving Russia its first constitution. As a boy, he had saved enough of his pocket money to buy the freedom of several serfs. As Tsar he decreed freedom for all serfs. On March 4, 1861, the day Abraham Lincoln took office, more than twenty-five million human beings gained their freedom. It casts a curious light on human affairs that Alexander was eventually murdered in the name of liberty by uncomprehending young radicals. After the

226

murder the tide turned and Alexander's constitution was revoked.

Most of these events still lay in the future when Strauss staked out a small preserve of charm and cheerfulness in the grim land of Russia. It is hardly surprising that quite a few women in his audience entertained special feelings for the virile creator of this entranced atmosphere.

Strauss's attractiveness sometimes caused him trouble. One morning two formal gentlemen presented themselves at Strauss's villa with a challenge to a duel. An army officer had found out that his wife had left an order with her florist to send a dozen roses to Strauss each day. He demanded satisfaction.

Strauss was temperamentally disinclined to settle an affair of the heart with bullets, the more so when he didn't even know the lady. He led the two gentlemen into a suite of three otherwise empty rooms filled to overflowing with the daily consignment of flowers sent by various admirers. "Would you pick out the ones you mean?" he said airily to his visitors, who looked at each other, clicked their heels, and departed without pressing the matter.

Now in his mid-thirties Strauss picked women—mostly very young ones—for charm and looks. Superficiality reassured him, and he failed to realize that by shying away from those elements that lend substance to a sexual attraction, he had set a trap for himself. Her name was Olga.

He called her *"l'Espiégle"*—imp—and indeed to Strauss, this sprightly and capricious girl, just turned twenty, may have seemed like one of his own more ephemeral melodies. For the first time he was helplessly, pathetically in love.

Olga had read enough novels to have an unusual emotional range for a Russian *jeune fille*. She, like all upper-class Russians, spoke in French—she called him "Jean"—and since she spoke it with a fine expressive flair, Strauss for the first time experienced the delights of open and precise communication with another person. Under her influence his own mode of expression grew more adequate to his thoughts.

"Have you noticed how sad I was during the concert?" he wrote to Olga one morning. "I was causelessly enveloped in melancholy

227

increased to a supreme pitch by the music of Schumann, so filled with agonized harmonies. Olga, how unhappy I am! I have never wept for inner pain before, but today—I would confess this to no one but you—it happened."

For Strauss, who never before had been able to put any feeling into words, this was a transformation. To every whim of Olga's he reacted with intense and unaccustomed pathos. After a trivial quarrel he suddenly rose to a harrowing level of emotional candour: "Let me know your selfishness, your pride, and the demon within you—so that I too may regain the balance of wholeness."

Olga was enchanted with her new power. A man had put himself in her keeping. With the fatal innocence of a cat playing with its prey, she tantalized a defenceless Strauss with her moods. "If you see me suffer," he wrote in his anguish, "why not tear my heart completely with just one scornful glance?"

But the kaleidoscope of her moods also held moments of radiant happiness. She lit his world with her smile, warmed it with hints of that ultimate generosity a woman can bestow on a man. June was an idyll. Olga and "Jean" lived their courtship like characters out of Turgenev: depositing letters for each other in the hollow of a tree, long walks, and secret rendezvous.

On July 31, 1859, the tree held this note: "I am more and more convinced that you are being destined for me by God, and there is no space within me that could harbour the thought of living without you. Jean."

This complicated matters. Olga's toy unexpectedly turned out to have a heart. It was breakable. And so, ultimately, she herself could be hurt. Now one had to be careful.

Even if she had returned Strauss's earnest and passionate love, there would have been obstacles. Olga Smirnitzki belonged to an aristocratic family, and it was unthinkable for her to marry a man whose name appeared on public placards. For all her romantic fancy, Olga had a tough sense of reality. She took refuge behind her family.

Strauss received an invitation to the Smirnitzki palace. Greatly pleased to be asked to Olga's home for the first time, he was in no

228

way prepared for his reception. Olga was not there to greet him. He was ushered into the formidable presence of her mother, who awaited him with a speech designed to discredit Olga in his eyes.

But she could not shake Strauss's devotion. As soon as he left the house he reported her action to Olga, characteristically unsuspecting that the girl herself might have initiated it. "When [your mother] said to me that I was not to believe a word you said, that all you did was designed to bring me to the point of madness; that all your wishes were inspired by the devil within you, then I conceived a positive hatred against your mother . . . who could say such insulting things against her own child."

Madame Smirnitzki demanded that Strauss hand over Olga's letters. Strauss refused—"For I need these letters to preserve my own life and I cannot do without them."

It is a mark of Olga's basic kindness that she permitted Strauss to go on believing that she loved him. She even put a few more letters in the hollow tree, hinting that only the surveillance of her parents prevented her from seeing him. Strauss tried to console her: "Do not let your parents' obstinacy burden your heart. I only want to know that you are not sad. Not a single moment should be shadowed for you."

The Russian summer was short. The gardens at Pavlovsk lay still and the music hall was locked. Johann Strauss braced himself for the long railway journey back to Vienna. He had no opportunity to take leave of Olga.

A few more letters passed between them, but these ceased soon after his return, when Olga married a man chosen by her parents. Strauss sought solace in work, but it was almost a year before the fires that lit his remembrance of Olga died down, and he at last found deliverance.

THE Vienna of the 1860s that welcomed Strauss after his Russian adventures was very different from that of his youth. Urban growth had altered its face, and the rise of industrial capitalism had poured new people with new money, new tastes and new attitudes into the city.

Outwardly it was an era of opulence for all of Austria, but beneath the gloss the nation was divided. For almost a millennium Austria had been a family of many nationalities sheltered under the paternal roof of monarchy. But after the revolution of 1848 the crown no longer inspired a unifying faith, and Austria's nationalities hoped to become independent nations.

Vienna reacted to the growing tension within the empire like a woman putting on her loveliest dress in the face of danger. The old city walls were razed and a great circling boulevard, the Ringstrasse, was built round the inner city. Nearly two hundred feet wide, it had a broad central road for wheeled traffic flanked by tree-shaded bridle paths and ample promenades. Magnificent buildings adjoined "the Ring", many of them set in spacious plazas between festive fountains. The Opera, the first to be completed, was soon followed by the Parliament, the City Hall, the Stock Exchange, the Imperial Theatre, and the vast museums of art and of science.

Emperor Franz Josef had given the most renowned architects of the day virtually limitless access to the state treasury. What inspired him to this extravagance was sound political intuition. Austria needed a spiritual binding force to strengthen the fading faith in the crown. By transforming her capital into an expression of generosity, dignity, and beauty, Franz Josef was asserting and validating the ideal of monarchic rule. The Ringstrasse was his way of countering the divisive forces of the new nationalism. Against an idea he posed a symbol.

East of the Opera the character of the Ring changed as public buildings yielded to private mansions—the homes of Vienna's *nouveaux riches*. The "Ring millionaires", as the old aristocracy contemptuously called the fashionable residents of the new street, were businessmen. Their money, often made by one man's enterprise, flowed into Vienna from the busy textile mills and machine shops of Bohemia, the Styrian mines and ironworks, from Moravia's sugar refineries, and from the private investment banks springing up everywhere to finance the belated burgeoning of industry in Austria.

230

In their social attitudes the Ring millionaires differed greatly from the rigid, land-owning establishment, and it was in their houses that, for the first time, Vienna's intellectual, artistic, and social worlds mingled on equal footing. It was here that Johann Strauss—by now fairly wealthy himself—found his new social *milieu*. Though the old aristocrats of the inner city would never have allowed a musician on their guest list, Baron Moritz Todesco, whose Ring mansion abounded with artists, writers, and an attractive sprinkling of débutantes, had no such scruples. In fact the charming, urbane woman who was the baron's companion and a gracious hostess to his guests was herself a famous singer.

Jetty Treffz was remarkable in many ways. That she was able, as Todesco's mistress, to assemble one of Vienna's most fashionable circles in itself attests to her charisma, for even the emancipated new society did not condone the open display of irregular unions.

Years on stage had given Jetty assurance, and though no longer young, she had retained her beautiful figure, and lustrous dark hair still framed her expressive face. Music critics had compared her to Jenny Lind, the "Swedish nightingale" who had enchanted Europe. Mendelssohn and Berlioz had dedicated songs to her. But at the age of forty she had abandoned her career for the companionship of Moritz Todesco.

They could not marry. The baron had promised his dying father never to abandon the Jewish faith, Jetty would not give up her Catholicism, and Austria recognized no civil marriage between persons of different faiths. So, even after the birth of two daughters, their union remained unsanctified.

In the baronial mansion on the Ring, Jetty led a sheltered existence. Only with Strauss could she recapture the stimulus of her former life as a musician. She saw to it that he came often to her house. And Strauss, still smarting from Olga's rebuff, responded to Jetty's warmth and to her deeply sympathetic knowledge of human nature. It didn't matter to him that Jetty was ten years older than he.

When the relationship between Strauss and Jetty could no

Left, Jetty Treffz
and Strauss, Jr.;
above, brother
Josef Strauss, and
right, younger
brother, Eduard.

longer be maintained within the bounds of discretion, Jetty asked
the baron for her release. He let her go without a word of
reproach. He must have loved her greatly. He settled a sizable
fortune on her, and he kept their two daughters to give them the
advantage of his position.

It was a quiet wedding. Aside from Jean and Jetty—she
preferred the French version of his name—only two witnesses
were present at St. Stephen's at eight in the morning on August
27, 1862. One was Carl Haslinger, Strauss's publisher. The other
was his mother. Neither was altogether pleased.

Haslinger worried about Jetty's money. With all economic
pressure removed, would Strauss remain productive? Anna Strauss
had other reservations. For all her artistic bent she retained the
outlook of a middle-class housewife, and her husband's defection
had narrowed her tolerance. To her, Jetty was a "fallen woman"
who had beguiled her dearest son into some alien world of
ingrained wickedness and ultimate perdition.

Yet if Strauss's marital prospects seemed doubtful it was not for

Angelika Strauss

Strauss, Jr., with Johannes Brahms

the reasons imagined by Anna. The real danger lay in the temper of the times and its effect on creative artists. It was actually Jetty's influence that enabled Strauss to escape the subtle morbidity that was slowly wrapping itself around Vienna's spirit. The break with Olga had made him susceptible to the melancholy and introspective aspects of the current romanticism, and occasionally he would spend whole days staring out of the window. Jetty was just the woman to give him the support he needed at this point in his life.

Deliberately, one suspects, she steered her marriage with Strauss into the safe and undemanding channel of cosy domesticity. She saw to it that their lives were basically routine, keyed to an even note of tranquillity. For Strauss this was a novelty as well as a need. The home Jetty created was a refuge. None but intimate friends came, and Strauss had few of those. His way of entertaining them was with a quiet game of billiards. For the most part Jetty had Strauss to herself.

With the money Todesco had given her, she bought a mansion

in Hietzing at the western outskirts of Vienna, adjoining the great park of Schönbrunn palace.

It was a two-storey building of golden-yellow sandstone, with a view from its rounded top scanning the entire city, with Schönbrunn in the foreground, the spire of St. Stephen's in the middle distance, and the Danube as backdrop. Towards the west one saw the gentle range of the Vienna Woods enfolding their vineyards between arborate ridges, and far to the south the eye met the gleam of the first Alpine peaks.

Jetty furnished the house in the latest fashion. All the walls were covered with brocaded silk. Strauss's study, for example, was lined in emerald green with wine-red stripes to match the velvet upholstery of sofas and chairs. Most of the other rooms were in deep red, a favourite colour in this opulent period. But in her choice of furniture Jetty resisted late Victorian massiveness, preferring the lighter and more graceful Biedermeier. Throughout the house the light from crystal chandeliers coaxed a pale reddish glow from waxed cherry wood and raised golden reflections in vermeil.

Strauss rarely went out of the house. By 1864, at the age of thirty-nine, he had fulfilled his contracts as a conductor, and his wife's wealth enabled him to retire from regular appearances and devote himself to composition. The Strauss orchestra, still the pride of Vienna and the mainstay of his family, was now wholly in the hands of Josef and the youngest brother, Eduard, who had also been groomed as a conductor. After Josef's fatal accident in 1870 Eduard carried on alone.

Unlike his brothers, Eduard was ordinary—a competent musician who lacked true musicality. As a conductor he was able to ape Johann's style, and for the audiences thronging to his concerts, that was good enough. It wasn't good enough for Eduard. He knew the difference, sensed his lack, and grew into a bitter, shallow man who cared more for good tailoring than anything else. In his foppish way "Edi" Strauss became one of Vienna's most fashionable men, always seen in the right places and at the right parties.

Edi was also a composer and successfully introduced his waltzes and polkas along with Johann's. They were neat and well-crafted, but Edi had no illusions. His were occasional pieces. Johann's work was timeless. Gradually this knowledge poisoned his relationship with his brother.

Johann tried to bridge the widening gap. "You see everything too darkly," he wrote to Edi. "You always suspect that I want to do you harm. I wish you would rid yourself of such foolish notions. When will you grow up enough to realize that your brother is not your foe?"

Although Edi rejected every conciliatory approach, Johann treated him with openness and generosity throughout his life.

Only after Johann's death could Edi vent his hate. In a macabre fratricidal gesture, he set a great fire, feeding it for two full days with all of Johann's unpublished manuscripts. No one knows what beauty and delight Edi burned. It is the measure of the man that he could turn music to ashes.

YET Edi's anger cast little shadow on Johann's life. Freed from the pressures of public performances, he settled into a creative routine. Dressed in his red velvet smoking-jacket, he would sit at his desk almost every night, filling sheet after sheet of music paper. Occasionally he would try a few chords on the piano— very softly so as not to wake Jetty. In the morning, after a late breakfast and a romp in the cobbled courtyard with his two Great Danes, he would walk in the still rural hills of Hietzing. After lunch he would play for Jetty the music composed on the previous evening. At times she suggested revisions, encouraging him towards increasingly symphonic structures, and Strauss trusted her advice. Jetty's competent, knowing participation in this growth gave their marriage a workable content.

This was the period in Strauss's life that prepared the ground for his great symphonic waltzes: "The Blue Danube", "Wine, Women, and Song", "Tales from the Vienna Woods", "Voices of Spring", "Artist's Life", and the "Emperor Waltz", to name but the finest. These works are liberated from subservience to the dance and attain validity in musical terms alone.

Long before he achieved this, Strauss had made his mark as a symphonic conductor. As early as 1856 he had conducted Liszt's *Mazeppa* in the composer's presence and to his explicit approval.

But his greatest coup of the sort was to conduct the Viennese *première* of excerpts from *Tristan und Isolde*, the most controversial score of its time.

The work had been scheduled at the Vienna Opera in 1861, but plans for the performance were dropped when the orchestra declared the music to be "unplayable". Strauss, an ardent Wagnerian, was incensed. He asked Wagner for permission to play orchestral excerpts from the score and, surprisingly, Wagner assented. He had once characterized Strauss as "the most musical mind in Europe". Apparently he had meant it.

Thus, on August 31, 1861, at a concert in the Volksgarten— the spacious park along part of the Ring—Vienna witnessed one of the strangest paradoxes in musical history: the most profound score of an era being introduced by the Waltz King.

Wagner's influence on Strauss became increasingly evident in his later waltzes. Within the limits of his medium he captured something of Wagner's mystic concept of a world filled with "endless melody", parts of which reach a composer's mind. Instead of stringing together contrasting waltz tunes like a multicoloured garland, Strauss now created endlessly flowing streams of related themes, gliding freely from one key to another in fluid Wagnerian harmonies.

Audiences responded readily to the surpassing beauty of these later waltzes, but some found them puzzling. Alexandre Dumas *père* observed in his journal: "It often happened that my partner and I, dancing to the magical music of Johann Strauss, would stop in order to follow into the infinite this inspired dreaming. It almost seemed to us a desecration to allow such melodies to be resolved into a physical pleasure."

The old waltz implied a feeling of happy, uncomplicated togetherness. To each couple the music said: "We". The new, far more subtle waltz says: "You and I", and the separateness, the ache of yearning, is the root of Victorian romance.

236

CHAPTER FOUR

THE UNIVERSE of the waltz can be epitomized in about fifteen minutes simply by playing "The Blue Danube". When its softly mysterious opening stirs the air with a rich, vibrant pianissimo that only a great orchestra can achieve, when the conductor retains a touch of lassitude even in the more exuberant phrases, the music takes subtle hold of the listener and makes him a living part of a vanished world.

A line in a love poem by a now obscure poet served as Strauss's inspiration for "The Blue Danube". The fluid sound of the phrase "by the Danube, beautiful blue Danube" captivated him, and he not only made it the title of a new waltz but transmuted it into the opening theme, which suggests the gliding flow of the great river.

Paradoxically the waltz that was to become Vienna's musical hallmark was one of Strauss's rare flops when it was first heard. Shortly after completing the score he turned it over to Johann Herbeck, the conductor of the Viennese Men's Choral Association, who had asked him to write something for that excellent group. But Herbeck had not considered the fact that the Waltz King was unaccustomed to writing for voice. That was the first portent of disaster. The second was the text. Since Strauss had not set words to the music, Herbeck handed the score to one Josef Weyl, a police clerk who sang in the chorus and occasionally wrote verses.

Weyl drew his inspiration for the lyric from the new electric arc lights that had just been introduced at Vienna's busier corners. The lamps were highly unreliable and often sputtered out. The opening lines of Weyl's poetry for "The Blue Danube" duly reflected these circumstances:

> *Vienna, be gay!*
> *And what for, pray?*
> *The light of the arc!*
> *Here it's still dark!*

It speaks well for the chorus that its members nearly rioted when they were obliged to sing out these inanities in antiphonal dialogue, one side exclaiming "The light of the arc!" and the other responding "Here it's still dark!" But they were persuaded to perform, and on February 13, 1867, at the height of the carnival season, a massed chorus of twelve hundred men bellowed forth this hymn to electric streetlights.

Strauss received the news of the disaster nonchalantly. It had been a good season for him. And just five days earlier, the public had cheered the first performance of "Artist's Life", a composition he considered one of his most beautiful. What did it matter if "The Blue Danube" was a flop? He is reported to have muttered, "Well, the hell with it."

"The Blue Danube" might well have lain forgotten among Strauss's papers, eventually to be burned by his brother, if he had not soon afterwards received a letter from the Comte d'Osmont, a well-known French patron of music, inviting him to Paris in the spring for the World's Fair. Apparently the Count had been in touch with the Austrian ambassador to France, Prince Richard Metternich—the son of the former chancellor against whom Strauss as a young man had written his revolutionary marches.

An astute diplomat, Richard Metternich had been persuaded that having Strauss in Paris at this time would be a smart political move. If he succeeded in captivating the Parisians, he might create an atmosphere favourable to the ambassador's own schemes, which aimed at allying France and Austria against Germany.

Just a year before, Bismarck had provoked a trivial border dispute with Austria. He had insolently pushed it to the point of war, and in just three weeks, his Prussian-drilled troops had trounced Austria's brave but bumbling forces. He had claimed no spoils. All he had wanted to do was to give the world a German lesson.

Stunned by this prophetic encounter, Austria was reaching for the hand of France. In terms of military prowess she had little to offer. Comparing Austria's army—a kind of permanent costume ball for its aristocracy—with the professionalism of the French

238

corps, Metternich quipped: "The Austrians make generals of their dukes; the French make dukes of their generals." But Austria's strategic location offered France a vital security factor. With Austria in the east and south and France in the west, a restraining ring might be forged against the stirring German monster.

To make Johann Strauss an instrument of such diplomacy had been the lucky inspiration of Richard Metternich's wife, Princess Pauline.

This vital and perceptive woman had seen that common denominators were needed if an alliance was to be achieved, and that music, better than anything else, might point up the natural affinity of Paris and Vienna, the two great cities that, in many ways, were products of the same joyful spirit.

Paris under Napoleon III was the city of the bourgeoisie. The stock exchange was like a great roulette wheel tossing fortunes from hand to hand. Speculation was a way of life. Reaching deep into the middle class, it undercut the traditional morality. Society was a pyramid of opportunists, topped by a matching monarch.

Louis Napoleon's paternity was questionable though he was generally recognized as the son of Napoleon I's brother. To strengthen his claim to the throne he sometimes went to considerable lengths. On one public occasion he is said to have signified his lineage by having a tame eagle flap about his head. The eagle was attracted to the imperial cause by a piece of bacon tucked into Louis Napoleon's hatband.

After the revolution of 1848 he became president of the new French Republic, but in 1852 he had overthrown his own government to proclaim himself emperor. Shortly thereafter he had made the beautiful Spaniard, Eugénie de Montijo, his empress, for when he had asked her the way to her heart, she had firmly replied: "Through the chapel, sir."

It was to this imperial pair that Johann Strauss was presented at a splendid ball at the Austrian embassy, arranged by Princess Pauline with a fortune of 167,000 francs she had wheedled from the Austrian government for just this evening.

Strauss could not have asked for a more auspicious introduction, for the pixie-faced Princess Pauline was the mildly scandalous darling of the Parisian *haut monde* and the confidante of the Empress Eugénie. She was the first socially prominent woman in Paris to eat in a public restaurant, she disdained the crinoline, and at home she smoked an occasional cigar. (But when one gentleman asked her if she would mind if he smoked, she answered icily: "I don't know, sir. No one has ever dared smoke in my presence.")

At her fête for Johann Strauss she may have felt a moment's consternation when the Prussian Crown Prince, in town for the World's Fair, crashed the party. It may also have been embarrassing that Johann Strauss, having as good an ear for language as music, spoke better French than the Emperor, who had been raised in German exile. But such concerns ceased to trouble the Princess as soon as Strauss, taking his place before the orchestra, launched into the first waltz.

That evening at the embassy Strauss proved himself Austria's greatest diplomatic asset, but he had yet to win over the wider Parisian public. It was his good fortune that the publisher of the newly launched paper, *Le Figaro*, decided to provide him with publicity. And when one of the editors suggested that a waltz new to Paris would add special interest to his forthcoming concert, Strauss remembered "The Blue Danube" and telegraphed to Vienna for the score.

Thanks to *Le Figaro*'s promotion, the French *première* of *Le Beau Danube Bleu* was anticipated as a major event at the fair. The fair itself was like festive music. This was the year that Paris earned its name as the City of Light. Gas jets flared from pipelines stretched along the endless railings of Parisian balconies. A million spots of flame illuminated the length of the great boulevards, turning the whole city into a luminous fairground. Across the Seine from the fountain-studded Place de la Concorde, the vaulted steel and glass exhibition halls themselves were marvels for their time, foreshadowing future architecture. Within, the new wonders of the age stood on display: puffing steam engines, chattering looms, whirling dynamos humming a promise of the electric era.

To a Danish visitor, Hans Christian Andersen, the fair was a fairy tale: "It's like a great Christmas display," he wrote home to Copenhagen, "with toys for grownups."

At the Cercle International, the fair's great auditorium, Johann Strauss now set forth his apotheosis of the Danube, this time in a purely orchestral performance. The audience, numbering thousands, had already heard such tuneful gems of his as "Morning Papers" and "Vienna Bonbons". Would the new waltz stand up to these standards?

The answer soon unfolded. Rising from its misty introduction, "The Blue Danube" flowed on like the river itself, swirling with exuberant melody, gaining momentum, vibrant with orchestral colour. Then once more it subsided into pastoral serenity. For a moment before the jubilant applause, the audience was silent.

Time and again Strauss had to repeat "The Blue Danube". Every orchestra in Paris eventually took up the tune. Parisians insisted on singing it, and one of *Le Figaro*'s facile hacks provided a text just slightly more palatable than the doggerel about streetlights.

Foreign visitors returning to their own countries couldn't get the melody out of their heads. Edward, Prince of Wales, went home humming. Later, at his invitation, Strauss went to London, where he gave six highly acclaimed concerts at Covent Garden. When he conducted the new waltz, even the formidable Queen Victoria nodded her pleasure, as at her coronation ball she had done to his father.

Back in Vienna a printing crisis had developed. Since the hand-engraved copper plates used for printing music wore out faster than they could be replaced, every available music engraver in the city was punching "The Blue Danube" into metal. Before the first printing was over, a hundred sets of plates had been worn down, and "The Blue Danube" had become the most profitable "property" in the history of music.

Only in one sense did Strauss and "The Blue Danube" fail. On June 19, 1867, hardly two months after Princess Pauline's magnificent party, Austria and France were torn apart by a salvo of shots in distant Mexico. Juárez and his revolutionaries had killed Emperor Maximilian, the brother of Austria's Franz Josef.

The news travelled slowly at first, riding with couriers across the desert towards the outpost of the telegraph in Texas. Twelve days after the event the tragic message finally flashed to Europe on the new undersea cable. Paris and Vienna were stunned. The Empress Eugénie, who was at the fair handing out medals, fainted when she received the news. All festivities were cancelled, and the Metternichs fled back to Vienna.

Hopes of an alliance between Austria and France were shattered; for it was the French who had persuaded the Austrian Archduke Maximilian to accept the crown of Mexico. In return for his protection of French interests in Central America, they had pledged him military protection. But they had broken their promise and abandoned him to his enemies. No music could heal the wound.

AN UNFORESEEN by-product of Strauss's sojourn in France was his eventual adaptation of the French operetta into a Viennese art form. At first Strauss was by no means willing to graft this patch of Paris to the Viennese stage. In Paris he had freely expressed his admiration of the form. Jacques Offenbach, composer of many popular operettas, in turn greatly admired Strauss, and on the occasion of a personal meeting had said to him, "You should write operettas." Strauss had shrugged off this suggestion. His experience with "The Blue Danube" had convinced him that his music could not properly unfold within the cage of text, and relating music to expressed ideas was the essence of Offenbach's work.

That the stage was linked to the world of literature was in itself enough to frighten Strauss. A man who never read a book and rarely a newspaper, he distrusted anything connected with words. Even among friends he rarely spoke anything but commonplaces. His charm resided in his manner, not his conversation. The only person in his life to whom he had ever talked at length was Olga. But that Russian interlude was long over.

Strauss himself was fully aware that language failed him. When he was asked by a publisher to write his reminiscences, he declined. "This has to do with words," says his letter. "For me words have always been tough and intractable stuff."

Strauss also realized that he had no sense of theatre. In Vienna, where the theatre was the central point of the cultural pattern, he almost never went to see a play. In this respect he stood in complete contrast to most Viennese.

Vienna's penchant for the theatre accounts for the almost riotous welcome Offenbach's works received when they were first heard in the Austrian capital. Immediately theatrical promoters began trying to grow a local crop of operettas. A few were composed. But it remained for Strauss, chiefly through his creation of *Die Fledermaus*, to give Viennese operetta its distinctive stamp.

IT WAS Maximilian Steiner, the impresario of the Theater-an-der-Wien, who finally overcame Strauss's steadfast refusal to have anything to do with the stage. He called on Jetty Strauss and asked her to steal some of her husband's manuscripts. He would have a text set to the tunes, he told her, and if Strauss liked the result, maybe something could be worked out with him after all.

Steiner, no doubt, played on Jetty's nostalgia for the stage, when he made this questionable proposal. And in the aging, isolated woman longing to enter once more the milieu of her youth, he found a receptive audience. She may also have hoped that a theatrical venture might bring her closer to Johann, who, after the first happy years of their marriage, had been neglecting her.

At any rate, on a subsequent morning, Jetty admitted a group of Steiner's singers to the house in Hietzing, and the nonplussed Strauss found himself listening to words he never dreamed of, set to his own unpublished melodies. He wavered between being intrigued and annoyed, but the outcome was an almost foregone conclusion, for he generally permitted himself to be manipulated by Jetty in business matters. Now, yielding to her persuasion, he agreed to compose for Steiner's theatre.

Steiner supplied him with three trivial operetta librettos in quick succession, and Strauss, for the first time in his life, wrote some thoroughly uninspired music. Because of casting difficulties he withdrew the first score, but the other operettas, *Indigo* and *Carnival in Rome* had brief runs at the Theater-an-der-Wien.

Only Jetty was unreservedly pleased. The smell of theatre air had revitalized her and all her energies were now bent on involving Johann more inextricably with the stage. He received her dictums with an air of indifferent submission. Then the descent into failure reversed itself. With a sudden rekindling of his creative fire Strauss achieved the joyful peak of *Die Fledermaus*, the one operetta ever to transcend its own genre to become a classic in the realm of musical theatre.

For once he had a libretto to match the spark of his music. *Die Fledermaus* was based on a proven German play that had run in Berlin under the title *Das Gafängnis (The Jail)*. Later it had been adapted for the French theatre, and through a French authors' agent the piece had come to the attention of the Viennese publisher, Gustav Lewy, an acquaintance of Strauss's. Lewy sensed that this brash, bubbling comedy had just the ingredients that Strauss's previous librettos had so notably lacked.

The operetta's title, *Die Fledermaus (The Bat)*, simply refers to one character's masquerade costume and gives no clue to the story, which is a preposterous *mélange* of mistaken identities, husbands inadvertently flirting with their own wives, chambermaids posing as ladies of fashion, devious lawyers, and sybaritic princes. What matters is that beneath its zaniness and spoof, the libretto of *Die Fledermaus* conveys a tough, unblinking portrait of Vienna's *nouveaux riches* with their aristocratic pretensions, their fashionably ambiguous sexual mores and stratagems, and insouciant attitude towards authority and law.

Strauss, whose social intuition was apparently sharp, immediately responded to these qualities in the script. He composed in a frenzy, barricading his room against interruptions, working day and night, eating and sleeping sporadically. Jetty, the only person to come near him during this period, later told friends that Strauss had sometimes wept with the joyful ecstasy of work. In forty-three days and nights he wrought his miracle—music that perhaps more than any other reaches towards the essence of laughter.

But on the evening of April 5, 1874, when *Die Fledermaus* was first heard at the Theater-an-der-Wien, Vienna could not laugh. The very stratum of the population that formed both the subject of *Die Fledermaus* and its most likely audience—the elegant, pleasure-seeking theatre buffs—had been cast into gloom by the great stock-market collapse of the preceding year.

When the Franco-Prussian War of 1870 had immobilized the Paris Bourse, Vienna had become the financial hub of the continent, and the sudden influx of capital had loosened an orgy of speculation not only among the rich but also among the wage-earning citizens. The stock exchange took on the atmosphere of a perpetual carnival, a mood entirely congenial to the Viennese temperament. For a couple of years sheer Viennese buoyancy supported unbelievable paper profits.

The sudden reckoning came on Black Friday—May 9, 1873. Stocks supported by nothing more substantial than cheerful temperament dropped almost one hundred per cent. Thousands of Viennese families waking in the morning to affluence were impoverished by nightfall. Some Viennese took the disaster with typical sangfroid. A former millionaire reduced to cooking his own meals would still pull on the bell before bringing his food to the table. "It's not so bad," he explained. "I get prompt service. I ring —and I come."

Since every disaster must have a plausible explanation, most Viennese blamed the Jews. Indeed, Viennese anti-Semitism, which was to reach its full bloody flower in a later era, had its most poisonous roots in the convenient assumption that Jewish brokers had manipulated the exchange to defraud Christian investors.

It took nearly a decade for the Austrian middle class to recoup its solvency and psychological composure. It is understandable, therefore, that the Viennese public was rather constrained in its response to the lighthearted fluff of *Die Fledermaus*. The economic basis for the champagne-doused life pictured on the stage had just been demolished. Instead of liberating laughter, Strauss's masterpiece evoked rueful reminiscence. It closed after only sixteen performances.

Die Fledermaus went into exile. Like "The Blue Danube", it finally won the world's heart not in Vienna but in Paris, where some years later it enchanted the French as *La Chauve-Souris* and flew off triumphantly to more than two hundred theatres throughout Europe, North America, India, and Australia. Twenty years later a young firebrand musician, Gustav Mahler, presented *Die Fledermaus* for the first time on the operatic stage, symbolically transplanting the work to a setting fit for enduring classics. His conducting of *Die Fledermaus* at the Vienna Opera is a musical legend.

Strauss went on to write a total of sixteen stage works. But aside from *Die Fledermaus* only *Der Zigeunerbaron—(The Gipsy Baron)*, a story of Hungarian village life, proved viable.

FOR STRAUSS, the 1870s were a time of transition. Among the adventures and misadventures that marked this passage, none was more picturesque than his journey to the United States, in 1872, when he had already begun to compose for the theatre but had not yet produced *Die Fledermaus*.

By then "The Blue Danube" had made the name of Johann Strauss a household word even in America, and the management of the Boston Peace Festival, a tribute to music as a symbol of world peace, invited him to conduct his works in Massachusetts. Fearful of transportation in any form, Strauss was terrified at the prospect of an ocean crossing. What finally changed his mind was the offer of an unprecedented fee of one hundred thousand dollars. In Austrian purchasing power it must have seemed closer to a million—enough to conquer even Strauss's fear of the water.

However, he still had reservations. Strange tales of American business ethics during the post-Civil War reconstruction period had reached as far as Vienna, and Strauss would not budge until the city of Boston had deposited the full amount in his account at the Vienna Anglo-Bank. He also demanded that the Bostonians pay all travel expenses for himself, for Jetty, for his valet, his maid, and his dog. All of which may explain why the Peace Festival nearly bankrupted its sponsors.

Contrary to expectations, Strauss greatly enjoyed the sea voyage. Of all the passengers aboard the S.S. *Rhein*, he alone was never seasick during the entire thirteen-day crossing from Bremerhaven. In rough weather he was almost the only guest in the dining room, and after dinner would watch with childlike amusement as his brandy snifter slid about the swaying table.

The New York he saw on his arrival on June 23 was not yet what was later to be described as "a city standing up". Like most European cities, New York was still "lying down". The graceful little spire of Trinity Church at the head of Wall Street marked the highest point on its horizon.

But if New York did not seem architecturally strange, other aspects of America induced in Strauss an acute case of culture shock.

Immediately on arrival he found himself encircled by newspaper reporters, concert agents, promoters, and curiosity seekers, who fired unintelligible questions at him in English and would not be silenced by the wave of his hand.

In Europe, at that time, a celebrated gentleman could assure his privacy simply by saying that he wished to be left alone. But in the boisterous United States of the Reconstruction period, voices were loud and the manners insistent. Word had got around that Strauss was a bigger sensation than General Tom Thumb, the Siamese Twins, or anything else in Barnum and Bailey's circus, and apparently nothing had been done to protect him from importunities. He was appalled at the gross familiarity with which strangers addressed him, at their probing questions, and at their suggesting all kinds of business propositions and schemes to him after only a few minutes' acquaintance.

He reacted predictably. Always inclined towards solitude, he simply locked himself in his hotel suites both in New York and in Boston and never went out except to rehearsals and concerts.

The Boston Peace Festival, which was in the hands of over-enthusiastic promoters, confirmed his grotesque impression of America. Appearing for the first rehearsal he faced a truly stagger-ing musical assemblage. His waltzes were attacked by a task force

of nearly two thousand musicians and a chorus of twenty thousand. These were augmented by anvils, firebells, "chimes" consisting of odd lengths of railway track freely suspended on wooden frames for convenient whacking, and a "Monster Bass Drum, 18 Feet in Diameter"

At the fore of this musical army, Strauss was stationed in a sort of lookout tower, watched by dozens of sub-conductors who followed his movements with binoculars and relayed them to the players. Strauss, who had always stressed subtlety of phrase, was in despair, especially since the downbeat—to get everyone started at the same time—was to be the belch of a cannon. His first impulse was to cancel his appearance. But somebody had warned him that Americans had been known to react with lynching to an acute disappointment. "A refusal to conduct would have cost me my life," he wrote back to Vienna. From then on he simply regarded the whole matter as a farce and conducted no less than fourteen concerts at the Boston Peace Festival in an enormous wooden shed that held an audience of a hundred thousand.

On one occasion the cannon marking the downbeat went off prematurely, and Strauss described the ensuing performance as "an unholy row such as I shall never forget." But the audience loved it, and for the remainder of his brief stay in America, Strauss was the hero of the day. Women besieged him for locks of his hair, and his valet obligingly handed out scented envelopes, each containing a black curl snipped from the shaggy pelt of Strauss's Newfoundland dog.

After the Boston series Strauss still found the courage to conduct three concerts in New York. At the Academy of Music on Fourteenth Street he was greatly relieved to find a normal orchestra of some seventy men, and in addition to some of his own works the programme included such sturdy concert fare as the overtures to Rossini's *William Tell* and Wagner's *Rienzi*.

American journalism was not yet paying much attention to the arts, and even *The New York Times* made no serious attempt to evaluate the concerts. Besides, it was a presidential election year and the paper devoted most of its space to Horace Greeley, who was fulminating against the incumbent Ulysses S. Grant, and referring to his political opponents as "murderers, adulterers, drunkards, cowards, liars, and thieves". In mid-July, as the campaign fever engulfed New York, Strauss and his entourage boarded the steamer *Donau* for their homeward voyage.

On arriving in Hamburg Strauss received news that a more ominous kind of fever—cholera—had broken out in Vienna. His mortal fear was immediately aroused. Instead of returning home he and his party headed for Baden-Baden, Germany's most fashionable resort, to wait for the cholera to subside.

Summer and early autumn passed in the leisurely routine of "taking the waters" and with long afternoon promenades in the Kurpark, usually in the company of the conductor Bülow and Johannes Brahms. Not until October did Strauss and Jetty return to Vienna—and the perils of the stage.

FOR Strauss the perils were not merely artistic. There were also young actresses. For the most part these were brief affairs and did not in themselves disrupt a marriage that had ceased to be intimate. But their fleeting nature left Strauss without real companionship, and with a deepening loneliness.

It is characteristic of Jetty's attitude towards him that in her letters she refers to him as "my Jeany-Boy". While Strauss was still emotionally attached to his real mother, Jetty's mothering of him was altogether satisfactory. But over the years his emotional needs changed and the relationship grew unworkable. The result was a silent rift. They had separate apartments in their house, and the collaborative spirit of their early years together vanished. Jetty continued to look after her husband in a concerned, motherly fashion. They did not quarrel, and, at least in the presence of others, their relations were considerate and polite.

The situation was resolved by Jetty's death. In the autumn of 1876 a young man presented himself at the house in Hietzing, addressed Jetty as "mother" and asked for money. Strauss did not know that Jetty had children other than the two Todesco girls, and she didn't interfere when he had the young man thrown out. But later she allowed herself to be blackmailed by her son. On April 9, 1877, while Johann was away, she received a particularly threatening demand, and when Johann returned in the evening he stumbled over her body in the dark. Jetty had died of a stroke, presumably induced by agitation.

To come suddenly upon one's dead wife would unnerve anyone. For Strauss it was a terror beyond his comprehension. It was as if in the fact of Jetty's death he had suddenly glimpsed his own. Like a panicked animal he took headlong flight to Italy. Towards the sun!

Eduard, his younger brother, was left to arrange for the funeral which Johann did not attend, and made no secret of what he thought of Johann's renouncement of responsibility.

It was months before Strauss found the courage to return to Vienna. Even then he avoided his house, and took an apartment at the Hotel Viktoria. The fear of death still clung to him and his former charm and sociability slowly gave way to remoteness.

It was at this period that Strauss, once a fiery and charismatic fiddler, stopped playing the violin. He never played it again. Strauss seemed to have turned against himself. Photographs of the time, as well as a famous portrait by Lenbach, show the changes in his face, the tension about his mouth, and something close to panic in his eyes. His love affairs now became symbolic, and the women he encountered were magic totems against his fears, against mortality. This lends a certain pathetic dignity to Strauss's relentless philandering and provides some basis for understanding his second marriage to a girl named Angelika. To the man whose music was a single love song, Angelika was the lyric sensuous presence of life singing on.

Angelika Diettrich had come to Vienna from Cologne in search of a theatrical career. No one ever remarked her talent, but she was pretty enough to get along without. Besides she had the advantage of being pale blonde with light blue eyes and Viennese men dreamed of blonde girls, wrote songs about them.

It may have been something of this yearning that drew the fifty-three-year-old Strauss to the twenty-six-year-old Angelika when they first met in the lobby of his hotel. Angelika, who had been drifting aimlessly in theatrical circles, was not going to discourage the attentions of Vienna's most famous composer. She permitted herself to be made the object of an intense and impatient courtship, typical of a man with a sense of time running out. There seems to have been little joy or spontaneity between Johann and Angelika, no ripening of affection. Each blindly used the other for private purposes, and on May 27, 1878, their mutual delusions culminated in marriage.

Strauss could not bring himself to return to the house in Hietzing where he had once lived so happily with Jetty. Instead the couple took up residence in the inner city at the elegant town house in the Igelgasse that Strauss had built shortly before with the belated earnings of *Die Fledermaus*.

At first Strauss took obvious pleasure in being seen with his lovely young wife, and for a while he and Angelika were the focal point of countless soirées in the bright whirl along the recovering Ringstrasse. But if they projected a public image of a kind of happiness, it soon had no counterpart at home. Childless and lacking the capacity for meaningful work or for friendship, Angelika fell into chronic boredom. She grew envious of Johann's talent, and mistook his sustained concentration on his work for deliberate inattention to her.

Embittered by her idleness and solitude she began to seek diversion elsewhere, mostly backstage at the Theater-an-der-Wien, where Johann's operettas were produced. This prompted the impresario, Maximilian Steiner, to involve himself once more in Strauss's private life. Glib and charming, Steiner seemed to Angelika the very image of the brittle glamour she had come to Vienna to find. And nothing in the character of either Steiner or Angelika prevented them from following their inclination towards each other.

Vienna, always avid for scandal, made the most of Angelika's liaison with Steiner. Strauss himself uttered not a single word about the matter, at least not before witnesses. The quality that saved him in these circumstances was his deep kindness. No matter what pain he endured because of her, he would inflict none of it on others—not even on her. As far as is known he did not reproach her and they did not quarrel. She quietly left his house.

The years with Jetty, though not always happy, had accustomed Strauss to domesticity and now, with the loss of Angelika, he once again faced the unsettling task of finding someone to marry. It was a coincidence, therefore, that about this time a young acquaintance of Strauss's died, leaving an attractive twenty-one-year-old widow, who incidentally was also named Strauss. In many ways Adele was Angelika's opposite. Small, fine-featured, with raven hair, she looked like a slender, rather wistful child, with warm dark eyes that promised solace. She was a banker's daughter, and like many well-brought-up women of her class, she combined assured competence and efficiency with delicacy of manner and an air of self-effacement. Strauss was enchanted with her, and Adele, feeling very much alone with her little daugher after her husband's death, gratefully accepted the love and solicitude of an older man.

Soon they decided to marry, but some legal difficulties had to be resolved. Divorce was almost impossible to obtain in Catholic Austria, and those who were divorced were not allowed to remarry. Fortunately Strauss was friendly with Duke Ferdinand of Saxe-Coburg-Gotha, who brought his dilemma to the attention of his uncle, the reigning duke of that German principality. If Strauss were to accept the Lutheran faith and citizenship in the duke's domain, he was informed, his difficulties could be resolved.

It was only with great reluctance that Strauss abandoned his formal allegiance to Austria and to Catholicism. But for Adele's sake, he did so. On July 11, 1883, Duke Ernst II personally pronounced his divorce from Angelika, and on August 15 of that year Johann and Adele were married in the royal chapel at Coburg. They spent a brief honeymoon at the palace, then returned to Vienna, now technically foreigners in their native city.

Strauss was fifty-eight at the time of this marriage, but his love for Adele rejuvenated him. In her presence his bearing and his gait were of a man half his age. Almost daily he wrote her little love letters. Before going to the theatre to conduct a performance, for example, he left her this note: "My dear Adele! I shall change the tempo from *maestoso* to *allegro* so I can hurry back to you all the sooner and kiss you a few minutes earlier. Your Jean." His scribbled notes to her ranged from little gallantries to exuberant declarations like: "You are the queen of my happiness, of my life!" Writing to her from Berlin, where he had gone to see his publisher, the normally inarticulate Strauss was moved to say: "I need my publisher to be able to adorn you. The publisher has an important part to play. There are arrows to be shot. Arrows of love—and they cost money. I am able to buy them through [my music which is] a love-token . . . Sleep well, you black-eyed Adele, the only woman on earth."

He wanted to be young for Adele. He dyed his greying hair and his moustache, and he kept himself trim by riding the fine horses he kept at his newly acquired country estate. If on occasion he still fell into a dark mood, just watching his horses canter would dispel his gloom. At this stage of his life he rarely accepted invitations for concert tours. But when a Russian impresario promised him two rare-blooded stallions if he would conduct a concert in Moscow, Strauss could not resist. He was so delighted with the Russian horses that he immediately gave them a workout. Later he wrote home: "Both the horses and I exerted ourselves too much. . . . The horses were too young for the work, and I was too old." It was the only time that Strauss, always conscious of mortality, ever mentioned his advancing years.

Despite his domestic happiness Strauss remained rather withdrawn. He seldom gave large parties and only a few friends visited him regularly. There was one main social rule: serious talk must be avoided. Strauss could not bear to hear anything of an intellectual or problematic nature discussed. It would upset him for days, making him unable to compose.

Among his acquaintances, Strauss's closest personal bond was with Johannes Brahms. Musically the two men stood far apart: Brahms probed music for ultimate depth; Strauss was as a public entertainer, always conscious of surface effect. Temperamentally, too, they were at opposite poles: Strauss always suave, while Brahms affected a gruff, bearish manner to hide the profound tenderness so evident in his music. Yet there grew an affinity between the two that allowed them to sit together in the garden for long afternoons, rarely speaking a word, each happy in the company of the other. At other times Brahms would go to the piano to play his own version of Strauss waltzes, enriching them with improvisations.

It was Adele, no less than Johann, who drew Brahms to the house. The old bachelor was an inveterate admirer of other men's wives, but always a respecter of marriage. To the arch-romantic Brahms, being in love—usually with unattainable women—was a creative necessity. He once quipped that he and Strauss were both "in service at the court of Adele—Brahms for fugues, Strauss for waltzes." Another time he inscribed Adele's fan with the opening bars of "The Blue Danube", signing it "unfortunately not by J. Brahms". He was not given to such self-effacement, almost invariably assuming a sarcastic defensiveness that eventually alienated most of his acquaintances. Johann and Adele Strauss were the exceptions, and he treated them with an affectionate courtesy and warmth shown to no one else.

For Strauss this was a time of contentment and respite. In the circle of his friends, nourished by Adele's devotion, he lived quietly into the acceptance of age. Adele had succeeded in arresting the tide of melancholy that had swept over him in the years just before he met her. Though he never recovered his former *élan*, it was through her that he attained a certain tranquillity. She gave him the emotional shelter he needed. She was his anchor in the sea of time and held him to the end of his life.

SOFTLY the rain fell. Now and then a gust of wind drove the water against the window-pane in the grey afternoon.

This was Strauss's favourite weather. Even in summer, at his villa in Ischl near Salzburg, he always hoped for rain. He liked to stand near the window, especially at dusk, his eyes tracing the drops running down the pane.

Adele

"I love this miserable weather," he wrote to a friend. "If only it keeps that way. Composing is so easy in the rain."

Occasionally he interrupted his work to play the newly written melodies for Adele on the piano, or he went into the kitchen to potter. "To clear my head from too much concentration," he said, "I like to pick peas from their pods or cut the ends of string beans."

His invasions of the kitchen often embroiled him in arguments with his cook, which he vastly enjoyed. The cook was a firm believer in the traditional Austrian five-course meal, with soup and fish before the roast. Strauss was all in favour of the fish. He loved fresh brook trout. But he firmly held that soup—especially an Austrian kind with chunks of lung hash or liver dumplings swimming in it—merely spoiled the meal, a heresy for which the cook never ceased to upbraid him.

When it wasn't raining he would play in the garden with his little stepdaughter, sometimes crawling around in his white flannel trousers to help her lay out some treasured seashells in decorative patterns among the flower beds. But his only true repose was work.

Late into the night he would scribble on his score sheets at his stand-up desk near the window, stopping at times to write a short letter to Adele, who was asleep in the next room. In the morning she would find messages like this piled on her night table:

"Dearest Adele! I wish you a very good-night, and a good sleep, and a good mood when you wake up! Let us be merry as we go through life. *On ne vit qu'une fois.* Especially women should always smile. . . . It looks so pretty on them and prevents wrinkles."

He had no hobbies now, no recreation. Ceaselessly he composed. Works such as *Blind Cow*, or *Waldmeister*—long forgotten except for their sparkling overtures—ran hundreds of performances on all the stages of Europe. Few of these scores maintained a consistent level of inspiration. With impresarios clamouring for new operettas Strauss now rarely found time to write orchestral waltzes. Yet in 1888 he made a notable exception. Franz Josef was celebrating the fortieth anniversary of his reign, and Strauss, the former revolutionary, was now the Emperor's official director of court ball music. As such, he wanted to pay special tribute to his sovereign, a unique figure in political history who was regarded by many as a saint rather than a ruler.

In his great and genuine modesty Franz Josef would have never encouraged such sentiments; yet something in his character invited veneration. He never was a heroic monarch. His was a different grandeur; a gentleness combined with unbending decency. Responsibility and a sense of duty kept him working at his desk each day as if he were just another government official. Even the humblest of his subjects could personally petition him in audience. He was unfailingly courteous, and those in contact with him were touched by his sense of compassion. He embodied gentlemanly correctness, justice, and probity—qualities he believed necessary to give moral sanction to the wielding of power. No historian has ever captured the essence of this rare and humble man, whose frail, stooped figure belied all vulgar notions of dominance. He had the natural majesty of a true monarch, an aura that stemmed as much from his humaneness as from his rank. This was the monarch whom Johann Strauss immortalized in "The Emperor Waltz".

It was the charisma of the Emperor, more than anything else, that kept Austria from crumbling. The various nationalities under the Austrian crown were agitating virulently for secession. Poles, Czechs, Hungarians, Serbs, Slovenes, and Slovaks had little love for each other, but they were united in their hate for Austria.

Nationalism was not the only rift in the failing empire. The rapid growth of industry, combined with total absence of adequate social legislation had created an exploited urban proletariat. In Vienna endless rows of slums now stood in shameful contrast to the splendours of the Ringstrasse. With an increasing portion of the population working twelve hours a day for a pittance, the *Gemütlichkeit* of the past was fast giving way to animosity.

The unthinkable question was whether an absolutist monarchy, suited to an agrarian economy, could survive in an industrial age. Like a spectre it lingered in the background, never allowed to interfere with the more visible pleasures and comforts of the Viennese. In the waning century Austria was a lovely baroque anachronism in the heart of Europe. Premonitions of its end made it seem even lovelier. "The atmosphere of Vienna," recalls the historian Cohen-Portheim, "was like that of Paris before the Great Revolution; there was that same incomparable refinement and elegance mixed with foreboding of disaster."

As Court Ball Music Director, a title which had finally been bestowed on him, Strauss had been repeatedly in Franz Josef's presence, both at the summer palace in Schönbrunn and at the Hofburg in the inner city. But in the last decade of his life he apparently also met Franz Josef at the villa of the actress Katherina Schratt, which lay in a quiet, tree-shaded street just outside the garden walls of Schönbrunn palace.

The Emperor's solitary morning walks usually took him in the direction of Kathi's villa, and during the summer it was his custom to have breakfast there. One morning, when he found Kathi's garden gate still locked, he simply stood in the street and waited. Since no door had ever been closed to him the Emperor did not know that one could ring a bell.

Strauss also frequently visited Kathi. His house in Hietzing, which he again was using, was just around the corner, and she often invited him for his favourite snack—crayfish and goose-liver pâté, served with very dry champagne. On such occasions, according to Viennese hearsay, Strauss and Franz Josef would meet informally—the King of the Waltz and the Emperor of the Realm enjoying each other's company in a summer garden.

The only authenticated conversation between Strauss and Franz Josef took place in 1894 when Strauss was celebrating the fiftieth anniversary of that now legendary night at Dommayer's, when he had defied his father by giving his first concert. In a week of nearly continuous festivities, one event was a gala performance of *The Gipsy Baron* at the opera. Just before curtain time all eyes turned in delighted surprise to the great, two-storey-high royal box. The Emperor himself had come to pay homage to the composer. Franz Josef had no ear for music and his rare attendance at the opera was a ceremonial duty. Since he usually left before the end of the second act, the stage manager asked him during the first intermission if he wished to receive Strauss at once. Unexpectedly the

Emperor replied that he intended to stay to the end of the performance and would talk to Strauss afterwards.

"This time I didn't want to leave," Franz Josef told Strauss after the last curtain and the thunderous ovation that followed. "I enjoyed myself immensely. It is strange, but your music ages as little as you do. You haven't changed at all in the long years I have known you. I congratulate you on your opera."

Strauss was beside himself with happiness. "Opera! The Emperor said opera!" he later exclaimed to his friends. It may have been nothing but an imperial malapropism, but for Strauss it was ecstasy.

Later that week the Vienna Philharmonic gave a banquet in honour of Strauss after which he delivered the only public speech of his life. It was hesitant and short:

"Gentlemen, I am not a talker. The honours you bestow on me today I owe to my predecessors—to my father and to Josef Lanner. They have indicated to me the way in which some growth may be attained: it is possible only through the expansion of form. That was my contribution—my small contribution. That is all I have done. I feel that I am too much honoured, one ascribes too much merit to me." He broke off abruptly: "I have talked too much . . . Nothing more . . . nothing more . . . It is already over."

An ovation drowned his embarrassment.

Later in the evening a gift from a group of American admirers was unveiled: a garland of fifty laurel leaves of solid gold—one for each year of his musical life.

His final years Strauss spent in the quietly ordered domesticity of his four residences: the town house in Igelgasse, the house in Hietzing at the outskirts of Vienna, the country estate at Schönau, and the summer villa in Ischl. He composed every day, and still enjoyed a physical vigour uncommon for his age. But now his withdrawals became more frequent, and again he went for days on end without speaking.

It was not that Strauss was unhappy. He would still on occasion enjoy the company of friends, though the death of Brahms in 1896 had taken from him his most cherished companion. Towards Adele he showed an invariable tenderness compounded of love, gratitude, and delight. But the sheer weight of time past foreshadowed for this silent man the border between living and no-longer-living.

May 22, 1899, was the Feast of the Assumption, Austria's traditional springtime holiday. On this cheerful occasion, a special performance of *Die Fledermaus* was given and Strauss himself conducted the overture, throwing himself into the music with the vitality of a youngster, and in the course of it sweating freely. To relax from the happy exertion and to enjoy the cool spring air, Strauss decided to walk home from the Opera instead of taking his carriage. It was the time of year when the fragrance of lilac and acacia sweeps through Vienna and the white-blossoming horse-chestnut trees along the streets are in full flower. Under their canopy and with his music still ringing in his ears Johann Strauss took his last walk.

The fever came in the morning and would not pass. This did not keep him from composing. For a few days he still worked at his desk, shivering in heavy robes, setting down note after note for the score of *Cinderella*. This was his first ballet music, and he was determined to go on with it despite the rising fever and the racking cough. Some days later he took to his bed. But as long as he could hold up his head he kept writing.

Because of the fever's obstinacy and the apparent involvement of bronchi and lungs, Strauss's physician called into consultation the famous Professor Nothnagel of the University of Vienna's medical faculty. When the professor laid his stethoscope against Strauss's back and asked him to cough Strauss did as he was told, then said with a smile: "Is that all I can do for medical science?"

There certainly was not much that medical science, at that time, could do for Strauss. Professor Nothnagel told Strauss that he had a severe cold. He told Adele that he had double pneumonia.

By June 1 Strauss was in delirium. Adele tells the rest:

"Suddenly he sat up in bed, and under his tortured breathing, softly, there was a song! An old song, which even my little daughter knew, but I had never heard him sing it. Now it came softly from his pale lips.

261

'My little friend, My little friend,
Now we must part . . . .
No matter how beautifully the sun shines,
Sometime it must set . . . .'

In the morning of June 3 he took my hand and kissed it twice without words. It was his last caress. In the afternoon at a quarter past four he died in my arms."

AT THE Volksgarten the long rows of roses were in bloom. There was a concert in the great park that afternoon. Between two selections, a man stepped up to conductor Eduard Kremser on the podium to whisper something to him.

Kremser stood quite still for a moment. Then he spoke briefly to the first violinist. From him the message passed in whispers through the orchestra. The men changed the sheet music on their stands. All the string players put mutes on their instruments.

The audience, murmuring, expected an announcement of a programme change. But the conductor said nothing. He raised his right arm for a downbeat, his left arm stretched out with the palm down to indicate *pianissimo*.

In a whisper the orchestra began the luminous opening of "The Blue Danube" much slower than usual. The orchestral volume never rose above a sigh. The audience understood and quietly dispersed.

It was so that Vienna learned of the death of Johann Strauss.

Hans Fantel

To meet Hans Fantel is to travel back to Vienna, that magical city by the Danube where, in 1922, he was born. In what he calls "the only nineteenth-century city left in Europe", horses' hoofs still clattered over cobblestones, and no café was without a violinist ready to break into a waltz. His father, a doctor, was devoted equally to science and music, and the Opera House was as familiar to young Hans as the school laboratory.

For the Fantel family, however, the music abruptly stopped with the Nazi invasion in 1938. Three harrowing homeless years later, a penniless refugee of nineteen, Hans arrived in New York. The beloved city of his youth was gone from his life.

America marked a new beginning. First there was a dreary job in a picture-frame factory, and nights crouched at a radio, teaching himself English. Then, with the help of a refugee-aid committee, came a scholarship to the University of Missouri and a degree in biology. Science was a family tradition, and in the years following he established himself as a researcher and a translator of German scientific treatises. Inevitably, he branched out and began to write articles of his own on both music and science, eventually acting as a music critic for *The New York Times*.

By now Hans Fantel was married—Shea Smith was her decidedly un-Viennese name and she was from Kansas. With the assistance of an architect friend, the Fantels converted a crumbling old building on the edge of New York's China-town into a comfortable residence, the living-room dominated by a grand piano. As he relates it, "I suddenly decided to take up the study of history. I felt if I could understand the terrible events that overtook Austria, it might make my memories of it less painful." The eventual happy consequence of this new interest was the writing of *The Waltz Kings*, which is as much the history of a city as of the music that was born there. In a sense, Hans Fantel had finally gone home again.

RENDEZVOUS – SOUTH ATLANTIC
Douglas Reeman

RENDEZVOUS—

Published by Hutchinson, Lon

SOUTH ATLANTIC

a condensation of the book by

DOUGLAS REEMAN

rated by Chris Maygar and Michael Grimsdale

"To the armed merchant cruisers *Rawalpindi*, *Jervis Bay*, *Laurentic*, *Dunvegan Castle*, and to all those other proud ships which sailed in peace but went to war when they were most needed."

This is the moving dedication to Douglas Reeman's latest and most exciting novel about fighting men and the sea. It tells of one of those ships—the *Benbecula*, previously a proud passenger liner plying between England and the Far East but now, beyond her prime in the darkest days of World War II, transferred to the Royal Navy. Her new captain, Andrew Lindsay, has the hard job of welding the disparate crew—merchant seamen who sailed with her in peacetime, men of the regular Navy and raw wartime recruits—into one fighting unit. Together, they face up to the challenges and dangers of patrols in the Denmark Strait, of encounters with raiders and submarines, of convoy escort duties through the South Atlantic to Ceylon.

Finally, in an unforgettable climax, these men prove that the *Benbecula* is none other than "The finest ship in the company".

chapter one

The battered staff car ground to a halt within feet of the jetty's edge, and the small Wren driver, muffled to the ears against the intense cold, made to switch off the windscreen wipers.

Her passenger said, "Don't switch them off. Not yet."

Commander Andrew Lindsay peered through the rain-slashed glass, his face expressionless.

Grey. Everything was grey. Islands, sky, and ships that tugged at their cables in the wind and rain. Scapa. That one word spoke volumes to thousands of sailors in two world wars. Damp and cold. Raging gales and fierce seas.

As his eyes moved slowly across the anchored ships he wondered what his new command would be like. H.M.S. *Benbecula*, an armed merchant cruiser, now lay awaiting her new captain.

And this was September. The third September of the war.

The Wren driver studied her passenger's profile. When she had picked him up at H.Q., she had felt a sudden throb of interest. There was something different about this one, she had decided. He was about thirty-three or four, with fair hair, longer than usual for a regular officer, and his blue eyes were level and grave. As if he was grappling with some constant problem. He had a touch of recklessness about him which appealed to her, but at the same time he seemed withdrawn. Even lost.

He said quietly, "You can switch them off now. Thank you."

Lindsay knew the girl was watching him and wondered idly what she was like under all those shapeless clothes and scarves. In her twenties probably. He smiled grimly. He had entered the navy twenty-one years ago, as a twelve-year-old cadet in 1920. All that time learning his trade. Just for this. Command of some clapped-out merchant ship which, because of a few guns and a naval crew, was classed as a warship.

"I think I can see a motor boat coming, sir."

He started. All at once he felt the returning anxiety and uncertainty. If only he was going back to sea in a destroyer again. Any destroyer would do, even one like the old *Vengeur*. But he must stop thinking like that. *Vengeur* was lying on the seabed in mid-Atlantic.

He had been given her just two days after the outbreak of war, and he had come to love her. She had served her company well, even at the last. She had been the senior ship of the escort to a west-bound convoy for the United States when a torpedo hit the port side of her forecastle. She went down in fifteen minutes, yet with dignity.

Only five men had been lost, the remainder being picked up from the boats and rafts by a Swedish freighter.

Lindsay dug his hands into his greatcoat pockets. Just one more sinking. It happened all the time. It was later. Later. He gritted his teeth.

The girl asked, "Are you all right, sir?"

He turned to her. "What the hell do you mean by that?"

She looked away. "I'm sorry."

"No." He removed his cap and ran his fingers through his hair. It felt damp with sweat. Fear. "No, I'm the one to apologize."

She looked at him again. "Was it bad, sir?"

He shrugged. "Enough." Abruptly he asked, "Are you engaged to be married or anything?"

She eyed him steadily. "No, sir. I was. He bought it over Hamburg last year."

"I see." Bought it. So coolly said. The resilience of youth at war. "Well, I'd better get out now. Otherwise the boat will go away without me."

270

"Here, sir. I'll give you a hand with your bags."

The wind slammed the door back against the car, and Lindsay felt the wind lashing his face like wire.

He said, "Maybe I'll see you again."

She squinted up at him, the rain making her forehead and jaunty cap shine in the grey light. "Maybe."

"What name is it?"

She tugged down the scarf from her mouth and smiled. "Collins, sir." She wrinkled her nose. "Eve Collins. Daft, isn't it?"

She had a nice mouth. Lindsay realized one of the seamen was picking up his bags, his eyes on the girl's legs.

He said, "Take care then." He hurried down the steps into the boat. As she backed the car away she saw the boat turning fussily towards the anchorage. Nice bloke, she thought, and let in the gear with a violent jerk, nice, but scared of something. Why did I give him my name? He'll not be back. Poor bastard. Like all the rest of us here.

LINDSAY remained standing as the boat dipped and curtsied across the water and past the anchored ships. Battleships and heavy cruisers, destroyers and supply vessels, their grey metal gleaming dully, the only colour their streaming ensigns or an occasional splash of dazzle paint on some Atlantic escort. All these ships, perhaps the best in the fleet, were here in Scapa, waiting. Just in case the German heavy units broke out again to try and destroy the convoys, scatter the defences and shorten the odds against England even more. Even now the mighty *Tirpitz* and several other capital ships were said to be lurking in Norwegian fjords or in captured French ports along the Bay of Biscay. Just gauging the right moment.

The seaman said gruffly, "There she is, sir. Fine on the starboard bow."

Lindsay held his breath. For a moment she was just one more shadow in the steady downpour, and then she was there, looming above him like a dripping steel cliff, huge and vulnerable.

Five hundred feet long from her unfashionable straight stem

271

to her overhanging stern, and twelve-and-a-half thousand tons, the *Benbecula* had steamed many thousands of miles since she first slid into the Clyde in 1919. Described in the old shipping lists as an intermediate liner, she had done well for herself and her owners. Almost constantly on the London to Brisbane run, she had pounded her way over the years, earning money, giving pleasure, making jobs.

After Dunkirk, she had done some trooping, but she was an awkward size. Not suitable for big cargoes, too small for large numbers of servicemen on passage, she had now been earmarked as an armed merchant cruiser, to patrol the seas, watch for blockade runners, report anything suspicious, but stay out of real danger. Any heavy naval unit could make scrap of an unarmoured hull like hers.

The motor boat cut across the tall bows and Lindsay saw the overhanging bridge wing, the solitary funnel and the alien muzzle of a six-inch gun below her foremast.

He said, "She seems to have a list to starboard."

The coxswain grinned. "'Sright, sir. I'm told she got a biff in some typhoon afore the war an' never got over it like."

The hull towered right over him now, the accommodation ladder stretching away endlessly towards peering faces at the guardrail.

As the bowman hooked on and Lindsay jumped to the grating, the boat's mechanic hissed. "Wot's 'e like, Bob?"

The coxswain watched Lindsay's slim figure hurrying up the side and replied through his teeth, "Straight-ringer. A regular."

The mechanic groaned. "Either 'e's blotted 'is copybook an' is no bleedin' good for nuthin' else, or we're bein' given some special, bloody-awful job! Either way it's no use, is it?"

The coxswain listened to the squeal of pipes from the top of the ladder and said unfeelingly, "Looks that way, so grab them bags."

LINDSAY looked at the assembled side party, anonymous in their glistening oilskins. The entry port was situated beneath the promenade and boat decks, and with the wind blowing across the opposite bow it was suddenly quiet.

"Welcome aboard, sir." A tall, heavily built officer stepped forward and saluted. "I'm Goss."

John Goss, the first lieutenant, was forty-five, but he looked fifteen years older. He had a heavy-jowled, unsmiling face, and in his oilskin he seemed to tower head and shoulders over everyone else.

Lindsay held out his hand. "Thank you, Number One."

Goss had not blinked or dropped his eyes. "I've got one watch and the second part of port watch ashore on store parties, sir. We ammunitioned at Leith before we came here." He added almost fiercely, "You'll not need to worry about this ship, sir."

Something in his tone, the hint of challenge or aggressiveness, made Lindsay reply coldly, "We shall have to see, eh?"

Goss turned away, his mouth hardening. He seemed very ill at ease, even hostile.

It had been a bad beginning. Lindsay blamed himself. They were all probably more worried about their new captain than he had realized.

He tried again. "Sailing orders will be coming aboard in the first dog-watch." He paused. "So there'll be no libertymen, I'm afraid, until I know what's happening."

Surprisingly, Goss smiled. It was more like a grimace. He said harshly, "Good. Most of the hands are more intent on *looking* like sailors than doing anything useful. Bloody shower of civvies and layabouts! If you'll follow me, sir." He gestured towards a ladder. "The books are ready for inspection in your quarters, below the bridge deck. Nothing's changed there yet."

Lindsay followed him in silence. Changed? What did he mean? Aloud he asked, "What about this list to starboard?"

Goss was already climbing the ladder. He did not turn round. "Always had it"—pause—"sir," was all he said.

The captain's quarters were spacious and ran the whole breadth of the bridge. There was a ladder which led directly above to the chart room and W/T office, the navigation bridge and compass platform, and from it the occupant could see most of the boat deck and forward to the bows as well.

Goss opened the door, his eyes watchful as Lindsay walked into the day cabin.

After the *Vengeur* it was another world. A green, fitted carpet and wood panelling. Good furniture, and some chintz curtains at each brightly polished scuttle. Above an oak sideboard was a coloured photograph of the *Benbecula* as she had once been. Shining green hull and pale buff funnel.

Goss said quietly, "There are, *were* five ships in the Company, sir." He took off his oilskin and folded it carefully on his arm. He had the interwoven gold lace of a lieutenant-commander in the Royal Naval Reserve on his reefer. "Good ships, and I've served in all but one of them."

Lindsay looked at him gravely. "Always with the one company?"

"Aye. Since I was fourteen. Would have been Master by now, but for the war, and the Admiralty taking the ships over."

"I see." Lindsay walked to the nearest scuttle and looked at the swirling water far below. Goss's comment was part of the reason for his attitude, he thought. *Would* have been Master. Of this ship perhaps?

He asked, "Was this your last ship, Number One?"

Goss nodded curtly. "I was Chief Officer. When she was taken over I stayed on."

Lindsay turned away. "Now if you'll arrange a sandwich I'll settle in while I'm reading the books."

Goss hesitated. "I hear you were in hospital, sir." His eyes flickered. "Lost your ship, I believe."

"Yes."

Goss seemed satisfied.

"I'll leave you then. Anything you want you can ring on those handsets or press the steward's bell, sir."

The door closed silently and Lindsay sat down behind the desk. He leafed through the books awaiting his scrutiny. Two hundred and fifty officers and ratings, most of whom were straight from the training depots. The nineteen officers aboard included a doctor, and for some obscure reason, a lieutenant of marines, most of them hostilities-only. *Civvies*, as Goss described them. A few, like Goss,

274

the engineer officers, the paymaster, Lieutenant Barker, and a Mr. Tobey, the boatswain, were Royal Naval Reserve, professional Merchant Navy seamen and well used to ships like *Benbecula*. That was something. The only Royal Navy regulars appeared to be the gunnery officer, a Lieutenant Maxwell, two pensioners, Baldock and Emerson, called back from retirement, and a solitary midshipman named Kemp. He would have to meet them, explore the hull from bridge to keel. Get the *feel* of her.

He lowered his face into his hands. Must do it soon. Waste no time in remembering or trying not to remember. He had got over the *Vengeur*, as much as anyone could who had seen a ship, his ship, die. But to get over the rest might take longer. He remembered the doctor's calm voice at the hospital. Avoid thinking about it, the doctor had said.

Lindsay stood up violently. How the hell could you?

A tall, mournful-looking man in a white jacket came in carrying a silver tray. He said, "I'm Jupp, sir. Chief steward. Nice to have you aboard, if I may make so bold."

Lindsay studied him. "Were you with the Company, too?"

Jupp smiled gently. "Twenty-three years, sir. We've 'ad some very nice people to deal with. You'll soon settle in, sir."

"Yes, thank you."

As the door closed behind Jupp, Lindsay took a sandwich from the tray. It was thin and beautifully cut.

There was a small card under the plate which read, *On behalf of the Aberdeen and Pacific Steam Navigation Company may we welcome you aboard the S.S.* Benbecula. Jupp had crossed out the ship's title and inserted H.M.S. with a pencil.

Lindsay sank into a chair and reached for another sandwich. Jupp at least was trying to help. So then, would he, he decided grimly, if only to hold on to his sanity.

JUPP walked around the captain's day cabin, checking that things were as they should be. It was still early in the evening, but the pipe to darken ship had sounded long since as it got dark quickly in Scapa Flow.

Lindsay sat at his desk, his jacket open as he pushed the last file of papers to one side. He had been working steadily for a full hour since his methodical tour around the ship with Goss.

The dockyard people at Leith had been ruthless with their surgery, he thought. Below "A" deck there appeared little left of the original hull. Massive steel frames in the main holds supported the main armament on the upper decks. There were four six-inch guns on the foredeck, two on either beam, and two mounted aft, one on either side. It was obvious that at no time could *Benbecula* use more than half her main armament to fire at one target. There was an elderly twelve-pounder situated right aft on the poop, a relic of the ship's short service as a trooper, and on the boat deck itself four modern Oerlikons. Altogether they represented *Benbecula*'s sole defence or means of attack.

Most of the original lifeboats had been replaced by naval whalers, two motor boats and a number of Carley floats and wooden rafts. The latter were the only things which really counted if a ship went down fast.

Magazines for the six-inch guns were constructed on the orlop deck below the waterline, with lifts to carry the ammunition to the mountings above. The guns were very old, First World War vintage.

He had met Lieutenant Maxwell, the gunnery officer, and a regular, about the same age as himself. Thin-featured, and very rigid in his carriage, he never seemed to relax. While they were speaking, Goss was called away, and Maxwell said quickly, "Pretty rough lot, I'm afraid, sir. But still we'll soon whip 'em into shape."

Unlike Goss, the gunnery officer was referring to the R.N.R. officers and ratings of the ship's company. Lindsay gathered that Goss and Maxwell rarely spoke to one another.

Later, on the way to the boiler room, Goss remarked sourly, "Did you know, sir, Maxwell was on the beach for five years until the war? Made some cockup, I expect. Damned unfair to have him put aboard *us!*"

Lindsay leaned back in the chair, his hands behind his head. Goss probably thought the same about his new captain.

Jupp paused by the desk. "I expect you'd like a drink, sir?"

"Thank you. A whisky, if you have it."

Jupp regarded him gravely. "I always manage to keep some for my captains, sir."

Lindsay watched Jupp busy at the sideboard. *There* is a man who is happy in his work, he thought wearily.

Then he remembered Fraser, the chief engineer. Lieutenant-Commander (E) Donald Fraser had taken him on a tour round the boiler and engine rooms. He was a small, almost delicate looking man with iron-grey hair, a sardonic smile, and a dry sense of humour. Lindsay had liked him immediately. Unlike most engineer officers he was almost insulting about his trade and about the ships he had served. He had been at sea since he was seventeen. He was now fifty.

When Lindsay asked him about his previous service Fraser said, "I was with Cunard for ten years. Now there was a company!"

"Why did you leave?"

Fraser ran a wintry eye around the mass of glittering dials and throbbing generators before replying slowly, "Got fed up with the wife. Longer voyages in this crabby company was the only peace I could get!" Then he said simply, "You and I'll not fight, sir. I can give you fifteen, maybe sixteen knots. But if you want more I'll do what I can." He grinned, showing his small uneven teeth like a knowing fox. "If I have to blow the guts out of this old bucket!"

The whisky glass was empty, and Jupp refilled it. Lindsay realized he had hardly noticed it going down, and that was a bad sign. The doctor had said . . . he shut his mind to the memory like a steel trap.

Jupp asked discreetly, "Will you be dining aboard, sir?"

He thought suddenly of the small Wren with the wind-reddened face. He could go ashore and give her a call. Perhaps take her somewhere for a drink. But where? Anyway, she would probably laugh at him.

He replied, "Yes." He thought Jupp seemed very pleased by his answer.

"I will try and arrange something special for you, sir." Jupp hurried purposefully away.

Lindsay switched on the radio repeater above the sideboard, half-listening to the smooth, tired voice of the announcer. Air raids . . . another setback in the Western desert . . . losses. . . . He switched it off angrily.

There was a tap on the door. It was Fraser. He held a bottle of gin. "I thought you might care to take a dram with me, sir?" His eye fell on the whisky decanter. "But of course if you were to offer something else, well now— "

Lindsay smiled and waved Fraser to a chair, thankful not to be alone on this first evening aboard. Goss, as first lieutenant, the link between officers and captain, the one man who could and should weld the ship into a tight community, should have invited the new captain down to meet the other officers.

Lindsay looked at Fraser. "Your health, Chief."

Fraser held the glass to the light and said quietly, "Ah well, we're both Scots, so there's some hope for this bloody ship!"

Beyond the tall sides of the hull the rain mounted in intensity, beating the black water like bullets.

chapter two

Andrew Lindsay woke from his nightmare, struggling and tearing at the sheet and blankets, gasping for air, and shouting aloud to break the torment. Hold it at bay.

In the pitch darkness he groped across the cabin to a scuttle and, cursing as he fought to raise the heavy deadlight, heaved it open. He thrust his head through, letting the rain drench over him. The scuttle was large. Big enough to wriggle through if you tried hard enough.

Breathing unsteadily he peered through the rain. The sky was lighter, but it was impossible to tell what time it was, or how long the dream had lasted. It was always the same.

Wearily he slammed down the deadlight and groped back to the bunk where he switched on the reading lamp and pulled on his dressing gown. He was shivering badly. Around him the ship was like a tomb. Not a footfall or a creak broke the stillness.

Face up to it. He filled his pipe to steady himself. Suppose it would never loosen its grip? Perhaps if it had not happened right after *Vengeur*'s sinking he would have been able to cope. Or maybe unknowingly he had already seen and done too much. Used up his resistance.

Throughout Lindsay's life the Navy had been everything to him. His father he could hardly remember. Wounded at Jutland, he had never really recovered, and his mother had remarried almost immediately after his death. She had married a Canadian with a thriving business in Alberta, and she had stayed only long enough to enter Andrew at Dartmouth, according to her dead husband's wish.

Denied a normal home life, Lindsay had given everything to the Navy. He wondered if that driving force, his inbuilt trust, had been the main cause of this breakdown.

Many times he had asked himself if any one thing could break a man. He sat down and stared at the glowing bowl of his pipe.

The Swedish ship had taken *Vengeur*'s survivors into New York. After a week Lindsay, some other survivors and a large number of civilian passengers, were put aboard a Dutch ship for passage to England. Lindsay, a passenger for the first time, had nothing to do. He found himself mixing more and more with the civilians. He needed to do something, to occupy his mind after the loss of his ship.

There was one family in particular. Their cabin was directly below his own. They were Dutch Jews, with two children, who had been caught in Italy when war began. They had finally reached America, and after delays, and with money almost gone, they got aboard the Dutch ship.

Lindsay had asked why they had not remained safely in America. The little man had shaken his head. He was a Jew, but foremost he was Dutch. In England he would seek work to help those who were still fighting the Nazis, and Holland was not far away.

The pipe had gone out. Lindsay stared fixedly at the closed scuttle, holding his breath.

It had been a fine bright morning. He had been in his cabin, wondering how to pass the day, and the tremendous explosion flung him on his back. When he scrambled to his feet he saw with shock that the sea beyond the scuttle was hidden in smoke; there were screams and running feet, shrill whistles and the clamour of alarm bells.

Two more explosions almost immediately shook the ship. Regaining his feet he found that the ship was already settling down. When he looked through the scuttle he saw one of the sights uppermost in his nightmare.

The sea had almost reached the next line of scuttles below him. At most of them there were arms and hands waving and clutching like souls in torment. It was then he realized that his own scuttle was just too small to climb through.

More violent crashes, the sounds of machinery tearing adrift and thundering through the hull. Escaping steam, and the banshee wail of the siren. He staggered to his cabin door and fought his way down companion ladders to the Dutch family's cabin. The door was open just a few inches, and he heard the woman sobbing, the children whimpering. The whole cabin bulkhead had collapsed, had sealed the door. They were trapped, with the sea just a few feet below the scuttle.

Lindsay said, "You must put the children through the scuttle." So calm and detached, even though every fibre was screaming inside him to run before the ship took the last plunge.

The little Dutchman asked quietly, "Will *you* look after them?"

Lindsay could not remember much more. The next scene had been on the ravaged boat deck. Shattered lifeboats and dangling falls. Two dead seamen by a ventilator, and an officer tumbling like a puppet from the upper bridge.

Down on the water, littered with rafts and charred wood, with bodies and yelling survivors, he saw the children float clear of the hull. Very small in their bright orange lifebelts. He jumped into the water after them. When he looked back, the whole line of scuttles had dipped beneath the surface. Here and there pale arms waved like human weed until, with a roar, the pressure forced them out of sight.

Lindsay swam with the children to a half-empty lifeboat.

The small convoy had scattered. When he stood up he saw the enemy, lying across the horizon like a low, grey islet, lit every so often by rippling orange flashes from her massive armament. About seven miles away, mercilessly she continued to drop her great shells on the sinking ships, on the boats and the helpless victims in the water, dying in agony under that clear sky.

Eventually, satisfied her work was done, the German raider had disappeared below the horizon. Lindsay had stayed five days in the boat with seven other survivors. Five men and the two Dutch children.

A corvette found them eventually, and the children were buried at sea the next morning. Lindsay had held them against himself for warmth and comfort long after they must have died from exposure, terror and exhaustion.

He sat now on the edge of the bunk and stared at the carpet. He had actually allowed himself to think about it. Just this once. What did he feel now? Despair, fear of what might happen next time? He rubbed his eyes, hearing a bugle bleating out reveille across the Flow. *Wakey, wakey! Lash up and stow!*

If he felt anything, anything at all, it was hatred.

The door opened an inch. Jupp asked, "Are you ready for some tea, sir?"

Lindsay shook himself. "Thanks."

Jupp padded to the table. "I heard you about, sir, so I thought to meself, ah, the captain'll like a nice hot strong cup of char, that's what I thought."

"Heard me?"

"Thought you was on the telephone, sir." Jupp's face was in shadow. "I was already in me pantry, an' the old *Becky*'s a quiet ship, sir."

He peered at the disordered bunk and pursed his lips. "Dear me, sir, you've 'ad some bad dreams, and we can't 'ave that." He grinned. "I'll fix you some scrambled eggs. Powdered eggs, I'm afraid, but there's a war on they tell me."

Lindsay stopped him by the door. "So I believe." He saw the man turn. "And thanks."

"Sir?" Jupp's features were inscrutable.

"Just thanks."

Lindsay walked to the scuttle, cup in hand. A new day. For him and the old *Becky*. Perhaps it might be good to both of them.

LIEUTENANT-COMMANDER John Goss stepped over the coaming of Lindsay's cabin and removed his cap. "You wanted me, sir?" His heavy face was expressionless.

"Take a seat."

Lindsay stood by a scuttle watching the rain sheeting across the forecastle. It was the forenoon. In spite of his bad night he was feeling slightly better. A good bath and Jupp's breakfast had helped considerably.

"I have sent round my standing orders, Number One, and I'd be obliged if you made sure that all heads of departments have read them." He paused, knowing what was coming. In the salt-smeared glass he saw Goss shifting his heavy bulk from one foot to the other. "Well, what's bothering you?"

Goss looked up. "There's this order about the accommodation."

"Yes. I want all the old titles removed or painted out, understood?" He saw Goss's eyes cloud over and added quietly, "To the ship's company as a whole, as a *whole*, do you understand, *Benbecula* must represent part of the Navy. It is a wardroom, not a *restaurant* as the sign says. A chief and petty officers' mess and no longer the cocktail lounge. Things like that can affect a man's attitude, especially a new, green recruit."

"I don't need to be told about war, sir."

Lindsay retorted angrily, "And neither do *I*, Number One, so do as I damn well say!" He could feel his heart pumping against his ribs. "A ship of war is only as strong as her people, d'you see that? *People!* And if we are called to action, I want a ship's company working as a team, do you understand?"

282

"If you say so, sir."

"Good."

He walked to a chair and slumped into it. "I know how you feel about this ship, at least I think I do. You may believe that by keeping up the old appearances you'll make them survive. Believe me, you won't, quite the opposite. Many of the new hands come from training depots which up to a year or so back were holiday camps. But after a while the trainees *believed* they were in naval establishments and progressed accordingly. Likewise this ship, so see that my orders are executed as of today."

"Aye, aye, sir." Goss sounded hoarse.

"I want to meet my officers today, too." He saw the shot go home. Goss looked suddenly uneasy. "I've read all I can about them, but that is as far as it goes."

"I'll arrange it, sir." Goss sounded in control again. "Eight bells?"

"Good."

A telephone buzzed on the bulkhead and Lindsay seized it. "Captain."

A voice said, "Signal from shore, sir. Guardboat arriving with sealed orders forthwith."

"Thank you. Inform the O.O.D. please." The phone went dead.

To Goss he said, "Perhaps we shall know now what we are to do."

Goss looked round the cabin, his face suddenly desperate. "They'll not be sending us to fight surface ships, surely?" When Lindsay remained silent he said, "One of our sister ships, the *Barra*, has got a nice billet at Singapore. She's an A.M.C. too, like us, but out there she'll be safe enough from those bloody U-boats."

Almost gently Lindsay replied, "Maybe you're right. But it's best to face the worst that can happen and plan from there."

He turned away, as a picture rose in his mind like some hideous spectre. Pale arms waving under the water, limp bodies pressed against his chest.

Goss opened the door. "I—I'll carry on, sir." Then he was gone.

Lindsay moved to the scuttle, and through the steady downpour saw a small boat chugging across the anchorage, several oil-skinned figures crammed together for comfort like wet seals on a half-submerged rock.

SHARP at noon Goss arrived to accompany Lindsay to the wardroom, which had once been *Benbecula*'s main restaurant and her pride and joy. As they entered the officers rose to their feet, their expressions a mixture of curiosity and apprehension.

Lindsay knew better than to expect a complete analysis at so brief a meeting. Some faces stood out, however. There was a Lieutenant Stannard, the navigation officer, a lean, beanpole of a man with skin like leather. An Australian reservist, he had served with the Company before the war.

As Lindsay shook his hand he drawled, "I sure hope we're going back to the Far East run, sir. The old ship can find her way there by now." He shrugged. "Otherwise I'm not too optimistic!"

The ship's doctor, Surgeon-Lieutenant David Boase, returned Lindsay's handshake, and in answer to a question said, "First ship, sir. I was at Guy's."

Then there was Lieutenant Aikman, R.N.V.R., past thirty and a bit flabby around the waist. Among his other duties he was responsible for deciphering Top Secret messages.

There were four very new sub-lieutenants. One of them, Dancy, a serious-faced young man, said quickly, "Actually, sir, I *have* done three months' watchkeeping before joining this ship."

Lindsay eyed him curiously. "What ship?"

"The *Valiant*, sir."

Lindsay was surprised. "I'd have thought this is a bit of a change from a big battleship, Dancy."

Dancy flushed. "Oh no, sir. Not *that Valiant*. Actually she was an armed yacht at Bristol."

The laughter broke the ice, and Goss said ponderously, "Shall I call the stewards over now, sir?"

Lindsay nodded and let his eyes move round the faces which would become so familiar, given luck and time.

Lieutenant Mark de Chair of the Royal Marines, a slim,

elegant figure with a neat, clipped moustache, said suddenly, "I expect you're wondering why I'm aboard, sir?"

Lindsay smiled. "Tell me."

"I was put here with my sergeant and thirty marines to man the ship's armament when we were trooping, sir." He shrugged. "The troops have gone, but their lordships in their wisdom thought fit to forget us."

"I've arranged for you to continue manning the after guns."

Lindsay took a glass from a steward and waited until they were all silent. He said quietly, "Well, gentlemen, I am sorry this has to be brief. I will have to get to know you better when we are at sea." The sudden expectancy moved round him like a small wind. "Our sailing orders have arrived. We will slip from our buoy at 0800 tomorrow and proceed on independent patrol."

He continued, "We will patrol the southwestern approaches to Iceland, to extend when required into the Denmark Strait." In his mind's eye he could see that raging desert of tossing whitecaps and dark-sided rollers, of shrieking gales and ice between Iceland and Greenland.

Stannard was the first to break the stunned silence. "Jesus, sir, they sure believe in pitching us into the deep end!"

Goss muttered, "We've had no time. No time to get things ready—" His voice trailed away.

Lindsay lifted his glass. "To the ship, gentlemen." As they drained their glasses he added, "And remember this. Our people will be looking to you after today. As I will. So let's not have too much despondency about, eh?"

He turned as a figure stepped into the wardroom. It was Kemp, the midshipman, the only officer he had not met. Kemp had been acting O.O.D. during the meeting.

"Signal from H.Q., sir." He proffered a soggy sheet of pad. "Would you report there at 1600, sir."

Lindsay glanced at the signal. "Affirmative." As the boy turned to go he added, "We're sailing at 0800 tomorrow. Iceland patrol."

Kemp simply nodded. "Yes, sir."

As the boy hurried away Lindsay noticed that one of the stewards had gone. The news would be all over the ship by now. He put down his glass. It was time to leave them to sort themselves out.

He said, "There will be no shore leave, so arrange for mail to be dropped tonight. After that," he forced a smile, "we are in business." He nodded to Goss. "Thank you. Carry on, please."

Despite the rain and chill wind he walked round the boat deck, past the hooded Oerlikons, and climbed slowly up to the bridge, spacious and now deserted. On either side of the wheelhouse the open bridge wings stretched out over the side, and he walked to the port gratings, his shoes squelching in rain puddles.

A petty officer was leaning over the wing, rain bouncing off his oilskins like hail. He swung round and saluted. "Ritchie, sir. Yeoman of signals." He had a round, homely face, but there was something remote about him.

"You've heard the news, Yeo?"

He nodded. "Aye, sir." Ritchie seemed oblivious of the rain. "I'm not bothered."

Lindsay asked quietly, "Had any leave lately?"

Ritchie looked away. "Last month, sir." When he faced Lindsay again there were tears running unheeded with the rain. "Bloody street was gone, sir! Nothing left."

Lindsay stared at him. Helpless. "Did you have—"

"Wife an' two kids, sir." He brushed his face with his sleeve. "All gone." He recovered and said, "Sorry about that, sir."

Lindsay remembered one of the children stirring in the lifeboat on the last night before the corvette found them. Dreaming perhaps. Like Ritchie's kids when the bomb had come down.

He touched Ritchie's arm. "If you want leave I'll see if I can arrange it."

"Thank you, sir, but no. You'll need a good signals department, I'm thinkin'." He hesitated. "'Sides, I'd like the chance to get back at those bastards!"

Later Lindsay went ashore to receive his patrol intelligence. The Chief of Staff, a serious-faced, urbane captain, was brief and to the point. "Things are bad, Lindsay, very bad. There is talk of more German raiders breaking out, probably from French ports.

However," he glanced up at the great wall chart with all its coloured ribbons and flags, "it is not unlikely they might try the longer way round."

"The Denmark Strait."

"Correct." Captain Lovelace eyed him distantly. "I want no heroics. Any sighting report can be used right here in Scapa."

Lindsay saw the great clusters of crosses on the chart, each representing a ship sunk by enemy action. There must be hundreds, he thought.

The captain said, "I know something of your experiences, and I'm sorry you've not been offered a command more fitting to your rank and knowledge."

A quick handshake, a fat envelope from a tired-looking lieutenant, and it was over.

The staff car was waiting to take him back to the jetty, but there was a different Wren behind the wheel. On his way out to the ship, a motor fishing boat packed with libertymen wallowed past in the gloom and he heard the sailors singing above the din of the rain and wind.

"Roll on the *Nelson*, the *Rodney*, *Renown*,
This one-funnelled bastard is getting me down."

If the men could sing like that, there was still some spark of hope. For all of them.

chapter three

Lindsay sat in his cabin, his legs thrust out in front of him, and peered at his watch. Half an hour to go before leaving harbour.

The cabin was dark, for the deadlights were tightly shut, as they would be most of the time. It would be strange to take *Benbecula* out of the Flow for the first time. Not that Lindsay was unused to handling big ships. He had served as navigation officer in a cumbersome submarine depot ship in Malta for two years. But he was going back to the Atlantic and all it had come to mean to him.

More sounds now. Wires scraping along the forecastle, the

distant bark of orders. Bells clanged overhead. Goss was testing the telegraphs, watching every move to make sure the captain would find no fault with his precious ship.

Lindsay stood up, patting his pockets automatically to make sure he had all he required. Pipe and pouch. And a small silver compass. He turned it over in his hands. Inscribed on the back was, *Commander Michael Lindsay*, H.M.S. *Minden – 1914*. It was just about all he had to remind him of his father.

There was a tap at the door and Goss looked in. "Ready to proceed, sir."

Goss followed him up the ladder and out to the bridge. Chief Petty Officer Jolliffe, the coxswain, a barrel of a man, was standing at the wheel. At each brass telegraph the quartermasters lounged with their hands on the levers. On either bridge wing the signalmen stood by their shuttered lights and flags, the yeoman, Ritchie, with his long telescope trained towards the shore.

Lieutenant Stannard saluted formally and said, "Wind's nor'westerly, sir. A bit fresh for my liking."

Ritchie yelled, "Signal, sir!" A light winked impatiently through the rain. "Proceed when ready!"

Lindsay tried not to lick his lips. "Ring down standby." He walked to the port door of the wheelhouse and peered towards the forecastle party. Maxwell was squinting at the bridge, his sodden cap tugged over his eyes, his party preparing to slip the final wire from their buoy. "Very well, Yeoman. Make the affirmative."

Seconds later a red flare burst against the leaden clouds and drifted seaward on the wind.

Stannard called, "That was the signal from the boom vessel, sir. Hoxa gate is open for us."

Lindsay lifted his hand and watched Maxwell point with his arm to indicate that the buoy was close up under the starboard side of the stern.

Once free, the wind would carry the ship abeam like a drifting pier. But there was plenty of room. Had wind and tide been against them, he would have had to contend with the nearby battleship and three anchored cruisers. He could see tiny figures watching him from the battleship's quarterdeck and her name gleaming dully in the morning light. *Prince of Wales.*

"Slow ahead together."

He made a chopping motion with his hand towards Maxwell in the eyes of the ship. A petty officer swung his hammer, there was the clang of steel as the slip was knocked away, and the buoy appeared immediately as if it had taken wings.

Jolliffe intoned, "Both engines slow ahead, sir. Wheel's amidships."

"Port ten."

He raised his glasses and watched the low humps of land beginning to drift across the bows. Faintly across the water he heard the shrill of a pipe. Somebody paying their respects to the *Benbecula* as she towered past on her way to the gate.

Overhead he heard Chief Petty Officer Archer bellow *"Pipe!"* And the answering squeal from his line of boatswain's mates.

Lindsay watched the land closing in on either bow where the humps of Flotta and South Ronaldsay guarded the Sound.

"Take her out, Cox'n."

Jolliffe was easing the spokes back and forth in his great red fingers, his eyes fixed on the channel, when a signalman said, "I think someone's calling us up, Yeo!"

Ritchie was across to the opposite bridge wing in seconds.

"Where, lad?" His telescope was swinging round like a small cannon. Then, "Gawd, you need yer eyes testin', it's a bloody car flashin' its lights!"

Lindsay walked to the open door as the yeoman exclaimed, "You're right, lad, it *is* callin' us." He looked at Lindsay. "He'll cop it if the officer of th' guard spots 'im!"

Lindsay raised his glasses as the signalman, mollified, reported, "He says *Good Luck*, sir."

A hump of land was cutting Lindsay's vision away even as he steadied his glasses on the distant lights. The battered staff car was parked dangerously close to the sea's edge, and he could picture her as she sat muffled to her ears, watching the old ship edge towards the boom gate.

He said, "Acknowledge." He knew they were staring at him. "And say *Thank you.*" The lamp started to clatter, then the car was lost from sight.

He walked out to the wing and rested his gloved hands on the screen. He thought of the girl in the car. She must have got up specially and wangled her work-sheet to get to that point in time to see them sail.

A telephone buzzed and Stannard called, "From masthead, sir. Ship closing port bow."

Lindsay watched the approaching ship as she loomed slowly and painfully out of the rain and spray. A cruiser, she was so low in the water aft that her quarter-deck was awash. Her mainmast had gone, and her after turret was buckled into so much scrap. She had received a torpedo which had all but broken her back, but she was fighting to get her people home.

In sudden anger Lindsay snapped, "Number One! Have the hands fall in fore and aft! And tell the buffer I want the best salute he's ever done!"

As seamen and marines ran to fall in on the *Benbecula*'s decks, Lindsay walked to the end of the wing and raised his hand to his cap as the cruiser moved slowly past.

The pipes shrilled and died and a solitary marine, his head bandaged, walked to the cruiser's signal platform and raised a bugle to his lips. The *Still* floated across the grey water, and above the neat lines of sewn up bodies on the cruiser's deck. Along the *Benbecula*'s side the lines of new, untried faces stared at the other ship in silence, until the bugle sounded again and Archer yelled, "Carry on!"

Stannard said quietly, "That was quite a scene, sir."

Lindsay looked past him at a young signalman who was biting the fingers of his gloves and staring at the listing cruiser.

"It will do them good!"

He had not meant to speak so harshly. Nothing had changed after all. Not the bitterness or the shock of seeing what the Atlantic could do.

Stannard said, "Time to alter course again, sir."

Lindsay saw the hurt in his eyes. "Very well, take the con."

By noon the *Benbecula* had turned her stern towards the land and headed west-northwest; she had the sea to herself. Lindsay remained on the open wing, his unlit pipe in his teeth, his eyes fixed on the tossing wilderness of waves.

He was in the North Atlantic.

He had come back.

STANNARD walked across the bridge, his lean body angled to the uneven motion.

"First dog-watchman closed up at defence stations, sir." He looked through a clearview screen. "I guess we've arrived."

Lindsay turned in his tall chair and nodded.

Eight days out, and the starting leg of the patrol area, Uncle Item Victor. A sprawling parallelogram which measured five hundred by three hundred miles. As far north as the Arctic Circle between Iceland and Greenland.

"Very well, Pilot. Bring her round to three-five-zero. Revs for ten knots."

When the ship turned slightly to port the motion became more unsteady and violent, waves piling up against the starboard bow before exploding high over the rails and hissing viciously across each open deck. It was almost pitch dark beyond the bows, with only the wavecrests to determine sea from sky.

Lindsay had been on the bridge almost continuously since leaving the Flow. He ran his fingers over the arms of the chair and recalled Goss's face when he had told him what he required. "I want a good strong chair, Number One."

That had been the first day out, and the shipwrights had built it during one watch from solid oak which had lain unnoticed in a storeroom. Bolted to the deck it gave Lindsay good vision above the screen and was within reach of the bridge telephones. But Goss had stared at it with horror.

"But, sir, that timber was being saved! You just can't get it any more."

But if he was to hold onto the vital reserve which might be

demanded in the next hour or minute, he *needed* a good chair.

In spite of the severe weather he had put almost every part of the ship through its paces. Gun and fire drill. Damage control and anti-aircraft exercises, until he had seen the despair, even hatred on the faces around him.

The gun drill had been the worst part. Pathetic, he had called it, and had seen Maxwell's rigid face working with something akin to shame. While mythical targets were passed down from the so-called control position above the bridge, the crews of the six guns tried to locate and cover them with minimum delay. But each gun was hand-operated, and valuable time was lost again and again while Maxwell and the assistant gunnery officer, Lieutenant Hunter, shouted themselves hoarse with frustration. In most warships, it was possible to train all major guns, even fire them, direct from the control and rangefinder above the bridge. But in *Benbecula* the six-inch gun crews crouched behind the shields, shivering and cursing as ranges and deflections were passed by telephone and then yelled to them above the din of sea and wind.

Also the big shells and their charges had to be manhandled and rammed home bodily. If the deck tilted the wrong way at the moment of loading, the massive breech block of a gun could swing shut, and bite off a man's arm like a horse snapping at a carrot.

A telephone buzzed at the rear of the bridge and the bosun's mate called, "Number Three Carley float is comin' adrift, sir."

Stannard crossed to the chair and said quietly, "Can't very well send the lads out in this, sir. Shall I tell the buffer to scrub round it until daylight?"

Lindsay tried to answer calmly. "Do it now. The boat deck is miles above the waterline. Pass the word for lifelines to be rigged. That should do it."

Stannard remained beside the chair, his dark features stubborn. "In my opinion, sir—"

Lindsay swung round.

"Just *do* it, Pilot! With the sort of results I've been getting since I took command, I think liferafts are about the most useful things we've got! By God, do you imagine *this* is bad?"

Stannard, angry, stood his ground. "I merely meant—" He shrugged. "I'm sorry, sir." He did not sound it.

"Well, listen to me, will you?" He kept his voice very low. "The weather is going to get much worse. We are up here to do a job as best we can. It does not mean being battened down below and weeping for mother every time it bloody well rains!"

Stannard turned and beckoned to Sub-Lieutenant Dancy. "Go yourself, Sub. Tell the buffer to take all precautions." He kept his back to Lindsay. "No sense in killing anyone."

Lindsay leaned back in his chair. He wanted to go out on the wing in spite of the weather and watch the men detailed to replace the lashings on the Carley float. At the same time he knew he must stay where he was. Allow them to hate his guts and so work better for it, if that was what they needed.

He peered at his watch. In fifteen hours they would officially relieve another armed merchant cruiser from this patrol. They would not see her, however, which was probably just as well. It would do no good for the ship's company to see what the other A.M.C. looked like at close range. How they would be looking themselves after a few weeks of this misery.

The telephone buzzed again.

"Float's secure, sir."

"Very good."

Lindsay rubbed his chin, feeling the bristles rasp against his glove. He felt strangely relieved.

Dancy entered the bridge, his face glowing with cold.

"Not too bad, sir." He sounded pleased with himself. "But by God it's parky out there!"

Stannard said shortly, "I'm going to the chart room, Sub. Take over."

Dancy stood beside the chair and rested his hands below the screen. Lindsay glanced at him curiously. He knew little about him. Young, serious-looking, nondescript.

He asked, "What were you before you joined, Sub?"

Dancy said vaguely, "I—I was a writer, sir."

Lindsay's own information described Dancy's previous calling

294

as bank clerk. But if he wanted to see himself as something else, what did it matter?

Stannard came back suddenly. "Sir? Sickbay has just called. The doc wants," he hesitated, "he *asked* if you could change course for about twenty minutes. A seaman's fallen down a ladder and broken his hip. Doc says he can't fix it with all this motion."

Lindsay could see the man's resentment building up. Waiting for him to refuse the doctor's request. He must think me a right bastard.

"Very well, Pilot. But work out the additional revs we will need to make up time, and inform the chief."

Stannard blinked. "Yes, sir. Right away."

As he vanished, Dancy said seriously, "Of course, I had to do other jobs as well. For a time, that is."

Lindsay slid from the chair, wincing at the stiffness of his legs. "Well there's a job for you now. Take over. I'm going to my cabin for a shave." He saw Dancy's face paling. "Just call Pilot if you can't cope. Call *me* if you like." He grinned at Dancy's alarm. "Good experience later on for your writing, eh?"

Dancy stared fixedly at his own dim reflection in the spray-dappled glass. He felt riveted to the deck, unable to move. Very cautiously he looked over his shoulder. The quartermaster's eyes glittered like stones in the dim compass light, the rest of the bridge party swayed with the ship, like silent drunks.

Nothing had changed, and the realization almost unnerved him. *He* was in sole command of this ship and some two hundred and fifty human beings.

He had always loved the sea and ships, but his parents' means and open opposition had prevented his chances of trying for Dartmouth. He sometimes told himself that but for the war he would have gone raving mad at the bank, and when he had gained the coveted gold stripe and been sent to the little armed yacht at Bristol, it had seemed quite natural to lie. "I'm a writer," he'd said. The officer had been impressed, just as Commander Lindsay was.

Stannard slammed back through the door and stared at him.

"Where's the Cap'n, for Chrissake?"

"He left me in charge," Dancy's eyes wavered under the Australian's incredulous gaze.

Stannard muttered, "Must be off his bloody head!" He looked at the quartermaster. "The Doc's finished. I'm going to alter course to zero-two-zero."

LINDSAY completed the shave and studied his face in the mirror. There were shadows beneath his eyes and his neck looked sore from wearing the towel under his duffel coat. But he felt refreshed, and perhaps later he might snatch some proper sleep.

The telephone buzzed, and when he clapped it to his ear he heard Stannard say tersely, "W/T office has picked up an SOS, sir. Plain Language. It reads: *Am under attack by German raider.*" He paused, clearing his throat. "Seems to be a Swedish ship, sir, probably a mistake on the Jerry's part—"

Lindsay snapped. "Keep on to it! I'm coming."

He bounded up the ladder and found Stannard waiting outside the W/T office door. Two operators were crouched below their sets, and Petty Officer Telegraphist Hussey had also appeared, his pyjamas clearly visible under his jacket.

He saw Lindsay and said awkwardly, "Was just having a nap, sir. Had a feeling something like this might happen." Old hands often found themselves called to duty by instinct.

Lindsay asked, "What do you make of it?"

From the door Stannard said, "She gave a position, sir. She's about ninety miles due north of us."

Hussey looked up from his steel chair. "Someone's acknowledged sir."

Lindsay bit his lip. "That'll be *Loch Glendhu*, the other A.M.C."

Hussey added after a pause. "Dead, sir. Not getting a peep now."

"Let me see your calculations." Lindsay brushed past Stannard into the chart room.

"*Loch Glendhu* should be pretty near there, sir, according to our intelligence log." Stannard's voice was detached.

Lindsay stared at the neatly pencilled lines and bearings on the chart. *Loch Glendhu* was bigger than *Benbecula* and better armed. But no match for a warship. Perhaps she would haul off and report to base for instructions.

"Keep a permanent listening watch for her. Tell Hussey to monitor everything."

What the hell was a Swedish ship doing up here anyway? Probably using the Denmark Strait as a matter of safety. Bad weather was better than being sunk by mistake in the calmer waters to the south.

"Lay off a course to intercept, Pilot."

He recalled Fraser's words. *"I can give you sixteen knots."*

It would take over five hours to reach the neutral ship's position. Longer if he waited for instructions from Admiralty. Five hours for men to die beyond reach or hope.

He was sweating badly, he could feel it running down his spine like iced water. Without effort he could see the low grey shape on the horizon, feel the breath-stopping explosions as the raider's shells tore steel and flesh to fragments all round him. He tried not to look at the nearest scuttle with its sealed deadlight. Tried to shut out a memory of pale arms waving like human weed.

Lindsay asked, "Have you got it yet?"

Stannard looked up from the chart. "Course would be zero-one-zero, sir."

Lindsay nodded. "Bring her round and get the chief on the telephone."

When Stannard got through, Lindsay took the phone quickly. "*Loch Glendhu's* in trouble, Chief."

Fraser sounded miles away. "I'll give you all I've got. When you're ready."

Lindsay looked at the others. "We'll see what we can do." To Stannard he added, "Right. Full ahead together."

The telegraphs clanged over, and far below, enshrouded in rising steam on his footplate, Fraser watched the big needles swing round the twin dials and settle on FULL. Then he forgot everything but the job in hand.

chapter four

Lindsay glanced at his watch. They should sight something soon. For hours the ship had rolled and crashed, pitched and battered her way forward into the teeth of sea and wind. Every strut and frame in the superstructure seemed to be rattling and protesting, and as the sea sluiced up and over the well deck Lindsay saw the foot of the foremast standing like an isolated pinnacle in the great frothing white flood.

There was a metallic scrape above the bridge, and he imagined Maxwell in his control position testing the big rangefinder, cursing his spray-smeared lenses. He glanced quickly round the bridge.

Stannard said, "Time, sir." He sounded alert, or maybe frightened like most of them.

Lindsay felt the sudden dryness in his throat. *As I am.*

He reached forward and thrust hard on the small red button. The alarm bells went screaming away through the ship.

As messengers and bosun's mates hurried to voicepipes and telephones the reports started to come in from every position. The mingled voices and terse acknowledgments sounded unreal.

Stannard said, "Ship closed up at action stations, sir."

"Good. Three minutes. Not at all bad."

He swivelled in the chair and looked at his team on the bridge. Jolliffe on the wheel, quartermasters and messengers, signalmen, with Ritchie adjusting his night glasses. Stannard and young Dancy, and Lieutenant Aikman.

Goss was in damage control, far enough from the bridge to survive and assume command should Lindsay fall dead or wounded, and the elegant marine lieutenant, de Chair, was down aft with his two six-inch guns and the feeble twelve-pounder.

Stannard replaced a handset. "Nothing from masthead, sir."

"Thank you." Another glance at his watch. "Reduce to half speed." No sense now in shaking the machinery to pieces.

The wavecrests were less violent, the troughs wider spaced, and he guessed the snow would be coming very soon now.

The telephone made him flinch, and Stannard snapped, "Very well. Good. Keep reporting." Then to Lindsay, "Masthead reports a red glow, sir. Fine on the port bow."

Before he could reply the speaker at the rear of the bridge intoned, "Control . . . Bridge." It was Maxwell's voice, unhurried and toneless. "Red two-oh. Range one-double-oh. A ship on fire."

Five miles. Lindsay swung his glasses to the screen. Nothing. Maxwell's spotters had done well to see it in such bad visibility. He picked up the telephone. "Guns, this is the captain. I'll not take chances. A diagonal approach so that you can get all the starboard battery to bear, right?"

Maxwell understood. "Starshell on One, sir?"

"Yes."

He heard the distant voices of the control team already rapping out ranges and bearings to the crews below. He had put his pipe in his mouth without realizing it and gripped it in his teeth so hard that the pain helped to steady him.

"Now, Pilot. Bring her round to three-two-five."

Even as the wheel went over the speaker said, "Range now oh-eight-oh."

"There it is!" Stannard craned forward. "Starboard bow, sir!"

Lindsay held up his glasses and saw the flickering glow for the first time. It was reflected more in the low clouds than on the water, and the thickening sleet made even that difficult.

Stannard added grimly, "The starshell'll scare the hell out of the poor bastards."

"Better that than make a bad approach. If the snow comes down we might lose her altogether."

Maxwell's voice sounded muffled as he spoke into his array of handsets. "Number *One* gun. Range oh-seven-five."

When the shell burst it was momentarily like some strange electric storm. The gunlayer had applied too much elevation so the flare burst in or above the clouds. Their bellies shone through the sleet like silver, and then as the flare drifted into view the sea was bathed with a hard, searing glare.

The ship was already well down in the water, her tilting hull shining, smoke from her blazing interior pouring downwind in one solid plume, black and impenetrable.

Lindsay could not take his eyes from the dying ship. Knowing he was right. Willing otherwise. Sweating.

He let the glasses fall on his chest. "That's *Loch Glendhu*. I know her."

Stannard said softly. "Oh, my God."

Tobey the boatswain, was staring past Lindsay at the flickering pattern of flames. "Sea's quietened a bit, sir. The whalers could be lowered."

Lindsay did not turn. "Starboard ten." He waited, his nerves screaming soundlessly. "Midships. Steady. Slow ahead together." Then he looked at Tobey's shocked face. "Yes. Whalers and rafts. Call for volunteers."

He swung round as a sharp explosion threw an arrowhead of fire high into the sky. A magazine perhaps. Not long now.

Ritchie said, "Shall I call 'er up, sir?"

Lindsay said flatly. "Just tell her to hold on. Keep trying. There'll be some left alive."

Another face emerged in the gloom. It was Boase, the doctor. He said to Stannard, "How many left, d'you think?"

It was too much for Lindsay's reeling mind. "Where the hell do you imagine you are?" He shouted. Boase was like those other doctors. Forget it. Don't worry. The stupid, heartless bastards!

Boase fell back. "I'm sorry, sir. I didn't mean—"

Lindsay shouted. "You never bloody well do mean anything! This isn't a Saturday night punch-up with a few revellers at your out-patients department while you play God." He swung round and gestured towards the sea. "Take a good look! There are men dying out there. Cursing the blind, ignorant fools who let them go to war in ships like that one. Like our own!"

A bosun's mate said hoarsely. "Boats ready for lowering, sir."

Stannard spoke first. "Tell them to watch out for burning oil."

Lindsay said, "Stop engines."

He wiped his burning forehead. It was not the doctor's fault. It was unfair to take it out of him in front of the others. Unfair, and cruelly revealing about his own failing strength and self-control.

The ship idled forward, her screws stopped for the first time since leaving the Flow.

More sounds rumbled in the darkness as the other ship started to roll on her side, the sea around her misty with steam and whipped spray. Small lights glittered in a deep trough, and Lindsay saw one of the whalers pulling strongly towards the sinking ship. He gritted his teeth as another crash from the forward gun hurled a starshell high over the scene. The show had started. There was not much time left.

Lindsay thought of the corvette's small quarterdeck on that morning. The line of corpses awaiting burial, and the two small ones at the end of the line. Like little parcels under the flag as they had gone over the rail. *Look after them.* Well, they had gone where there was no more hurt. No persecution.

Stannard said loudly, "She's going!"

More frothing water, and the last flame extinguished with the suddenness of death. Then nothing.

It seemed an age before Stannard reported, "Boats returning, sir."

He walked to the starboard wing and peered down through the snow flurries. The boats were crammed with bodies. Shining with oil. A familiar enough sight in the Atlantic. Others clung round the sides of the boats, treading water. Here and there a red lifelight shone on the water, others floated away unheeded, tiny scarlet pinpricks, each marking a corpse.

Lindsay turned to see Lieutenant Aikman staring at him.

"Go and make sure everything's all right! If they need more hands, take them from aft. I want those boats hoisted and secured without delay." The officer scurried for the ladder.

Dancy said hoarsely, "If I have to die, I hope it's like that, sir."

Lindsay felt his anger giving way to a kind of madness, with wild, uncontrollable laughter ready to burst out. Then he patted Dancy's arm. "Then we shall have to see what we can do. But before you decide anything definite, go and visit the survivors in the sickbay. Then tell me again."

301

Stannard called, "Ready to get under way, sir."

"Very well. Slow ahead together. Bring her round on course."

Goss appeared through the rear door and said thickly, "We've picked up thirty, sir."

He saw Ritchie thumbing through a manual, then holding his torch steady above one page. He said, "She 'ad a company of three 'undred sir."

"Thank you, Yeo. Thank you, Number One. We will remain at action stations for another hour at least. Pass the word for a good lookout while visibility holds."

He heard Goss slamming out of the wheelhouse. Probably cursing me. The iron-cold captain that no pain, no sentiment can reach. God, if he only knew.

One hour later the snow came down, and as the men left their action stations and ran below, Lindsay heard a sailor laughing. Horror of what they had witnessed was giving way to relief at being spared. Later it would be different, but now it was good that someone could laugh, he thought.

OVERNIGHT the sea lost much of its anger, as if eased by the growing power of the snow.

Goss clumped into the wheelhouse, shaking snow from his oilskin and stamping it from his heavy sea boots.

"Ready, sir."

Lindsay slid from his chair. Apart from a few short snatches in his chair, he had not slept, and as he stood by the door he could feel the chill in his bones, the inability to think clearly.

"I'll be about ten minutes, Number One."

He clattered down the ladder, boots slipping on the slush, hands cold on the rungs, for he had forgotten his gloves. When he reached the after well deck he had to steel himself before he could climb down the last ladder where Maxwell and Stannard were waiting to assist with the burials. There were eight of them.

He returned Maxwell's salute. Beyond the gunnery officer he saw Lieutenant de Chair with some of his marines.

God, how could he do it? Just ten minutes, he had told Goss, but

302

he was already cracking. He could feel his reserve stripping itself away like a protective skin. He cleared his throat.

"Let's get on with it."

As he pulled the little book from his pocket, de Chair said quietly, "Very well, Sarn't. Off coats."

He stared, dazed, as the marines obediently stripped off their shining oilskins and formed into a tight, swaying line behind the canvas-covered bodies. They were all in their best blue uniforms, and somehow they were shaved. In spite of everything.

Blindly he thumbed open the book, then removed his cap. Maxwell shouted towards the bridge, and the engines fell silent. With sudden resolution Lindsay thrust the book back into his pocket. He did not need it any more. He had spoken and heard the words too often to forget even if he wanted to.

"Forasmuch as it hath pleased Almighty God . . . to take unto himself the souls of these our brothers here departed, we therefore commit their bodies to the deep. . . ."

The marines edged forward, raising the neat bundles beneath the two large ensigns.

One of the bodies was of *Loch Glendhu*'s captain, who had died within thirty minutes of being carried aboard. By rights he should have died back there on the bridge. Hit by several shell splinters, savagely burned, blasted into the sea by an explosion, even then he had refused to die. Perhaps he needed to stay alive just long enough to tell his short, bitter story to Lindsay who had watched the other captain's mouth through the bandages as he had gasped it out.

There had been no neutral under attack. Just the big German raider, waiting for them like a tiger shark. She had looked Swedish, with her painted flag and neutral colouring, but as *Loch Glendhu* turned to offer help, the enemy's guns opened fire from a dozen concealed positions, smashing through the hull, blasting men to pulp who seconds before were preparing to give aid.

The dying captain had said, "It was my fault. Should have been ready. Expecting it. But it was something new." Then he had died.

Lindsay was speaking the familiar words even while his mind

relived those last moments. When he looked again the flags were being folded, the bodies gone.

He nodded to Maxwell, and within seconds the big screws had started to churn the sea into a busy froth. He replaced his cap, and Stannard fell into step beside him as they walked forward along the promenade deck.

"I will make a signal to Admiralty now, Pilot. Can't tell them much—" Lindsay shrugged, knowing Stannard was looking at him. Thinks I don't care, or that I am past caring.

As they started up the last ladder he heard voices, harsh with anger. On the open wing, he saw Goss hunched in one corner, towering above Fraser, who was glaring up at him, his white overalls coarse against the swirling snow.

Lindsay snapped, "What the hell is going on?"

Goss whirled round. "Nothing, sir!"

Fraser exploded, "Nothing, hell!" He hurried towards Lindsay. "I came on deck. Just to watch quietly when—" he glanced briefly aft—"when the engines stopped." He added slowly, "I heard something, sir."

Goss said harshly, "You can't be sure, for God's sake!"

Fraser looked at Lindsay. "I've been too long in my trade not to recognize a winch, sir." He pointed into the driving snow, beyond the bows. "There was a ship out there, sir. I *know* it!"

Stannard was still on top of the ladder, unable to get past Lindsay. He called, "But surely no raider would still *be* here?"

"Why not?" Lindsay's voice was quiet and calm. "He's done pretty well for himself so far. He's probably sitting out there in the snow preparing for *Loch Glendhu*'s relief."

Goss stared at him incredulously. Stannard fell back as Lindsay thrust him aside and wrenched open the wheelhouse door.

As he tore off the dripping oilskin and dropped it to the deck he snapped, "Back to your engine room, Chief. I want *dead slow*, right?" He looked at Stannard. "Pass the word quickly. I want the hands at action stations on the double. But no bells or pipes, not a bloody sound out of anyone. Understand? Send them in their bare feet if necessary!"

304

Midshipman Kemp emerged from the chart room and Lindsay seized his arm saying, "Get the gunnery officer yourself, lad, and be sharp about it!"

He walked to the front of the bridge. The deck was trembling very gently now. Fraser must have run like a madman to reach the engine room so quickly.

Five minutes later Stannard said, "Ship at action stations, sir."

Lindsay turned and ran his eye over the others. Jolliffe had certainly been fast enough. He was still wearing old felt slippers and there were crumbs on his portly stomach.

"I need three good hands up forrard. Right in the eyes of the ship. Yeo, send some of your bunting-tossers. They'll have keen ears and eyes. If," he checked himself, "*when* we run this bastard to ground I want to see him first. So he'll know what it's like."

Ritchie buttoned his oilskin collar. "I'll go meself, sir." He beckoned to two of his signalmen. "It'll be a pleasure."

Like a towering ghost the *Benbecula* glided forward, her decks and superstructure already inches deep in snow. Apart from the gentle beat of engines, the occasional creak of steel or the movement of feet above the bridge, there was nothing to betray her.

Lindsay took out his pipe and put it between his teeth, his eyes on Ritchie's black figure as it hurried between the anchor cables. Perhaps Fraser had been wrong. There might be nothing out there in the snow.

He gripped the side of his chair and waited.

chapter five

Petty Officer Ritchie was in position as far forward in the bows as he could reach. Aft, the bridge was almost hidden by snow, with only the wheelhouse windows showing distinctly, like square black eyes. Occasionally the wind twisted the snow into nervous, darting patterns, and he saw the sea moving slowly towards him, dark, like lead.

He held his breath as a shadow lifted through the snow, and

then relaxed. The wind had cut a path just long enough to reveal an open patch of water which, for a few seconds, had become a ship. If there was a ship out there, he knew she could just as easily be listening and waiting for them.

The deck was steady. Hardly an engine vibration reached him, and in the handset earpiece he could hear Lindsay breathing. A good bloke, he thought. Not condescending, but genuine, maybe a bit too much so. Like someone nursing an old hurt. Something which was tearing him apart, so that when he heard of other people's troubles he felt it all the more. Like at that burial service, for instance.

He had witnessed it as the captain spoke the prayer over the corpses. The same expression he had seen in London at the mass burial. Almost the whole street. The faces had been frozen, like Lindsay's.

He stiffened. There it was again. His head swivelled round as he heard the faint but distinct clang of metal.

"Green four-five, sir. As far as I can tell. I 'eard metal."

Lindsay said, "Keep it up, Yeo." Cool, unhurried, as if he was reporting on a cricket match.

Ritchie felt the sweater warm against his neck. Madge had made it for him from an old jumper she had unravelled. The snow whipped against his cheek in a wet mould. He dashed it from his eyes, and when he looked again he saw the other ship. She lay diagonally across *Benbecula*'s line of advance, the stern towards him, her tall upperworks and poop gleaming like icing on a giant cake.

He said hoarsely, "Ship, sir! Fine on the starboard bow! Range about two cables!"

She was big right enough, probably a liner, with two funnels and a large Swedish flag painted on her side. As he watched he saw part of her upper bridge move and realized it was being lifted bodily by one of her forward derricks. The chief *had* heard a winch. The Germans were changing their appearance already, preparing for their next victim.

He rasped, "Down, lads! She's seen us!"

LINDSAY had seen the other ship's blurred outline with something like disbelief. The snow gave the deceptive impression of leaving one opening, an arena just large enough to contain the two ships, while all around the downpour was as thick as before.

"Port fifteen! Full ahead both engines!" The sharpness of his voice broke the shocked stillness in the wheelhouse.

"Midships! *Steady!*"

Jolliffe muttered, "Steady, sir. Course three-five-five."

Voicepipes and handsets crackled. He heard Maxwell shouting, "Commence! Commence! Commence!" And the instant reply from the fire gongs.

By turning slightly to port Lindsay had laid the enemy on an almost parallel course some four hundred yards away. With bare seconds between, the three starboard side guns opened fire. Number Three, which was farthest aft fired first; the marines had been quicker into action.

"She's turning away!" Lieutenant Aikman almost fell as Number Three gun hurled itself inboard on its recoil springs and sent another shell screaming across the grey water.

The deck was quivering violently now as the revolutions mounted, and the bow wave ploughed away on either beam like a solid glass arrowhead.

"Starboard ten." Lindsay dropped his eye to the gyro. "Midships. Steady." He saw droplets of his sweat falling on the protective cover.

When he raised his head again the enemy was nearer, the bearing more acute.

A bosun's mate shouted, "Number Three gun 'as ceased firin', sir. Unable to bear!"

It could not be helped. If he hauled off again to give the marines a clear view of the enemy the other ship would escape in the snow. She was big. About seventeen thousand tons, and with the power to move at speed.

The two forward guns fired again, the long orange tongues leaping from their muzzles as the shells streaked away towards the enemy.

Through the snow flurries Lindsay saw a brief flash, like a round red eye, and heard Maxwell yell, "A *hit*! We hit the bastard!"

She was pulling away, her funnels already hidden by the snow. Lindsay waited, counting the seconds, until the guns fired once more. Longer intervals now, as cooks, stewards, and supply ratings struggled to feed the guns with those great, ungainly missiles while the hull shook round them. The snow lifted and writhed above the enemy ship, and Lindsay saw the telltale orange flash. The other captain had at last got one of his after guns to bear.

The shell hit the *Benbecula*'s side like a thunderclap, the shock hurling men and equipment about the bridge, while above the starboard bulwark smoke came billowing inboard in a solid fog.

Lindsay gripped the voicepipes, heard splinters ripping and ricocheting through the hull, and tasted lyddite on the cold air.

But the guns were still firing, and above the din he heard layers and trainers yelling like madmen, the rasp of steel, the clang of breech blocks before the cry, "*Ready!*"

Aikman called, "Damage control reports a fire on 'A' deck, sir. Two casualties."

Lindsay raised his glasses and studied the enemy. Nearly gone. now, her shortened outline was just a murky shadow in the snow.

He had to chance it. "Port ten." To Aikman he snapped, "Tell the gunnery officer to bring Number Three to bear."

He watched the ticking gyro. "Midships." He strode to the starboard window, feeling the icy wind clawing his face.

De Chair's gun reopened fire even as the enemy settled on the *Benbecula*'s starboard bow, and the shell hit her directly abaft the bridge. This time the explosion was more dramatic. The shell had probably ignited a small-arms magazine or signal flares.

The enemy fired again. The shell hit *Benbecula*'s side farther aft, exploding deep inside the hull and sending white-hot splinters scything in every direction. Some burst upward through the boat deck and cut a whaler in half, leaving bow and stern dangling from the davits.

Stannard said hoarsely. "Snow's getting heavier again." He ducked involuntarily as a shell exploded alongside, the flash

310

masked instantly by a towering white waterspout. Bridge and wing were buried under cascading water.

Lindsay peered after the enemy in time to see her fading completely into another squall. Only the glare of her fires was still visible, and he heard several small explosions as de Chair's last shell spread its havoc between decks.

Aikman reported, "Damage control have 'A' deck fire under control, sir. Second hit was also 'A' deck. No fire, but four men wounded."

Another telephone jarred the sudden stillness and Stannard said, "It's the chief, sir. He asks if he can reduce revs. Starboard shaft is overheating. Nothing serious, he thinks, but—"

"Thank you, Pilot. Reduce to slow ahead."

No sense in tearing the engines to pieces for nothing. The enemy would not come back for another try. Not this time.

He added slowly, "Get a signal coded up right away. To Admiralty. Advise on our position, course and approximate speed of enemy. Tell them we have engaged enemy raider and obtained two hits. Extent of damage not known. Mention that *Loch Glendhu* has been sunk, and check with the sickbay for a list of survivors."

Lindsay leaned over the wing to watch some of the damage control team scurrying along the forward well deck, bowed against the wind. He was shaking uncontrollably, yet his hands seemed quite steady. Perhaps it was in his mind.

Goss appeared suddenly in the wheelhouse door. "Nobody dead, sir." He sounded accusing. "One man's lost a foot, but the doc says he'll live—" He swung round as Ritchie pushed his way to the door.

Ritchie said harshly, "There was *one* killed, sir." He paused, recalling the astonishment on the boy's face, the eyes glazing with drifting snow. He said, "Ordinary Signalman Cummings, sir. Shell splinter got 'im in the spine. I didn't realize he'd bought it till I told 'im it was all over."

Lindsay nodded. "You did bloody well, Yeo."

Goss cleared his throat noisily. "About the *damage*."

"Yes?"

"It's a dockyard job, sir."

Lindsay could feel his nerves dragging. He said flatly, "No, it isn't, Number One. It's *yours*, until we hear to the contrary."

Goss spoke between his teeth. "If the snow hadn't eased at that moment we might have run straight into that German!"

Lindsay swung on him. "Well, at least we'd have sunk the bloody thing! Now, for God's sake get on with those repairs!"

Dancy poked his head through the door. "The chief says everything's all right, sir."

"Thank him for me, Sub. And fall out action stations."

Dancy withdrew, and seconds later the upper deck tannoy grated, "Fall out action stations. Starboard watch to defence stations." The merest pause, then "Up spirits!"

"Good advice, Yeo." Lindsay walked towards the wheelhouse again. "I think we deserve it!"

Ritchie watched him and then shook his head. You'll do, he thought. For me, and this poor old ship. You'll do.

SUB-LIEUTENANT Michael Dancy pushed aside the heavy curtain and stepped into the wardroom. With only half the deckhead lights in use the wardroom looked cosy, the oak panelling gleaming softly in welcome. Just over an hour to midnight, and as Dancy had the middle watch he saw no point in trying to sleep.

By the fat coal stove he saw the paymaster in conversation with Boase, the doctor. Normally Dancy did not drink much, but tonight he felt like it.

He sat in a deep chair with his back to the others and stared unseeingly at the swaying curtains which partitioned off the dining space. He tried to assemble his memories to capture each moment, as a writer should. But it was difficult. It had been so swift. And all the while this great ship—and she was enormous after the armed yacht—had wheeled and pounded through the snow, guns blazing.

The door opened. It was Kemp, the midshipman, the only officer over whom Dancy could exercise his scanty authority.

The boy said quietly, "I—I was just looking to see if—" His voice trailed away.

Dancy frowned. "Sit here if you like."

Kemp was slightly built, extremely pale, but he possessed one glittering asset which Dancy could never claim. He was a regular and had been to Dartmouth. Dancy had already discovered that he was one of a family of naval men. He seemed to epitomize all Dancy's peacetime dreams, yet at the same time did not really fit the role.

He asked casually, "Your old man's pretty senior I believe?"

Kemp replied, "He's a captain. Shore job at Rosyth." He sighed. "He was beached between the wars for several years."

Dancy nodded gravely. "I'll bet he's glad to be back."

Kemp looked sad. "Glad? That's an understatement."

Dancy was getting irritated without knowing why. "You sound as if you're unhappy about the ship or something."

"I am." Kemp shrugged. "Not the ship exactly. It's the Service. I hate it. I never wanted to enter the Navy, but he kept on at me."

"But surely he knew the Navy well enough to understand, eh?"

Kemp stood up violently. "My father understands nothing about me, and cares less! He's a stupid, pompous bigot, so stop asking about him will you, *please*?"

Dancy was aghast. "There's no call to speak like that! By God, if I'd had half your chances in life—" He checked himself hastily. "What I mean is, if I'd not taken another profession I'd have wanted to enter the Service."

Kemp's hands were shaking. "Well, you got there in the end, didn't you, *sir*!"

As he ran for the door he almost collided with Stannard. He watched the midshipman run past and said dryly, "That young fella's keen to go somewhere."

Dancy said angrily, "Doesn't know when he's well off. I'll be watching him in future."

The Australian grinned lazily, "You do that, Admiral, but in the meantime shift yourself to the bridge, chop, chop!" He gestured to the clock. "*Our* watch, I believe?"

313

Dancy's frown faded. Stannard was a bit coarse at times, but he was all right. Never got in a flap. Dancy buttoned his bridge coat and followed the lieutenant to the ladder.

JUPP stopped beside Lindsay's littered desk and placed a large china mug carefully on a mat before removing its lid.

"'Ot soup, sir. Just the job before you turn in."

Lindsay leaned back in his chair and smiled wearily. "Smells fine." It was midnight, and Lindsay realized he was ravenous. It had been a long day. Inspecting damage between decks, checking the progress of repairs, burying Signalman Cummings.

It was quite impossible to learn anything about the damaged raider. The Admiralty had merely acknowledged his signal. It was unlikely anything could be done. It had been too stormy for flying off aircraft, and the sea was a big place. The German was probably steaming like hell to some secluded Norwegian fjord where she could lie up and lick her scars.

The chief steward said, "The lads took it right well, I thought, sir."

Lindsay nodded, "Yes."

There was a tap at the door and Maxwell peered in. "You want me, sir?" The gunnery officer's face was red from the wind, but as usual his uniform was impeccable.

"Yes, Guns. Sorry to keep you from your bunk after you've been on watch."

Maxwell removed his cap. He had a very sharp, sleek head, like a polished bullet.

Jupp slid from the cabin as Lindsay looked at the lieutenant thoughtfully. An odd bird. Maxwell had made some error or other before the war and been allowed to leave the Navy without fuss.

He said, "The gunnery this morning was erratic. The marines got off two shots to every one from forrard. Not good enough."

Maxwell said swiftly, "My assistant, Lieutenant Hunter, is R.N.R., sir. Keen without proper experience." He let the words sink in. "But I'll get on to him first thing tomorrow."

"You deal with it, Guns. It's your job."

314

Maxwell's mouth tightened into a thin line. "I did not mean to imply—" he stopped.

"Carry on then."

As the door closed Lindsay stood up and walked slowly into the other cabin. He lay down on the bunk fully clothed, and after a few seconds kicked off his sea boots, then fell into a deep sleep.

How long he slept he did not know. He was fighting with the blanket, kicking and gasping as the nightmare flooded round him more vividly than ever.

He rolled on his side, and as the madness retreated he heard a voice, remote but insistent. "Officer of the watch."

It was Stannard, and Lindsay stared at the telephone as it swung back and forth on its flex. He must have knocked it off in his nightmare. He seized it and said, "Captain."

Stannard said, "I'm sorry, sir. I thought you were calling me."

Lindsay fought to keep his tone even. "It's all right, Pilot. What time is it?"

"0350, sir. I'm just calling the morning watch." A pause. "Visibility as before. Wind's still north by east."

"Thank you."

He lay back again. God, what had he been saying?

Up on the bridge Dancy was standing beside the voicepipes as Stannard replaced the telephone.

"All right?"

Stannard did not look at him. "Sure. Just the skipper asking about the time."

He should not have listened. It was like laying bare something private or shameful.

Heavy boots thumped on the ladder as Goss mounted to take his watch. Stannard thanked God he and not Goss had heard that desperate voice. They needed Lindsay, whatever it was he was suffering.

Goss waited until Stannard had made his formal report. Then after a small hesitation he climbed into Lindsay's chair.

Stannard walked slowly to the ladder. Goss's action was symbolic, he thought.

315

Throughout the ship the watch had changed, and in bunks and hammocks men slept or lay staring at the deckhead reliving the fight. Drowsy cooks tumbled cursing from their blankets and made their way to the waiting galley with its congealed grease and dirty cups left by the watchkeepers. In the stokers' mess-deck, Stripey, the ship's cat, lay curled into a tight ball inside someone's metal cap box, his body trembling gently to the steady beat of the screws, as the *Benbecula* pushed slowly across a steep beam sea, her shape as black as the waters which were hers alone.

FIVE WEEKS later *Benbecula* headed south-east away from the patrol area. The relief armed merchant cruiser steamed past less than a mile distant.

Lindsay sat in his tall chair and watched her. Winter had tightened its grip. Each dawn found *Benbecula*'s superstructure and gun barrels gleaming with ice, the signal halyards glittering like a frozen waterfall. Once they had ridden out a Force Eleven gale, and during the whole time they had sighted just one ship, a battered little corvette which had been ordered to rendezvous· with them to remove wounded and the handful of survivors from *Loch Glendhu*.

Tempers among the ship's crew had become frayed, fights erupted without real cause, and Lindsay saw resentful faces across the defaulters' table, much of the hatred, of course, directed against him. But now they were heading south.

Lindsay sat back and looked at the hard, dark horizon line. The afternoon watch was almost finished, and the sky was dull with a hint of more snow. He heard the signalman talking quietly with Ritchie, the occasional creak of the wheel and Maxwell's clipped voice.

The duty bosun's mate was saying, "Beg pardon, sir, but Number Six gun 'as just called up. They say one of the life rafts is workin' adrift again on th' poop."

Maxwell spoke. "Right, tell Lieutenant Aikman to deal with it."

The man stared at him.

"But you sent 'im to the chart room, sir."

Maxwell nodded jerkily. "Oh, yes." He turned to Lindsay. "He's fixing the plot."

Lindsay asked, "What about young Kemp?" He had appointed the midshipman to Maxwell's watch for the experience.

Maxwell nodded. "Yessir." To the seaman he barked, "Mr. Kemp is up in control. Pass the word for him to lay aft, chop, chop. Get a move on!"

BY THE time Midshipman Kemp had made his way aft to the poop daylight was almost gone. As he groped along the guardrail, the sea looked very dark, with deep swells and troughs.

Beside the covered twelve-pounder he found Leading Seaman Swan waiting for him with weary resignation.

Kemp asked, "Where are the others?"

Swan was a big man, made even larger by several layers of woollens beneath his duffel coat. He had already done several repair jobs about the upper deck in the freezing weather and was just about ready to go below. The cold, damp air was playing havoc with his patience. Kemp's arrival did nothing to help ease his irritation. Normally quite tolerant of midshipmen in general, just this once Kemp's obvious uncertainty filled Swan with resentment.

He replied offhandedly. "They'll be here any second." He waited for Kemp to pull him up for omitting the "sir".

Kemp shivered and said, "What's the trouble anyway?"

The leading seaman gestured with a massive, leather-gauntleted fist towards the nearest raft. It was poised almost vertically on two wooden skids, so that in an emergency it could be released straight down over the port quarter.

"Some idiot has slopped paint all over the lines, and in this sort of climate it makes 'em fray more easily." He saw Kemp peering doubtfully at the heavy raft and added, "Not that it matters much. What with paint and the bloody ice, I doubt if the thing would move even if Chatham barracks fell on it!"

Two seamen loomed up from the poop ladder and he barked, "Where the hell have you been?"

The first seaman said, "The officer of the watch 'ad me on the rattle for smokin'." He looked at Kemp. "That's wot."

Swan waited for Kemp to say something. Then he said angrily, "Well, just you wait here. I'm going to get some new lines. You can start by checking how many of the old ones are frayed, right?"

As he stamped away one of the seamen muttered, "What's up with Hookey then? Miserable bastard."

Kemp gripped the guardrail with both hands, willing himself to concentrate on the raft. He knew the two seamen, like Swan, were testing him.

He heard one of them duck behind the twelve-pounder gun-shield and the rasp of a match. He thrust himself away from the rail. "That's enough!"

The two seamen stared at him with mild surprise.

"Start working on those lines!"

One of them said, "Which lines, sir? Can't see much in this light."

Kemp felt despair rising like nausea. He seized the nearest seaman's sleeve and thrust him towards the raft. "Get up there and *feel* them one at a time!" He swung on the second man. "And you start freeing the ice from the metal slips. Swan will probably want to splice them to the new lines."

Behind his back the seaman on the raft made an obscene gesture.

Kemp was shivering uncontrollably beneath the oilskin. He knew it was partly because of the cold, but also due to his inability to play out his part as he knew he must if he was to keep his sanity. In the beginning Kemp had been prepared to try and see his father's point of view. Perhaps if he had known what he had wanted to be, then his father might have relented. But at eighteen Kemp was still unsure.

He looked up startled as Swan bounded up the ladder carrying a huge coil of line.

Swan shouted, "What the *hell* are you doing up there, Biggs? Come down immediately and fix a lifeline, you stupid bastard!"

Even as he spoke the other seaman inadvertently cut through a lashing with his knife. The end of the severed lashing, complete

318

with a metal shackle, slashed upward, cutting Biggs full in the face as he made to scramble back to the deck. Kemp stared horrified as the man swayed drunkenly. Then as Swan flung himself on the raft Biggs fell outboard and down.

Swan pushed Kemp aside and groped for the handset by the twelve-pounder. But the canvas cover was frozen iron-hard and with a sob he ran for the ladder, yelling as he went.

Kemp gripped the rail and peered down into the churning white wash. But he did not know where to look. Where would Biggs be? Below, staring up at his ship as she faded into the darkness? Or already far astern, choking and crying out in terror? He began to fumble with a lifebuoy as Swan came aft again.

Swan said hoarsely, "Forget it. He'll have been sucked into the port screw."

The other seaman, who was still standing transfixed with the knife in one hand, said brokenly, "We're turning!"

Kemp stared at the ship's pale wake as it began to change into a wide sweeping curve. It was a mad dream. It had to be.

Right in his ear Swan said, "They'll have to go through the motions. Even if he missed the screws he'll be a block of bloody ice in minutes!"

A marine corporal from Number Six gun clattered onto the poop and snapped, "Captain's compliments, Mr. Kemp, and he wants you on the bridge right away." He looked at Swan. "You, too."

The man with the knife said in a small voice, "Worn't my fault Hookey!"

Swan looked at Kemp with savage contempt. "I know. You were obeying orders!"

Kemp tried to speak, his mind reeling with shock. "I—I'm sorry —I was only trying to—"

All the way along the upper deck Kemp was vaguely aware of silent, muffled figures watching him as he passed. No matter what had really happened, he was already condemned in their eyes.

As they reached the door at the rear of the bridge Kemp heard Lindsay's voice, very level, as if from far away.

"Another five minutes, Pilot, then bring her back on course."

chapter six

The Chief of Staff looked up from his desk as Lindsay entered the office, and then waved to a chair.

"Take the weight off your feet." He shot Lindsay a smile as he groped in a drawer and took out two glasses and a bottle of Scotch. "The sun, had it been out today, would be well over the yardarm by now, eh?"

Lindsay relaxed slightly. The whisky was neat and very good.

Captain Lovelace said, "I didn't call you over until now because I thought you'd have enough to do. Anyway, it gave me time to study your report. You did damn well to have a crack at that raider. Against all sane instructions, of course, but I'd have done the same."

Lindsay replied. "I wish I could have finished him off."

"I dare say. We had a couple of clear days recently and the R.A.F. got a reconnaissance flight going. Your raider is holed up in Norway. She's the *Nassau*, seventeen thousand tons, and fairly new. Used to run in the East African ports. Intelligence have reported she's completely converted as a raider." He added wryly, "Of course, they didn't tell us anything about her until a few days ago."

Lindsay nodded. He had been expecting the captain to attack him for taking independent action. No heroics, Lovelace had said at their other meeting. Now it looked as if heroics were just about all they had.

As if reading his mind the captain said, "We're tightly stretched. Things are bad in the Med and we've had heavy losses in Western Approaches. My operations staff will let you have all the backlog when you're ready for it." He looked grave. "We have not released the news of *Loch Glendhu*'s loss to the public as yet. The less the enemy knows about our meagre resources the better."

Lindsay felt suddenly depressed. The endless strain, the continuous effort needed to pull his new command into a fighting unit were taking their toll.

He said, "It all sounds pretty hopeless."

Lovelace paused with the bottle in mid-air above Lindsay's glass. "Hard luck about losing that chap overboard. What have you done about the midshipman?"

"Nothing, sir. It was an accident due more to ignorance than carelessness. I doubt Kemp will ever forget it."

Lovelace nodded. The telephone buzzed and he snapped, "I will see the commanding officer of *Merlin* in three minutes. Tell him to warm his backside on your fire until I'm ready."

Lindsay stood up. "Any orders for me, sir?"

"Soon. I'm afraid a week for maintenance is about all you can expect, so work along those lines. I hear you've completed refuelling, so you can allow local leave whenever it suits you."

Lindsay picked up his cap. "Thank you for the drink, sir."

Lovelace grinned. "My pleasure. I hear so much gloom that it's a real prize to meet somebody who's achieved something at last!"

As Lindsay walked through the adjoining room he saw the officer who was waiting for the next interview. A full rank junior to Lindsay, yet he commanded the *Merlin*, a new and powerful destroyer lying near to *Benbecula*'s buoy.

He watched Lindsay pass, his face curious. Lindsay could imagine the picture in his mind. The captain of that old A.M.C. looked all right, but with a command like her he must have something wrong with him.

Lindsay stood stock still in the deserted passageway, spent and despairing.

Damn them all to hell.

"Are you all right, sir?"

Lindsay swung round and saw the girl standing by the main entrance. As before she was muffled to the ears.

He stared at her. "Yes, thank you." He tried to smile, seeing the doubt and concern in her eyes. "A bit bushed, that's all."

She took off her jaunty cap and shook out her hair vigorously. "I saw you come in this morning. We all heard about what happened."

Another Wren passed Lindsay. As she reached the door the

Wren called Eve Collins tossed her an ignition key and said, "Thanks for relieving me early, Sue. Watch out for ice."

The other girl paused. "Do it for me sometime." Then she was gone, the blackout curtain swirling in a jet of cold air.

She said quietly, "I'm glad you made it back all right, sir."

Lindsay recalled the flashing headlights on the shore. "One of the bunting-tossers read your message when we left Scapa. It was nice of you to see us off." He added abruptly, "I wonder if you'd care to have a drink with me? Maybe we could get a meal or something?"

She replaced her cap slowly. "I'm sorry. I really am. I've *got* a date." She looked away. "I can break it though—"

"No. It's all right." He thrust his hands into his greatcoat pockets, trying to sound casual. He did not know why it had all become so urgent and important. "Forget it."

The curtain swirled inward again and an R.A.F. flight-lieutenant blundered in. "I guessed you'd take half the night to get changed! I've got a car outside. I'll run you to your billet." He saw Lindsay. "Oh, sorry!"

She said, "Jack, this is Commander Lindsay." Then she turned to him again. "The fighter boys are giving a dance at the field. Why don't you come, too?" She looked at the flight-lieutenant. "It would be all right, wouldn't it, Jack?"

"Of course." He did not sound very enthusiastic.

Lindsay smiled. "I must get back to my ship. But thanks again. Enjoy yourselves."

Then he was outside in the darkness, the icy wind making his eyes water like tears. He quickened his pace and turned once more towards the sea.

LINDSAY was working at his desk when Goss, followed by Fraser, entered his day cabin.

"Sit, gentlemen." He looked at the two men. "I have just received our orders. We are at forty-eight hours notice for steam."

Fraser muttered, "A week and a day. That's all they've given us." Then he grinned. "Generous bastards!"

322

Lindsay turned to Goss. "What about you, Number One? Are you all buttoned up?"

Goss had taken the time in harbour badly, arguing with engineers and workers from the repair shop, following the mechanics and welders between the *Benbecula*'s decks like an old hen trying to protect its chickens from a pack of rampaging foxes. But for Fraser's excellent work on damaged platings and frames while the ship had been returning to the Flow it was hard to see how they could have managed.

Jupp padded into the cabin and opened the drinks cabinet as Goss replied, "I've done my best, but it's nowhere near ready."

Lindsay said, "I believe we may be at sea for Christmas." He had been at sea for nearly every Christmas he could remember, but this was different. Most of the ship's company had not, and after the misery of the last patrol, Christmas in the Arctic wastes might seem like a final disaster.

Fraser asked mildly, "Is it definite, sir?"

Lindsay glanced at Jupp's stooped shoulders and smiled, "The chief steward informs me so."

Jupp eyed him calmly. "I saw the turkeys meself, sir. Bein' stacked up ready to be collected. A sure sign."

Goss did not seem to be listening. "Same patrol?"

"No. Farther south-west than Uncle Item Victor. But that's just between us."

Goss shuddered. "Nearer Greenland. There'll be ice about."

The three of them lapsed into silence. As Jupp filled his glass, Lindsay wondered if the chief steward had noticed he was drinking more. He should have gone ashore, if only to find a change of scene. But apart from two official visits to headquarters he had remained on board, immersed in the business of preparing his ship for sea again. He had stayed too much alone.

He realized too that something had to be done to break the gloom which hung over his command. The scope for enjoyment in Scapa was almost nil.

He said suddenly, "I thought we'd have a party before we sail. It will help make up for Christmas." He was watching Goss. "It's rather up to you, Number One. If you think you've too much on your plate we'll scrub round it, of course."

Goss stirred in his chair. "I *am* very busy, sir." He was pondering, his eyes far away as he continued. "Who would be coming?"

Lindsay kept his tone matter of fact. He said, "Oh, all the usual. Base staff, some of the people who have been helping us. That sort of thing."

Fraser said over the rim of his glass. "I think it might be too difficult. Number One's people have still got a good bit of clearing up to do. In any case, who'd want to come to a ship like this? There's a damn great carrier here now and—"

Goss swung towards him angrily. "That's all you bloody well know! How many ships like this one have *you* seen then, eh? A carrier, you say? Most people are sick to death of warships up here!"

Lindsay asked quietly, "You're in favour?" He saw Fraser drop one eyelid in a brief wink.

Goss recovered his dignity. "Well, if you think—" He darted a glance at Fraser. "Yes, I am, sir."

"That's settled then. I'll leave it to you. Two days is not long to arrange it, but I expect you'll manage."

"Manage?" Goss frowned. "I've seen the main saloon filled to overflowing in my day. A prince, his whole retinue, and some of the richest passengers we've carried, all eating and drinking fit to bust." He stood up. "We'll show 'em. So if you'll excuse me, I'll start making the arrangements." He left the cabin with unusual speed.

Fraser said quietly, "I've not seen him like that for years. My God, sir, you don't know what you've sparked off."

Lindsay smiled. "I hope you're right, Chief. This ship needs something, so we'll make a start with the party, right?"

Fraser grinned. "Right."

LINDSAY did not have much time to think about the party. Almost to the hour of its starting he was kept busy dealing with the ship's sailing preparations.

It was dark in the Flow when Goss came to Lindsay's quarters. "Ready for you in the wardroom, sir." He was wearing a new uniform and his cheeks were glowing from a fresh shave and bath.

When they reached the wardroom Lindsay was astounded. It was difficult to believe he was in the same ship. Everything shone with polish and small coloured lights, and two long tables were groaning under a weight of sandwiches and canapés. The stewards who had been with the Company before the war were wearing their old mess jackets and maroon trousers, and three other stewards waited self-consciously with violins and a piano which had certainly not been present before.

Goss faced him grimly. "Well, sir?"

Lindsay kept his face impassive. "It's not Navy, Number One." Then he touched Goss's forearm. "But it's bloody marvellous! I knew you'd do your best, but this is more than that!"

Goss stared at him uncertainly. "You like it then?"

"I do." Lindsay saw Jupp making towards him with a tray. "It's what we all need in this bloody war!" And he meant it.

Goss snapped his fingers at a steward and said, "I heard a boat alongside. The first guests are arriving." Then he strode away.

Fraser, who had joined Lindsay, said, "You've made his day." He looked at Lindsay. "That was a damn nice thing you did."

In no time at all the wardroom was crowded with visitors. As the din of conversation and laughter mounted, Lindsay was conscious of the impression Goss's party was having. He, too, could sense a kind of pride for the way this old ship was hanging on to her past and so giving pleasure to the present.

Faces swam around him, handshakes and slaps on the shoulder. There were officers from the base and other ships, some nursing sisters and the wives of senior officers and officials, and several Wrens, too, but not the one he was waiting to see.

Jupp said quietly, "There has just been a telephone call, sir. Captain Lovelace will be coming aboard shortly."

But Lindsay was looking past him towards the door. Boase, the doctor, was greeting several latecomers. One of them was the Wren called Eve.

Without her scarves and baggy coat she looked quite different. She was much smaller than he had imagined, and her hair was cut very short, giving her a sort of elfin simplicity.

He pushed through the press of figures. Boase stiffened and said, "Oh, this is the captain."

She held out her hand. It was small and very warm. "I know."

Lindsay said, "I'm glad you could come."

She had hazel eyes, very wide. And she was studying him with that same mock gravity he remembered so vividly from the first meeting in the staff car.

She said, "It's like nothing I've ever seen. She's a beautiful ship."

He realized he was still holding her hand and said, "Here's Jupp with a drink for you. Take it and tell me what you've been doing."

She smiled up at him. "Not much." She lifted the glass. "Cheers."

Boase had drifted off, but Lindsay had not noticed. "I'm sorry I was a bit stupid the other night. You must have thought—"

She interrupted. "I thought you looked worn out. I was sorry, too, about that dance."

Lindsay glanced round. "Have you brought him with you?" He forced a smile. "He seemed a nice chap."

"You hated him, and it showed!" She laughed at his confusion. "But he's not with me."

Lindsay guided her to the bulkhead. "We're leaving tomorrow, but I imagine you know. About the meal I promised you . . ."

She looked at him with concern. "Oh, I forgot to tell you. I've been drafted."

"*Drafted?*" The word hung between them like a shutter.

"I've been trying for ages to go on a signals course. Well, at last I'm being sent on one." She faltered. "In Canada."

Lindsay looked away. "I'm very glad for you."

"No, you're not." She rested a hand on his sleeve. "Neither am I. Now."

Canada. Not even where he could visit her. He cursed himself for allowing his disappointment to show.

He said, "You didn't come aboard to be miserable. Come and meet the others."

She shook her head. "I can only stay a little while. They're shipping me out of here tonight. I expect I'll be joining a convoy at Liverpool quite soon. Rotten, isn't it?"

"Yes." He wanted to take her away. Free himself and her from the noise which hemmed them in like a wall. "I shall miss you."

She studied his face for several seconds. "You mean it, don't you?"

Maxwell's polished head moved from the crowd. "Sorry to interrupt, sir, but Captain Lovelace is here. He has an important visitor with him."

"Tell him I'll be right over." As Maxwell hurried away he said urgently, "You won't leave the ship without saying good-bye?"

She shook her head very slowly. "No. Of course not." She tried to bring back her cheeky grin. "I'll go and yarn with your delicious doctor."

Lindsay found Lovelace speaking to Maxwell, his serious features breaking into a smile as he said, "Ah, Lindsay, I'd like you to meet Commodore Kemp."

The other guest was a thickset man, who nodded abruptly and said, "Quite a party. Never think you'd been in action, what?"

Lovelace said, "You've done a marvellous job, Lindsay."

Lindsay watched the commodore. There was something aggressive about him. Intolerant. Like his words.

"Are you joining the base, sir?"

The commodore took a glass from a steward. "I'm here to co-ordinate new strategy." He embarked on a long dissertation.

Lindsay felt increasingly angry, as he thought of the girl, of the fading, precious minutes. Then the commodore said abruptly, "Where's that son of mine then?"

Kemp. Of course. He should have guessed.

"I'm afraid I don't know, sir."

"*I* would want to know where every one of my officers was, at any time of the day or night."

"Come along, sir, why not meet some of the other guests?"

Lovelace sounded tense. "I'm sure the captain doesn't bother about one more midshipman, eh?"

Kemp stared at him bleakly. "I *want* to see him."

Lindsay sighed. "I'll send for him."

It was his own fault. After all, Kemp had come a long way to see his only son.

He heard the commodore say, "Young fool. When I heard about his latest failure I thought I'd explode!" He stared round at the shining panels and glittering lights. "Under these circumstances, however—"

Lindsay turned sharply, "Are you here on official business, sir, or as a guest?"

Kemp looked at him with surprise. "As a guest of course!"

Lindsay said quietly, "Then, sir, may I suggest you start acting like one!"

He turned and walked away.

The commodore opened and closed his mouth several times. "The impertinent young—" He turned to Lovelace again. "By God, there will be a few changes when I'm in control, I can tell you!"

Lindsay almost collided with Jupp as he pushed between the noisy figures by the door.

Jupp said, "Beg pardon, sir, but the young lady's gone. There was a call from the shore. Something about 'er draft bein' brought forward an hour." He held out a paper napkin. "She said to give you this, sir."

Lindsay opened it. She had written in pencil: *Had to go. Take care of yourself. See you in Eden. Eve.*

He hurried out to the promenade deck, where the gangway staff were huddled together in their thick watchcoats. The quartermaster said, "Can I 'elp, sir?"

"The last boat, Q.M. Can you still see it?" Beyond the guardrail, the night was pitch black.

The quartermaster shook his head. "No, sir. Shoved off ten minutes ago."

Back in the noisy wardroom, Lindsay noticed Commodore Kemp speaking to his son in a corner. He reached Goss's side and said,

"I'm going to my cabin, Number One. You take over, will you?"

Goss nodded. "Good party, sir."

"Yes." Lindsay looked at the door, as if expecting to see her there again. "Very good party."

He walked out of the wardroom and climbed the deserted companion ladder.

chapter seven

The telephone above Lindsay's bunk rattled tinnily. He reached up for it. "Captain."

"Time to alter course, sir."

Lindsay held up his watch. Four in the morning. Another day.

"Very well, Pilot." He dropped the handset on its hook and lay back on the pillow.

What a way to fight a war. Mile upon wretched mile. Empty, violent and cold. He heard feet overhead, the muffled clatter of steering gear as Stannard brought the old ship round on the southernmost leg of her patrol. At this moment the cross on the chart would show the *Benbecula* almost five hundred miles southwest of Iceland, while some seven hundred and fifty miles beyond her labouring bows was the dreaded Cape Farewell of Greenland. It was not a patrol area, he thought. It was a freezing desert.

One more day and they would be in December, with still another month to go before they could run for home. The deadly monotony and discomfort was affecting almost every man aboard.

He turned on the bunk and heard the small pill jar rattle beneath the pillow. Enough to make you sleep deeply for four hours at least, Boase had said. Yet he was afraid to take even one of them in case he was needed. He rolled over and thought instead about opening a new bottle of whisky. It was no use. He could not go on like this. He was slowly destroying himself, and knew he was a growing menace to all those who depended on him.

Whenever he fell on the bunk for even a few moments the nightmare returned, and he would awake, sweating and frightened.

The telephone jarred his thoughts. It was Stannard again.

"Sorry to bother you, sir. There's a west-bound convoy altering course to the south-east of us, approximately five hundred miles away."

"Anything else?"

"Admiralty reports a deployment of seven plus U-boats converging ahead of the convoy's original course, sir."

"Very well. Keep a good listening watch."

As he lay back he tried to dismiss it from his mind. The convoy was not *Benbecula*'s concern. Like all others, it must depend on its own resources. But he could not put aside a sudden feeling of uneasiness.

He switched on the light and swung off the bunk. It was no surprise to hear the discreet knock at the door and to see Jupp's mournful face peering in at him.

"Will you be wanting an early breakfast, sir?" His eyes flickered across the disordered bunk.

Lindsay shook his head. "I think I'll make do with coffee for now."

Jupp vanished and returned in minutes with the coffee. "Blowing a bit up top, sir." He glanced with obvious disapproval at Lindsay's soiled and crumpled sweater. "I could get you some more gear from my store."

Lindsay smiled. "Later."

He swung round as the handset rang again. "Captain."

Stannard said, "W/T office has just received a signal for us, sir. Top Secret. I've got Aikman on it right away."

Lieutenant Aikman had the chore of decoding the more secret and difficult signals.

Lindsay swallowed some coffee and then asked, "Any news of the convoy?"

"Six more U-boats reported to the south of it, sir. I've marked 'em on my chart, so it also gives us a fair idea of the convoy's position."

Lindsay nodded. "Good." As he buttoned his jacket he was thinking of those submarines. Seven plus ahead of the convoy's

330

previous course. Now six more to the south. It was a formidable force, but fortunately there was still time to take avoiding action.

Jupp handed him his cap and glasses and he hurried up the companion ladder. Inside the chart room Stannard was working with dividers and rulers. He straightened his back and said, "Oh, good morning, sir. As far as I can make out the convoy has made a really drastic alteration of course. They are steaming almost nor'west and really cracking it on."

Lindsay knew what the convoy's commodore was doing. He had already passed out of effective range of air cover from England and was heading farther north in the hope of getting help from the long-range bomber patrols from Iceland. There were so many dead patches where aircraft could not reach. Like the vast area now covered by *Benbecula*'s endless vigil.

Stannard said, "I looked at the intelligence log, sir. Seems it's a fast west-bound convoy of only ten ships."

The door banged open and Aikman, his pyjamas covered by a duffel coat, stepped over the coaming.

"Bloody hell, Pilot! Can't you let a bloke get some shut-eye!" he saw Lindsay and flushed. "Sorry, sir."

Lindsay smiled. "I know how you feel. What does the signal say?"

Aikman ran his fingers through his tousled hair. "Three German heavy units have left Tromsö, sir. Last reported heading south along the Norwegian coast. Further information not yet available. There's a list of deployments too, sir."

Lindsay read the long signal slowly. The enemy could be moving three important warships south to Kiel or the Baltic for use against the Russians. They had been *seen* steaming south, but that could easily be a ruse. Perhaps they were going to make another attempt to break into the Atlantic.

He ran his eyes over the deployment information. A cruiser squadron was already on its way from Iceland, and more heavy units had left Scapa Flow. The picture began to form in his mind. Almost every available ship was being sent to forestall anything which the three German units might attempt.

He looked at Stannard. "I want you to make notes on this signal. I'll stay on the bridge."

Stannard nodded. As Lindsay walked towards the wheelhouse he was thinking that apart from *Benbecula* and two patrol vessels in the Denmark Strait there was hardly a single ship within five hundred miles of the convoy and its escorts.

Stannard entered the wheelhouse a few minutes later. "If those three jokers make a go for the Atlantic, which way will they come, d'you reckon, sir?"

Lindsay shrugged. "They'll know they've been seen on the move and will not waste time trying for the Denmark Strait this time. My guess is they'll head for the Rose Garden, the area between Iceland and the Faroes."

"It'll be hard to slip past our ships, surely?"

"Over four hundred miles?" Lindsay looked away. "It's a pretty wide gap."

He settled back in the chair. He did not want to talk. He wanted to think, to try and explain why he felt so uneasy.

This was a very bad time of the year. Visibility was hopeless and air cover restricted accordingly. It was just possible the Germans might make it. Or was this a carefully planned ruse by the German heavy units to draw off the Home Fleet's reserves and allow a fourth unknown vessel to enter the Denmark Strait?

Aikman entered the wheelhouse. "Another signal, sir. Two more U-boats reported south of the convoy."

Stannard snapped, "Give it to me. I'll put it on the chart."

Lindsay's voice stopped him by the door. "While you're there Pilot, get me a course and speed to intercept the convoy."

Aikman asked, "They'll never come right up here, surely, sir?"

Lindsay looked at him. "Wouldn't you if you had fifteen odd U-boats coming after you?"

Aikman nodded glumly. "I suppose so."

Stannard came back. "Course to intercept would be one hundred degrees, sir. Revs for fifteen knots. We should make contact at 2000 tonight." Then he added slowly, "Of course, sir, we'd be out of our allotted area by noon if you decided to act on it."

"Yes."

The convoy's original track was straddled by U-boats. To the south the gate was also closed. But if the convoy came farther north and the German heavy units burst through the patrol lines, they would need all the help they could get.

He said, "Very well. Bring her round to one-zero-zero. Call up the chief before you ask for maximum revs, but warn the engine room what to expect."

He could feel the sudden expectancy amongst the shadowy figures around him.

"Port fifteen. Midships." Stannard had his eye down to the gyro. "Steady."

"Steady, sir. Course zero-nine-five." The quartermaster sounded breathless as the ship rolled heavily across a steep trough.

"Steer one-zero-zero." Stannard looked up as a telephone buzzed. "For you, sir."

Fraser sounded irritable. "What's all this I hear about full revs, sir?"

Lindsay quietly spoke into the mouthpiece. "There may be a convoy coming into our pitch, Chief. There are three bandits at large from Norway and a whole pack of U-boats to the south. I thought our presence might cheer 'em up a bit."

There was a long pause. "Aye, sir. Ring down when you're ready. I'll give you everything I've got."

Lindsay handed the telephone to Stannard and said, "I'm going below. I have a feeling this is going to be a long day."

Two hours later Jupp stood beside Lindsay's table and eyed him with grave approval. Lindsay was eating his first complete breakfast since taking command. There was a tap at the door and Petty Officer Ritchie stepped over the coaming. He looked brighter than Lindsay could remember. Perhaps, like himself, he craved to be doing something, if only to keep his inner hurt at bay a while longer.

"Good morning, Yeoman. Anything new?"

"Some more information about the convoy, sir. Ten ships and three escorts. It's a fast convoy apparently. Mostly tankers in ballast and two personnel ships. One of them has got a complete signal course of Wrens aboard."

Lindsay stared at him, suddenly ice cold. It was more than a coincidence, surely. The nagging feeling that something was wrong.

He stood up. "Get back to the bridge, Yeo, and tell the W/T office I want every channel open. *Anything* they hear I want to know about."

Jupp watched the door close and asked, "More coffee, sir?" When Lindsay remained staring at the bulkhead he added gently, "She'll be safe, sir. They'll not take chances with a ship full of women."

Lindsay turned slowly and looked at him. He said quietly, "I expect you're right. And thank you."

IN HIS private office below the bridge Lieutenant Philip Aikman locked the secret cipher books inside his safe. Unlike most of the other officers aboard, he really enjoyed his appointment to the ship. *Benbecula* was not involved with complicated fleet manoeuvres and she was remote from all but the rarest chances of air or U-boat attack. In civilian life Aikman had been manager of a travel agency in the London suburbs. His education was scanty, but he made up for it by his sharp attention to detail and manner. When war came he volunteered for the Navy, and was asked if he was interested in a job on Contraband Control. Without a blush he had completed his forms, adding a list of languages which he spoke fluently. In fact he spoke only his own, but his supreme confidence somehow carried him through. But when he was transferred to a troopship and later to *Benbecula* he felt relief.

Luck could not last forever, and here he was really safe. His first job had been as boarding officer, searching neutral ships in the early days of the war to make sure no war materials were being smuggled to the enemy. Now the captain had made him cipher officer as well.

He stepped over the cabin coaming, and as the wind smashed him back on the wet steel, he had to run like mad to reach the bridge ladder without getting soaked. In the chart room only Midshipman Kemp and Squire, the navigator's yeoman, were working.

Aikman said casually, "I've just deciphered that last Top Secret." He laid the pad on the chart. "It states, two repeat two of the German heavy units have entered the Skagerrak, so you'd better note it in the pilot's log."

Kemp looked up, his eyes red with fatigue. "Just two of them?"

Aikman gave a grave smile. "It stands to reason that if two of them have gone to earth the other will be close behind. If not, I imagine the Home Fleet can take care of that bastard!"

Kemp thrust the pad to Squire. "You do it, will you?"

Aikman yawned hugely and walked to a salt-stained scuttle, to watch spray running down the glass and freezing into small distorted worms.

Behind his back Squire paused, his pencil in mid-air. He said quietly, "These two Jerry ships, sir. How can they be in the Skagerrak? If three of them left Tromsö last night, they can't have reached as far south as Denmark in that time, unless they grew wings!"

"What?" Aikman smiled. "That's bloody rubbish, lad." He crossed to the table. "If their lordships tell us they've got there, then who are we to question them, eh?"

"I think you should check the original signal, sir."

Aikman felt a sudden twinge of alarm. "As it happens, Squire, I do not require any advice on my department!"

Squire said stubbornly, "When the navigating officer returns, sir, I shall have to tell him."

"You *do* that small thing, Squire!" Aikman shot him a withering stare. "I may have some things to tell him too!" He stamped out of the chart room and slammed the door.

At that very moment Stannard was standing beside Lindsay's chair.

He said, "Well, sir, I have to tell you that we should make a turn. Even allowing for dead reckoning and little else, I'm sure we're miles over our patrol line."

Lindsay nodded slowly. Stannard was right, of course. The convoy had made another turn to westward, its commodore apparently satisfied the U-boats had given up the chase. There had been several reports of ice near Cape Farewell.

Aikman hurried onto the bridge and reported. "Two enemy units have been sighted in their own waters, sir. The third is still unaccounted for."

Stannard grinned. "That settles it then. I'll go and lay off a new course."

Lindsay glanced at Dancy. "Ring for half-speed."

He settled down again in the chair and thought of the party of Wrens who were probably quite unaware of their momentary danger.

He realized that Aikman was still beside him, deathly pale. "What's wrong?"

Aikman spoke between his teeth. "There's been a mistake, sir. Not important now as the enemy ships are back in safe waters, but—"

Lindsay asked, "What sort of mistake?"

"I was called here this morning and told to decipher that first signal. I was tired, sir, and I must have confused the time of origin."

Lindsay gripped the arms of the chair. "You did what?"

"Well, sir, it was just a small slip." A bead of sweat ran from under Aikman's cap. "But the three German ships left Tromsö twenty-eight hours earlier than I calculated."

"But two of them are back in their own waters." Lindsay forced himself to speak gently. "Is *that* part right?"

Aikman nodded. "Yes, sir."

The door crashed open and Stannard said harshly, "'Own waters!' Those ships are already in the Skagerrak, and that was how Squire knew *he*," Stannard pointed angrily at Aikman's rigid shoulders, "had made a cock of the deciphering!"

"Easy, Pilot!"

Lindsay slid from the chair, his mind working wildly. In twenty-eight hours quite a lot might have happened. He looked over at Stannard, "See what you can find out about the convoy." Then he looked at Aikman. "I just hope to God I'm wrong. If not, you'd better start praying!"

When Stannard came back from the W/T office he said quietly, "Convoy is now steering two-seven-five, sir. Should pass within fifty miles of our southernmost leg at 2000."

Lindsay waited, knowing there was more.

"A Swedish freighter reported sighting an unidentified ship in the Denmark Strait the night before last, sir. That is all the information available."

Lindsay walked past him and gripped the rail. Almost to himself he said, "So while every available ship is out searching for the three from Tromsö, one other slips quietly through the Denmark Strait. He's been there, sitting patiently while the U-boats did the hard part for him." He swung round on Stannard and slammed one fist into his palm. "Driving the convoy up to him like beasts to the slaughter!"

Stannard stared at him. "Oh, my Christ!"

Lindsay turned away. "Bring her round to your new course. Maximum revs again, and the hands to exercise action stations in thirty minutes before the light goes!"

Aikman, who had gone back to his small office, gripped a knuckle tightly between his teeth to keep himself from sobbing aloud. He still did not understand what had happened, but knew it was far more terrible than he had imagined.

chapter eight

Lindsay sat very still on the bridge which, apart from the shaded compass lights, was in total darkness.

The *Benbecula* had turned in a great arc, so that she was now heading once again towards the southern extremity of Greenland. All afternoon they had listened to the crackle of Morse from the W/T office. The third German ship had at last been sighted entering the Skagerrak like her consorts. The carefully planned German ruse to draw off the Home Fleet's reserves had worked, and by now the fourth ship could be anywhere. If only Lindsay had known of the twenty-eight-hours delay things might have been very different. He could have taken *Benbecula* at full speed to the northern span of her patrol area, where there was the best chance of contacting any ship which might come through the Denmark Strait.

Benbecula had received more signals giving details of the convoy's approximate position. The ten ships and their escort were now on *Benbecula*'s port bow, possibly thirty, possibly one hundred miles away. The sea was much calmer, evidence that ice was near.

Lindsay thought of the girl out there in the blackness. She was probably in her lifejacket, listening to the unfamiliar orders and sounds around her. One good thing was that the convoy consisted of fast ships. It was not much but . . . . He turned and rapped, "Time?"

A signalman said, "2100, sir."

Lindsay darted a quick glance round the bridge. Dancy and Petty Officer Ritchie, Stannard by the rear door, and the signalmen and messengers at telephones and voicepipes. The coxswain was leaning over the wheel, his heavy face set in concentration. The tension was almost a physical thing.

A telephone buzzed. Stannard snatched it and then said quickly, "Signal from convoy escort to Admiralty, sir." He paused, listening. "Am under attack by German raider. One escort in sinking condition. Am engaging." He swallowed hard. "Require immediate repeat immediate assistance."

Lindsay did not turn. "Full ahead both engines."

Stannard shouted above the jangle of telegraphs. "Admiralty to *Benbecula*, sir. Act as situation demands. No assistance is available for minimum of twelve hours."

Another telephone buzzed and Lindsay heard Dancy say, "Masthead. Yes. Right." Then he said, "Gunflashes at Red-two-oh."

The bridge was beginning to vibrate savagely as the revolutions mounted.

Dancy called, "Masthead reports he can see more flashes, sir."

"Very well."

338

Lindsay willed his mind to stay clear. The flashes were a guide, but with low cloud and the possibility of ice about it was impossible to gauge the range. He pounded the screen slowly with his gloved fingers. Come on, old girl. Come on.

Dancy asked quietly, "D'you think it's the same one that sank *Loch Glendhu*, sir?"

"Yes. That last effort was just a rehearsal. Maybe this is, too."

A bright orange light glowed suddenly in the blackness ahead. It hung like a tall, brilliant feather of flame, then vanished.

Stannard said, "That's one poor bastard done for."

Another bright flash against the unmoving backcloth. This time it seemed to last for several minutes so that they could see the underbellies of the clouds shining and flickering as if touched by the fires below.

Out there ships were burning and men were dying. It had been planned with the methodical accuracy of an assassination.

Stannard took the handset from a messenger before it stopped buzzing. "To us from Admiralty, sir. The convoy has divided. The two personnel ships with the commodore aboard have turned north. The tankers and remaining escort have headed south. Enemy has ceased fire." He sounded surprised.

Lindsay walked slowly across the violently shaking gratings. Of course the German had ceased fire. He had destroyed two or more in the convoy. The U-boats would be waiting for the tankers now. The raider could take his time. Follow the two helpless ships as far as the ice and then. . . .

He swung round, his tone harsh. "Come to the chart room, Pilot. We'll alter course immediately to go after them."

Ritchie crossed to the gyro. "What d'you think, Swain? Will we make it?"

Jolliffe's face remained frozen in the compass light like a chunk of weatherworn carving. "I'll tell you one thing, Yeo. If we gets stuck up there in the bleeding ice it'll be like shooting fish in a barrel."

Dancy heard the words and gripped the rail and shivered uncontrollably. Knowing he was at last afraid.

339

LINDSAY peered at his luminous watch. Six o'clock. He walked to the port side to watch as fragments of broken ice materialized out of the black water and swirled playfully along the side. Nothing dangerous. . . .

A telephone buzzed and a messenger said urgently, "It's the doctor, sir."

Lindsay swore silently and groped across the deck to the handset. "Captain. Can't it wait?"

Boase sounded edgy. "Sorry, sir. It's Lieutenant Aikman. He's locked himself in his cabin. I think he's upset."

"*Upset?*" The word hung in the air. "What do you want me to do, for God's sake?" Lindsay made an effort to steady his voice. "Do you really think he's in trouble?"

Boase replied, "Yes, sir."

As Lindsay stood with the telephone to his ear, the hands of the bulkhead clock showed eight minutes past six.

At that precise moment several small incidents were happening. Small, but together they amounted to quite a lot.

Able Seaman Laker was being relieved from the crow's nest by a seaman called Phelps. As they clung together on the swaying iron gratings outside the pod Laker was shouting in the other man's ear about the stupid, bloody maniacs who had fitted such a piddling little heater for the lookout. Neither of them was paying much attention to the sea beyond the bows.

On the forward well deck a seaman fell from a bollard and slithered like a great black crab across the ice and came up with a thud against a hatch coaming.

The lookouts on Numbers One and Two guns turned to watch his clumsy efforts to regain his feet, while the rest of the deck party paused to enjoy the spectacle as well.

On the bridge Dancy was remembering Aikman's stricken voice, his pathetic self-defence under Stannard's anger and the Captain's questioning. He turned to peer at Lindsay's vague outline at the rear of the bridge.

All small incidents, but as Dancy turned back to his clearview screen he saw in that instant, looming out of the darkness, a

340

solid wedge of ice. For several seconds he was totally incapable of speech or movement.

Then he yelled, "Hard astarboard!" He heard the wheel going over, the gasps of alarm, and added wildly, "Ice! Dead ahead!"

Lindsay dropped the telephone and hurled himself towards the screen, his voice sharp but level as he shouted, "Belay that! Wheel amidships! Both engines *full astern!*"

Then he gripped the rail and stared at the oncoming ice. It was difficult to estimate its size. Probably ten feet high, and some eighty feet from end to end. Against the dark backcloth of sea and clouds it appeared enveloped in vapour. He felt the engines shaking and pounding in growing strength to stop the ship's onward dash, and counted the seconds as the distance shortened. Dancy should not have put the helm over. If the ship hit an ice ledge with her bilge it would slit her open like a huge can. But if he had not even seen it the ship would have smashed into it at full speed, with terrible results.

Stannard came running across the bridge, then stood stockstill beside him, his voice strangled as he said, "We're going to strike, by Jesus!"

It seemed to take an eternity for the ice to reach them. The engines were slowing down, dragging like great anchors even as the ice became suddenly very close, its jagged crest looming past the port bow as if drawn by a hawser.

The crash, when it came, was muted, but the sensation transmitted itself from the keel to the flesh and bones of every man aboard.

"Stop engines!"

Lindsay hurried to the unprotected wing, and watched the ice moving away while the ship idled forward sluggishly.

Stannard called, "First lieutenant's on the phone, sir."

Goss was brief. "Flooding in Number Two hold, sir. I've got the pumps working, and I'm waiting for a report from the boiler room. Their main bulkhead is right against that hold." He paused and then said, "I knew something like this would happen."

"Any casualties?"

"I don't know yet." The question seemed to catch Goss off guard.

"Well, get on with it and let me know."

Lindsay knew what Goss was thinking. What most of the others were probably thinking, too. That their captain had been stark, staring mad to drive the ship like that with ice about. He felt pain and despair crowding his brain.

Jolliffe said, "We're drifting, sir. Ship's head is now three-three-zero."

A messenger called, "Engine room reports no damage to the bulkhead, sir."

Then Ritchie snapped, "Listen! I 'eard a ship's siren!"

Lindsay went out into the freezing air on the starboard wing with Ritchie and Stannard.

"And there's another!" Ritchie peered over the wing.

Stannard said quickly, "Same ship." He was listening intently. "Once I did a spell in a whale factory ship. Some masters used their sirens to estimate the closeness of heavy ice. Bounce back the echoes, so to speak."

Lindsay heard it again. Mournful and incredibly loud in the crisp air. The echo threw back its reply some ten seconds later.

Dancy joined them by the screen. "I—I'm sorry about that helm order, sir. I lost my head."

"You were quite alone at that moment, Sub." Lindsay knew how Dancy was suffering. "And if we had not stopped the engines we would have drowned out that siren."

"Damage control says the pumps are holding the intake, sir. No apparent danger to boiler room bulkhead." A seaman waited, gasping in the cold air. "And only one casualty—a broken wrist."

Lindsay nodded. "Good. We'll try and close on that siren, Pilot. And we'll have some extra lookouts on the boat deck."

Stannard's face suddenly lit up in a violent red flash. The savage crash of gunfire echoed across the water.

Lindsay dashed through the open door, glasses hanging against his chest as he shouted, "Half ahead together!" Around him men were slamming the steel shutters, and he added, "Leave the centre one!" As he cranked it open he heard the sudden surge of power from the engines as once more the ship began to push forward.

"Steer for the flashes, Cox'n!"

A ball of fire exploded and fanned out to reveal the outline of a ship less than two miles away, her superstructure burning fiercely. There was ice all round her, jagged prongs enclosing her like a trap. Another ripple of flashes came from her opposite beam, and Lindsay saw one more bright explosion below her bridge. The siren was bellowing continuously with probably a dead man's hand dragging on the lanyard. It sounded like a beast dying in agony.

Crisp and detached above the din, a metallic voice intoned, "Control to all guns. Semi-armour-piercing, load, load, load."

More thuds and clicks below the bridge, and somewhere a voice yelling orders. "Target bears Green two-oh. Range oh-five-oh."

Lindsay raised his glasses. Five thousand yards. Maxwell's spotters had done well to estimate the range on the flashes alone.

"Port ten." He watched the ticking gyro. "Midships. Steady."

More flashes blasted the darkness aside and joined with those already blazing on the helpless ship. Lindsay could see her twin funnels, great pieces of wreckage falling into the fires and throwing up fountains of sparks. Not long now.

Maxwell's voice again. "Starboard battery stand by."

Lindsay lowered his glasses. "Open fire."

Maxwell waited until the hidden raider fired again and then pressed his button. All three starboard guns roared out together. Lindsay held his breath and counted.

"Up five hundred. Shoot!"

Again the guns belched fire and smoke.

"The other ship's going down, sir!" Dancy was shouting.

Lindsay watched as the stricken ship began to tilt over. She must have been hit deep inside the hull. He could see the gaping holes, angry red, and found himself praying there was nobody left to die in such horror.

More distant flashes, and this time he heard shells pass high overhead, whispering like birds on the wing.

Maxwell's bells tinkled again, and seconds later Lindsay heard him shout, "One hit!"

A fire glowed beyond the sinking ship, just long enough for the guns to get off another round each. Then it died. The enemy had turned end on, either to close with this impudent attacker or to run.

"Enemy has ceased fire, sir." Maxwell seemed out of breath.

"Very well." Lindsay watched the other ship's hull getting closer to the sea. "Tell Number One to prepare rafts for lowering."

A sullen explosion threw more wreckage over the other ship's side, then, with a great roar of inrushing water, she dived, the fire vanishing and plunging the sea once more into darkness.

"Prepare both motor boats for lowering, Pilot. Each will tow a raft. Number One will know what to do."

The enemy had gone. Lindsay did not know how he could be sure, but he was. Slipped away again. Leaving blood on the water.

He stood up suddenly. "Yeoman, use the big searchlight. Tell the gunnery officer to expect an attack, but we'll risk it."

As the beam fanned across the heaving water, where the two boats and their tows stood out like bright toys, Lindsay saw the endless litter of charred wreckage, with here and there a body, spreadeagled face down in the water or bobbing in a life jacket, its eyes like small stones as the beam swept low overhead. There was a stench of oil and burned paint.

Stannard strode onto the gratings and said, "The first lieutenant reports that Aikman has tried to kill himself. Cut his wrists with some scissors."

Lindsay nodded. "He couldn't even do that properly, could he?"

He was watching a motor boat as it gathered way towards a dark clump in the water. The other personnel ship was probably farther to the north-west, waiting for light before attempting to brave the ice and the possibility of a new attack.

A torch stabbed across the water and Ritchie said, "One boat 'as got eleven survivors, sir." He turned as the second boat's light winked over the lazy swell. "She's got eighteen, though Gawd knows 'ow she's managed to cram 'em in."

Entry ports in the hull clanged open and ready hands were waiting to sway the survivors inboard.

Goss came to the bridge and said, "Boats secured, sir. I've had to

344

abandon the two rafts. They're thick with ice. I'd never get them hoisted." He added, "There are five women amongst the survivors. I don't know if they'll live after this."

Lindsay gripped the screen. So the Atlantic had cheated him after all. He said, "Take over the con and get under way. I'm going below."

By the time he reached the sickbay he was almost running. As he stumbled past huddled figures cloaked in blankets, Boase looked across at him and said tersely, "We'll do our best, sir."

Lindsay ignored him, his face frozen like a mask. Slowly he stared round at the survivors. Then without a word he turned and began the long climb to the bridge. The engines were pounding again, leaving the fragments bobbing in their wake. She was with them. Back there in the Atlantic.

Take care, she had said. Will see you in Eden.

He reached the bridge. "Take over, Number One. I'm going below for half an hour." He left without another word.

Goss grunted and walked to the empty chair.

LINDSAY tucked his cap beneath his arm as he stepped into Boase's sickbay. A week had passed and in that time the doctor and his staff had done wonders. Three of the survivors had died, two more were still dangerously ill, but it was a miracle any had endured the fires and the freezing cold.

Biggest surprise of all, the five girls had survived. Four of them were sitting in chairs now, dressed in a colourful collection of clothing which the ship's company had gathered. A fifth Wren was in a cot, her burned face swathed in bandages.

Lindsay looked round the long sickbay. He cleared his throat. "As you know, we've been ordered to proceed direct to Liverpool, where you will be landed and my ship can receive repairs."

He looked again at the watching faces. "I have also received a signal that the Japanese have invaded Malaya, and yesterday morning carried out an air attack on Pearl Harbor in the Pacific." He tried to smile as they stared at each other. "So the Americans are in the war with us. We're not alone any more."

Two days after the attack, *Benbecula* had sighted the second personnel ship edging through some drift ice. She had been ordered to Iceland and would be in Reykjavik by now with another escort. *Benbecula* had not been short of company either. As she turned and steamed south once more she had been watched by two long-range aircraft, as well as a destroyer on the far horizon. But it was all too late. And the evidence of it lay and sat around him listening to him as he said, "And remember, you'll all be having Christmas at home." He turned to leave, the words coming back to mock him. Christmas at home.

The Wren with the burned face plucked at his jacket. As he bent over her, she said, "Thank you for coming for us."

Her voice broke Lindsay's careful guard. He took her hand and asked gently, "Did you know Wren Collins? Eve Collins?"

"I think so. I think I saw her by the lifeboats when—" She could not go on.

Lindsay released her hand and said, "Try and sleep." Then he swung round and hurried from the sickbay.

He returned to his day cabin and found Goss and Fraser waiting for him. "I just wanted to go over the docking arrangements at Liverpool." He remembered the other thing and added quietly, "By the way, Number One, you told me that one of *Benbecula*'s sister ships was an A.M.C. in the Far East."

"The old *Barra*, sir. That's right."

"Well, I'm afraid she's been sunk by Jap bombers."

Goss's face crumpled. "That's bad news, sir."

Goss had been third officer in the *Barra* many years back. Her picture hung in his cabin. Now she was gone. *Benbecula* could go like that, in the twinkling of an eye.

Lindsay was saying, "And there's the matter of leave. We should get both watches away for Christmas with any luck."

Goss said, "I'd like to stay aboard, sir."

Lindsay made a note on his pad. "Right then. Now about Number Two hold—"

In his pantry Jupp listened to the muted conversation, and hoped Fraser at least would remain with the captain. He had seen what

346

the girl's death was doing to Lindsay and knew he must not be left alone. He had heard him in his bunk, fighting his nightmares and calling her name like a lost soul in hell.

The bell rang, and with a flourish he picked up his coffee pot and thrust open the pantry door. Something might turn up. And until it did, Lindsay would have his help.

chapter nine

The wardroom stove glowed cheerfully as *Benbecula*'s officers waited for the stewards to open the bar. The ship was moored to a wharf awaiting the move to dry dock and some of the officers glanced repeatedly through the rain-dashed scuttles as if unable to accept the fact. Murky grey buildings instead of a tossing wilderness of angry waves.

As the stewards opened their pantry hatch, Dancy tried to think of some special, extravagant drink to mark his return to safety. Stannard crossed to his side. "Well, Sub, we've made it. All snug and safe. Until the next bloody move!"

He sounded relaxed, and Dancy envied him for it. "What do you think about the Japs, Pilot?"

Stannard looked at him thoughtfully. "God knows." He shrugged. "Still, I guess they've got it in hand by now." He brightened and added, "Now, about that drink. Have it on me."

Dancy frowned. "A brandy and gin."

Stannard stared at him. "*Mixed?*"

"Mixed."

"You greedy bastard! I hope it chokes you."

The door banged open and Goss marched towards the fire. Turning his back on it he barked, "Just pipe down a minute, will you!"

They all paused, suddenly aware of the harshness in his tone.

Goss said, "We've just had news from the Far East. The Japs are still advancing south into Malaya." He swallowed hard. "And they've sunk the *Prince of Wales* and *Repulse*." He did not seem able to believe his own voice. "Both of 'em. In less than an hour! They had no air cover and were overwhelmed by enemy bombers."

"Jesus." Stannard stared at Dancy. "What's the matter with our blokes out there?"

Dancy looked at his glass. Goss's news left him confused and feeling vaguely cheated. They had done so much, or so it had seemed. The quick, savage gunfire in the darkness, the handful of gasping, oil-sodden survivors, it had all been part of something special. The brief announcement about the two great capital ships sunk in some far off, unknown sea had changed it in an instant. It made his own part in things appear small.

Stannard was saying, "My brother's out there in an Aussie battalion. To think his life depends on those stupid Pommie brasshats!" He smiled at Dancy. "Sorry about that. You're quite a nice Pommie, as it happens."

"Thanks." Then he said quickly, "What about coming home with me, Pilot? My people would love to fuss over you. Christmas is pretty quiet but—" He hesitated. All his carefully built up disguise as the intrepid writer would be blown when Stannard met his parents.

"No can do, Sub." Stannard was thinking of the girl he had met in London. He would spend his leave with her. Have one wild party and make it last until the leave was over. He added, "But thanks all the same. Maybe next time, huh?"

Dancy nodded, relieved and saddened at the same time. "Maybe we could meet up somewhere for a drink?"

"Yeah, why not." Stannard grinned. "I'll give you a shout on the blower when I get fixed up." She would probably have forgotten him by now anyway. But she was a real beaut.

A steward called, "Ambulances 'ave arrived to take your people away, sir." Boase extracted himself from the group by the bar.

Dancy said, "Let's go and see them leave, Pilot."

They grabbed their caps and hurried to the promenade deck. There were plenty of the ship's company with the same idea. A ragged cheer greeted the first of the survivors, as on stretchers or walking with attendants they moved towards the gangway.

348

Stannard muttered quietly, "There's Aikman."

The lieutenant was walking slowly along the deck, a suitcase in his hand, a petty officer following him at a discreet distance.

Stannard bit his lip. Aikman was going ashore for medical observation. That was typical of Lindsay, he thought. Most other skippers would have slapped him under arrest to await court martial for negligence, but Lindsay seemed to realize Aikman could not be punished more than he was already.

He said impulsively, "Poor bastard."

Dancy looked at him, recalling Stannard's anger on the bridge, his contempt for Aikman's pathetic efforts to cover his mistake.

Stannard strode forward and asked, "You off then?"

Aikman stopped as if he had been struck. His face was very pale. He said thickly, "Yes. I—I'm not sure quite what—" He looked terrible, far worse than immediately after he had tried to kill himself.

Stannard thrust out his hand and said quietly, "Good luck, mate. I'm sorry about what happened. Could have been any one of us."

Aikman seized his hand and said brokenly. "But it wasn't. It was me."

There were tears running down his cheeks, and the petty officer said cheerfully, "Come along, sir, we don't want to keep 'em all waiting, now do we?"

Dancy said quickly, "So long, sir." Then he saluted and watched Aikman being led down the gangway.

DURING the forenoon of 2nd January 1942, *Benbecula* was warped from dry dock and made fast to her original jetty. All leave for the ship's company was due to expire at noon, and as officers and ratings returned to Liverpool, they could only stare at their floating home with a mixture of surprise and apprehension. The old ship had shed her drab grey, and now rested at her moorings with an air of almost self-conscious embarrassment. From stem to stern, from the top of her single funnel to the waterline, she was covered with dazzle paint, green and ice-blue, black and brown. Only her list remained to prove her identity.

When he returned from his leave, Lindsay sat in his cabin studying the piles of stores folios, signals and the latest Admiralty Fleet Orders.

For Lindsay the leave had been a strange and frustrating experience. He had gone to London and after several attempts had obtained an interview at the Admiralty with a fairly senior intelligence officer. He took with him a lengthy report he had compiled on the raider, and stressed his belief that the Germans were planning another series of widespread attacks on Allied commerce. The officer had been courteous but unhelpful. He knew very little about the raider, other than that she was the *Nassau* which had sunk *Loch Glendhu* and was responsible for other recent losses. She had not returned to Norway, and nobody had heard or seen anything of her.

When Lindsay persisted with his theory, the officer was more definite. There was no evidence to suggest that Lindsay was right. And anyway, the war was quite difficult enough without adding to it with ifs and maybes.

Lindsay groped for his pipe, remembering London. The ruined buildings, the gaps in small terraced houses where the bombs had carved a path like some giant axe. Sandbags around stately Whitehall offices, the blackout, and the wail of air raid sirens, night after night, with hardly a break.

The people had looked tired and strained, as with each new day they picked their way over rubble and firemen's hoses to queue with resigned patience for buses which still somehow seemed to run on time.

When not waiting in an Admiralty lobby Lindsay had walked the East End and dockland, Green Park and the scruffy gaiety of Piccadilly. Quiet, faceless streets south of the river, and the proud skyline of the city etched against the night sky with its criss-cross of searchlights and sullen glow of burning buildings. Once, he had been bustled into an air raid shelter by an indignant warden who had shouted, "Who do you think you are, mate? God or something? You'll get your bloody head blown off if you walk about while there's a raid on!"

He had sat on a bench seat, his back against the cold concrete, while the shelter had quaked and trembled to the exploding bombs. And inside the crowded shelter he had found the same patience, the sense of oneness which had made such a mark on his memory.

From the day he had entered the Navy as a cadet Lindsay had been trained in all matters of the sea and, above all, sea warfare. But nobody had said anything about the other side of it. At Dunkirk and Crete, Norway and North Africa, the lessons had been hard and sharp. Terrified refugees on the roads, scattering as the Stukas had sliced through them with bombs and bullets. Soldiers queueing chest-deep in the sea to be taken off devastated beaches by the Navy, which like London buses always managed to reach them in time. But at what a price.

The loss of his own ship, the agonizing memory of the sinking transport which refused to leave him in peace, had all left their scars on Lindsay. But this last visit to London had shown him more than anything else that he knew nothing of the other war at all. It was not a battle to be contained in a gun or bomb-sight, with an enemy beyond reach or personality. It was right here. It was everywhere. No one was spared, and he knew that if these people with whom he had shared an air raid shelter and all the others like them were to lose faith and hope the end was even closer than some imagined.

Yet in the battered pubs with their watery beer he heard plenty of optimism. On the face of it he could find no reason for it. The war was going badly, and the first relief when it was learned that the Americans were now firm allies, was giving way to an awareness that the real struggle had not begun.

There was a tap at the door and Goss walked in.

"Eight bells, sir. Still seven absentees, but there's been a train delay. They might be on that."

"Thank you. We will be taking on fuel and ammunition this afternoon. We'll work into the dog-watches if necessary."

Goss said suddenly, "I've made it my business to find out where we're going next. I did hear we might be going south."

Lindsay nodded. He had already noted the extra fans and

351

ventilation shafts, and the bright dazzle paint pointed to something more than another Icelandic patrol. He realized too that he did not care where it was, except for one thing. The faint, impossible chance of meeting that raider again.

Goss said, "If we do, I don't think we'll ever get back." He was deadly serious, more troubled than Lindsay had ever seen him.

"While you were away, sir, they got the old *Eriskay*. Only three left now." Goss moved restlessly to a scuttle, his face very lined in the grey light. "They've no right to put them where they can't survive. It's not bloody fair!"

Goss's outburst was both vehement and moving. Lindsay knew he was hitting not only at the nameless warships but at the Service which controlled them.

"I've seen people in London, Number One, who are in much the same position. They've no choice." He hardened his voice. "Any more than we have."

Goss recovered himself. "I know that."

"Well, carry on, Number One."

IMMEDIATELY after lunch, the ship's company turned to briskly loading stores and ammunition.

Fraser stood by the guardrail above the oiler, watching his chief stoker checking the intake, and thinking of his family. For years he had been almost a stranger in his own home, and this time he had been shocked to find his wife suddenly growing old, and his two children like strangers. There had been no tours around the pubs as in the past. Instead, for three whole weeks he had tried to rediscover what he had never known he possessed, and it had been a close, warm Christmas.

The chief stoker squinted up at him. "That feels better, eh, sir? The old girl'll take us anywhere!"

Fraser regarded him dourly. "She'd bloody well do that, Usher! I'll not forgive her if she conks out now."

Above, on the boat deck, Lieutenant Maxwell stared up at the twin mounting abaft the bridge superstructure.

His assistant, Lieutenant Hunter, was saying, "I've checked the communications, sir, and the siting of the mounting is quite good, too."

Maxwell bobbed his bullet head. "Good. Fine. As it should be." He had hardly heard a word.

He still could not accept it. If he had telephoned first he would never have known. Decia, his wife, always seemed to be home, anyway. She had money of her own, and was content to entertain her friends rather than go visiting.

On the last link of his journey down to Hampshire the train had been held up for several hours because of a derailment farther along the line. Then when at last he reached his station there was no taxi, so he had to walk the five miles to his house.

The house was as quiet as a grave, and for a few minutes he imagined she might be away. Then he heard her laugh. A long, excited, sensuous sound. He did not remember running upstairs. In his mind he could only picture the scene captured in the bedside lights.

Decia sitting up and staring at him, her naked body like gold in the lamplight. And the man, open-mouthed and transfixed, one hand still thrust against her thigh. He tumbled from the bed, groping for his trousers, sobbing with terror as Maxwell crossed to his side.

The worst part was that Maxwell had been unable to hit him. The man was paunchy and ridiculous. Not even young.

Maxwell heard him stumbling downstairs, the sounds of his feet across the gravel drive, and then silence.

In the bedroom there was no sound either. Just her breathing and his own heart pounding into his ribs like a hammer.

"Why? In Christ's name, *why?*"

Instead of trying to cover her body she leaned back, her eyes calm. "Why not? Did you imagine I'd be able to go on living like this without a *man?*"

"You bitch!"

Still she did not flinch. "What did you expect? That I could just sit here while you go playing the little hero again? But for this war you'd still be living on my money, pretending to be the retired gentleman, when we both know you were thrown out of the Navy!"

"I was not thrown out. It was an accident. Someone else—"

"Someone else? Oh, it would be. It always is when you fail."

Everything else had been lost in a blur. He could still hear himself screaming down at her, saw her amused contempt change to sudden fright as he struck her across the mouth. He could see her doubled over the side of the bed, her cheeks puffed and swollen, her beautiful lips running with blood.

That last sight chilled his fury. Hesitantly, almost timidly he put one hand on her quivering shoulder.

She turned and looked up at him, her hair disordered across her bruised face.

"Better now, little man?"

Maxwell remembered only vaguely leaving the house. Even as he closed the front door he heard her call after him. *"Bastard!"*

The leave had been spent in a small hotel. He had almost gone mad in his room drinking and going over the scene with Decia again and again. And he had thought about the incident which had ended his Naval career before the war.

He had been young and newly-married to Decia when it happened.

As gunnery officer in a destroyer, he was in charge of a practice shoot. His assistant was a sub-lieutenant, a spoiled, stupid man whom he should never have trusted. Perhaps he was thinking about his new bride. Whatever it was, it had not been the shoot. The sub-lieutenant made a serious mistake with deflection, and instead of hitting the towed target, the shell ploughed into the tug and killed seven men.

The sub-lieutenant had been dismissed the Service with dishonour. But Maxwell was recognized as the true culprit. Only his excellent record had saved him from the same fate. To be required to resign was a lesser punishment in the court's eyes, but to Maxwell it had spelled disaster.

Hunter was watching him carefully. He asked, "Everything all right at home?"

Maxwell turned, his face screwed up with sudden anger.

"You mind your own damn business, right? Do your job and keep the guns in order, that's all I want from you!" He swung away towards the bridge.

A SIGNAL had arrived saying that the commodore would be visiting the *Benbecula* that afternoon. At 1400 hours a staff car drove towards the main gangway, the car door opened and a stocky figure climbed out to stare up at the ship's side, the dull light glinting on his oak-leaved cap and the single broad stripe on his sleeve.

In the captain's cabin Commodore Martin Kemp sat down. Without his cap he became just as Lindsay remembered him from the wardroom party at Scapa. He looked like a man who took pains over his appearance. His features were very tanned, so that his keen blue eyes and the few remaining wisps of grey hair stood out as if independent from the rest of the mould.

He said briskly, "I expect you're wondering why I've come bursting in like this."

Lindsay watched him impassively. "I would be ready to receive you at any time, sir. Would you care for some refreshment?"

Kemp shook his head. "No time. But if you feel *you* would like a drink, don't let me stop you."

Lindsay sat down and tried to relax. He must not let Kemp get under his skin.

"What is it you want to see me about, sir?"

Kemp interlaced his fingers carefully across his stomach. "I have been doing a good deal of work on co-ordination, Lindsay."

"I did hear something about it, sir. But I've been away for several weeks, and of course there has been leave for the whole ship since we came to Liverpool."

Kemp's eyebrows lifted. "Away? Oh yes. The patrol."

Lindsay took out his pipe and gripped it until Kemp's casual dismissal of the patrol faded into perspective.

Kemp continued, "That was a bad show about the convoy." He shrugged, "Past history now."

355

Lindsay said quietly, "It was murder. In my opinion, our people will have to start thinking like the enemy and not acting out the war as if it is a game." His hands were trembling. "To see men die and be helpless to aid them was bad enough. To know it was because of failure to watch the Denmark Strait and the fjord where that bastard was anchored makes it all the worse."

Kemp smiled. "You are still on your hobby horse? I've been hearing about your assault on the Admiralty. No matter. I came to tell you your new assignment. Not partake in amateur strategy."

Lindsay replied, "You don't believe that ships and men's lives are important then, sir?"

Kemp smiled again. "Look, Lindsay, you've had a bad time. I make a point of knowing everything there is to know about my officers. Especially *commanding* officers."

Lindsay looked away. *My* officers. So Kemp was taking the reins.

He said, "I am involved, sir. I cannot just ignore it."

"Of course not. Admirable sentiment. However, you must allow me to understand the overall position and what must be done to contain whatever the Hun intends to do."

Lindsay watched him with sudden realization. There was something old-world about Kemp. The *Hun*, for instance. It had a First World War, *Boys' Own Paper* ring to it. God, if Kemp thought he could introduce cricket into the Atlantic he was in for a shock. He felt anger rising like a fever.

"Drastic situations call for drastic measures, Lindsay. I will be speaking to everyone concerned tomorrow, but I felt you should be put in the picture first." He stood up and walked to a scuttle. "The situation in Malaya is grave, but one thing is certain. Singapore will be held. We can soon retake the initiative on the mainland."

Lindsay massaged his eyes. What was Kemp saying? That *Benbecula* was to go to the Far East?

Kemp became very grave, so that his eyes seemed to sink into the wrinkles like bright buttons.

"Reinforcements are to be sent out forthwith. A fast convoy, under my command, will sail in four days. Armoured vehicles and anti-aircraft weapons, troops and supplies, and everything else they'll need for a siege."

Lindsay tensed. "Around the Cape, sir?"

"Of course. Non-stop to Ceylon. From there the troops and supplies will go on in smaller ships with fresh escorts." He rubbed his hands. "That will keep the moaning minnies quiet when they see what can be done with a bit of initiative."

Lindsay said, "It's thirteen thousand miles to Ceylon, sir. Even allowing for minimum changes of course to avoid U-boat attacks, breakdowns and delays, it will take nearly seven weeks to get there."

Kemp's eyebrows rose a full inch. "I am glad you have such a quick grasp of routes and distances. But I hope you are not suggesting that Singapore will have sunk without trace before that time? We will have a heavy escort, and will go through regardless of what the Hun can throw in our way."

Lindsay stood up. "Look, sir, my idea about this German raider was not just born on the spur of the moment. I believe it is the start of something which could put our convoy into real danger. We're fighting on two oceans now. The Americans can't be expected to help us until they've replaced some of their losses at Pearl Harbor."

Kemp picked up his cap. "I am not concerned with the American Navy, Lindsay. That is hardly my worry." He smiled grimly. "I know you're fretting about having this old ship to command. With any luck I may be able to help towards something better." His smile vanished. "But I do not expect to hear any more of this defeatist talk."

Lindsay followed him from the cabin and saluted as Kemp hurried down the gangway. If he was coming along for the ride he might at last realize what he was up against. Or kill all of them.

Lindsay remembered Goss's words. *I don't think we'll ever get back.* Then he thought of the commodore and quickened his pace towards the bridge. I'll get them all back, if it's only to spite that pompous fool, he thought.

Jupp was waiting for him and said, "South Atlantic then, sir?"

Lindsay sat down wearily. "Who says?"

Jupp showed his teeth. "Some fur-lined watchcoats 'ave just arrived, sir." He spread his hands. "If they sends us that, then we just 'ave to be goin' to the sunshine, it stands to reason."

Lindsay nodded. "Except for the word *reason*, Jupp, I'm inclined to agree."

chapter ten

"Forenoon watch closed up at defence stations, sir." Stannard saluted formally.

"Very good, Pilot."

Lindsay lifted his glasses to study the regularly spaced lines of seventeen ships.

The convoy had been at sea for four days, steaming in three columns, the centre one being led by the *Madagascar*, a heavy cruiser, mounting twelve six-inch guns. She was followed by two oil tankers and then the most hated member in the group, a large ammunition ship which steamed directly ahead of the *Benbecula*. Troopships, one of which was the *Cambrian*, with the commodore on board, led the two outer columns of freighters carrying aircraft and armoured vehicles of every kind.

Lindsay readjusted his glasses to watch one of the destroyers zig-zagging, fast and aggressive and graceful, some five miles ahead of the convoy. All around them the horizon was bare, with the enemy-occupied coastline of France some thousand miles away on the port beam.

"Signal from commodore, sir." Ritchie was wide awake. "Alter course in succession to two-two-zero."

"Acknowledge."

Ritchie steadied his telescope. "Execute."

Like ponderous beasts the ships moved slowly onto their new course. A destroyer swept down between the lines, signal lamp flashing at a rust-streaked freighter which had edged badly out of station. As she dashed abeam of *Benbecula* her loudhailer echoed across the churned water, "You have a bad list, old chap!"

Stannard snatched a megaphone and ran to the open wing. "You have a loud voice, old chap!" He sounded angry.

He came back breathing hard. "Stupid sod!"

Lindsay asked, "Have you heard how your brother is getting on?"

"Not much." Stannard stared gloomily towards the nearest ship. "My dad will miss young Jason, I guess. It was bad enough for my folks when I scarpered off to sea."

Ritchie called, "Signal from *Merlin*, sir! Aircraft bearing zero-eight-zero!"

Lindsay strode to the port wing and levelled his glasses over the screen at the black splinter etched against the sky.

"It'll be a Focke Wulf reconnaissance plane. Long-range job. It'll not come within gunshot unless by accident."

The Focke Wulfs were like great eagles. They could cover many hundreds of miles of ocean, where there were no fighter planes to pluck them down and no guns to reach them as they circled round a convoy, their radio operators sending back vital information to the U-boats.

"Signal from commodore, sir." Ritchie stood in the doorway. "Maintain course and speed. Do not engage."

Do not engage. Lindsay felt despair like pain. What did the bloody fool imagine they could do?

Dancy said, "Is it bad, sir?"

"Bad but not critical, Sub. We will be altering course at dusk. That may throw them off the scent. If we can keep up this speed we should soon be out of range. Keep an eye on him, Sub. I'm going to check the chart."

Dancy turned to Stannard. "With an escort like ours we *should* be all right."

"Too right. The destroyers can cope with the subs. And the cruiser can beat the hell out of the captain's raider."

"Is that how you see it?"

"The raider?" Stannard shrugged, remembering Lindsay's agonized voice on the telephone as he relived his nightmare. "Every man has to have something in a war. Something to hate or hope for. A goal, personal ambition, who knows?" He glanced round quickly to make sure the nearest lookout was out of earshot. "Sorry I couldn't give you a ring, Sub. Got a bit involved. You know how it is. Still, I expect you had some little sheila to keep the cold out, eh?"

Dancy tried to grin. "I did all right." He did not want to think of his leave, of his mother complaining about rations, his father telling him how the war should be waged.

Stannard raised his glasses and studied the ammunition ship for several seconds. "Check her bearing again, Sub. I think she's off station."

I must be losing my touch, Stannard thought. He had never believed in love at first sight, but it had happened to him. Just like that. And there was no future for either of them.

He had taken a taxi to the flat, and it was all exactly as he remembered. But another girl opened the door. When he identified himself she said calmly, "Oh, *she* left some weeks back."

Stannard had been taken aback. He left without a word.

And then, a few days later, as he was walking aimlessly down a London street, an air raid had started, and he had run into a shelter. When, thirty minutes later, he emerged, it was almost dark and pelting with rain.

It was then he noticed her, a girl standing in the doorway of a bombed shop clutching a paper bag and staring at the rain in dismay. Without hesitation he took off his greatcoat and slung it across her shoulders before she could protest.

"Going far? Well, I'll walk you there, if you like. We'll be company for each other if there's another raid."

And that was how it had all begun. She lived in a small house close to Putney Bridge. At the door she looked at his dripping uniform and said quietly, "Would you like to come in for a minute?"

Her name was Jane, and she was married to an Army captain.

As Stannard gave her his greatcoat to hang by the fire he saw her husband's picture on the sideboard. A nice-looking chap standing with some other soldiers in front of a tank.

"I'd offer you a meal but I'm afraid I've only got some Spam."

She was dark and very attractive. She opened the rain-splashed parcel and took out a small, brightly coloured hat.

"I was being extravagant. I wanted everything to be just right."

Stannard glanced at the photograph but she said quickly, "No, it's not that. But he'll not be coming home yet. He's in the Western Desert. I've not seen him for two years."

Stannard reached for his greatcoat. "I've got something better than Spam. I was bringing it for—"

Then she smiled. "So we were both let down?"

Try as he might, Stannard could not remember the exact moment which brought them together. All he could recall was her fierce passion as she had given herself, pulling him to her as if there were only minutes left before the world ended. Once, as Stannard lay awake, he felt her crying against his shoulder, very softly, like a child. But she was asleep, and he wondered if she was thinking of that other man, somewhere in the desert with his tank.

The next day he checked out of his hotel and stayed at the little house near Putney Bridge until the end of his leave.

She had said, "I'm not sorry for what we did. You know that, don't you? It wasn't just because you, *we* were lonely. You must know that, too."

On the crowded train he tried to rationalize his feelings. It was over. An episode, inevitable in this bloody war. He had wanted her. She had been starved of love for two years. That was all there was to it.

When Lindsay told him of the convoy and the long haul round the Cape to Ceylon he tried again. Time and distance would end it. But in his heart he knew he would have to see her again.

Feet moved on the gratings and Lindsay said, "We've had a signal from Admiralty, Pilot. Four plus U-boats in our vicinity. You'd better put your plotting team to work." He glanced at his watch. There was still plenty of time. The hunters and the hunted knew their skills, just as they knew how easily their roles could be changed.

"I'm going below. Call me if you hear anything," he said.

361

IT WAS dusk when the first torpedoes streaked into the convoy. Aboard the *Benbecula* the hands had been sent to action stations, with nothing to do but listen to the thundering roar of the *Merlin*'s depth-charges and watch tall columns of water bursting skyward as the destroyer swung round for yet another run-in across the hidden submarine. She had been joined by the other wing escort, while the other destroyers tore back and forth like nervous dogs around a valuable flock of sheep.

Merlin reported she had lost contact. The U-boat might have been damaged or it could be a ruse to allow for evasive action. Either way, *Merlin*'s attack had given the convoy more time.

Lindsay sat on his tall chair and watched the ships on either bow as darkness closed in. They were moving faster now, making a good fourteen knots.

Dancy said, "It looks as if we may have given them the slip this time, sir."

Lindsay shrugged. "If the escorts can keep them down, yes. But if they surface they can make a fair speed, too."

Stannard snatched up a shrilling handset. He swung towards Lindsay. "Masthead reports torpedoes approaching on the port quarter, sir!"

Lindsay jumped from his chair. "Full astern!"

When he reached the bridge wing he saw the pale lines cutting across the dull water. His brain recorded their bearing and speed even as he noted the flash of signal lamps, the muffled squawk of the R/T speaker as the alarm ran like wildfire along the lines of ships.

He craned over the screen, straining to watch the nearest track as it sped for *Benbecula*'s port bow. Nothing happened. The torpedo must have missed the ship by less than twenty feet.

"Resume course and revs, Pilot!"

There was a single, muffled explosion which seemed to come from miles away. As he ran to the starboard wing he saw a searing column of fire, then a billowing wall of smoke completely hiding the victim from view.

The torpedo must have run diagonally right through the convoy, hitting a freighter just astern of the commodore's ship. He guessed the U-boat commander had fired at extreme range, fanning his torpedoes in the hopes of getting a lucky hit.

Depth-charges boomed across the water, and over the R/T Lindsay heard an unemotional voice say, "Have contact. Am attacking."

The *Pole Star*, the freighter astern of the torpedoed ship, was already swinging wildly out of line, her tall hull glowing scarlet in the reflected flames.

A destroyer was charging down the lines of ships, and faintly above the grumble of depth-charges and engine room fans Lindsay heard her loudhailer bellowing. "Keep closed up, *Pole Star! Do not heave to!*"

Stannard said thickly, "God, look at her."

The stricken freighter was beginning to heel over, and in the leaping flames and sparks it was possible to see the deck cargo of army lorries starting to tear adrift and go crashing through the tilting steel bulwarks as if they were matchwood.

The destroyer swept down *Benbecula*'s side, her wash surging against the hull plates like a great wave breaking on a jetty.

Dancy called, "*Pole Star*'s stopping, sir."

Someone else said hoarsely, "He's going to try and pick up survivors!"

Lindsay watched the sinking freighter swinging helplessly abeam in the heaving water. The *Pole Star* obviously intended to ignore the escort's order, and already he could see a boat jerking down its falls.

"Starboard ten." For a few seconds nobody moved or spoke. Then Lindsay watched the bows swinging very slowly towards the burning ship. "Midships." The bows edged round until the motionless *Pole Star* suddenly appeared in direct line with the stem.

"Steady." Lindsay hurried out on the wing again. Over his shoulder he snapped, "Yeoman, make to *Pole Star*. Resume course and speed. Do not stop."

He heard Ritchie's shuttered lamp clicking busily but kept his eyes fixed on the ship ahead.

Stannard exclaimed, "We'll ram her if we keep on this course, sir!"

"Exactly." Lindsay did not move.

Ritchie said, "*Pole Star* requests permission to pick up survivors, sir."

"Denied!"

"*Pole Star* is under way again, sir."

"Port fifteen."

Lindsay stayed by the screen, his heart pounding in time with the engines. The *Pole Star*'s master had ignored a necessary signal to try to save a few lives. It had taken the sight of *Benbecula*'s massive bows to make him change his mind. As the freighter turned heavily onto her proper course the sinking ship drifted into view. Lindsay watched the blazing hull fixedly as if under a spell. Most of the freighter was ablaze now and she was going down by the stern.

A signalman called, "Sir! There's men in the water!"

Ritchie said harshly, "Just you watch the commodore's ship, Bunts!"

But the signalman turned towards him, his voice breaking. "But Yeo, there's blokes down there! I saw one wavin' at us!" He sounded close to tears.

Ritchie strode across the gratings and gripped his arm. "Wot d'you want us to do, lad? Bloody well stop and get blown up ourselves? Up at the 'ead of the convoy there's two troopers with Gawd knows 'ow many squaddies on board, see? We've got to stick together!"

The signalman was little more than a boy. "I know that, Yeo." He dashed one hand across his eyes and picked up his Aldis lamp. "It's just that—"

Ritchie interrupted gently. "You don't 'ave to spell it out, lad." He sighed as the signalman moved slowly to the opposite side of the bridge. Away from the dying ship.

The bosun's mate by the voicepipes said bitterly, "Look at the skipper. Just standin' there watchin' 'em fry!"

Ritchie pivoted on his heels and thrust his face within inches of

364

the seaman's. "If I 'ear you talk like that again I'll 'ave you on a charge! The skipper's worth twenty of your sort, an' you'll eat your bloody words if you lives long enough!"

Lindsay heard none of it. He watched the other ship's bows begin to rise slowly above the litter of drifting flotsam, heard the dull roar of inrushing water as she slid steeply under the surface. Then nothing.

A messenger said, "Sir, from W/T office. Six plus U-boats in convoy's vicinity."

Stannard snapped, "Very well. Tell my yeoman in the chart room."

He walked out to the wing, sucking in the cold air like a man brought back from drowning. He said, "Poor bastards. D'you think the escorts will be able to find any of them, sir?"

Lindsay's shoulders sagged. "Listen." Astern the depth-charges were rising to a drumming crescendo.

Stannard had seen many hundreds of dead and gutted fish left in the wake of a depth-charge attack. Men in the water would fare no better, except they would know what was coming.

Lindsay continued to stare astern, his mind cringing from the suddenness of death. He should be hardened, as his half-trained company imagined him to be. But you never were. Close the ranks. Don't look back. His mouth twisted in a tight smile. That was the most important bit. Don't ever look back.

Stannard saw the smile and said quietly, "I'm sorry, sir. I didn't understand."

Lindsay turned his back on the sea and looked at Stannard.

"Stop thinking about those men, Pilot." He saw Stannard stiffen and added coldly, "Another few feet and it would have been us."

An hour passed with nothing to break the regular beat of engines, the sea noises beyond the bridge. Ritchie found Lindsay in his chair. "From escort, sir. No survivors."

"And no U-boats sunk."

"No, sir."

Lindsay turned in the chair. "Pass the word to get some hot soup and sandwiches for all hands."

As Ritchie beckoned to a messenger, Dancy called, "The first lieutenant's on the phone, sir, wants to know if he can fall out action stations."

"No." As Dancy turned back to his telephone he added quietly to Stannard, "Cold and uncomfortable it may be. Cursing me they most certainly are. But if we catch a torpedo I want as many people as possible on deck, where they've got a chance."

Stannard walked to the starboard side where Dancy was peering through his night-glasses at the ship ahead.

Dancy lowered them. "He cares, doesn't he?"

Stannard nodded slowly. "By Christ, and how he cares. I saw his face when we steamed through those wretched devils in the drink back there. I've sailed with some skippers in my time, but never anyone like this."

THIRTEEN days out of Liverpool found the convoy steaming due south, with the Cape Verde Islands some three hundred miles on the port beam. Instead of leaden grey the sea was now a deep blue, and above the spiralling mastheads the sky was of paler hue with a few frayed banners of cloud.

Not only the weather had changed. The convoy was steaming now in two lines. The day after the first ship had been torpedoed the *Pole Star* had been attacked and had sunk in minutes. That same day one of the escorts had been hit and sunk.

Encouraged by their success the U-boats made a surface attack under cover of darkness, only to be caught and pinned down by starshells from a destroyer which had dropped astern of the convoy. In the eerie glare of drifting flares she opened fire. One U-boat managed to dive without being hit, but another received several shells so close alongside it was unlikely she would ever reach home. The destroyer had rammed the third just abaft the conning tower, riding up and over the low whaleback of her casing with a scream of rending metal. Like a gutted shark the U-boat rolled over, breaking apart as the destroyer continued to grind and smash across her.

When daylight came the men on the rearmost ships of the

convoy lined the guardrails to cheer the victorious destroyer as she turned away for the dangerous passage to Gibraltar. With her bows buckled and her forecastle gaping open she would be out of the war for some time to come. She had made a sad but defiant sight as her low silhouette had finally faded astern, and there were few men in the convoy who had not prayed for her survival.

chapter eleven

Thirteen days. Two escorts gone and three merchant ships. The two remaining lines were led by the commodore's troopship, *Cambrian*, and the cruiser *Madagascar*. Just four ships in each line, with *Benbecula* now steaming directly abeam of the ammunition freighter. The early dislike and fear of her had given way to a kind of nervous admiration. Day in, day out, she was always there. Big and ugly like her name, *Demodocus*, she was a coal-fired ship, and usually on the receiving end of some caustic signal about making too much smoke, but either her master didn't give a damn or her chief engineer had his work cut out just to keep the boiler from bursting.

Lindsay sat in his chair thankful that for the past twenty-four hours there had been neither an attack nor any more reports of U-boats. The hands had been able to get some rest, enjoy a properly cooked meal, and above all be spared the jarring clamour of alarm bells.

Lieutenant Maxwell had the forenoon watch, and he was out on the port wing staring at the ammunition ship, his cap tilted over his eyes against the glare. Lieutenant Paget, Aikman's replacement, stayed on the starboard side, unwilling to stray out of Maxwell's vision in case he was needed.

Petty Officer Hussey, the senior telegraphist, walked to Lindsay's side and saluted. "The usual bulletins, sir. No U-boats. The Japs are still advancing, though. They've reached a place called Batu Pahat." He grinned. "Could be in Siberia as far as my geography is concerned, sir."

367

The rear door slammed back. "What was that?" Stannard came out of the chart room, his brass dividers grasped in one hand. "Batu Pahat's only sixty miles from Singapore, for God's sake! It can't be true."

Lindsay watched him. "I expect your brother has been pulled out by now anyway. If Singapore Island is to be the real holding-point it would be the obvious thing to do."

Stannard nodded. "I guess so. But surely to God the people in charge out there can see what's happening?"

A signalman shouted, "Signal from escort, sir! *Merlin* has strong contact at zero-nine-zero. Closing!"

Lindsay snapped, "Sound action stations!"

As bells shrilled through the ship he walked to the port wing. Ritchie was already here, brushing crumbs from his jacket and still chewing as he snatched his telescope and shouted, "From commodore, sir. Alter course to two-five-zero!"

"Acknowledge."

Lindsay gripped the screen, feeling the ship vibrating under his fingers as voicepipes and telephones burst into life.

Ritchie's telescope squeaked as he readjusted it on the leading ships. "Execute in succession, sir!"

Stannard was already at the gyro compass, his face expressionless while he studied the column wheeling slowly to starboard.

Ritchie said, "*Merlin*'s got 'er black pennant 'oisted, sir! She's goin' in for a kill!"

"Starboard ten." Stannard's mouth twitched as a pattern of depth-charges exploded somewhere on the port quarter. The *Merlin* was moving at speed and swinging in a wide arc.

"Midships." Stannard watched the *Demodocus* following round obediently. More explosions, and a second escort came tearing down the column, racing for the great spreading area of churned water where the last charges had exploded.

As she ploughed through the white froth Lindsay saw the charges fly from either beam, while two more rolled from her quarterdeck rack into her own wash. Even though he was expecting it he flinched as the charges detonated.

"*Madagascar*'s signallin', sir!" The man's voice was shrill. "Torpedoes approachin' from starboard!"

Already the cruiser was turning her grey bulk towards the torpedoes, while far away across the commodore's bows a destroyer was racing in to give additional cover.

"Must be two of the bastards, sir!" Stannard raised his glasses and added sharply, "Watch the ship ahead, Cox'n. Follow her like a bloody sheepdog, no matter what!"

"Aye, aye, sir." Jolliffe eased the spokes and kept his eyes fixed on the oil-tanker.

"Missed her anyway!" A double explosion rattled the bridge screen and brought down flecks of paint.

The freighter astern of the cruiser had been hit. She was already staggering to port, thick smoke billowing from her side. There was a sudden internal explosion; the bridge superstructure appeared to lift, the funnel buckling and pitching into the smoke as if made of cardboard. She was certainly sinking, but as the convoy fought to maintain formation she was a very real menace.

"Commodore's signalled *Rios* to take evasive action, sir!"

The *Rios* was astern of the torpedoed freighter, and with something like a prayer Lindsay watched her turn unsteadily and head diagonally from the broken column.

"Torpedo to port, sir!" Dancy had the masthead telephone gripped so tightly his knuckles were white. "Two cables!"

Lindsay saw the flurry of excitement on the ammunition ship's bridge. It must be running straight for her.

A man screamed, "If she goes up we'll go with her!"

"Silence on the bridge!" Jolliffe's voice was like a saw, but his eyes stayed on the ship ahead.

It was more of a sensation than a sound. Lindsay saw the *Demodocus* stagger, her foremast and derricks falling in tangled confusion even as the telltale column of water shot violently above her fore deck.

Nobody spoke or moved. As she slowed down and fell past *Benbecula*'s port beam, to those watching her it felt as if there were just seconds left to live. The sea and sky, the sinking freighter, the depth-charges and fast-moving destroyers, none of them counted for anything now.

Lindsay rubbed his eyes. The old *Demodocus* was still there. There was plenty of smoke, and he heard the discordant grinding of her port anchor cable running out. The explosion must have blasted away a capstan or sheered right through the forepart of the lower hull.

"They're callin' us up, sir." Ritchie watched a small winking light from the other ship's bridge.

"Have fire in forrard hold. Am holed port side but pumps are coping." He shuttered an acknowledgment before saying thickly, "An 'e says that there *is* a God after all!"

A telephone had been buzzing for some seconds. Or minutes.

A messenger said, "W/T office reports the escorts have sunk another U-boat, sir. Definite kill."

Lindsay wiped his face. "That will keep them quiet for a bit." He felt unsteady on his feet.

"From the ammo ship, sir." Ritchie smiled grimly. "Can't never pronounce 'er name, sir. She's tellin' the commodore she can only manage five knots till they've carried out repairs. But the fire's almost under control. There was no ammo in *that* 'old, sir." He watched the slow winking light. "But the next 'old is filled to the brim with T.N.T."

Lindsay looked at Stannard. "She may still have to abandon. Tell Number One to warn the boat crews and lowerers."

The *Merlin* was edging past the *Demodocus*. As she moved into full view, her loudhailer boomed into life. "I have a message for you, Captain!"

Lindsay trained his glasses on the slow moving destroyer. Her captain's face swam into the lenses, reddened by sea and wind, but the same man he had seen in the office at Scapa. He, at least, had something to be proud of. He had sunk a U-boat and damaged at least one other.

Lindsay picked up the megaphone and shouted, "Well done, *Merlin*!"

As he said the words he felt a new upsurge of resentment and despair. To this young destroyer officer *Benbecula* would be seen as nothing more than a big, vulnerable liability.

The loudhailer continued, "From commodore. You will stand by *Demodocus* and act as her escort. The risk to the troopships is too great to slow down." He added almost apologetically, "The cruiser too is somewhat naked under these conditions." The destroyer gathered speed. "By dawn tomorrow you should be joined by other escorts. But I'm pretty sure there are no more U-boats in the vicinity now. If there are, they'll keep after the convoy."

Lindsay lifted one hand to him. "Good luck!" He turned his back on the other ships. "Signal *Demodocus* to take station astern. Find out her exact speed and reduce revs accordingly."

The escorts re-formed and the cruiser altered course to lead the single line of merchantmen away. In an hour there was little to see.

Ritchie said quietly, "Now 'ere's a fine thing, Swain."

Jolliffe darted a glance at the officers and nodded. "I know. A D.S.O. for the commodore, D.S.C. for the escort commander, and medals all round, I shouldn't wonder." He grinned. "An' us? We'll be lucky if we sees the bloody dawn tomorrow!"

Ritchie called, "Ammo ship 'as R/T contact now, sir."

Lindsay strode quickly to the W/T office where Hussey and his telegraphists slumped wearily in their steel chairs.

Hussey said, "Here you are, sir." He handed a microphone to Lindsay and added, "Permission to smoke, sir? My lads are just about dead beat."

Lindsay nodded and snapped down the button. "*Benbecula* to *Demodocus*. This is the captain speaking. How is it going?"

A tired voice replied, "Thanks for staying with us. We're not doing too bad. The collision bulkhead is weeping a bit and there's still a fire in the forrard hold. We've no breathing apparatus, so nobody can work down there for more'n minutes at a time." They heard his sigh very loud on the speaker. "Can't make much more'n four knots. If that bloody bulkhead collapses the hold will flood." He laughed. "Still, better that way than how the Jerry intended, eh?"

Lindsay said, "Keep a good lookout astern, Captain. I'm going

371

to drop a boat and send you some breathing gear and extra hands."

"I'm obliged." A pause. "A doctor too if you can spare him. Mine was killed by the blast and I've twelve lads in a bad way."

"Will do." Lindsay saw Ritchie in the doorway. "Tell the first lieutenant. Quick as you can."

All afternoon the work on the burning hold and the clearing of débris from the fore deck of the *Demodocus* continued while the two ships ploughed across the blue water at a snail's pace. The last dog-watch had almost run its course when a signalman said sharply, "There's someone callin' us up, sir!"

Ritchie was across to the open wing before Lindsay could move from his chair.

The signalman pointed. "There. On the upper bridge, Yeo."

One of the ammunition ship's officers was dimly outlined against the outdated compass platform, his arms moving very slowly like a child's puppet.

Ritchie raised his telescope, gasped and said, "'E says there's somethin' astern, sir. Five miles or thereabouts." He looked quickly at Lindsay. "Could be a submarine."

Lindsay lowered his glasses. "That captain is a very clever man, Yeoman. Most men as tired and worried as he must be would have used a lamp, or even worse, the R/T."

To Goss, hurrying from the chart room, he added, "Reduce to dead slow and close the gap. We *must* keep visual contact. Their lookouts may be able to see the U-boat, but if we try and turn they'll know we've spotted them."

A messenger called, "W/T office reports no signals, sir."

As the U-boat hadn't fired, nor made any signal, it was possible it had been damaged in that last attack. Maybe she could not dive, or her torpedo tubes had been put out of action by depth-charges. But she was back there all the same. Limping along like a wounded wolf, and every bit as dangerous. Lindsay stared at the dipping sun. It was too high. The slow-moving ships would stand out against the horizon as perfect targets for another half-hour, maybe longer.

"I think the U-boat is going to close and use his deck gun."

372

Goss stared at him. "But if they get one shell into that bloody ship—" He could not go on.

Stannard said tersely, "Shall I signal them to abandon, sir? We could drop all our boats and rafts and maybe come back for them later."

"Leave her, you mean?" Lindsay spoke very quietly. "Run away?"

Goss said, "It's not that. We've our own ship to consider."

A signalman called, "The Yeoman says that the ammo ship can still see the U-boat. On the surface, full buoyancy."

No U-boat would chase after its prey fully trimmed to the surface. It *must* be damaged. It was their only hope.

"Tell the Yeoman to use his Aldis. It should be masked from the U-boat by the other ship. I want the *Demodocus* to start another fire. It'll be damn dangerous, but her captain will know the risks. I want plenty of smoke."

He pushed past the others and snatched up the engine room handset. "Chief? This is the captain. I want you to make smoke, produce the biggest fog in creation! Just as soon as I give the word!"

"Aye, sir." Lindsay heard Fraser yelling to his assistant above the roar of fans. Then he asked calmly, "Might I be told the reason, sir?"

"Yes. We're going to engage a surfaced U-boat."

He dropped the handset as Stannard said, "They've got a fire going already."

Lindsay saw the pall rising rapidly astern. "Sound action stations." He grasped Goss's arm. "I'm going to go hard astarboard in about ten minutes. The fact that the U-boat's made no W/T signals doesn't mean she won't very soon. Her radio may be damaged, but if they once get it going again we're done for." He had to yell above the alarm bells. "So go to damage control, and *pray!*"

Dancy called, "Ship at action stations, sir."

"Very good. Tell control to stand by. Maxwell will have to engage with the starboard battery."

Chris Mauger

He looked at Stannard. "Inform the chief. Make smoke now."

He turned to watch the thick greasy cloud which started to gush over the funnel's lip almost before Stannard had replaced the telephone.

Lindsay took out his pipe and thrust it between his teeth.

"Stop starboard. Full ahead port." He felt the deck shuddering violently to the added thrust on one shaft. "Hard astarboard!"

He glanced through the stern scuttle at the dense smoke. Already the angle was changing. "Starboard engine full astern!"

He turned to face the empty sea beyond the bows. Perhaps it could not be done.

"Midships! *Full ahead together!*"

Heeling steeply, the *Benbecula* thrashed round on a reverse course. Lindsay waited for a first sight of the enemy as, caught by down-draught and change of direction, the wind fanned Fraser's fog screen over the ship in a solid wall. They must be passing the *Demodocus* somewhere to starboard, although her improvised smokescreen was so thick she could have been a mile away.

"Steer zero-one-zero!"

He kept his eyes fixed on the thinning pall of smoke across *Benbecula*'s line of advance. Soon he would know if he had been right. If he were not, and the U-boat was undamaged, one salvo from her bow tubes would be enough. With *Benbecula* working up to her maximum revolutions the effect would be terrible.

Maxwell's voice came over the bridge speaker, detached and toneless. "Starboard battery stand by."

Lindsay saw the two guns moving their muzzles slightly, like blind things in the swirling smoke. Slivers of spray spurted over the bows, and he knew that Fraser's gauges were well into the danger mark now. The old ship was shaking and groaning under the strain.

Maxwell's voice cut the other sound. "Submarine on the surface at Green-two-five! Range oh-eight-oh!"

Lindsay gritted his teeth, willing the smoke to clear so that he could see what Maxwell had seen from his precarious position high above the bridge. There was a brief flash beyond the smoke and

376

seconds later the sound of a shellburst, then another flash, the sullen bang of an explosion.

Lindsay glanced at Stannard and said, "He's shooting at the ammunition ship!"

When he turned again he saw the U-boat. Even at four miles range her austere silhouette was exactly as he had pictured it, the dying sunlight so bright on the slim conning tower that it looked as if it was made of pure copper.

Then the bells rang below the bridge and both six-inch guns fired in unison. Two columns of water burst astern of the U-boat, very white against the darkening horizon.

"Over. Down two hundred." Maxwell sounded so cool he could have been at a practice shoot.

The U-boat was turning, steering almost on a converging course now. She was high on the water. The bells sounded once more and both guns lurched back on their springs as the shells ploughed into the sea to the right of the target.

There was an answering flash from the U-boat's deck gun and Lindsay felt the hull shudder as the shell ploughed alongside and exploded, hurling up a great column of water and smoke.

He felt very calm. Whatever happened in the next few moments would decide the fate of his own ship and the *Demodocus*. But one thing was certain. The German captain could not dive, nor could he use torpedoes. He would have done both by now if it were possible.

Smoke funnelled back from the bows, and Lindsay heard the screeching crash of a shell exploding between decks.

"Range oh-six-two."

He banged the rail by the screen with his fist. The U-boat showed no sign of turning and her gun was firing with greater rapidity. Just one good shot and *Benbecula* could be slowed or stopped while the German manoeuvred to a more favourable position—right ahead of the bows where not a single gun would bear.

A shell ripped past the bridge and Lindsay heard a man cry out. Maxwell snapped, "First aid party on the double!"

377

Stannard yelled wildly, "We've straddled the bastard!" He was almost sobbing with excitement as two waterspouts bracketed the U-boat, burying her after-casing beneath tons of falling spray.

Two tiny figures pitched forward from the bandstand abaft her conning tower, and vanished into the falling deluge of water. One of the shells must have exploded close enough to rake the stern with splinters.

The bridge speaker intoned, "Target is moving right. Number three gun stand by to engage!"

Lindsay said, "I think his steering is damaged."

The U-boat's forward gun flashed once more, and he felt the deck jump beneath him as a shell exploded inside the hull.

The two forward guns belched fire again. A tall waterspout shot skyward beyond the German's hull and the other shell exploded directly against her side.

Lindsay steadied his glasses. "She's going over. Look, Pilot, the gun's crew are baling out." His voice was flat, empty of excitement.

Dark shapes tumbled from the conning tower which was already tilting towards him. Gigantic air bubbles were exploding on the surface alongside, like obscene glassy creatures from the depths.

"Reduce to half-speed. Starboard ten."

Another shell exploded alongside the U-boat's listing hull. Greedily the sea was already clawing along her buckled after-casing, dragging a corpse with it as it advanced.

Lindsay watched without emotion. The Atlantic was having another victory. It was as impartial as it was ruthless.

Dancy called, "Damage control reports flooding in Number Three hold, sir. There's a fire on 'B' deck, too."

"Is Number One coping?"

"Yessir. But one man has been killed, sir. Twenty more wounded by splinters or burns."

"Very well. Make a signal to *Demodocus* and request they send the doc as soon as possible."

There was a yell, "There she goes!" And Lindsay heard wild cheering as the submarine began to slide under the surface. For just a few more seconds she hung with her raked stem pointing straight at the sky, holding the last tip of sunlight. Then she vanished, and a patch of oil spread across the water.

"Slow ahead both engines."

Lindsay walked slowly to the open door and stared at the shattered gyro repeater. Stannard joined him. "Stop engines, sir?"

Lindsay watched the dark shape of a power boat approaching from the ammo ship. "Yes. Put a party of our people in the boat and send it to pick up survivors."

He gripped the rail until the pain steadied him as the ship began to slow down. They had been made to steam past sinking ships. Now there *was* time, so they would obey the code. Except that this time the survivors would be German and not their own.

Goss came to the bridge and said, "Fire's out, sir." He sounded incredibly tired. "The pumps are holding the intake in the hold but the marines' messdeck has been destroyed. God, it looks like a pepperpot on the starboard side!"

Ritchie called from the wheelhouse, "Ammo ship 'as just called us on R/T, sir. That one shell the Jerry slung at 'er seems to 'ave put 'er shaft out of line. 'Er chief says 'e don't reckon on bein' able to get even steerage way now."

Lindsay removed his cap and turned to face the cool evening breeze. After all, they would have to abandon the other ship.

Aloud he said, "If I'd known that before, I think I'd have let those Jerries drown."

Goss watched the motor boat as it started back for the *Benbecula*'s tall side. "Not many of 'em left anyway. The *bastards!*" He went on, "Could we stand by *Demodocus* till morning, sir?"

"Yes." Lindsay replaced his cap. "It would be safer than trying to transfer her crew in the dark."

"I wasn't thinking of that." Goss sounded strangely calm. "We could take her in tow."

Lindsay stared at him. "Do you mean that?"

"I know we're not rigged for it." Goss spoke very quickly, as if he had made up his mind despite inner arguments. "But with some good hands I could work all night and lay out a towing cable. There's not much aft to help secure it, but I thought—"

"The twelve-pounder gun?"

"Yessir. It'll probably never fire again, but it'd make a damn fine towing bollard."

There was so much to do, but all Lindsay could think of now was Goss and his obvious conviction. It was even more than that. It was the first time since he had taken command that Goss had openly shared their mutual responsibility.

He nodded. "Then we'll have a damn good try." He beckoned to Stannard. "Tell *Demodocus* we will stand by until first light. Tell them what we are going to do."

Lindsay watched the motor boat riding on the swell against the ship's rough plates.

"Number One."

"Sir?" Goss paused.

"Tell doc to make some arrangements for the German survivors. His sickbay must be getting rather crowded."

"I'll lay it on." He waited, knowing Lindsay had something more to say.

"And thanks, Number One."

Goss squinted at Lindsay's silhouette dark against the sky, then without a word he vanished down the ladder. He had his pride. It was unshakable, like his faith in this old ship. Just for a few seconds he had almost overcome it. But not quite.

Lindsay walked into the wheelhouse. "Slow ahead both engines. Take the con, Pilot, until we can work out the drift. We don't want to ram the poor old *Demodocus* after getting this far."

Stannard walked to the compass. He had heard most that had been said. He knew what it had cost Goss to make his suggestion about towing. He could have remained silent, but if he had to tow that hulk with his bare hands to prove what his *Becky* could do, then no doubt he would attempt that, too.

A telephone buzzed and the bosun's mate said, "Sickbay, sir. The doctor says there's one Jerry lieutenant amongst the survivors. 'E sends 'is thanks for us pickin' 'im up. Any reply, sir?"

"Tell doc to do what he can for them." Lindsay walked towards the chart room. "But keep that bastard lieutenant off my bridge!"

As the seaman spoke rapidly into the telephone Lindsay added from the doorway, "What do they expect? All pals again now that it's over for them?" His voice in the sudden stillness was like a whip. "Well, not for me, Pilot. But if you happen to bump into this polite German lieutenant on your rounds, you may tell him from me that I only picked them up for one reason. And that was to see what they *looked* like."

He realized they were all staring at him and added curtly, "We will remain at action stations, but make sure the watchkeepers and lookouts are relieved as often as possible. Gun crews can sleep at their stations. And see what you can do about some hot food. There could be another U-boat about, although I doubt it."

Stannard replied quietly, "I'll do that, sir." Lindsay staggered against the open door. "And congratulations, sir. That was a bloody fine piece of work!"

Lindsay remained in the doorway, his face in shadow. "You did well, Pilot." He looked slowly around the darkened bridge. "You all did." Then he was gone.

Jupp came into the wheelhouse. "I've brought some sandwiches for the cap'n, sir."

Stannard strode to the chart room and pulled open the door. Lindsay was sprawled across a locker, his cap lying on the deck. He closed the door gently.

"Leave him, Jupp. Let him rest while he can. He's earned it."

The watch continued, and in the dimly lit chart room Lindsay slept undisturbed either by dreams or memory, his outflung arm moving regularly to the motion of his ship.

AT first light the next day the business of passing a towline was started. It took hours of backbreaking work and endless patience, while Lindsay conned his ship as close as he dared to the drifting *Demodocus*, and Goss strode about the poop yelling instructions until his voice was almost a whisper. Twice the tow parted but the third time it worked.

When two destroyers found them on the following day both ships were still on course, the cable intact.

The senior destroyer made a complete circle round the two ships and then cruised closer to use a loudhailer.

"Glad we found you! It looks as if you've had a bad time!"

Lindsay raised his megaphone. "Have you a tug on the way?"

"Yes!" The other captain brought his ship closer. "You're damn lucky to be afloat! There was a report of a surfaced U-boat shadowing the convoy. But we'll take care of the bastard if she comes this way!"

Lindsay said quietly, "Bring them on deck, Sub."

The German survivors were hurried onto the forecastle and lined up in the bright sunlight. Lindsay waited a few seconds and then called, "We met up with her. But thanks for the offer."

Another day passed before a salvage tug appeared to take the crippled *Demodocus* in tow. Lindsay would probably never meet the ammunition ship's master. But as she wallowed slowly abeam while the tug's massive hawser brought her under control Lindsay saw him standing on his bridge, his hand raised in salute. Along the upper deck his men waved and cheered as the strange ship with a list to starboard and her dazzle paint pitted with splinter holes was lost in a sea haze.

Goss came onto the bridge, his uniform covered in oil and rust. He shaded his eyes to watch the little procession as it turned eastward and then said gruffly, "Well, *that* showed 'em." He turned to Lindsay, "I don't reckon you could have done better, even if you'd been in the Company." He held out his hand. "If you wouldn't mind, sir."

Lindsay took it. He could see the faces round him, blurred and out of focus, just as he could feel the power of Goss's big fist. But he could not speak.

Goss added slowly, "We've had differences, I'll not deny it. She should have been my ship by rights." He stared up at the masthead pendant. "But that was in peace. Now I reckon the old girl needs both of us."

Lindsay looked away. "Thank you for that." He cleared his throat. "Thank you very much." He strode into the wheelhouse and they heard his feet on the ladder to his cabin below.

382

chapter twelve

Lindsay stood on the starboard bridge wing and watched as very slowly the *Benbecula* touched against the massive piles of the jetty. The whole of Trincomalee was packed with shipping of every description, so that the two tugs sent to assist had not found the last few cables easy. Lindsay could see white uniforms on the jetty amidst the hundreds of Ceylonese dockyard workers, faces raised to watch as *Benbecula* handed over her safety to the land once again.

After leaving the ammunition ship they had continued in something like a holiday atmosphere. They had crossed the Equator and all work stopped for the usual boisterous ceremony of Crossing the Line. They paused in Simonstown to replenish the fuel bunkers, and the ship's company swarmed ashore to see the sights. Then they were at sea again, and into the Indian Ocean for the last long haul of the voyage.

All at once their small world changed. The war came crowding in again. The news broke that Singapore had surrendered, and with it, every man unable to escape on the few vessels left afloat by Japanese bombers.

The remains of Commodore Kemp's fast convoy still lay in Trincomalee with other ships which had been expecting to go to Singapore's aid.

Stannard came out to the wing and saluted. "All secure, sir. Permission to clear the bridge?"

"Carry on." Lindsay hesitated and then said quietly, "Look, Pilot, your brother may have been one of the lucky ones."

It was impossible to read Stannard's expression. "I don't know whether I wish him dead or a prisoner. You've heard what the Japs have been doing to prisoners. I'll carry on then, sir." He swung round and hurried into the wheelhouse.

Lindsay ran lightly down the ladders to "A" deck where an entry port had been opened to receive the heavy wooden gang plank from the jetty. He paused and looked at the smoke-grimed

383

paintwork, the scars of deflected splinters, and was suddenly moved. After a destroyer, he had seen this ship as the end of the line. But when the U-boat's last shell had shaken the bridge beneath his feet he had felt something more than anxiety. Affection, love, there was no proper word for it.

Maybe most of his officers had been appointed to her because they were not much use for anything better. The majority of the ratings were untrained, so they too had been sent to make up the required numbers.

But somehow, back there over the hundreds of miles from the Arctic Circle to Ceylon, they had come together, and that was more than could be said for many ships.

Goss was waiting by the entry port, an elegant lieutenant in white drill at his side.

The latter saluted smartly and announced, "Commodore Kemp sends his compliments, sir, and would you join him at his residence for dinner?"

Lindsay nodded. "Very well."

The lieutenant gazed at the splinter holes. "The wires were fairly humming about your U-boat, sir." He sighed. "But we are rather involved with this other unhappy affair at present."

Boots clumped on the planking as the German prisoners marched towards the entry port. Their lieutenant, seeing Lindsay and the others, threw up a stiff salute which was returned with equal formality by Kemp's lieutenant, but Lindsay turned away.

He heard the lieutenant say testily, "That man over there! Don't you know you should stand to attention when an officer passes, enemy or not?"

"*That man there*" was Fraser. Hatless, his boiler suit almost black, he was leaning against a ventilator shaft, bowed with fatigue.

He straightened up slowly and stared at the angry lieutenant.

"*One*, I don't salute any bastard who's been trying to blow my backside off! And *two*, I don't take orders from some snotty-nosed little twit like you!"

Goss said gravely, "This is Lieutenant-Commander Fraser. The chief engineer."

384

The lieutenant blushed. "I—I'm sorry, sir. I didn't understand."
He turned to Lindsay. "I have to go now, sir."

Goss looked down at Fraser and said, "Amazing. I'm surprised
he didn't recognize a real gentleman when he saw you like that."

Fraser eyed him with equal gravity. "In my book a gentleman is
someone who gets out of his bath to have a pee."

Goss turned to Lindsay. "Now you see why we used to try and
keep the engineers away from the passengers in the Company, sir?
Their *refinement* might have made some of them feel inferior."
Then he turned and walked towards the bridge.

Fraser gaped after him. "Well, I'll be damned! He made a
joke!"

Lindsay smiled. "And you asked for it, Chief. If you insult
another up-and-coming admiral I may not be able to save you."

Fraser shrugged. "When the likes of that upstart are admirals
I'll either be tending my garden at home or six feet under it." He
chuckled. "But fancy old John Goss cracking a joke."

COMMODORE KEMP'S temporary residence was a tea-planter's
house, very attractive, white-walled and fringed with palms. A
staff car delivered Lindsay to the door and a houseboy in white
tunic and scarlet sash took his cap and ushered him into a cool,
spacious room. The commodore was standing with his back to a
large portrait showing a bearded Victorian with arms folded and
one foot on a dead tiger.

Kemp offered Lindsay his hand. "Good to see you safe and well."
He snapped his fingers to the servant. "You'll have a drink before
dinner, I imagine."

"Thank you, sir. Scotch."

Lindsay tried to relax. Kemp certainly appeared to be enjoying
his new role, as if the house and all it entailed were his by right.

"I was damn glad to hear about your U-boat. *Merlin*'s captain
was pretty sure he'd done for that one, otherwise I'd never have
left you without another escort, naturally."

"But your ships got through all right, sir."

Kemp shrugged. "Lost the other freighter, I'm afraid. She had a bit of engine trouble." He poured himself another drink. His hand was shaking. "But I *knew* there was no real risk of more U-boats attacking us, so I pressed on."

Lindsay watched him over his glass. "You left him behind."

Kemp looked uneasy. "It should have been safe enough. But the destroyers could find no trace of the poor chap. Must have had an explosion aboard."

Lindsay swallowed his drink. Kemp had abandoned the freighter. Just like *Benbecula* and the ammunition ship.

Kemp walked to one of the wide windows. "Well, there's damn all we can do about it now." He turned, his face set in a smile again. "Now, about you. I gather you've had the repair yard hopping like mad all day. They'll do what they can, of course, but it'll have to be a patch-up job. I've been informed your damage is largely superficial."

"We'll manage, sir." He tried to hide his bitterness. "I was wondering about the next assignment, sir."

"Well, we can't talk shop tonight, eh? This is a welcome break for you." He became serious. "Of course, with Singapore in the enemy's bag there's nothing for all these reinforcements we brought out from U.K. I gather we'll be expected to help get them back in another convoy. But you shouldn't complain. I'll not be surprised if you get a decoration for saving the ammunition ship and sinking the U-boat. Promotion, too, I wouldn't wonder."

"There are several of my people I'd like to recommend for—"

Kemp frowned. "Well, we must wait and see. Everything's in turmoil here. *Merlin*'s captain is being promoted to one of these new killer-groups. Nice young chap. But for your early setback I daresay you'd have been on the list for something of the sort, too."

Lindsay replied calmly, "I lost my ship, sir. I was blown up in another. Many have suffered the same fate." His voice hardened. "Many were less fortunate."

Kemp nodded gravely. "I know, Lindsay. We who face death and live to fight again rarely realize how narrow the margin can be."

Lindsay began to see not merely that Kemp was drunk but that he needed to be so. *We who face death.* Kemp had not been at sea in wartime before this last convoy. Had it really been the vital need of ships and men for Singapore which had made him drive them without letup? Or was it his own fear?

A houseboy appeared in the doorway. "Dinner served, sir."

Kemp lurched to his feet. "The Admiral would like to see you tomorrow. You'll be informed of the time. I'd be obliged if you'd not mention your ideas about commerce raiders. He's quite enough on his plate at the moment."

"Even if it means saving ships and men, sir?"

Kemp seemed to have difficulty in holding him in focus. "That last freighter sank by accident, Lindsay!" He was shouting. "And that's all there is to it!"

Lindsay stood stockstill. He had not even been thinking about that unfortunate ship, except for the fact Kemp had left her unaided. But now, as he followed Kemp's thickset figure to the dining room, his mind was already working on a frightening possibility.

The terrible news about Singapore could be all that was needed to make the Germans take full advantage of their ally's victory. For the next few months naval resources would be stretched far beyond safety limits as troops and supplies were re-deployed to meet the new dangers.

Inside the tea-planter's cool house it all seemed so clear he was almost unnerved. It must be just as plain to those in real authority. Unless. . . . He looked at Kemp's plump shoulders. In past wars it had always taken several years to rid authority of men like him. Admirals, for example, who had scoffed at the trivial consequences of submarine warfare.

He was surprised to find that he was not the only guest for dinner. A bearded surgeon-commander from the admiral's staff and his wife, the commodore's aide, and an elderly major of artillery were already standing round a well-laid table. Midshipman Kemp was also present.

In spite of the fans it was very hot, and the ample helpings of varied curries did little to help matters. There was too much drink. Lindsay was astonished at the way the commodore could put it away, his voice growing louder and more slurred.

Beside Lindsay the midshipman ate his meal in silence until his father suddenly said, "By God, Julian, don't pick at your food! Try and *eat* like a man, if nothing else!"

Lindsay recalled the boy's face after the action. Tight-lipped but determined. Stannard had told him how the midshipman had worked with his plotting team. How he had been sick several times but had kept going. And all that time he had probably been picturing his father speeding to safety, leaving him alone, as he had always done.

Lindsay leaned back in his chair. He felt light-headed but no longer cared. "Actually, sir, he did very well on this last trip."

The commodore said flatly, "You don't know my son or you might think otherwise."

He signalled for more wine, unaware of the sudden tension around the table.

"My son does not like the Service. He would rather sit on his backside listening to highbrow music than do anything useful."

"I think he's old enough to know his own mind." Lindsay could feel his anger returning. "When the war's over he'll be able to make his choice."

"Is that what you think?" The commodore leaned forward, his eyes red-rimmed. "Well, I'm telling you, Commander Lindsay, that I will decide what he will or will not do! No son of mine is going to bring disgrace on my family, do you hear?"

"Perfectly, sir." He gripped his glass tightly to prevent his hand from shaking. "But at present he is under my command, and I will assess his qualities accordingly."

The commodore snapped, "We will take our port in the next room."

Lindsay stood up. "If you will excuse me, sir. I would like to be excused."

The surgeon's wife said hastily, "You must be worn out, Commander. I think you should get some rest."

The commodore only succeeded in rising to his feet with the aid of a servant's arm. "You *are* excused. And as far as I'm concerned you can—" He turned and walked unsteadily to the door without finishing.

Lindsay left the room and waited for a houseboy to fetch his cap. He heard footsteps and saw the young midshipman.

"I'm sorry, sir. I'd not have had this happen for anything."

Lindsay forced a smile. "Forget it. My fault entirely."

"You don't understand, sir." Kemp's face was tight with concern. "I *know* him. He'll try and get his own back on you." He dropped his eyes. "He's not like you, sir. If he were, I'd never have needed to be told to enter the Navy."

The boy's sincerity, his shame and humiliation, made him appear even more defenceless than usual.

Lindsay said quietly, "That was a nice compliment. One which I happen to value very much."

By the time a slow lurching taxi had carried Lindsay back to the jetty a moon had appeared, and in the pale light he could see the *Benbecula* resting against the piles, the dazzle paint vivid and garish. It was very still, and after lighting his pipe Lindsay walked the full length of his ship.

As he passed Stannard's cabin he heard the crash of breaking glass. Dancy was leaning against the rail. "I'd leave him, sir," he said. "There was a message sent aboard just after you left. Pilot's brother is aboard one of the hospital ships. He went across right away. He's been back in there drinking ever since." Dancy rested his elbows on the rail and added, "He saw him all right. But he'd got no arms! And he can't see either, sir!"

Lindsay stared past him towards the distant buildings, so white in the moon's glare. "You've been here all the time?"

Dancy nodded. "Just in case, sir."

Lindsay touched his arm. "I'll not be turning in yet. Come and have a drink in my cabin when he's asleep." He waited. "If you feel like it."

Dancy straightened his back. "Thank you, sir."

Lindsay walked on towards the bridge ladder. In just one evening he had learned a lot about his officers. And himself.

chapter thirteen

For three days no fresh instructions were sent to *Benbecula*. Lindsay had not had the expected interview with the admiral, but at first this omission did not trouble him. He was being kept more than busy with his ship's repairs.

But it was *Benbecula*'s repairs and general replenishment which at last gave him a hint that something odd was happening. Lieutenant Hunter called on him to complain of his inability to secure any six-inch shells, although plenty were available. Goss was perturbed by the lack of attention being paid to his list of repairs by the dockyard staff. Stores were difficult to obtain, and apart from the basic rations of food and clothing, very little seemed available for the *Benbecula*.

Added together, Lindsay felt it was more than mere coincidence.

The ship's company on the other hand accepted the situation with obvious delight. Trips ashore, strange sights of native women and rickshaws, elephants and snake charmers, all made each day an event.

Stannard had been ashore very little. In fact he hardly left his cabin.

Lindsay saw him alone after the night of the commodore's dinner party and asked if he could do anything.

Stannard replied, "Jason's being sent up to a hospital at Karachi tomorrow, sir. After that, they say it'll take time." He looked at Lindsay with sudden anguish. "Just tell me how I'm to write to the old man, sir."

On the morning of the fourth day the summons to naval H.Q. was received, and Lindsay changed into a white uniform which he had not worn since the outbreak of war.

At the gangway Goss had to shout above the rasping rattle of a rivet-gun. "You won't forget about my paint, sir? We're getting very low, and I'm not happy about the port anchor cable."

Lindsay smiled briefly. "I'll do what I can."

Then with one hand to the oak-leaved peak of his cap and the unfamiliar feel of his sword in the other, he hurried down the brow to where a car was waiting.

But at H.Q. he was met by a harassed flag-lieutenant who explained that the admiral had been whisked away to some important conference.

Lindsay spent a further twenty minutes in a small room before the lieutenant reappeared to usher him into an adjoining office. The Chief of Staff came round a big desk and shook his hand.

"Sorry about this mix-up, Lindsay, but no doubt you have seen enough of admirals, anyway. We've been waiting for instructions from Admiralty. Certain recommendations have been made, and it's my duty to inform you of them." He studied Lindsay thoughtfully for a moment.

"The war's speeding up. Increased submarine activity and long-range aircraft have made previous ideas obsolete. Almost overnight, in a manner of speaking."

Lindsay tensed. Something in the Chief of Staff's tone acted like a warning. The man was troubled. No, he was embarrassed.

"My staff are arranging your orders, Lindsay. But I think it best if you know without any more delay. *Benbecula* will return to U.K. as soon as the dockyard say she is seaworthy."

Seaworthy. Not ready for action or patrol duty. She merely had to be able to make the passage home.

Lindsay asked tightly, "And then, sir?"

"Rosyth. I gather they want her as a sort of depot cum accommodation ship for incoming drafts, replacement personnel and so forth." He flicked over some papers. "Your first lieutenant will be promoted to commander upon arrival there. He will also assume command from that time." He tried to smile. "It seems very likely your promotion is already on its way here. I'm glad for you. You've more than earned it."

Lindsay felt as if the walls were moving inward. "And *my* appointment, sir?"

The Chief of Staff did not look up. "The Navy's growing every day. Recruits are flooding the depots like ants. We're having to cut courses rather than lengthen them, and they need the very best help they can get." He plucked at the litter of papers. "I detest this job. I entered the Service to feel a ship around me. I know this work is important and I'm doing more good here than I would be on the bridge of some cruiser in Scapa Flow." He shrugged. "But I still find it hard to take." His eyes lifted to Lindsay's face and he added quietly, "As you will, at first."

"Shore job?"

"They're putting the finishing touches to a new training depot on the east coast. You are to take command."

Lindsay was on his feet. East coast. Shore job. Probably a converted holiday camp or hotel. A white ensign on a flag mast. A ship's bell by the main gate. A temporary illusion for temporary sailors.

He said, "I thought I was going to get—"

The Chief of Staff watched him sadly. "I know. You can appeal against the decision of course, but you know as well as I do what weight it will have."

Lindsay crossed to the window and stared blindly at the courtyard below. Most of the officers who commanded such establishments were old, retired and brought back to the Navy to help spread the load. Men like Commodore Kemp.

He heard himself ask, "I take it this was Kemp's idea, sir?"

"You know I cannot discuss confidential reports." The Chief of Staff added, "But you may draw your own conclusions."

"I *will* appeal."

The other man gave a brief shake of the head. "It is your privilege. However, on the face of things you are being given a just promotion, and I think you should be warned against such a course of action."

A telephone rang and the Chief of Staff snapped, "No. *Wait*." He slammed it back before adding quietly, "I do not know Kemp very well. I would go farther. I do not *wish* to know him very well. But from what I hear of him I would say he is not the sort who would act without apparent justification."

Lindsay strode to the desk and leaned on it, his voice almost pleading. "But there must have been signals, sir?"

392

"Again, they are confidential. But there was a full report made to Admiralty." He looked away. "Including one from the staff medical officer."

Lindsay straightened up, sickened. He recalled the bearded surgeon at the dinner party. Kemp must have planned the whole thing. Must have worked on his first dislike which their meeting at Scapa had begun, in order to destroy him.

Now even the *Benbecula* was being taken. That realization most of all was more than he could bear.

"Look, Lindsay, try not to take this too badly. The war is not going to end next week. And who knows, you may find new orders in England which will make all this seem like a bad dream."

Lindsay thrust out his hand. "I will leave now, sir." He met the other man's troubled gaze. "I would not have been in your shoes for this. Thank you for trying to spare my feelings."

The Chief of Staff smiled. "I feel like an executioner, nonetheless."

Lindsay picked up his cap and walked slowly to the door. It was over. For him and the ship. Outside, the flag-lieutenant handed him an envelope and said, "Here's a brief rundown on appointments, sir. It will be all right to mention them to your people if you so wish."

Lindsay walked through the building and headed for the parked staff car.

He must hold on. Just long enough to reach his cabin. Hide, like Stannard. But he knew it was only a deception. There was nowhere he could hide from himself.

GOSS stood a few paces from Lindsay's desk, listening.

"So you will have the ship after all, Number One. And with promotion, you should be well placed after the war with shipping companies." Goss's silence was like something physical. "Aren't you pleased? I thought it was what you wanted?"

Goss clenched his big hands. "I've always wanted the *Becky*. But not like this."

"She'll be safe as a depot ship. No more convoys."

Goss said quietly, "A ship dies when she's inactive." He seemed to be struggling with his words. "A ship should be at sea. It's her life, her purpose."

Lindsay saw the emotion on his heavy features. "I'll leave it to you to tell the others. Stannard's to go on an advanced navigation course, de Chair and his marines are to be sent to Eastney Barracks for re-allocation, and Maxwell's to get his half stripe. He'll be going to Whale Island for an instructor's course. Young Dancy is going on a navigation course, too."

Goss asked abruptly, "What about Fraser?"

"The chief is transferring to a fleet repair ship."

"I see." Goss walked a few paces and stopped. "Isn't *anyone* staying from the old Company?"

"Dyke will take over the engine room." He added, "I thought you disliked Fraser?"

Goss said vaguely, "Dyke can't do the job. It takes a proper chief engineer. She must have proper care." He added with sudden fierceness, "No, I've never liked him much. But he's the best chief in the Company, and no matter what he's told you, he bloody well cares about this ship!"

"I know that, too." Lindsay stared at the papers on his desk. They were blurred.

Goss stood looking down at Lindsay. "And *you're* on the beach, sir. I know a lot of people'll only see your extra stripe and envy you. But I know different. I'm not a clever man. I sweated blood to get where I am, and saw many a useless bastard get promoted over my head. There's not been a captain in the Company I've not envied, nor one whose job I've told myself I couldn't do better given the chance." He rested his hands on the desk. "But I've not envied you, because I couldn't have done what you've had to do. No matter what I've kidded myself, on that score, I know that."

Lindsay did not look up. "Thank you." He heard Goss moving restlessly to an open scuttle.

Goss added slowly, "Christ, she can feel it already. Poor old girl, she can *feel* it."

Lindsay lurched to his feet. "For God's sake, Number One, we

394

have to carry out orders. Ships don't feel. They're only as good as the men who control them."

The other man shook his head. "It's no use talking to me like that, sir. You don't believe it either."

Somewhere a tannoy bellowed, "Hands to dinner. Leave to port watch from 1400 to 2300. Ordinary Seaman Jones muster at the quartermaster's lobby for mail."

Goss moved to the door. "Can you see her tied up to some stinking pier, sir? With nothing to do, no use any more?" He stared at Lindsay's lowered head. "No, and no more can't I."

As the door closed behind him Jupp entered the cabin and asked, "Will you be wantin' your lunch now, sir?"

Lindsay shook his head. "Fetch some whisky, please."

Jupp picked up the dress sword from a chair where Lindsay had thrown it. "If you'll pardon the liberty, sir, it's not fair."

"Just the whisky."

Jupp hurried away. For once he could think of nothing to say or do which would help.

LINDSAY could not remember how he reached this particular restaurant. It was evening, the sun already hidden beyond a towering white temple on the opposite side of a dusty square.

A board creaked as he thrust through some bead curtains and dropped into a chair at one of the small cane tables. Lindsay stared at the menu proffered by a smiling waiter. He had been drinking heavily since noon, and the thought of food seemed impossible.

"Perhaps the commander would wish to order later?"

He looked up. Either the newcomer was cat-footed or Lindsay was more drunk than he imagined. It seemed impossible he could have missed such a man. He was gross, his huge body impeccably covered in a cream linen suit, his girth encircled by a crimson sash. A chair groaned loudly as the man sank into it.

"A drink first, maybe?" He snapped his fingers. "I am the owner." He waved a plump hand, several rings glinting in the coloured lanterns overhead. "And bid you welcome."

The waiter was pouring out two glasses of neat gin. The owner sipped and smiled. "My religion regards gin as an evil. However, one must adapt to the country's ways, eh?" He watched Lindsay unblinkingly and continued in the same gentle tone, "I am Turkish. Once, I was in the Grand Cavalry. A Captain of Horse." He chuckled, the sound rising from a great depth. "Now it would take more than one beast to carry me, you are thinking?"

Lindsay smiled. "I am sorry. I am bad company."

"Only loneliness is bad, Commander."

Lindsay felt the gin scraping his throat like fire. "I really must go."

The man shook his head. "Not yet. It is not time."

"*Time?*"

The man smiled gently. "Do not play with fate, Commander. You will have one more glass, and then, perhaps, it will be time."

Lindsay stared at him. He must have finally taken leave of his senses. He sighed and raised the glass to his lips.

The massive Turk stood up. He held out one fat hand. "Now, you may leave. Somehow, I feel that your hurt will be easier to carry."

Lindsay thanked him and walked out into the purple gloom, dazed by the encounter. Perhaps the man was crazy. He lurched against a shuttered shop front and gasped. The gin was real enough.

At the end of the street he saw bright lights and hurrying crowds.

"Hey, mate, got a light?" Two Australian soldiers were clinging to each other for support. Lindsay took out his matches and waited while one of them made several attempts to light their cigarettes. Then they staggered away, alien against the coloured lanterns and bazaars, and Lindsay realized they had not returned the matches. He was still patting his pockets when a taxi scraped against one of the nearby stalls and sent a mountain of fruit crashing. A crowd gathered. He tried to free himself from the growing crush but it was impossible. He decided to make for a doorway to wait till the crowd cleared. Two white figures were already in the doorway and he was being pushed slowly towards another shop front when through the excited babble he heard a voice. It was like part of a dream.

"Commander! Commander Lindsay!"

All at once he was fighting his way back through the crowd. A policeman grabbed his arm, yelling, but he knocked him aside, blind to everything but the doorway and the two figures in white.

In those last desperate moments he imagined he had at last gone mad. Gasping, almost sobbing, he burst from the crowd into the opening. Then he stood quite still.

She said, "I *knew* it was you!"

Slowly he reached out and put his hands on her shoulders. "Eve." He felt her shiver under his grip. "Eve. I thought—" The other Wren moved away as he murmured, "Oh Eve. All this time."

She said quietly, "You're not well." To the other girl, "Marion, tell that policeman to get us a taxi." Then she pressed her face into his chest and whispered, "It's a miracle. We were trying to get back to the base. Then this crowd, and I saw you. I had no idea you were here." She trembled. "I still can't believe it." She looked up at him again, her eyes very large in her face. "You didn't get my letter then?"

He stared at her. "We've had no mail except local letters."

"And you thought I was in Canada!" She laughed, her eyes shining with sudden tears. "There was a last minute mix-up. My medical report got confused with another Wren's, and by the time it was sorted out the convoy had sailed without me. So they sent me here instead."

She touched his face. "You're like ice! What happened?"

"The convoy." He was trembling violently. "It was attacked. The ship with the Wrens aboard was destroyed. I was there. I saw it." He felt her hair with his fingers. "Burning. I tried to find you."

A policeman shouted, "What's going on here?"

The other Wren replied just as loudly, "Get a taxi and don't be a bloody fool!"

Lindsay was conscious only of the girl pressed against his body. He had to hold on to her.

397

She asked, "Is the taxi coming, Marion? We must get him to his ship quickly. He's ill." She touched his face again gently. "It'll be all right now. My poor darling. I'm so sorry!"

"Here's the taxi!"

Lindsay remembered very little of the journey. There was some sort of argument at the dockyard gates, a pause while the other Wren hurried away to make a telephone call.

Then she said, "We can't come any further. Regulations. We've been on leave, or else I would have known your ship was in."

The other girl came back and peered into the taxi. "I got the sentry to put me through to the ship."

Feet scraped in the darkness and Jupp loomed above the girl's shoulder. "Ah, there you are, sir!" He saw Eve and nodded gravely. "I'm so glad for you, Miss. For you both."

She said, "Take good care of him." As Lindsay tried to keep hold of her arm she added, "It will be all right, darling, I shall see you tomorrow, I promise."

"Come along, sir."

Jupp helped him from the taxi. At the far end of the gang-plank Lindsay could see the quartermaster.

Jupp said evenly, "Just a few more paces." He moved back. "On your own, sir." He followed Lindsay, willing him on.

The quartermaster had been joined by the O.O.D. It was Stannard. He saw Lindsay and Jupp's set face behind him and snapped, "The captain's coming aboard!" Then he stepped between the quartermaster and the entry port and said quietly, "Welcome back, sir."

Jupp smiled but kept his eyes on Lindsay.

"I think some 'ot soup might do the trick, sir."

Stannard watched them fade into the shadows.

Jupp succeeded in getting Lindsay to his cabin without meeting anyone else. He waited until he had dropped on his bunk and then said, "I'll fetch the soup, sir."

Lindsay's eyes were closed. "Don't bother. I'm all right."

"I 'ad it ready. It's no bother."

He opened his eyes. "You saw her, didn't you?"

"'Course I did, sir!" He grinned broadly. "Don't you worry, she'll see you tomorrow, if I 'ave to fetch 'er meself, an' that's a fact."

Lindsay's eyes closed again. "There was this Turk. He made me stay there. Said it wasn't time. Something about fate."

Lindsay grew quieter and more relaxed. "Was trying to find some matches. And then I heard her call my name."

"That's right, sir." Jupp watched him sadly. "I don't understand a word of it but I'm sure you're right." He snapped off the light and padded from the cabin.

In his pantry he sat down on a stool and stared at the soup. He'd not be wanting it now. Then he groped in a locker and took out a bottle of Drambuie. It was for special occasions. Jupp poured himself a generous measure.

chapter fourteen

Petty Officer Ritchie stepped into the cabin. "Good mornin', sir." He handed Lindsay a sealed envelope. "Just arrived from H.Q., sir."

Lindsay opened the envelope, and then said, "Orders. You'd better ask Number One to come and see me as soon as he's finished with Morning Colours." He stared at the carefully worded instructions. Four days time. It was not long.

The bulkhead telephone buzzed and Jupp announced, "Just the O.O.D. About requestmen and defaulters."

"I see."

He tried to concentrate on his written orders. Work to be completed before sailing time, leave for the ship's company at the captain's discretion.

Goss appeared in the doorway. "You wanted me, sir!"

"Orders, Number One. Four days notice."

"Not much. Still a lot of work undone."

"Well, do what you can. They might still cancel the orders."

Goss shook his head doubtfully. "I went ashore last night and met an old mate. He says there's a big convoy being assembled."

It made sense. Every available escort would be required if the convoy was a large one. The telephone buzzed again. Jupp's face was expressionless. "It's the Signals Distribution Office, sir."

He handed over the phone and said breezily, "Now, Mr. Goss, what about a cuppa while you're 'ere?"

Her voice seemed right against his ear. "Sorry about the deception, although this *is* the S.D.O." Then she asked quickly, "Are you all right?"

"Yes. Never better." Goss, Jupp and the cabin faded away. "When can I see you?"

"Now, if you like. I must see you as soon as possible." She added very clearly, "There isn't much time, is there?"

"No. I'll be at the gates right away."

Goss was watching him, a cup like a thimble in his large hand.

".I'm going ashore, Number One. Not for long."

Goss nodded. "I can cope, sir." He studied Lindsay over the rim of the cup. So that was it. Well, bloody good luck to him.

Jupp asked, "Nice coffee, Mr. Goss?"

Goss stayed poker-faced. "Very nice." Surprisingly, he winked. "Better for some though, eh?" He followed Lindsay from the cabin. "By the way, sir, if, and I say *if* you were thinking of taking a bit of leave, we can manage quite well. After all, the sooner I get used to carrying the weight on my own the better."

"Yes. Thank you. I may hold you to that." Lindsay saluted and ran quickly down the gangplank.

She was waiting outside the gates, looking very young in her white uniform. She said, "There's a little Chinese restaurant just up the road. It's quiet."

In the restaurant they were ushered to a table and he said, "My God, you're even more beautiful than I remembered."

"It must be darker in here than I thought!" Her voice was husky, and for a few moments neither of them spoke.

Then she removed her cap and shook out her hair. "I'm working in the S.D.O. So I know about your orders. Four days." She fell silent until the waiter had brought some tea. "I will be going back too." She grasped his hand. "Maybe we'll be in the same convoy. Don't worry. It won't be like that other one."

"No. But why are you going back so soon?"

"I was sent here with some others for the Singapore operation. We were to work here." She tightened her grip on his hand. "There's something I must tell you. I don't know what you'll think but I must say it."

He waited, suddenly tense.

"You remember my friend Marion? Last night? Her father's a lord and terribly rich." She seemed nervous. "He has business here. There's a place down the coast. We stayed there during the last leave." Her hand trembled slightly. "I can get leave again now that I'm on draft." She looked directly into his eyes. "If you'd like that."

"You know I would, Eve. If you're sure—"

She stared down at their hands on the table. "I'm sure. It's just that I'm afraid of losing you again." She tried to laugh. "I was also scared you'd think I was in the habit of taking all my commanders to a coastal villa!"

"When can you leave?"

She looked up again, her eyes very bright. "Today. And you?"

He remembered Goss's words. "This afternoon. How do we go?"

"I can get a car. We'd better go now. There are things I must do."

Outside the sunlight was almost blinding. He touched her bare arm. "I love you."

A working party of seamen marched along the road, and as they passed the petty officer bawled, "Eyes left!"

When he turned again she saluted him too and said, "And I you, *sir*!"

In his cabin as he threw a few things into a case he kept one ear for the telephone. He was still expecting something to go wrong. A change of orders. Some crisis which would hold him aboard.

Jupp helped him pack, and as he was about to leave said, "Perhaps you'd take this too, sir." He held out a tiny silver replica of the *Benbecula*, less than two inches long but perfect

402

in scale and detail. He added awkwardly, "It was made by the *Becky*'s boatswain many years back. Shouldn't be tellin' you this o' course, but 'e 'ad to melt down four silver teapots from the first class dinin' saloon to complete it."

Lindsay stared at him. "But you'll want to keep this!"

"I was savin' it, sir." He shook his head. "Maybe this is what for. Anyway, I reckon she'd appreciate it."

Lindsay placed it inside the case. "She will. As much as I do."

Jupp followed him to the ladder. It was strange to be parted from the little silver ship after all these years. But the girl for whom it had been intended had not waited for him. He heard the trill of pipes and gave a deep sigh of relief. Lindsay had got away all right. He loped into the cabin and picked up the telephone. "'S all right, Bob. You can reconnect the phone now. All's well."

Then humming cheerfully he went to his pantry to find the bottle of Drambuie.

THE car was a very old open M.G. but the engine sounded healthy, and when they had cleared the town limits the miles passed quickly. Lindsay rested his arm along the back of her seat, his fingers touching her hair as it ruffled in the wind. He had never seen her out of uniform before. Her dress was pale green and very simple. It was, she explained, straight off a stall.

Green hills with trees above the road changed to long open stretches with only an occasional building or bungalow, then another narrower road. The sea was never far away.

They stopped eventually on the crest of a small hill. Below, Lindsay saw a crescent of beach and a house painted white and partly screened by a line of trees. It looked very cool and inviting.

She said, "An old chap and his son look after things most of the time." She let the car move forward, and halted outside the gates. "Ah, here he is."

The head servant was grey-bearded and extremely wrinkled. He said as they got out of the car, "Welcome back, Missy. My son will get your luggage."

403

The girl looked at Lindsay. "You'll be wanting a telephone?" She gestured to a door. "In there." For an instant her face clouded over. "Don't go back, even if the base is on fire!" She ran her fingers through her hair. "Ugh, the dust! I'm going to have a swim. Then we'll have something to eat."

Lindsay walked into a low-ceilinged room. There was a little, old, hand-carved furniture and an unlikely brass telephone. The line was surprisingly clear, and after a short delay he was connected to the ship.

"This is the captain. O.O.D. please." He tried to control a pang of apprehension.

But it was not the O.O.D.

Goss sounded calm and matter-of-fact. "Everything's all right this end, sir. Two marines just brought aboard drunk." He paused. "A normal day, in other words."

Lindsay gave the telephone number to Goss. Then he said, "Thanks for holding the fort."

"No bother, sir!" There was the sound of someone murmuring in the background. Goss said abruptly, "Just heard where I can lay my hooks on some paint. Can't stop, sir." The line went dead.

"I take it from your smile that the base is *not* on fire?"

He swung round and saw her framed in the doorway. She was wearing a black swimsuit which made her limbs appear very tanned.

He walked towards her. "You're very lovely. Especially today."

She tried to frown. "My mouth is too wide, I'm covered in freckles and I've got a figure like a boy. And I love you even if you are a liar."

He put his hands on her shoulders. Her skin was very smooth. She pushed him away. "Get your trunks, and join me on the beach."

She ran out into the sunlight, her bare legs like gold against the nodding palm fronds.

The old man was waiting at the door of an end room, the swimming trunks in his hands. He said impassively, "The young missy is very much alive. It pleases me to see her so."

Lindsay threw off his soiled shirt. "Was she unhappy?"

404

"I think lonely. But that is gone now." He picked up the shirt and added, "I will have the women attend to this for you."

Lindsay looked round the room. The green dress lay on a chair beside the bed. He touched it. It was still warm. Then he opened the case and took out the silver model. On a teak table was the girl's wristwatch. He put the little ship beside it.

He turned and ran down the hallway, the floor cool under his bare feet.

When they finally emerged dripping and gasping from the sea the light was already fading. She threw him a towel and began to rub another one vigorously over her hair.

She said suddenly. "I haven't asked yet. How long?"

"Two days." He saw her shoulders stiffen, the skin still shining with droplets of spray.

Then she replied quietly, "We'll make it last, won't we?"

They ran up the shelving beach and into the house. Lights were already burning, and in the low-ceilinged room a table was laid and a bottle of wine stood chilling in a silver bucket. He slipped his arm around her shoulders.

She said, "It's quite marvellous. I didn't know things like this could happen." She moved away. "I'm going to change. I shall try and look like a lady, just for you."

Lindsay was stooping at a drinks cabinet when she burst in on him again, holding the silver ship in her hands.

"This is a wonderful present, darling!" She ran to him and kissed him impulsively on the cheek. Her face was wet, but it was not spray this time.

"It was Jupp's. He wanted you to have it."

"Bless him." She stood back and studied him for several seconds. "And you." Then she walked away again, holding the ship like a talisman.

The dinner, like everything else, was perfect. While Lindsay was changing into shirt and slacks, candles appeared on the table, and while the old man and his son waited on them, he and the girl, wearing a dress of soft yellow, sat facing each other, aware of nothing beyond the circle of candlelight.

When the table was cleared, the coffee cups empty, Lindsay could see yet another change in her mood. She walked to the door. "Don't look at me. I—I don't want to make a fool of myself. But there's so little time." Her lip quivered. "And I want you so badly." When he made to speak she added quickly, "Just give me a few minutes. I'm a bit fluttery inside!"

Lindsay sat in the quiet room listening to the insects against the screens. Then he blew out the candles and walked from the room. She was lying in the bed, a black nightgown across a chair. "It belongs to Marion, but I don't want anything belonging to anyone else. You don't think I'm silly?"

"No. Of course I don't." He leaned over and kissed her forehead. "I think you're very special."

As he pulled the sheet gently from beneath her chin, she closed her eyes and lay still. He sat looking at her, his hand moving gently across her body. She did not move until he had slipped out of his clothes and lay down beside her. Then she opened her eyes and watched him, her breath warm against his face.

"Two days and three nights."

Her body went rigid as he moved his hand across the gentle curve of her stomach. Her fingers gripped his shoulders with sudden urgency as she whispered, "Oh, God! I do love you!"

AND that was how it continued for the next two days and nights. Moments of peace and intimate silence. Swift, exploring passion which left them breathless. The perfection of sun and blue sea and isolation was a backcloth to their happiness. And for Lindsay the nightmare seemed to have gone. Had it found the one unmatchable strength and left him at last in peace?

When they climbed into the old car again Lindsay said quietly, "I will never forget this place. One day I'll remind you of it. When you start getting fed up with me."

They hardly spoke on the return journey. Once when he saw a tear on her cheek she reached out for his hand, saying, "I'm all right. Don't worry, my darling."

She dropped him at the dock gates.

He said, "I'll ring you as soon as I know what's happening." She kept both hands on the wheel.

"You're not sorry."

"Grateful. And happy."

She revved the engine. "Me too, as it happens."

The car moved away into the traffic and Lindsay walked towards the gates.

He returned the sentry's salute. "Good morning."

The marine watched him from the corner of his eye. "Good for some," he said.

chapter fifteen

The day prior to sailing Lindsay attended a conference at H.Q., and from it gleaned the importance of the convoy. Troops, munitions, oil and food, it was to be organized like a vast relay race.

The first leg across the Indian Ocean was more or less straightforward, as Japanese submarines had so far made little impression there. Once around the Cape, escorts would be joining and leaving the convoy, like guards changing on a valuable treasure, and a powerful cruiser squadron would be at sea the whole time, to give support against heavy enemy units.

Off Gibraltar some ships would slip under the Rock's own defences with supplies for the fleet and the desert army. Others would head westward to America. The bulk of the ships would press on, and run the gauntlet of U-boats and German long-range bombers.

Because of the convoy's changing shape and size it was necessary to retain one naval officer in sole charge, in a ship which would be employed for the whole of the voyage. *Benbecula* was that ship. Commodore Kemp was that senior officer.

Maybe Kemp was unsure of Lindsay's reaction, or unsure of his own popularity with higher authority. Either way, he appeared content to keep his contact with Lindsay to a minimum.

When he first came aboard he said, "You command the ship. I will control the overall pattern of events."

Now, four days out, Lindsay walked to the port wing and stared astern at the great panorama of ships, twenty-four of them in all. *Benbecula* was leading the starboard line, while one of the big troopers led the centre, and a dazzle-painted cruiser the third. There were oil-tankers, grain ships and ore carriers, while in the centre four stately liners carried the most precious cargo of all, the troops. The second troopship, with Eve aboard, was partly hidden by the leader. He wondered where Eve was at this moment. Peering at *Benbecula*? Resting in her cabin or chatting to the irrepressible Marion?

Stannard walked out on the wing and stared at the ships. "Quite a sight, sir." His eyes moved to Lindsay's shoulder straps. The fourth gold stripe was very bright and new against the others. "How does it feel, sir?"

Lindsay smiled. "I don't feel any different."

Stannard seemed surprised. "It's just that I've never seen you looking so well, sir."

Lindsay looked at the ships. "I am getting married when we reach the U.K."

Stannard gasped. "Well, Jeez, that is, I am very glad, sir." He held out his hand. "Hell, that's good news."

"You're the first to know." He wondered why he had told Stannard. Seeing his obvious pleasure made him glad he had.

EIGHTEEN days out of Ceylon the convoy was off the Cape of Good Hope and heading north-west into the Atlantic. The leading destroyers had been relieved by another pair from Cape Town, and a Royal Indian Navy sloop had returned to her own country.

As the forenoon watch took stations round the ship, Lindsay climbed to the bridge and found Commodore Kemp sitting in his chair. He had hardly shown himself throughout the voyage so far. He had a large cabin aft, formerly a stateroom for very important passengers.

Kemp turned as Lindsay saluted formally. "I've just had a top secret signal from Admiralty." He sounded hoarse, and Lindsay wondered if he was drinking. "A freighter has been sunk off the Cape Verde Islands. Believed to have been shelled by a surface ship. Not our problem, naturally, but it's as well to know these things."

Lindsay watched him narrowly. "Was that all, sir?"

"Admiralty appears to think there may be some connection with another report. A cruiser was badly damaged by a mine. Too far out in the Atlantic for a drifting one. Dropped with some others apparently, on the off chance of hitting any stray ship."

Lindsay clenched his fists to steady himself. "It must be that raider again. Has to be."

Kemp replied evasively, "We don't know that for certain. Anyway, if the two attacks *are* connected, the Hun is in for a shock. This convoy is on the top secret list and so is our additional cruiser screen. If the enemy tries to tangle with us, I can whistle up enough heavy guns to cut him into shreds!"

"Was there any other information from the freighter before she was silenced?"

"She was a Greek. Said she was going to the assistance of a Spanish merchantman which was in difficulties."

Lindsay bit his lip. How long would it take people to see through this simple trick? But Kemp was right about one thing. If the raider came upon the convoy, even the one cruiser in company should be more than a match.

Kemp added curtly, "In another week, we'll be meeting with a heavy additional escort from Freetown." The thought seemed to give him new confidence. "Like a clock, that's how I like things."

Jupp came from the port wing carrying a tray covered with a napkin. He saw Lindsay and showed his teeth.

"Coffee and a sandwich, sir."

Kemp said coldly, "What about me?"

"Sir?" Jupp placed the tray down carefully. "I will inform your steward you wish 'im to fetch somethin' for you." He looked at the man's angry face. "Sir."

The commodore rose and stalked to the door. As he disappeared down the ladder Lindsay saw the quartermaster give a quick wink at the signalman.

He said, "It won't do, Jupp. And it won't help either."

Jupp folded the napkin into four quarters. "I'm not with you, sir? Did I do anythin'?"

Lindsay grinned at him. "Get back to your pantry while you're still alive!"

LINDSAY began to see more of the commodore as news was received from Admiralty of a changing pattern in enemy activity. A German raider was at large, and, more to the point, it was the same one that Lindsay had last seen off Greenland. Her captain appeared to care little for his own safety. Several times he had barely missed the searching cruisers, and the net was closing in on him rapidly.

Two days before the anticipated meeting with the Freetown escorts Kemp sent for Lindsay in his quarters. He seemed to have aged in the past week. The deck around his feet was covered with signals.

"Another sinking report."

Lindsay nodded. He had seen it. A Danish tanker sailing without escort had been sunk barely a hundred miles from the previous sinking, which had been three hundred miles northeast of Trinidad.

"The German's working south, sir. Trying to catch the Americas' trade as much as possible. He'll sink a few more poor devils before he's run to earth." He did not try to hide the bitterness.

Kemp picked up another signal, his eyes blazing. "They've ordered our cruiser screen westward. Taken it away from my support!"

Lindsay watched him coldly. "They've no choice. If the raider continues to move south or south-east the cruisers will have him in the bag. He can't run forever."

"This is a vital convoy. It's wrong to expect me to take all the responsibility."

Lindsay kept his voice level. "When you are in charge of any convoy there is always the risk of sudden alteration in planning."

410

There was a tap at the door and Stannard stepped into the cabin. Kemp glared at him. "Well?"

"Signal from Admiralty, sir. Request you detach the cruiser *Canopus* and destroyer escort immediately, to leave with all speed and join in the search." He shrugged. "It seems that the net is tightening."

Kemp nodded. "Execute." As the door closed he muttered, "Now there's just this ship until the Freetown escorts arrive."

Lindsay returned to the bridge. The cruiser was already moving clear of her column, and far ahead of the convoy he could see the two destroyers gathering speed to take station on her.

"Signal the freighter *Brittany* to take lead ship in the port column. It seems we're in charge of things, Yeo."

Ritchie, who was keeping an eye on his signalman, nodded. "'Cept for the Yank, sir." He jerked his thumb over his shoulder. "She's still with us, more or less." The ship in question was the *John P. Ashton*, an old American destroyer, which had already had engine trouble.

Lindsay smiled. There was no real danger but it was strange that in a matter of hours their strength had melted away to leave the two oldest ships as sole protection. "Signal the *John P. Ashton* to assume station ahead of the convoy."

Ritchie said, "She'll blow 'er boilers, sir."

"Her captain will know he's the only one now with submarine detection gear. He won't have to be told what to do."

Later, as the elderly destroyer thrashed past the other ships he saw her light blinking rapidly and heard Ritchie say, "Signal, sir. 'This must be Veterans Day'." He shook his head. "He ain't kiddin' either."

When darkness fell over the three columns the American destroyer had retained her position well ahead of the convoy. Lindsay was lolling in his chair dreaming of a sunlit beach and the girl, wet with spray and warm in his arms, when Stannard roused him.

"Just decoded an urgent signal, sir. Admiralty. R.A.F. reconnaissance have reported a large German unit at sea. Out of

411

Brest, sir." Stannard sounded apprehensive. "Won't affect us, will it? I mean, this is a top secret convoy."

Lindsay slid from the chair. "Nothing's that secret. How can you hide twenty-four ships?" He added sharply, "Send someone to tell the commodore."

As Stannard hurried to a telephone Lindsay walked out onto the port wing. Just suppose it was part of a plan? That the raider's attacks on *Loch Glendhu* and the other convoy had been a working-up for all this? At best, it would mean the Germans had been right in assuming that a single raider could tie down a far greater mass of ships than her worth really suggested. At worst. . . . He gripped the screen. Then it would mean that every available cruiser had been withdrawn from this convoy to search for a red herring. The raider would be caught and sunk, but in exchange the Germans might hope for the greatest prize of all. A whole convoy. . . .

THE following morning was another fine clear one. Maxwell was officer of the watch, and as Lieutenant Hunter started the daily check of the columns of ships nearby, Maxwell stayed by the screen. He glanced at Lindsay but he was asleep in his chair. He returned to his thoughts, unconsciously clasping his hands behind him as if on parade.

Soon he would be getting his half stripe. Without effort he could see himself at the gunnery school on Whale Island. It would be like picking up the threads all over again. With luck, further advancement would follow automatically, and people would forget the one mistake which had cost him so much.

He swayed back on his heels. When he reached Whale Island again no one would sneer or cut him dead. He would be the man who had sunk a U-boat and made history with ancient six-inch weapons and half-witted conscripts.

Then he thought of Decia. It would all be too late. He would not have her. Not see the admiration and envy on the faces of brother officers when he entered a room with her on his arm.

The telephone by his elbow buzzed. "Officer of the watch?"

It was the lookout. "Aircraft, sir. Green four-five."

Lindsay was awake. "What was that?"

Maxwell covered the mouthpiece. "Bloody fool says there's an aircraft on the starboard bow, sir." He frowned. "Fifteen hundred miles from the nearest land and he sees an aircraft!"

Lindsay moved from the chair and took the handset. "Captain here. What exactly can you see?"

The seaman sounded flustered. "Can't see nothin' now, sir." Then more stubbornly, "But it was there, sir. Like a bit of glass flashin' in the sun. Very small, but no doubt about it."

Lindsay handed the telephone to Hunter. "Inform the commodore that I would be grateful for his presence here. Very well, Guns. Now you can sound off action stations."

For a moment nobody moved. Then Maxwell asked, "But, sir, *why?*"

"It may give us," he paused, recalling the gross Turk in the restaurant. "It may give us *time*."

Without another word Maxwell pressed hard on the red button.

THE SHIP had been at action for two hours. The commodore heaved himself from the chair and snapped, "Chart room." He waited until Lindsay had followed him and added, "You, too, Pilot."

In the chart room it was very hot with every scuttle and deadlight clamped shut.

The commodore said, "Nothing."

"The lookout was certain about the plane, sir." Lindsay seemed very composed. "He is an experienced rating."

"I see. What do you suggest?"

Lindsay relaxed slightly. "If I'm right, sir, it would be inviting disaster to make a radio signal for assistance. One, we know the Freetown ships will not make contact before tomorrow at the earliest. Two, if there is an enemy ship out there, it might be in total ignorance of our position."

"Well?"

"I suggest you should alter course to the east'rd, sir. Or turn one hundred and eighty degrees and *then* call for assistance. Increase to maximum speed. It would give us time and room to manoeuvre."

413

"Do you know what you are asking?" Kemp's voice trembled. "For me to run away from a shadow! You must be out of your mind!"

Lindsay said patiently, "That aircraft was probably catapulted from its parent ship. If so, you can expect the worst." He added with sudden sharpness, "What is the alternative? Head on into destruction?" He spoke faster as if to break Kemp's resistance. "Think, sir, of the effect it will have if we allow this convoy to be decimated."

Kemp took a few paces to the bulkhead. "Can't do it. It's too big." He added hesitantly, "We have to take the risk."

"I do not see you have any choice but to take evading action *now*, sir."

Kemp faced him abruptly. "Leave me to think."

Stannard followed Lindsay into the passageway. Under his breath he muttered, "Stupid bastard!" He slammed the door behind him.

Above the bridge in his armoured control position Maxwell heard the door slam. His shirt was wringing with sweat, and the backs of his spotting team and Lieutenant Hunter immediately below his steel chair looked as if they had just emerged from the sea. There was no defence at all against the sun.

Hunter twisted round. "No more aircraft. No bloody anything. So why can't we fall out action stations?"

Because that stupid commodore can't make up his mind, that's why. But aloud Maxwell replied sharply, "Don't you start!"

Hunter shrugged and reached out to open a small observation slit on the port side. For a split second he imagined an aircraft had dived from the sky. The screaming roar pressed down on him. Then came the explosions, and as he stared incredulously at the nearest troopship he saw towering waterspouts rising beyond her, higher and higher, until they shone like white silk in the sunlight, then the telltale pall of black smoke, growing like a filthy stain. A ship on the port column had been hit. But with what?

Maxwell yelled, "Don't gape! Start tracking!" He punched the shoulder of the nearest seaman. "Come on, *jump* to it!"

414

He pressed his eyes to his powerful sights. Nothing. He felt a chill run down his spine as he picked up the handset and reported, "Captain, sir. Those shells came from below the horizon." He heard Hunter gasp. "No target, sir."

Lindsay ran to the wheelhouse door. The ship which had been straddled by three or more heavy shells was falling out of line, her upper deck burning fiercely.

He snapped, "Make the signal." He scribbled a brief addition before Ritchie dashed to the W/T office. "At least someone will know what's happening."

The commodore pushed through the bridge watchkeepers, his voice shaking as he called, "What was it? Where is the enemy?"

Again that screaming roar. Three columns of water shot above the far line of ships.

Lindsay shouted, "I've reported we are under attack." He glanced at the other man's stricken face. "I'm afraid we can't rely on luck any more."

Then he entered the wheelhouse. It was too late to turn the convoy now. At any second the other ship would show herself. But to shoot this far and with such accuracy she must be very big.

He saw the faces of the men around him, watching, waiting for his decision.

He said quietly, "As soon as we know the enemy's bearing we will make a signal to the convoy to scatter."

Kemp's shadow filled the doorway. "I did not order that!"

"Do you have any objections, sir?"

Kemp dropped his eyes. "I suppose some will get away. There's nothing we can do."

Lindsay eyed him calmly. "When the convoy scatters, *your* control will be at an end."

Kemp stared at him. "There's still the American destroyer!"

Lindsay did not bother to hide his contempt.

"You'd send *her*, would you?" He turned his back. "She'll be needed anyway, to shadow the enemy when it's all over."

As if to mark the finality of his words, the tannoy speaker intoned, "Control to bridge. Enemy in sight!"

415

chapter sixteen

The burning ship had dropped a mile astern of the convoy when the port column of ships wheeled away in response to Lindsay's signal.

"From *John P. Ashton*, sir." Ritchie steadied his telescope. "Request permission to engage the enemy."

The bridge shivered as another salvo came screaming out of the sky, to explode in an overlapping line of spray and dirty smoke a mere cable from the leading troopship.

"Negative." A near miss would sink the elderly destroyer. "Make to the second column to scatter *now*."

Stannard muttered fiercely, "They can't get far. God, those bastards are shooting well."

Lindsay slid open a shutter on the starboard side and raised his glasses. He saw only haze and the clear blue sea below the horizon. Behind him he heard Hunter's voice on the speaker.

"Green three-oh. Range one-eight-oh."

Then quite suddenly he saw the enemy ship. She was a darker blur in the horizon haze, but as he watched he saw the ripple of orange flashes which momentarily laid bare her superstructure. A cruiser at least. He heard the screaming whine of shells as they tore down over the scattering ships.

"Make the signal to our column. Tell them to be as quick as possible."

The enemy fired again, and the rearmost ship in the column was straddled by three shells. As she steamed stubbornly through the falling torrents of spray he saw she was badly mauled.

"All acknowledged, sir." Ritchie scribbled automatically on his pad. Not much point. Nobody would ever read it.

There was a sudden silence in the wheelhouse as Lindsay said, "Give me the mike." He took it from Dancy, seeing in his mind the men throughout his command.

"This is the captain speaking. We are under attack by a heavy enemy warship which is now about nine miles off our starboard

416

bow. She is big and therefore fast. With bad visibility or darkness the convoy might have been saved by scattering."

He paused, then continued. "To have even a hope of escaping, these ships must be given time."

Lindsay snapped down the button and looked at Ritchie. "Very well, Yeoman. Hoist the battle ensigns."

The commodore swung round and shouted, "*Stop!* I order you to—"

Lindsay interrupted harshly, "I intend to give the convoy as much time and chance as possible. With or without your help, sir." He stooped over the gyro. "Starboard ten. Midships. Steady."

"Steady, sir. Course three-four-zero."

"Full ahead both engines."

As the ship heeled onto her new course Lindsay saw a dark shadow fall briefly across the screen. He looked up at the great ensign climbing the foremast. When he turned again the sea astern seemed full of ships moving away on differing bearings.

"Aircraft, sir. Dead ahead."

He watched the sliver of silver above the horizon as it moved in the sunlight. The enemy's eye, reporting each fall of shot. Standing by to pursue and guide the cruiser. Too fast for Maxwell's ponderous guns. Out of range for the automatic weapons.

But as yet nobody aboard the enemy ship appeared to have noticed the *Benbecula*'s challenge. Maybe they imagined she was out of control or trying to escape in the wrong direction.

Stannard said tightly, "Maxwell's guns will never even mark the bastard at this range."

Lindsay picked up a handset. "Guns? Captain. Commence firing with the starboard battery." He waited, shutting out Maxwell's protest. "I know the marines can't get their guns to bear. But we *must* draw the enemy's fire from those ships. I will try to close the range as quickly as possible."

He replaced the handset and heard the fire gong's tinny call, the immediate crash of guns.

"Short."

417

He lifted his glasses in time to see the thin feathers of spray falling in direct line with the enemy's hazy outline. But she was much clearer now, her turrets already swinging as if to seek out this sudden impudence.

Dancy watched transfixed and then felt himself falling, Stannard and a signalman entangled round his legs, as the whole bridge shook to one terrible explosion. He pulled himself upright and then almost vomited as he stared at the bloody shape beneath the starboard door.

Lieutenant Paget had been almost cut in half by the explosion. Yet as his hands worked like claws across his torn body his screams grew louder.

"Starboard twenty!" Lindsay locked his arm around the voicepipes as the helm went over. "Stand by, the port battery!" He wiped paint dust from the gyro with his elbow. "Midships. Steady."

"Steady, sir. Course zero-three-zero."

Jolliffe gritted his teeth as a signalman wrapped a bandage around his arm. A small splinter had laid it open.

The port guns hurled themselves back on their springs, their muzzles angled towards the sky in their efforts to hit the enemy.

Lindsay made himself ignore the screams until they became fainter and suddenly stopped. A stretcher party had entered the bridge but he did not turn his head as he concentrated on the other ship.

"Range now one-six-oh."

Eight miles separated the armoured cruiser and the garishly painted ship with the list to starboard. The enemy had got the message now all right. She had turned towards *Benbecula* using her two forward turrets alternately.

As the gunfire mounted Lindsay changed course at irregular intervals. Starboard battery and then port. Two by two against the German's six.

Maxwell remarked over the speaker, "She's the *Minden*. Eight-inch guns, twelve torpedo tubes." A brief sigh. "Estimated speed thirty-three knots." A miniature battlecruiser.

A telephone buzzed, the sound muffled by explosions. "W/T have received a signal, sir. Raider sunk. All available assistance on way to help you. Cruiser *Canopus* calling us, sir. What is your position?"

Lindsay saw the sea erupt again. Much closer this time. "Tell her our position is *grim!*"

All four guns were firing and reloading as fast as they could, with Maxwell's spotters yelling down bearings and deflexions with each veering change of course.

In the engine room Fraser clung to the jerking platform and watched his men swarming round the pounding machinery like insects. In damage control Goss sat unmoving in his chair. Throughout the ship, every man waited for the inevitable.

Far astern, and spread fanlike towards the horizon, the once proud convoy had long since lost its shape. The first ship to be hit had sunk, but the others still managed to maintain their escape.

Aboard the second troopship the decks were crammed with silent figures in lifejackets.

A deck officer at his boat station said suddenly, "God, look at the old girl. I'd never have believed it!" He took off his cap and waved it as he called, "Good luck, old lady!"

The small party of Wrens packed at the after end of the boat deck huddled closer as the distant ship was again straddled by waterspouts.

Marion slipped her arm round her friend and said, "Don't cry, Eve."

She shook her head. "I know I'm crying." She tried to see the ship with the stubborn list and outdated stern. "But I feel like cheering!"

Something like a sigh transmitted itself through the watching soldiers. A voice called, "She's hit!"

Marion tightened her grip. "But they're still firing!"

Eve was seeing the little villa, the table in candlelight. And him sitting on the bed. Looking at her. Holding her.

Another set of explosions rumbled across the sea's face. More muffled now as the distance steadily mounted between them.

A man said, "Direct hit that time. Must be."

"Would you like to go below?" Marion stared sadly at the great spreading smokestain far astern. "They've made it safe now."

"No." She shook her head. "I'm sure he'll know I'm here."

They stayed by the rail in silence.

"SHOOT!"

Maxwell was hoarse from yelling into his mouthpiece. The compartment seemed full of smoke and the din was unbearable as time and time again the ship rocked to the enemy's salvos.

"Why can't we *hit* her?" Hunter shouted. "We're down to six miles range, for Christ's sake!"

The starboard guns crashed out again and Maxwell cursed as his shells exploded into the haze.

"Up two hundred!"

He was still speaking when the next salvo straddled the ship. He saw Hunter lurch in his chair to stare up at him in horror even as the blood gushed from his mouth and his eyes lost their understanding forever.

Two seamen were also down, and a third was crawling up the side of Maxwell's chair holding his hip and sobbing with agony.

"First aid party to Control!" The line had gone dead. Maxwell hung his microphone on the chair, then, giving the wounded seaman a vague pat on the head, climbed out into the sunlight.

Figures blundered past him in the smoke and a man yelled, "Up forrard! Starboard side!"

Number One was still firing when Maxwell arrived, and he found Baldock, his elderly warrant officer, giving local orders to its crew. The other gun was in fragments, hurled inboard above a deep crater round which human remains lay scattered.

Baldock shouted. "Both quarters officers are done for on this side!"

Maxwell nodded, feeling very detached. "You carry on then."

He strode to the opposite side where he found the young sub-lieutenant in charge sitting on a shell locker, an arm across his face like a man in the sun.

"All right, Cordeaux?"

The officer stared at him. "Yes, sir."

Then he saw a spreadeagled corpse at the opposite gun. Headless, it still wore a jacket. A shell whimpered close overhead but Maxwell did not flinch. "Luck of the draw, my boy. I'm going aft to see the marines. Keep at it, eh?"

The youth groped for his helmet. In front of him the gunlayer and trainer, the gloved seamen who worked the breech were waiting as before. They were going to die. All of them.

The gunlayer said thickly, "We're turnin' again, sir!"

Cordeaux said, "Stand by, Number Two." Then with the others he watched the bows start to swing to starboard.

"MIDSHIPS!" Lindsay had to yell to make himself heard. The enemy gunners were shooting rapidly and he knew that *Benbecula* had been badly mauled. But, as he conned the vibrating ship, he was conscious only of the distance which still separated the ill-matched enemies.

"Wheel's amidships, sir!" Jolliffe was clinging to the wheel, his face ashen from loss of blood.

Lindsay swung round as sunlight lanced through the smoke and he saw the spotter plane flashing down the starboard side less than half a mile distant. Somewhere aft an Oerlikon came to life, making the seaplane veer away. Too far away for good shooting, but Lindsay could understand the Oerlikon gunner's gesture. Strapped in his harness, vulnerable and helpless as the ship came apart around him.

Stannard shouted in his ear. "The ships'll be safe now!" It was more like a question.

"There's still too much daylight left."

He watched the seaplane turning for another run. But for the plane the ships would have been beyond reach by now. But once *Benbecula* had been destroyed the German captain would be in pursuit again.

The deck canted violently and a wall of flame shot skyward from the forecastle.

Telephones buzzed and he heard men yelling over the remaining voicepipes.

"Bad fire forrard, sir! Number One gun knocked out. Mr. Baldock has been killed."

A savage explosion tore down the ship's side, filling the air with splinters and heavier fragments. The funnel was streaming tendrils of smoke and steam from countless holes.

Lindsay saw that his chair was empty. The commodore had gone below. He shrugged. It did not seem important now.

He raised his glasses again. The range was less than six miles. The cruiser was still coming for them, moving diagonally across the bow, her turrets tracking *Benbecula*'s approach.

A pencil rolled across the counter beneath the screen and for a second Lindsay stared at it. The list which had defied owners and shipyards for years had gone at last. Goss had probably flooded the magazine nearest the fires, the weight of water bringing the old ship upright with a kind of stubborn dignity. How would she appear to the enemy and the German gunnery officer? This battered, half-crippled ship, limping towards destruction but refusing to die?

He clenched his jaw. The German must be held off until help arrived.

"Where's *Canopus* now?"

Stannard glanced at him. "W/T office is badly hit, sir. Can't be sure what's happening."

Lindsay opened his mouth to speak and then found himself face down on the gratings with someone kicking and struggling across his spine. There was smoke and dust everywhere.

Near his face small things stood out with stark clarity. Rivets, and pieces of his watch which had been torn from his wrist, a man's fist. It belonged to Jolliffe. The coxswain had been blasted from the wheel and lay with his skull crushed against the binnacle.

Lindsay lurched to his feet. Stannard was on his back, blood running between his legs, and Dancy kneeling over him.

Ritchie was already dragging himself to the wheel and managed to croak. "Got 'er, sir! Steady as she goes!" He grinned. "To 'ell!"

422

Stannard opened his eyes and stared at Dancy. "Easy, mate. I'm all right. Christ, I can't feel much of anything!"

Midshipman Kemp and Squire, the navigator's yeoman, entered the smoke-filled compartment, slipping on blood and broken panels, groping for handholds.

Lindsay said, "Man those voicepipes!"

Kemp nodded wildly. "I've sent for the first aid party, sir!"

Dancy crouched over the Australian, holding him as the deck jerked to another shellburst.

"You'll be fine. You see. We can be in England together and—"

Stannard's head lolled to one side and Lindsay said, "He's gone, Sub."

Dancy stood up, shaking badly. Then he said, "I'm O.K., sir." He tried not to look at his friend on the gratings.

Boase, with two stretcher bearers, ran into the wheelhouse. In an unexplained lull of gunfire young Kemp shouted wildly, "Go on, Doc, show us what you can do! You're bloody good at offering advice to others!"

Lindsay snapped. "Get a grip on yourselves!"

Kemp's face crumpled. "He was helping my father to ruin you, sir. Was giving a bad report so that you'd be finished." Fury came back to his face as he yelled at the stricken doctor, "You rotten, bastard! You're like my father, so why don't you run down and hide with him?"

Boase was standing with his arms at his side, his face deathly pale, and his steel helmet awry.

Squire took him by the wrist and pushed him towards the grim-faced stretcher bearers. "Get him away, chum."

A bosun's mate said, "First lieutenant on the phone, sir."

Lindsay took it. "Captain."

Goss sounded far away. "Forrard bulkhead is badly cracked. If it's not properly shored the whole thing will go." He coughed harshly and added, "There's a bad fire here, too."

"You want me to reduce speed?"

"Yes. At full revs she'll go straight to the bottom if this lot caves in." A pause. "We'll need fifteen minutes."

Fifteen minutes. He could as easily have asked for a week.

Dancy was watching him, another telephone in his fist.

"It's the chief, sir. Two pumps out of action. Engine room is flooding."

A shell exploded somewhere aft. Lindsay heard heavy equipment falling between decks, the tearing scrape of splinters ricocheting from the ravaged hull.

"Yes, Chief."

Fraser seemed very calm. "I can still give you full speed, sir. But I'm warning you that things could get dicey down here."

"Yes." Even the one word seemed an effort. "Get all your spare hands out right away and put them in damage control. It may not be long now."

"Aye." Fraser shouted something to his assistant and then added, "She's not doing so badly though." The line went dead.

Lindsay said, "Ring down for half speed."

Dancy swung the telegraph. "They'll have us cold now, sir."

Another shell ploughed into the forecastle. Rigging and spars vanished through the broken plating, smearing the remains of Cordeaux and his gun crew as they passed.

Lindsay felt someone tying a dressing around his forearm and realized he had been hit by a small splinter. There was no pain. Just numbness.

"Enemy's ceased fire, sir." The remaining bosun's mate leaned against the screen as if about to collapse.

Lindsay moved automatically to the port door. When he wrenched it open he found he was looking straight down at the deck below through a tangle of blackened, twisted steel and wood. The shell which had killed Stannard, Jolliffe and the others on the bridge had carved the wing away like so much cardboard. How he and Dancy had survived was a miracle.

He felt the salt air driving the smoke from his lungs and tried to steady his glasses on the enemy. The ship was so slow now. She must be filling badly, he thought. Nearly finished.

He heard Goss clattering through the bridge but kept his glasses on the enemy. The cruiser had all but stopped too, less than four miles away. He could see the scarlet flag at her gaff.

Behind him Goss muttered, "The bastard's picking up his seaplane, sir."

The little aircraft, bobbing on its floats, manoeuvred delicately towards the ship's massive grey hull. A derrick had been unlimbered by the mainmast and was swinging outboard.

Perhaps the sight of these calm, practised movements did more to break Lindsay's reserves than any act of expected violence. The cruiser was confident of the victory. She could afford to ignore the blazing, shell-pitted ship without masts or ensigns, and would soon be off again after the convoy. Because of *Benbecula's* challenge many of those ships would survive. But some would not, and with sudden anger Lindsay shouted, "Stop the starboard engine!"

He hurried to the wheelhouse. "Stand by to abandon ship. Get the wounded on deck and cut loose the rafts." They were all staring at him. "Jump to it!"

The telegraph clanged, and with a brief shudder the starboard screw spun to a halt.

Dancy called, "The enemy are training their tubes on us, sir!"

Lindsay ran to the shutters. Even without glasses he could see the gap in the cruiser's silhouette where one set of torpedo tubes had been swung out across the side.

Goss muttered, "There's not time to get the lads off, sir."

He had guessed Lindsay's intention and was surprised to find he could understand and meet the inevitable. He had been chasing after his damage control parties, plugging holes, dragging the sobbing wounded out of mangled steel, repairing obsolete pumps and trying to stay alive in a prison of screaming splinters and echoing explosions. His cabin had been torn apart, his pictures and relics just so much rubbish. Anger, despair, resentment; for a few moments he had known them all. It was like seeing his life lying there amidst the wreckage. Carefully he had unpinned the Company flag from the bulkhead, and crunched out of the cabin.

And now the noise and din were all but over. With narrowed eyes Goss watched the little seaplane etched against the cruiser's side.

425

Then he said, "I'm ready to have a go if you are."

Lindsay met his gaze. "It's only a faint chance."

"Better'n sitting here waiting to be chopped." Goss walked aft. "I'll tell de Chair. Maxwell, too, if he's still in one piece."

"Stop port."

Before the last clang of the telegraph he had the telephone against his ear.

"Chief? Listen." Through the open shutter he saw the seaplane rising up against the grey steel.

Lindsay joined Dancy by the voicepipes and said, "Hold this phone, and when I give you the signal just tell the chief to let her rip." He added to Ritchie, "Just keep her head towards the enemy's quarter. I'm going to give the after guns a chance. Only one of them will bear. But if we miss I'm going to turn and try again." He smiled grimly. *There'll be no second go. By that time we'll be heading straight down.*

Aft on the well deck Goss found Maxwell squatting on the side of a gun mounting. Between the two guns the wounded lay in ragged lines. A few exhausted stokers and seamen waited in little groups, and de Chair lay in the shadow of a shattered winch, his face enveloped in bloody dressings.

His hands moved slightly as Goss said, "You are to engage with Number Six gun. Captain's orders."

The marine sergeant standing by said, "Right, sir."

But as he moved Maxwell bounded over the coaming and threw himself against the big six-inch gun.

"*No!*" He thrust the gunlayer aside and crouched in his seat as he added petulantly. "Check your sights!"

A young marine bugler at Goss's side said shakily, "Anything I can do, sir?"

Goss tore his eyes from Maxwell's frenzied movements. "Yes. Why not." Carefully he unfolded the Company flag and added, "Bend this onto that radio antenna. We've no ensigns and no bloody masts. I guess the old *Becky* would rather end her days under her right colours anyway!"

Another marine had found a telephone which was still connected

426

with the bridge. Only his eyes moved as he watched the little bugler clamber up to the boat deck and seconds later the big flag billow out from its improvised staff.

Goss found Lindsay on the bridge just as he had left him. "Ready, sir."

Lindsay nodded. "Chief says the engine room is flooding faster. Without those two pumps—" He broke off as the seaplane rose out of the cruiser's shadow and swung high above the rail.

He looked at Squire. "When I drop my hand."

Squire swallowed hard. "All right, sir."

Lindsay concentrated on the distant warship. How slowly the seaplane was moving on its hoist.

He held his breath and then brought his hand down in a sharp chop.

Squire gasped, "Now!"

Along the remaining telephone wire and into the ear of the motionless marine. Across the littered deck and pitiful wounded, to where Maxwell was poised over his sight like an athlete awaiting the starter's pistol.

This was the moment. His moment.

"*Shoot!*"

He felt the sight-pad crash against his eye, the staggering lurch of the gun recoiling inboard, and was almost deafened by the explosion.

The shell exploded directly on target. There was one blinding flash, and where the seaplane had been hanging above its mounting there was a swirling plume of brown smoke. It was followed instantly by another, darker glare, the flames spreading and dancing even as the breech was jerked open and the next shell rammed home.

On the bridge Lindsay had to hold down the sudden surge of excitement. The seaplane had been blasted to fragments and the whole section below it was ablaze with aero fuel.

He shouted, "Now, Sub!"

The gun crashed out again and drowned Dancy's voice, but far below them Fraser had heard, and as he threw himself on his throttles the screws came alive, churning the sea into a great welter of spray, pushing the old ship forward again, shaking her until it seemed she would come apart.

The sudden fire on the cruiser's deck had done its work. The torpedo crews were being driven back while their comrades with hoses and extinguishers rushed in.

Maxwell's next shell was short, the explosion hurling the spray high above the enemy's side, the flames dancing through the glistening curtain like bright gems.

Lindsay pounded the screen with his fist. He could see the cruiser's forward turret turning in a violent angle to try and find the hulk which had returned to life.

On his steel seat beside the one remaining gun which would bear, Maxwell took a deep breath as he concentrated on the column of smoke forward of the cruiser's mainmast. Just the one set of tubes would do. Six torpedoes in a neat row, all set and ready to deal *Benbecula* a death blow. Except that now they were unmanned because of his first shot. In spite of the tension he could feel the grin spreading across his face. If Decia could see him now. If only—

"*Shoot!*"

The two ships fired almost together. Maxwell did not see what happened next. His gun, the crew and most of the marines at the opposite mounting were blasted to oblivion from the explosion. In seconds the well deck and poop were ablaze from end to end, the scorching heat starting other outbreaks below and as high as the lifeboats.

Lindsay felt the shock like a blow to his own body. He knew that the ship had done her best and could fight no more. So great was the onslaught of metal that he was totally unprepared for the wall of fire which shot skyward above the billowing smoke. Then as a down-eddy parted the huge pall he saw the cruiser's raked stem moving steadily into the sunlight, the forward turret still trained towards him.

As she emerged from the smoke, Lindsay saw that her bow wave was already dropping and her stern was awash. The torpedoes

428

had blasted her wide open with greater effect than if they had been fired into the hull.

Lindsay felt Dancy gripping his shoulders and Ritchie croaking in either joy or disbelief. Throughout the battered hull men were cheering and embracing each other, and even some of the wounded shouted up at the sky, crazed by the din but aware that despite all they were still alive.

The cruiser was slewing round, her bilge rising to blot out the chaos on her decks as she started to roll over. More explosions echoed across the water, and even at such a distance Lindsay heard heavy machinery and weapons tearing adrift to add to the horror below decks.

There was no hope of saving lives. *Benbecula* was devoid of boats, and most of her rafts were either lost or destroyed in the savage battle.

Steam rose high above the cruiser's bows as very slowly they lifted from the water, a black arrowhead against the horizon and clear sky. Then she dived, the turbulence and spreading oil-slick marking her last moment of life.

Dancy asked thickly, "Shall I get our people off, sir?" He seemed stunned. "We could build rafts."

Fraser, without orders, had already cut the speed to dead slow.

"Yes." Lindsay touched his arm. "And thank you."

But Dancy did not move. "Sir! Listen!"

Feebly at first. Little more than a murmur above the hiss of flames, the occasional crackle of bursting ammunition, Lindsay heard the sounds of Fraser's pumps.

He took the handset. "Chief?"

Fraser was chuckling. "The old cow! I told you, didn't I?" He sounded near to tears. "Bloody old cow judged it right to the last bloody moment—" His voice broke completely.

Lindsay said quietly, "If we can get these fires out and hold the intake we might keep her afloat." He lowered the handset.

Then he walked out onto the remaining wing. Slowly he looked down and along his command. The death and the terrible damage, even the leaping fires on the well deck could not disguise the old

429

ship's familiar outline. Hoses which had been lying smouldering came to life again, and men emerged like rats from their holes to control them. He saw a stoker, his head bandaged, carrying the ship's cat and standing it down by a full cup of water. Then he stood back to watch the cat's reactions, as if witnessing the greatest miracle in the world.

Three hours later, as the ship struggled forward at a dead slow speed, her hull cloaked in smoke and escaping steam, a lookout reported another vessel on the horizon.

It was the *Canopus*, hurrying back in the hope of saving some of the convoy.

The sight of the riddled, fire-blackened ship with an unfamiliar flag flapping jauntily above the destruction made her captain believe the worst had happened.

Ritchie lowered his telescope and reported, "'E wants to know, sir. What ship are you?"

Goss, bare-headed and black from top to toe, was sipping tea at the rear of the bridge. He looked at Lindsay's tired face and winked.

Then he said to Ritchie, "Make to *Canopus*. This is H.M.S. *Benbecula*." He turned away in case Lindsay should see his eyes. "The finest ship in the Company."

Douglas Reeman

One of the occupational hazards of being a distinguished author is that you get bombarded with invitations. Often the events themselves turn out to be a dreadful waste of time—but sometimes, for instance when Douglas Reeman was crossing the Atlantic on the QE 2, they turn out to be not only entertaining but also professionally rewarding. On this occasion there was the customary (for important passengers) invitation to sit at the Captain's table and the more unusual invitation to attend a party given by the ship's stewards. Both were signal honours but it was the party that provided the highest dividend. One of Reeman's hosts asked him why he had never written about armed merchant cruisers and proceeded to elaborate on the subject with such interest and intensity that, by the time the party ended, *Rendezvous—South Atlantic* was already halfway to being written. . . .

From its moment of publication, it was hailed as a first-rate addition to Reeman's fleet of highly successful novels about sea warfare. As one can easily guess from any of these novels, the author writes with first-hand experience of his subject and indeed, during World War II, he served in the Navy in all the major theatres of operations, mostly aboard motor torpedo boats. No less than three ships were sunk beneath him. After demobilization, he served with the Metropolitan Police for nearly five years, mostly in the East End of London, attached to the C.I.D. Planning marriage, he felt that the lot of a policeman's wife would not be a happy one, and so he became a social worker in Battersea. Still devoted to boats and sailing, he and his wife, Winifred, lived for some time on a boat, though now they live on dry land in Surrey, sailing whenever they can.

While he was doing social work he tried his hand at writing, and had a number of short stories about the sea published. His first full-length novel, *A Prayer for the Ship*, was accepted immediately by the first publisher who saw it, and had a great success. Since then he has devoted himself full-time to writing, dividing his talents between modern novels and tales of Captain Bolitho, a sailor in Nelson's navy, written under the pseudonym of Alexander Kent.

His success has established Reeman as the undisputed successor to the great C. S. Forester.

THE UNEXPECTED MRS. POLLIFAX
Dorothy Gilman

The
Unexpected
Mrs. Pollifax

A CONDENSATION OF THE BOOK BY
Dorothy Gilman

ILLUSTRATED BY JOHN FALTER
PUBLISHED BY ROBERT HALE, LONDON

Sweet and grandmotherly, the rose on her hat slightly askew, Emily Pollifax confronted the young CIA man. He *did* seem a bit startled by her idea. Yet she could see no good reason why she shouldn't become a secret agent.

She was widowed, her children grown and married. She was weary of her humdrum, purposeless routine and, besides, no one in his right mind would ever suspect her of anything sinister.

At first there was official resistance to her plan, but fate joined her one-woman conspiracy and she found herself with an assignment.

So begins a delightful tale of suspense in which everything—almost—inevitably goes wrong.

Soon the CIA, as well as the enemy, has every cause to wish that Emily Pollifax had stayed at home and left both sides to fight the cold war in peace.

T HE NURSE WALKED out of the room and Mrs. Pollifax looked at the doctor. He was a very *nice* young man, with very white teeth, and horn-rimmed glasses which he now removed. "Well, Mrs. Pollifax," he said pleasantly, "for a woman of your age you're in fantastically good health. I congratulate you . . . yet I do note certain signs of depression. You're not quite the same Mrs. Pollifax I saw last year. Anything troubling you?"

Mrs. Pollifax hesitated, wondering if he could possibly understand. He was so absurdly young. "Well, I think one can sometimes have too *much* time." She paused. "It sounds terribly frivolous when people are starving, but I can't help feeling I've outlived my usefulness." There, the words were out and curdling the air.

The doctor returned his glasses to his nose. "I see. Your two children, Mrs. Pollifax, are . . . ?"

"Grown and far away. And visits aren't the same, you know."

He was listening attentively. "You said you do a great deal of volunteer work. Do you enjoy it?"

Mrs. Pollifax blinked at the unexpected question, then suddenly smiled. "Actually I suppose I loathe it," she said.

He could not help smiling back; there was something contagious about her smile, something conspiratorial and twinkling. "Perhaps it's time you looked for more congenial outlets," he suggested. "It's terribly important, at any age, to live to your full potential. Otherwise a kind of dry rot sets in."

"Yes," she said simply. "I agree, but what is one to do? After my husband died I set out to make a very sensible life for myself so that I'd never be a nuisance to my children. It's just that—"

"It's too sensible, perhaps?" he supplied. "Isn't there something you've always longed to do that you've never been free to?"

Mrs. Pollifax looked at him. "When I was growing up—oh for years—I planned to become a spy," she admitted.

The doctor threw back his head and laughed, and Mrs. Pollifax wondered why, when she was being her most serious, people found her so amusing. Her husband's favorite form of endearment for her had been "lovable little goose," which was his way of forgiving the odd bent in her that he didn't quite understand, and as they grew older the children, Roger and Jane, had also acquired the habit of thinking her just a little absurd. She could hear Jane now: "But Mother, why on *earth* . . . ?" and to her astonishment she found herself thinking, I don't suppose that I *am* a very sensible person actually. Perhaps the doctor's right. I can't be happy trying to be what I'm not.

But the mood of confessional had ended with the doctor's roar of laughter. They chatted a few minutes longer but without further rapport, and Mrs. Pollifax left his office.

I wasn't joking, she thought indignantly. I really *was* going to be a spy. She had worked hard at it too, going to the town dump every Saturday morning with her cousin John to watch him shoot rats, and proving such a persistent tagalong that he had condescended to let her shoot with him. There were the maps too, that she had pored over in her room with such devotion that when the Second World War began she was still able to announce the longitude and latitude of obscure little islands nobody else had ever heard of. What a funny child she had been, she thought with affection, a lonely but very happy child. She was lonely now but so— so *unused*, so *purposeless*. Last Monday when she had carried her geraniums to the roof of the apartment building, she had stood

438

at the edge of the parapet looking down, her mind searching for one good reason why she should not take a step forward into oblivion. Even now she was not sure what would have happened if young Mr. Garbor hadn't called out, "Mrs. Pollifax! For heaven's sake step back!" When she obeyed him she saw that he was trembling.

She hadn't told the doctor this. Obviously she must find a way to instill novelty into her life or she would be afraid to carry her geraniums to the roof, and she loved her geraniums.

She walked up the steps of her apartment house. Miss Hartshorne was standing by the elevator and she immediately felt herself shrivel. It was not Miss Hartshorne's fault that she reminded Mrs. Pollifax of her algebra teacher, but Mrs. Pollifax illogically blamed her for it nevertheless.

"Mrs. Pollifax," boomed Miss Hartshorne in her quartermaster's voice. They stepped inside the elevator and Miss Hartshorne pressed the button. "Warm today," she announced.

"Humid too," contributed Mrs. Pollifax. Pulling herself together she added, "Planning a trip this summer, Miss Hartshorne?" Miss Hartshorne was always either planning a trip or showing colored slides of one. At times Mrs. Pollifax felt that her neighbor did not really see the countries through which she traveled until she came home to view them in her living room.

"In September," said Miss Hartshorne crisply. "It's the only month for the knowledgeable traveler." The elevator door opened. "Good day," she said dismissingly.

"Yes—to you too," mumbled Mrs. Pollifax, and went into her apartment with a feeling of escape. As she passed her desk she stopped to glance at her engagement calendar. This was Monday. On Tuesday she wheeled the bookcart at the hospital, on Wednesday she rolled bandages. Thursday there was the art association, and on Friday the garden club. Saturday the hairdresser and tea with Elise Wiggin, who talked of nothing but her grandchildren and how joyously they embraced toilet training.

Mrs. Pollifax picked up the newspaper and leafed through it; it was important to be well informed. On page three the photo of a woman caught her eye. FINDS CAREER AT 63. Mrs. Pollifax, captured, sat down to read. Mrs. Magda Carroll had turned to little theater groups after her children married, had been discovered by a Broadway agent and was now in a play that had opened to rave reviews in New York. "I owe it all to my age," she told the interviewer. "The theater world is teeming with talented young things, but there is a dearth of sixty-three-year-olds. They needed me—I was unexpected."

" 'They needed me—I was unexpected.' How perfectly wonderful!" Mrs. Pollifax whispered. She stood up, walked to the hall mirror and stared at the woman reflected there: small, feminine, somewhat cushiony in figure, hair nearly white, eyes blue. A nice little woman unsuited for almost everything practical. Wasn't there any area at all in which she too might be unexpected?

Nonsense, she told herself. Absolutely out of the question. But nothing ventured, nothing gained, she reminded herself timidly. And "Isn't there something you've always longed to do?" It wouldn't hurt to ask. Just looking into it would be a nice little vacation from volunteer work. I haven't visited Washington, D.C., since I was eleven. . . . It was insane, utterly. "I'll go!" she announced out loud, and feeling positively giddy she opened the closet and pulled down her suitcase.

THE first thing Mrs. Pollifax did in Washington after registering at a hotel was to visit her congressman. The next day she spent sight-seeing and restoring her courage, which had a tendency to rise in her like a tide and then ebb, leaving behind tattered weeds of doubt. But the following day she resolutely boarded the bus for the twenty-minute ride to Langley, Virginia, and the headquarters of the Central Intelligence Agency. She had discovered its address in the public library, glancing over her shoulder discreetly as she copied it down. But now she was astonished to see signs along the road directing everyone, presumably Russians too, to the CIA. Nor was there anything discreet about the building itself. With its towers, penthouses and acres of glass it fairly screamed for attention.

440

Mrs. Pollifax walked through the gates and approached the guards. Her courage was on the rise today. Only Miss Hartshorne could have squashed her. "I would like," she said, consulting her memo pad, "to see Mr. Jaspar Mason."

She was given a form to fill out; then a guard escorted her down the corridor. Mrs. Pollifax walked slowly, reading all the signs on how classified wastepaper should be prepared for disposal, and at what hours it would be collected. She was ushered into a small, bright, impersonal room. From its contents—several chairs, a couch and coffee table—Mrs. Pollifax deduced that it was a repository for uninvited visitors. Mr. Mason contributed to this impression when he joined her—a man capable of classifying and disposing of people as well as wastepaper with tact and skill. He shook her hand, glancing at his watch. "I'm afraid I can give you only ten minutes," he said. "Tell me how I can help you."

With equal efficiency Mrs. Pollifax handed him the introduction which she had extracted from her congressman (she had not of course told him her real reason for wishing to interview someone in the CIA). The young man read the note, glanced at Mrs. Pollifax and frowned. He seemed particularly disapproving of her hat, and Mrs. Pollifax guessed that the single fuchsia-pink rose that adorned it must be leaning again, like a broken reed.

"Ah—yes, Mrs. Politflack," he murmured, obviously baffled.

"Pollifax," she pointed out gently.

"Oh—sorry. Now, Mrs. Pollifax, you are a member of a garden club and are gathering information . . ."

Mrs. Pollifax glanced around to be sure the door was closed. She leaned toward Mr. Mason and said in a low voice, "Actually I've come to inquire about your spies."

The young man's jaw dropped. "I beg your pardon?"

Mrs. Pollifax nodded. "I was wondering if you needed any." He seemed obtuse—perhaps he was hard of hearing. Enunciating clearly, she said, "I would like to apply for work as a spy."

He closed his mouth. "You're not serious."

"I've come to volunteer," she told him warmly. "I'm quite alone, you see, with no responsibilities. It's true that my only qualifica-

441

tions are those of character, but when you reach my age character is what you have the most of. I've raised two children and run a home. I know first aid, never shrink from the sight of blood and I'm very good in emergencies."

Mr. Mason looked dazed. "But spying these days is not bloody at all, Mrs.—Mrs.—"

"Pollifax. I'm relieved to hear that, Mr. Mason. But still I hoped you might find use for someone—expendable, you know—to preserve the lives of your younger people. I don't mean to sound melodramatic, but I am quite prepared to offer my life or I would not have come."

Mr. Mason was shocked. "But Mrs. Politick," he protested, "this is simply not the way in which spies are recruited. By volunteering. It's a matter of your country looking for *you*."

Mrs. Pollifax was gently reproving. "But how on earth could my country find me in New Brunswick, New Jersey?"

Someone tapped on the door and a young woman appeared. "Mr. Mason, I'm sorry, you're wanted on the phone."

"The phone? Yes." Mason jumped to his feet. "I must excuse myself, Mrs. Politick."

"Pollifax," she reminded him forgivingly, and leaned back in her chair to wait for his return.

BILL Carstairs was lean and tall, with graying hair and a tanned, weather-beaten face. His secretary, Bishop, had no idea how he managed to maintain his outdoor façade. Carstairs spent long hours in his office—a very special room equipped to bring him into contact with any part of the world in a few seconds—often worked until midnight, and when something unusual was going on he would stay the night. He was OSS-trained, but Bishop still thought it was inhuman the way he kept his calm—he himself was apt to hit the ceiling if his pencil point broke.

"Anything from Tirpak?" Carstairs had asked Bishop the first thing that morning.

"Nothing from him since Nicaragua."

"That was two days ago. No word from Costa Rica?"

442

Bishop shook his head and Carstairs leaned back in his chair. "Damn . . . well, I'll arrange for Mexico City anyway. If there's any word I want to hear immediately. I'll be in Higgins's office."

Higgins, of cherubic face and fantastic memory, presided over "Personnel": thousands of names in top-secret files. "Good morning," said Carstairs, peering into Higgins's room.

"Actually it's cloudy," Higgins said mildly. "That's the trouble with this modern architecture. But what can I do for you?"

"I need a tourist. A very particular type of tourist."

Higgins sighed. "Tourists I can supply by the droves, but a particular type—well, go ahead."

"Someone inactive, absolutely unknown. That's vital."

"Go on. For what type of job?"

Carstairs hesitated. He hated divulging information, but then Higgins was not likely to meet with torture during the next twenty-four hours. "There's a package coming into Mexico City. This particular tourist must, on a certain date, stop in at a specified place, pick up said package and bring it here."

Higgins lifted an eyebrow. "A regular courier won't do?"

"Couriers are pretty well known to them," Carstairs pointed out gently. "And to mail it is far too risky."

"Have you considered someone absolutely new—a fresh face?"

"That would mean someone totally unseasoned, wouldn't it?"

"Would it matter? Better that than having someone met in Vienna in 1935 suddenly pop up in Mexico City."

"What are your possibilities? Very little is demanded of my tourist except accuracy, but he or she must look exactly right."

From the files Higgins drew out photograph after photograph. Some were instantly withdrawn with an "Oh no, he won't do, he broke his tibia in the Balkans," or "Sorry, this lady's been loaned to the Orient." When Carstairs left it was with only four pictures.

"Nothing on Tirpak yet," Bishop greeted him.

"Damn," said Carstairs again. Bishop, bless his heart, had left some coffee on the desk and Carstairs took a grateful swallow. Tirpak was one of his best men, and should have reported before now. For eight months he'd been on this job, and from the bits and pieces he'd sent out of South America by wireless and coded mail they had been fruitful months. Visually Tirpak was only a photograph in the top-secret files to Carstairs, but Carstairs knew his mind well—that of a computer, a statistician. Months ago he had been fed all available tips, stories and rumors about Castro's secret operations in the hemisphere, and now he was sending back neat, cold facts. But alone facts were nothing; most vital of all was the proof he was bringing to Mexico City, so concrete that each nation in the Alliance for Progress would know in exactly what form the Trojan horse of communism would appear in its country.

Coffee in hand, Carstairs stared moodily at the ceiling-high map on the wall. The most difficult phase of Tirpak's job was to get that proof into the right hands and move it north, country by country, to Carstairs's desk. It was only to be expected that somewhere the wrong people would get wind of it, so it was no surprise that Tirpak's informants had begun to disappear. But time was now against Tirpak and Carstairs was worried.

He knew the shape this phase ought to take if everything went perfectly: the shabby photographic studio in Costa Rica where Tirpak's bulky packages would be reduced to microfilm; then the trip into Mexico to leave the microfilm with DeGamez, for Tirpak was persona non grata in the United States—a myth that had to be perpetuated for his safety. From Mexico it was up to Carstairs and his tourist. Restlessly, Carstairs lit a cigarette. Was Tirpak being followed? Had he been killed, and all that documentation lost?

The door opened. Carstairs rearranged his features into their habitual mask, but Bishop was smiling. "Tirpak's in Costa Rica."

Carstairs's reaction was fervent and brief. "Thank God," then savagely, "What took him so long?"

Five minutes later he was frowning over a decoded message. Castro's Red Chinese pals were interested in him, Tirpak reported: he had decided it was time to go into hiding. The documents would arrive in Mexico City, suitably camouflaged, between August 12 and August 18. Tirpak planned to remain in Costa Rica for a week or two.

444

If Tirpak said the microfilms would arrive in Mexico City between the twelfth and the eighteenth, they would be there. It was time to get the tourist moving. "Bishop," Carstairs said, arranging the photos on his desk, "which one?"

Bishop said, "They all look like true-blue tourists to me."

Carstairs sighed. "Nobody should be judged by face alone, but this man looks too eager for me. Might get carried away and do some bragging—it's amazing what can come over people in a foreign country. This chap was in China during World War II. If the Chinese are pursuing Tirpak we can't risk him."

"And this woman?" Bishop asked.

"No. I want someone over forty-five." Carstairs studied the fourth face. "Humorless type. She'll do the job; probably won't talk to a soul. Charlotte Webster, age fifty-eight, Washington, D.C. Bishop, I'd like to take a look at her, without being seen."

"I'll ask Mason to set up an appointment with her in the first-floor interviewing room. You can stop in and look her over."

"Inspired, Bishop. See if Mason can get her here at two o'clock."

At two Carstairs finished lunch in the cafeteria and hurried toward the first-floor interviewing room. "Mason's appointment in there?" he said to the guard outside.

"Yes, sir. A woman."

The woman was seated alone in the room and she was so utterly right for the job he could scarcely believe his eyes. He had always been extremely intuitive, able to separate pretense from authenticity at once. His glance first noted the really absurd hat, with one rose completely askew; it then traveled over the wisps of white hair that refused to be confined. He marked the cheerful mouth, and when he met a glance that was as interested as his own he felt the triumph of a casting director who discovers the perfect actress for a pivotal role. He strode across the room with hand outstretched. "I'm Carstairs," he said warmly. "We want you for a job. Have you been talking with Mason?"

"Mr. Mason?" For just a moment she appeared bewildered. "Oh yes, but he was called to the telephone, and—"

445

"It doesn't matter. I realize that you're inexperienced but this is the simplest of jobs. The important thing has been to find someone absolutely right. I think you'll do very well indeed. Are you free to work from August third to August twenty-second?"

"Quite free," she gasped, pink with pleasure. "I'd be delighted!"

"Excellent. Have you ever visited Mexico?"

"Mexico! No, never. You'd like me to go to Mexico?"

He appreciated her radiant response. "You'll be paid the usual courier fee, and of course expenses. You'll be an American tourist, use your own name. The job is to visit a place in Mexico City at a specific date; for the rest you'll be on your own." Miss Webster, Carstairs thought happily, was not only right but perfect—though an extremely bad photographer must have taken her picture. "You can handle this?" he added with a smile.

She drew a deep breath. "That's why I came—because I thought I could. Yes, I'm sure I can. I'll do my *very* best."

He said, "Do you mind coming to my office to fix an appointment? I won't have time to brief you now. Would tomorrow morning be convenient?"

"Perfect." Beaming, she fumbled in her purse and extracted a card. "I don't believe you know my name. I always carry these."

Carstairs, amused, dropped the card in his pocket and escorted her down the hall to his office. "Let's look at my calendar. Nine tomorrow? Sorry to bring you back but I always insist on thorough briefings."

"I think you should," she told him approvingly. "And really, you have been so kind. So *unexpectedly* kind. Thank you."

"Kind?" echoed Carstairs when she had gone. "Well, Bishop, I found my tourist. She's so congenitally innocent she'd baffle Mao Tse-tung himself."

Bishop's jaw dropped. "But, sir—Mason has only this minute called to say Miss Webster has arrived."

"Nonsense. Miss Webster just left."

"No, sir, Miss Webster has just arrived."

Carstairs began, softly and vehemently, to swear. "Then do me the kindness, Bishop, of asking Mason just who the hell was waiting for me in his interviewing room? On the double, Bishop." He drew Mrs. Pollifax's card out of his pocket and reached for the photograph of Miss Webster. There was a superficial resemblance— Miss Webster was a dehydrated version of Mrs. Pollifax. "Well?" he growled as Bishop returned.

"Her name was Politick or Politflack. Mason says she came here to apply for work as a secret agent."

Carstairs stared. "Nobody just walks in and asks to be an agent." Then the corners of his mouth began to twitch. "Preposterous. But damn it, Bishop, order a top-priority security check run on" —he consulted the card—"Mrs. Virgil Pollifax of New Brunswick, New Jersey. I want the results before eight a.m. And then start praying."

"Praying, sir?"

"Yes. Pray that she's never unwittingly entertained a Red for dinner. And tell Mason to send Miss Webster home."

2

FLIGHT NUMBER FIFTY-ONE to Mexico City loading at Gate Four. Flight Number Fifty-one loading at Gate Four. . . ."

Mrs. Pollifax was suffused with almost unbearable excitement. For days she had been practicing the inscrutable look of a secret agent, but now it was impossible to sustain—she was far too enraptured by the thought of her first visit to Mexico. And it was just as well, she told herself, for Mr. Carstairs had emphasized that she was only a tourist. "If I thought you capable of being anyone else I'd never have given you this job," he'd told her firmly.

Mrs. Pollifax had listened with shining eyes. "Your tickets and other papers will be mailed to you. Reservations have been made at the Hotel Reforma Intercontinental on August third for Mrs. Virgil Pollifax, who will be visiting Mexico for three weeks. Where you go is up to you; I assume the usual tourist places—Taxco, Acapulco. But on August nineteenth at ten a.m., *without fail,* you will visit this bookstore in Mexico City." He handed Mrs. Pollifax a slip of paper. "Memorize this address," he had said quietly, and Mrs. Pollifax's heart beat faster. "You will be visited before you leave by a man who will make certain you remember it."

Mrs. Pollifax began memorizing the words at once:

El Papagayo Librería (The Parrot Bookstore)
Calle el Siglo 14,
Mexico City
Senor R. DeGamez, Proprietor—Fine Books Bought & Sold

Carstairs had continued. "In the bookshop you will ask for Dickens's *A Tale of Two Cities.* Senor DeGamez will regret that he does not have a copy at the moment." Mrs. Pollifax waited breathlessly. "Whereupon you will tell him—with an apology for contradicting him—that there is a copy in his window. You will say, 'I think Madame Defarge is simply gruesome, don't you?'" Mrs. Pollifax repeated the words. "These identifying phrases are a nuisance," Carstairs had told her, "but it is wiser to have a double check set up. Asking for *A Tale of Two Cities* and reference to Madame Defarge are the important things to remember."

Mrs. Pollifax nodded. "And whatever I'm to bring you will be in the book? Oh dear, I should never have asked that!"

Carstairs smiled. "No, and I would not in any case tell you. Although in honesty," he added dryly, "I don't know myself what he will give you. As soon as you have paid for the book, you will leave and not return again. You will continue your sight-seeing for two more days and return by jet late on the twenty-first."

She nodded. "What about Customs when I come home?"

"Let's just say that there will be no problems."

"Oh," Mrs. Pollifax said sadly. "It doesn't sound dangerous in the least."

"My dear Mrs. Pollifax, there is always risk, but if real danger were involved I would never allow an amateur to do this. This is simple courier work." He had stood up, smiling. "I hope you weren't insulted at the lie-detector test?"

"Oh no, it was terribly interesting," she told him, beaming.

"Good. It's routine for everyone here." He shook hands. "I won't be seeing you again, Mrs. Pollifax—have lots of fun."

She shrewdly suspected that he had used the word "fun" deliberately, to rid her of any lingering fancies. Well, she *was* going to have fun. Her children's reactions to her trip had been very different. "But Mother," Jane had wailed over long-distance, "if you wanted to travel, you could have come out here to Arizona."

Roger had told her to be careful about drinking the water, but had added, since there was a great deal more of his mother in him than in Jane, "I was getting worried about you, Mother. You haven't erupted in years. Godspeed. If you get in a jam, wire."

Dear Roger. She leaned forward to look out the window as the plane began to taxi. I do hope I'm going to like this, she thought with jarring abruptness when with an overwhelming burst of sound the landscape moved away like a streak.

THE Hotel Reforma in Mexico City proved luxurious beyond Mrs. Pollifax's dreams—almost too much so, but she recalled that the choice was not hers; this was where *tourists* stayed. So the next morning she was first in line for the tour bus. By the end of the day she had made two friends—American schoolteachers, Miss Lambert and Mrs. Donahue—had learned a great deal of Mexico's history, and remembered the name on each street sign they passed. But she had not seen the Calle el Siglo.

The next day she bought a map and after an hour's study set out to find the Calle el Siglo and The Parrot Bookstore, for she did not feel she could really enjoy herself until she knew precisely where to present herself on August 19. To her surprise it was in easy walking distance of the hotel, in a perfectly respectable side street full of tourists, and neither shabby nor neglected, as she romantically imagined, but a smart, modern store.

The following afternoon, after a visit to the National Palace, she steered her two friends up the Calle el Siglo, saying with a ruthless lack of conscience that it was a direct route back to the hotel. This time they passed the very door of The Parrot, and Mrs. Pollifax glanced inside. The man at the counter looked pleasant, with white hair, and a white mustache that was striking against his swarthy skin. Like a Spanish grandee, she decided.

During the days that followed, Mrs. Pollifax found so many opportunities to pass the place that she began to think of it as her own bookstore. At the end of a week she went to Taxco for several days and wandered alone around the crooked, cobblestoned alleys. Everywhere she found people charming and friendly. On the bus back to Mexico City she was entertained by a widower from Chicago. From his conversation she guessed that he was a professional gambler, but this in no way curtailed her interest—Mrs. Pollifax had never met a professional gambler.

The first thing she did after she had checked back into the Hotel Reforma on August 15 was to walk down the Calle el Siglo to reassure herself about her store. Senor DeGamez was there, looking so pleasant that she thought, Surely it wouldn't hurt to buy something? I haven't a thing to read. As she paused, considering, a party of tourists came out of The Parrot laughing and carrying packages. Mrs. Pollifax crossed the street and went in.

Senor DeGamez was wrapping books for a customer. Unfortunately, however, he was speaking Spanish, so Mrs. Pollifax could not eavesdrop. She leaned over a pile marked LATEST BOOKS FROM USA, selected a volume of memoirs by a well-known actress and was groping in her purse when a strident voice screeched, "Old books, new books, read a book!" Mrs. Pollifax turned in astonishment to see a parrot in a cage nearby.

"You like my parrot?" Senor DeGamez's customer had departed and they were alone. "Come see," he said, walking over to the cage. "You know parrots? This one is exceptionally fine."

"So brilliantly colored," said Mrs. Pollifax in a hushed voice.

Senor DeGamez patted the cage. "I named my store after my Olé. She has been with me twelve years. What I do when she dies I don't know."

Mrs. Pollifax nodded sympathetically. "People would say, find another parrot; but it's never the same, is it?"

"Si, you are very wise. My wife is dead five years now, and my sons are grown and away. You have children too perhaps?"

451

Mrs. Pollifax gave him money. "Two," she told him, "both grown. I've been a widow for eight years."

"I am so sorry. But you have not come to Mexico alone?" Mrs. Pollifax nodded. "Then you are courageous. That is good."

"It's sometimes a little lonely," she admitted.

"Do you play solitaire, senora?" Mrs. Pollifax shook her head. "You are missing a delight. I myself treasure the solitaire. It is so mentally healthy."

"I remember trying a few games when I was a child—"

"Si, but you are grown-up now," he told her, smiling. "Please, allow me"—and cutting off her protest he handed her 77 *Ways to Play Solitaire*. "Because you like my parrot."

Mrs. Pollifax, charmed, began to laugh. "I'll try it."

"Good." He nodded to a man and a woman who had entered the store and finished tying up the book she had purchased. "This has been a pleasure, senora. May you have a beautiful visit."

Mrs. Pollifax felt touched and warmed by his friendliness. "Thank you so much," she said, starting for the door.

"Oh, senora," he called to her. "How can you play solitaire without cards?" Mrs. Pollifax turned and he tossed a deck of playing cards the length of the room to her.

"Oh but . . ." she exclaimed, and reached up and caught the cards in midair. Her son would have been proud of her.

"As you Americans say, 'on the house!'" he called gaily.

How nice he was. But she had gone less than a block when she stopped, aghast. That charming gentleman was no other than Mr. Carstairs's Senor DeGamez! She had meant only to walk in, discreetly make a purchase and leave. Now what on earth would he think when Mr. Carstairs's courier turned out to be her! How awful, she thought. This is not the way secret agents behave at all. She resolved not to go near the place again until *The Day*.

She made a list of Things To Do during the next four days: get souvenirs for Roger, Jane and the grandchildren; send postcards. *Dear Miss Hartshorne, Mexico is lovely. . . .* But it was all too dull, so she opened the book Senor DeGamez had given her, and she discovered, to her surprise, that solitaire not only relaxed her nerves but entertained her mind, and she wondered if she ought to mention this to Senor DeGamez when they met again. Better not, she decided regretfully; she must on the nineteenth play the part of secret agent, cool and impersonal.

On the eighteenth she ventured out to complete her shopping for the family. When she retired that night there were serapes draped across the bureau and chairs. Not the very best, she reflected, but buying six at once is expensive, and of course I'm paying for these myself. She had kept a conscientious account of every dollar spent, recalling how grimly Jane's husband talked of waste in Washington. Already she had been here for nearly three weeks . . . for the first time it occurred to Mrs. Pollifax that her visit to The Parrot Bookstore might be more important than Mr. Carstairs had led her to believe. Nonsense, she thought, he just wanted to be sure everyone knew her as a tourist.

WHEN Mrs. Pollifax opened her eyes the next morning she knew it was *The Day*. She zipped the skirt of her best navy blue suit, and because it was cool this morning, added the gorgeous Guatemalan wool jacket that she had given herself as a gift. Then she tucked the playing cards into her purse to carry with her. Her purse contained an astonishing assortment of odds and ends: a pocketknife for her grandson's birthday, two chocolate bars, some handkerchiefs, Band-Aids, travelers' checks, two new lipsticks and one old one that was worn flat, and a memo pad and pencil. She would have to clear all this out soon. But not now.

At 9:45 she turned into the Calle el Siglo. The door of the bookstore was open. She walked in with what she believed to be exquisite casualness.

"*Buenos días,*" said the man behind the counter, looking up with a smile. After a second glance he added, "Good morning."

Mrs. Pollifax glanced around uncertainly, but no one else was there. "Good morning," she said. He was not Senor DeGamez.

"May I be of help?" suggested the man with a bow.

Mrs. Pollifax decided there was no alternative but to ask when Senor DeGamez would be back. "When I was here before," she told the man confidingly, "the proprietor was so helpful. Will he be in soon?"

"But I am the proprietor, senora. The other man was my cousin who comes in to help. He is DeGamez too."

"He was so kind," explained Mrs. Pollifax. "He gave me a book on solitaire—oh dear." She gasped. "Perhaps I shouldn't have mentioned that—but I'd be happy to pay you for it—"

"Yes, that is José," said the man with a rueful smile. He shrugged, his gold tooth gleaming. "If the store were his we'd be bankrupt in a month. Still, his charm brought you back, no?"

"Yes indeed—to buy *A Tale of Two Cities*," she told him boldly. "I believe there's a copy in your window."

"Si?" He said it with just the proper note of surprise. She walked with him to a low curtain that divided the window from the store. They both looked, but Mrs. Pollifax could see no copy of *A Tale of Two Cities*. With a sinking sensation she realized that she ought to have looked for it before coming inside. Nothing seemed to be going well; it was as if fate were testing her. "It was here the other day, I ought to have stopped then. I think Madame Defarge is simply gruesome, don't you?" She waited, her eyes alert.

Senor DeGamez looked at Mrs. Pollifax and his eyes grew thoughtful. "It is not there," he said. "But I think we understand each other nevertheless, you and I."

"Pardon?"

"I mean that I have been expecting you. Please—a cup of tea in my little back room while I get what you have come for."

Mrs. Pollifax said cautiously, "That's very nice of you." She wasn't sure that it was, and the absence of the book made her feel like a fool. Yet the man said he had been expecting her. Perhaps the book had been mislaid—even spies must have their bad days. "Very kind indeed," she added more firmly, and since he was holding back the curtain that separated the back room from the shop, there seemed nothing to do but walk past him into the rear.

"Forgive the untidiness," he said with a sweeping gesture.

It was indeed untidy, with cartons of books piled to the ceiling and the floor littered with paper. But Senor DeGamez was not luring her behind the curtain to hit her over the head. Tea really was brewing on a sterno, and at the sight of it—there was something so cozy about tea-making—her confidence returned.

"Milk, lemon, sugar?" he asked, leading her to the desk.

"Milk and one sugar, please," she said, sitting down in the swivel chair. "Although really I mustn't stop more than a minute."

"No, of course not, that would be most unwise," he agreed, bringing her a steaming cup. "I'll be back in a minute."

He disappeared behind the curtain and Mrs. Pollifax sipped the tea. He was certainly polite, but he lacked the warmth of his cousin. She wondered what he would bring her—another book or a package? What a stuffy room this was! It would have been kind of him to open a window. She drained the cup and as she stood up an odd shape caught her eye: domelike and covered with a cloth. She pulled the cloth aside. It was a birdcage, empty now but for one vivid blue feather.

The parrot! she thought in astonishment. The other Senor De-Gamez had said, "I named my store after my Olé. She has been with me twelve years. . . ." *My* store . . . But she could not think clearly now, for it was very close and her head was beginning to ache. She tried to force herself to think: if the parrot belonged to the first senor . . . There was a conclusion to be drawn but Mrs. Pollifax could not draw it. Something was terribly wrong and it *wasn't* the heat. It was the tea. "There was something in that tea," cried Mrs. Pollifax, taking a step toward the door, but she took no more than one before she sank, unconscious, to the floor.

3

MRS. POLLIFAX opened one eye, dimly aware that someone was methodically slapping her face, first the left cheek and then the right. She closed her eyes and the rhythmic slapping began again. When she next roused she made an attempt to focus on a looming face. "Fu Manchu," she murmured wittily, and giggled.

"You will wake up, pliss," said a voice.

Mrs. Pollifax sighed. "Very well. Only stop slapping my face." This time she made a distinct effort to keep her eyes open, but the sight that confronted her was not rewarding. She and the cheek slapper appeared to be sharing a small, windowless tar-paper shack. A kerosene lamp sent grotesque shadows over the rough walls, there was a smell of mustiness and wet earth, and she saw why she had burbled in her sleep about Fu Manchu: the cheek slapper was Chinese. He was neatly dressed in Western clothes and looked like a young student. "Where am I?" she asked indignantly.

"I wouldn't bother asking if I were you," said a voice behind her. The voice was male and definitely American. Mrs. Pollifax squirmed in her chair to look but discovered that she couldn't: her hands were bound tightly behind her with wire. "We're tied together," explained the voice. "Back to back, wrist to wrist—very chummy. Farrell's my name. Who the devil are *you*?"

She said stiffly, "Mrs. Virgil Pollifax from New Brunswick, New Jersey. Look here, young man," she told their guard firmly, "I know first aid. You will have to amputate my left hand if you don't allow it some circulation."

The guard said calmly, "Soon you will eat and be given an opportunity to exercise the hands."

The door opened and a man with a tray of food walked in. Glancing beyond him Mrs. Pollifax saw that it was dark outside. I've been unconscious all afternoon! she thought in astonishment. The cheek slapper leaned over to free her wrists with a pair of pliers. She kept her eyes hungrily on the food: tired-looking tortillas, dry gray bread and two cups of coffee. It was just as well that she had food to divert her because her captor was none too gentle; tears rose in her eyes as he worked. When her numbed hands were free she placed them in her lap and tried not to notice the blood trickling into her palms. The young Chinese said, "Eat," and went out with the other man. A key grated in the lock and Mrs. Pollifax turned to look at the man behind her. He was staring at her incredulously.

"Bless my soul," he said, his jaw dropping. "Where do you fit into this? No, don't touch the coffee," he added quickly, "it's probably drugged."

Mrs. Pollifax regarded him with suspicion. He was not the type of man that she could approve of. He had a lean, hard face with a Hollywood kind of handsomeness about it—the type of face that lent itself to caricature. Draw a perfect, deeply tanned oval, square it a little at the jaw, cap it with a line of straight black hair, add a black mustache, and there would be Mr. Farrell—a tough inhabitant of a world that she knew would shock her. Perhaps he even dealt in the drugs that he mentioned so lightly. "Where are we," she demanded, "and who are these dreadful people?" She picked up a tortilla and resolutely chewed on it.

"These are Mao Tse-tung's boys," said Farrell. "And I definitely heard a plane land outside while they were trying to bring you back to consciousness."

"What airport can this be?" said Mrs. Pollifax falteringly.

He shrugged and sat down to eat his tortilla. "I've heard they have secret airfields in Mexico."

Mrs. Pollifax said stiffly, "You certainly seem well informed. How do you know all this unless you're one of them?"

He grinned. "Don't trust me? Now that makes me suspicious of you for the first time. I'm being abducted too, in case you hadn't noticed. Whisked away from a theater date with the beautiful Miss Willow Lee, who has very high connections in Peking."

Mrs. Pollifax was astonished. "And you were going to take her to the theater?"

He grinned. "My dear lady, I knew all about her when I met her. What I didn't realize was that she knew all about me too. Now just how did *you* land in this?"

Suddenly Mrs. Pollifax laughed. I'm here because I carried geraniums to the rooftop one day, she thought to herself. And I don't have the right to be afraid. I asked for a little adventure and it's precisely what I'm having. She felt calmed at once. She said, "I think I'm here because I walked into a little shop in Mexico City to buy a book."

Farrell looked at her strangely. "Not El Papagayo!"

His face swam toward her, then receded. She heard him say in a thick voice, "Damn it, they put it in the tortillas."

Mrs. Pollifax nodded wisely. Just enough new drugs in the food to dope them again. Very clever, she thought, and this time took the precaution of sitting down so that she would not fall to the floor. I'm becoming quite experienced, she reflected proudly, and even smiled a little as blackness descended.

BILL CARSTAIRS had spent most of the morning of August 20 conferring with a State Department official about a revolution that had erupted in a small South American country. When Bishop brought his coffee, he had also a slip of paper from the teletype marked CARSTAIRS URGENT. It read: BODY IDENTIFIED AS RAFAEL DEGAMEZ FOUND IN CANAL LAST NIGHT STOP POLICE ESTIMATE DEATH OCCURRED AUGUST 17 STOP INVESTIGATION UNDER WAY.

Carstairs felt hot rage grow in him. It would in time be supplanted by ruthless efficiency; but now he allowed himself a moment to mourn DeGamez, whom he had known and liked. It was no way for a man to die—even if he did know the risks.

"Get the message verified by the Mexico City police, Bishop, and tell them to keep us in touch. Oh God," he added suddenly. "Mrs. Pollifax! She was to visit DeGamez yesterday. Get the Hotel Reforma Intercontinental too."

"Mrs. Pollifax is being paged," Bishop reported in a few minutes.

"Now get me Johnny at the Galería de Artes in Mexico City," Carstairs barked.

But Johnny had not yet come into the Galería de Artes; Carstairs picked up the connection, began speaking in fluent Spanish. Had this happened before? When had the owner of the Galería last been seen? Grimly Carstairs hung up. "Take this down, Bishop. 'Temperature 102 in Mexico City. Worried about health of Aunt Josephine. Suggest complete rest in hospital.'" He wrote names on a sheet of paper. "Translate and send out at once, top priority, to these people."

By two o'clock messages had begun filtering in. Mrs. Pollifax had not been seen in the hotel since the morning of the nineteenth.

There was no news of Johnny. If he had been snatched, the whole thing had blown higher than a kite. DeGamez's knifed body had been discovered, weighted with cement, in a canal which the sanitation department had begun to drain under a new insect-control drive. The peculiar thing was that DeGamez's store had been open through August 19. The police were checking on the man who had been running it. Now the hotel detective reported that clothes belonging to Mrs. Pollifax still hung in the closet of her room, but all coat linings had been slit open, as had her suitcase and her pillow. From Johnny's apartment came word that nothing had been touched except a safe in the kitchen. This had been tidily blown open with nitroglycerin.

Carstairs swore savagely. "They've got Johnny, and the code as well. Take this telegram. 'Regret to inform you Aunt Josephine died five o'clock. Kindly acknowledge at once.'" He had to face the fact that they might have Tirpak too. "Get Costa Rica."

At five o'clock a description came through of the man in De-Gamez's shop. No one in the neighborhood had ever seen him before. It made Carstairs thoughtful. "I only hope I'm wrong," he said to Bishop. "Get me File Six-X."

The file arrived and Carstairs scowled at two photographs of the same man: one an enlargement showing him standing next to Mao Tse-tung, the other a snapshot taken secretly in Cuba. "Take away the glasses and who do we have?" he said. Bishop whistled. Carstairs nodded. "Our brilliant and ruthless friend General Perdido. Mao's handpicked man for South America—the person responsible for bringing Castro closer to Red China than to Red Russia." Now he knew they must have found Tirpak. "There's one feeble hope. Perdido was in Cuba last week, wasn't he?"

"Seen there on August fifteenth," Bishop said.

Carstairs said slowly, "He just might take one of them—Johnny or Tirpak or Mrs. Pollifax—back to Cuba with him." He glanced at Bishop and smiled faintly. "Go have lunch or whatever it's time for. You can bring me back some coffee and a chocolate bar."

Carstairs, relieved at being alone, lit a cigarette. His face was like granite as he weighed all angles. Eight months of Tirpak's invaluable work gone up in smoke, three top agents missing and presumed dead. He thought of the years that DeGamez and Johnny had spent in building up their reputations in Mexico City as cover for their real work. They had been good, very good.

But in this game these things happened. Tirpak, DeGamez and Johnny had all—he was already using the past tense—been seasoned agents. They knew the tricks of the enemy, they had their own tricks, and if all else failed they knew how to kill themselves quickly. It was Mrs. Pollifax who was on Carstairs's conscience. She had been so exactly right, that preposterous hat, those little absurdities that gave her so much character. She had been given the most routine of jobs, yet the fact remained that he had sent her off totally unprepared. She had not even been given a cyanide pill. She was not aware of General Perdido's kind of world. He had sent a lamb into a wolves' den—and the wolves would make short work of devouring his lamb.

God help her, Carstairs thought devoutly.

"WONDER if they'll try to brainwash us," Mrs. Pollifax was saying cheerfully. "Do you know anything about brainwashing, Mr. Farrell?"

"Uh—no," Farrell said politely.

"It might prove interesting." She was remembering the lie-detector test. Life was really very scientific these days. She had been alert for an hour now, it was still night, and they were flying through the air. Her wrists were unbound, but around each of her ankles was a medieval-looking shackle chained to a ring set into the seat. It was not uncomfortable, but it did give her a perverse longing to cross her legs now that she couldn't.

"You didn't answer my question," Farrell said suddenly. "About that bookstore you walked into. Was it El Papagayo?"

"I'm afraid I didn't notice its name," Mrs. Pollifax lied smoothly. "I seldom do. Of course I know when I'm in Macy's or Gimbels but this was a very *little* store."

There was a glimmer of amusement in Farrell's eyes. "A very *little* store. And what happened there?"

"I went in," said Mrs. Pollifax, "and asked for a book. This man was very friendly and invited me into his back room for tea. The next thing I knew I was tied up with you in that shack." She suddenly remembered that the best defense was an offense. "And how did *you* come to be here? Are you a tourist too?"

"I've lived in Mexico since 'forty-five—I run the Galería de Artes in Mexico City. John Sebastian Farrell's the name."

Mrs. Pollifax was relieved. "Oh, I thought you might be a dope peddler, or . . ." she said.

He grinned. "I've done some rum things in my life, but no one's ever taken me for a dope peddler before."

Mrs. Pollifax at once apologized. "I've lived a sheltered life, but you do *look* as if you'd done some rum things."

"It's beginning to show? Well, at forty-one it's bound to. Pity."

Mrs. Pollifax paid his mockery no attention. "What are some of the rum things you've done?"

"Heavens, should you be interested? You're not planning to write a book on your travels?" He was still grinning.

She considered this seriously and shook her head. "No, it had never occurred to me, although I'll be very interested in seeing Cuba. You still believe it's where they're taking us?"

Farrell said irritably, "In all probability, but it's taking us a hell of a long time to get there. Sorry—what were you asking?"

"You were going to tell me what a rum life consists of."

He grinned. "You don't think I'd dare give you an unlaundered version, do you? I've bummed around Mexico since 'forty-five, when I was discharged from the Marines. Ran a charter boat out of Acapulco till I lost it in a poker game. I've also given painting lessons to debutantes—I do occasionally move in the best circles."

"As well as the worst?" Mrs. Pollifax hoped he wasn't going to disappoint her.

"As well as the worst. For a year I smuggled guns in to Castro before he won his revolution. Rather a friend of mine although I've not seen him lately," he added with a roguish glint. "And I might add modestly that women constantly fall at my feet."

Mrs. Pollifax could not allow this weakness in her sex to go

461

undefended. She said blandly, "Like the Chinese woman you were going to take to the theater?"

Farrell gazed at her for a moment. "Duchess—I hope you don't mind if I call you that—you surprise me. You're not a member of the DAR after all."

"No, but I *am* a member of the garden club and—"

"If General Perdido knew these things he'd turn pale."

"General who?"

"Just someone I know." He leaned forward to the window. "We're still very high but I thought I saw some lights down there." He added savagely, "You understand what you've gotten yourself into, don't you? You know what the odds are?"

Mrs. Pollifax was tired of feigning innocence. She said quietly, "Yes. I'm aware that I've been abducted by dangerous people."

"It doesn't bother you?" he demanded.

Mrs. Pollifax wanted to tell him that of course it did. She would like very much to be flying home to a hot tub. She did not want to die in a strange country, and she did not labor under any illusions about Mr. Carstairs coming to her rescue. It was a lonely situation, but Mrs. Pollifax was acquainted with loneliness and it did not frighten her. What did frighten her was the thought of losing her dignity. She had never met with cruelty before. If her life had to end soon, she only hoped that it could end with dignity. She must be very careful not to display any unsteadiness; it was the least that the old could do for the young. Her gaze fell to the seat beside Farrell and she gasped. "Look—my purse! They haven't taken it away. It's squashed down between your seat and the next."

"Thoroughly searched, of course. What's in it?" he asked as he handed it to her.

She felt as if it were a Christmas grab bag. "It's a good deal emptier," she agreed, opening it. "Oh dear, my aspirin's gone. And Bobby's pocketknife—he's my eleven-year-old grandson."

"No, they wouldn't approve of that at all."

"But the Band-Aids are here, and my memo pad and pencil and lipsticks—oh, and look," she cried happily, "they've left me my playing cards!" She slipped them tenderly out of their box.

"Small comfort," growled Farrell.

"You don't know how comforting they can be," she told him with the enthusiasm of a convert. "I already know twenty-two games. It's so relaxing and it will give me something to do." She was already laying out cards in a circle on the seat beside her for a game of solitaire. "They left the chocolate bars too," she said absently. "You can eat one if you'd like."

Her eyes on the cards, she heard him say in a funny voice, "We ought to be hungry, you know. Terribly hungry."

"Why, so we should be." She frowned. "I had that man's tea, and nothing until night, then only a slice of bread and a tortilla."

He said quietly, rolling up his sleeve, "Wonder if you have needle marks on your arm too. I think we've been fed intravenously so we wouldn't die on their hands." He leaned forward and said in a low voice, "The plane I heard landing back in Mexico was a propeller job. The plane we're in now is a jet. They must have landed somewhere and switched. I think we've been unconscious for a whole day instead of a few hours."

Mrs. Pollifax put down her cards. "But jets travel very fast. And if we've been traveling for such a long time—"

He nodded. "I don't think that you are going to see Cuba."

"Not see Cuba," she echoed. "But where . . . ?" On second thought this question was much better left unsaid. Instead she said in a voice that trembled only a little, "I certainly do hope Miss Hartshorne is remembering to water my geraniums."

4

It was still night when they began their descent. Mrs. Pollifax felt the flutter of excited dread she had experienced as a child when the dentist beckoned, saying it was her turn now. She stared in amazement at the heaving landscape below.

"High mountains," said Farrell, but he did not say where the mountains might be. "We're landing," he said suddenly.

A scattering of lights increased, and suddenly the earth rushed past with dizzying speed and they taxied to a very bumpy stop. Mrs. Pollifax put her playing cards in her purse as the cockpit door opened and two Chinese they had not seen before walked in, one of them carrying a revolver. The other unshackled their ankles and indicated that Mrs. Pollifax and Farrell were to climb down a ladder propped against the side of the plane. The two men waiting for them in the oppressively warm night were not Orientals; to Mrs. Pollifax they looked—perhaps Greek. She saw Farrell glance from them to the mountains and then at the stars. She said anxiously, "Have you any idea *where* we may be?"

He said grimly, "If my guess is right, Duchess, I should say, Welcome to Albania."

"*Albania!*" gasped Mrs. Pollifax. "But I don't know anything *about* Albania. The idea's preposterous!"

"Nevertheless," said Farrell, "I think it's where we are."

A long car, white with dust, drew up and they were ushered into the rear. "A Rolls," Farrell whispered, and Mrs. Pollifax nodded politely. The two Greek-looking men climbed in and sat facing them on drop seats, guns in hand, as the car began to move at reckless speed over incredibly bumpy ground. Soon they entered a town, threading narrow streets. The houses that showed briefly in the headlights looked inhospitable, their rooftops barely seen over the tops of high walls guarded by huge gateways with iron-studded doors. Then they left the town behind and Mrs. Pollifax saw that they were heading toward harsh, craggy mountains.

"But why Albania?" Mrs. Pollifax said. "Surely you're wrong!"

"Because it's not China, and one has to think of the few parts of the world where the Red Chinese are welcome. That town looked Balkan. These mountains could be the Albanian Alps, and certainly these men are Europeans."

Mrs. Pollifax nodded. "Greek, I thought."

"If this is Albania then Greece is only a few hundred miles away," Farrell pointed out. "Albania is the only country where the Red Chinese can come and go at will. Until 1960 Russia was Albania's big brother. Then Stalin was denounced and that rocked Albania—they're Stalinists here, you see. When Russia withdrew

464

its aid, Red China moved in. It gave them a toehold in Europe."

"But why such trouble to bring us here?" asked Mrs. Pollifax.

"Perhaps they feel we're worth it," Farrell said.

"Oh," said Mrs. Pollifax in a small voice, and was silent.

The car climbed a steep road that appeared to be carved out of the side of a mountain. Higher and higher it climbed until at last it stopped and their two guards came to life, jumped out and gestured at them to leave the car. Once outside, they found themselves in a vast basin of desolate gray rock. Dawn was near, and quite absurdly Mrs. Pollifax recalled her son Roger telling her to wire him if she found herself in a jam.

One of the guards went off and reappeared leading four donkeys. To Mrs. Pollifax's consternation he signaled that she mount one of them. "I can't," she said.

"I believe you're going to have to," Farrell pointed out in amusement.

She eyed the animal with distaste and in turn it eyed her with suspicion. Farrell moved forward to help, and a truce was accomplished because, once she was on its back, the donkey could no longer see her. Farrell and the guards also mounted donkeys.

The wilderness path was desolate beyond belief. The sunrise brought heat, and Mrs. Pollifax was soon extremely uncomfortable. They had traveled for perhaps an hour when Farrell said suddenly, "Psst—look."

Mrs. Pollifax reluctantly lifted her eyes. They had come out upon a small plateau literally carpeted with stones, like a dry brook bed. At the very edge of a cliff straight above stood a fortress-like stone building with black slits for windows. As her donkey picked its way over the stones Mrs. Pollifax saw that they were heading for a second, smaller building precisely like the other except in size. If she were a tourist, she thought wistfully, this would be a wild, romantic scene; but she was a captured American spy—and no one on God's earth knew where she was. For a moment she allowed herself to think of her children. It seems so *unreal*, she thought unhappily.

"Journey's end," commented Farrell dryly.

"I don't think you need put it in just that manner," Mrs. Pollifax said crossly. "I have always found that in painful situations it is sensible to take each hour as it comes. But oh how I wish I could have a bath!"

The iron door of the smaller building opened; a man stepped out with a rifle under his arm but Mrs. Pollifax was too busy separating herself from the donkey to pay him any attention. No sooner was she upright, all her bones protesting, than the guard grasped her arm and led her into the building.

The door was at one end of a thirty-foot rectangle; they entered a room that occupied the precipice end of the structure. On their left was a dark hall, and looking down it Mrs. Pollifax saw two iron cell doors. The entrance room contained a desk, a chair, a water cooler, a gun rack, a small switchboard and a gray-haired man dressed in a uniform. He greeted them curtly in English.

"I am Major Vassovic." Brandishing a huge key, he led them to the first cell door and opened it. "In, please."

"I don't suppose you have an aspirin," Mrs. Pollifax told him hopefully. "I have the most ridiculous headache. I don't mean to complain, but I've been doped twice, and it's been a rather exhausting plane ride—"

The major looked at her in astonishment, then wiped all expression from his face. "I have no orders to give you anything."

The door clanged shut behind them and Mrs. Pollifax said, "I don't see how one aspirin . . ." Her voice died away at sight of their prison. It was quite decent in size, but lighted only by the two slits in the wall. There was to be no privacy. There was an iron cot at each end of the room, with a night chamber under each, and there were two small tables, but no chairs, screens, lavatory or clothes pegs.

"Well," said Farrell, and sat down on a cot.

They stared at each other through a silence that was becoming much too dismal. "Well," Mrs. Pollifax said briskly, and spread out her playing cards.

"Not again," groaned Farrell. "Not *here*."

"Whyever not?" she said, glad to see him diverted.

She had played three games when the door opened and a guard gestured that she was to come with him and Farrell to stay. "Good luck, Duchess," Farrell said lightly.

Mrs. Pollifax did not look back. Her knees trembled as she was led out into the blazing sun, over the stones, to the larger building and into a large room of whitewashed stone. There were two men in uniform in the room and a man seated at a desk. "Why, Senor DeGamez," Mrs. Pollifax gasped. "How did you get here?"

His gold tooth flashed in a smile. "In the same manner that you did, Mrs. Pollifax."

"Except," she went on, "that I realized as soon as I saw the empty parrot cage that you weren't Senor DeGamez."

"Actually I am General Raoul Perdido. Allow me to present General Hoong, who is in charge of the—uh—buildings here." The Chinese at the window bowed, and Perdido continued, "Do sit down, Mrs. Pollifax, we have a few things to discuss. Pleasantly or unpleasantly, depending upon your attitude."

Brainwashing, thought Mrs. Pollifax contemptuously, suddenly unafraid. She had endured other crises without losing her dignity—births, widowhood. She knew now that everything worthwhile took time and loneliness. She told herself, I refuse to be frightened by a man whose only weapon over me is the cessation of life. Aloud she said, "May I ask just why you had to abduct me like this?"

He leaned back in his chair, lit a cigar and impaled her with a sharp glance. "Mrs. Pollifax, I abhor pretended innocence."

"And I have a great deal to complain about," she told him coldly. "You have flown me across the world to ask questions that could have been asked in Mexico. I don't know what country you work for, General Perdido, but your taxpayers have every right to be furious."

The general's face darkened. "I see that you are going to deny you are an American spy."

"*Spy?*" said Mrs. Pollifax scornfully. "Is that what you take me for? This is one more grievance I must hold against you, General. And I wish you'd tell me where I am. Albania—is this true?"

"Never mind," he shouted. "You are far from home and no one knows where you are. I have methods for extracting truth from you—all painful. I am extremely accomplished in them."

"I'm sure you are at the top of your profession," she said tartly, "but I do not find it a very admirable profession."

General Hoong turned from the window and spoke rapidly. Then Perdido said reluctantly, "Let us try to be reasonable, Mrs. Pollifax. You visited The Parrot Bookstore on a day when, you told me, the first Senor DeGamez made you the gift of a book?"

"Yes, he was very kind." On this Mrs. Pollifax could be completely frank. "We began talking—about his parrot and about traveling alone. That's when he gave me the book. He told me that solitaire was something I would enjoy. Have you tried it?"

The general opened a desk drawer and brought out two books. "Then it is the book on solitaire that he gave you!"

Mrs. Pollifax gasped. "Why—you *stole* my books!"

"Yes, but one of them was presented to you by an extremely dangerous man." The general studied her. "You are being a little ingenuous, Mrs. Pollifax. So far we have found nothing. For the moment it is sufficient to learn that it is *77 Ways to Play Solitaire* that he gave you. We shall examine it many more times."

Mrs. Pollifax said stiffly, "That book was given to me out of kindness, which seems a very feeble reason for my abduction. If you insist that it is full of messages in invisible ink, or whatever you people use these days—"

The general interrupted, staring at her with dislike. "If you are innocent you chose a most inauspicious morning to visit the bookstore, Mrs. Pollifax."

"On the contrary," she said coldly. "The sun was shining and I wanted a book to read."

"But you did not so much as demur when I suggested I had something to give you. Why did you accept tea from me? Just what were you expecting?"

"A chat," said Mrs. Pollifax. "Is that so difficult for you to believe? My government expects us to be traveling ambassadors abroad. I was *trying*," she added piously, "to know you better."

General Perdido exploded in what sounded like an oath. "You may go back to your cell."

Mrs. Pollifax nodded and arose. "There is one other matter," she said. "Please could I be given one aspirin?"

Farrell sprang to his feet as soon as the door slammed shut behind Mrs. Pollifax. "Are you all right?" he asked.

His concern deeply touched her. "Yes, really. I was asked questions by that man I met in a bookstore in Mexico City." She sat down and shuffled her cards. "Are we being bugged?"

"There must be some kind of listening device—it's why they put us together—but where on earth did you get that term?"

"One learns a great deal about life at the hairdresser's." She whispered, "Farrell, I must apologize. The reason they brought us here is that they believe I'm a dangerous American spy."

"You?" The corners of his mouth twitched. "You're not, are you?"

Mrs. Pollifax hesitated. "In one sense, no . . . in another, yes. But certainly not *dangerous.*" Then, still whispering, she told her story. "General Raoul Perdido," she said. "You mentioned his name once—quite lightly—on the plane. Do you know him?"

"Nobody mentions Perdido lightly; if I did I ought to have my head examined. He's a cruel, vicious bas— Sorry." A smile lit up his eyes. "Duchess, let's not be gloomy. You've outflanked him for the moment. You've bought time. . . . Oh-oh, company again."

The door swung wide and a man walked in carrying a tray of food, followed by a guard who dramatically covered them with his rifle. Mrs. Pollifax thought it extremely ill-bred of him. The men exited and she examined the odd-looking food which lay on her dish like a piece of melted rubber. "Is it drugged, do you think?"

"Not likely. They'll be questioning me soon, and I'd be no good to them drugged. It's some sort of cheese dish. Not bad."

They ate quietly. There was strong coffee and cakes drenched in honey. When they had finished Farrell said, "And now, Duchess, there is something I should tell *you.* General Perdido already knows it. I too work for Carstairs." Mrs. Pollifax drew in her breath sharply. "I've been an agent in Mexico since 'forty-seven when the CIA was formed. I did a job once with DeGamez but I hadn't seen him for years until on the afternoon of the nineteenth I received a crazy, garbled message from him and I went at once to his bookstore. You see, inserted into the message was a code word meaning SOS. By reacting to that code word I had proved I was just who they thought I was—an agent they'd been looking for for years. The first thing they took from me was the cyanide pill I'm never without. The second thing they took from me was my freedom. So here I am, full of information, a real Christmas present in August for General Perdido."

Mrs. Pollifax stared at him. "You are very brave."

He lifted an eyebrow mockingly. "Not at the moment, Duchess. You see, I can't allow General Perdido to question me. You understand what I've got to do, don't you?"

"What do you mean?" faltered Mrs. Pollifax.

"I mean that no one can hold out indefinitely against the general's methods. I mustn't be taken alive into that building."

Mrs. Pollifax became very still. Farrell began pacing. "For me it's part of the job," he said, "but I hate leaving you in the lurch."

"You mustn't concern yourself with me at all. *Please*. But what do you intend to do?"

He shrugged. "Try to break away between here and the other building and hope they'll shoot me. Throw a rock at somebody."

She averted her eyes so that her compassion need not embarrass him. Men like him must have been dying for years in queer parts of the world without her ever knowing of their existence. She was extremely grateful to have known Farrell.

"I hate deserting you," he continued. "But Carstairs would never approve of my staying alive; I know too much." Hearing the door open he gravely shook her hand. Two guards, heavily armed, and Major Vassovic had come to superintend Farrell's removal.

"God go with you," whispered Mrs. Pollifax.

Major Vassovic coughed. "The—uh—order has been received now. One aspirin, to be taken in my presence. Come."

Mrs. Pollifax, her headache redoubled, followed the major into the guardroom. He brought her a cup of water and the pill. As she took it, she noticed on the wall guns and knives with beautiful silver ornamentation. They belonged in an art museum and she told the major so.

"The long guns are called *pushkas,*" he said gruffly. "The sabers we call *yataghans* in this country."

There was also an assortment of undecorated, lethal-looking pistols and revolvers but Mrs. Pollifax ignored these, her glance falling to the three drawers set into the base of the gun rack. One of them held a key in its lock; a brass key, really quite distinctive. She kept her glance riveted to this. I am admiring a brass key, she told herself. Presently Farrell will be killed and I mustn't think about it. She did not have long to wait. Harsh shouts came from outside the building, then the sound of guns being fired. Mrs. Pollifax very carefully placed the cup of water on the major's desk and was pleased to see that her hand was not trembling.

At the sound of firing Major Vassovic uttered an oath, glanced from the window, said, "Back—back," and pushed Mrs. Pollifax roughly down the hall to her cell. The door slammed upon her, and there was only silence now. Mrs. Pollifax sat down on Farrell's cot and said quietly, "I didn't look." For some reason this was very important to her. "I didn't look," she repeated. Fumbling in her purse, she brought out a handkerchief and angrily blew her nose. Then she resolutely laid out her cards for a game of spider.

The silence was like a shroud in the stone cell—like Farrell's shroud, she thought bitterly. Then she heard a small noise from the wall behind her. It sounded like someone rhythmically striking the stone. Remembering the second iron door in the hall outside, she knelt on the cot and tapped back. Immediately the sound stopped, then just as Mrs. Pollifax decided that it was someone repairing a drain, the fist beat an excited staccato reply. This fist had a personality all its own, thought Mrs. Pollifax, for now it was replying with joy. Yes, with joy. She reflected that if this were anything but real life they would now exchange urgent messages in Morse code. Unfortunately she knew no Morse. She tapped again, but it was like communicating with someone who spoke only Swahili; after the initial greetings there wasn't much more to say.

Besides, her mind was on Farrell. She sadly returned to her cards.

It seemed a long time later when the building filled with noise again. She heard booted feet and Major Vassovic irritably issuing orders and she waited for the inevitable grating of the key in the lock—a sound she was beginning to dread. Then the door swung open. *"Farrell!"* she gasped.

He was propped between two guards, one leg dangling uselessly, his clothes smeared with blood. At her cry he opened one eye. "Goofed again, Duchess," he said, and as the men dropped him on the cot he added peevishly, "Damn cliff. If *you* jumped from a hundred-foot cliff wouldn't *you* expect to be killed?" Unconscious, he fell back on the bed.

5

IGHT FELL and Mrs. Pollifax sat beside Farrell, listening as he slipped in and out of feverish dreams. His leg was broken in two places and she had neither water nor bandages for him. Apparently only one bullet had hit him; it was embedded in his right arm above the elbow. She had stanched the bleeding by using her blanket as a tourniquet. When General Perdido arrived with Major Vassovic she was in a cold fury.

Major Vassovic inserted a candle he carried into a metal ring set in the wall; the general glared down at Farrell contemptuously. "I have asked for water and bandages and no one has brought them," Mrs. Pollifax said icily. "If I may make a suggestion, General, why don't you shoot Mr. Farrell? He is making a great deal of bothersome noise and bleeding all over your furniture."

Perdido turned on her angrily. "You are insolent, Mrs. Pollifax."

"Then perhaps you would like to shoot me as well."

For a moment she thought General Perdido was going to strike her. She hoped he would, so uncontainable was her rage. But he turned on his heel. "Give the woman what she wants," he said to Major Vassovic. "Perhaps she can revive the prisoner for questioning." With this he marched out.

The major brought strips of cloth and a water pitcher and watched while Mrs. Pollifax moistened Farrell's lips, untied the tourniquet and removed two wooden bed slats from her cot.

"What you do now?" asked Major Vassovic curiously.

"I intend to set his leg. I hope you will help me."

He said stiffly, "I have no orders. No orders," and went out.

Mrs. Pollifax knew she would bungle the job alone. Gritting her teeth she ripped away his trouser leg. She looked at his leg, already swollen and red. "I will not faint, I will not."

The door behind her opened quietly. One of the guards stood there, his finger to his lips. "My name is Lulash." He closed the door gently. "The major has gone for the night," he said. "I have worked in hospital. I can set this leg. *Zot*, but it looks bad."

Mrs. Pollifax's eyes filled with tears. "He was trying to kill himself, Mr. Lulash," she explained in a strangled voice.

Lulash only nodded. "I do my best. I bid you sit on the man's chest and hold him down." Numbly Mrs. Pollifax obeyed.

Ten minutes later the leg was set and Mrs. Pollifax, shaken and ill, watched Lulash bind it with the bed slats. After one enraged scream Farrell had lost consciousness again. Lulash mopped his brow with a soiled handkerchief.

"We are Americans," said Mrs. Pollifax. "Is this Albania?"

The guard shrugged. "We call it Shqiperia—Land of the Mountain Eagle. But yes, it is Albania."

"Do all Albanians speak such fine English?"

"No. They searched for those of us in the Sigurimi—the name of the secret police—who speak your language."

Mrs. Pollifax gasped. "Then you are—"

He shrugged. "The time is difficult. Those who do not join the Sigurimi can be seen on the roads. They smash rock, have no hope."

"I'm sorry," said Mrs. Pollifax, unable to see anything in the dark, secretive face to explain his kindness to Farrell.

"Albanians are a proud, fierce people," he said. "But without luck. First the Turks ruled us, then the Russians, now the Chinese. You know nothing of our country?"

"Nothing at all, I'm afraid."

"I have book I show you about it," he said. "The most beautiful country in the world. Ah, your friend is stirring. I find an aspirin."

At the door he stood waiting for her. Surprised, she followed him out, touched by his trust. In the guardroom he opened a desk drawer and brought out a flask of what looked to be brandy. Mrs. Pollifax's glance again took in the gun rack behind the desk. The little brass key to the drawer was still in its lock. If that drawer contained ammunition, a person could steal the key and later hope to come back. Then perhaps a gun could be taken. . . . While Lulash bent over the bottom drawer, she stepped backward until she felt the gun rack between her shoulder blades. Fumblingly she slid the drawer open; it was filled with neat stacks of bullets, cartridges and clips. She slid it closed, placed her fingers around the key. I can't do it, she thought bleakly. Lulash would be punished. I am an utter failure as an agent. These people plan to kill me and still I can't steal this key because this man has helped me.

Lulash stood up, brandishing a bottle of white pills, and she accompanied him back to the cell.

"What goes?" asked Farrell shakily.

"This gentleman set your leg," she told him. "We've brought you brandy and aspirin. Could you sit up just a little?"

He struggled to one elbow. "I hope I haven't given away any secrets. I have the feeling I've been talking like an idiot."

She smiled faintly. "But not like any friend of Mr. Carstairs."

"What are the prospects?" he gasped, lying back after gulping down aspirin with a huge draft of brandy.

"Dim," replied Mrs. Pollifax dryly. "You infuriated General Perdido by injuring yourself so badly that he couldn't question you." She whispered so Lulash could not hear, "It might be wise to keep talking as wildly as possible."

Lulash turned to leave. Mrs. Pollifax reached for his hand. "Thank you," she said warmly. "We thank you very much."

"Is all right," he said, nodding and smiling.

When he had gone Mrs. Pollifax sat down abruptly on her cot. "You look exhausted, Duchess," Farrell said, "For God's sake get some sleep. I'll try to limit my ravings for a while."

Mrs. Pollifax looked at him in the flickering eerie light of the candle and realized how very fond of him she was becoming. And lying down she fell at once into an exhausted sleep.

On the twenty-third of August, Carstairs sat in his office with Bishop and a man who was an expert on Mao Tse-tung and one of the few Americans to have known General Perdido personally.

"There hasn't been a sign of Farrell or Mrs. Pollifax being smuggled into Cuba," Carstairs said, "though that doesn't exclude their being there. But I think we can say without doubt that Perdido is not in Cuba at the moment." He handed a paper to the expert, whose name was Peattie. "We know of two secret Russian landing strips in Mexico, and as you will see by this report, activity has been observed at one in Baja California. A four-engine, Russian-made prop landed there the night of August nineteenth—the day that Perdido vanished from sight and the day that Farrell and Mrs. Pollifax disappeared."

"Mmm," murmured Peattie. "Two people carried aboard on stretchers. Has beautiful Miss Willow Lee also left Mexico City?"

Carstairs nodded. "She's in Hong Kong. Destination Peking."

Peattie mused. "I hate to say this, for I assume you're grimly hoping to regain those two agents. But if General Perdido is not in Cuba, I fear he has headed for Red China."

"This department does not grimly hope," said Carstairs in a hard voice. "Farrell and Pollifax are crossed off our lists."

"Then I don't think I understand," said Peattie.

Carstairs hesitated. "You might call our investigation fifty percent precaution and fifty percent conscience. We don't want any international incidents. We *have* to be sure these people are dead. We have to have *proof*."

Peattie nodded. "I'll send out feelers on Perdido. Within a few days I can tell you whether he is or has been in China." He gave Carstairs a curious glance. "The fifty percent conscience—?"

Carstairs sighed. "I'm thinking of Mrs. Pollifax. The late Mrs. Pollifax, I fear. A comfortable little woman in her sixties, with a charmingly direct way about her. Asked Mason if there was some-

476

thing she could do for us; naïve, but so patently right for what I needed that I gobbled her up, so to speak."

"I see," Peattie said quietly. "She knew the risks?"

"Oh yes. But she left without indoctrination or training or cyanide. And now I must wire her relatives explaining why she is not en route home; and then think up some plausible death for her in Mexico."

"A boating accident perhaps. Mexico is being very helpful," put in Bishop.

Peattie stood up. "I can promise you information within the week. I wish it could be sooner but China still moves by oxcart."

"Thanks—we'll take anything we can get."

When Peattie had gone Carstairs lit a cigarette and said wearily, "Tirpak is dead. Knifed in Guatemala, just identified."

Bishop sighed. "What you'd call a clean sweep then."

"There's more. Our contact in Costa Rica put all the information Tirpak brought him on film and burned the papers. Six microfilms. Tirpak left with them in a plain white envelope."

"Ouch," said Bishop.

Carstairs nodded. "I would assume he planned to insert them into something printed—say a book. I believe they reached The Parrot Bookstore and DeGamez was killed because of them."

"So General Perdido has the microfilms then."

Carstairs frowned. "I'm not so sure. If so, why would he have kept the bookstore open or searched Mrs. Pollifax's room? And their including Farrell bothers me. His only link with the Chinese was Miss Willow Lee. He had no knowledge of Tirpak or the microfilms."

Bishop nodded. "Snatching him *does* imply desperation."

"Yes. That's why I'm reasonably sure Perdido would choose to keep Farrell and Mrs. Pollifax alive for a day or two. And that, my dear Bishop, is why I am not sleeping well these nights. The general's methods of extracting information are neither polite nor pretty."

"But Mrs. Pollifax had no information to extract."

"Bishop, do you think Perdido would believe that?"

There was a long silence. "Well if Perdido doesn't have the microfilms, that's something, isn't it?"

Carstairs gave a short laugh. "Oh yes. It means they're lost to everyone. If they were appended to a book sold in DeGamez's shop then someone at this very moment may be reading that book, never realizing it's the repository for secrets costing eight months' work and the lives of several people. And that is what I call waste. Where is the telegram sent to Mrs. Pollifax's children?"

Bishop drew copies from his file. "Here they are, sir. They went off late yesterday from Mexico City to Roger Pollifax in Chicago and Mrs. Conrad Kempf in Arizona."

Carstairs read them with irony: HAVING WONDERFUL TIME STOP POSTPONING RETURN A WEEK OR MORE STOP MEXICO CHARMING STOP LOVE TO ALL MOTHER.

PERDIDO returned to the cell the next afternoon. Mrs. Pollifax had heard him coming so he found her playing a quiet game of solitaire and Farrell thrashing feverishly on his cot.

"Take the green ones away, for God's sake!" shouted Farrell.

Both the general and Mrs. Pollifax looked at him, one with exasperation, the other with admiration. Mrs. Pollifax said bitingly, "I have set his leg but the bullet wound in his arm is infected."

"Senor Farrell," Perdido said harshly.

"Carmelita?" Farrell said tenderly, and then, hopefully, "My darling?"

There was a sickening sound as General Perdido's fist crashed against Farrell's cheekbone. Mrs. Pollifax turned away, thinking, I really can't bear this. But there was, for the next few minutes, a great deal more to bear. The general was determined to find out whether Farrell was shamming. When at last he desisted she was more calm than he—Perdido's face was distorted with fury. "You may tell Mr. Farrell that I look forward to his speedy recovery." He opened the door and turned back dramatically. "As for you, Mrs. Pollifax, you have inconvenienced me so greatly that I resent your very existence."

The door slammed and only then did she dare look at Farrell.

"I think the general has been seeing too many B movies," she said lightly, and wanted to cry over Farrell's battered face.

Farrell said evenly, "Did he break my nose, damn him?"

Mrs. Pollifax sat down beside him and they took inventory. The list was encouraging: bruises, two loosened teeth—both molars— and a split upper lip; but there appeared to be no bones broken. She said gently, "Have you endured this sort of thing before?"

He glanced away. "Once, during the war. That was when I knew Carstairs. There are limitations, you know, after the first time. The mind knows what to expect. It can become a worse enemy than the pain. But this was brief—mercifully."

Mrs. Pollifax felt his forehead and sighed. "You still have a fever, you know. About a hundred and one, I'd guess."

"But not the raving kind." He tried to smile.

"No, not the raving kind. You put on a very good act."

He said gratefully, "Duchess, I've known an incredible number of young and beautiful women—but I nominate you as the Woman I Would Most Like To Be Captured With In Albania!"

"Ah, you are feeling better," said Mrs. Pollifax with a twinkle.

At mealtime a new prisoner arrived, pushed in ahead of the trays by a swearing Major Vassovic. A third cot was brought in and placed along the third wall. Mrs. Pollifax was too busy feeding Farrell with a spoon to pay much attention, but while she ate her own meal she eyed the man curiously. He lay on his side, and all she could really see of him was the top of a bald head fringed with white about the ears. Farrell was also studying the man. "My name's Farrell. Speak English?" he asked.

The man responded with a jumble of unintelligible words.

"He doesn't speak English—that's good," said Mrs. Pollifax.

"Look at the candle!" Farrell said suddenly.

Mrs. Pollifax's glance went at once to the candle on the wall over the newcomer's head—then she realized that the new man too was looking at the candle and had understood Farrell perfectly. Apparently the general had unearthed another English-speaking member of the Sigurimi.

Tonight it was Lulash who came to remove their trays. "We

are late tonight in collecting your tray. General Perdido had to be driven to his airplane." He deposited two aspirins on her table, then in a low voice, "For you, to read about my country." With his back to the new prisoner he slipped a book under her pillow.

Mrs. Pollifax had to content herself with a grateful glance. When at last Farrell fell into a restless sleep and the stranger filled the air with rhythmic snores, she lay down. She pulled out Lulash's book. *Albania: Land of Primitive Beauty.* It was an old volume, copyrighted in 1919, and she was touched that it was still treasured by Lulash. She thumbed through it, recalling books in her childhood with the same gray photographs of people in national costume. And then she came face to face with a map—a very clear map. There was Albania, fitted neatly between Greece to the south and Yugoslavia on the north. And there was the Adriatic Sea. . . . Water, thought Mrs. Pollifax, feeling her way toward an idea not yet expressible. Thoughtfully she began looking for mountains. In the south a thin line of them faced the sea, but these were hardly fifteen hundred feet in height. She and Farrell had been brought to a very high range of mountains. "Ah," she breathed as she spied the North Albanian Alps running from east to west across the top of Albania like a necklace—a necklace extremely close to Yugoslavia and not far from the Adriatic Sea. "Let's see," she mused. They had landed by plane in an old town, driven toward the mountains, traveled for one or two hours by donkey. Would it be possible to figure out the direction?

"The sun," gasped Mrs. Pollifax. From the heaving back of her donkey she had watched the sun rise and spread across the valley in a flood of gold. Yes, the sun had definitely risen in front of her and slightly to the right. Therefore they had been traveling northeastward. If she reversed this, moving her finger westward on the map, there was only one real city: Scutari. The other towns were small. If the plane landed in Scutari, we must be about *here,* she decided, scratching an X with her fingernail. It was a point surprisingly near the Adriatic. And across the Adriatic lay Italy. . . .

She placed the book under the mattress and lay down, almost frightened by her thought. It was a long time before she slept.

"Y OU MAY come out," said Lulash the next afternoon. "General Hoong has said you may have a little walk."

Mrs. Pollifax nodded and went to look at Farrell. If he was to survive the bullet would have to be removed from his arm. His temperature must be 104 or 105 and he was not always lucid. She leaned over him and said gently, "I'll be back in a few minutes."

Farrell opened one eye and grinned weakly. "Have fun."

Before leaving Mrs. Pollifax picked up the Guatemalan jacket which, an eternity ago, she had worn when she left her Mexico City hotel room. She had lived in the same skirt and blouse for six days and nights, but the jacket she had not worn. During the day it was spread carefully on her pillow; at night it was folded across the small table on which she played her card games. As she plucked it up now, her hand groped under the pillow for the book on Albania. Without a glance at the Gremlin—the nickname bestowed on their stool pigeon by Farrell—she walked out.

"Did you like my book?" asked Lulash in the hall.

She nodded with vivacity. Lulash led her outside, and on the way she saw that the key to the ammunition drawer had again been left in the lock. After the darkness of the cell, the sun seared her eyes and she gasped and covered them with her hands.

"Here." Lulash handed her his dark glasses.

"Really you are so kind." She put them on and was able to look around without discomfort. "I am to walk?" she asked.

He nodded, and lowering himself to the bench beside the door he explained, "Better today if you walk within my eye, understand? From there to there." He indicated boundaries.

Nodding, she made her way to the edge of the cliff and began what she hoped looked like an aimless stroll. From this height she could look far across the valley. She traced the winding skein of a riverbed that ran from east to west across the plain; by it were four small towns. The floor of the valley was almost a checkerboard of symmetrical lines dividing field after field—possibly rice paddies.

Below the cliff was a rocky pasture full of goats, and below that still other sloping pastures. Off to the west a road ran toward her into the mountains, and on its surface she could see men at work, so tiny they resembled little black insects. Beyond Lulash and the stone house the mountain towered above her. Of one fact she was certain: there could be no escape over that peak into Yugoslavia. The only possibilities lay to the west, along the route they had come, or through the valley.

Escape . . . for the first time she acknowledged the direction of her thoughts. The idea was mad, but surely some effort had to be made. Always Mrs. Pollifax had found it difficult to *submit*, and it struck her as characterless to sit around waiting for execution. She waved at Lulash, sat down on a rock and opened the book to the map. A valley, an alp, a river . . . yes, there *was* a river. "The river Drin," she exclaimed in a pleased voice. About fifteen miles away, according to the scale of the map, it flowed westward into the Adriatic Sea.

Walking back to Lulash she said pleasantly, "The city with the airport, is that Scutari, your capital?"

His face lit up. "Ah, you did read my book. No, it's not the capital, and it's now called Shkodër. But yes, the airport is there."

"You are a mine of information about your interesting country," said Mrs. Pollifax with complete honesty. "Forgive me, but I think I will go inside now. This heat . . ." Lulash let her into the stone building and closed the door behind her. Major Vassovic was kneeling in a corner of the guardroom. "Oh—I beg your pardon!" she said. "Is that some form of yoga you're practicing?"

"Zot, no," he said heavily. "There is only the one electric wire— ah! I have it." The major climbed laboriously to his feet. "For my heat brick. The electric is difficult here. We have, what you call it, big machine in the other building."

Mrs. Pollifax brightened. "Oh yes, a generator. And that is your heat brick? We call it a heating pad at home."

"Yes, for the back," he said. "My back very sore."

Mrs. Pollifax was genuinely concerned. "You mean a cold has settled in your back. You poor man! Have you tried massage?"

He stared at her, uncomprehending, and she said firmly, "Take off your shirt. Have you rubbing alcohol?"

"Alcohol?" From a drawer he dubiously pulled a brandy flask.

"Yes, why not?" she said cheerfully. "Now if you'll lie on your desk I'll rub your back." He retreated in alarm. "No, no, you don't understand." She went to the door. "Mr. Lulash," she called, "could you please translate for me? I want to rub the major's back. Please ask him to remove his shirt and lie across his desk."

With a grin Lulash entered and translated the words. Major Vassovic said, "Ah!" then, "Oh?" and removed his shirt.

Mrs. Pollifax poured brandy into the palm of one hand, then pummeled, kneaded and slapped the major's back with enthusiasm. His small shrieks of protest presently became sighs of joy.

"He needs a blanket," Mrs. Pollifax told Lulash. "He must lie still for several minutes before getting up." Lulash got a blanket and Mrs. Pollifax threw it over the major and collapsed into a chair. "I haven't done that in years."

The major grunted happily from the desk and Lulash said, "Allow me," and poured brandy into two paper cups.

Mrs. Pollifax said doubtfully, "I suppose I could call it a late afternoon cocktail?" She accepted the drink and very casually dangled her other hand over the ammunition drawer, feeling for the brass key. Lulash was seated on the other side of the desk and she exchanged friendly smiles with him across the prostrate form of Major Vassovic. "*Skoal!*" called Lulash, lifting his cup.

"*Skoal!*" returned Mrs. Pollifax gaily, pulling open the drawer behind her. She filled her hand with cartridges and pushed the drawer closed again.

The major sat up. "Was good, good. You do again sometime?"

Mrs. Pollifax beamed. She now had four cartridges in her lap. "Of course, until they dispose of me." Lulash looked surprised and she added cheerfully, "Oh, they'll eventually have to kill me."

"But you cannot be dangerous," he protested.

Mrs. Pollifax shrugged. "Does anyone care? This isn't a democracy, you know. In a democracy it takes a jury of twelve people to decide on anyone's guilt."

Major Vassovic stared at her. "Twelve officers, you mean?"

"Oh no," said Mrs. Pollifax. "Twelve ordinary working people."

The two men stared at her. Vassovic said, "But then no one would ever be found guilty. Who instructs them?"

"They make up their own minds from the evidence."

The major looked alarmed. Lulash looked interested. "Explain to me how it works," he said.

Mrs. Pollifax hesitated, not from any lack of articulateness but because of the four cartridges she was holding. "First I must put on my jacket, I'm cold," she said, and walked over to the stool where she had put her jacket and the copy of *Albania: Land of Primitive Beauty*. Slipping the cartridges into the pocket, she shrugged on her jacket and squeezed the book tightly under one arm. "It works like this," she began, and from the doorway a voice said coldly, "Good afternoon, Mrs. Pollifax."

Mrs. Pollifax turned. She had not realized before how very much General Hoong's face resembled a fresh brown egg. There was something sinister about a man who showed not a single line of laughter or of sadness. "Good afternoon," she said.

His nostrils quivered fastidiously. "Lulash, Vassovic, have you been drinking?"

"I was allowed a short walk and I had a touch of sunstroke," intervened Mrs. Pollifax. "They offered me brandy for medicinal purposes. I'm glad you are here, General Hoong. I need permission to extract the bullet from Mr. Farrell's arm. He will die otherwise. This would make General Perdido quite angry, don't you think?"

The general's left eyebrow lifted. "I will need a knife," she continued recklessly, "boiling water and a bandage. This is possible?"

"There is nothing else?" It was the most delicate sarcasm.

"I don't believe so," Mrs. Pollifax told him, ignoring it. "Your food is quite good and I'm growing accustomed to the mattress."

He bowed slightly. "I am so glad."

"And now I believe I'd like to go back to my cell and lie down."

Major Vassovic led her down the hall. As he swung the cell door open for her he whispered, "Tomorrow, same time?"

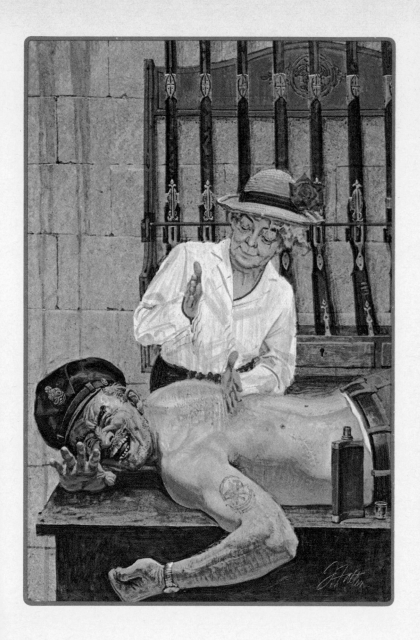

Feeling like a paramour making an assignation Mrs. Pollifax told him gravely, "Tomorrow, yes."

She returned to the cell to discover that Farrell was asleep and the Gremlin had disappeared. She hid the book on Albania under her mattress and then examined the items she had stolen from the ammunition drawer. Two, she found, belonged to a Beretta pistol, and two to something called a Nambu. Very good, she thought. She placed one cartridge in her purse, another inside her underclothes, a third she trusted to a hole in her mattress and the fourth she put into Farrell's mattress. Since he was still asleep she took out Lulash's book and turned again to the map.

"What, no solitaire?" asked Farrell suddenly.

"Lulash has loaned me a book on Albania," she told him absently. "It has a very good map of the country."

"Good God. You can't possibly be thinking of escape!"

Mrs. Pollifax said calmly, "Why not? I don't want to spend my sunset years in Albania. The winters are extremely cold, the book says so. There must be a way to get us out before Perdido returns."

"Us?" echoed Farrell in astonishment.

She looked up from her map in surprise. "You can't possibly think I'd leave you behind. I've asked for permission to cut the bullet out of your arm, then your temperature should go down."

"Leaving only a broken leg," rasped Farrell.

"The simplest way would be to lower you over the cliff," Mrs. Pollifax went on, "but we'd need a hundred feet of rope. We ought to have a gun too, and clothes for disguise, and food. And I suppose to be really efficient we ought to have a compass."

"How about ordering a limousine?" It was their first quarrel and he said scornfully, "You're off your rocker, Duchess; if you'll forgive me I'll go back to sleep, which is the best escape *I* can think of."

"Coward," said Mrs. Pollifax with a sniff, and was sorry as soon as the word left her lips. Farrell's eyes closed, a gentle snore issued from his half-open mouth, and Mrs. Pollifax thought how very striking his beard would be in a few more days.

The boiling water, a penknife and a towel arrived at dusk with Major Vassovic, who had been ordered to help. Gruffly he addressed the Gremlin, now returned to their cell. "His name is Adhem Nexdhet," he told Mrs. Pollifax. "I have asked him to hold the candle for you. Lulash is not on duty tonight."

Hold the candle for *me?* thought Mrs. Pollifax. Her knees were suddenly wobbly and she tried to recall the dozens of splinters and broken glass she had extracted from small knees and fingers in her lifetime. She remembered a bit of advice given her by a doctor: never bleed for the patient, just get the job done. She glanced only once at Farrell's open eyes. He must manage his own hell, as she must somehow manage hers. She quickly probed the rotting flesh for the bullet, and with one swift, cruel turning, lifted it and heard it drop to the stone floor. Not knowing how else to complete the job she poured the hot water over the infected skin, and this at last brought from Farrell a yelp. "They'd never hire you at Mount Sinai Hospital, Duchess."

"Really? And I was planning to apply next week. What a pity!"

He grinned weakly and turned his face to the wall. Mrs. Pollifax realized what he had endured and her resolve to escape hardened. It was at least a cleaner way to die than whatever the general was planning. It was now a matter only of *when* and *how*. She wet the towel and began swabbing blood from Farrell's mattress.

"You did that well," said Nexdhet suddenly. "Without emotion."

Mrs. Pollifax stepped back. "You really do speak English."

He smiled wryly. "You already knew this. Allow me," he said, taking the towel from her. "You must be tired."

"I suppose you're also in the secret police?"

"I am Colonel Nexdhet of the Sigurimi."

Mrs. Pollifax winced. "That makes you the major's superior. It also makes it especially kind of you to help."

"There is one thing that General Perdido does not know about you, Mrs. Pollifax—how well you perform under pressure."

"Oh?" Nexdhet's stare made Mrs. Pollifax distinctly uneasy.

"To Perdido you are an embarrassing mistake," he continued. "But I wonder if you are not more than you appear to be."

Mrs. Pollifax spread out her cards, aware that the colonel was watching her with both speculation and amusement.

THE NEXT MORNING Mrs. Pollifax began to plan in earnest. When Nexdhet left the cell, presumably for exercise, she brought from her purse everything that could be used as a bribe or trade: three lipsticks, two of them in smart bejeweled gold cases; the Band-Aids; travelers' checks; the small memo pad with its gold pencil. To these she reluctantly added her Guatemalan jacket, but she kept the memo pad. On one of its pages she had jotted down a few Albanian words from *Land of Primitive Beauty*. After an hour's effort she managed to write a message in Albanian with four of the words and carefully copied it out on a sheet of memo paper. Night —Sleep—Bring Voice. She added hopefully in English, since everyone here seemed to speak it, "We are two Americans here; who are you?"

"What's up?" asked Farrell from his cot.

"Nothing, nothing at all. How are you feeling? Your temperature is almost normal, I felt your forehead while you were asleep."

"You look like a cat planning to swallow the canary, Duchess. Whatever you're up to, it won't work."

The cell door groaned open and a guard appeared. "I believe it's time for my walk now," she told Farrell, and swept out.

The door had no more than closed behind her when a voice said, "Mrs. Pollifax! We can walk together. I've been waiting for you." It was Colonel Nexdhet.

"To guard me?" she inquired coldly. Major Vassovic was in the guardroom. "Good morning. How is your back today?"

"Ah, *Zogë* Pollifax," said the major, beaming. "Still sore, yes, but last night I sleep like baby."

"Mrs. Pollifax," cried Lulash, holding the door for her. "Take my sunglasses, please. Remember you and I are jurors."

"What did that mean?" asked Nexdhet.

"Nothing important. There are so many of you here to guard so few of us, it seems such waste."

"We will go to the east," said Nexdhet, gesturing. "No, it is not waste. There are other prisoners in the larger building."

"I didn't know that. How long have you been here, Colonel?"

"Oh, several months. I was brought here to be second-in-command

488

to General Hoong. It is very bleak at times, but I enjoy my walks. I fancy myself as a bird watcher." He carried binoculars.

"And do you enjoy being in the Sigurimi?" she asked.

"It is my job." He looked at her and smiled as they began to climb toward the forest. "You question everything, and this is good. But you doubt nobody, and this is weak. I observe in you the desire to trust, to lean on others."

Mrs. Pollifax was aware of a tired wisdom in his eyes. She said, "I honestly don't think I agree with you. I don't lean on people; it only comforts me to know they are there. You trust no one at all?"

He helped her over a fallen log. "I have watched too many knives in the back. I served Albania under the Turks, then under King Zog. We were friends with Mussolini, then Mussolini turned on us. Then Russia was our friend. Now the Red Chinese help us. It is the way life is. Nothing endures except the idea, the mind. This alone is pure, not soiled by change." He shrugged. "One adapts." With a wry smile twisting his preposterous mustache he asked, "Politically you are what?"

"Republican," acknowledged Mrs. Pollifax. "Although I did vote for Adlai Stevenson once—*such* a charming man."

He smiled. "Then you too adapt." He touched her arm. "We will follow the cliff back. There is a good view of the valley."

There was indeed. "Beautiful, is it not?" said Colonel Nexdhet, standing beside her. "Those men below—how small, like ants. They are building a missile site." He said it without interest.

Missile site? A shock of excitement moved down Mrs. Pollifax's spine. If she could take news of a Chinese missile site to Mr. Carstairs she would not have failed as a spy after all. Obviously Nexdhet would not have mentioned it if he was not absolutely sure that Mrs. Pollifax would remain in Albania. Aloud she said disapprovingly, "They would do better to build roads. Why do you need a missile site?"

Colonel Nexdhet gave her his arm. "Shall we start back? The Chinese are very patient, Mrs. Pollifax; they build for the future."

"I have not seen any birds, Colonel Nexdhet," said Mrs. Pollifax to change the subject before she gave away her profound interest.

He said gravely, "That is what makes bird-watching so fascinating—there are so few of them up here on the cliffs," and presently the stone buildings lay ahead.

IT WAS A quarter past five when Mrs. Pollifax returned to her cell, flushed from a string of small, happy accomplishments. She found Farrell livid. "Don't you dare go off again like this," he sputtered. "I've been out of my mind picturing you shot or being tortured. And now you have the gall to walk in looking happy."

She kissed the top of his head fondly. "Bless you, I'm sorry."

"Then try to look sorry. Where have you been?"

"Oh, walking with Colonel Nexdhet," she said airily, "picnicking with Lulash, rubbing Major Vassovic's back. We even discussed having a party in the guardroom tomorrow night. Lulash knows some old mountain songs, Nexdhet plays an instrument, Vassovic has volunteered something alcoholic."

Farrell stared. "All right, what *have* you been up to, Duchess?"

She drew a sheet of onionskin paper from her pocket and put it in his lap. "For tracing the map in Lulash's book," she whispered, then drew out a metal case. "I won't have to tell you what this is."

"A compass!" Farrell whistled. "How on earth—"

"I traded with the major after I rubbed his back. It was quite fun. I said I was getting rid of my effects early. It cost me two new lipsticks. Does it work?"

"It may," Farrell said, frowning over it. "It moves."

"East," she told him, "would be toward the guardroom."

He looked up. "And just how do you know that?"

"We traveled into the rising sun when we came here—so we arrived from the west, from Shkodër, where our plane landed. And according to the map the river Drin flows west, into the Adriatic."

He said quietly, "You'd better tell me exactly what you're thinking of, Duchess."

"What I would have told you at once if you hadn't been in such a state is about the person in the cell next to us." She described the striking she had heard on the wall. "I've heard nothing since, but this afternoon I dropped a note through the window slit of that cell. It was made up of scraps of Albanian from Lulash's book, but I hope he'll get the point that we'd like to hear from him again."

Footsteps echoed in the hall. Mrs. Pollifax stuffed the compass and paper into her purse and was shuffling her deck of cards when Adhem Nexdhet walked in. "What is this game you always play?" he asked.

"Different kinds," she told him. "Solitaire is very healthy for the mind and the nerves. Has General Perdido returned yet?"

"He comes late Thursday," Nexdhet said absently, his eyes on the cards she was arranging.

Mrs. Pollifax managed a laugh. "I don't know what today is!"

"Tuesday." Nexdhet abruptly sat down on her cot. "Show me," he said. "The cards in a circle, what is the key to this?"

"It's called clock solitaire," replied Mrs. Pollifax, and began to explain. But her heart was thudding. *Thursday*. This was Tuesday. . . . The general's face came clearly to mind: impassive, only the eyes betraying shrewdness and cruelty. She glanced at Farrell, who was chewing reflectively on his mustache, and hoped he did not recall what lay ahead of him. Then something occurred to her and she said in shocked astonishment to Nexdhet, "But why so soon? Did you tell him Farrell was well enough to be questioned?"

"I warned you to trust no one," he pointed out gently.

On Wednesday, during her walk along the cliff, Mrs. Pollifax selected two fist-sized rocks, took them back to the cell and hid them. But what they needed most was a crutch for Farrell. Lulash was sunning himself on a bench while he cleaned his gun. "Lulash, I've had the *nicest* idea," she said to him. "But I'll need your permission and your help. Mr. Farrell cannot take walks, as I do. He's shut up all day in that cell. Lulash, I should so like to hang some green branches in the cell. Surely no one would mind?"

Lulash smiled. "Every woman, she likes to make pretty, eh? I'll ask the major's permission."

Vassovic not only gave permission but announced that he would come too, and the three of them set out for the scattered firs, with Mrs. Pollifax talking mercilessly until they reached the trees, whereupon she became reverently silent for so long that the men became restive. Then, with apparently spontaneous inspiration, she asked, "Could we take back a very small tree?"

"Tree?" said Lulash.

"Tree?" echoed Vassovic in astonishment.

"This little Christmas tree." Ruthlessly Mrs. Pollifax delivered the coup de grace. "I—I will not see another Christmas."

That did it. Lulash angrily tightened his lips. "She shall have little tree," he said.

"Of course," and Major Vassovic nodded.

"Lovely," murmured Mrs. Pollifax, and with the tree between them like a fourth member of the party they marched back.

"Isn't it beautiful? Christmas in August," said Mrs. Pollifax to Farrell with a warning frown—Colonel Nexdhet was seated on his cot reading. But presently, with a nod, he got up and went out.

Mrs. Pollifax sat down on her cot and said tartly, "I have just given the most nauseating performance of my life. I, Emily Pollifax, was girlish! Kittenish! I nearly had them weeping for me."

"Not over this—this ragged evergreen, I hope," Farrell said.

Mrs. Pollifax said crossly, "That ragged evergreen, my dear Farrell, is the crutch that will help you walk to the Adriatic Sea. No crosspiece, but we can use pieces of mattress and blanket to wad the top and protect your arm."

"Oh, something else happened, fortunately while Nexdhet was out. *This* fluttered through the window."

"Our neighbor! He did reply after all!"

"In a fashion," said Farrell, and watched as she held the paper to the light. On it had been printed a message in Chinese script!

7

THAT EVENING Nexdhet followed their dinner trays out of the cell. As soon as he had gone Mrs. Pollifax sat down on Farrell's cot. He looked brighter-eyed than she had seen him in days. "All right," he said, "let's go over the list."

Mrs. Pollifax nodded. "One tree. But no earthly way of cutting it down to a crutch." On the memo pad he wrote *knife.* "Four cartridges for Beretta or Nambu pistols, but no pistols." Farrell winced. "Cheese and stale bread for two days. No water. One compass, if it works. One tracing of a map of Albania. Two rocks."

"Ah, the rocks!" Farrell brightened. "But first the tree. I don't suppose you've seen a knife lying around anywhere?"

"There are half a dozen in the guardroom gun rack, locked under glass. You could ask to shave, but they'd want the razor back."

He nodded, but without appearing discouraged, which pleased Mrs. Pollifax because she was very discouraged indeed. "How do we manage to cut the tree at all with Nexdhet in the cell? I picked up those rocks thinking we could hit him over the head at the proper time but . . ." She shivered. "I couldn't. Could you?"

Farrell smiled faintly. "Yes. I haven't been completely idle, Duchess. At night while you and Nexdhet were asleep I've been doing crazy exercises to get my strength back. Look." He got to his feet and stood, his weight on the good leg. "I don't get dizzy anymore. I've been exercising my arms too. I could hit our friend over the head, if he gets close enough to me. Let's see whatever's left of your trading goods for friendly natives."

"One lipstick, one handkerchief . . ."

"Men's handkerchiefs?"

"Yes, they were my husband's, and so much more substantial."

"Excellent gags." Farrell took her lipstick case apart, ran a finger over the rim of the metal tube. "Let's see those rocks."

"You mean we may have found a cutting edge?"

"A peeling edge. Maybe I can chisel a sharper point with the rock. Bring a few more back tomorrow. But without a gun . . ."

Mrs. Pollifax said reasonably, "But if we escape as far as the guardroom we can steal as many guns as we want."

"Yes, but we'll have to manage the crutch sooner, preferably after our spy has been rendered unconscious."

"You *will* hit him gently," mourned Mrs. Pollifax. "It'll have to be a time tomorrow when someone unlocks the cell and comes in, like Lulash with a tray. We hit him over the head too, I suppose."

"Everybody. Major Vassovic too—somehow."

"I could scream or something to bring him in," suggested Mrs. Pollifax, getting into the spirit of the thing. "About six o'clock."

"Too early, too light—people in the big building might see us."

"But if we wait until they bring in the candle, Perdido may have returned. I'm sure he'll want to see us right away."

Farrell said firmly, "I'll think of something. Don't worry."

"Not worry!" Mrs. Pollifax felt a trembling deep inside her. It was absolute madness and none of it was real—Albania, Farrell, Perdido, this ridiculous cell—and tomorrow evening they were going to try to escape with two rocks and a Christmas tree.

Farrell was staring at their pathetic heap of treasures. "Not bad. Their letting you out for walks and these rocks you picked up are two miracles. Nobody can ask for *more* than two miracles."

"*I* could ask for another," said Mrs. Pollifax tartly. "A *knife!*"

Farrell grinned flippantly. "Maybe someone will start throwing knives at the party and you can catch one between your teeth."

Unfortunately not a knife was to be seen at the party. There were forks, though, and Mrs. Pollifax at once secreted two. Lulash and Vassovic had obviously begun sampling what they had filched from the wine cellar. "Join us," said Lulash with shining eyes.

Mrs. Pollifax startled them by emptying her glass. "It is so sweet of you to have a party for me," she told them. "Ah, and olives! Have you a knife? Americans eat olives with knives."

Vassovic shook his head. "We have no knives. Try a fork."

Mrs. Pollifax was on her second glass of wine when Colonel Nexdhet arrived bearing what looked like a zither. "General Hoong will be coming too," he said. "He enjoys parties."

"Then I will sing before he comes," said Lulash, and promptly sat cross-legged on the floor. The colonel plucked his peculiar-looking instrument and Lulash began a song about love and springtime. "A Russian in Tirana," he said softly, "once sang to me those words. Where is she now?"

Major Vassovic noisily blew his nose and Mrs. Pollifax wondered why love songs had to be so sad. The wine had left her a little belligerent. "Colonel Nexdhet," she said with unsteady dignity,

"I've decided it was immoral of you to give your country to China."

Lulash looked appalled. "*He* gave us to China?"

The colonel said firmly, "Not personally, Lulash. Russia moved out, China moved in. We wanted China to help us."

"I had nothing to say about it," Lulash said. "What this country needs is a George . . . George who, Mrs. Pollifax?"

"Washington."

"That's right, George Washington! To democracy!" shouted Lulash as the door opened and General Hoong entered in full-dress uniform. He said distastefully, "Private Lulash, you are drunk." To Mrs. Pollifax he bowed. "I have brought a bottle of vodka."

"And a knife to open it?" she asked eagerly.

"A knife? No, a corkscrew. Vassovic, open it." Taking out his pistol, General Hoong fired six shots into the ceiling "The party may begin now," he announced, seating himself next to Mrs. Pollifax and resting his pistol on his knee.

"What an interesting-looking gun, General," Mrs. Pollifax said.

"It is Japanese, a Nambu. Since it is empty you may look at it."

Mrs. Pollifax held it to the light admiringly, then placed it carefully on the desk between them. The general offered her some vodka. "Oh, a very little," she said, and as he leaned forward she neatly slid the Nambu into her pocket. Lulash began another song and Mrs. Pollifax moved closer to Hoong. "It is so very kind of you to join us."

His empty eyes looked at her. "A general is always alone."

"But soon General Perdido will be back."

He said fastidiously, "Perdido is a barbarian."

Mrs. Pollifax thought about this. "Yes, he is. I quite understand. You live a very isolated life here. Have you hobbies?"

"I have a mistress."

Mrs. Pollifax gamely nodded. "Yes, that would help."

"And I write poetry."

"Do you really! Will you please recite one of your poems?"

The general did so—about pale moons, white clouds and a grieving heart.

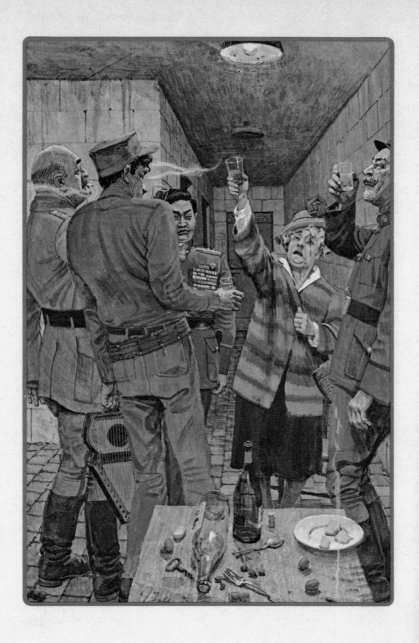

"Charming," said Mrs. Pollifax, "and so sensitive. You really must find a job where you don't have to shoot or torture people."

"Job?" he said, and drained his vodka. "There is nothing wrong with my job. It is my mistress who causes me torment."

"I TRIED," she said to Farrell back in the cell, "to steal a knife, but all I got was a pistol."

Farrell was admiring the Nambu. "Duchess, the odds against our escaping have just shrunk by about five hundred. I feel much more secure now. Get me the cartridges." She gave him the two cartridges and he grinned. "How was the party?"

"Dismal, except for Lulash. He would like a George Washington for Albania."

He patted the pistol lovingly, slipped it beneath his mattress. "Been planting seeds of insurrection, Duchess?"

"Well, it's a change from geraniums," said Mrs. Pollifax. The effects of the wine were wearing off, leaving her depressed. But then Colonel Nexdhet walked in and she realized that she must face the next day if not with equanimity, at least with stoicism. Farrell was pointedly staring at her, then deliberately at Nexdhet, who was removing his jacket. Mrs. Pollifax's eyes widened. Nexdhet was wearing a knife strapped to his belt.

"Our third miracle," said Farrell very quietly.

Mrs. Pollifax could scarcely believe it, but being of a practical mind she whispered, "You?" Farrell gestured helplessly toward his leg and she nodded. She yawned elaborately. "Good night, Colonel Nexdhet," she said sweetly. "It was a lovely party."

"Oh yes. Good night." He nodded curtly and stretched himself out on his cot. Mrs. Pollifax lay on her side with her eyes fixed upon the knife and tried, through the gloom, to figure out just how it was affixed to his belt.

Farrell began to snore gently—and Nexdhet began to snore loudly. Mrs. Pollifax slowly sat up, the mattress rustling even more than usual. She remained sitting for a few minutes to make certain the snores continued. Then she stood up and waited again before easing herself toward Nexdhet's cot. Nearly there, she was attacked

497

by an almost irrepressible urge to giggle. Firmly she controlled herself and leaned over Nexdhet. She drew the sheath up and out. Then she sank to one knee, and with one hand steadying the sheath she pulled on the knife with the other. It came out easily. Nexdhet did not stir and Mrs. Pollifax glided to Farrell's cot.

He was snoring softly but a hand reached out, open-palmed, to accept the knife. Then he turned on his side, his back to her, and Mrs. Pollifax knew he was hiding it under his mattress. She returned to her own cot and sank upon it with relief, to sleep.

8

I N THE MORNING when Mrs. Pollifax awoke she remembered at once that a fateful day was beginning. In every life, she thought, there eventually came a moment when the shape of the future was out of one's hands, to be decided by chance, by fate or by God. There was nothing to do but accept it and do one's very best.

Farrell was sleeping soundly. Nexdhet was sleeping too, and suddenly she was afraid. He would wake up, find his knife gone and know that she or Farrell had taken it. Last night it had seemed like their third miracle. But it might prove their undoing.

As if he had felt her thoughts Nexdhet sat up and rubbed his eyes. Meeting her gaze he nodded, and Mrs. Pollifax fought to keep her eyes from the empty sheath. Nexdhet stood up and stretched. He lifted his jacket off the foot of the bed and shrugged his arms into the sleeves. He had not *seen* the empty sheath, thought Mrs. Pollifax wildly, and waited for him to feel for the knife's presence. Instead, he began tying his shoes.

Farrell sat up and glanced quickly at Colonel Nexdhet, then anxiously at Mrs. Pollifax, who shook her head. At that moment steps echoed in the hall, and a guard named Stefan walked in carrying breakfast trays. Nexdhet spoke curtly to him and walked out.

"Bathroom privileges," muttered Farrell darkly.

Mrs. Pollifax thought yearningly of all the hot tubs taken for granted during her long life. Not a long life if it was to end today, she amended, and began to feel angry with these people.

Stefan backed out and Farrell whispered, "Now that Nexdhet's out of here he can't blame the knife on us." He stood up, wobbled dangerously but waved Mrs. Pollifax away. "Look what I did while you slept." He limped to the tree, grasped it at the top and neatly removed the last twelve inches. "Can you find some padding?"

Mrs. Pollifax nodded. "There's a very nice hole in my mattress." She was already extracting horsehair from the mattress and making a bundle to fit the top of his crutch. "I'll wrap it in my slip. I never was good at sewing, both straps are pinned together."

"Bless your charming lack of housewifery," said Farrell.

"Now if you'll turn your head . . ." said Mrs. Pollifax. Then, "You can turn around now," and she presented him with slip, pins and horsehair. They sat down to breakfast, the bread and cheese disappearing automatically into Mrs. Pollifax's handbag, leaving them only a thin porridge. But this was the day they were going to do something. Mrs. Pollifax had faced her fears—anything was preferable to submission. She said, "Which direction shall we head at first? They'll expect us to leave the way we came."

"Yes, but can you think of anything better?" asked Farrell.

It would be clever to head away from the sea, she thought, to throw Perdido off. But then they would have to double back, and Farrell could never endure the extra miles.

"All we need is darkness and a great deal of luck." He smiled at her. "It's not too late to change your mind, you know, about including me in your wild venture."

"Absolutely not," said Mrs. Pollifax flatly. "If I made it alone, which I doubt, I would only be extremely unhappy when I got there." She rose to her feet as the door swung open and Lulash walked in. "Good·morning, Lulash. May I go outside now?"

"Yes, Zoëe Pollifax. Was good party last night?"

"Every minute of it," she told him with more cheerfulness than she possessed. "You make us feel like human beings again."

From his cot Farrell said, "Beware, Lulash. That is a very bad way to feel in a place like this."

THERE WAS NO ONE to guard her today, and it occurred to Mrs. Pollifax that she might try to observe the missile site more closely.

Life never seemed better than when death might be imminent, and she looked long and ardently at earth, sky and clouds. She climbed doggedly toward the slanting pines in the wood and there stopped to recapture both her breath and her sense of direction. She had moved only a few hundred yards more on the course she had taken with the colonel when she heard a very peculiar noise, a feverish crackling sound which came from between two large boulders up ahead. Deeply curious, she tiptoed across the fallen pine needles. A voice now broke the stillness of the woods but the crackling sounds continued. Static! thought Mrs. Pollifax. A radio!

The canned voice stopped speaking, and to her amazement a live voice began. She poked her head between the rocks. "Why, Colonel Nexdhet!" He was speaking into a walkie-talkie, and at the sound of her voice he dropped it as if it were a live coal.

"*Mrs. Pollifax!*" Eyes blazing, he picked up the walkie-talkie and spoke a stream of foreign words into it, then put it in a hole in the rock. "Why are you allowed in the woods?" he barked at her.

"If you come out here secretly to report to General Perdido," she said, "you must inform not only on us but on General Hoong as well. A paid informer, Colonel Nexdhet! Shame!"

He grasped her by the arm. "I'll take you back to your cell."

Both Lulash and Vassovic were in the guardroom but the colonel did not so much as look at them. He marched Mrs. Pollifax straight to her cell. Then she heard him issuing curt orders.

"He sounds peeved," said Farrell pleasantly.

Mrs. Pollifax said indignantly, "Colonel Nexdhet is a paid informer. A spy on his own men and not to be trusted."

"But I never did trust him," pointed out Farrell logically. "He's a colonel in their secret police, isn't he?"

Mrs. Pollifax sat down forlornly on her cot and stared into the long, nerve-racking day that lay ahead and wanted to cry. Instead she got out her playing cards and shuffled them.

A guard who did not speak English brought lunch. No one else came and, hour by hour, the afternoon wore on. Mrs. Pollifax played every one of the games of solitaire she knew, until she was tired to death of cards. Senor DeGamez could not have foreseen the conditions under which she would play his cherished game. Remembering his kindness she hoped he was in good health, because obviously he was a spy too; Mr. Carstairs's friends were very poor insurance risks.

The dinner trays arrived, and with them Colonel Nexdhet. "Good evening," he said pleasantly, as if nothing had happened. "General Perdido should be with us by nine."

It would be quite dark by then—good! "What time is it now, Colonel Nexdhet?" asked Mrs. Pollifax politely.

"Half past six."

She looked at him in surprise. "I always thought we ate at five."

He said primly, "Yes, but we are late tonight. General Hoong and Lulash have gone to meet General Perdido, leaving only myself, Vassovic and Stefan here, plus two guards in the other building." He paused and added casually, "And when you have finished your crutch—and I advise you to at once—I would appreciate your returning my knife to me. I am very fond of it."

Farrell and Mrs. Pollifax stared incredulously—it was a full minute before the colonel's words were absorbed. "You know?" said Farrell in a stunned voice.

"Of course." Nexdhet shrugged. "It is my business to know."

"And you're not going to give us away?" Mrs. Pollifax gasped.

"Give you away? How can I? I know nothing of any escape plans," he said blandly. "And if I did I am quite weaponless, whereas you have my knife as well as a loaded Nambu pistol."

Mrs. Pollifax took a deep breath. "Colonel Nexdhet, just what *were* you doing in the woods this morning?"

"I am extremely sorry you saw that, Mrs. Pollifax. It would have been much safer for all of us if you had not."

Farrell studied the man intently. "What *did* you see, Duchess?"

Mrs. Pollifax faltered. "He was hidden under two rocks listening to a voice on the radio, then he talked back into the radio."

"Radio!" Farrell repeated. "Over these mountains lies Yugoslavia, and to the east is Bulgaria—" Suddenly he began laughing. "My

501

God, Nexdhet, you're a Russian agent. They left you behind to
report on the Red Chinese!"

"Would you do me the kindness to speak in a lower voice?"

"My apologies." Farrell smiled. "Don't you see, Duchess? Those
bird-watching walks!" To Nexdhet he said, "But why help *us?*"

"I strongly dislike the word help. I am *not* helping you."

Mrs. Pollifax blurted out, "But you *have* been helping, Colonel.
You deliberately wore that knife last night—and it was you who told
us when General Perdido was coming back. Why?"

The colonel sighed. "Very well, I will say this much." He chose
his words carefully. "You are here because you are suspected of
knowing the whereabouts of a missing report on Communist ac-
tivities in Latin America. Red China will do anything to prevent
the United States from learning exactly how heavily involved it
has become in Latin America. Red China would also like to learn
what Russia is up to in Latin America, and Russia in turn would
enjoy knowing what Red China is secretly doing in Latin America. But if there is a choice between Red China or the United States
having that report, Russia would infinitely prefer the United States
to. The balance of power must be preserved at all costs."

Farrell nodded. "Yes, but what guarantee have we that Russians
aren't waiting somewhere to capture us?"

Nexdhet shrugged. "No guarantees at all, Mr. Farrell."

Farrell considered. "We'll have to trust him," he said finally.

Mrs. Pollifax smiled. "You advised me to trust no one, Colonel."

His answering smile was grave. "Nor should you, Mrs. Pollifax.
Remember, I will be in the party that hunts you down."

Mrs. Pollifax thought about this and nodded. "Then could you
do one more thing for us—shoot to kill?"

"If you are caught, I could not afford to let you survive."
Nexdhet stood up. "In return I ask only that when you hit me
with your rock, do not hit me here." He pointed to the back of his
skull. "I have already a small steel plate here from an old wound."

Farrell took out the knife and began to slash branches from
the tree. "Better than that, we'll only gag you."

"The missile site," Mrs. Pollifax burst out. "Colonel, you *wanted* me to see it!" She turned to Farrell. "The Chinese are building a missile site only a mile from here."

"Good God," he gasped.

Nexdhet looked apologetic. "A small but vital detail, lest your country underestimate Red China." He smiled wryly.

"You've known our plans that long then?" asked Farrell.

Nexdhet smiled. "It was after I saw Mrs. Pollifax remove the bullet from your arm that I decided you were worth the risk. And it is to my interest that neither of you is questioned by Perdido."

Mrs. Pollifax's eyes fell on the window slit and she jumped to her feet. "It's already twilight," she said in a shocked voice.

Farrell was padding the crutch. He stood up. "Not bad."

Mrs. Pollifax, suddenly appalled by the meagerness of their preparation, brought out the rocks, collected cartridges, map and compass from their hiding places and added the cheese from dinner. Farrell said quietly, "They're coming for the trays."

To conceal the rocks she sat down on top of them just as Vassovic walked in rattling his keys. "Evening," he said.

Farrell had hidden his crutch but the tree's absence was conspicuous, and Mrs. Pollifax decided she must divert the major's attention. "How is your back?" she asked, and then saw the candle he was carrying. "But you're not going to light our cell so early?"

"Busy tonight," Major Vassovic said. "No time for it later."

Farrell looked up, appalled, while Nexdhet eyed Mrs. Pollifax with sardonic amusement. She now realized with a sinking heart that the moment had come to knock the guard unconscious and that neither of them was prepared for it. The candle had never been brought in so early! It couldn't be more than eight o'clock, but the cell door wouldn't be opened again unless to admit General Perdido, and here she sat like a brood hen on the rocks Farrell needed to hit the major. Because Farrell was of course the one to do it. But Farrell was across the room. I can't, she told herself—what would the garden club or the pastor of her church think?

Major Vassovic, his back turned toward them, struck a match to light the candle and Mrs. Pollifax watched it flame into life. I've never hit anybody in my life, she remembered. Quietly, rock in hand, she walked up to Vassovic and hit him on the head. "For heaven's sake," she said, staring down at him where he lay like a suit of old clothes. "I hope I didn't hurt his back again."

"Good girl." Farrell reached under the cot for his crutch and hobbled over to the major. He plucked the huge keys from the floor and dropped them into Mrs. Pollifax's purse. "Now we'll call in the other guard and I'll try *my* skill. Help me arrange Vassovic so we can say he's fainted. I do beg your pardon, Nexdhet. Damn funny doing all this in front of you."

Nexdhet said politely, "Not at all, I'm sure. What next?"

Farrell took up a position behind the door. "Now?" Mrs. Pollifax asked. He nodded and she gave a penetrating scream.

Footsteps hurried down the hall. Stefan walked in and Farrell hit him. Stefan also sank into a heap.

"I'll get some rope," said Mrs. Pollifax, and hurried to the guardroom. It was not until she arrived there that she realized it might not be empty; she made a mental note to develop more cunning. Rummaging through the drawers she found what she needed and hurried back to Farrell.

"You'd better tie me up too, before I change my mind," Nexdhet said. "It surprises me, how alarmed I'm beginning to feel."

Farrell grinned. "It's the Duchess who gives this such a delightful, amateur quality. Lie down, chum." Nexdhet gratefully did so and Farrell linked him by rope to Vassovic and Stefan. "I'll gag you. Are you a good actor?"

"No, but I'm known as a very good Sigurimi man."

"Let's hope it protects you. And Nexdhet—thanks."

"Just spare me the trouble of shooting you, that's all."

The gag went into his mouth and Farrell knotted it securely while Mrs. Pollifax left again for the guardroom, this time to strip it. With the major's keys she found a Beretta pistol and another Nambu. Then she decided to load up on cartridges, but the drawer that for a week had held a key in its lock would not budge. Now she had one thing to do that Farrell might not approve of. She tiptoed past their cell door and inserted one of the major's keys into the lock of the neighboring cell and opened the door. She stood uncertainly peering in, and suddenly the darkness of the farthest corner expelled a gray genie of a man in flowing gray robes who began a repeated bowing as he chattered in a singsong voice.

Mrs. Pollifax interrupted him. "Please, we are going to try to escape. Would you like to come with us?"

He regarded her with interest, his face surprisingly long and Gothic for an Oriental. He looked like a happy child in the guise of a man, all twinkles, smiles and curiosity. "Come," Mrs. Pollifax said, as if to a child, and pulled him by the sleeve. When they reached the cell she said to Farrell firmly, "Look what I found."

"Good heavens," said Farrell. "Who on earth is this creature?"

"The man next door. Ask Colonel Nexdhet who he is."

Farrell loosened the gag. "I will not tell you," Nexdhet said harshly, "and you must absolutely not take him."

Comprehension dawned upon Farrell. "Duchess, you're not thinking of— He may be a Commie worse than Perdido."

"Then why would he be in jail?"

"He's Chinese, isn't he? He had to *be* somebody to get here."

"Trusting, always trusting," pointed out Colonel Nexdhet from the floor. "Now you are crazy."

"He may not *want* to escape," Farrell said in exasperation.

"Everybody wants to escape," said Mrs. Pollifax scornfully.

"Put him back in his cell," warned Nexdhet. "I know who he is."

"You absolutely won't tell us?" They both regarded him thoughtfully. Farrell said, "Oh, to hell with it, this whole thing is insane, anyway. Bring him along, Duchess, damn it."

Mrs. Pollifax wordlessly handed him the two pistols and helped stuff the gag back in the colonel's mouth. "Okay, let's go," Farrell said crisply, and they moved out into the hall. Farrell locked the cell door and restored the keys to Mrs. Pollifax's purse. "Get rid of them later," he told her. "What do we call this—this mistake of yours?"

"Our Genie," said Mrs. Pollifax. "He reminds me of Aladdin's."

"Our Genie with the light brown hair," quipped Farrell. Leaning on his crutch he unlocked the door to the outside and pulled it open. "Only two lights shining in the big building. Shall we go?"

Gallantly he held open the door for Mrs. Pollifax and her charge, and they walked into the sultry night air. We're out! We're free! thought Mrs. Pollifax, when a voice said, "Well! My three prisoners, and no guard in sight."

General Perdido had come back.

9

"I'LL HAVE Vassovic's head for this," barked General Perdido, drawing his gun from his belt holster. "Lulash, see what they've done with him."

He shouted orders, his attention distracted for a second, and Mrs. Pollifax lifted her arm and threw the cell keys far into the night. She winced at the sound of metal against rock, but the general didn't notice and somehow this proved that he was not superhuman. Her courage began to revive. These particular keys to the cells were gone, and it would take time to find duplicates.

Now, ignominiously, the three of them were back in the guardroom, standing like naughty children before the general. Desperately Mrs. Pollifax tried to think: the electricity was primitive —only one line, the major had told her; it would be marvelous if she could hurl herself at the one power line and plunge the building into darkness. Unfortunately she was totally without knowledge of power lines.

"What fools," hissed General Perdido. "I will take delight, Mr. Farrell, in punishing you. As for you, Mrs.—yes, Lulash?"

Lulash looked anxious. "I can't get in. The cells are locked."

The general irritably opened one desk drawer after another. "One of the three must have them. Search them!"

Mrs. Pollifax's heart sank: a search would reveal the pistols. She said, "I had the keys. I threw them away. Outside."

The general stood up and walked to Mrs. Pollifax. He lifted one arm and with precision struck her across the cheekbone.

Farrell gave a cry, Lulash looked stricken, and Mrs. Pollifax, reeling, heard the general promise that this was only the beginning. The Genie spoke then, and Perdido answered in Chinese.

"Lulash—search them," said Perdido harshly.

Lulash gave Mrs. Pollifax a long glance, but she could not tell whether apology or a plea was in it. He moved over to Farrell. "Turn to the wall, please, and place your hands against it."

It took a second before Mrs. Pollifax realized that Lulash stood squarely in front of Farrell, concealing him from Perdido as well as protecting him from the general's gun. There was a curious smile on his lips. "Faster," he said, "or I will shoot you."

Farrell understood. One hand moved swiftly to his pocket, the other seized Lulash. Over Lulash's shoulder he fired his pistol at the general, then tapped the guard on the head with the butt. Both fell to the floor.

"Let's go," said Farrell, heading for the door on his crutch. The Genie reached it first and the three of them fled into the night, Farrell stumbling and muttering oaths. "Damn it, I only winged him," he said furiously. "A few minutes and he'll be after us."

"Yes," Mrs. Pollifax said grimly, realizing that without Farrell to slow them down they would already have reached sanctuary in the fir trees. She measured the difference it might have made, then put the thought aside forever. "Here we are," she said with relief as they reached the thin cover of firs.

"My God," gasped Farrell. "Look!" Two donkeys were tied to a tree. Farrell hobbled toward them. "Plain bloody miracle, except of course they had to be somewhere, with the general arriving." He untied them, then the Genie put out his hand for the ropes, gesturing to Mrs. Pollifax and Farrell to mount. Behind them came the sound of a gunshot and Mrs. Pollifax froze. "Don't panic, it could be Perdido signaling for help," Farrell said. "Just jump on."

Mrs. Pollifax unfroze. "No, I will *not* mount one of those beasts again. The Genie will. Besides, I believe I know the way to go. I'll do the leading." So with the two ropes in her hand Mrs. Pollifax set out to find the cliff. Already shouts were being exchanged behind them; the donkeys moved with maddening slowness; the cliff, which they ought to have reached by now, failed to materialize. Mrs. Pollifax wondered if in skirting the boulders she might have begun circling back—at best they were less than a mile from the main building. Where *is* that damn cliff, she thought—and was appalled at her choice of language.

She tugged on the donkeys' halters and quickened her step, which proved ill timed. Her right foot moved out into space, came down in anticipation of earth or rock and found neither. With a startled gasp she catapulted into space, men and donkeys dragged with her. It was not a long fall and was suddenly broken when Mrs. Pollifax discovered herself ignominiously straddling a creaking tree branch that threatened to break at any moment. She had found her cliff. But where she was to go from here, and where the others had gone, she had no idea.

"*Well!*" exclaimed a voice nearby.

"Farrell!" she gasped, and at the same moment she heard the Genie and the faint, anguished bray of a donkey.

Farrell told her fervently, "I think you'd better try to join us here where there's rock. What's under you?"

"A tree branch and—*air*."

"Keep talking so I can find you. Damn this darkness."

Mrs. Pollifax was reciting *The Rime of the Ancient Mariner* when she felt a hand clutch her ankle. A little sob of relief escaped her. Farrell said, "Now *very* carefully start shinnying backwards. I'll keep my hands on your ankles. If the branch starts to go I think I can still hang on to you."

"Think?" repeated Mrs. Pollifax, and felt like laughing hysterically. But she obeyed, and thereby learned how sinuously a person can move if his life depends upon it. After what seemed like hours her toes met the solid rock on which Farrell was kneeling. Then she knelt beside him and allowed herself the luxury of feeling faint.

"It *seems* to be a small ledge we fell onto," Farrell explained. "The Genie and I both landed on donkeys. I'd say we fell only about twenty feet or so."

Suddenly they heard voices above. "Back," Farrell whispered. "There's a small overhang, and a hollow in the cliff. Find one of the donkeys and hold his mouth shut. I'll take the other."

The donkeys had crawled into the shallow indentation of rock,

508

leaving no room for humans; Mrs. Pollifax all but climbed on top of them as she heard Perdido shouting orders above. A searchlight was directed downward, and Mrs. Pollifax closed her eyes, hoping this would make her even smaller as she pressed against the donkeys. Then the light moved along the cliff's edge and the voices of the men diminished. Mrs. Pollifax relaxed, and presently fell asleep, her head pillowed on the abdomen of a donkey.

It was the Genie who awakened her with a tap on the shoulder. She was startled to discover she had slept through the night. The sky was perceptibly lightening and now she could see the appalling smallness of their ledge—a bare seven feet wide, above a drop that turned her blood cold. Farrell, noting her face, grinned. "The gods were with us, eh?" Mrs. Pollifax shuddered and he went on, "The Genie donated his sleeves to tie up the donkeys' mouths. Perdido's probably wirelessing news of our escape all over Albania by now. We'd better move in a hurry, before it gets light."

"Move! Move where?" asked Mrs. Pollifax.

"Well, we absolutely can't move *up*," he said mockingly. "Besides, I'm getting hungry."

"Hungry?" Mrs. Pollifax automatically groped for her purse, but Farrell shook his head. "It's gone. Down *there,* presumably."

Mrs. Pollifax leaned forward just a trifle—heights made her dizzy—and looked down into the valley. Farrell was suicidal—they could never negotiate such a cliff; but then her resistance turned to curiosity. The cliff slanted down over avalanchelike beds of gravel and rock, short drops and more gravel beds, to a pasture below. "But you couldn't make it with your leg," she protested.

Farrell smiled. "Look, walking's hard, but nobody *walks* down a cliff. One slides, using arms and hands. Come on, let's go."

Oh, these happy young, thought Mrs. Pollifax, feeling unutterably weary and ancient. "All right, who leads the way?"

Farrell said casually, "Which brings up another subject. I don't trust the Genie and I won't have you trusting him. Who knows what he said to Perdido? All I know is, we're stuck with him. So you go first, then the Genie. I go last with the gun."

Preposterous, decided Mrs. Pollifax. Gritting her teeth she

inched forward and dangled her feet over the edge of the cliff. "No," Farrell told her. "Hang from the branch with your face to the cliff and reach for a toehold below."

"Great. I can join the circus when I get home."

"*If* you get home," Farrell pointed out. Recklessly she placed both hands around the tree branch and let her body swing in space —a great deal of space, in which she hung for a sickening moment, with Farrell hissing directions from the ledge. "There—you've got it," he said.

What she had got, as he put it, was one foot on an outcropping of rock. She glanced below her and clung harder to the branch. "That rock will *not* support me!"

"It will if you move your hands to that stubby little root growing out of the rock to your right," Farrell said.

Mrs. Pollifax saw that since either course could bring about her violent demise, she might as well try going down. She felt for the root and closed her eyes. "One for the money . . ." she whispered. Cautiously she opened her eyes and discovered that her position had vastly improved. Her body was now pressed tightly against the face of the cliff wall. She even noted a small hole in the rock into which her hands could fit for the next move.

Inch by inch the three of them descended into the valley. The sun discovered them as they reached the last slope, a charmingly easy hill of pebbles. They stopped to catch their breath and take stock. This was the rocky pasture, usually alive with goats, that Mrs. Pollifax had seen on her walks along the cliff. It lay just above another pasture, and then another, each terrace tipping down a little drunkenly toward the flat dry valley. There were no goats now, but looking to the right she saw a small rock-walled building that must be the goatherd's home. Then Mrs. Pollifax drew in her breath sharply: a woman stood in the doorway watching them.

"What is it?" demanded Farrell.

Wordlessly she pointed, and Farrell reached into his pocket. "No, you mustn't shoot her," Mrs. Pollifax said. "Anyway, there may be others inside."

"It's her or us, Duchess."

"Let's be sure she's alone. Then we could just tie and gag her—a gunshot would be heard for miles."

"Woman to woman, eh? Have it your way, Duchess."

The woman looked as ageless as the rocks around her, nothing but her eyes alive in a watchful, sunburned face. Nervously Mrs. Pollifax led the way toward her. Two feet from the doorway she stopped with a wan smile and pointed to the top of the precipice, then to herself and Farrell. "*Inglese*," she said.

The woman's impassive glance moved to the cliff above, then returned to Mrs. Pollifax, Farrell and the Genie. She made a turn back into the hut and Mrs. Pollifax's heart constricted. But she merely held back the goatskin at the door and gestured them to follow. Mrs. Pollifax saw Farrell's hand slip back in his pocket.

It was like twilight inside, with a fire burning in the center of an earthen floor. The first object that caught Mrs. Pollifax's eye was her lost purse lying beside the fire, and she realized that their progress down the cliff must have been observed for some time. The woman spoke to two males squatting near the fire: a boy of fifteen or so, and a tall, well-built man with smoldering eyes. The three conferred for several minutes, and Mrs. Pollifax wondered if Farrell and the Genie felt as edgy as she did at being discussed with no knowledge of what was being said. These people now had the power of life or death over them. Would they have to kill the family? I'm too soft for all this, she thought.

Suddenly the man stood up and went out, and Mrs. Pollifax and Farrell exchanged alarmed glances. The boy also jumped to his feet, but only to bring stools for them to sit on. The woman gathered up three wooden bowls and dished something into them that resembled lumpy oatmeal drowned in oil. Mrs. Pollifax accepted hers with a polite smile. "What do you think?" she asked Farrell in a low voice.

"I don't know," he replied, seated next to the Genie.

Mrs. Pollifax spooned up the honeyed grain, scarcely aware of its taste. Where had the man gone? Her fate was no more than a slender thread loosely held by indifferent strangers.

It was the woman who made the next move. She walked to a

chest in the corner and began pulling from it an assortment of clothes. Astonished, Mrs. Pollifax wondered if possibly these people were going to help them. She turned and saw the look in Farrell's face: the confusion of a suspicious and desperate man confronted by hope. The woman took out a cone-shaped felt hat which she clapped on the Genie's head; then she held against Farrell the loose-flowing clothes and sash of an Albanian mountain man. To Mrs. Pollifax she handed two petticoats and a voluminous woolen skirt with inserts of handmade lace. She gestured toward the blanket hung across one corner of the room.

"Well!" beamed Mrs. Pollifax at Farrell, and she retired.

A few minutes later they reassembled around the fire. Farrell, with his unshaven jaw, looked a fiercely authentic bandit. The Genie still appeared birdlike, yet somehow transcending the absurdity of his costume. Mrs. Pollifax had no idea how she looked but she knew she felt very warm indeed under so many layers.

The woman held out Mrs. Pollifax's purse. On impulse Mrs. Pollifax opened it, extracted the pistol and its cartridges, the compass, the map, the food and her playing cards, and gave the purse back to the woman. "Keep it," she said, smiling. "There are plenty of pockets in these new clothes. One in each petticoat," she told Farrell. She snapped and unsnapped the purse, a feat that brought surprise and delight to the woman's face. Her smile was beautiful and Mrs. Pollifax realized that she was still a young woman. She pressed the Guatemalan jacket on her, hoping she would not wear it outside the hut for a good many months.

Now the boy flung back the skin at the door, and Mrs. Pollifax saw that his father had merely gone to assemble his goats for the day. They were milling about the door, bleating. With his crook the man prodded them even closer. The boy now eagerly began explaining in pantomime what the family had decided. First he pointed to the cliff and grimaced, so that they understood that Perdido's eyrie was disliked in the neighborhood. Then he pointed to the sun and appeared to be urging them to go quickly. In their new clothes—he pointed to them—they might be able to reach the road. He indicated cars on a road.

513

Mrs. Pollifax nodded. "I spotted a road from the cliff. It runs across the plain, south to north, about five miles from here."

The boy had not finished. The pastures could be seen clearly from the cliff, and someone might be watching with binoculars. His father had decided to drive his goats down to the pasture nearest the valley. If Mrs. Pollifax and the Genie could move with the herd they would not be seen. He dropped to his hands and knees and crawled into the herd to show them. "Good heavens," said Mrs. Pollifax faintly. Scrambling up again the boy pointed to Farrell's leg, seized his father's crook and placed it in Farrell's hand. The father now got down on his hands and knees.

Farrell grinned. "Duchess, do you get the same message? From the cliff it will appear that Mac here and his son are taking the goats out, as they do every morning. But going out I will be the goatherd while he joins you and the Genie with the goats. In some convenient place we'll be left behind."

Mrs. Pollifax made only one comment, "Damn."

"They'll be blackballing you at the garden club this winter," said Farrell, grinning. "Hurry now, they're waiting."

The Genie was already crouched down among the goats, his eyes twinkling. Gingerly Mrs. Pollifax crawled in among them too. "For heaven's sake move them slowly," she cautioned.

Farrell grasped the crook, the boy called out something in the high clear air and the herd, with Mrs. Pollifax, the Genie and the goatherd in it, began to move.

Mrs. Pollifax had not crawled since she was a child, but it was the goats that proved unnerving. They stepped on her, bleated alarmingly, playfully nipped her. Each time the procession halted for a rest they stumbled over her. And how they smelled! As the ground slanted more and more, the soft grass was replaced by pebbles that cut Mrs. Pollifax's knees, and once they left the shadow of the cliffs the sun beat down mercilessly. As their queer progress continued, every thought faded from Mrs. Pollifax's mind, but after a long time she became aware that the herd had come to a standstill and that she was being lightly touched on the shoulder. She looked up at Farrell. "You can stand up now, Duchess," he said. "We're hidden from the top of the cliff. We've reached the valley."

He looked drained and white and Mrs. Pollifax realized that a goatherd's crook was not the same as a crutch; he must have had to place his weight on a leg broken in two places, poorly set and unmended yet, and all this on rocky downhill terrain.

The Genie popped up from among the goats looking so cheerful that Mrs. Pollifax began to feel almost hostile. She took a step forward and almost fell; but she had always been a gracious hostess. She tottered forward to wring the hand of the boy and his father who had helped them at so much risk to themselves. "*Det, det,*" the man was saying, pointing westward.

Mrs. Pollifax recalled that this meant "sea," and nodded. Farrell shook their hands and the Genie went into his bowing routine. Then the man handed Farrell his crutch, took back his crook and he and the boy strolled away. Mrs. Pollifax, Farrell and the Genie were alone. They were standing in a dry creek bed. In front of them stretched the valley, shimmering in the morning heat. To the south, barely visible, lay objects that might be tall rocks or a village. There were almost no trees. Because it all seemed so overwhelming Mrs. Pollifax suggested that they sit down and rest.

"Not on your life," said Farrell flatly. "They must be combing the mountains for us. They'll get to the valley next." She nodded wearily. There seemed nowhere to hide in this naked countryside and she was bone-tired, but she glanced at the Genie and he smiled vivaciously. Farrell said, "Not a brain in his head, is there? An intelligent man would be scared stiff. Well, let's go."

They clung to the security of the creek bed, for although they wore native clothes they were three in number, and it was three for whom the general would be searching. The sun was searingly hot; stumbling along in the prison of her woolen skirt and two petticoats, Mrs. Pollifax longed for water—they had none—and for something green to look at, anything but this rocky landscape.

They came in sight of the road so suddenly that Farrell gave a hiss and dropped to the ground behind a rock. The Genie and Mrs. Pollifax promptly imitated him. The road was overrun by men wearing striped prisoners' suits, spread out for maybe a mile, listlessly splitting rocks. An alarming number of guards with rifles were posted near them, and several were sprawled in the shade of a large black car. The road ran straight from the cliff in the north toward the airport in the south. Rimmed by so many people, it might as well have been an insurmountable wall. "What can we do?" whispered Mrs. Pollifax helplessly.

Farrell ran a dusty hand across his bloodshot eyes. His face had a dreadful pallor and his hand trembled. Mrs. Pollifax shuddered at what he must be enduring. "We'll have to wait until dark," he said in a cracked voice. "A whole rotten day without water."

Poor Farrell, she thought, and then she glanced beyond him and stiffened. Her look of horror caused Farrell and the Genie to look too. Half a dozen men were crossing the plain behind them. What had caught Mrs. Pollifax's eye was the flash of a mirror that was shortly answered from a treelined foothill up on their right. The search was under way—one group combing the cliffs, another the valley. Then the Genie stood up.

"Hey," yelped Farrell.

"Down—get down!" cried Mrs. Pollifax.

But the Genie ran on, toward the road and the guards.

"I told you I didn't trust him," snarled Farrell, drawing out his pistol. Mrs. Pollifax, befuddled by thirst, exhaustion and panic, watched him try to steady the gun on the rock and made no move to stop him. Because it had been her idea to bring the Genie along, it made his betrayal the more personal. Farrell groaned. "Too late. My hand shakes, damn it."

Mrs. Pollifax stared ahead at the Genie, who was now conversing with the guards. Of course—he's Chinese, she remembered bleakly; perhaps the guards were too. She glanced behind her—within a few minutes their pursuers would converge upon them.

"Well?" said Farrell grimly, holding up the pistol.

She said steadily, "Yes—yes, it's really the only thing left to do, isn't it. But I'm afraid you'll have to be the one—the one to—"

He said harshly, "I understand. But you realize it's only to spare you worse. I've grown damnably fond of you, you know."

516

"Thank you," she said gravely.

The Genie and a guard with a rifle were now in the big black car, the guard in the driver's seat, the Genie beside him. With a jerk, the car left the road and bounced toward them.

Farrell ran his tongue over parched dry lips. With one hand he lifted his gun, trying to steady it as he aimed at Mrs. Pollifax's heart. "Isn't the brain faster?" she asked curiously.

"Oh for heaven's sake," groaned Farrell, the pistol wobbling. "Just don't talk, will you do me that favor please?"

Mrs. Pollifax sat up straight, primly folded her hands in her lap and waited patiently for oblivion. She did wish Farrell would hurry because the car was racing toward them. He lifted an elbow to clear perspiration from his eyes. It was too late. The car was upon them. The Genie leaped out, knocked the pistol from Farrell's hand and, brandishing it, gestured them both into the car.

Mrs. Pollifax regarded him without expression. If he was Chinese he could not really be called a traitor. Wearily she whispered to Farrell, "Come. I still have the Beretta, you know," and climbed into the back seat. It was a Rolls, she noticed: a very ancient one, highly appropriate for funerals. Farrell sank beside her and the guard slammed the door. This time the Genie slid behind the wheel. He turned and smiled, his eyes bright and fathomless, at the guard beside him.

Snake in the grass, thought Mrs. Pollifax.

With one smooth, effortless movement the Genie lifted the pistol and shot the guard between the eyes. Then he opened the door and pushed the body into the dust. In clipped, perfect English, he said, "I think we'd better get the hell out of here, don't you?"

"Who the devil are you?" demanded Farrell.

"And why didn't you tell us you spoke English?" asked Mrs. Pollifax.

"Didn't dare trust you. Sorry." Abruptly the Genie backed and turned and regained the road. "I don't know how long we can stick with this car. Only about four hundred in the country, but there are radios and things like roadblocks. Also, I'm not very good at driving the bloody thing."

Mrs. Pollifax noted the speedometer and reached for Farrell's arm. "We're going one hundred miles an hour."

"That's kilometers, not miles. Only about sixty." Farrell spoke with his old briskness. "This road leads into Shkodër. Hell, we don't want to go there, do we?" he said.

Mrs. Pollifax, surrounded by so much masculine profanity, said firmly, "Hell, no."

The old debonair smile crossed his face. "Duchess, *absolutely* no more swearing—a car's following us, damn it!"

"Three, maybe four miles behind us," said the Genie, his eyes on the rearview mirror. "At least this car moves faster than six legs, one of them broken." He peered at the dashboard panel. "Plenty of gas, thank heaven." He shoved the accelerator down. The car surged ahead in a burst of speed and Mrs. Pollifax wished she dared close her eyes. Now the Genie was braking to avoid an oxcart. Next they swerved around a sheep baaing in the center of the road and shot through a cobblestoned village street.

Moments later a small plane zoomed over them, banked, flew over them again. "They've heard about us in Shkodër too," Farrell said grimly.

"We'll have to ditch the car," the Genie said. "Where and how I don't know."

Mrs. Pollifax didn't know either, but she grasped at once that just ditching the car wouldn't be enough, not with pursuers behind them and their progress observed from the air. "An accident," she said suddenly. "Can't we tip it over and set it on fire? They would think for a few minutes that we were still inside."

Both men were silent, fumbling with the idea, and then the Genie said, "You haven't any matches, have you?"

"Two," said Farrell.

"And there's a lake to the west of us, on our right?" With a squeal of brakes the Genie turned right down a cart track and plunged toward a grove of trees. "You'll need a head start, Farrell," said the Genie. "Start running when we stop. I'll try to ram the car into a tree." He braked the Rolls among the trees. "Out! Hurry, that way," and to Mrs. Pollifax he said, "Wait. I'll need help."

Mrs. Pollifax watched Farrell hobble away for dear life. Dear *dear* life. What things people did to remain alive—that is, physically alive, she amended, for to remain alive inside was far more intricate and difficult. There was a roar from the Rolls engine and, aghast, she watched the car head at top speed toward the largest of the trees, the Genie leaning half out the door. Car and tree met and the Rolls crumpled like an accordion. The Genie, shaken but whole, had leaped out and now was fumbling for the matches. She ran to help.

He was wrestling with the cover to the gas tank, his hands trembling. Mrs. Pollifax gave it a twist and lifted it off. "Start running," said the Genie and, obeying, Mrs. Pollifax did not look back until she heard the explosion. The Genie caught up with her at the edge of the grove, where they found Farrell looking very ill. It was obvious that he could go no farther.

The landscape offered no hope of concealment, and Perdido would soon discover that no bodies were in the Rolls. Mrs. Pollifax could see the roof of a hut, and back of it a pen of some kind. In the corner of that pen was a two-wheeled wooden cart filled to the brim with hay.

"Look," she whispered. A slim hope, but it was the only object in sight that could possibly shield them. Farrell and the Genie looked at it; rather stupidly, she thought, until she realized they were exhausted and that as the senior member of the party—rather like a scout leader—she was going to have to assume command. As if to emphasize the urgency, she heard the plane flying back to scour the countryside.

"Into the cart," she cried, pulling out tufts of hay. "Quickly, both of you." There was barely room for the two of them.

"What about you?" demanded Farrell.

"They don't know I'm in peasant clothes," she pointed out, devoutly hoping this was true and piling hay on top of them. "For heaven's sake don't move." There was a sneeze. "Or sneeze either."

The plane was circling now over the woods where the Rolls was burning. Presently its remains would be cool enough to examine. Mrs. Pollifax regarded the cart speculatively, then kicked the rock from under one of the wheels. Bracing herself she moved between the shafts and tugged. Oddly enough the cart moved quite easily, and the earth sloped conveniently downward. She felt rather like a ricksha boy. Having achieved a precarious speed, she marched sturdily on, the cart at times pushing her in front of it, toward a wood less than half a mile away. The pastureland they were crossing now was of greener grass, which led Mrs. Pollifax to hope they were nearing the coast.

She was in the middle of the pasture when she heard another plane roar overhead, then head west. It ought to have alarmed her, but instead her heart quickened. Pontoons! A seaplane, she thought. We must be near water.

THE GROUND, after thoughtfully slanting downhill, had begun to slant uphill, and in their path directly ahead lay a field of corn. Mrs. Pollifax had to concede that she was not an ox. "I just can't pull anymore," she said in an anguished voice.

It was the Genie who emerged first from the straw. "Quite so. I suggest we crawl into the corn and rest a few minutes."

It was a bad idea, but what else could they do? "Yes," she said.

Farrell came up out of the hay looking utterly ghastly. "I'll move the cart and cover your trail as I join you," said the Genie.

In among the cornstalks Farrell and Mrs. Pollifax sank wordlessly to the ground. Mrs. Pollifax roused enough to explore the pocket of her first petticoat. She drew out the pistol, map and compass, then one slice of stale bread and a small amount of cheese. "There isn't much and we have to save some for later." They could hear the Genie looking for them. She carefully put aside his portion of food and picked up the pistol to put it away. Hearing the Genie's footsteps, she glanced up smiling.

But it was not the Genie standing there. It was the guard Stefan, with a look of blank stupidity on his face. For just the fraction of a second Mrs. Pollifax shared his stupidity; then she realized that she was holding the pistol and without thinking she lifted it and aimed. The noise was deafening and she watched with horrified fascination as Stefan, bleeding, began to crumple. Mrs.

Pollifax said blankly, "Farrell, I've killed him. I've killed a man."

"He'd have gladly killed both of us," gasped Farrell. "Don't just sit there, Duchess, they must have heard that shot for miles."

Certainly the Genie had heard it. He was with them again, kneeling beside Stefan, removing his pistol, checking his pockets. She stuffed pistol, map and compass away and stood up. "Madness, every bit of this," she muttered under her breath.

Farrell said grimly, "God how I wish I could run."

The Genie was tugging at Mrs. Pollifax's arm to get her away from the dead man.

"Don't ever look back," Farrell told her harshly.

So he understood in his rough way. With an effort Mrs. Pollifax pulled herself together and they hurried to enter a forest of pines that lay beyond the cornfield. The shadows brought only meager relief but it was peaceful and Mrs. Pollifax yearned to sink to the ground. The Genie said suddenly, "I smell water," and moved ahead.

Farrell's pallor alarmed Mrs. Pollifax; he looked already dead, like someone embalmed and strung up on wires by a fiendish mortician. Then she realized that she, too, smelled water—there was a freshness in the air. If it was the lake, they must be near Yugoslavia and freedom. The Genie was ahead of them waving his arms, but it seemed an eternity before they reached him. "Look," he said. She lifted her head to see water glittering in the sunshine, water to bathe in, to cool parched throats. She wanted to stumble to the shore, but the Genie clutched her arm and she heard the sound of the plane again. "This way," he said, and led them back among the pines.

Lake Scutari, she remembered, was about two hundred square miles in size, half of it in Yugoslavia. . . . When the plane disappeared to the north the Genie stopped, one finger on his lips, removed his shoes and began retracing their steps.

Mrs. Pollifax wanted to fall to the ground, but she knew that Farrell couldn't sit down—mustn't, in fact, lest he never get up again—and innate courtesy kept her upright. Presently she saw the Genie wading in the shallows of the lake. He appeared to be searching for something, and some minutes later he beckoned Mrs. Pollifax and Farrell to the bank of the lake. They jumped into the shallows and then he guided them toward an old tree that hung over the lake, its roots exposed and rotting. Here the water over the years had brought an accumulation of debris. The Genie parted the branches of a sumac that had grown from the gnarled tree roots and said, "It's not dry, but there's room here for three people." He pushed aside a log that had been caught in the flotsam and helped Farrell crawl into a tiny cave under the bank. Mrs. Pollifax followed, and the Genie squeezed in after her, taking care to pull the log back into its original position.

It was wet, but it was a curiously womblike place—dark, quiet and cool—and Mrs. Pollifax's eyes simply would not remain open. Fatigue won and she slept from exhaustion.

It was not the sound but the awareness of danger that awakened her. She lifted her head to hear the roar of a motorboat running near the shore. It passed their hiding place, water in its wake rushing into the cave, submerging them. They had barely caught their breath when the airplane came again, and then from above they heard men shouting. The launch came back, then sped away sending fresh waves to torture them in their cave. The men's voices above moved away, growing distant in the forest. But the plane returned. It soon became obvious that not one but a number of police launches were on patrol. Whole centuries seemed to pass—and twilight deepened. In what other world had she yearned for water to drink and bathe in? Mrs. Pollifax asked herself.

Farrell said to the Genie, "I suggest we float that log and hang on to it all the way across the lake. If the wind isn't against us, we might land in Yugoslavia."

"Police boats," the Genie pointed out wanly.

"We'll just have to watch out for them."

Mrs. Pollifax turned to the Genie. "We still know nothing at all about you. You haven't told us even your name."

"Smith will do nicely if you'd like a name."

"Nobody's named Smith," growled Farrell. "Not in my circle."

"It's much, *much* better you don't know my name if you meet

General Perdido again," the Genie replied. "Much safer. He'd never appreciate your knowing."

"I was thinking of next of kin," Mrs. Pollifax said reproachfully, and something like a chuckle came from him.

"Bless you, they held my funeral two years ago. I've been dead a long time, Mrs. Pollifax," he said, which puzzled her.

She grimly began the job of moving a body that had lain on its stomach for hours, and after considerable manipulation managed to climb to her knees and squeeze through the opening. Farrell followed slowly, pushing his damaged leg and crutch ahead of him. The darkness outside was broken only by a scattering of stars and half a dozen lights across the lake. The air was soft as velvet. The Genie wrestled with the log, which had the advantage of being large enough and high enough out of the water to give them sufficient cover; on the other hand this made it harder to cling to from the water. "Straddle it," suggested the Genie. But for three exhausted people to mount a wet, round log proved nearly impossible. No sooner had one of them climbed on than the others fell off. Finally they brought it back to shallow water and climbed on together at the same moment.

"Everybody ready to set sail?" asked the Genie. Gingerly they paddled, with hands and feet, out from the shadows and into a breeze that sprang up from the north, destination Yugoslavia.

10

In Washington, D.C., that same day, the man named Peattie notified Carstairs that he had received information from Peking. "It seems," he said, "that General Perdido *has* been there, but alone and not until August twenty-fourth, five days after the kidnapping of Mrs. Pollifax and Farrell. Also, and this you may find interesting, he arrived in China on a jet that collected him in Athens."

"Athens!" Carstairs was visibly electrified. "The Balkans—Albania! But I never thought he'd take them so far—"

Peattie went on. "He remained in Peking until the middle of

the week, leaving yesterday in a private plane that was said to be heading for Albania." Peattie smiled with the pleasure of someone holding a very interesting card up his sleeve. "I have something more. I took the liberty of—well, after all, since Albania has become the prodigy of the Chinese Reds it has naturally fallen into my province. So I made inquiries. Perdido's plane came in at Shkodër last night, and the car that met him took off immediately for the mountains."

Carstairs frowned. "So five days after the kidnapping the general flies back to Albania. It could mean a great deal. Or nothing."

Peattie nodded. "We know frustratingly little about Albania since the Red Chinese moved in, but there have been reports of a primitive stone fortress somewhere in the North Albanian Alps where a few top-secret political prisoners are kept. The countryside is almost inaccessible—cliffs, gorges, crags—and it was into these mountains that the general disappeared."

"Any chance of pinpointing the place's whereabouts?" Carstairs crossed the room to the wall map.

With a shrug Peattie joined him. "Anywhere from here to there," he said, tracing the line of the mountains in the north. "We know the road ends about *here*," he added. "But roads are constantly coming to a crashing halt in these countries and life still goes on, by mule, donkey, bicycle, oxcart."

Carstairs shook his head. "There's not a chance they could be alive, but can we confirm that they were taken there?"

"Very difficult making inquiries," Peattie said. "Foreigners are suspect and the few allowed in as tourists see very little. A good many Albanians are connected with the secret police, through relatives or marriage—the usual trick, you know, to keep the citizenry terrorized. I'm not sure . . ." He hesitated, then said firmly, "I'm *very* sure our agents over there wouldn't be allowed to endanger themselves for the sake of—"

Carstairs bluntly completed the thought. "For the sake of two agents who have been at the mercy of General Perdido for more than a week. Quite right. I wouldn't allow it myself."

Peattie looked away as he added, "I think I should tell you that this mountain eyrie has a most unsavory reputation. It's spoken of in whispers, and they say no one has ever left it alive."

"I'm curious about that fortress," Carstairs said. Excusing himself, he went out to confer with Bishop. When he returned he explained, "I've asked for a private seaplane to get lost over the Albanian Alps. They should have it there in an hour."

"Reconnaissance?"

Carstairs nodded. "Unofficial, but we'll share any information we get with you people. If Perdido's going to go on snatching Americans we'd better find out where he's tucking them in."

When Peattie had gone Carstairs went back to his paper work. He lunched, and it was after two o'clock when he returned to his office to be handed a radiogram by Bishop. The seaplane had made a sortie over the Albanian Alps. No building of Carstairs's description had been seen with the naked eye but the reconnaissance photographs would be dispatched as soon as they were developed. What had intrigued the pilot, however, was the activity going on in the area bounded by the Alps, the town of Shkodër and Lake Scutari. He had seen a large number of men scouring the area on foot, a stream of black smoke rising from a wood—obviously something containing oil or gasoline had been set afire—and an unusual concentration of police launches patrolling the lake.

Carstairs wondered what the devil this could mean. He wondered if Peattie would know, and was about to pick up the phone when Peattie himself was ushered in again.

"This just came through," Peattie said without preamble. "Something's up all right in the north of Albania. One of our agents broke silence to send it—damned risky of him. Here, read it yourself, it's fresh from the decoding room."

Carstairs picked up the sheet and read:

PERDIDO MYSTERIOUSLY SHOT AND WOUNDED DURING NIGHT STOP TODAY DIRECTING LARGE SEARCH PARTY FOR ENEMIES OF STATE ESCAPED MOUNTAIN HIDEAWAY IN CAR STOP ONE RUMORED AMERICAN STOP GROUP ASSUMED STILL ALIVE AND HEADING TO COAST STOP

Carstairs leaped to his feet to look at the map. "We've got to give these people every possible help," he sputtered. "The rumored American could be Farrell; even if he isn't, they can give us valuable information. Yugoslavia has to be where they'll head; it's their only chance. Bishop," he bellowed into the intercom, "get me Fiersted in the State Department." To Peattie he said, "If Fiersted will clear the way with the Yugoslav Government, we can have men to watch the border by midnight."

By midnight Mrs. Pollifax, Farrell and the Genie were no longer adrift on Lake Scutari, but they were not in Yugoslavia either. An ill wind had blown them south, and at the stroke of midnight they were huddled behind a stone wall in the city of Shkodër. High above them stood a grim-looking medieval castle. A fuzzy, pink moon shed a faint light on the scrap of wet paper that had once been their map, and by this light Mrs. Pollifax was now trying to make some sense of the lines that had not been obliterated.

The Genie was angrily regarding the unidentifiable body of water in front of them. "It *looks* like a river," he said.

It had *felt* like a river too, and if the moon had not emerged from clouds they'd have sailed right down it. Now, having barely managed to propel the log to land, they were hiding in the shadows of the cobbled alley, back in the city where they had first entered Albania.

"There *is* a line," said Mrs. Pollifax, peering at the map. "It goes from Shkodër to the Adriatic, but it has no label." She passed the scrap of paper around, and the two men took turns squinting at it.

"It *appears* to be a river," Farrell said, nodding. "Nameless, unknown and confusing."

"There's this to consider," Mrs. Pollifax said softly. "To go from Lake Scutari to the coast on foot is quite a distance, ten to twenty miles, I'd say. But if one had a boat, and if this truly is a river, and if it empties into the Adriatic—" She broke off and sighed. "So many *ifs*. A terrifying gamble."

"But that is precisely what life is," the Genie said soberly.

"Everything is a matter of choice. We gamble on its being a wise choice, and it is free choice that makes individuals of us." He was silent a moment. "Stay here," he added, standing up. "I will try to find a boat for us."

Mrs. Pollifax was deeply relieved. It was bliss not to move, and even greater bliss to be ordered not to, since this eliminated all sense of guilt. But Farrell was already asleep, so with a sigh she forced her eyes to remain open. Someone had to be on guard. To occupy herself she began figuring how many hours ago they had escaped. They had left their prison around nine o'clock Thursday night, and it had been roughly nine p.m. this day, Friday, when they had set their log afloat. . . . Only a little more than twenty-four hours had passed. Incredible. It seemed a lifetime of nightmares. She heard the quiet drip of an oar and put out a hand to waken Farrell. She placed a warning finger across his lips and they both turned to watch the silhouette of a long boat move across a path of weak moonlight. "Come aboard," said the Genie, bowing, with his old twinkle. Mrs. Pollifax, wondering how he had found this craft, helped Farrell in—it was necessary for him to sit on the side and tumble in backwards because of his bad leg. She too half fell into the boat and lay on the floor too exhausted to move or speak. The Genie took off, giving the water quick, short jabs with his oars.

"It was tied up, not far away," he whispered over his shoulder. "Sleep a little. The current helps."

Mrs. Pollifax's gaze traveled high above him to Shkodër's castle, outlined black against the deep blue sky. There was a solitary star, and with her eyes upon it she fell softly asleep. When she awoke both the castle and the star had disappeared and the sky looked a shade lighter. But what had awakened her was the sharp crack of a pistol shot from along the shore. She sat up at once.

"Down," whispered the Genie violently. "It's someone on the shore. I think he wants us to stop. He was waving his arms but I looked away. I pretended to see nothing."

"He may hit you the next time," Farrell pointed out.

The Genie said pleasantly, "Yes, I know. But we are moving

faster. The river is growing wider and there is a change in the air. Smell it?"

Farrell and Mrs. Pollifax sniffed. "Salt water!"

The pistol fired again and something plunked against the side of the boat. "He's a damn good shot in this light," said Farrell.

"He can't question a man going toward the sea in a boat if the man refuses to stop," the Genie said casually. "He'll either find a boat or telephone to people on the coast to stop us."

Mrs. Pollifax looked around her. Ahead were a number of birds. "Sea gulls!" she cried as the darkness rolled back.

"We've got to know where we're going, what we're to do," Farrell said in a brooding, desperate voice. "My God, we don't even have a dry gun!"

The Genie said, "Yes, we have. I took Stefan's pistol, remember? His holster was waterproof. Check it. It's in my pocket."

Farrell did so. "Five cartridges," he said.

The Genie nodded. "And you?" he asked of Mrs. Pollifax.

She began emptying the pockets in her petticoats. Out came the playing cards. "Not those!" Farrell exclaimed. "Duchess, I'll never see a deck of cards for the rest of my life—if I have one—without thinking of you."

"Well, that's one form of immortality." She drew out the pistol, the cartridges, the map, the compass. "If I'm captured again perhaps they'll spare me time for a game of solitaire instead of the usual last cigarette."

"It's getting lighter," Farrell said gloomily. "Too light."

Mrs. Pollifax said to the Genie, "Wouldn't you like me to take a turn? The current's so strong now there's really no need to row."

"There's still need for steering," he pointed out dryly. "And I think we're very near the Adriatic. Near enough to walk to it if this river decides to turn and go elsewhere."

Farrell said, "If they know about our boat, perhaps we *should* walk," and Mrs. Pollifax knew by the pride and the fury in his voice that his nerves had reached a breaking point.

Suddenly a gaudy, bloodred sun cleared the cliffs behind them. Mrs. Pollifax thought, Why, this is the morning I was sure I'd never see! Caught by the magic of life, its brevity and unpre-dictability, she stared at this world as if just born into it—the distant snowcapped mountains, the cliffs tawny with shadows—and felt a sense of freedom she had never known before, as if she stood at the very core of life and felt its heartbeat. It came of being alive when she ought to be dead, and of the unquenchability of the human spirit.

She heard Farrell say, "You all right, Duchess?"

Mrs. Pollifax started. "Yes, I'm fine, thank you."

Ahead of them the ground mist rolled away and they saw the sun shining on the clear, sparkling Adriatic. Almost simultaneously Farrell cried, "Look!" A police boat was setting out toward them from the shore, flags flying from bow and stern, the spray rising majestically in an arc behind it.

THERE were two men in the boat, faceless from this distance, but well armed, it could be assumed. The boat was too old to move with speed and its motor kept cutting out, but even so it would make progress against one man with a pair of oars. The Genie, his face grim, was churning the water frantically.

Mrs. Pollifax glanced around, hoping for some concealment to present itself, but behind them the river was empty, and ahead the sea was open and boundless, furnished only with buoys at the river's entrance. Buoys . . . no, nothing could be done with buoys. Her gaze swerved to the left bank and she gave an exclamation. "Look! A wharf and a sailboat!" She leaned forward and clutched the Genie's arm. "Do look," she begged. "The man's going out, the sail's up. We have that gun and we can make him take us to sea." She found herself standing and helping the Genie push and pull at the oars. "Faster! Faster!"

They were rowing crosscurrent now and the police launch was gaining on them with shocking speed. The wharf was a float, really, with a narrow catwalk leading to the land. The boat was roughly twenty-five feet long, its sunlit sail flapping gently as a man secured the halyards. Behind them the whine of the motor launch grew louder, and now Mrs. Pollifax could see the two men clearly, one thin and dark-faced, the other fleshy and bald. She began to tremble. "For God's sake faster!" Farrell said.

The man in the fisherman's clothes seemed completely oblivious to the race being run nearby. In leisurely fashion he untied his mooring lines. He gave the tiller a thrust, the sails filled with wind and the boat swung free of the wharf. The Genie had been aiming for the wharf; now he swerved to follow the boat, and both he and Mrs. Pollifax began shouting, "Wait—wait for us." Startled, the fisherman turned. They were very close to him now, but the launch was even closer behind them. "Wait," shouted Mrs. Pollifax, waving violently. Undecided, the fisherman brought his boat about into the wind, sails luffing, bow pointed at them. The Genie viciously thrust one oar back through the water and shot across the sailboat's bow. Then, dropping both oars, he jumped aboard.

"Zot!" The fisherman stood up and roared his indignation.

The Genie ignored him and leaned over the water to Mrs. Pollifax's outstretched hand and pulled their boat alongside. He shouted to Farrell, "Aim your gun at this man! Climb aboard before he kills me with his bare hands!" There were shouts from the police launch behind; it was ramming straight into the sailboat, but the Genie had pulled his boat into position as a buffer. "Hurry!" he told Mrs. Pollifax, and she stumbled toward Farrell to help him drag his useless leg over the side.

The fisherman, no longer indignant, stood with opened mouth, his stare moving from the gun in Farrell's hand to Mrs. Pollifax. His eyes narrowed as he recognized the uniforms in the police launch and he very sensibly chose to jump overboard and swim toward the wharf. The deserted tiller moved idly to one side; then abruptly, savagely, the sails filled with a wind that sent the boom crashing, lifted one side of the boat and sent buckets skidding across the deck.

"Grab the tiller!" screamed Farrell from the bow.

"What's a tiller?" screamed back Mrs. Pollifax hysterically.

"That thing." Farrell pointed and she retrieved the long arm of smooth wood and clung to it. The boom nearly decapitated the Genie, the sails flapped erratically. What saved them was the

531

boat, which the Genie held captive and on the other side of which the two policemen had attached themselves like barnacles. The bald man had started to climb across it to the sailboat—now, as the sailboat lurched in the wind, he was caught with one foot in it and one in the launch. He waved both arms wildly in a fight for balance, then fell to the floor of the middle boat. The thin man pulled out a revolver and fired at the Genie. Farrell returned the fire, the man slumped over, and Mrs. Pollifax screamed, because now the bald man was climbing to his knees and aiming a gun at Farrell. "Shoot!" she screamed, pointing, and Farrell and the policeman exchanged shots simultaneously.

The Genie's clutch on the buffer boat loosened. With nothing to hold them now, the rigging tightened, the sails went taut and the wind carried them zooming across the water with an abruptness that sent Farrell sprawling across the Genie on the deck. Mrs. Pollifax, holding tightly to the tiller, screamed for help.

"Drop it!" shouted Farrell, and she was mystified when, as she let the tiller go, the boat came about into the wind and ceased its reckless caroming. Then she saw that Farrell had lifted himself up and was staring in horror at the Genie.

"Oh no," she whispered, and knelt beside him. "Is he dead?"

Farrell very gently placed the Genie's head in his lap. "Not dead but *very* badly hurt."

She saw blood welling out of Farrell's sleeve at the shoulder. "Oh God, you're hurt, too."

"Not badly but I can't risk moving either myself or the Genie. Duchess, you're going to have to sail this boat."

"I?" gasped Mrs. Pollifax. "Me?" She thought back to the night on the precipice, to the goats and the wild chase in the Rolls Royce, to the cornfield, the hours in the cave and the night floating across Scutari on a log. Surely there must be a few ounces of overlooked iron in her soul. "I'll try," she said, and wiped a tear from what must be a very raddled cheek by now.

"I can tell you what to do," Farrell said. She crawled drearily back toward the tiller, and he added casually, "Any idea whether I winged that bald chap?"

Mrs. Pollifax looked back. "The boats are still bobbing around. No head showing in either."

Farrell nodded. "Two boats, each carrying a wounded or dead policeman, will set off a merry chase." He seized a tarpaulin with which to keep the sun off the Genie. "Okay, Duchess, full speed ahead. We can't risk heading north to Yugoslavia and running into more police launches. We'll have to head straight out to sea."

Mrs. Pollifax gaped at him. "Out to sea!"

Farrell grinned weakly. "We've done everything else the hard way, why stop now? Give me that compass and turn the tiller to starboard—to the right. Brace yourself first."

Mrs. Pollifax tossed him the compass and turned the tiller to the right. At once the wind seized them like a gigantic hand, the sail tightened, and the rigging creaked. "Easy does it," Farrell shouted over the wind. "Keep the tiller in the center. Excellent, keep it that way. If you hit a squall and get scared let the tiller go, the boat'll come about by itself. The important thing is to get the hell out of sight of land as fast as possible." With his one useful arm he was pulling the tarp over his head and shrugging it into position so that it would shade the Genie.

"Yes—oh *yes*," gasped Mrs. Pollifax. Tiller in hand, she dedicated herself to getting them the hell out of sight of Albania as fast as possible.

11

Toward five that afternoon the first mate of the *Persephone*, a seagoing tug making its way southward from Venice, sighted a sailboat in which someone was waving what looked like a white petticoat. "Damned tourist," he growled, but he reported it to the captain, who ordered their course slowed, and presently the sailboat drew alongside. The first mate gasped, for seated at the tiller was one of the wildest-looking women he had ever seen: white hair in shreds, face filthy and blistering from sunburn. He recognized her voluminous skirt as Greek or Albanian, but the woman's features did not match it. Then he saw the tarpaulin lift. The way the two men looked flashed his memory back to the war years and to lifeboats found in the Mediterranean. Both men looked as if they'd had it and it was plain that a doctor was needed. The first mate hurried to report again to the captain.

Mrs. Pollifax, gazing up at the tug from below, wondered why the sailors were staring with such horrified fascination. For the first time she realized how tattered and bizarre she, Farrell and the Genie must appear to these well-scrubbed seamen.

Then the spell broke. A sailor shouted, "Inglese! Welcome!" Cheering broke out, and Mrs. Pollifax had to look away to conceal her tears.

"Well, Duchess," said Farrell, smiling at her.

"Well, Farrell." She smiled back, wiping her eyes.

"You look like hell, Duchess, but you're safe."

"Safe!" Mrs. Pollifax tasted the word on her tongue, then a rope ladder was flung over the side of the tug and an officer was descending to assist her upward. On board the ship, Mrs. Pollifax was escorted to the captain, and after identifying herself she said, "If you would be so kind as to contact Mr. Carstairs at the CIA in Washington, please."

The captain's eyes flickered. "It's that way, is it? You will write the message. I ask only that I see it before it is sent."

Mrs. Pollifax sat down gratefully at his desk, then looked up. "What ship is this, and where are you going?"

"The *Persephone*, due to land at Otranto in two hours, or at nineteen hundred hours."

Mrs. Pollifax chewed on her pencil and wrote:

.Sir: Rescued from Adriatic Sea this afternoon by SS *Persephone* arriving Otranto at 1900 hours. Farrell and second companion in need of medical attention. Have no passport or money and must request some help otherwise it has been a most interesting trip. Sincerely yours, Emily Pollifax.

The captain read it through and nodded. "I will also send word to Otranto that a doctor is needed. We do not have one aboard.

And you," he added to Mrs. Pollifax, smiling faintly, "you would perhaps like to wash a little and comb the hair?"

Mrs. Pollifax's eyes widened. "Wash a *little?*" And she laughed.

AT Otranto, before the *Persephone* had docked, a harbor launch drew up and two men came aboard. Both wore business suits; one carried an attaché case up the rope ladder and the other a medical bag, and they were escorted at once to the cabin where Mrs. Pollifax, Farrell and the Genie were resting.

The doctor hurried to the berth where the Genie lay, while the second man stood looking appraisingly at Farrell and Mrs. Pollifax. "Ben Halstead's my name," he said, his scrutiny completed. "I believe we have a mutual friend named Carstairs."

Mrs. Pollifax brightened. "Yes, indeed. I am Emily Pollifax and this is Mr. Farrell. He has a broken leg and bullet wounds in his shoulder and his arm; and this man . . ." She glanced toward the Genie, whose eyes were vacant as he gazed at the doctor. "We don't know who he is but we brought him along anyway—a very peculiar and resourceful Chinese who speaks English, though he kept that a secret for quite long."

"Oh? That's interesting." Halstead moved to the berth and over the doctor's shoulder looked down at the Genie.

"You don't know anything at all about him?"

"Actually we didn't trust him at first, nor he us," put in Farrell. "But he rescued us from a very sticky situation."

Mrs. Pollifax said slowly, "When I asked him about next of kin, he chuckled and said they'd held his funeral two years ago."

The doctor removed the stethoscope from his ears. "Well, he can't be questioned for a day or two. He needs the best of care. It'll be tricky removing this bullet."

"Will he survive?" asked Mrs. Pollifax anxiously.

"Considerable patchwork will be needed, but barring anything unforeseen—yes, he'll survive." The doctor tucked a blanket around the Genie. "From the sound of it we're docking now. I'll arrange for a stretcher and then I'll take a look at you, Mr. Farrell."

Farrell said cheerfully, "No need to hurry; I wouldn't feel

comfortable without a bullet in me somewhere." He was watching Halstead, who kept staring at the Genie. "You recognize him, don't you." It was a statement, not a question.

"Not recognize . . . more a feeling of familiarity." Halstead didn't turn. Then he snapped his fingers and exclaimed, "Good grief! Dr. Lee Tsung Howell!"

"I beg your pardon?" faltered Mrs. Pollifax.

"Considerably thinner . . . that's what fooled me. Disappeared two years ago. Memorial service was held for him—every bit of evidence pointed to his murder by the Red Chinese."

"Who *is* he?" asked Mrs. Pollifax.

"Dr. Howell, the scientist. Born in China; father English, mother Chinese. English citizen. Made the mistake of traveling to Hong Kong two years ago. That's when they snatched him."

Farrell said incredulously, "You mean he's *the* Dr. Howell? The protein man?"

Mrs. Pollifax said, "But why on earth would a protein man be locked up in a cell in Albania for two years?"

"Food," said Halstead. "Can you think of anything China needs more desperately? At the time of his disappearance Dr. Howell was at work on a method for extracting protein from a common weed—a protein that would feed hundreds of people for only a few pennies. We knew they'd kidnapped him but we were told he was killed fighting for his life. What a break for the world that you found him! The presses will be humming all night long."

Farrell grinned. "Duchess, do you recall—and it pains me to do so—my suggesting that the Genie was mentally retarded?"

Halstead laughed. "To be charitable, I might add that he's known as quite an eccentric." They were silent as the stretcher was brought in by two orderlies, who lifted the Genie gently onto it.

As they carried the stretcher out Mrs. Pollifax said suddenly, "Will I be able to send him get-well cards? I should like very much to have the hospital's name."

Halstead said, "You can learn that simply by reading your newspaper tomorrow morning in Washington, D.C."

"Washington!" exclaimed Mrs. Pollifax.

"My orders are to fly you there at once. You can eat and sleep on the plane, you know, and Carstairs wants to see for himself that you're alive." He glanced at his watch. "We leave as soon as the doctor has pumped Farrell full of anti-infection and anti-pain shots." Then he added with a grin, "It isn't everybody who has a jet plane specially commandeered for them. You'll be in the air within the hour."

THEY sat facing Carstairs across his broad desk. After four injections and seven hours of drugged sleep on the plane, Farrell still looked frail. After one glance at him Carstairs said flatly, "I won't keep you long. The important thing is to put this on tape before you forget; it will surprise you how unreal it will seem once you've recovered." His face softened. "And may I congratulate you both on rescuing Dr. Lee Tsung Howell?"

"You may," said Farrell with a grin.

"And on coming back yourselves," added Carstairs. "I don't mind telling you that I gave you both up long ago."

"Did you really!" exclaimed Mrs. Pollifax in a pleased voice.

"I'm going to call in Bishop now," went on Carstairs. "He'll take a few notes but the bulk of it will be put on tape. I think we'll give Johnny the rest he needs by letting Mrs. Pollifax do most of the talking. Johnny, you join in when it suits you, agreed?"

Bishop had come in, and Mrs. Pollifax noticed that his nostrils looked pinched during the introductions. "It's the goats," she told him. "Just don't sit too near me." It was obvious that only a complete change of clothes and a vast amount of hot water and soap would ever make her acceptable to society again.

"*Goats?*" said Carstairs, startled.

She nodded. "Goats. Where would you like me to begin?"

"Begin with your meeting Johnny. That would be the nineteenth of August."

She nodded and, awkwardly at first, then with increasing absorption, she told of the flight to Albania and their time there. Farrell joined in occasionally, and Carstairs did not interrupt until Mrs. Pollifax mentioned the missile site.

"Missile site?" he exploded. "Are you *sure* it was a missile site?"

"No," she said, "but Colonel Nexdhet was."

Farrell grinned. "Let her go on; it gets even more interesting."

Mrs. Pollifax continued, eventually concluding ". . . so we sailed west, straight out to sea. . . ."

Carstairs smiled and flicked off the tape recorder. "I'd like that missile site pinpointed on a map if humanly possible. All this can wait, though."

Farrell said soberly, "You've avoided the beginning. Mexico City. I take it the whole thing blew up. They got DeGamez?"

Carstairs sighed. "One thing lost, one thing found. Let's not underestimate what you accomplished in getting Dr. Howell back, as well as yourselves." He looked directly at Farrell. "Yes, Johnny, DeGamez was murdered on August seventeenth."

Farrell swore savagely and Mrs. Pollifax felt a tremor of shock. She said quietly, "I'm terribly, terribly sorry. He was so kind, such a *gentleman.*"

Carstairs suddenly became very still. He said at last, very softly, "Mrs. Pollifax, how could you possibly know that, when you never met the real Senor DeGamez?"

"Oh, but you see I did," she told him eagerly. "I had to be sure I could locate his bookstore, don't you see? And after finding it I passed it nearly every day. And that's why—well, after passing it so many times I thought I'd stop in one morning and browse around a little. I didn't think it would hurt," she added anxiously, suddenly noticing the intensity of Carstairs's gaze. "So I went inside and we had a lovely chat."

"When?" Carstairs's voice was urgent.

"It must have been—let's see, four days before the nineteenth—August fifteenth. We chatted about traveling and being alone, and did I play solitaire. He gave me a book called 77 *Ways to Play Solitaire,* and—"

"Mrs. Pollifax," interrupted Carstairs in a strangled voice, "De-Gamez was given your photograph on the ninth of August. When you walked into The Parrot Bookstore, he knew who you were. Do you understand? *He knew who you were.* He must also have strongly suspected by then that he was being closely watched. Now, I want you to tell me every word he said, and just where I can find that book."

"Oh, but there was nothing in the book," she assured him. "General Perdido had it examined many times. They found nothing."

Carstairs sat back and looked at her. "If DeGamez had the microfilms, he would have found some way to give them to you. I want you to go back and reconstruct *everything* that happened."

Carefully Mrs. Pollifax began. The book of memoirs. The parrot's shout. The conversation about Olé. The book on solitaire. "He wrapped my purchase in white paper," she added, frowning. "But by then two other customers had come in, so I left."

"Try again," said Carstairs.

Again Mrs. Pollifax described her visit, and once again uncovered nothing. "The two other customers walked in, and he said something about wishing me a beautiful visit in his country. And then I—*oh*," she cried, "the *cards!*"

"Cards?" Carstairs leaned forward.

"It was just as I reached the door," said Mrs. Pollifax. "He called out, 'How can you play solitaire without cards?' and he threw them to me. Surely he wouldn't throw anything of value so casually?"

"That is precisely the way a man under surveillance would dispose of something dangerous. *What happened to those cards?*"

She said, "I have them right here in my pocket."

Carstairs stared at her in astonishment. "You mean you carried then *with* you? You mean you still *have* them?"

Farrell began to laugh. "Have them! Carstairs, the Duchess played solitaire with those cards endlessly, right under the guards' noses, and in front of Perdido too. She drove everybody nearly crazy with them."

Mrs. Pollifax gave him a reproachful glance. Reaching down to her second petticoat she brought out the deck of cards and placed them on the desk. Carstairs picked them up and ran his fingers over them. He said softly, "They're enclosed in plastic. Bishop, take these to the lab on the double. It's microfilms we're after."

"Yes sir," gasped Bishop, and the door closed behind him.

Carstairs sat back and stared at Mrs. Pollifax with a little smile tugging at his lips. "And I believed I had sent an innocent lamb to a den of wolves. You have great resources, Mrs. Pollifax."

"It's my age," said Mrs. Pollifax. "I can't think why I forgot about the cards, though. Is that what's called a mental block?"

"If those cards turn out to be . . ." The phone buzzed. Carstairs picked it up and grinned. "Right. Thanks, Bishop." He hung up. "They've found the first microfilm. Tirpak used two packs of very thin playing cards. He cemented the back of one card to the front of another, with the film between." He added fervently, "If that was a mental block, Mrs. Pollifax, then bless it. Perdido would have sensed at once that you were concealing something. It saved your life when you were questioned, and it's recovered for this country a great amount of invaluable information. Mrs. Pollifax, we are in your debt."

She said gently, "If I could have a bath and clean clothes . . ."

"I'll make certain you have both within the hour. And for you, Johnny—a bevy of beautiful nurses."

Farrell stumbled to his feet and walked to Mrs. Pollifax. He bent over and kissed her. "I won't say good-by, Duchess. Don't you dare leave town without coming to see me on my bed of pain."

Mrs. Pollifax beamed. "I'll bring roses, my dear Farrell. And a deck of playing cards to teach you some games of solitaire."

He said gravely, "A small price to pay for my life, Duchess. . . . God bless you and have a *wonderful* bath."

Mrs. Pollifax put down her suitcase in front of the door to her apartment and groped in her purse for the key. As she inserted it into the lock a door across the hall flew open, spilling sunlight across the black and white tiles.

"Mrs. Pollifax, back at last! You must have had a *marvelous* trip to stay so long."

Mrs. Pollifax turned. "Yes, marvelous, Miss Hartshorne."

"I've a package for you. Came this morning and I signed for it." Miss Hartshorne held up one hand dramatically. "Don't go away, don't even move, I'll be right back."

Mrs. Pollifax waited, and presently her neighbor appeared with a box wrapped in brown paper and covered with seals. "Special delivery all the way from Mexico City! Here's last night's paper too, so you can catch up on our news."

"How very kind of you," said Mrs. Pollifax. "Won't you come in and have a cup of tea with me?"

Miss Hartshorne looked shocked. "Oh, I wouldn't dream of it. As an experienced traveler myself I know how exhausted you must be. But I hope you'll invite me in soon to see your slides."

Mrs. Pollifax said quietly, "I'm afraid there'll be no slides." She saw the stern disapproval on Miss Hartshorne's face. But Mrs. Pollifax smiled and said gently, "I didn't take any snapshots, I was too busy. In fact it might surprise you how busy I really was." She added firmly, "Now I insist that you come in—we've never had a cup of tea together, have we?"

Miss Hartshorne looked shaken. "Why—why, no. I don't believe we have."

Mrs. Pollifax pushed wide the door and walked inside. "Do sit down, I'll put the water on to boil." She put her suitcase down, left package and newspaper on the couch and hurried to the kitchen to fill the kettle. "There," she said, returning, "that will take only a minute." From where she sat she could see the headline on the newspaper: RESCUED SCIENTIST GAINS STRENGTH, DR. HOWELL TO MEET PRESS TOMORROW. Mrs. Pollifax smiled contentedly.

"Your package," insisted Miss Hartshorne. "Aren't you curious?"

Mrs. Pollifax eyed the box beside her. "Yes, I *am* curious." She fetched scissors and cut the strings. The box bore the label of an expensive shop near the Hotel Reforma Intercontinental. Eagerly she opened it. "Serapes!" she gasped.

"How beautiful," said Miss Hartshorne in a hushed voice. "A gift? How many friends you must have made."

Mrs. Pollifax lifted out first one and then another until the couch was aflame with brilliant colors.

"Six!" cried Miss Hartshorne.

Mrs. Pollifax beamed. "One for each grandchild, and one for Roger, Jane and myself." Then she saw the card that had been slipped between the folds of the last serape. It read simply, "With mingled gratitude and apologies, Carstairs."

Carstairs . . . He must have had her room searched, found the ones she'd bought, her only tourist presents . . . A great warmth filled Mrs. Pollifax at the thoughtfulness of such a busy man. She glanced around her apartment at the sunshine striping the rugs, the atmosphere of quiet security, and just for a moment a procession of people trouped through her thoughts: a goatherd and his wife; a Genie who talked of life's choices; Colonel Nexdhet of the extraordinary mustache; Lulash; Major Vassovic and a man named John Sebastian Farrell who faced pain with gaiety. She said with a smile, "I met a great many unforgettable people on my trip, Miss Hartshorne."

Simultaneously the tea kettle began to sing and the telephone rang. Mrs. Pollifax said, "Oh, Miss Hartshorne, would you fix the tea? The tea bags and cups are in the cupboard over the stove."

It was the first time that Mrs. Pollifax had ever heard Miss Hartshorne laugh. "How casually you live, Mrs. Pollifax. This takes me back to my college days." Over her shoulder she said, "Call me Grace, won't you?"

But Mrs. Pollifax was already on the phone. "Why, Roger!" she exclaimed with pleasure. "How wonderful to hear from you. Worried about me?" Mrs. Pollifax laughed delightedly. "Roger dear, what possible trouble could I have gotten into at my age and in Mexico of all places." Her gaze fell to the serapes lying on the couch. With a small, very private smile Mrs. Pollifax picked up the card that had arrived with them and slipped it into her pocket.

Dorothy Gilman

"I suppose we all tend to assume that an author resembles her heroine, and I was surprised to find Dorothy so young and attractive," recalls John Falter, the famous illustrator who drew our pictures for *The Unexpected Mrs. Pollifax*.

And that is but one of many unexpected things about Dorothy Gilman. Although she won her literary spurs at the age of eleven, when she carried off first prize for a newspaper short story, she set out in life to be an artist. Indeed, she trained at an art school and the urge to write did not reassert itself until, at the age of twenty-two, she wrote her first stories for young readers. Years later she decided to try her hand at a novel for adults. She says, "When I began *The Unexpected Mrs. Pollifax* I thought, why not write a story about a woman who has everything happen to her that I want to happen to me?"

At forty-seven, Dorothy Gilman was a long way from the "sixtyish" Mrs. Pollifax, but that didn't worry her at all. She had grown up in a New Brunswick, New Jersey, parsonage, where her father was a Baptist minister, and had always been fascinated by the elderly eccentric Victorian ladies of the parish, who seemed, delightfully, to lose many of their inhibitions in old age and take off suddenly on new careers. So Dorothy Gilman distilled their characters into one unforgettable personality whom she sent off to live out her own dreams.

It worked like a charm. The novel was an international success and was made into a film starring Rosalind Russell. For Dorothy Gilman, the profits have enabled her to travel the world looking for backgrounds for more adventures concerning the unexpected Mrs. Pollifax.

Picture credits. Pages 184 left, 185 left, 232: The Bettman Archive. Page 184 right: Culver Pictures, Inc. Pages 185 right, 220 left: Historisches Museum der Stadt Wien. Pages 220 right, 221 left: Worcester Art Museum, Worcester, Mass. Pages 221 right, 233 right: New York Public Library. Page 233 left: Picture Archive of the Austrian National Library.

PP. 73